KENTUCKY
BLUES

Derek Robinson

KENTUCKY BLUES

CASSELL&CO

Cassell & Co
The Orion Publishing Group
Orion House
5 Upper St Martin's Lane
London WC2H 9EA

A catalogue record for this book is available
from the British Library

ISBN 0-304-36182-8

Designed by Goldust Design

Printed and bound in Great Britain

F - ROBINSON

For Connie and Al

A GUARD AGAINST
THUNDERBOLTS

His wife said, 'Be sensible, now,' and Joe Killick ignored her. He took a pistol from the wagon and loaded it. His rifle was in its saddle-scabbard. 'At least leave me the blessed map,' she said. 'You get killed and I'll never find my way out of this wilderness.' He rode off and left her with the wagon, four slaves and a dog.

Judith Killick was nineteen, married less than six months, on the trail nearly half that time, except it usually wasn't trail, it was mostly animal tracks or dried-out streambeds. And rightly speaking the map was hers. She'd given Joe the twenty dollars to buy it.

No point in trying to argue with him when he was angry. She knew he was raging as soon as he saw smoke further up this valley. Back when they found the valley, he had been happy; jubilant. He had said: Now it's just a matter of picking the best land. Then, up ahead: smoke. Not a wisp from a camp-fire. Big smoke, black.

Killick left her and followed the river for a mile or more, and then he heard the chink of axes. The sound led him another mile, to a clearing. A dozen slaves were felling timber, hauling logs, burning out the stumps. The sight astonished and infuriated him. Nobody knew of this valley except Killick and the old trapper who'd sold him the map. That was why he'd sweated and toiled all the way from Virginia. Now look: he was cheated. Robbed.

Unless these niggers were runaways. Fugitives. Outlaws.

One way to find out. Use the damn gun. See if they keep running.

He fired at a crow. The bang bounced off the hillsides. Everyone stopped work. Nobody ran. 'God damn you all to hell,' Killick said. There had to be a white man somewhere. Sure enough, in the shade of a big old oak, getting onto a horse, cantering into the sunlight,

1

waving his hat at the slaves, ordering them back to work.

Killick knew he had to go and meet the man. If he didn't, if he turned and went back to the wagon, the bastard might follow and kill him. Of course that might happen in any case. This day was rapidly falling to pieces. He walked his horse forward.

They both stopped when there was still forty yards between them. 'Henry Hudd,' the man called. 'This is my land. Was that your shot?'

'Saw a bear. Scared him off.'

'We get all sorts of beasts in these woods. Some dangerous. Some not.'

Killick thought about what that might mean. He nudged his horse and it ambled closer. From what he could see, this Hudd fellow carried no weapon. 'Joe Killick,' he said. 'I got a piece of paper here says I got first claim on any land either side of the upper Flint River.' He took out the old trapper's map and held it high. Maybe Hudd couldn't read. Plenty men couldn't.

'That so.'

They were close enough to get a good look at each other. Killick saw a big-chested man, relaxed, sure of himself, about his own age, twenty-two. Hudd saw a man tired from too many weeks in the saddle, wearing a permanent frown. 'Wish I could help you,' Hudd said. 'Fact of the matter is, you got the wrong river. This is the Cameron.'

'Cameron.' Killick looked at the map. 'Where am I?'

'Dundee County, Kentucky. Any further south, you'd be in Tennessee.'

Killick took off his hat and tucked the map inside the lining. His face looked as if he'd just bitten his tongue.

'I don't know of any Flint River,' Hudd said. 'Upper, lower or middle. Never heard of one.'

Killick took a good look around. Level ground, no rocks, dirt as black as soot. 'I guess you took the best land here.'

'Well, Providence was kind. Seemed the right thing to do.'

Killick looked at the toiling slaves, sweat gleaming on black skin. 'Providence decides to drop a thunderbolt smack on top of you right now, then I guess all these niggers and all this land would be mine.' Killick had his hand on his pistol. All he wanted was for Hudd to laugh. Smile, even. Just give an excuse. Killick had his gun and his anger but he needed help.

2

Hudd didn't help. 'Providence put my brother up in the branches of that oak tree there, with a rifle,' he said. 'Just to guard against thunderbolts.'

Killick went back to his wife and his wagon. He found the second-best stretch of land – sandy in some parts, marshy in others – and set the slaves to clearing it.

That was in 1832. He didn't speak to Henry Hudd again until 1840, when he needed to borrow a slave. By then he knew that Hudd never had a brother, in or out of an oak. Something else he could never forgive Hudd for.

A HALF-SIZE BULLWHIP

The Cameron valley was so fertile that the second-best stretch of river bottom land should have made a good farm. The river was big and the valley floor was flat. Even in the longest summer the river never failed. When it was in spate it looked like cold beef soup, there was so much rich muck in it.

Joe Killick boasted to visitors that his land would grow anything. *Anything.* Plant a row of laces, tomorrow you'd get a crop of shoes. 'See them trees?' he said. 'That's where I fenced a field with green timber. Posts began to sprout in a week. Now look: I got a line of oaks fifty feet high.' They weren't oaks. Joe Killick never made much effort to understand the land he farmed or the stuff it grew. He didn't see himself as a farmer. Landowner, that's what he was. Leave the work to the slaves, leave the crop to the dirt, which was how God intended, otherwise He wouldn't have given them both to the Killicks. It was a seductively simple formula. Often it failed. When the visitors had left, Judith Killick said, 'We got trees for supper tonight. How you want yours? Fried or boiled, with a little sawdust on the side?' Joe sniggered, but his crops that year were no joke and they both knew it, and his wife made him suffer for it.

When it came to making things grow, Joe had only one, small talent and he worked it hard. Judith bore him seven children, not counting a few that failed the course. For the first half of their married life she was almost permanently pregnant. It wasn't pleasant, but Judith knew she had to breed if the farm was to survive. Joe could help with the breeding. He couldn't do much else. Especially, he couldn't make his land grow slaves.

The Killicks – father and sons – sowed beads of black sweat in plenty, but they never harvested a fresh crop of niggers. The opposite, in fact: year by year they lost slaves through sickness or exhaustion

4

or sudden death, which sent Joe to the auctions down in Tennessee. He begrudged paying top price for a new nigger when he blamed an old one for dying on him, so he always came back with poor stock. There were never more than twelve Killick slaves. Upriver, Henry Hudd never had fewer than twenty. Killick hated that. It was common knowledge in the valley that Hudd got the work of thirty out of his twenty. That deepened Killick's hatred. He kicked and whipped his slaves as hard as any man, and still Hudd got all the luck. That rubbed Killick sore.

Henry Hudd's luck was based on sound husbandry. He treated his slaves like animals, and he treated his animals well. Stupid to buy a good cow and feed it bad hay. Foolish to have a fast horse and not tend it if it went lame. Same with slaves. Henry Hudd allowed his stock of slaves enough plain food, and he doctored them, outside and in, whenever an ailment weakened them. He stabled them in dry cabins, clothed them warmly in winter. 'A nigger can't shiver and work both at the same time,' he told his son. 'Ain't made that way. You can whip him, of course. That warms him up some, gets him moving. But it don't stop the damn weather, and soon he gets cold again, thickens his blood, gives him the shivers. Another thing to remember: all that time you spent whippin' him was lost time, no work got done then, except by you. So you give your nigger a wool coat, pants an' hat, a good pair of nigger brogans, keeps the wind an' rain out, pays off handsomely in the long run.'

Food, shelter, doctoring, clothes. That wasn't good nature, it was good husbandry. Joe Killick was too cheap to understand the difference.

～

Geography makes history. About midway between the two farms, the Cameron broadened and yet – by some trick of the ground – the river kept its depth from shore to shore. When the first steamboat explored, in 1842, this was as far as the captain cared to go. From here on up, bluffs and cliffs crowded and cramped the river. A side-wheeler needed space to turn. If a boat couldn't turn, it had to back downstream until it found space. Awkward, slow, dangerous. This bulge in the Cameron was God's gift. A place like that deserved a name. They called it Rock Springs.

On its next trip, the steamboat carried a bunch of pioneers, including a man called Flub Phillips. He was a failed pig-farmer from New Jersey, slim and good-looking and glib, and he had drifted through Delaware and Maryland, into Virginia and Tennessee, making a living out of courteous bigamy. He gave each new plain and dumpy wife a memorable honeymoon and then moved on with her savings. He felt it was a fair exchange. But he became like an actor always playing the same suave role in the same play. He needed a change. Newspapers said there was gold in Oregon. Should be good opportunities there.

When the boat slowed and turned and eased into the bank, he was the last man down the gangplank. 'Which way's the town?' he asked a deckhand. All he could see was brush and forest.

'Any way you like. Ain't built yet.'

'I was expectin' a hotel, or somethin'.'

'Yeah, sure, hotel, that would be nice.' They moved aside to make space for stores being unloaded. 'I guess these folks brought tents to live in while they stake out their farms, if that's what they're aimin' to do. You could sleep in a corner of a tent, maybe.'

'Good Christ.'

'Keep your boots on if you do. Snakes everywhere.'

The settlers hauled their stuff away, taking a narrow track through the brush. Nobody showed any interest in Flub, and he was too dismayed to ask for help. The steamboat cast off and churned downriver. He took his bag and sat on a fallen tree and pictured the hotel he would be staying in if this place had a hotel. After a while he realized he was looking at a small white boy, very dirty, wearing torn cotton pants and a tattered straw hat that rested on his ears. Flub was dressed in a seersucker coat and pants to match, French cuffs, a bootlace tie and a curly-brimmed beige hat with a high crown. The way the boy looked at him, he felt like the king of Spain. 'Hey,' he said.

The boy said nothing. He was the Killicks' eldest child, George, nine years old, scrawny body, no expression, never been more than three miles from the farmhouse in his whole life. Flub was the most colourful creature George had ever seen, and that included six Cherokee that went up the valley three years ago. At least, pa said they were Cherokee. George had his doubts about pa. To pa, anything in bright feathers was either Cherokee or kingfisher. Saved a lot of argument.

'This is Rock Springs, right?' Flub said. No response. 'Where's the rock and where's the springs?' Flub asked. George picked his nose while he thought about that. 'Forget it, kid,' Flub said. 'The answer's not up there. Which way's Oregon?' Foolish question. But it made him check the sky. Afternoon was wearing on, sun was going down, making the Cameron glitter. West was beyond the river. He was on the wrong bank. 'Hey!' he said. 'Where's the damn ferry?'

'Ain't none,' George said. He felt pretty sure about that. He had a voice like a young crow.

'You got a home?' Flub asked. George nodded. He was absolutely certain of that.

They went to the farm. Judith Killick said Flub could stay for 50 cents a night, grub included. 'You share a bed with George,' she said. Flub agreed. Anything was better than sharing with snakes.

Joe showed him the farm, starting with the house. The chimneys were stone, the rest was wood. Squared-off logs for the walls. Few windows, and they were small. 'Keeps the weather out,' Joe said. Began with just one level, then children kept coming, so he put a second level on top of the first. 'I'm what you'd call potent,' he said. 'Go forth an' multiply, the good book tells us. I must be the most Christian man in Dundee County, Kentucky. You got family?'

'Possibly.'

There wasn't much else to see. Additions had been tacked onto the back and sides of the main building. It looked more like a cluster of barns than a home. The slave cabins were downwind, out of sight. 'Don't want to see 'em, an' I sure don't want to smell 'em,' Joe said. 'Niggers are a lot of work, don't let anyone tell you different. They got more ways of goin' sick than warts on a warthog.'

Flub was surprised. 'You ever see a warthog?'

'Saw a picture, once.'

They sat on the porch and sipped home-brew whiskey.

The children watched and scratched, fought and whispered. 'You met George,' Joe said. 'He came first. Then there's Dan, Stanton, JoBeth – she'll look better when she gets some teeth – and Jessica's inside probably, she's still at the tit. More on the way. I ain't done yet.'

'Quite a family.'

'George is the smartest. Gets that from me. George can whup a nigger just like a grown man. I showed him how. Has to use a half-size bullwhip, y'understand. I made it special.'

'You have a lot of trouble with your slaves?'

'Oh … they need remindin', time to time. That boy's a great help. I seen him whip a black ass so clean, criss-cross, you could play tic-tac-toe on it.'

'Remarkable.'

'Want to see him do it? I could fetch – '

'Thank you, no. Black flesh …' Flub touched his stomach and winced.

'Yeah.' Joe poured more whiskey. 'Causes a man to wonder. The Almighty made slaves, He got that right, so why'd He make 'em so goddamn ugly?' He raised his drink to heaven. 'No offence meant, Lord. Oregon, you say.'

'That's where the gold is. So I'm told.'

'Must be the worse part of two thousand miles. And you haven't crossed the Cameron yet.'

'Steamboat people said this was a terminus, so I reckoned there must be a stagecoach I could use.'

'Stage? In Kentucky? Nothin' but creeks an' mountains. Come winter, we haul everythin' by sled.'

'Well, I certainly don't reckon on *walking* to Oregon. There really is no ferry?'

'Nope.'

They watched the sun go down.

'Course, you could always build one,' Joe said.

'I wouldn't know where to start.'

That was all. The sun vanished as if swallowed. They went inside and ate.

A GROWL AS DEEP
AS A GROAN

The steamboat was back again in five days.

Henry Hudd heard its whistle, so distant that it got lost on the wind and he had to listen twice before he was sure. 'Saddle up,' he told his son. 'I'll show you what a side-wheeler looks like.' Charles was twelve, and he never left the farm except with his father. This trip excited him.

There was one job to be done before they could go. They rode into a field and Henry said, 'Fetch me a nigger. Any nigger.'

Charles stood in his stirrups. Nine or ten slaves were working, chopping weeds. He knew them all, could recognize each one, even far off, just by the back of his head. 'What's wrong?' his father growled. 'Can't you count up to one?' Charles pointed.

'Adam,' Henry called. The man straightened up, looked, laid down his hoe, walked towards them, taking care not to tread on the crop. Henry opened his mouth but he was too late; Adam was already taking off his shirt. He reached them, and stood where he knew he must stand, a tall, thin, grey-haired negro, and without dismounting Henry Hudd whipped him across the back, three strokes each way, making the leather crack like a snapped branch. The weight of the lashing forced Adam to this knees.

They rode away. The chink-chink of hoes had never stopped.

'What was that for, sir?' Charles asked.

'Nothin'. I like to discourage idle thoughts in the others while I'm away. Keeps them busy. Now tell me: what is your book at present?'

'Just started *The Last of the Mohicans*, sir.'

'Very sound. Cooper knows about Indians. What else?'

'Last week I finished the Book of Job, sir.'

His father laughed. 'That's more than I ever did. Too much belly-achin' for me. I admire the style, it's plain and simple like good furniture, but Job was good for only one thing and that's failure. Some men make a career of it.'

They talked about books all the way to Rock Springs. Charles Hudd was proud of American writers and he planned to introduce his son to Longfellow and Washington Irving. He kept in touch with British writing too. 'There's a man called Dickens who's making a mark. I'll get his books. And Sir Walter Scott's. They'll teach you about chivalry and honour and suchlike. Remarkable man, Scott. Owned a publishing house but it went bankrupt. Read about that in a newspaper, years ago. Enormous debts, hundreds of thousands of dollars. Scott wrote books until he'd paid off every last cent. Didn't sit around and bleat about his bad luck, like Job. No, sir. Scott valued his name and reputation. Knew what was right. Sense of decency. True gentleman.'

Henry Hudd spoke of other authors, and his son nodded dutifully, but he was thinking of Sir Walter Scott, a knight in shining armour, going about and defending decency so that people said, 'Sir Walter Scott is a true gentleman.'

The steamboat was unloading when they reached Rock Springs. Young Charles went to stare at it. Henry looked at the passengers. A scruffy bunch. After a while he noticed another man watching them, a man dressed for the city; so he went and introduced himself.

'I was hoping there would be a ferry,' Flub Phillips said. 'I'm aiming for Oregon.'

'My advice is get on that boat and go back and start again.'

'No, I can't do that.'

Hudd nodded. It was impolite to ask a man his reasons for not returning somewhere. 'You won't find much excitement here, Mr Phillips. See these people? Runts of the litter.'

'What lies beyond your farm, Mr Hudd? Upriver?'

'Virgin forest.' He looked at Flub's polished boots. 'I could lend you an axe.'

'I need a regiment of engineers, to build a ferry.'

Henry Hudd lost patience with Flub's helplessness. 'I hope you find a way to Oregon, Mr Phillips,' he said, 'and I hope these dregs follow you. I know their sort. Atheists and agitators. I don't need them upsetting my slaves with their blasphemous opinions. My farm

10

is an island of peace and obedience in a wicked world, and I intend to keep it so. Good day to you.'

He found his son. Charles was fascinated by the size and smell and mechanical ingenuity of the boat. They stayed long enough to see it depart in a lather of foam and triumphant whooping from its steam-whistle, a performance that left Charles speechless. This amused his father.

Flub Phillips went back to the Killick farm.

'I've been thinking,' he said. 'Now the steamboat's on a regular run, people on the other side of the Cameron will need a ferry to get them across to here so they can … See what I mean? Trade both ways. Running a ferry would be an honest living for someone.'

'You need a big strong raft,' Joe Killick said. 'You hire two of my slaves, a dollar a day each, they'll build you the biggest, strongest raft in Dundee County.'

Nine-year-old George chose the slaves and walked them to Rock Springs, slashing at their legs with a switch from time to time. 'You got to remind them,' he told Flub. 'Otherwise they forgets.' At Rock Springs he gave Flub the switch. 'Don't take no lip,' he said. 'They give you lip, you lay it on 'em strong. On the legs is best. But don't bust 'em up. Pa says if you bust a nigger you pay for him. Niggers ain't cheap.' Then George went home.

It took a week to build the raft. The two slaves preferred working for Flub. He waved the switch a couple of times; that was all. Years of hog-farming had cured him of any wish to draw blood.

It was as big and strong a raft as Joe had promised. The slaves poled it across the Cameron, and Flub landed. Within ten yards he was knee-deep in swamp. He struggled out and they poled him upstream and he landed again. More swamp. Went downstream. Swamp again. Everywhere he tried to land: swamp.

Joe Killick was not surprised. 'Always thought that land looked kind of wet. Too green to be true. You see any alligators? Heard tell there's alligators over there. Better get them pants off and check your legs for leeches. You owe me fourteen bucks.'

'Now I know why the steamboat lands on this side and not on the other,' Flub said.

'I could've told you it was all swamp over there,' Joe said, 'if you'd asked me.'

The lack of a ferry made a difference to Rock Springs, good and bad. It meant the place could never become a crossroads town. As much as the Cameron brought travellers, it also stopped them moving on. Swamp to the west, cliffs and gorges to the north, bad trails to the east, Tennessee to the south. They'd just come either from the east or from the south, and they had no stomach for going back that way. So they mostly settled at Rock Springs. Within a year Flub Phillips was teaching school and serving hooch. Sometimes at the same time. Sometimes to the same people.

The first building in town was an inn. When Flub ran out of money to pay Judith Killick he took up teaching. That wasn't much choice: he couldn't find anyone worth marrying, and educating children seemed slightly less distasteful than raising hogs, the only other thing he knew to do. He taught in the open air, until winter came and he moved his class of seven into the inn. There was nowhere else to go. The owner, a failed lawyer named Slattery, had no objection, and Flub picked up an occasional extra pupil when a customer wandered over to watch a lesson and stayed to learn the alphabet. Slattery had no objection to that, either, provided the customer kept on drinking. Slattery didn't enjoy his work. Building the inn had pleased him. Running it bored him, therefore he expected his customers to drink hard, otherwise Slattery was wasting his time by being there. Often he said to hell with it and went hunting in the woods.

When that happened, Flub ran the bar and taught class at the same time. 'A whiskey, a pickled pig's knuckle and a plate of grits,' he told his pupils. 'How much is that? Write it down, add it up.' Spelling and sums and bartending, all combined.

Late the next spring, a wolverine was ripping into a deer carcass when Slattery came around a bend and startled them both. Slattery was four times its size but the wolverine had a mouth like a black bear and teeth like a timber wolf and it feared nothing and nobody. Its growl was as deep as a groan and the hair on its back rose in a thousand fine spines. It moved forward. Slattery's legs were empty. He tried to turn, stumbled, dropped his rifle butt-first and it shot him through the head.

The wolverine waited for a minute and then got on with the

deer. Eventually it went and sniffed the other body, but decided it could eat no more; so it turned its back and raised its tail and sprayed Slattery with a liquid so disgusting that now only a wolverine would touch this meat. Then it ambled off to find a place to sleep.

A couple of trappers found the body. The stink persuaded them to bury it where it lay. By general consent, Flub Phillips inherited the inn. Nobody else really wanted it.

That year, Rock Springs began to take shape. It got a general store, a blacksmith's shop, a place where you could have teeth pulled or boils lanced or horses doctored, and two houses. The steamboat company built a landing. Next year someone opened a laundry and bathhouse. Flub sold the inn to a woman called Maggie, and built a schoolhouse. A corn and seed business arrived. You could buy clothes in Rock Springs. It had a Main Street, which was mud and horseshit, and sidewalks, which were not. Flub missed the warmth and noise of the inn. He gave the schoolroom to his oldest pupil, who was fourteen and ready to shave, and told him he was the teacher now. A rooming-house had just opened. It wasn't full of drunks, and you could get food that wasn't pickled pig's knuckle. Flub became manager. Soon there was a bank, a church, a gunshop. One day, Flub opened the front door and looked out and saw strangers who were obviously at home. It came as a little shock: there were more people living in Rock Springs than he could easily know. Now it was a town.

The first elected mayor of Rock Springs was Joe Killick. His wasn't much of an election, but then he wasn't much of a mayor. The job paid nothing. Nobody else wanted it. Joe gave away a lot of whiskey and a show of hands did the rest.

'Flim-flam,' Henry Hudd said when his son told him.

'He got elected, sir. It was legal.'

'Votes don't change a man. It's like suds and beer. Suds rise to the top, don't they? But they're still just suds.'

'Cream rises to the top, too,' Charles said. He was fifteen, and an inch taller than his father, and beginning to have opinions of his own.

'Cream.' Henry laughed. 'You don't know the Killicks, do you?

Joe has failed as a farmer. That's why he wants to be mayor. He'll fail again, you'll see.'

'But ...' Charles was still too young to enjoy cynicism. 'They reckon he's best man for the job, sir. He deserves a fair chance.'

'*Deserves*? A man deserves what he earns. Killick fails because he's more comfortable with failure. It doesn't demand so much. From the day he came through those trees and saw I'd got here first, taken the best land, he decided he'd been cheated. What could he do? Had a choice. Could work twice as hard, got the most out of what God gave him, create a place, not as good as this, but still a place to be proud of. *Or* he could sit on his ass and bellyache about poor crops, which makes him feel better because it proves he got cheated. So now it's *my* fault.' Henry Hudd turned his head and spat. 'See? Killicks give me a sour mouth.'

'Is that why you never ask them to visit us, sir?' Charles asked. Henry nodded. 'Seems strange,' Charles said. 'Two biggest farms in the valley, not visiting. Not speaking.'

'Killicks and Hudds don't talk the same language.'

Charles thought: *Father feels good when Joe Killick fails. He likes to be superior.* But he was not brave enough to say so. Instead, he said, 'Would it not be a Christian act to offer the hand of friendship, sir?' He had been reading the Letters of St Paul. 'Nobody is so low that he can't be raised.'

'So I've heard.' Henry Hudd was tired of talking about the damn Killicks. 'If you want to do some raising, go ahead. New mayor probably needs a clerk. Go and offer yourself, see if you can improve the man's manners. But don't bring him here.'

Charles was away for a week. Henry was lonely without him. His wife was sick and often bedridden. She'd never been strong after the boy was born, certainly not strong enough to bear any more children, whereas the Killicks had bred like rabbits. Henry felt badly let down by his wife.

Charles came back after a week. 'Mr Killick needs no assistant,' he told his father, 'because he does no work. He's always in Maggie's tavern. Just drinks whiskey and plays cards.' He was frowning like a hanging judge.

Henry pretended to be surprised. 'That's too bad. What about the hand of friendship? Any luck there?'

'He accused me of spying on him.'

'An unkind remark.'

'He was foul-mouthed. He lied, and he cheated, and he tried to humiliate me. So I left.'

'Well,' Henry Hudd said, 'now you know.'

~

The Hudds despised and ignored the Killicks, and the Killicks hated and blamed the Hudds, and they went on doing this for the next fifteen years. This would have been a great test of silent endurance and perseverance, but for the Ridge between them.

It was more than five miles by water between the two farms, less than two if you climbed over the Ridge. The Cameron was that sort of river, curling like a snake. Nobody ever climbed over the Ridge. It was that sort of Ridge.

Even to save four miles, nobody would take on such a climb. It wasn't just the steepness and the undergrowth – chest-high and stiff with thorns and briars – and the deep, sudden streambeds that slashed across your path and forced a change of direction; it was also the animals. Hudd Ridge belonged to bear and panther and rattlesnake. Always had. It was true wilderness up there.

Everything separated the Hudds from the Killicks – wealth, competence, ambition, taste, education, manners – but the best barrier was the Ridge. It did a find job of keeping the peace.

But nothing lasts for ever.

A DISH OF FIRE

In the fifteen years that passed after Joe Killick got elected mayor, everyone changed. Everyone always does. Joe got kicked out of the mayor's job. Rock Springs was growing into a prosperous little town with two bars and a lawyer and a weekly newspaper, run by Flub Phillips. It didn't need a mayor who was drunk by noon and couldn't button his fly properly when he was sober. Joe went back to the farm, where he had three boys he could boss about. They were not nearly as respectful as Henry Hudd's boy had been, and that annoyed Joe. With the years, this problem got worse.

And always, the Hudd farm prospered. It would have required hard work for it not to: rich dirt, slaves to work it, good prices for crops. Henry's son married when he was twenty-three, the lawyer's daughter from town, a perfect creature, cheerful and attentive, and within a year she died, nipped in the leg by a rabid dog and gone in a week.

The shock aged Charles. When he turned thirty he looked like his father, except that of course by then his father had changed: he was stout and bald and increasingly angry. The older Henry Hudd got, the more he became convinced that only two things mattered. One was the economic value of sound and regular thrashings: to him, an unmarked nigger was a nigger not working hard enough. The other was the Bible. He developed a huge enthusiasm for certain chunks of the New Testament. These compensated somewhat for his disappointments, which were many. He had given his life to finding and creating the richest, most handsome farm in Dundee County, and what thanks had he got? His wife quit childbearing after one son. Then his son went and picked the wrong wife, and after that failure Charles lost interest in all women. Henry Hudd owned a house that some people said was as fancy as the Governor's mansion, and all for what? A weak wife and a widower son. A lesser man wou[ld have] despaired, but Henry had those two great props, those twin pi[llars of] righteousness: the lash and the Bible. Especially the New Testa[ment.]

Whenever the family and the slaves assembled for worsh[ip he] raised the brass-bound Bible, thick as a brick and three times the weight, holding it one-handed to show that his whipping arm hadn't weakened, and let the pages fall open wherever Providence thought fit. This was always at the same place. Without looking, he read aloud: '*Servants, be obedient to them that are your masters according to the flesh, with fear and trembling, in singleness of your heart, as unto Christ.* Ephesians, six, five.' *Bang*, the Bible slammed shut and he searched for a black face foolish enough to be looking at him instead of at the ground. He never saw one. Every day, for years and years, he told his slaves to be obedient with fear and trembling and by God they all bowed their heads and trembled, especially in the winter. Until the day when one didn't.

Henry Hudd stared down at him. He was a boy aged about twelve, uncommonly tall and well made, strong enough to be a field hand already. His name was Alonzo. Everyone called him Lonzo. His head was tilted and he was taking a good long look at his master. Even when their eyes met, Lonzo did not lower his head. Well, you couldn't whip a nigger during family prayers, not even a little nigger, so Henry just gave a snort to let Lonzo know what was coming and got back to business. He said a short prayer, something to do with the crops. While they mumbled their amens he glanced at his wife, who had been getting kind of tetchy lately. He opened the book at its marker, and read out: '*Let the woman learn in silence with all subjection. But I suffer not a woman to teach, nor to usurp authority over the man, but to be in silence.* First Timothy, two, eleven and twelve.' The Bible slammed again. *Pick the bones out of that, madam,* he thought, and dismissed the lot of them.

Lonzo was an unusual slave.

On a bright May day in 1848, a Virginian farmer named Dr Douglas Fox had mated a female negro with a male Cherokee. It was done on a pile of straw in a corner of a field, during the meal-break: Dr Fox saw no reason why science should interfere with good husbandry.

He had first made a close examination of both sets of sexual parts. When he was sure there was no obstacle to complete and satisfactory copulation, he told the Indian to start. It took two minutes and seven seconds. Dr Fox entered the time and other details in his journal. He had paid the Indian in tobacco and he wondered whether he had perhaps been too generous. 'If the Union be not Fruitful,' he wrote, 'I shall require another Coupling for no charge.' Business was business. Farmers had developed bigger turnips, taller wheat, fatter sheep. Now Dr Fox was experimenting, trying to breed a stronger slave. It worked. As he grew, the child's physique combined the best of both worlds: strong as a nigger and hard as a Cherokee. Fox sold Lonzo to Henry Hudd at an auction in Danville, sold him on the stump for five hundred dollars. The boy was seven years old. Hudd didn't want the mother. Fox sold her south, Mississippi or Alabama or someplace. Sold her cheap, she was all dried-up inside, useless for breeding.

Now, five years later, Henry sat in the rocker on the porch, his feet on the rail, and sent for the boy.

Lonzo was sparkling with sweat when he arrived, and his hands and wrists were red with soil. 'Stand on that block, boy,' Henry ordered. It was an oak stump that he like to use for whippings; it added a touch of ceremony. Besides, it had been sawed steeply on the slant, so whoever stood on it was easily knocked off balance. The wood was bleached white except at the top. The top was black, partly from the scuff of feet but mainly from the drip of blood. Lonzo climbed on the block.

'You were lookin' at me, boy,' Henry said.

Lonzo said nothing. It wasn't a question, and he knew better than to talk back to a white man. He picked bits of dry clay from his fingers and wondered whether or not to clench his teeth when the whip burned his back. Some said Master Henry like to hear a good loud scream, it made him happy. Some said no, screaming made him angry. Lonzo had seen him lay on the lash when he was smiling and when he was frowning. It was hard to know what to do for the best.

'Why did you look at me, boy?' Henry Hudd asked.

Lonzo heard whip in that voice. He looked at Henry's boots, which was safe, and said, 'You said to.'

That was not what Henry expected, and he laughed. For a big man, Henry had a little laugh. Like a squeak from a barn door. He didn't care what his laugh sounded like, he wasn't the one to hear it. 'I said to look?'

Lonzo nodded. The effect of standing straight on the slanted block made his stomach muscles tense up and ridge like a washboard.

'I said to look.' Henry stood. He took a buggy whip and flicked it at Lonzo's ankles. 'When did I say to look?'

'Yesday. You was readin' prayers for us all. You said … You said we got to look out for the master of the house, an' stuff.'

'What stuff?' The buggy whip stung like horseflies.

'Like not sleepin' when we should be workin'.'

'Ah.' Henry rested his elbows on the porch rail. He played with the buggy whip as if it were a fishing pole, making the lash coil softly around Lonzo's neck. 'That stuff, eh?' He propped the whip and went into the house.

Lonzo stooped and smeared clay onto his right ankle where it was bleeding. The clay would keep the flies off.

Henry came out with the big old Bible. 'If you're playin' games with me, boy,' he said mildly, 'I'll score your black hide like corduroy.' Pages flickered under his fingers. Lonzo's gut grumbled from a mixture of hunger and fear. 'You don't say,' Henry said. The pages stopped and his forefinger began searching. 'Hot damn!' he said. '*Suffer the little children to come unto me … Suffer.* That's what it says. *Suffer*. Can't argue with that. *Suffer*. You ready to suffer, boy?' His finger moved on. He turned a page. 'You ain't wrong, boy. *Watch ye therefore: for ye know not when the master of the house cometh, at even, or at midnight, or at the cockcrowing, or in the morning: Lest coming suddenly he find you sleeping.* Mark, thirteen, thirty-five and six. That what you mean, boy?'

'Yessir.' Lonzo looked him in the eye. 'Good book say watch for the master, so I watch for the master. Can't watch without lookin'. Nossir.'

'Hunh,' Henry said. It was an odd experience, looking into the eyes of a boy-slave. He had never done it before. Grey, they were. 'Hunh,' he said.

'You the master here,' Lonzo explained. 'Yessir.'

'Get down. Get back to work.' Henry's head felt tired; he wasn't accustomed to holding long discussions with his slaves; he wanted to lie down in a cool room. 'And don't do any more watchin' during prayers. You hear me clear enough. Don't need to see me as well.'

Later that day, in the cool shade of an oak, Henry thrashed an old slave called Matt, but it did not give him the satisfaction he wanted, not did it seem to make much difference to Matt, whose back was armoured with old scars.

After a dozen lashes Henry grew bored. 'Oh, get out of my sight,' he said. 'You're worse than a dead mule.' Old Matt wiped his eyes and shuffled away. *Jesus wept*, he thought, *Jesus wept, Jesus wept, Jesus wept.* He had been whipped many times, and he knew that nothing stopped the pain; but those two words gave his mind a comfort and a distraction. He had tried other words, but nothing worked like *Jesus wept*.

After supper, Henry told his son about the unusual incident with young Lonzo.

'Well, I'm not surprised,' Charles said. 'Lonzo's a smart boy.'

'Don't be a bigger fool than you can help,' Henry said.

'One of these days ...' – Charles was lighting a cigar – '... you're likely to say that and I'm likely to hit you so hard you'll bounce twice before you feel it.'

It had been a difficult day. First Lonzo, then Matt, and now his own flesh and blood. 'You raise your hand to me,' Henry said, 'and it's the last thing you'll do on my farm.'

'You're right there, father. If I knock you down you'll stay down, and then it'll be my farm.'

Henry Hudd's eyebrows went up like sash windows. 'You threatenin' me, son?'

'Damn right.' Charles blew a smoke ring and watched it wobble away. 'I'm not your boy any more and you haven't run this place for at least five years. Why? Because you don't know how.'

Henry's heart was thudding hard: hammers falling on a hot anvil. 'When I came here this land was – '

'When you came here the land was free for the taking and it was so rich that any fool could plant nickels and grow silver dollars.'

'So I'm a fool too, am I?'

'You're a fool if you think the best fertilizer is nigger sweat and nigger blood. That's a waste of good nigger brains.'

'Good nigger brains?' Henry's voice climbed until it cracked. 'Good nigger brains! Sweet Jesus, I never thought to hear such horseshit in my house!' He was talking to himself. His son was halfway upstairs, to bed.

Next morning Charles rode out into the fields and found Lonzo chopping weeds. 'Leave that and come with me,' he ordered. 'You're going to learn how to read and write.' Jacob, who was the slave in charge of that field, saw them go and ran to intercept them, striding long because his feet were heavy with dirt. 'These weeds don't get chopped, Mister Charles sir,' he said, 'somebody gonna get whipped, sir.' The *sirs* were unusual. They meant Jacob was really anxious. Matt had been whipped the day before because he broke a spade handle. The spade was twenty years old and the handle had cracked twice and been mended twice, but Matt got whipped just the same.

'Nothing to worry about,' Charles said. His horse's tail slashed at the flies. 'Nobody's gonna get whipped. In fact if Mister Henry touches you or anyone because Lonzo's with me, you come straight and tell me. Straight, you hear?'

'Aw, Mister Charles,' Jacob complained. They both knew why he was upset: to make a fuss about one whipping was to invite a second.

'Mister Henry knows what's happening. Do as I say. If you don't, I may come back and whip you myself.' He trotted off, with Lonzo holding a stirrup. Jacob stood, his arms like jug-handles, and watched them go. *Fuck*, he thought. *Fuck fuck fuck*. If he listened hard he could actually hear the goddamn weeds growing.

Henry did nothing. At breakfast Charles had bet him fifty dollars that Lonzo could be taught to read, write and do sums, all in the space of one year, provided of course that Henry did not interfere in any way. Henry had to accept. 'You educate that little nigger,' he said, 'and I'll guarantee to teach a blue-assed baboon to play polkas on the piano, using the black notes, the white notes, and the cracks in between.'

Charles taught the boy for one hour every day except Sundays, longer if the weather was bad. Henry did not interfere; nor did he punish Jacob or any other field hand if Lonzo's allotted work was not completed. This did not mean that his whipping arm got any rest. There were plenty of other slaves, male and female, who demanded correction. They were all lazy and slovenly, of course, but in addition some were insolent. This had never been the case when he was younger, but his son had loosened the bonds, and that was a fatal folly. Henry Hudd despised any slave-owner who flinched at cruelty. He knew that slavery and tyranny went hand in hand. Obedience was not natural to a slave. It had to be constantly enforced by a rigid discipline. The older he got, the more convinced Henry became of the value of chastisement. Remove fear from a negro, and in its place came laziness, mischief and impudence. He knew when a nigger was giving him an insolent look, even if he was fifty yards away. He got whipped. He knew when a bunch of niggers was telling an obscene joke about him, even though he couldn't hear the words. They got whipped. A slave deliberately stumbled and slopped a pail of milk, or took too long to catch Henry's horse, or failed to say Amen at the end of prayers: he whipped them all. It was exhausting but it had to be done or the whole damn farm would go to hell. Nobody helped. Then his wife died on him. No warning: went to bed and died in the night.

Henry mourned briefly and went straight back to work. He didn't spare himself. In the hottest hour of the hottest week he found four slaves skulking behind a wagon of logs they should have been unloading. They said one of them had broken a finger and they were attending to it, which was just the sort of thing you expect darkies to say, and he ordered their shirts off their backs instantly.

The first staggered at each bite of the lash but he made no sound. Henry was always surprised by the vivid red of negro blood. The second man did not flinch and at the end of his punishment Henry was running wet with sweat, and gasping for breath. He prayed for strength and did his best by the third man. The lash felt as heavy as an anchor rope and he could not split the skin. Sparks fizzed across Henry's vision and his chest felt as tight as barrel-hoops. The man looked at him with contempt. Henry was furious: furious at these idle slaves, at his own body, the pounding heat, the whole damn world. His whipping arm hung like a pump-handle and felt ten times heavier. The sparks had turned to soft red and yellow blotches. The fourth man was standing, waiting. The others were watching, insolently. He couldn't see them but he knew they were insolent. Insolence could not be tolerated. He forced his arm to lift the whip and suddenly the barrel-hoops tightened, grabbed, squeezed. Pain rushed from his chest and flooded his mouth. He had never tasted such pain. It was like a dish of fire.

JUNGLE IN THEIR BLOOD

Henry Hudd was the first man to be buried in the new grave-yard at Rock Springs. The town had grown so much that the old church was too small, and a bigger church was built on a mound at the top end of Main Street. Its graveyard was untouched. Henry got a prime slot.

The burial attracted quite a crowd, but mainly for its novelty, for half the mourners had never met Henry. 'Tragic, truly tragic,' they said to his son. 'A great man taken in his prime. We shall not see his like again.' 'Uh-huh,' Charles said. 'Uh-huh.' They moved on, touched by his stoicism.

But a distant cousin turned up, and to him Charles said, 'The old bastard flogged himself to death. Dug his own grave with his whip. God knows best.' Jake overhead this and disapproved strongly. That was no way to speak about your father. Master Henry had been the Lord's agent on Earth, said so in the Bible. '*Let as many servants as are under the yoke count their own masters worthy of all honour, that the name of God and his doctrine not be blasphemed.*' First Timothy, six, one. Jake knew it by heart. Heard it often enough. If God told the niggers to honour Henry, then Charles ought to honour him too. But Jake kept his black mouth shut. Another verse had been pounded into his brain year after year: '*Servants, be subject to your master with all fear, not only to the good and gentle, but also to the froward.*' First Peter, two, eighteen. And Jake knew for sure there was nothing in the Bible that allowed a nigger to be froward. Whatever that meant.

After the funeral everyone got asked back to the Hudd place for refreshments. It was worth the hot ride. Word had got out that Charles had not spared himself and there was honey-glazed ham, beef cooked three ways, glazed tongue, some kind of fancy turkey

23

dish, chicken with hot biscuit, sweet potatoes and various greeneries, plus seven different sorts of fruit pie, fresh lemonade by the tub and even wine for those who had mourned most strenuously and needed reviving.

The entire Killick family came. Few had ever seen the Hudd house before and they were impressed. It was a fantasticated three-storey affair, hung with balconies and verandahs and topped with ambitious eaves and gables. It made the Killick place look like a jumble of shacks. Mrs Judith Killick, eating hard, complained to her married sister of the injustice: Look here, Charlie Hudd had all this and no family, she said, while the Killick outfit was smaller and poorer and God had sent her all these children.

'Maybe He wouldn't have sent 'em if you and Joe hadn't spent so much time bouncin' about in bed, prayin',' her sister said.

'The Lord gave me a fertile womb, Sarah.'

Her sister took some fried pepper rings. 'Oh, sure,' she said.

'You can't argue with Divine Will.'

'Can't you? I sure did.'

'That's blasphemy, then.'

'Maybe so. There was one night when Arthur kept on wanting his oats until I put my knee in his nuts. Plenty of blaspheming took place, as I recall, but nobody got knocked-up.'

'Oh well,' Judith Killick said. 'Too late now. What kind of pickles are those? Gimme some anyway.'

'I don't believe it. You eatin' for two already?'

'It's a safe bet,' Judith said complacently.

Charles Hudd moved through the crowd, joking with the men, flattering the women. Nobody mentioned his father. Henry was history now, part of the terrain, like the woods on the hills beyond the Cameron, red maples and cedars that trembled in the slow breeze following the river.

The best place to take your plate was under the shade trees around the house, some of them taller than the roof, and it was at a table beneath a massive old oak that Charles Hudd found Joe Killick with cranberry sauce on his chops. Charles sat beside him. His legs were beginning to ache.

'I'll give you this,' Killick said, turning a turkey leg to find any overlooked meat, 'you got a bunch of smart niggers.'

'Indeed?' Charles Hudd hadn't noticed; his slaves were part of the setting, like the gates and wells. It was like being complimented on having clever livestock.

'Yessir. I been watchin' your niggers and they don't drag their black asses all the time, they don't fall asleep and wait to be told. I mean, look at this nigger here now.' A female slave called Polly was bringing a crystal jug of lemonade and some tumblers to the table. 'Real smart ...' As she poured the lemonade he said, 'Tell you what I'll do. I'll swap you a sow in litter ...' He picked his back teeth and sucked his forefinger. Charles sipped lemonade. 'And my best pair of mules.' Charles shook his head. He was uncomfortable: this was the wrong time to do business, and he wished Killick would wipe the sauce off his chops. 'Throw in a bottle of whiskey,' Killick offered, and grinned to show it was all in fun. He was a stocky man, too short in the legs for such a powerful body, and his red hair was fading. The top half of his forehead, always shielded by his hat, was white as a new mushroom. The grin pushed his face out sideways until it looked as wide as it was long. 'Prime whiskey,' Killick said. 'I always give a slug to a nigger that gets snake-bit. Don't cure 'em but they die smilin'.'

'You can go, Polly,' Charles Hudd said. He wanted to move on but it would be ill-mannered to walk away without having finished his lemonade.

'Smart *and* handsome,' Joe Killick said. 'White blood in there somewhere?'

'No.'

Killick worked his lower lip in an amused manner. 'Ain't no crime for a man to improve his stock.'

'So you say.'

'A duty and a pleasure, some might think.'

'No doubt. But not here.'

'Still and all ... Just look at the nose on that nigger there. Straight as an arrowhead. And the mouth, you can't tell me that mouth came out of Africa, Mr Hudd.'

'Cherokee,' Charles said. 'I understand some Cherokee blood may be present.' He finished his lemonade, got to his feet and saw a startlingly pretty young woman coming across the grass, carrying a dish of blancmange with peaches sliced into it. He pretended to have stood up in order to reach for the jug. She was a Killick: flaming hair escaped from a straw bonnet in a froth of curls. But her face was

25

different from the family's broad muscularity. It was slim, and the eyes were alert. That was what Charles Hudd saw: a lively mind behind a vivid face. Or maybe a vivid mind behind a lively face. He was too surprised to care. He refilled his tumbler, and smiled as she put the dish in front of Joe Killick and gave him a spoon.

'You've not met my JoBeth, Mr Hudd?' Killick said. 'Ugly, ain't she?' For a moment, pride washed his face clean.

'As the dawn. As the dewy rose.' Charles amazed himself by his eloquence. 'No, I haven't had the pleasure.' They shook hands. 'My loss,' he said, and shut up before he overdid things.

'I've been livin' down in Tennessee,' she said. 'Near Nashville. Gettin' myself educated.'

'Whatever *that* means,' her father said.

'It means learnin' not to eat soup with your fingers,' she said. 'Can I fetch you some dessert, Mr Hudd?'

'Most kind of you.'

They watched her walk away. Her summerweight skirt moved like a blue shadow of the limbs inside it. 'Haven't seen that girl bucknaked since she was thirteen,' Killick said thoughtfully, 'but from memory she got legs could break a grown man's heart and a sweet little butt like two halves a honeydew melon.'

'Allow me to restore your glass,' Charles Hudd said. He spilled a little. It could happen to anyone.

'Brains, too. From her momma's side, I guess.' Killick spooned down blancmange. 'My problem, Mr Hudd, is I am the stupidest member of my entire family.' He chuckled. Charles Hudd could think of nothing to say, so he smiled. 'Take young George,' Killick said. 'Not so young any more. Just a few years behind you. In a fair world, he'd of gone to college. If God hadn't meant him for college, why give him the brains? I don't mean you to answer that. There ain't no answer.'

'Puzzling, I agree.' If he cocked his head, Charles could see JoBeth returning through the crowd.

'Maybe the good Lord is testin' me out, see if I can't help George somehow.' Killick scraped out the corners of his bowl and licked his spoon clean. 'This is a big, big place you got here now,' he said. 'A lot of land for just one white man to manage. *Lot* of land. Think you might get lonely?'

Charles Hudd nearly said no and then nearly said yes. Either way seemed wrong. 'Might do,' he said. He cranked up a smile for JoBeth.

'You ever consider takin' on an overseer,' Killick said, 'I'd certainly appreciate it if you'd think on my George first of all.'

'Uh-huh.' JoBeth was getting closer. But for the presence of this mob he would have taken her hand and led her into his house, up the staircase and onto his feather bed, this very minute. Or so his loins dreamed. 'Excellent,' he said. 'Admirable.' She put the dessert in front of him, and dropped a hint of a curtsy, almost mockingly. 'You are far too considerate,' he said.

'Just a passin' thought,' Killick said. 'Still, if it's any use to you I'm glad to have been of help.'

She picked up his bowl. 'If Pa's bein' helpful, you'd better lock up your spoons,' she said.

'Mr Hudd's thinkin' of takin' on George as his overseer.'

'Only thinking,' Charles said quickly. 'Maybe next time I'm over your way I might stop by and talk to him.' And see his sister again.

'Stay to supper,' she said. 'Make a change to have someone civilized in the house.'

'I'll be pleased to.' For a funeral, he thought, this was turning out a most enjoyable day. He whacked a nosy wasp with his spoon and began to eat.

Next day he rode over to the Killick place, and stayed for supper. The meal was plain but he hardly noticed. And before he left, he had hired George as his overseer.

~

If he had lived, Henry Hudd would probably have been fifty dollars richer. Young Lonzo was bright but not brilliant, and he did not take readily to learning. In particular he did not take to reading the Bible, which Charles reckoned would be a good English primer because most of the words were short.

At first they made slow but steady progress. Charles's method was to tell Lonzo to open the book anywhere, it didn't matter where, put his finger on the page and start reading. One day his finger landed on Genesis, nineteen, twenty-six.

He studied it in silence for a couple of minutes. 'Dunno,' he said gloomily.

'Try it.'

Lonzo squared his shoulders. 'But,' he began, 'his wife ...' He glanced up. Charles nodded, and said, 'Wife, right.'

'But his wife ... looked ... back ... from ... From behind him ... and she ...' He was defeated.

'Became,' Charles said.

'She became ... a ... I dunno this word.'

'Pillar. Sort of thing that holds a house up. Round like a tree. You've seen 'em.'

'Pillar. Became a pillar ... of salt.' He rubbed his nose. 'That right? Salt?'

'What it says, Lonzo.'

'This woman ... real woman, flesh an' blood an' all ... an' then she's all salt.'

'According to the Bible.'

'Salt all through. Not just salty on the outside.'

'Solid salt. It was a punishment. She was Lot's wife. The Lord told Lot and his family to escape from Sodom and Gomorrah and not ever to look back. They escaped, but ...' He shrugged.

'Mrs Lot done took a look.'

'Yes.'

'So the Lord done killed her.'

'I guess so.'

'Jus' for turnin' her head, she's made a pillar of salt.'

'Uh-huh.'

'You believe that, Mistah Charles?'

'The good book says so.'

'Good book says Methuselah lived nine hundred an' sixty-nine years.'

'Indeed it does.'

'Says Samson killed a thousand men with the jaw of an ass.'

'That too.'

Lonzo closed the big, heavy Bible, taking care not to crease the page. 'Seems like anything' the Lord wants,' he said, 'the Lord gits.'

'Time you did some writing.' Charles was beginning to feel angry and defeated: Lonzo was not the absorbent pupil he had expected. 'Remember, don't press too hard.'

'That Mrs Lot,' Lonzo said. 'I guess she musta bin a white lady.'

Charles had to think fast. 'Seems probable. Why?'

'Can't see the Lord makin' a pillar of *black* salt. No use to nobody, *black* salt.'

A week later Lonzo chanced to open the Bible at First Kings, twelve, eleven: *My father hath chastised you with whips, but I will chastise you with scorpions*; and that was the end of the Bible as a reading primer, for a while, at least. Instead they used newspapers: the *Frankfort Yeoman, Bowling Green Bugle, Dundee County News*. Lonzo enjoyed the crime reports, the bloodier the better. Soon he was stammering and charging his way through stories of hold-ups, of shoot-outs, of the fearful damage inflicted on honest citizens who tried to resist burglars, and (less often) of the battering given to incompetent burglars by citizens who kept clubs at their bedside. Lonzo enjoyed it all. It came out of a world he had never seen. His world was one of monotonous toil, dull food and niggers who lived and died with one thought in their heads: obedience. Now here was Mister Charles showing him that somewhere out there, over the hill, up or down the river or both, there were people who did bad things to each other, really terrible bad things, like whacking someone on the head and stealing all his money, or sticking him full of holes with a knife because he ran off with your wife (this baffled Lonzo; white folk never ran anywhere; any running needed done, the niggers did it), and the most amazing part about these crimes was *the feller didn't always get caught!* Lonzo had been raised to believe that the whip followed the crime as sure as night followed day. Sometimes the whip had come *before* the crime, if Mister Henry gave you a few licks on account you looked like you might do something bad tomorrow or the next day. Now Lonzo was reading in these newspapers about folk who were free to do exactly what they wanted, such as the blacksmith in Tompkinsville who split his neighbour's head with an axe because he didn't like the way the feller combed his hair. Last seen, the blacksmith was rafting down the Cumberland River. 'He gonna get away?' Lonzo asked. 'Nobody chasin' him too hard. Not so the paper says, anyways.'

Charles Hudd looked at the date. 'My guess is he's gone west by now. Missouri, Kansas, Alabama, maybe Nebraska Territory even. Plenty of call for good blacksmithin' out west. What did the other feller do? The one got hit?'

Lonzo searched the report. 'Irish.'

'That's not a job. That's a misfortune.'

The remark passed over Lonzo's head. He read on. 'Sez he was a waiter in the ho-tel.'

Charles grunted. Lonzo understood *that* sound. Whatever an Irish waiter was, and Lonzo had not the slightest idea, his end was no loss, not according to Mister Charles's reckoning. 'Irish,' he said. 'Is Irish same as white folks?'

'They ain't niggers,' Charles said. 'And that's about as far as I can go. Now, you got your pencil? Start copyin' out this seed catalogue. Try and keep your letters all the same size this time.' Lonzo licked the lead and tried.

While he was trying he was thinking: you didn't have to be a nigger to get whopped by a whitey. The thought was encouraging. He began to hum as he worked. Charles heard him, came over and seized him by the ears. 'You enjoyed that terrible killin', didn't you? Know what you are? Just a brute an' a savage! How can you take pleasure in such sufferin'?'

'As long as that blacksmith's whackin' another feller's head,' Lonzo said, 'he ain't whackin' mine.'

The logic was irresistible. Next day Charles produced the *Farmer's Almanack* and told Lonzo to read the section on Hog Diseases and Their Treatment. It was heavy, sweaty weather. The breeze was fitful; it came and went as if to irritate by reminding what it could do if it wished. Lonzo blinked at the technical terms, and grew drowsy. Charles gave up. 'To hell with the goddamn hogs,' he said wearily. 'Get a newspaper.' What worked, worked.

～

The first gunshot blew a hole in the silence of the morning. Out of that hole emerged the clamour of birds. By the time Charles Hudd reached the front porch the noise was settling, like the birds themselves. He could see them, circling a distant patch of woods on the uphill edge of the farm. Then came the second shot and that was too much for the birds; they fled, screaming – black swirls climbing against the smooth blue bowl.

Wrong time of year for professional hunters, wrong weapon for any kind of hunter. Pistol shots. Charles got his horse and rode over to see.

George Killick was up a shagbark hickory. He saw Charles

approaching and climbed down to meet him, finding handholds in the fissured trunk and reaching with his long legs from branch to branch. Standing at the base of the tree was an old slave called John. George's horse grazed nearby.

'Trouble?' Charles called.

'Couple of rascally-lookin' types,' George said. He brushed down his moleskin vest, green with powdery tree-moss. 'White fellers, not from these parts. Tryin' to take Old John away.'

'Abolitionists.'

'Reckon so.'

'What did they say?'

'I was too far off to hear, Mr Hudd. Old John was lookin' for a strayed sow. This pair was tryin' to hustle him off, so I fired an' they left in a hurry.'

'Which way?'

George pointed to the woods. It was all rocks and ravines up there, no place for a horseman. All wild vines and brambles, too. No place for a man on foot if his feet were in riding boots.

Charles turned to the slave. He was picking bits of dead skin from his fingers. His hands were his tools; they were constantly getting worn away. 'You all right, John?' Charles asked and got a nod for an answer. The slave had a cleft palate and he was deaf in one ear. No point in trying to talk to him unless you had twenty minutes to spare.

'Couldn't see them from up the tree,' George said. 'Guess they hid in the wood.'

'Abolitionists,' Charles said. 'I'll be damned.' The word had appeared often enough in newspapers, usually in reports of fanatics in the North who organized protection of runaways, which was contrary to the Fugitive Slave Act and clearly illegal. But this was the first time Abolitionists had actually shown themselves in Dundee County. 'They've got a brass gall, just walkin' in like that.'

'Worse'n horse thieves,' George said. He had the strong, square face of the Killicks. As he looked at Old John his jaw was clenched and his brow was lined.

'You did well,' Charles said. 'Nothin' like a bullet up his ass to speed a man on his way.'

'Wish I'd hit 'em. Too far off. Besides, Old John was standin' right nearby.'

That afternoon JoBeth came over to visit her brother. It was the fourth visit in a week and she didn't care all that much for George; Charles knew this for a fact because she'd told him so. When she arrived at the house, George was in some remote field, overseeing the endless weed-chopping. Charles invited her to freshen up. She came back looking, he thought, as lovely as a flower. She kissed him on the cheek. 'Sweet Jesus!' he said.

'Heavens,' she said. 'That was just being friendly.'

'I was surprised.'

'Wait till you get a real kiss on the lips. You'll be astonished.'

They went into the drawing room, cool and dark with half the shades drawn. 'How is your family?' he asked.

'Dead drunk in a ditch.' That made him stare. 'Well,' she said, 'you don't care a tinker's cuss how my family is, so let's not waste time on them.'

'You're in a very curious mood today.'

'No, today I'm normal. The times before when I came here I was acting like a proper, well-brung-up young lady, which I am not, and it near to killed me.' She smiled with a tomboy twist to her mouth that made him suddenly afraid that perhaps all his flies were undone. One of the house slaves came in, a woman called Sarah, bringing cold mint tea. Charles took the opportunity to stroll to a window and secretly check his buttons. They were fastened, but he still felt insecure. For no reason that he could think of, he said, 'I don't want to be disturbed for the rest of the afternoon, Sarah. Miss Killick and I have business to discuss.'

Sarah nodded, and closed the door behind her.

'Well, now you've ruined our reputations,' JoBeth said.

'Nonsense. How can you say that?'

'Niggers know better than to leave two white folks together. White folks still got all that jungle in their blood. Dey ain't dun got noooooh self-control, no suh.'

Charles handed her a glass of tea. 'What balderdash you do talk,' he said, and he contrived to touch her fingers.

'Balderdash?' She was very amused. 'That's a genuine three-dollar word, that is. That's the kind of word you keep locked away with the best china.'

'Why are you making fun of me?' he asked. 'What have I done?'

'Nothing. It's time you did something, Charlie Hudd, before you die like your father.' He was lost for words. Nobody had ever talked

32

to him like this. He felt the blood come pounding up an artery in the side of his neck. *Hell's teeth*, he thought, *maybe that's how father died*, and he forced himself to sprawl in an armchair and smile. It felt like an amiable grin. He caught sight of himself in a mirror. His lips were barely curled.

'How long since your wife passed away?' she asked.

'Seven years.'

'How long since you bought a new suit of clothes?'

'Seven years.'

'What I thought. Bet you wore the same clothes to both funerals.'

'None of your business.' He was about to get up when she came and sat on the arm of his chair. 'Suit still fits,' he said.

'Sure it does. You still got the same shape body. Nothing wrong with that. Why dress it up in gloomy old clothes?'

He looked down at himself. 'Plenty of wear left in these. Anyway, I thought grey flannel was fashionable.'

'Wrong. It went out just before the codpiece came in.' That startled him. He looked up and realized what a thrusting bust she had. He blinked. There was a gap down the middle big enough to eat strawberry fool out of. 'Why don't you get yourself a bottle-green corduroy coat?' she asked. 'And white linen pants?'

'This is a farm. White linen isn't practical.'

'You don't do the laundry. How many house-slaves you got?'

'None of your damn business.' He felt like he was being chased around a field, and it was *his* damn field. 'Anyway, you don't know what a codpiece is.'

'Men's long johns with half a turnip shoved down the front to make the company believe he's loaded for bear.'

He made an effort to frown, and found himself laughing. 'Is that what they taught you in Tennessee?'

'They didn't teach me much,' she said, 'but what little I learned, there was no make-believe in it. Stand up.' He stood. She put her hands inside his coat and slid them up and down his ribcage. 'You have a fine body,' she said. 'Far too good to waste on grief.'

'Um,' he said.

The action turned into a hug. 'Also,' she said, 'you grow handsome turnips.' She released him.

'This is crazy,' he said. 'We hardly know each other.'

'Does that matter?'

'Perhaps not, but … What will people think?'

'Does *that* matter?'

'No.'

'What matters?'

'Being happy.' The answer came so fast that he had to stop and think again. 'Yes, being happy,' he said.

'Well, we're agreed on *that*. Come on, take me to my brute of a brother so I can say I've done my duty.'

On their way across the fields he told her about the foiled Abolitionist raid. 'George saved me five or six hundred dollars right there,' he said.

'Down in Rock Springs, lot of talk about secedin'.'

'They'll talk and they'll talk. It's a handy threat to make the North keep its agitators in line. We don't need secession. We got the Constitution on our side.'

ALTOGETHER LOVELY

The more Charles Hudd taught Lonzo, the less he liked him. The boy was clever and determined but he lacked humility. He lacked gratitude. Charles didn't expect great thanks but a little obvious respect, some deference, some acknowledgment that this was rare and privileged treatment, would have pleased him.

As it was, Lonzo treated the lessons like part of his daily toil. He came straight from the fields, seeds in his hair, broken fingernails, dried snot on his nostrils, stinking of sweat. Charles was used to nigger sweat, it was part of the scenery, sweeter than the smell of a lathered horse and a whole lot sweeter than a tomcat's squirt. He put his feet on the porch rail and listened as Lonzo ploughed through the crime columns. The boy's thumbs made dirty imprints on the paper when he found an especially bloody murder.

Later they did simple arithmetic. Lonzo followed instructions and sometimes got the right answer. He couldn't see any point in it. Multiply eight dollars fifteen cents by six, Mister Charles said, and when Lonzo finally got it, forty-eight dollars ninety on the nail, Mister Charles was so bright-eyed you'd think the money just fell out the sky. Lonzo sucked his pencil. He wasn't ever going to see eight dollars fifteen cents, not this side of heaven, and probably not the other side either, unless God turned out to be a nigger, and if He *was* a nigger then old man Henry Hudd must've died a second time, right there at the Pearly Gates.

'Not bad,' Charles said. 'Now multiply nine dollars ninety-nine by four.'

Lonzo sighed. He began writing the numbers, slowly and heavily, his thumb squashed against the pencil, the nail white with gloom.

'You can do it in your head,' Charles told him. 'Nine ninety-nine is a penny short of ten dollars. Right? What's four tens?'

'Forty,' Lonzo said. He made it sound as if Charles had beaten it out of him.

'Now take off four cents.'

Lonzo hunched his shoulders and screwed up his eyes. The harder his mind worked, the more figures it had to hold. Too many. He lost some. The rest were useless. Forget them all. Go back, start again. His head hurt and he groaned.

'You got to *think*,' Charles urged. 'It's easy.'

Lonzo thought. Through the jumble of numbers clogging his brain, one idea emerged. 'Give the man the four cents,' he suggested. 'Then everyone happy.'

Charles hooked his foot under Lonzo's chair and tipped it and sent him sprawling. 'Uppity nigger,' he said. 'Get back to your field.'

Lonzo went. He couldn't figure what he'd done wrong. Four cents didn't mean a damn thing to Mister Hudd. White folks were peculiar.

~

After the invasion of the Abolitionists came the whiskey-bottle fire.

Charles saw smoke as he was riding home from town. It was in a hay-meadow near the river, and the smoke was as rich as grey velvet and just about as motionless, it being a hot and heavy afternoon. He got there in one long gallop and by then the smoke had mostly gone. George Killick was organizing a dozen slaves with rakes and sticks and buckets of water. Half a haystack was broken down and scattered. Here and there small spurts of flame lived and died. 'Keep that water comin'!' George bawled. 'I want all this stuff wetter'n wet!' Charred bits of hay dotted his hair. His hands and forearms were black.

Charles dismounted. 'Could have been a lot worse, I suppose.' Now the fire was out he could afford to seem casual.

'Awful shame, Mr Hudd.' George's chest was heaving. 'That was real good hay.'

'Yeah. You got here quick.'

'Uh-huh. Not quick enough.'

'I'm not complainin', George. Half a stack's better'n no damn hay. What worries me is *why*. I've known a stack take fire before, but never this time of year.'

They walked over to it. The ground was so hot it was steaming.

'Water here!' Charles shouted. George stepped on something that clinked. 'Hey, hey,' he said. He poked around with his boot and kicked out half a whiskey-bottle.

'That's your fire-lighter,' Charles said. 'Sun plus glass equals flame.'

'Someone lookin' for a soft bed where he could drink hisself to sleep, left us this little keepsake.'

'Trapper? There's plenty on the river.'

'They're worse'n animals themselves.' George was thoroughly disgusted. 'Shouldn't be allowed on a decent man's property.'

~

Usually she rode over in the afternoon, but for once she arrived in mid-morning and nobody at the house knew where Charles was. An old slave called Martha was washing the windows. She had cataracts in both eyes, so the glass ended up smudged and smeared, but Martha always washed the windows, would be miserable if someone else did it. Sarah went round later and wiped away the smears while Martha was out looking for eggs, which she could find by feel. 'You want to wait, Mizz Killick?' Martha asked. 'Fix you some coffee.'

'I think I hear him. Ain't that him? Never heard him sing before.'

The voice led her to a cluster of barns and sheds around a cobbled yard. There was a pump in the middle. The slave Jacob was keeping it gushing, Charles Hudd was grabbing bucket after bucket and flinging the water at Lonzo, who was naked and standing with hands on his hips and delight on his face. '*Let us gather at the river,*' Charles sang, '*the glorious,*' – another couple of gallons crashed against Lonzo's chest – '*glorious river!*'

She sat on her haunches in the shade, and watched. Naked little niggers were not an unusual sight, she passed them every day, but Lonzo was not little. His chest and arms were big enough to heave a sack of meal. Each time the water hit him, his stomach muscles outlined themselves like an anatomical drawing. His calves and thighs had grown strong through walking and working all day, every day. Bright morning sunlight on sharp water made his skin look not black but dark bronze. He was like a statue of a young athlete. Charles was singing and swinging buckets, but she wasn't watching Charles.

It was Jacob noticed her and stopped pumping. Charles looked where Jacob was looking. He threw an old flour sack at Lonzo; it had holes cut out for head and arms: nothing comes cheaper than free. He walked over to her.

'This is no place for you. Why didn't you wait at the house?' He tried to speak softly. Embarrassment skewed his face and gave his words a harsh edge. He tried to steer her away but she slipped his grasp.

'I've got eight brothers,' she said. 'Nothin's likely to come as a big surprise to me now.'

'That's not the point. This kind of thing's dangerous. Suppose Lonzo thinks … You know what I mean.'

'What? That I like his body?'

This time Charles grabbed her arm and hustled her around the corner. 'You crazy?'

'No. Just human. The way that boy's put together is enough to make any natural young woman want to jump out of her clothes and into the long grass.'

'That's tar-and-featherin' talk.' They were walking back to the house.

'Because I say it don't mean I'd *do* it. Anyway, you should be flattered. I wouldn't say it anywhere but here. You don't know what it's like bein' a Killick. Heaven for Killicks is ownin' a plantation where the whiskey comes out of a fountain, and the women slaves lie on top and do all the work and say thank-you nicely. Pa reckons a nigger's like a mule except he'd rather have a picture of the mule hangin' on the wall.'

'Hey, hey, slow down.' This line of talk made Charles Hudd uncomfortable. If he had to choose, he'd sooner look at a mule too.

'I'm not goin' fast. I'm not goin' anywhere.'

'Just remember the Bible tells us God put the negro race on Earth to serve as beasts of burden. Bible says that.'

'Bible says not to eat pork. Don't see too many people around here payin' attention to *that*.'

'You defying Holy Writ?'

'You givin' up bacon?'

They stopped, and took a long look at each other. A small part of him was flickering with anger, for no woman had ever spoken to him like that, but mostly and overwhelmingly he was intrigued and enchanted by someone who not only was so pretty but also had such a smart mind. She looked and saw a man who was worth all the Killicks rolled into one, not saying a whole lot but still a pleasant, even an exciting experience. 'Not here,' she said. 'Too hot.'

They moved under a shade tree, a giant sycamore, and kissed on the lips, first cautiously, then firmly, and finally with a drunken, swaying recklessness that ended in laughter and a slow collapse onto the cool ground.

'His mouth is most sweet,' she said cheerfully, 'yea, he is altogether lovely. This is my beloved, and this is my friend, O daughters of Jerusalem.' He rested on his elbows and stared. 'See, the Good Book ain't all junk,' she said. 'Song of Solomon, five, sixteen.'

'Altogether lovely.'

'Well, maybe not *altogether*.' She reached out and rubbed his chin. 'Ever think of buyin' a new razor?'

'Haven't got time for fuss an' feathers.'

'You got time to wash your boy-slave. You do that every mornin', or just when it don't rain?'

He explained. Lonzo had turned up for his lesson stinking of cow manure. The farm kept a small herd of milk cows and Lonzo had been shovelling their muck out of a stall. He was up to the knees in filth and well spattered above that level. The stench hung about him like an evil steam. Around the stench hung a flock of flies. Lonzo was surprised by Charles's loud displeasure. 'You want me to go wash my han's, Mistah Charles?' he said. Charles ordered him to the pump, collected Jacob on the way, and she knew the rest. 'Fun,' he said. 'And I needed the exercise.'

'You need a son, is what you need. And believe me, you ain't never gonna wash that one white.'

Charles was ready to send Lonzo back to work but she protested: she wanted to see him being educated. Charles refused. She would distract the boy, fluster him. No, no, she said. 'Look,' he said, suddenly impatient, 'it's too damn hot, an' that dress of yours is too damn loose. I can see your nipples and I'm not even *tryin'*.' That silenced her. He was taken aback by his own candour. 'Well, all right, sit indoors if you like,' he said. 'You'll hear everything through the jalousies just as loud.'

Lonzo was waiting on the porch. He almost groaned when he saw the brass-bound Bible.

'This is just for once,' Charles said. He pointed out the place.

'Behold …' Lonzo said tentatively. 'Behold?' Charles nodded. 'Speak up,' he said. 'Behold is right. Speak up loud.' Lonzo took a run at it. 'Behold, thou art fair, my love,' he said. 'Behold thou art fair … Hey, this is easy.'

'Verse five,' Charles said. 'And speak up!'

Lonzo found it. 'Thy two …' His lips framed the word several times before he attempted it. 'Breasts,' he said. Charles nodded. Lonzo shrugged. 'Thy two breasts are like two young roes …'

'Kind of deer. Let's hear it again. Tell it to the whole world.'

'Thy two breasts are like two young roes!' Lonzo cried, 'that are … twins, which feed among the … the lilies.' He looked up. 'This kinda stuff always been in the Bible, Mistah Charles?'

Charles took the book from him and read aloud. 'Thou hast ravished my heart, my sister, my spouse. Thou hast ravished my heart with one of thine eyes, with one chain of thy neck.' He slammed it shut. 'Understand?'

'Nossir.'

'Me neither. It's all a mystery. Here, find yourself some original sin.' He tossed a newspaper at him.

Lonzo knew where to look. 'Man Shot Three Times In Tavern,' he announced. This was good. This was better than shovelling cowshit.

~

Every week, after the Abolitionist raid and the whiskey-bottle fire, George Killick did something that proved his worth as an overseer.

He shot a bobcat that had been killing the chickens. Charles had never even seen a bobcat before, dead or alive, although he knew they were up in the Ridge, along with a dozen other wild beasts, from black bear to ringneck snakes. Why a bobcat would come down from the Ridge, where there must be rodents and rabbits for the taking, was more than Charles could understand, but George had the evidence with feathers still on its chops, so that was good enough.

In fact, George was vigilant and hard-working and efficient; and soon Charles let him get on with running the farm. The slaves knew what to do, and how, and when: if George didn't understand anything, they explained it.

His sister visited regularly and often never saw him; it was a big farm and he was off in some far corner, overseeing things. At first Charles suggested they ride out there, take George a jug of lemonade.

'Is he fit and well?'

'Was this morning.'

'Good. He can last until tomorrow. You want to be kissed right here where everyone can watch, or were you plannin' on waiting till sundown?'

She spoke pleasantly. She always did; it was one of the things that Charles found most delightful. His experience of women was small. His late wife had lived briefly and died swiftly. He had found that discouraging. Why argue with Providence? God always won: Lonzo was right about that. In any case, because he was a widower, women had treated Charles like some kind of emotional cripple: they were kind and gentle and bloody boring. JoBeth wasn't boring. She had a voice like butter and a mind like a hot knife. She was worth listening to.

They went inside. 'Everybody knows about us, anyway,' he said.

'I do believe you're right. You know about us, don't you, Sarah?' she said to the house slave.

'I know nuff to keep my big black mouf shut.' Sarah was sweeping the floor. The broom whisked dust vigorously, left and right, spreading it fairly so there would be some to sweep up tomorrow.

'Leave that now, Sarah,' Charles said.

'You don't approve of me,' JoBeth said pleasantly. 'You don't think I'm good enough for your master.'

'Ain't *nobody* good enough for Mister Charles.' Sarah's feet slapped. The door banged.

They embraced, and his lips enjoyed her mouth as greedily as if he had been a sailor home from a year at sea. Finally both were sated, the kissing stopped, the heads slid apart, and he released a long, shuddering breath, a sound of pure animal gratitude. 'Keep your feet still,' she murmured into his ear, 'Sarah's downstairs listenin' to every creak of the floorboards.' He laughed like a schoolboy, a natural explosion of happiness, and their bodies shook together in his laughter.

~

JoBeth flattered herself. The Hudd slaves neither approved nor disapproved. They didn't care what Charles got up to with her: that was his business, and at the end of the day they were too weary and too

41

hungry to think of anything but food and sleep. You try it: you bend your back for ten, twelve hours in a field under a sun that's fit to bake you blacker than you are, if it could, and see at the end if you're much interested in other people's fun and frolics. You try it. Look out, here comes tomorrow, another day's toil. Killick woman? What Killick woman? She was not of their world. She was invisible.

Lonzo was another matter.

His getting lessons surprised and puzzled the other Hudd slaves. White people were always acting peculiar, that was what having empty days and full pockets did to a man's brain, added to which some were filled with strange notions, all delivered by God himself: Mormons, Quakers, Baptists, Shakers, Methodists, Catholics, Lutherans ... The Hudd slaves heard rumours of them, how they sometimes fought each other to keep God happy. Or maybe God made them fight, it was His world, He could do what the hell He liked with it. But Charles was not educating Lonzo for God's sake, and the other niggers couldn't figure out his reason.

A slave called Josh had an idea. Josh had ideas about everything. He'd lost three fingers when the front wheel of a wagon ran over his hand, and then the back wheel had crushed a few toes, leaving him worth only about sixty cents in the dollar, and he made up for it by trying to impress. 'I know what's goin' on,' he said. 'I see right clear through it like it was a glass window.'

'Smart nigger,' Nat said. Nat was twice his age. They were sprawling in the shade, a dozen of them, chewing and drinking, taking their midday break, the time when time went by twice as fast. Nat was ready for some foolishness to help lighten the rest of a hard day. 'Say what.'

'Why, it's obvious,' Josh said. 'Mistah Charles plannin' to save himself some money. Lonzo gonna be overseer here one day.'

That got a laugh.

'Nigger overseer'd be real cheap,' Josh said. 'Half what this Killick fellah gets. *Less*'n half.'

'Hey, Lonzo!' called an old woman named Ruthie. 'You hear that? Josh just cut your wages *twice*.'

'Overseer don't get no wages,' Lonzo said.

A few hoots and lazy whistles went his way. It was too hot for loud derision. Lonzo grinned.

'He knows,' Josh said. 'The li'l nigger knows.' Lonzo was as tall as Josh, and a lot stronger.

'Tell you when you'll see a black overseer.' This was Bettsy, resting back-to-back against Ruthie. 'When hell freezes an' I get a piece a the ice to suck on. That's when.'

'Ain't a terrible hard job, overseer,' Josh pointed out. 'You got to read and write some, an' figure dollars an' cents enough so you know when cheatin's goin' on. Lonzo's halfway there now.'

'He gets to be overseer,' said Jacob, 'Killick man's out of a job. White folks don't do things that way.'

'So what's goin' on?' Nat asked. He yawned, and felt the seductive tug of fatigue. 'Mistah Charles workin' awful hard on Lonzo.' He shut his eyes and took pleasure in the free play of colour on his eyeballs.

'I know why,' said Buck. He sounded as if he was talking to himself: a whispery voice softening into a lisp. Buck's teeth didn't fit his mouth; never had. He didn't care. People always listened. He was the biggest and strongest man on the farm. Nobody else could lift an anvil. Buck felt he deserved more respect than he got: also more affection. 'Yeah, reckon I know why,' he said.

'Fine,' Nat mumbled. 'Rest of us can forget it, then.' Buck irritated him.

Nobody much cared what Buck thought, nobody except Josh. 'Aincha gonna tell us?' he asked.

'Why, Lonzo's a pretty boy,' Buck said. 'Mistah Charles likes to have a pretty nigger boy to play with.' The words were split and splintered by his teeth.

'You're prettier'n me, Buck,' Lonzo said. 'I quit. You be Mistah Charles's pet nigger. We're all proud of you, boy.'

That was the funniest yet. Bettsy and Ruthie laughed so much their backs slipped and they fell off each other. Buck did not laugh. He was on his feet and lunging at Lonzo in two strides. Lonzo ran. If he tried to fight Buck he'd get a lot of lumps and no respect from anyone. When you couldn't win, you ran. He ran just slow enough to let Buck think he could catch him.

Jacob stood up, slowly and painfully, his knees feeling like rust. 'Work,' he said. Everyone rose.

THE GNAW OF ACID

J oe Killick was angry all morning. Came noon and his anger made him bolt his dinner. This upset his stomach. In the afternoon the gnaw of acid worked on his anger to make him nervous and unsure. Everyone on the farm was glad to see him saddle up and ride away.

He was angry because mice had got into a corn store and feasted, taking a nibble here and there, tainting the crop with their stinking droppings and leaving some fungus that spread and smelt like death. He brooded over this curse every mile to the Hudd place. The corn was spoiled: he'd been robbed, cheated. He could feed it to the hogs but it might make them sick. He should burn it, probably. Roast the fungus to death. That was like burning money. He tasted bile, and spat until there was blood in his spit.

One slave took his horse, another his hat. A third led him to a big, bare room where Charles Hudd was standing with one foot on a stool and his thumbs hooked inside his belt. He was wearing white linen pants, a bottle-green corduroy jacket and a dark red bow tie that hung to his lapels. Killick was startled to see that Hudd was having his portrait painted. The easy, neighbourly greeting Killick had prepared went clean out of his head. 'Damn me if you don't look like you're runnin' for President,' he said.

'Which party?'

'Uh …' Killick couldn't think of a safe answer. 'Not the Know-Nothings, anyway,' he said at last. The Know-Nothings were an anti-Catholic party. At election time they went about beating up recent immigrants who tried to vote. Joe Killick approved of this. A few years ago, when an election in Louisville had ended in gunplay, with twenty dead and a large part of the city in flames, he had thought of starting a branch of the Know-Nothings in Rock Springs. The thought passed. Occasionally he remembered it and wondered if it was worth the effort.

Hudd was silent. He still had not moved his head. *I say something wrong?* Killick thought. *He hates the Pope too.*

Hudd was not looking at Killick because the painter had told him to keep absolutely still, but he heard the flat, hard strain in the man's voice and knew that something troubled him. 'I'm sorry there is no chair,' he said.

Killick wandered around the room, reached a window, looked out. Not a weed, not a broken fence. The hot, green shimmer of money everywhere. And all for one man.

'Have you come to see your daughter, Mr Killick?' Charles asked. 'Because she's not here.'

'No, no.' It came to Joe that his answer should have been 'The winning party'. Smart answer. Too late now. 'Way things are goin'', I reckon *you* might be comin' to see *me* about her, soon.' Charles was silent. Joe chuckled as he walked to another window. He trod on a loose board that made the easel shake and the painter glare, but Joe was never going to apologize to a man smaller than he was, particularly a man who wore eye-glasses and oiled his hair. 'Truth is, I rode over here to give you first bite at the cherry,' he said.

'Cherry season's over.'

'Figure of speech.'

'Oh. You want to borrow some money.' That came out more crudely than Charles intended, but Joe Killick's swagger offended him. Also Killick hadn't shaved. Shouldn't swagger if you haven't shaved, not in another man's house.

'You got two problems, Mr Hudd. First, you jump to conclusions and second, you're not in touch with the great big world of the United States. Amazin' things are happenin' out there, y'know. Amazin' opportunities.'

'You want to borrow some money.'

'See what I mean? Lucky I stopped by, or you could wake up one day an' find you're the last man in Dundee County farmin' without a McCormick's Patent Virginia Reaper.'

'Oh,' Charles said. 'That thing.'

'You got another problem too.' Joe was looking over the painter's shoulder. 'Wrong-colour eyes. This here is blue, yours is grey.' The brush halted. Charles's head jerked. Joe knew he had blundered.

45

'Only joshin',' he said, fast, and moved away.

'I don't grow wheat,' Charles said. 'Don't need anybody's patent reaper.'

'You grow some barley. Oats, sometimes. This McCormick contraption can harvest them ten times faster than your fastest nigger with a sickle or scythe.'

'Till it busts. Leg's getting stiff.'

'Five minutes,' the painter said.

'Hire a mechanic,' Joe Killick said. 'See, the clever part is, you rent it out to your neighbours. Less than a year, they've paid for it. You win, comin' and goin'.'

Charles clenched his feet and stretched his toes. 'Lucky me,' he said.

'Sure.' It felt like walking on a rope bridge that swayed at each step but you had to keep going. 'Play your luck,' he said. 'Buy two reapers. Buy three. Sit back an' watch me turn 'em into rollin' goldmines.'

'Yes,' Charles said, 'you want to borrow some money.'

'Your funds, my brains. Can't fail.'

'So go to the banks.'

'They're rich already. Thought I'd share this among friends.'

'Truth of the matter is, Mr Killick,' Charles said, 'you've borrowed so much from them – '

'This is different,' Joe said. 'You and me, hell, we're almost kin.' He heard himself begging and felt sick to his angry stomach.

'Listen,' Charles said, 'because I'm never going to say this again. You sow cheap seed, and you get poor crops. You neglect your fences, and you lose your animals. You abuse your slaves, and they rejoice in your failure. No machine made by McCormick or any other man will save you from yourself.' He took his foot off the chair, knowing he had said too much, had let his contempt show, but he was too stubborn and self-righteous to unbend.

They went into another room. Martha brought tea. Killick longed for liquor. Hudd sipped, and thought of JoBeth. He was hard on the father because the daughter kept trying to get into his pants. She was a bewitchingly seductive creature and she often went away leaving him with aching balls. It was difficult, being a man protecting his virtue against a hungry woman. He wanted her, but not outside marriage; and he was not entirely convinced he wanted to marry her. Or not yet.

They were outside, waiting for Sarah to bring Killick's horse, when Charles Hudd said, 'How much did you want to borrow?'

'Thousand dollars.'

'So why deny it? I knew from the start that's why you were here.'

Killick said nothing. His face looked as if a mule had trod on his foot.

When he got home nobody was surprised that he was too mad to speak, eyes stained with rage. It had been a bad mistake to try to do business in that state of mind. Typical Killick behaviour. First make it bad, then make it worse.

Hudd went back to the empty room and put his foot on the stool, and the artist got back to work. After five minutes of silence, Hudd said, 'I want you to make a portrait of the woman who will be my wife, but she's not to know you're doing it.'

'A surprise?'

Hudd wondered about that. 'Can you do it?'

'I'll have to see her, make some sketches. I can do it ... discreetly.'

'She'll visit here tomorrow.'

The painting of JoBeth was ready a week later. Hudd was startled at the fee. 'If you don't want the work,' the artist said, 'I'll happily take it away. I've no doubt I can find a buyer for a face like that.' Hudd paid him. Later he hid the portrait in his bedroom.

A hot summer month passed, day after day when the Hudd farm seemed to tremble under the heat of creation. JoBeth visited almost every day.

She taught him to dance, and slowly waltzed him around the drawing-room. His left hand was too high, she kept telling him, and their bodies must be closer. How else could she know where he wished her to move? 'You wish us to move to my bedroom,' he said.

'No, my sweet,' she said, her fingers seizing a handful of shirt. 'You may take me now, right here, if you wish.'

'But the floorboards creak.'

'Tell the servants it was a polka.'

'You are a wicked, wicked woman.'

'I know. I have to be wicked for us both. It is very hard work.' They danced on, Charles dogged and deliberate, JoBeth swift as her own shadow.

When it was impossibly hot they stayed indoors. If there was a breeze they strolled in the orchard. Always they talked. It delighted him that conversation was so easy: she always had something to say, and usually it came as a surprise. Not always a pleasant surprise. Once, she kissed him so generously that he felt a surge of affection. It would have been so easy then to say that he loved her, she was wonderful, splendid, his darling creature. The words were lined up, ready and eager. He sent them packing. 'I wonder how you will feel,' he said, lightly, his arms around her, 'when your daughter is old enough to do that to a man.' And he smiled.

She looked sad. For a moment she looked hurt. 'Why should I have a daughter?' she asked, without emotion. It was a plain question. 'Or a son?'

'The usual outcome of marriage. Someone to inherit all this.'

'If men died in childbirth they would not be so blithe about the whole messy, bloody business.'

That silenced him. They walked on. He felt badly jolted; he wanted her for her fun and liveliness, and now he felt punished by that sudden shaft of suffering. Punished for being a man. It was damned unfair. He searched for an answer to an accusation he didn't understand, let alone deserve, and found nothing, which depressed him, and it was all a waste of time because in a minute she was chattering cheerfully about something different and frivolous. He did his best to smile but inside himself he was asking: *What happened to death? You're too fast for me!*

That night, when he was holding a newspaper and trying to read about this ambitious lawyer Lincoln, who had grown up in Kentucky and now had his hands full, up North, trying to rein in a bunch of Republicans hell-bent on freeing every slave this side of the Rio Grande, Charles saw only the face and figure he was in love with. She would fall into bed with him whenever he said the word. What was he waiting for? A decent span of courtship to end? Or was it just the vanity of being able to say that no young beauty could hustle him into bed? Marriage now might look like the triumph of lust. Was it lust? Jesus, his loins were chuckling with multiplication, he could feel it, damn near *hear* it … He flung the newspaper aside and stamped out, shouting for his horse. Rode at a gallop nearly all the way to Rock Springs. Turned and let the horse walk back, leaving his mind to think for itself; he was weary of working it. Maybe she was right.

Maybe it was a crime to be a man. Well, he was damned if he would be a monk, just to please her.

He almost fell off his horse, he was so tired. Sarah led it away. He yawned and stretched. Being a monk wouldn't please her, for God's sake. That was the last thing she wanted. What in hell's name was he thinking? He stumbled off to bed.

SAYS SO IN BLACK
AND WHITE

Came market day, and it rained fit to choke all the fish in the
Cameron River.
Rock Springs's market day was first Tuesday in the month.
Not a big event, even on a clear day, but a chance to talk to people
you never saw otherwise. Now there was a stream running down
Main Street big enough to take a ten-man canoe. Market day was a
wash-out. Nothing left to do but splash over to Maggie's tavern and
get drunk.

At noon Job Sims, the town blacksmith, gave up waiting for trade
and draped an old tarpaulin over his head and walked to the tavern.
The rain hammered on him like a mad drummer. He was looking
forward to a comfortable chair, a drink and maybe a game of cards.
Instead he walked into a large, hot argument. Men twenty feet apart
were shouting, stabbing with their fingers, turning away in disdain
or disbelief.

'Politics,' Maggie said wearily as she gave him his beer. 'Election
year. Everybody hollers, nobody listens.'

'Well, that's democracy,' Job said.

'Listen, you jackass,' a farmer named Ryan Kidder was shouting
down the bar, 'I'll vote for anyone who destroys this damned underground railroad. I'd vote for a goddamn baboon.'

'So vote for Lincoln,' said a pedlar. 'He looks like a gorilla.' That
got a laugh. It was true: Lincoln had huge hands and a shaggy head.

'It's no damn joke when Abolitionists sneak in and steal your slaves
and railroad 'em north,' Kidder said angrily. 'That's not funny.'

'Who'd you lose?' Job asked.

'Oh, a couple or three, I guess. Lost Tom, a good strong field hand, two weeks ago. Then last week they got a nigger of mine called Bettsy. Tell you, this underground railroad, it's gonna ruin the South.'

'Theft!' declared a man called Dunbar, the town's cooper. 'Plain and simple thievery.'

'Horse-thieves get hung,' the pedlar said. 'So should nigger-thieves.' The uproar was dying down. It had been mostly the whiskey talking, since everyone was agreed on voting against goddamn Lincoln and his gang of Republican crooks in the North, and the pedlar wanted to revive it. Nothing else was likely to provide any fun today. 'I could sell you some good rope,' he offered.

'Lost Tom, did you?' Job Sims said. 'Thought you told me he fell in the river and drowned, him being a one-armed cripple and all.'

'Never found the body,' Ryan Kidder muttered. He didn't want to talk about it.

'I know where your nigger Bettsy is,' said another farmer, Hoke Cleghorn.

'New York?' the pedlar said. 'Boston? Canada, even?'

'Shut up. Your Bettsy's in Natchez, Tennessee,' Hoke said. 'You sold her husband down South. Natchez is where he went and Natchez is where she is now. Betcha.'

'That nigger wouldn't dare,' Ryan Kidder said.

'You don't whup 'em enough,' the pedlar said, but Kidder had moved away to the other end of the tavern, gone to pick a fight with a wheelwright called Stackmesser who had recently arrived in Rock Springs. Stackmesser was German and from the North, probably Illinois where Lincoln lived, so Stackmesser was to blame for everything. 'He don't whup 'em enough,' the pedlar said. 'I got some handsome bull-whups I can recommend one hunnerd per cent.'

'Shut up, you shitty little asshole,' Job Sims said mildly. He quite liked the pedlar but if the man kept opening his mouth one of these drunks would soon put his fist in it. Rock Springs had a new dentist, but the only reason the man took up working teeth was because nobody would hire him as a carpenter. 'What you sayin', Hoke?' Job asked. 'Sayin' there ain't no underground railroad?'

'Maybe there is.' Cleghorn shrugged. 'Anythin's possible.' He walked to the door and looked at the rain, pounding so hard that it threw up a high, brown spray. He came back to the bar. 'Just saw a dead elk get washed down the street,' he said. 'Anybody here lose an elk lately?'

'Underground railroad's a fact,' Charles Hudd said.

'Been stung?' Hoke Cleghorn asked.

'Would have been,' Charles said, 'if my overseer hadn't scared 'em off. They ran into the woods, an' got away.'

'Send for me next time,' Cleghorn said. 'I'll find the sons-of-bitches for you.' He stretched his suspenders and let them slap his chest.

'That so.' Charles hadn't intended to get into conversation with anyone, he only came to Rock Springs because he needed ink and also he knew JoBeth wouldn't ride over in this weather, but when he got the ink he found himself reluctant to return to a house he knew would be dank and silent, so he dropped into Maggie's to kill some time. Now he found himself talking to Hoke Cleghorn, a man he didn't much like. Cleghorn wore buckskin pants, fringed down the sides, and he carried a Bowie knife at his belt. He was known to fornicate with his female slaves once a week, maybe twice, even though he had a good-looking wife. Charles disapproved of that knife. Kentucky was not the frontier. A blade that size was grotesque, vain. 'You'll find them, will you?' he said. 'Is that a guarantee?'

'I rode with Kit Carson from Mexico to the Rockies and beyond. Kit was the finest scout any army ever had. He could track a mouse over a mountain, and he taught me all he knew.'

'Kit Carson came in here once,' Maggie said, mopping spilt beer from the bar. 'He never spoke of you.'

Cleghorn nodded. 'That's Kit all right. Never said a word more than he had to.' He hiked up his pants and took his belt in a notch.

Across the room, three mule-skinners and a charcoal-burner were quarrelling over cards. Accusing arms collided, the table rocked, drinks spilled.

'Shit and corruption,' she said. 'Ain't men got no brains at all?'

'Just mule-skinners,' Dunbar said. 'Just passin' through.'

'Faster than they expected. That table cost me three bucks.' She dried her hands on her skirt, and her arm-muscles moved about like sleeping animals. Carrying booze all day is work.

'Well, I got to get back,' Charles Hudd said. He could see Ryan Kidder returning, and two of the Killick boys were with him.

'That Yankee Stackmesser,' Kidder said, loud with disgust, 'he won't fight for the North and he won't fight *against* the North.'

'That's right,' said one of the Killicks. Hudd couldn't tell them apart: they were both red-haired and square-faced and drunk.

'How can the feller fight *against* the North in here?' Job Sims asked. 'Ain't nobody to fight.'

'Could fight *me*,' the other Killick brother said. 'I'm for the Union. I told Stackmesser, I said secession's … uh …'

'Unpatriotic,' his brother said.

'Yeah. Unpatriotic. That's my opinion.'

'No, it ain't,' his brother said. 'You're lyin'. You're red-hot for secession.'

'Yeah, but *he* don't know I'm lyin'. Stackmesser don't know that. So why don't he fight?'

'Cus he's a damn Yankee,' Ryan Kidder said. 'They won't ever fight. Got no guts.'

One of the mule-skinners cursed, and swung a fist. The table rocked. Maggie grunted. 'Mind the bar, Job,' she said.

'Poker must be an exciting game,' the pedlar said. 'Any of you gentlemen care to explain the rules?'

'I'm not exactly red-hot for secession myself,' Charles Hudd said. 'I'll stay with the Union if it honours my rights under the Constitution, which includes the right to own my personal niggers and have them sent back if someone steals them. That's the law. Says so in black and white.'

'Black and white!' the pedlar said. 'I like your wit, sir.' Nobody laughed. Everyone was watching Maggie throw two mule-skinners into the street. They raised a splash. She stood in the doorway, arms folded, examining the soaking sky for any sign of a break. One mule-skinner crawled back. 'We got nowhere to go, Maggie,' he pleaded. Blood mingled with mud to give his face a rusty coat. 'We'll drown.' She thought about it. 'Yeah, that's a good idea,' she said.

Job Sims was pumping beer. 'I never owned a slave,' he said, 'Ain't gonna start now. You gotta feed 'em, an' doctor 'em, an' hear their worries, an' tell 'em where to go and when to start and how they're doin' it wrong, an' then they're too old and weak to work, but you can't sell 'em cus who wants 'em? But still you got to feed 'em and all that. At least with a mule you can shoot it and make a dollar on the skin.'

Hoke Cleghorn blew the froth off his beer. 'You'd better be a good blacksmith,' he said, 'because you make a truly sorry bartender.' His belly hurt, and he let his belt out a notch.

'That true, you rode with Kit Carson?' one of the Killick brothers asked.

'I did,' Cleghorn said.

'How big's his dick?'

Cleghorn was startled. 'What you say?'

The other brother said, 'Some folks reckon Carson is a woman.'

That brought silence, apart from the endless throb of rain and the snores of a few trappers who had begun drinking at breakfast.

'Kit Carson was my friend,' Cleghorn said to the brothers. 'State your point or shut your mouth.'

'The point is ...' The Killick brother turned to Charles Hudd. 'You know the difference between a bull and a cow, don't you?'

'Never been a problem.'

'Tell at a glance, right?'

'Mr Hudd don't waste his time just glancin',' Ryan Kidder said heavily. 'Mr Hudd believes in gettin' to know his stock real well.'

Charles Hudd felt his face redden. 'A farmer can't know too much,' he said, and drank to hide his face.

'Damn right,' the Killick boy said. 'A man would be a fool to buy a mare without sittin' astride her and ridin' her hither and yon, test out her stride, know what I mean?'

'Then he's got to think about it a piece,' his brother said. 'Go back and ride her some more, just to be sure.'

'Could take weeks to decide. Months an' months, maybe.'

Cleghorn had been paying no attention to all this. 'Kit Carson was the manliest man ever rode West,' he declared.

'Then why did he always squat down to pee?' one of the Killicks asked.

Maggie reached for her club as Cleghorn threw a punch that was so telegraphed, the Killick boy swayed backwards and watched the fist make an arc that was completed by the pedlar's head. The others scattered. She whacked the club on the bar, and shouted: 'Any more fightin' an' I'll double the prices!' The Killick brothers backed off, laughing so hard they were gasping for breath. Cleghorn, spitting obscenities, raged after them. They overturned tables and threw chairs at his feet. 'If I could run, I'd kill 'em,' Maggie said wearily. 'These goddam knees ... Go bleed in the rain, fart-face,' she told the pedlar. His nose was broken. It pumped blood that sprayed and spattered with each convulsive jerk of his head.

Charles Hudd slipped away. Rock Springs had no sheriff – the last one had been bitten by his horse and died of blood poisoning – and he had no wish to be involved in a killing. He rode home, eyes almost shut against the pelting, slanting rain, while mud splashed the horse's chest and belly. All the way, he wondered about Ryan Kidder's heavy words: *Mr Hudd believes in gettin' to know his stock real well.* That was a joke. Rock Springs was mocking him. *Ride her some more, just to be sure* ... Rock Springs believed he was fornicating. Rock Springs was jealous, it wanted him wed. Well, to hell with Rock Springs.

NOTHIN' SPECIAL

Entertainment had always been scarce on the Killick farm. Nobody played a musical instrument, and the only book was a Bible that had been nibbled all round by rats until most of the verses made no sense. When he was a boy, George Killick made his own entertainment by hitting the niggers. Now that he was a man it still gave him pleasure. Unfortunately, Charles Hudd had forbidden it on his farm: the overseer, he said, must not strike a slave unless he, Charles, approved the punishment first. So when George came home to visit for a day, he had a lot of catching up to do.

'How is it over there?' his father asked.

'It's good.' They were sitting down to dinner: Joe and Judith; George; JoBeth and several brothers and sisters. 'You seen his dirt: it's black as sin,' George said. 'How is it here?'

'Not good.' They bowed their heads. 'Lord God,' Joe said, 'You better get me a good price on them hogs are ready for slaughter, cus I can't afford to go on feedin' the sons-a-bitches, an' that goes for all them hens ain't layin', God knows this ain't a zoo I'm runnin' here, amen, pass the pertaters.'

Dinner was salt bacon, potatoes, cabbage and cornbread. The bacon gave Joe a sour and burning stomach but he was damned if he was going to change his meals just to please his stomach. He drowned it in milk. An hour from now, he knew his tubes would be writhing in knots. Too bad. Let 'em suffer.

'Your memory's slippin', Pa,' JoBeth said as she sawed the bread. 'You forgot to ask the Almighty to empty the outhouse.' The two red-headed brothers hooted and their mother, forestalling the wrath of God, rapped their heads with a ladle; but they were too old to be hurt much. Dan was twenty-four, Stanton twenty-one.

'I hoped you'd be married by now,' Joe said. 'That feller annoys me.'

'He propose yet?' George asked.

His sister made them wait for her answer. 'Not in so many words,' she said.

'What's holdin' him up, George?' Joe demanded.

'Heck, Pa, don't ask me. I'm out in the fields. Nobody tells me a damn thing.'

'When I was in town, I heard Flub Phillips exercisin' himself about Hudd's nigger,' Stanton said. 'The one he's been learnin' to read an' write.'

'Lonzo,' George said through a mouthful of cabbage.

'Flub's an old bag of wind,' JoBeth said.

'Best Baptist preacher in this county,' her mother claimed. She had a generous figure, and a sweet, kind face, and a voice like a club. 'I heard Flub Phillips preach two full hours by Ryan Kidder's watch, and the sinners were so thick at his feet, repentin', you couldn't see the floorboards for humility.' She tore a piece of bread in half to teach it a lesson.

'Flub's a dangerous man to repent to,' JoBeth said. 'He'd promise you salvation an' then he'd lead you up in the trees so you can show him exactly how your sinnin' was done, on account of he doesn't want to take any chances with your eternal soul.'

'Did that include male sinners too?' Dan asked.

'This ain't fit conversation for the dinner table,' Joe Killick growled. He took more potatoes. He sucked at a fibre of bacon until he got it out of his back teeth. 'Well, did it?' he asked JoBeth.

'Oh, Flub ain't fussy,' she said. 'Hot sin excites him whether it's got its pants on or not.' One of her young sisters found that so funny she wet herself and had to go out.

Joe Killick's mind was taking one pace forward and two back. He kept wanting to know but he was afraid to ask. Eventually he scratched his ribs and said, as if he was bored, 'What was old Flub complainin' about, anyway?'

'Reckoned Hudd didn't ought to teach the nigger stuff,' Stanton said. 'Nigger who's educated gets uppity. So old Flub was sayin'.'

'Don't need sayin',' George said, 'everyone knows. Look at that Nat Turner. Some fool showed *him* how to read the Bible, next thing he's leadin' a slave army all through Virginia, massacrin' white folks in their beds. Killed five hundred.'

'Hogwash. They killed sixty or seventy,' JoBeth said. George glared. 'It was thirty years ago,' she said, 'and the number gets bigger every year. Pretty soon Nat Turner will have slaughtered the entire state of Virginia.'

'What in hell d'you know about it?'

'After that,' she said, 'he'll start wipin' out both the Carolinas and half of Georgia. I swear, that Nat Turner's a bigger killer dead than alive.'

'You reckon it's funny?' her father said. 'Harper's Ferry wasn't no joke, an' that wasn't no thirty years ago, neither, it was last year.'

'And John Brown wasn't black.'

'Makes it worse. He stirred up the niggers an' before it was over plenty of decent white blood got spilt.' He had stopped eating. His stomach was sending messages of grim rebellion.

Dan knew the sign. When his father put his fork down like that, it meant a foul temper the rest of the day. Dan enjoyed making trouble but not with his father. That was one fight he could never win. 'What's holdin' Hudd back, anyway?' he asked. 'JoBeth ain't bad-lookin'.' Let Hudd take some stick for whatever was going wrong.

'Grown white man shouldn't favour a nigger boy,' his mother said. ''Tain't natural.'

'Don't fuss on that account, ma,' JoBeth said. 'The man has his faults but unnatural vice ain't one.'

'Maybe this Lonzo ain't a nigger-boy at all,' Stanton said. 'Maybe Hudd found himself a real pretty nigger-girl. I mean, *real* pretty.'

She knew the suggestion was meant to sting; all the same it *did* sting. 'I seen both you two naked,' she said, 'and I seen this Lonzo naked, and he's got twice the manhood of you two put together.' *Oh shit,* she thought. *Wish I hadn't said that.*

Nobody moved. For a moment it was like funeral. Then her father spoke, in a voice that dragged like a blunt saw. 'I seen you naked, girl,' he said, 'and I strapped your bare ass plenty too, but not often enough, it seems. Get out this room now.'

She left.

'That man Hudd has a twisted mind,' Mrs Killick said. 'Nigger-lover ain't natural. By rights half that farm should be ours already.'

'Well, I'm doin' my best,' George said.

'You be careful,' his father ordered. 'You be damn careful, you hear me?'

Nobody sat long around the table. George found himself alone, with an afternoon to kill. He went to the door and squinted into the bleached blaze of sun, so white it hurt. The air was saturated with heat until it trembled and quivered under the pressure. Hounds were sleeping in the dust beneath a shade tree. Occasionally one awoke to snap at a trespassing fly. Then its head would droop and droop until its jowls flattened on the dirt again.

George got his squirrel rifle and a handful of bullets. He went down to the cellar and filled a little narrow-neck jug with whiskey from the barrel. He went back up and looked for a wide-brimmed hat. The only thing he could find was a monstrously floppy straw with a kingfisher-blue bow, obviously belonging to one of his sisters. He looked strange in it, both handsome and grotesque, so he took it. Nobody would see him, anyway.

The hounds trailed after him, disgruntled. It was a stupid time to go hunting and they knew it.

George strolled from tree to tree, resting often to take a sip of whiskey and enjoy the shade. He was making for a bend where the river had cut steeply into the opposite bank. A fine stretch of trees overhung the water: beech, white oak, poplar, maple, some sycamore. Good place for squirrels. Hit one, it would fall in the river, then a hound could swim out and get it. Not that George meant to do anything with the squirrels. Some people ate them, said they tasted better than chicken. Not the Killicks. The eating wasn't worth the skinning. Couldn't trust a slave to get the meat out, either, not properly. Your average squirrel had more brains than your average nigger.

As he walked, George saw blemishes in the farm that he would not have noticed before he went to work for Charles Hudd. Crops were slow because they had been planted at the wrong time, or in the wrong field, or with the wrong seed. Drainage wasn't always good; there were patches of bog and patches of desert. He saw rat-runs and rabbit droppings everywhere. George saw this and ignored it. As soon as he could save some money he was off to Lexington. Or Louisville. Chicago, even.

He sat on the river bank. George was good at doing nothing. He watched the river go by and waited for the squirrels to forget he existed. The hounds found some shade and went back to sleep. Birds flew: a cardinal, a pair of mockingbirds, some wood thrushes, warblers, a red-headed woodpecker. He kept his head still and tracked them with his eyes. Nearby, a hidden rock made the river bulge and in the swirl below it, a big fish sometimes swam out and sucked down a hatching fly. George saw the rings in the surface, and thought *I could kill you*. But then the fish made him wait so long that he forgot it and drank some whiskey instead.

JoBeth. Last time he saw her naked she was thirteen and already then she had bumps on her chest. Now, when she went into Rock Springs, men fifty yards away stopped talking. George had seen the looks in their eyes: slack regret in the old men, hot yearning in the young. Even thinking about it brought the taste of desire to his throat. A swig of whiskey washed that away. How could Charlie Hudd keeping kicking her out of bed? Maybe Flub was right. Lonzo had nigger skin but he had that Indian face, arrowhead nose, straight lips, clear grey eyes. Maybe Hudd was a bigger nigger-lover than just teaching Lonzo to read and write. A deer swished its tail high on the top of the opposite bank, and George glimpsed its shape in a lucky gap between the trees. Without thinking, he aimed and fired.

Birds came clattering out of the branches in a panic. The deer vanished. Stung, perhaps, but not dead, unless the little bullet had nicked an artery.

In a moment the sky was empty and the echoes had died. George reloaded. Stupid shot, the range too great, the beast too big for a squirrel rifle. Now every damn squirrel would be hiding. Stupid shot. He drowned his mistake with a sip. Or two.

The river bulged over its hidden rock. George stared, held his stare for a minute, two minutes. The fish never rose. He hurled some pebbles at the place, *splash-splash-splash*. Fuck the damn fish.

He was sick of this spot. He got up and kicked the nearest hound and walked upstream. Away to one side, something moved. A row of slaves, working in a field. He changed direction.

They were bent double and moving slowly. When he got close enough, George shouted: 'What you doin', boy?' The nearest slave half-straightened and called back, 'Pickin' bugs offa the crop, Mister George.'

'Bugs, huh.' That bad rain must have bred a crop of caterpillars. 'Get to it, then.' The man's head went down.

George sat on a stump.

It was the hottest part of the afternoon. The air shimmered and wobbled above the fields. Even doing nothing, even under his crazy girl's hat, George felt the impact of the sun. It sucked out his sweat. He drank from the jug, but the sun was always one pace ahead.

That fool deer annoyed him. It had surprised him, made him shoot without thinking, and now there was nothing to kill. He'd carried this damn rifle for nothing. On the far side of the field he saw a jug on a fence post. Well, he could shoot that. It wavered in his sights and he belched just as he fired, so the shot missed by a mile. That made him angry, especially as the niggers all looked up, and he reloaded fast. Second shot bust the jug in a hundred pieces.

They howled. He thought that was very funny. Must have been full of some darkie jungle-juice. 'Pick bugs!' he shouted. 'I see anybody slackin', I'll blow his black ass off!' Their heads went down in an instant.

After that there was nothing to do but watch, and sweat, and sip, and watch some more. The niggers never stopped work. This was even more tedious than the river.

The hounds wanted to go home. Some of them began whining, and he whacked them with the butt of the rifle. Trouble with whiskey was it made you thirsty. A horsefly bit him on the back of the neck. It stung like punishment, and that really infuriated George. In the middle of the field a nigger started to stand up, to ease his back, or that's what George thought, and he lifted the rifle, but then he saw it was just Moses.

Moses was tall, taller than any of the Killicks, and when he moved forward his rump stuck up higher than any of the other slaves. Moses wasn't shirking. Just moving. George took aim at his rump just the same. Rifle was raised, might as well take aim. Next thing he knew he'd fired and Moses was knocked over.

〜

The pain made the slave's legs collapse. It burned into his butt and raged there, a tiny fire but so hot it melted his knees. He let out a shout, high-pitched and hoarse. The other slaves thought he'd been snake-bit.

'Sixty yards if it was an inch,' George said aloud. 'Hot damn! I should be in the U.S. Army, killin' Indians. Sixty? More like seventy.' He re-loaded. 'Back to work!' he roared. 'Moses ain't hurt, I just clipped him, for God's sake …' But they crowded around Moses and jabbered like crows.

'Shit,' George said. Some days nothing goes right.

He walked over to the group.

Moses was being helped to his feet. Blood soaked the seat of his pants and kept spreading. 'That ain't nothin',' George said. 'You can go wash that in the river.' They were still holding him up; he looked ready to faint. 'Let me see,' George said.

He pulled down Moses's pants. The hole in his buttock was badly torn at the edges. George knew what had happened: the bullet had wobbled in flight and smashed sideways into the flesh. 'Huh,' he said. 'Looks like you were standin' too far away from me, boy. Next time, get your black ass up close an' I promise, you won't hardly feel nothin'.'

That was a joke. Being niggers, they wouldn't laugh unless the white man laughed first, so George gave a good, loud chuckle. Still nobody laughed. 'Fun's finished,' he said. 'Get back to work. Somebody got a knife better pick that slug out. Here, I'll wash it clean.' He emptied the jug over the bullethole. Raw whiskey met raw flesh and Moses screamed. One of the slaves holding him up cursed and kicked the jug out of George's hand, which hurt George's fingers, so he cursed and slammed the rifle butt into the slave's ribs. The others scattered and ran.

In the evening, George rode back to the Hudd farm. Charles saw him arrive. 'Have a good day?' he asked.

'Well, you know,' George said. 'Nothin' special.'

SATAN'S BATHTUB

Upstream from the Hudd farm, the Cameron River ran through beautiful country that had not changed in ten thousand years. As the valley narrowed, so the cliffs became steeper: but they never closed in enough to make a gorge, and the river was always flanked with trees. Many were huge. White oaks were so massive, their roots ran so wide and deep, that no storm could bring them down. Higher on the slopes were chestnut trees: canopies of shimmering leaves enclosing armies of squirrels. Topping them all were the yellow poplars, ten feet across at the base, booming up arrow-straight a hundred and fifty dizzying feet, sending out flowers that looked like an almond tulip. Between these giants grew bitternut hickory and sugar maple, patches of hemlock and pine. Below them, flowering dogwood and silver birch and crab-apple filled in the gaps. For those with eyes to see, the forest floor was rich with flowers: jack-in-the-pulpit, the butter-coloured woodland sunflower, a rust-red lily at the water's edge, a pinkish bog-rose, the scarlet cardinal flower, even an orchid called lady's slipper, delicate and yellow. The river trail upstream from the Hudd farm passed through this splendid, startling scenery. Charles Hudd and JoBeth Killick had grown up with all that stuff. It was like an Alp to a Swiss: just wallpaper. In any case, they had other things to think of.

JoBeth was thinking of marriage, and wondering why Charles was being so contrary about it. Foolish, even. Sometimes, if they had been apart for a day or two, there were tears of longing in his eyes when they met again. And his kisses told their own story. So why couldn't he go one more step and propose marriage? What was stopping him?

And if he was just being contrary or foolish, did she really want to marry a contrary fool?

However hot his kisses. However broad his acres. A wedding would be fun but afterwards you were a long time wed. Look at ma and pa. Hard to believe *that* was ever fun.

Charles, riding ahead on the narrow track, was pleased to be going on a picnic. It had been her idea, and she'd chosen the place: Satan's Bathtub. A picnic when everyone else was working in the fields was an act of total self-indulgence, the sort of thing he'd forgotten how to do. How she brightened up his life! He couldn't imagine a future without her. They would marry, he was certain of it. They would marry just as soon as her family and the entire nosy community stopped holding its breath, because he was damned if he would do it to satisfy *them*. There had not been much affection in his life: a shadowy mother, a wife too soon dead, a father who gave him books instead of love. Charles had learned to be hard on himself, and therefore hard on everyone else. Now JoBeth had got under his guard but the rest of the world was still his enemy. He was comfortable that way.

Satan's Bathtub was two miles from the farm boundary. It was a geological quirk. A strip of black basalt held up the Cameron and made a thumping waterfall. A hundred thousand floods had pounded out a deep basin, scoured it until it was polished and round. The wet edges shone in the sunlight, black as coal and sleek to the touch. Hoke Cleghorn reckoned Satan's Bathtub had been a sacred Indian site; said his father had seen the Shawnee practising human sacrifice on the big boulder beside it and pitching the body into the pool, which was thought not impossible.

Charles unsaddled the horses so they would cool off. The horses found a place to drink at, and then ambled under the shade of a big cedar. They stood head to toe, swishing flies from each other's face.

It was a simple picnic: sugar-roast ham, sliced fine; cherry tomatoes; cold boiled potatoes, newly dug; a dozen mushrooms, picked at dawn before the heat could hit them; some fluffy biscuits, fresh-baked; a bottle of French white wine, shipped from New Orleans. And a peach pie.

They were both hungry. They ate, and watched the waterfall tumble and foam.

The food was spread on a checked cloth. Charles sprawled, propped on one elbow, wondering whether to have another piece of pie, when a splendid butterfly arrived and settled on a red square of the cloth. It uncoiled its tongue and tried to taste the colour.

'Not smart,' Charles murmured.

She nodded. It was as big as a young sparrow, vividly coloured and velvety. It walked all over the red square, tasting.

'You'll starve to death,' Charles told it, 'and then you'll be sorry.'

'Sorry for what?' she said.

'Sorry you didn't stay in butterfly school and get some learnin'.'

'School,' she said, in a voice as dead as chalkdust.

He rested his head and closed his eyes, but he made himself stay awake in case he snored. Snoring was vulgar and unattractive. She shook his arm. 'Look,' she said.

Another butterfly had landed and it was trying to mount the first. They staggered and stumbled, their wings clashing, until they suddenly took off, the male in hot pursuit of the female, and were gone.

'Smart,' she said. 'I bet those two aren't sorry for anythin'.'

He shaded his eyes and looked at her. 'I get the feeling that was one of Aesop's Fables,' he said, 'only I missed the moral.'

'Do as the butterflies do. Live.'

'They'll be dead by next week.'

'So might we be. All the more reason.'

He sighed, and smiled. 'You have a worrying way of making everything sound simple,' he said.

'Well, it is simple. Either you live to enjoy or you live to regret what you didn't enjoy while you had the chance.'

'Life may be simple for you, my sweet, but it's more complicated for me. The Hudds have some standing in this part of Kentucky. I have a reputation to protect.'

She sat up straight. Her eyes were wide with surprise. 'Is that why you won't bed me?' she asked. 'To protect your shiny reputation?'

'I'm old-fashioned. First marriage, then bed.'

'God speed the plow!' Impatience brought her to her feet. She went over and sat on his chest, with a knee on each arm, grabbed his ears and shook. 'You haven't got a reputation, Charlie! You lost it weeks ago! Everyone in Rock Springs believes you and me have been banging like a barn door in a blizzard every since I started coming out here without any chaperone.'

'That hurts,' he said.

'I'm sorry.' She kissed his ears, and then his mouth. 'Listen, dummy. You've lost your precious reputation, so why not enjoy what you've paid for?'

'Can't. Not now.'

'There's nobody here to see us but the birds!' she cried in exasperation, bouncing hard.

'Got hiccups,' he said.

'Oh.' She stopped bouncing. Air exploded up his throat and flung his head back. 'Sweet Jesus!' she said. 'I'm sorry. What can I do?'

'Get up.' Another detonation ravaged him.

She helped him to his feet. 'Poor Charlie!' she said. She held his hand, desperate to help. 'Does it hurt a lot?'

'Not a lot.' He stood absolutely still, trying to make himself invisible and therefore invulnerable, until suddenly his body convulsed again. 'Oh God,' he groaned. 'If you don't mind, dear, I'll go away, and …' He walked into the woods, treading carefully. Distant hiccups reached her, like the call of some strange and solitary bird.

He sat on a rock and waited until his stomach grew bored of its practical jokes. Half an hour later he strolled back. 'Never hit a man when he's down,' he said. 'It upsets his innards.'

She smiled, sleepily. She had been lying in the sun and now she felt baked. 'I'm going for a bathe in Satan's Bathtub,' she announced.

The Cameron had run off its floodwater but the pool was still deep. 'Can you swim?' he asked.

'Not very well.' She began unbuttoning. 'Come on, Charlie. If I wear my shift and you wear your shirt, God won't strike us dead.'

The coolness of the water climbed as they stepped down and it claimed their bodies in a rush of pleasure. The shift and the shirt floated like lily-leaves. 'Don't tell God,' he said nervously. Before he could drag his shirt down, her arms were around his neck and he had to work at keeping them both afloat.

'Hey, don't skin feel good on skin?' she said into his right ear.

'You can't swim a stroke, can you?'

'Feel this,' she said, pressing and wriggling, 'Feel *that*! Wheeeeee!'

'Don't let go, damn you.' This was huge fun and huger folly, and Charles didn't know whether to grin or to groan. 'We're going across,' he said.

They were in the middle of the pool, Charles swimming on his back, JoBeth riding happily on his chest, when the horses bolted.

Their whinnying reached him faintly because his ears were mostly submerged. Treading water, upright, trying to look over the bank, he heard the drumming of hooves. It soon faded.

No point in talking. Both knew something or someone had scared the horses. They were strong, stolid animals, unafraid of raccoons or deer or snakes or even a wondering coyote. Maybe a drunken trapper had tried to steal them. Or a lost Indian. Unlikely. Indians never got lost. Abolitionists? Runaway slaves? In fact it was a black bear.

JoBeth saw it first: just the head. Charles immediately began swimming again, softly and quietly. By the time they reached the far side of the pool they could see the whole bear. It was shorter than Charles but much heavier and far stronger. It had claws like knives; if threatened it might make a bloody mess of a large animal, especially one clad only in a wet shirt. Or shift. It was finishing the picnic.

They sat near the edge, where they were up to their necks in water, and waited.

'Bring a rifle?' she asked softly.

'Under the saddles. You want to get it?'

The bear found the peach pie, which had been wrapped in muslin. The water was starting to chill them.

'Wonder what the butterflies would do,' he said. 'I mean, if they were us.'

She thought about it. 'No,' she said reluctantly. 'Not right now.' She was shivering.

'Wise decision. Wouldn't want to work up a froth. Might attract the bear.'

The bear finished off the left-over biscuits and licked out a pot of mustard. It got its head stuck inside the picnic basket and ripped the thing apart like a paper bag. It ambled upstream and had a long drink and ambled back. It searched the picnic site in case it had missed something, tried eating the muslin because it smelled of peach pie, took a bite out of JoBeth's hat because it was yellow, chewed on Charles's boots for God-knew-what-reason, yawned, scratched itself, and finally headed off into the trees.

By then they were shuddering with the cold. Clambering out was toil. Just to sit in the heat of the sun was a reward beyond price. The bear had missed the bottle. It held a mouthful of wine each. She was shivering so violently that he had to hold the bottle to her mouth.

He found the horses a mile away and led them back.

She was combing her hair. The rifle lay beside her.

'You know, if we'd just shouted,' he said, 'it might have run away.'

'Maybe.' She showed him her hands: deeply wrinkled. 'I feel like a bushel of walnuts.'

'Me too. I think my sweetmeats climbed up and hid inside me for good.'

They laughed. 'Not a very romantic afternoon,' she said.

They rode home. He wondered whether she was right, that he had lost his reputation, all for nothing. If he had, did he really care what people thought about him? And if he didn't care, then his reputation didn't matter, did it? Except that if he bedded her because everyone expected it, and married her for the same reason, he wasn't in command of his own life, and he wasn't going to let *that* happen, damned if he would. Yet what did waiting gain for him? Respect? Who from? A bunch of people whose opinion could be bought for a shot of whiskey? It was all very difficult. You were damned if you did and damned if you didn't. 'Oh, hell,' he said. 'Who cares?' He hadn't meant to speak aloud, but she heard him. 'That's the big question,' she said. She sounded sad.

~

At the end of a day, if he wasn't too tired, if there was nothing better to do, if he felt ambitious, Lonzo practised his reading and writing. It made Josh jealous and it irritated Buck. Lonzo enjoyed that. Also he could daydream about living in power and luxury and idleness like a white man. He wasn't fooling himself: he knew it was a dream. Reading and writing a few words weren't going to do Lonzo any good. Born a slave, he'd die a slave. He didn't expect different, so there was no room for regret. That never entered his mind.

Charles had given him paper and pencil and some printed stuff to copy. He was sitting against a stump, steering the pencil and thinking that his letter 'y' looked sort of like a cat's tail so he made it longer and then tied a knot in it. Looked funny. The farm had a few cats. Maybe he could catch one and tie a knot in its tail. He wrote another 'y'. Maybe catch two and tie their tails together …

Ruthie came by. 'Whatcha doon, Lonzo?' she asked.

Every time, same question. Well, Ruthie was old and she never had been much of a thinker. Still: every damn time, same dumb question. He gave her a real hard sneer. Ruthie's eyes weren't too good any more. Waste of a good sneer. 'Watcha think?' he said.

'Jeez, I dunno.' Ruthie had a good chuckle. Nothing disturbed her. She never complained, never celebrated, never criticized, never praised. Sold from the auctioneer's block when she was six. Three masters – one cruel, one loud but lazy, one dying and therefore indifferent – before Henry Hudd saw her at a bankruptcy sale, told her to strip, poked and prodded and squeezed her until he was sure she could breed, and got her at a knockdown price of two hundred dollars, with a lame mule that nobody wanted thrown in too. Three good husbands, all dead now. Seven children, all sold south, never seen again. Snakebit once, nearly died but didn't. All luck, all chance. Nothing agitated Ruthie. What she didn't understand made her chuckle. She chuckled a lot.

'I'm writin',' Lonzo said. 'Same as always.'

'Yeah?' Ruthie was impressed. Well, he expected that. They were all impressed, even Josh and Buck, who pretended otherwise. 'Writin', huh?' she said. 'What for, Lonzo?'

'Writin' to the President.' He bent over his work.

'President, huh?' Now she was very impressed.

'Tellin' him to get his white ass down here, an' bring plenty of corn whiskey.' She giggled from shock: niggers never used that sort of talk. 'If he don't,' Lonzo said, carefully copying the word *boll-weevil*, 'Kentucky's goin' to secede on him.' He didn't know what it meant but he'd heard white people say it.

'I always knew you was the most cleverest little nigger,' Ruthie said.

'Aw, anybody can write,' he said. ''Tain't so hard. You could write if you wanted, Ruthie.' She laughed and shook her head. 'Sure you could,' he said. 'Gimme your hand.'

She knelt beside him and he put the pencil in her fingers. He held her hand and steered it. The writing was big and shaky. 'What have I writ?' she asked.

'You jus asked Old John to marry you,' he said. That was the funniest thing ever. Ruthie could scarcely walk for laughing. Lonzo put her words in his pocket.

WHOLE HOUSE SHOOK

After an hour or so, the yellow stain in the river had worked its way almost as far as Rock Springs.

The stain began where one of the Hudd cows had got stuck in the stream and was now stuck worse than ever, tiring fast, and looking to be dead through drowning before sundown. It was stuck in what people called quicksand but was really mud, an umber-coloured gruel that gave little support to the animal's weight. The more it struggled, the more it trapped itself. An hour ago it had been bellowing, a strident, screeching din. Now it was too hoarse to bellow. Its nostrils blew blood-tinged bubbles. Its eyes rolled like marbles. The river was up to its neck and sometimes lapping over its back.

When Charles Hudd arrived, most of his slaves were already there, glad of a good excuse for quitting their fieldwork and in no hurry to get back to it, so they made a lot of noise and ran about, pointed, gave each other orders, and hoped to string out the entertainment indefinitely.

Charles did three things, fast: sent for George Killick, sent for rope, and sent Lonzo into the river with orders to hold the cow's head up. The river wasn't deep but the mud was. This wasn't the first time a beast had got itself stuck. Charles had once seen an elk go down in twenty minutes and any elk must be three, four times stronger than this cow.

'Keep swimmin'!' he shouted. 'You're no damn use to me if you get bogged too.'

That amused the slaves. 'Hey, Lonzo!' Josh said. 'You get bogged, you write us a letter, you hear me, boy?'

'You!' Charles said to Josh. 'Get on that cow's tail and when I say twist, you twist!'

'Aw, Mistah Charles,' Josh complained. But he swam out to the cow and caught its tail.

'Hey Josh, you do your stuff, now,' shouted Bettsy. 'That cow worth more than two wet niggers.'

Charles ignored that. She was wrong, but only by about a hundred dollars; Josh had come cheap, born in the Hudd slave compound. 'Keep that beast's head *up*,' he called. 'Treat it gentle. Where's that damn rope?' A piece of rope was coming but it was short, barely long enough to reach the cow. Charles, exasperated, seized the slave who brought it and shoved him in the river, where he made a great splash. 'Idiot!' he bawled. 'You, Buck, go get more rope, *long* rope!' Buck trotted away. 'Run!' Charles roared, and flung a stone at him. Buck ran until he was out of range and then slowed to a trot again.

No sign of George.

'Still sinkin', boss,' Lonzo said.

'Damn. Damn.' Charles, fists on hips, stared. 'How in hell's name did you get in this fix?' he asked, savagely. The cow produced a groan. 'That so?' he said. The slaves laughed. One laughed so much, he fell in. The others whooped and hollered. This was better than a revivalist meeting. Charles lost his temper. A good cow likely to get drowned, that wasn't funny. 'Tie that rope around the horns!' he shouted, and kicked the nearest nigger, to underline the order. 'Do it, blast you! Do it now!'

With a loop tight around the horns, there was just enough rope for two men on the bank to pull. 'Get a grip,' Charles told them. 'You ready to twist, Josh? When I say go … Go! Go! Go!' Everyone took up the chant. Charles encouraged the rope men, gesturing hugely. For a moment it looked and sounded like a tug-of-war. A sharp spray jumped out of the tightened rope. Josh twisted, the cow lunged for the shore, screeching with pain. It went nowhere. The attempt failed completely. Worse: the cow had sunk another inch or two. 'Stop, stop!' Charles shouted. The rope slackened. The slaves fell silent. Lonzo struggled to keep the heavy head above the surface. The sour yellow stain drifted away with the stream.

Charles began to loathe the cow. If the niggers hadn't been there he would have walked off and left it, so he hated the niggers too. And he raged silently against the river, which just went on its stupid selfish way and never gave a damn for anyone or anything.

Two empty, angry minutes passed. The slaves sat and watched.

Josh stumbled ashore, too tired to swim. Charles sent Nat out to replace him.

'Let's try again,' he said. Despair made him sluggish: try what again? The same thing that had failed already? That was when Buck came in sight, loping along with a coil or rope around each shoulder. All at once, the impossible seemed possible again. With three ropes on the horns, the cow would come out like the cork out of a bottle.

Charles got every spare hand on the ropes, and this time it was worse than before. The ropes held the head up but as soon as the cow started to kick, it sank some more.

'Go and get my gun,' Charles told Bettsy. 'This foolishness has gone on long enough.' He had forgotten about George Killick, and was surprised to see the man riding towards them. 'Where you been?' he demanded. 'Hell, never mind, it's no matter. This here is hopeless.'

George dismounted and studied the scene. 'Cow's still livin',' he said.

'More we pull, deeper it sinks.'

'Yeah. Thing is, how to keep its feet out the mud.'

'That surely might help,' Charles said. 'What you gonna use? Blasting powder?' It was sarcasm and it was feeble.

'Need some cord,' George said. 'Got some in my saddle.'

He cut four lengths, each a yard long. 'Every time that cow tries to kick out the mud, it raises one foot, an' puts all its weight on the other three, so now you got three legs goin' down for every one that's comin' up. Maybe, if I can tie up all four legs …'

'Damn cow'll go straight down.'

'Might not. We get a long rope around its hindquarters, just might keep it afloat.'

George shed his boots and his shirt while they fixed the rope. He swam out, clung to the cow, took a deep breath. He went under and pulled himself down the left foreleg until he felt mud and raked out a channel behind the leg. He came up for air, went back, got both hands on the hoof and doubled the cow's leg. A looped cord was on his wrist; he slipped it over the leg, hauled it tight and knotted it.

The cow was too exhausted to resist. It took him about a minute to release each leg and another half a minute to tie it back. As he tied the last knot he could feel the ropes hauling the animal like a great sled. When he waded ashore it was sprawling at the water's edge, looking disgruntled. Lonzo lay next to it, muscles twitching.

'I wouldn't have believed that,' Charles said, 'if I hadn't seen it.'

George spat out some yellow water. 'Trick of the trade,' he said. He'd learned it from a bored cowboy returning east who'd been eager for company on a dull night in Maggie's tavern; but he wasn't going to tell Hudd that. 'Can't fight a quicksand. Got to out-think it.'

'You look Chinese. Ain't they all yallery? Goddamn, that was slick!' Charles was so pleased he couldn't stand still. 'If that wasn't worth openin' a bottle of good bourbon, I don't know what is! You drink bourbon, George?'

'No, but I've heard it's right agreeable,' George said. They rode back to the house together, trailing the rich stink of river-mud.

~

That was the most excitement in the Cameron valley for a couple of weeks.

Elsewhere, passions were getting raised. Men in the North said the institution of slavery was cruel, barbaric, wasteful, unChristian, intolerable. Well, it certainly wasn't intolerable: the United States had tolerated it all these years. Thomas Jefferson had had slaves, and it hadn't troubled his conscience, had it? Well, then.

What was truly intolerable was the North being stampeded by a bunch of rabid radical immigrants who'd never seen the South and didn't understand it. Their demands were a direct assault on States' Rights. If a State couldn't run its own affairs, then the Union became a tyranny, and wasn't that exactly what the War of Independence was fought to overthrow?

In Maggie's tavern they argued the point back and forth, mainly for its entertainment value. It was an old fight and everyone knew how it came out. Once in a while the politicians in Washington stubbed their toes on slavery and got in a lather, but in the end they always put their fat heads together and found a compromise. They'd do it again, that's what politicians were for. Besides, Kentucky wasn't the deep South. This wasn't plantation country. Niggers here were part of the family, better off slave than free. Well-known fact. Ask anybody. The North would bluster but they'd see sense in the end. The North *needed* the South. They couldn't abolish slavery without breaking the Constitution. Simple as that.

Joe Killick had his own personal answer to the slave question: sell 'em. It got him a black eye and fat ear. But not in Maggie's.

He had spent a bad evening over his account books. The farm was deeper in debt, third year in a row. He had crops not yet harvested where the yield wouldn't even touch his hands: it would go straight to pay off interest. There was a barn trying to fall down: bang goes another bundle of money. And that was just the start. What it came to, his niggers were working mornings for him and afternoons for people just waiting to see him fail, so they could move in and claim the pieces.

He left the sorry columns of figures and walked to a window. The moon was full; when he was younger he'd enjoyed a stroll around his land on nights like this. Now he lacked the energy. A bat flickered by and his eyes changed focus, too late. What he saw instead was his own reflection in the glass. It looked like his father's face, the year he died: grim, tired, beaten.

For the first time, Joe Killick knew he was in the last few years of his life, and he felt bitter. A man deserved comfort, leisure, a little luxury in his old age, not this constant worry. He went back to the desk and leaned on his knuckles until they ached. That was when he saw the solution, and went to his wife. 'I'm gonna sell the slaves,' he said.

'Oh no you're not,' she told him, and punched him in the eye with a straight right. 'You get that idea out of your head now and forever.'

They were in the bedroom. One eye had closed, the other was full of tears. He felt blindly for a chair, missed it and sat on the floor, hard. In a long marriage, Ma Killick had often hit him, but always in the middle of a quarrel, and usually after he had struck her first. This new unfairness made him feel older and more helpless than ever. 'I quit, I quit. Just leave me alone to die.'

'You ain't bloody dyin', either,' she said, and whacked him on the ear because it was the closest part. 'An' you ain't sellin' a single slave. Now go wash your stupid face.'

He did not move. 'It's the only way we got left to raise money,' he said.

'You're drunk or mad. Who'll cook an' clean? You expectin' me to wash floors and peel taters?' Her scorn was massive.

'Slaves are all we got left to sell.' He wiped his mouth and found blood: must have bit his tongue when she walloped him. 'Clear the debt, start again. Hire some hands and – '

'Muleshit.'

'You find the money, then. I can't.'

'I done my share. Gave you a family, didn't I?'

'All they do is eat, an' grow out of their goddamn clothes,' he said bleakly. His ear was singing like a tuning-fork.

'You'd send me into Rock Springs without a nigger to carry my purchases, wouldn't you? You'd let folk say, There goes Mrs Killick, not a nigger to her name, husband sold their slaves, every last one, you can see she does her own laundry, look at her hands, red as cherries, that's her husband, ain't he a disgrace, why'd she marry him, a man who'd sell his slaves before he'd give up whiskey? That's what they'd say.'

'Whiskey's got nothin' to do with it.' He was so drained he could sleep on the floor.

'Shut your mouth. I heard enough of your foolishness.' She put her nightgown on. 'JoBeth's gonna marry Charlie Hudd, and Hudd's got enough money for all of us, so keep your crazy ideas to yourself.' The bed bowed and groaned under her weight. The candle went out. Killick closed his eyes and prayed to be taken by his Maker, painlessly, in his sleep. For all anyone knows, God gave the application His serious attention and decided there were other candidates with better qualifications. When Joe came down to breakfast, he had an eye like a sick clam. 'You think that's bad,' Stanton said to Dan, 'you should see the other fellow.' His father hit him full in the face with a bowl of hot grits.

'No more than you deserve,' Ma Killick told Stanton. 'Honour thy father, like the Bible says. Jessie! Make some more grits,' she shouted to a house-slave.

'Don't want no goddamn grits,' Joe said.

'Now see what you done?' she told Stanton. 'You put your father off his breakfast. Jessie, get someone to clean up here.'

'Man can't open his mouth no more,' Stanton mumbled. He was slightly stunned. Grits were falling into his lap. 'Can I leave the table?'

'Don't ask me. Your father's master of this house.'

'Leave the goddamn State,' Joe said. His head was in his hands.

'You children don't know how lucky you are,' she announced. 'And that's the everlasting truth. What you smilin' at, JoBeth?'

'Was I smilin'?' JoBeth said. 'I guess it's my natural sunny disposition. I take after you, Ma. Everyone says so.'

'That Charles is a lucky, lucky man,' her mother said.

~

'In the fall,' Charles Hudd said. 'That suit you?'

'Uh-huh,' JoBeth said.

They were sitting on a broad branch of a cedar. Its limbs hung so near the ground that it made a natural tree-house, cool and fragrant.

'I don't hear anybody cheering,' he said.

'Well, I don't see anybody down on his bended knees.'

He thought about that. 'Lumbago,' he explained.

'Oh.' She nodded, gloomily. 'As long as it's somethin' real romantic.'

He looked away. 'Beginning to sound like we're married already.'

'Could have been married a month ago. You havin' second thoughts? Better speak up now. There's a boy over at Slade's Crossing wants me so hard he splits his pants just thinkin' of it. If you're foolin', he's liable to come over and cut your heart out, see if it's true to me or not.'

She wasn't smiling. He couldn't decide how serious she was. 'So then they hang your friend,' he said, 'and you end up an old maid.'

'He ain't my friend. Ain't my lover, either. In fact I never even had a lover.' That got his attention. 'You got a virgin bride waitin' for you. I hope your lumbago stands the strain. Hate to see a grown man break down and cry on his wedding night. We had a stud bull once, couldn't find the target with a pair of eyeglasses on. Kept slippin' and fallin'. Weak ankles, they said.'

'Us Hudds are famous for our strong ankles. Watch this.'

He jumped down, and then caught her when she jumped. Their hold slipped easily into a hug, the hug into a kiss. 'No second thoughts,' he said. 'And no second-best. It's you or nobody.'

They strolled away, arms around each other's waist. Her hand found its way into his coat pocket, and something rustled. 'What's that?' he asked. She pulled out half a sheet of paper.

He unfolded it, and they stopped to read the big, sprawling writing: *nsiD th Bern OK.*

'What's *nsiD*?' she said, and knew as soon as she heard herself. 'Inside. And that's *the*.'

'Yes. *Inside the* ... Who's Bern? I don't know anyone called Bern. And what's OK? Bern OK. Sounds foreign.'

Again she saw it first. 'Oak. O plus K spells oak.'

'Ah. Forgot you went to school in Tennessee ... *Inside the Bern oak*. Could that be *burned*?'

'Sure.'

'Nigger writing,' Charles said. 'Except there's only one nigger here can write and this ain't his. Lonzo's writing ain't marvellous, but that scrawl looks like a drunk in a thunderstorm did it.' They walked on. 'This old coat of mine hangs on fence posts half the day,' he said. 'Most anyone could slip that paper in.'

'You burn much oak around here?'

'In this heat?' He made a thin, high-pitched grunt, as if he had remembered something surprising, and his head jerked. She looked up at him, thinking maybe he was in pain. 'Happy,' he said. 'I felt happy right then. Damn ... That hasn't happened to me since ... Whooo, I can't remember when. Not just, you know, glad. Happy! For a moment there I was floatin' like a balloon.'

She was amused and touched. A barrier between them had vanished. 'If it's as simple as that, we can fix up to get married more often.'

'Something I want to show you.'

He took her back to the house, up three flights of stairs, through the attic and onto the roof. Where a pair of gables met, the builders had added a belvedere: a gingerbread-trimmed turret with a pointed, round-shingled roof. All four sides were open; they revealed a panorama of the Hudd farm. Never in her life had JoBeth been so far above the ground. The view was splendid; just looking was exhilarating; she hurried from one side to the next, greedy for sensation: this really was like floating in a balloon! Charles leaned against a corner-post and smiled, pleased that he had pleased her. 'There's George,' he said. The horseman was a small, soft blur, slowly drifting past a line of smaller blurs.

She was reluctant to leave. 'Can we come back?' she asked. 'Promise me we'll come back.'

'Sure. After the fall you can come up here as often as you like. This will be yours too.'

She rode home late in the day, when the air had a calm, cool touch and the swallows feasting on insects raced back and forth as if they were an overhead escort. Charles rode with her.

'Ma whopped Pa a good one last night,' she said, sombrely. 'He came down to breakfast with a black eye.'

'Good heavens.' He could think of nothing more to say.

'It's always in their bedroom. They never whop each other in front of the family.'

'Oh. So it's not ... something new.'

'Been doin' it for years. Pa's supposed to be the boss but when they go to bed she whops him. Sometime he gets his licks in first. Not last night, though. Ma flattened him. Whole house shook.'

'Hard to believe.'

'Don't let her sugary smile fool you. She like hittin' people. Well, they both enjoy it, but Pa's slowin' down, an' he gets caught. Reason I'm telling you this is ...' She looked away. Charles was startled: JoBeth was finding it hard to speak. *That* had never happened before. 'Let's not you and me whop each other,' she said.

'I'll agree to that.'

They rode in silence for the best part of a mile. Then she suddenly said, 'Burned oak. Look.'

It was the blackened trunk of a lightning-struck oak, still green in its branches. It stood thirty or forty yards from the trail.

'I've seen that tree a thousand times,' he said. 'Never noticed it.'

They parted near Rock Springs. On the way back he stopped and examined the oak. It was hollow at the base where the lightning-strike had burned it out. He stood inside it and stretched his arms. The air smelled of charcoal and corn meal. He caught a whiff of something else too but couldn't put a name to it. He stood there so long, thinking, that his horse grew stiff and began to stamp. He came out of the tree, and swung up into the saddle and jogged home. It had been a good day. Just as well. There weren't going to be many more.

THE BEAUTY OF IT

The Hudd place was pretty well self-sufficient in the day-to-day necessities. They had a mill where they ground their own corn, a smokeroom where they cured their own pork, a dairy where they made their own butter and cheese. They made soap; they made candles. Most produce got sold to various merchants in Rock Springs.

George Killick liked to drive the wagon to town; he said it made a change from overseeing. He never took anyone with him: the merchants had slaves of their own to do the carrying. It took George a good ten minutes, going hard at it, to remove part of the load and hide the stuff inside the burned-out oak: four sacks of cornmeal, three sacks of smoked hams, a box of soap and three 14-pound cheeses. He was gasping and sweating as he ran in with the last cheese, and he squatted on his heels while he recovered. That was when Charles said, 'Now put it all back.'

If George hadn't been so relaxed he might not have wet himself. As it was, the top of his left pant's-leg got a brief drenching. He stood, and saw the other man watching him, and would have killed him if he could. Not as an antidote to guilt – guilt was a luxury the Killicks couldn't afford – but because Hudd had made such a fool of him, hiding behind a tree while he slogged back and forth, resting while he laboured. But Hudd had a rifle and George had to swallow his humiliation.

He said nothing. He lugged everything back to the wagon: cheese, soap, hams, meal. There was no hurry. It was sweaty, grubby labour. When he heaved the last sack onto his shoulders, Charles followed him. George stacked the load tidily and locked up the tailgate and walked away. He knew he was fired. Might as well go home and get some dinner.

Charles, driving the wagon at a sharp clip, passed him without looking. 'Greed,' he said. 'Greed and stupidity.' He went on to town.

Joe Killick was exercising a rocking chair on the porch when his son walked across the yard. Joe had his belt unbuckled and one hand inside his shirt, the fingers digging into the pain, while the other hand gripped the arm of the chair. He had found that regular rocking took some of his mind off the arson attacks going on in his stomach. Only some. The rest of his mind soaked up the suffering and braced itself for more. Joe was at war with his body and he was never going to surrender. He'd kill it first.

'He found the tree, Pa,' George said emptily. 'He was hidin' in the woods. Saw me dump the stuff.'

'Jesus! Think he knows?'

George sat on the steps. 'Be your age, Pa. Course he knows.'

'Hold on, hold on, could be other reasons.' Joe Killick sent his mind hunting for escapes. It was an old familiar chase. His conscience knew better than to interfere. 'Wagon could've been overloaded, couldn't it? Maybe an axle cracked, or ... Somethin' wrong with a horse. Went lame. So what you did, you – '

'Pigshit, Pa. He *knows*. He ain't gonna go to law, is my guess, so don't bust your nuts over nothin'.'

His father grunted. 'I'd swap my nuts and ten dollars for a fresh set of innards.'

'You bin eatin' that sour pickle again?'

'Had fried chicken. What's chicken without pickle?'

George yawned. 'They're your innards, Pa. Give 'em hell if you want.'

Joe Killick brooded. The pain was fading: it couldn't fight the competition of bad news, which just went to prove that if you stood up to your body, gave it orders and kicked its ass, eventually it did what it ought to do. 'Might've bin worse,' he said. 'I might've bin waitin' there too. Anybody else see you?'

'No.'

Joe stood and put his hands in his pockets to keep his pants up. 'If Hudd keeps his mouth shut, it never happened.'

'I got fired. *That* happened.'

'Some bastard must've told on you. You got pay comin'?'

'Forget it, Pa.' George took his boots off. One heel was blistered. He wasn't accustomed to walking. 'Ain't goin' back. Just forget it.'

'Forget nothin'! If you'd had a goddamn written contract – '

An upstairs window banged. 'Can't a person sleep in this house?' Ma Killick demanded. Pigeons clattered out of a distant tree.

'Oh shit,' her husband said.

'George! What you doin' here?'

'Gettin' up strength to eat,' George said, knowing she wouldn't listen. The window slammed over his last words.

'Royal imperial shit,' Joe said grimly. 'Now what we gonna tell her?'

'Tell her I got fired. Which I did.'

'Won't be enough.' There was a gruff edge to his voice that made George look up. For the first time he saw the black eye.

'Jesus, Pa,' he said 'I mean, for Christ's sake.'

'She means well, son.'

'Yeah. Her aim ain't bad, neither.'

The thump of her feet as they hit the stairs, and the rasp of her voice giving orders to house-slaves, attracted several children. Soon George faced an interested audience, black as well as white. When his mother asked him again why he wasn't at work, he knew he wasn't going to tell the whole truth. The atmosphere was all wrong for that.

'Well, I guess I got fired, Ma,' he said.

'Fired? *Fired*? That I do not believe. How could Charlie Hudd do that?' She set off along the verandah. 'You saved his cow from drownin'. You put out that fire! Had that gunfight with them Abolitionists! You been *runnin'* that entire farm single-handed!' She reached the end of the verandah and the end of her breath: her chest was heaving, her nostrils flared, she was the picture of fighting motherhood. 'What for, fired?' she cried.

George had seen the question coming from a long way off. Now everyone was looking at him, and he knew he had to please these people. He turned his imagination loose.

'I guess it must've been because I went in the hay barn kind of unexpected, and found him in there with that pretty little nigger-boy,' he said. He shrugged one shoulder.

'The one called Lonzo?' his father asked. He made it sound like a bad habit.

George nodded. Having started, he had to go on: the ring of eyes demanded it. 'Nigger was buck-naked,' he said, 'and Hudd wasn't too well dressed himself. Looked to me like … stuff was goin' on. You know.'

End. Some of the eyes were disappointed.

'What stuff was goin' on?' the youngest son asked, but George ignored him.

Ma Killick was down on her knees. 'From fornication, and all other deadly sin, and from all the deceits of the world, the flesh and the devil, Good Lord deliver us.'

'Is Mr Hudd the devil?' the youngest son asked. It was a reasonable question. Nobody answered.

'Not fornication,' Joe said to his wife. 'I don't think George was talkin' about fornication.'

'Well then, it says thou shalt not commit adultery,' she told him, 'and Hudd's an adult. Exodus, twenty, fourteen.'

'You see any adultery?' Joe asked. George shook his head.

Ma Killick's knees were starting to hurt. 'Abstain from fleshly lusts,' she said. 'First Peter, two, eleven.'

'I guess that covers it,' Joe said.

'Covers what, Pa?' his youngest son asked. Waste of breath. The boy kicked the nearest nigger on the ankle and ran into the house.

'Get up, Ma,' George said. 'It's too hot to pray.'

'He that diggeth a pit shall fall into it,' she said, 'Ecclesiastes, ten, eight.' She stood up, sweating with righteousness. 'Hudd lusts, and George pays the penalty. That ain't right. What you goin' to do about it?'

Joe felt trapped. He looked to George for help; after all, George's lies had built the trap; but George was cleaning his nails with his pocketknife. 'I reckon I know my fatherly duty,' he said, 'and I intend to honour it. I shall save my daughter from that lustful beast. JoBeth ain't gonna marry no nigger-lover. JoBeth's goin' back to live with my sister in Tennessee.' He buckled his belt and jutted his jaw.

Ma Killick was shocked. She'd asked for retribution and Joe had provided it. Too late to argue.

JoBeth was out visiting friends. When she got home the news made her furious. She told George he was a liar and she told Joe he was a fool if he thought she was leaving Rock Springs. By that stage of the day, Joe had taken enough whiskey to stun his stomach and dull his brain. He meant to cuff her lightly and instead knocked her down with a blow that loosened one of her back teeth. He and

George tied her to her saddle and within ten minutes George was taking her to Tennessee. By bedtime Ma Killick had had second thoughts about the cancelled marriage. Nobody was perfect and it was a Christian's duty to forgive. Besides: someone was going to marry Hudd. Now her husband had made a blundering idiot of himself and ruined all their prospects. She turned on him and smacked him in the eye: the same eye. He never saw the punch coming. For the rest of his life, that eye was never much good. But it was too late to send for George and JoBeth. They were on a riverboat, heading for Nashville, and everyone in Rock Springs knew why. Or thought they did.

~

Charles didn't expect her to visit him next day. He'd just fired her brother for thieving; best let the dust settle.

He was writing a letter to her – trying to explain events and making hard work of it because stating the facts looked like making a condemnation but anything less seemed apologetic – when he looked through the window and saw two horsemen coming to the house.

It was the red-headed Killick brothers, Dan and Stanton.

He went out. 'If you're lookin' for George's belongings,' he said, 'I sent a nigger with them this morning.'

'We got that,' Dan said. 'Somethin' you forgot to send.'

'What's that?'

'Two things,' Stanton said. They had not dismounted, which was discourteous. Charles moved so that he did not have to squint into the sun.

'You forgot your apology,' Dan said. 'We came to collect it. Thought we'd save you the ride. Us Killicks are famous for good manners. You could take a lesson from us.'

'Also five hundred dollars,' Stanton said. Both men seemed calm and serious.

'Well, now,' Charles said. These jokers were on *his* land, giving *him* orders. He felt the kick of anger and promptly suppressed it. 'I'm not a man to hold a grudge – ' To his surprise they laughed, and Dan spat a stream of tobacco juice. It hit a whitewashed rock in the border of a flower-bed and left a spreading stain. 'You're easily amused,' Charles said. 'I'm not. I'm sorry things worked out the way they did – '

'Good. Now put it in writin',' Dan said.

'I have nothing to apologize about. After what your brother did to me? You've got some gall!'

'He saved your farm,' Dan said. 'Saved your cow, your nigger, your hay.'

'I paid him.'

'Not in full,' Stanton said, fast. 'George has wages comin'. You owe him.'

'Five hundred,' Dan said.

Charles had a slim gold watch in his vest pocket. It was on a gold chain, and when he took it out, it just about filled his palm. 'I'll give you boys sixty seconds to turn around and start for home,' he said. 'After that – '

'Hey!' Stanton said. 'You got half your debt right there in your hand, Mr Hudd.'

'We'll take it,' Dan said. They both dismounted.

Charles found himself suddenly short of breath. It was twenty years since he had been in a fist-fight. He had never had to fight two strong young men, both at once. 'What you're proposin' is a crime,' he warned.

'What you did is a crime,' Dan said. 'We're just squarin' things up.'

They were advancing on him, and he was backing off, slipping the watch chain from its buttonhole as he went. 'You Killicks,' he said. 'You are a corrupt family.'

That, too, made them laugh. 'Take your hat off, Stanton,' Dan said. 'We're bein' preached at by the professor of corruption in these parts. Show some respect.' Then they rushed him.

Like most brawls, it was a clumsy affair. Charles flailed at them with his watch and was lucky: it missed Stanton's upflung arm and smacked his mouth, cut his lips and chipped a tooth. His chin ran blood, and he recoiled as if he had run into a tree. Dan kicked Charles on the leg but there was no power in the blow. They swung at each other, huge scything punches that missed and left them stumbling, unbalanced. Stanton said, 'Hey.' The blood on his fingers was vivid and sticky, and now he could taste it too. 'Hey!' he said. Dan turned to look and Charles dodged away. He ran towards the nearest tree, a sycamore dense with leaves, whirled his gold watch like a slingshot, and let it fly. The tree swallowed it and kept it.

After that they were fighting because none knew how to stop. Mainly it was charging and lunging and cursing. Stanton did most of the cursing. He wasn't sure how badly damaged his mouth was, but his lower lip was a banana and there seemed no end to the blood. He was proud of his face. The thought of being scarred for life upset him, so apart from some hurried kicks he kept his distance. The fight lurched and staggered, watched in awe by black faces at the windows. A few lucky blows got through, but it was too damn hot to keep up this toil. Fatigue set in; the punches became wilder. Everyone was gasping and wheezing, sweat in the eyes, clothing twisted, wondering how in hell to stop, when Lonzo came around the corner.

It was time for his lesson. For a short while he watched, fascinated. He'd read about white men fighting but this was the first time he'd seen it done. They looked drunk. Every time he got taken to Rock Springs he saw drunks falling over their own feet. He moved closer and recognized the Killick brothers and realized it was two against one; so he moved closer still and called out: 'Mister Hudd, you want me to fetch you them horse pistols, Mister Hudd?'

The fight came to a ragged, stumbling halt.

Charles tried to answer but his lungs wouldn't let him. All he could do was raise a hand in acknowledgment.

Stanton could talk, although the words emerged in a thick lisp. 'That's Hudd's pretty nigger-boy,' he told his brother. 'Reckon he's worth five hundred dollars?'

'Sure,' Dan said. He was sitting on his heels, sucking on scraped knuckles.

Charles tried to tell Lonzo to get away. It came out as a meaningless croak. Lonzo stepped forward to find out what Charles wanted.

The rest was just a matter of speed and obedience.

'Hold my horse, boy!' Stanton shouted. Lonzo obeyed. Whitey shouts, nigger jumps. All his short life Lonzo had been jumping; now was not the time to argue and get a crack on the head. He ran and held the horse. In three strides Stanton was beside him, yanking a rifle from the saddle-scabbard, touching the barrel against Lonzo's bare neck. 'Now jump up,' Stanton told him.

The rifle barrel stayed with Lonzo as he got into the saddle. Stanton swung up behind him and shoved him against the horn. Dan was walking towards his horse. Charles was trying to run towards the house but the best he could make was a stumbling trot.

By the time he had got the horse-pistols and someone had brought his horse, the Killicks were gone, were out of sight. He had to follow, not because it was a smart idea but because a dozen niggers were standing around staring at him like he was Davy Crockett and anyhow why keep a pair of loaded pistols on a shelf over the front door unless you're willing to use them? And so Charles, bruised and bad-tempered and unsure of himself, galloped off.

The Killick brothers were sure he would come after them. It was a long ride back to their farm, Hudd would have a good horse, he was bound to catch them. They didn't want another fight. They had his favourite nigger. That was a sort of a victory since it would make Hudd mad. They left the trail and hid behind a canebrake.

They sat on a fallen tree with Lonzo between them.

'I could handle a bucket of cold beer right now,' Dan said.

'Don't talk like that,' Stanton said. 'Talk like that just makes it worse.' Flies kept buzzing near his swollen lips, crazy for a taste of blood, and all he could do was flap his hands at them. If he touched his mouth it hurt like fire.

'Who'd of thought Hudd was so tight with a dollar?' Dan said.

'I reckon George was lyin',' Stanton said. 'George is a terrible liar. He'd tell you gators eat taters, just to keep in practice.'

'Well, maybe they do. Hungry gator'd eat anythin'. Just cus you never saw – '

'Forget it,' Stanton said. 'Just forget the whole damn thing.' Talking had worsened the split in his lip. His tongue found it and it felt like a ravine.

'I heard tell of a gator in Louisiana walked into a man's house, ate the man and his wife and their whole dinner clean off the table.'

Stanton, rather than risk speaking, tensed his buttocks and manufactured a small, unimpressive fart.

'Mighty big gator, boss,' Lonzo said respectfully. He was in no danger. Nobody would harm a fit, strong slave. As pointless as damaging good farm machinery.

'Bigger'n this old tree we're sittin' on, boy,' Dan said. He was in a good humour: they had revenged George, and he personally had caught Hudd a satisfying whop on the nose. Now this nigger could work off Hudd's debt on the Killick farm, which would take two or three years. 'Big appetite! That poor man was set to eat a quart of oysters, big old ham, fried tomatoes an' onions, bowl of sweet per-taters, and enough carrots to stuff a hog. Gator ate the lot an' licked the plates clean too.' Dan began feeling big. Maybe he would take this nigger for his own personal slave. 'You done any inside work, boy?' he asked.

'Yes boss.' That was a lie but it made Dan smile so Lonzo knew he'd said the right thing.

'You ain't worked till you worked for us, boy,' Stanton muttered. It hadn't taken him long to forget to keep his swollen mouth shut. 'Pa's gonna kick your sweet black ass so hard he'll need new boots twice a month.'

It was not a clever remark, but afterwards Stanton was never able to figure out what he had said wrong. He'd treated Lonzo like any other slave. It baffled Stanton. He was to brood over it, and in later years it helped make him bitter and pessimistic. He used this attitude as an excuse for not thinking, so he ended up even stupider than he began, and Stanton had never been the brightest boy in the family. He was seven before he could tie his bootlaces, and fourteen before he attempted simple joined-up writing, and even at twenty he wasn't always confident which was his right arm and which his left. He didn't see why it mattered anyway. He knew he was handsome and women liked his looks whichever side they stood. All that was to change on this day of the fight and kidnapping. Stanton soon learned his right from his left in a flash, and never forgot it.

'I bet George lied,' Dan said. 'I bet Hudd never owed him no five hundred. Hell, George ain't worth two-fifty neither. Hundred dollars, that's my guess ... Well, he ain't gettin' this nigger. I won me this nigger in a fair fight. George can go whistle up his ass.'

Stanton was not listening. Dan's ramblings bored him. He was still thinking of the Louisiana alligator that ate the couple. 'Who says that gator did what you said it did?' he suddenly demanded.

'Well-known fact,' Dan told him. 'Now shut up.' He cocked his head.

'Hell, no. If that gator ate them people, *and* it ate all their grub,' Stanton persisted, 'how did anybody know for sure just what there was for it to eat in the first place? Jesus, Dan – '

'Shut up and listen. Horseman comin'.'

Lonzo was thinking about what Stanton had said. He sat quiet and peaceable like a good nigger should, but his brain kept working.

He thought: I could end up hid somewhere on the Killick farm and be made to sweat blood and eat what the hogs left and suppose someone killed me, they'd just roll my body in the river, nobody'd ever know, plenty other black bodies went that way, why waste diggin' a hole on a dead slave?

He heard the pattern of hooves and saw the flicker of a rider through the fringes of the cane, and knew it was Charles Hudd. He turned his head. Stanton's ear was only inches away, a good, shapely ear with a fine, flat lobe. Lonzo struck like a snake and bit Stanton's ear. He had strong jaws and sharp teeth. They sliced through most of the ear like fat bacon. Stanton screamed so loud his brother fell off the log in surprise and at the same time the pain made Stanton jerk his head. This finished the damage. The bottom half of his ear was left hanging by a tatter of skin. Lonzo spat blood, then ducked and ran. The wrong way.

He blundered into a patch of bog and sprawled on his hands and knees. When Hudd came riding around the back of the canebrake, Lonzo was on his feet and Stanton had one hand around his throat. Stanton was cursing in a high-pitched monotone and trying to punch the slave. Shock had drained the strength from Stanton's arm. His legs wavered like tall grass in a breeze.

Dan had the rifle but before he could think of using it, Charles Hudd slid off his horse and was rushing at Stanton with a pistol in each hand. 'Release that nigger!' he roared. 'Release him instantly!' The words sounded curiously formal, but those were the words that emerged from his mouth. 'You!' Now he was addressing Dan. 'Disarm yourself, sir! Ground your weapon, I say!' Again, his words sounded odd, but much of that was because his nose was so badly bent.

Dan put down the rifle. Hudd was talking peculiar and acting mad: it was time to quit. 'Let the sonofabitch go, Stan,' he said.

But Stanton did not. His fingers were dug hard into Lonzo's neck: it was his only contact with reality. If he let the nigger go, he could never get his ear back; that was how he thought. Pain licked his ear like a flame and his brain could not compete.

So he clung to Lonzo and he stared at Hudd's face as if he'd never seen it before. In a sense, he hadn't: under the broken nose, a moustache and beard of blood had dried black in the galloping air, and fury gave his eyes a wild flicker.

Hudd was furious, not at Stanton, but at the foolishness of this confrontation. Stanton didn't know that. He saw a crazy man trying to rescue a wild nigger who'd just maimed him. 'You can take this black bastard,' Stanton said, 'after I've killed him.' His voice kept splintering. More betrayal, more treachery.

'You stole my nigger.' Hudd's voice was thickly nasal. 'Give him back.' He reached out with the pistol and prodded Stanton's hand, the hand that gripped Lonzo.

'This ain't fair,' Stanton said. His mouth got smashed and his ear chewed off, and for why? Because he tried to get some justice for George. 'This ain't fair.' He couldn't see clearly for tears. 'My goddamn ear,' he said. 'He bit off my ear.'

'Give me back my nigger!' Hudd shouted, straight into Stanton's face. Lonzo, not hurting from the grip, stood with his thumbs hooked inside his pants and thought: *Hey! Everyone wants Lonzo! This nigger's valuable!*

Stanton could not release him. The more Hudd shouted, the less Stanton heard. So in the end Hudd lost all patience and raised one pistol and shot Stanton through the left arm.

That worked. The bullet made such a God-awful mess that Stanton went down unconscious. A tidal flood of heat swamped his arm and overwhelmed his brain so fast that he didn't feel the first jolt when his rump hit the ground, or the second when his head bounced. By the time Dan got to him, Stanton's face was the colour of skimmed milk. His ear had stopped bleeding. A knitting of spittle linked his lips.

'You shot my brother,' Dan said, amazed. 'Over a *nigger*.'

'He made me. You saw it.' That was a lie, but Hudd was still stunned by how simply the problem was solved. It was the first time he had shot anyone. You shot and they fell. That was the beauty of it.

'One stinkin' little nigger,' Dan said, 'and you had to go and shoot my brother.'

'He ain't dead. Put a tourniquet on that arm, get him to the doctor. And stay off my land.'

Charles Hudd rode away, with Lonzo running alongside. The echoes of that shot were still ringing in his ears.

DEAF, DUMB AND BLIND

D oc Brightsides had one of the most lucrative practices in Chicago until a suspicious husband kicked in the consulting-room window at the height of a very thorough examination, and the doctor escaped through the door only slightly ahead of several bullets.

He had long, slender fingers, developed by piano-playing. Early in his medical career he had been gently feeling the breasts of a beautiful young woman, Mrs Flynn, who had complained of unusual sensitivity in that region, and he had found nothing unusual apart from her exquisite contours, when he noticed that her eyes had closed, her lips had parted and her breathing made little gasps in time with his touch.

Two days later she was back. He applied an aromatic ointment, quite harmless but so effective that she had to lie down and recover. Later that week she returned and asked for a complete physical examination: apparently the ultra-sensitivity had reached other parts of her body. His long and slender fingers massaged various oils and unguents into various places. He enjoyed giving the treatment, she gained enormous if temporary relief, and the fee was hefty.

As word of mouth spread news of his skills among the rich young women of Chicago, Doc Brightsides realized that treating the healthy paid far better than healing the sick. Heal the sick and they go away. Treat the healthy and they keep coming back.

Soon he had to work surrounded by thick screens to muffle the tiny shrieks of ecstasy, and his fingers were too tired to play the piano in the evenings. Then the window-glass shattered and he was legging it down the hall.

Her husband was an angry man and he pursued Doc Brightsides deep into Ohio before he quit. Brightsides just kept on going into

Kentucky. To be on the safe side, he went up the Cameron as far as the steamboat would take him. Rock Springs needed a doctor. Brightsides stayed.

That was how he came to be in Charles Hudd's living room, straightening his broken nose with a teaspoon handle and a bottle of brandy.

'You done this before?' Charles asked.

'Hundreds of times. Keep your head absolutely still and it won't hurt.' He gripped the back of Hudd's skull and eased the teaspoon handle up a nostril. There was an agonizing crunching and Charles howled. 'See? You got to pay for your pleasures in this world,' Doc said. He worked on the other nostril. Pain drained all strength from Charles until he felt like a cardboard cut-out. His nose was being levered into shape with a red-hot crowbar. 'Best I can do,' Doc said. 'You can take a drink now, if you want.'

Charles collapsed into a chair. Blood swamped a hand towel. 'Don't worry about that,' Doc said. 'Your blood pressure was too high anyway.' He poured himself a brandy. 'Lie down, put your head back. That blood should stop running in five or ten minutes. If it keeps up, you'll probably die. Mind if I play your piano?'

When he left, Charles felt worse but looked better. Blood had clotted inside his nostrils like bottle-stoppers. 'I expect you had to stitch up that Killick boy,' he said densely.

'Did what I could, which wasn't much. Bullet hit the bone. You know that?'

'No.' And at that moment, Charles was suffering too much to worry about Stanton's problems. 'If you're going back to the Killick place soon, you might take a message to Miss JoBeth. I'd be obliged.'

'You'd be obliged, and I'd be gone for a month. JoBeth's in Nashville.' Doc Brightsides shook his head. 'Everyone in this county knows that but you, Charles. Nashville, Tennessee. You could go and fetch her, but you'd have to fight George when you got there. Don't let him hit your nose. It won't stand mending twice.'

Charles Hudd went out in the fields and did some bad-tempered overseeing until even he knew the slaves would get along better without him. He couldn't go into Rock Springs, not with a nose so swollen it reduced his eyes to slits. He rode up river, to Satan's Bathtub. Where the track was broken, or if his horse stumbled, pain flooded his head and made him gasp. But it was so much less than what the Doc had inflicted with his teaspoon handle that Charles despised it. 'You can't hurt me,' he said aloud. 'Nobody can hurt me.' His horse pricked its ears at the strange, cracked voice.

When he reached Satan's Bathtub he knew the visit was a mistake: everything he saw reminded him of her.

'Idiot,' he said. 'Stupid imbecile fool idiot.'

He dismounted and stood looking at the place where they had crawled ashore and he had seen her in a wet shift that clung like a wrinkled skin.

Too late now. He'd had his chances. She'd offered him every chance. 'Unbelievable brainless idiot,' he said aloud. 'Deaf, dumb and blind.'

He soaked a handkerchief in the pool, then led his horse up into the trees. He found a flat rock and stretched out on it, with the handkerchief over his ruined face to keep the flies off.

Nashville, Tennessee. Well, he could easily go there but he knew he wouldn't, not because he was afraid of George Killick but because it was not a fitting thing for a man of his age and standing to do. A man in his position couldn't just leave his farm and go chasing off into the next state in pursuit of a much younger woman he wasn't even formally engaged to. That would be like announcing to the world that he was infatuated.

Which he was. Wasn't he?

'Oh, Christ,' he groaned. Everything had gone wrong: everything. He had done his best to behave properly and the result was betrayal, threats, brutality, kidnapping, gunshot, bloodshed. Now she expected him to go to Nashville and save her.

No. That was too much to ask. He fell asleep.

A gusting breeze snatched the handkerchief away and he awoke to see lemon-yellow streamers of sunlight. It was late afternoon. He rode home, feeling dull of brain.

The weather was changing: rain on the way. He looked at the house and wished it would burn down. Every room he entered would shout memories of a woman who would never be his wife, and that was not his fault. He went inside, got a bottle of whiskey, and climbed slowly and heavily to the belvedere.

He was drunk by the time the rain came. Very soon there were blasts of wind, blinding stabs of lightning, thunder that crashed like doom. He sipped steadily and prayed for the storm to end all his troubles in one well-aimed flash. But when dawn came he was alive. Stinking of booze and riddled with self-pity, but alive.

Two months later he married Mary Boyd, the schoolmistress who ran Rock Springs school. She was a widow, neat and stocky and clean-cut, only a year younger than Charles, and with two strong boys nearing puberty. She knew he was going to propose, and when he did she agreed at once, without fuss. It was a very quiet ceremony.

By then, Stanton Killick's arm had been amputated just below the elbow. He didn't want it done but the wound was poisonous. You could smell it twenty yards away, upwind. Dan got him very drunk and Doc Brightsides used his surgical saw, with a friend or relative holding Stanton down at each corner. His father had already sworn to kill Charles Hudd but everybody in Maggie's tavern had heard him say it, including the new sheriff, which made vengeance difficult, even when the operation wasn't a success and Doc Brightsides had to come back next month and take off another nine inches.

That was about the time the country elected Abe Lincoln president. As much by bad luck as bad judgment he had to preside over a civil war.

Kentucky chose to be neutral, which was a high-minded way of dodging the issue. In fact Kentucky was far from neutral. The Mississippi was the main trade route from North to South. As the rebel states stockpiled for a fight, Kentucky sent huge boatloads of goods down the river, and made a fat profit out of the conflict. At that stage, the South had all the romantic appeal. Almost to a man, the Kentucky state militia rode south and joined the Confederate Army. Often they came back to skirmish and raid; often, they settled old grudges while they were at it. This created new grudges, and so it went. Kentucky was never neutral. It was incurably split. Towns were divided, streets, families. Here was a war within the war; as if one wasn't enough.

MEN! BRACE
YOURSELVES!

The Killicks backed the rebels. Hudd was for the Union. It figured.

Dan went out one morning, saw the Lexington Rifles riding south and looking as smart as new paint, ran back to get his horse and didn't even wait to tell his parents he was going. He saw Stanton sitting in the sun – that was about all Stanton did nowadays – and went over to hug him goodbye. Stanton shook his brother's hand so vigorously that Stanton's stumpy arm bounced about. 'Hey, kill a Yankee for me,' Stanton said.

'I'll kill you a dozen.' Dan hated the way the stump flopped. Why didn't Stanton tie it down? 'Damn Yankees can't fight. Soft as shit. You'll see.'

Charles Hudd thought Lincoln was a crook but nevertheless, the Union must be above politics. 'This country could fall apart if it ain't wired together,' he told his wife. 'We only just got California and Oregon organized. Texas came in, what was it, fifteen years ago? Now all of a sudden South Carolina wakes up with a bad headache and the whole South wants to be its own nation. Suppose everyone in Wisconsin gets drunk and decides to quit and join Canada? We can't afford that way of thinking. It's …' He searched for a word. 'It's frivolous.' Now that he was safely married, Charles Hudd despised frivolity. 'The Union is a serious matter.'

'What do you intend to do?' she asked. Mary Hudd was not a woman to dodge the issue.

'Don't know,' he said.

He thought about it for a week. During that week he became increasingly close to her two boys. He took them fishing, hunting.

They all went to an auction and he let them bid for a few items, a scythe, two spades, some lanterns, that sort of stuff. Mary was there, and she took pride in their maturity. She knew by then what he had decided.

'Well, I'll miss you,' she said. 'We haven't had long together, have we?' No point in tears. Theirs had not been a grand passion. Still, she couldn't stand to think of losing a second husband so soon.

~

He rode into Ohio and joined the Federal army at Dayton. The officer who interviewed him came to the conclusion that he was not a natural leader but he was tall, fairly handsome and quite well educated, and so he gave him a captaincy and the command of a recruiting unit. Good decision. Charles Hudd's Kentucky accent made a favourable impression all across Pennsylvania and into New York State. Here was a Southerner who opposed the rebels, so obviously the South must be divided against itself. Hooray for the war and a weak enemy! Enlist, now, while stocks of glory last!

'I can tell you this,' Hudd said to the crowds of potential recruits as he held his pistol by its barrel and whacked the butt against his palm, 'from my own personal experience, all it takes is a bullet in the right place and your average rebel goes down looking strangely surprised.' That usually won a respectful laugh. Stanton Killick hadn't been a rebel at the time, not strictly speaking, but he was the only man Charles had shot, so he had to do.

It was a soft life. The recruiting party rode from village to village, rarely covering more than ten miles a day. Captain Hudd made a speech, ate a civilian meal, slept in a comfortable bed, rose late, moved on. A couple of sergeants kept records and directed the recruits to the nearest army camp.

Then a bundle of three letters caught up with him.

Dear Charles, the first began, *I and the boys are well but I am sorry to say that Ruthie died three days ago. There has been fever around Rock Springs and I think Sarah may be infected – she is in bed and very weak ...*

He tore open the second letter. No mention of fever.

... the Confederacy has been here! Not a big force, only fifty mounted men led by Capt. John Hunt Morgan, but big enough to

take Rock Springs. Morgan made a loud speech on the courthouse steps, all the time waving his hat which was full of feathers like a Cherokee chief. They lived in Maggie's tavern, drank it dry and galloped off, nobody knows where. We are all alarmed ...

The third letter was dated a week later.

Morgan's men came back, although not so many – they have been in a fight. Stayed here on the farm two nights, made us feed them, stole all the hams, preserves, etc., stole all the horses, tried to burn the barns but Lonzo told them Federal troops were near and this frightened them so they quit. Mr Dan Killick was one of them ...

Charles stuffed the unread pages in his pocket. Before the day was out he was riding south with written orders to join General Buck T. Masterman, a lawyer turned politician with no military experience to speak of. Lincoln had made Masterman a general because his family owned a couple of influential newspapers in Illinois. Anyway, Lincoln was short of generals. At that stage of the war he was short of everything except failure and critics. Masterman was eager. Maybe he would turn out to be the Napoleon of North America.

Charles Hudd found Masterman's army in camp near Waynesburg in southern Pennsylvania. A Confederate force was just over the border, in Virginia, looking for trouble. This wasn't Kentucky, where Hudd wished ideally to be, but it was the next best thing, and there was the promise of real action.

At first he couldn't find anyone to report to. All too damn busy. Come back after the battle. Very discouraging. Then he came across Buck T. Masterman's tent. 'Think I might speak to the general?' he asked.

'Sure,' the guard said. 'Every other bastard has.'

Four journalists were arguing over a large map. The general was alone, seated on a stool, chewing at a pen. Hudd saluted. 'What's another word for 'enemy'?' Masterman asked.

'Foe?' Hudd suggested.

Masterman disliked it. 'You see, what I got so far, I got *Men! Brace yourselves! The enemy is at hand.*' He shook his head. 'Lacks punch. Got no kick to it. Who are you?'

Hudd told him.

'Find yourself a job. Organize the ammunition. I got my battle all planned out, that wasn't difficult, but writing the Order of the Day, this is the tough part of being a general.'

Hudd said he was glad to find the general in such a confident mood.

'Find 'em and lick 'em, captain, that's all there is to it. Find 'em and lick 'em.' Masterman returned to his Order of the Day. 'Foe, you said. No, that's no good.'

Next day Masterman's army advanced into Virginia, and the day after that it attacked the rebel force, and by sundown he knew he was useless as a general. From first to last he bungled the battle. He had no idea how to direct large bodies of men. He told them to attack, and soon they were lost in the smoke of battle. When he sent fresh orders, this company was dead, or that squadron had vanished altogether. He panicked. He screamed abuse at his staff officers. The enemy was heavily outnumbered, and by mid-afternoon it had slipped quietly away. Long before then, Masterman was emotionally spent. He fell asleep in his tent. At dusk, Charles Hudd saw him on the battlefield, watching his men bring in the dead. By Civil War standards it had been a small battle, no more than a few hundred killed. 'I did my best,' Masterman said, over and over again. 'I did my best.' It was true. He spoke clearly, but his face shone with tears. Charles Hudd watched carefully. He had never before seen a man cry like that: weeping but not sobbing. But then, of course, Hudd had never watched himself in the belvedere, in the storm.

~

'Hey,' Dan said. 'This ain't right, George.' He stopped and rested his bad knee.

George went on for perhaps ten yards down the dry creek bed. It was all rounded, polished rocks; you had to walk carefully or your boots skidded off them. He looked back and was surprised at how thin his brother had become: the grey uniform was baggy, the face was sunken, the jawbone and cheekbones suddenly sharp. Couldn't be sudden, must have been like that for days, but George hadn't noticed the change. Too much else to worry about, George being a sergeant and all. 'Christ's sakes, Dan,' he said in a voice like a handful of gravel, 'stop your fuckin' whinin' and shift your fuckin' ass.' The army had altered George's style of speech.

'Yeah, but this ain't right.' Dan took a pebble and threw it at the scoured, baked, empty landscape. 'I mean, look. This ain't worth fightin' over. Hell, this ain't worth fartin' over.'

'Bragg knows better'n you.' General Bragg had led his Confederate army deep into Kentucky. Now it was in the Knobs, a long, hillocky strip shaped like a battered horseshoe that contained the Bluegrass country. If Bragg knew why they were here, he hadn't told them.

'Bragg knows better, does he?' Dan said. 'Ask him where the goddamn water is, then.' His voice had the squeak of self-pity in it. That was new, too.

George moved on. Dan followed, limping like an old man. He had slipped and gashed his right knee. If they found water he promised himself he would soak it for an hour. 'We should have stayed with Morgan's Marauders,' he grumbled.

George was thinking: this is a damnfool place to fight a war. Knobs is what it is, just picayune hills as far as anyone can see, nothing growing except trees too stupid to die, no water and heat hot enough to bake a man's brains. 'You get lost, Dan, I ain't comin' back to look for you,' he said, not bothering to look around.

'Whole damn army's lost,' Dan said. It was nearly true. Many of Bragg's troops were out wandering the Knobs, searching for water. 'Damn musket's damn near broke my damn shoulder off.' He switched it to his other shoulder. Soon that was aching too.

He was stumbling along, dreaming of beer, big foaming jugs of cold beer, jugs that never emptied no matter how much you poured into your cracked salty grateful mouth, when he followed George's footprints across a patch of sand and around a boulder that stuck out like a peaked cap.

'Way I see it,' George said, 'there's enough for all of us.' He was talking to a young blond soldier in a blue uniform. Water dripped from the soldier's chin. His legs were braced and his carbine kept wavering as if he were facing a high wind. His eyes were grey as woodsmoke and huge with fear. One tooth was missing, an upper tooth on the left, and his tongue kept seeking and leaving the gap.

'Stay back,' the soldier said. But Dan came on, fast, straight at the pool of water in the shadow of the boulder, fell to his knees and stuck his face in it.

'Idiot,' George said to him. 'Look, you gone and stirred up all the muck.'

Dan sat on his heels. He looked at the soldier and he squirted a long stream at his boots. 'That's a Yankee,' he said. 'First I seen up real close. On the small side, ain't he?'

George laid down his musket and took his bayonet from his belt. 'You stay away,' the soldier said, gruff as he could, which wasn't much. 'I just want a drink,' George said. He squatted by the pool and used the bayonet to skim aside the worst of the slime that Dan had disturbed.

'Where you from, boy?' Dan asked. He had poked the end of his musket in the sand when he drank. 'Shit,' he said. 'Now I got to clean this bastard.'

'I'm from Spendthrift,' the soldier said, trying to make it sound tough. Spendthrift was not a tough name. 'Up near Lexington.'

'I got friends from Lexington,' Dan said. He went back to the pool for another drink.

'We're from Rock Springs, him an' me,' George said. 'Rock Springs ain't near anythin'.' He laughed. 'Maybe Tennessee. Fall in the river, you'll float clear to Tennessee. Take a month or three. Cameron twists an' turns so much, it goes through Rock Springs three times 'fore it knows where it's headin'.'

'John Hunt Morgan,' Dan said. 'I raided with him all up and down this state. You ever met John Hunt Morgan?' He was washing his cut knee in the scummy pool.

'You're worse'n a hog!' his brother said. 'Ain't that disgustin'?' he asked the soldier. To Dan, he said, 'Next person to drink there is gonna get your blood an' scabs an' stuff, ain't he?'

'Lucky fellah. People been after my blood for years.' The joke was out before he realized he'd made it. He grinned with pride.

'I seen Morgan a few times, in Lexington,' the soldier said. 'His family are rich, real rich.' He had lowered the carbine. His hair pushed curls out of the sides of his cap. Below his ears, at the corner of the jaw, a fuzz that had never seen a razor made a pattern like the nap on velvet. Now that he knew they weren't going to kill each other he became curious. 'What's the grub like in your army?' he asked.

'Mules eat better'n we do,' Dan said. 'You?'

'We're eating the mules, is what it tastes like. Never enough, anyway.'

'Armies are all the same, I guess,' George said. 'Who called the cook a bastard? Who called the bastard a cook?'

The soldier grinned, and felt guilty. These men should be his prisoners. 'I reckon I better be going,' he said. George's face changed: it twisted with anger, and he reached for his musket. *Oh Jesus*, the soldier told himself. Then George fell on his rump, hard, as if someone had put a hook around his neck and yanked it. The soldier heard a crisp neat bang, and he turned. Two men in blue uniform stood in the streambed, fifty yards away. Then there was an almighty deafening bang, and he turned again. Dan was lowering his musket and squinting through its blue-black smoke.

George groaned, an inhuman sound, more like a slowly splitting plank, and he slumped over sideways. The soldier caught up with what was happening. He ran. He ran so fast that one foot clipped the other ankle and he tumbled, lost his carbine, fell and cracked his mouth against the barrel.

It was the greatest pain he had ever felt, or ever would feel. Dan heard terrible sounds coming from his brother. He snatched up the bayonet and fell on the young blond soldier like a stabbing machine.

The two Unionist soldiers were running away, looking for something to hide behind. Dan sat next to the leaking corpse and got his breath back. George was watching him.

'You ain't killed, then,' Dan said.

'Shoulder,' George said. 'Felt like I got whomped by a ten-pound sledge.'

'Yankee bastards. Sneakin' up on us.'

The dead soldier twitched. Dan stood up and kicked him in the head.

'You got a terrible temper,' George said. 'Come on, brother. You killed him three times over. Take his money and his gun and help me out of here.'

The shots had attracted others from their regiment, and now that the enemy had been found, the two armies drifted into battle. The more they fought, the more they fought. Eventually about 28,000 men were shooting and being shot at. About a quarter of them got hit. At the end, General Bragg pulled his men out and went back to Tennessee, so he lost; but the Unionist army failed to chase him, so it didn't win. Nobody won, least of all a seventeen-year-old from Spendthrift, who had only joined the army to prove to a neighbour's daughter how brave he was. How brave was he? About average, it turned out.

General Buck T. Masterman went home and concentrated on drinking himself to death. This was something he had a natural talent for, and he achieved it in only one year and forty-seven days, at the time a record for southern Illinois.

Masterman's army, or the remains of it, was distributed to other Yankee generals.

Charles Hudd, now a major, went to General Grant and did tedious, essential staff work – the mechanics of slaughter: ensuring that tens of thousands of men arrived on time and got fed and watered and properly armed, in exactly the right place to kill and be killed. One of the things that Hudd learned from watching Grant was the absolute necessity of accepting large-scale death as a fact of war. Grant never lost any sleep over it. And he never rested. When an opponent quit and retreated, Grant drove his great military machine hard at the enemy and battered him some more. Hudd admired that. He was never in the fighting, he was just one of those who made the fighting possible; and because he knew he wasn't a brilliant staff officer, he made himself work harder to compensate.

Grant went off to Virginia, to fight Lee. That was when he gave Hudd to Sherman.

Sherman was in Chattanooga, Tennessee, preparing for his great march on Atlanta. Ninety thousand men take a deal of organizing. Hudd worked all day and night. Sherman stormed across Georgia and burned Atlanta. Then he learned that a Confederate force had circled around behind him. It was raiding his supply lines; worse still, it threatened Tennessee.

Sherman detached an army under General Schofield and sent it to meet the threat. Hudd went too. Schofield fought a Rebel force at Franklin, Tennessee, and won a clear victory. Hudd contributed to this success. He worked around the clock; around too many clocks. As Schofield celebrated, Hudd collapsed from exhaustion.

Schofield had more Rebels to fight, so he left Hudd behind, with a corporal to take care of him. Two weeks later they got news of a crushing Unionist triumph at the Battle of Nashville. What Confederate soldiers had survived were making a long retreat to Mississippi, and they were unlikely to return.

Hudd had been in uniform for almost four years. When he felt strong enough to get on a horse, he decided he deserved some leave. They set off for Kentucky. 'By way of Nashville,' he told the corporal. 'There must be a military hospital there. I'll get an army doctor to examine me.'

It was late December 1864, well into winter, a hard time to ride across Tennessee just to find a doctor. When they got to Nashville it wasn't worth the ride. The town was half-empty. Hudd rode in and saw gravediggers and garrison troops, a few weary civilians, a lot of wounded. The doctors were overworked, up to the elbows in surgery.

Hudd said it didn't matter, he felt greatly restored, and he could take care of himself now. He sent the corporal back to his unit.

~

'I think I'll go and live in New Zealand,' the mayor of Nashville said. 'Do you know anything of New Zealand, sir?'

'Not a thing, sir,' Hudd said.

'This country is ruined. Finished. Look around you. We Americans have a knack for self-destruction. A taste for it, perhaps. Land in New Zealand is quite cheap, would you think?'

'Possibly.'

They were in the mayor's office, sitting in a corner to avoid the rain that dripped monotonously from holes in the roof. 'This town will never be the same again. Canada is another possibility. Is it as cold as men say, d'you think?'

'Probably.'

All this time, the mayor was looking at the portrait which Hudd had given him. The mayor was grey-haired, slim, about fifty, and his face was too tired to show the feeling of his words. He sighed. 'Not Canada, then ... No, don't know this lady.' He gave the painting back.

'Not a face a man is likely to forget,' Hudd said gently.

'True, major.'

'My information is that she came to Nashville, or near Nashville, just before war began.'

'Many have left. Because of the war.'

'Of course.' He took great care as he rolled up the portrait. 'Well, thank you for your time.'

The mayor got up and emptied a bucket of rainwater out of the window, and replaced it under a drip. This drip made a hard, metallic rap, unlike the plops in the other buckets. The noise formed a ragged rhythm that was always out of step. 'You are not the first officer in a blue uniform to come in search of a civilian,' he said.

Hudd thought about that. 'You're referring to spies?' he said. The mayor shrugged. 'Nobody is looking for spies, sir,' Hudd said. 'There is no work left for any spy in Tennessee or Georgia. Nor, from what I hear, in Virginia. Believe me, sir, I take no pleasure in saying this. The war has been a tragedy for our country, on both sides. I'm only relieved that it's almost over.'

The mayor watched him slide the portrait into a leather tube, much scuffed and scratched, and secure the end with a strap.

'You have carried that picture a long way, major?'

'In four years I have never been without it, sir. The case was made for a telescope. Ideal for this purpose.'

'You will forgive any impertinence if I ask: your inquiry was not of a military nature?'

'I was to marry the lady, sir.'

'Ah. Miss Killick.'

'Yes.'

'I congratulate you. Many a Nashville man dreamed of a similar fate. The last I heard, Miss Killick was staying at the Henderson Farm. You'll find it without difficulty. It's in the middle of the battlefield.'

The rain that kept the mayor busy emptying buckets also discouraged Charles Hudd from riding into the battlefield. At least, that's what he told himself. It was a heavy rain, and cold, and the sky was dark grey with the gloom of low-hanging cloud to the horizon, so there was plenty more of this misery to come. *You've been rained on before,* he thought. *What's so terrible about this?* Back came the answer: *That battlefield must be a swamp by now.* But he knew his reluctance had nothing to do with the rain. He had carried the portrait for four years, unrolled it and re-rolled it a hundred times, and now that he knew she was less than an hour's ride away, he was afraid. Love frightened him. It was easier to dream about her picture, and dream about meeting again one day in warm, sunny surroundings, blue sky, birdsong, happiness. Not this bleak, broken, sodden countryside.

Charles Hudd shivered. Standing around wasn't solving anything. He could either stay, or go. It was unthinkable to leave Nashville without seeing her, so he might as well get on with it.

He found a heap of oilskin capes in a corner of a barracks, and took one. It was torn and bloodstained, so he took a second, and wore both. Rain penetrated them by the time he reached the battlefield. Soon it had soaked through his uniform.

The mayor was wrong when he said Hudd would find Henderson Farm without difficulty. The fighting had left most buildings in ruins. Hudd saw no civilians. The few soldiers he met were no help. After a couple of hours' searching, Hudd was so chilled he was clenching his teeth to stop them chattering. His stomach was growling with hunger. His horse was weary from dragging its feet through mud. He hated Tennessee, and Nashville, and occasionally he hated JoBeth Killick. When he saw smoke rising from what was left of a farmhouse, he turned his horse towards it. He found a barn. The barn was full of black soldiers, all wounded, some dead. The sick sweet smell made Hudd cough. Nobody spoke, nobody moved. It was a week since the battle.

A fire made a dull glow. He walked carefully between the bodies. They sprawled, and the light was poor. He trod on a hand. Its owner made no sound. 'Forgive me,' Hudd murmured, and looked at the man, and wished he hadn't.

He knelt by the fire and absorbed its heat. All his limbs relaxed in a rush of surrender. His eyes closed. Warmth had never been so warm as this. 'Get some goddamn wood,' someone said. It was a voice charred by overwork, as harsh as bad whiskey. Hudd sighed. A boot kicked him in the ass. That got him up. It was a woman, dirty, haggard, so tired she couldn't stand straight, and it was the woman he was looking for. 'For the love of Christ,' he said.

She studied him as if he had fouled his breeches. He was startled to see how thin she was, how red and raw her eyes. 'The love of Christ won't help that fire,' she said. 'Get some goddamn wood.'

He went out and found broken timbers in broken buildings, and carried some back. 'More,' she said. He fetched more. She was doing things to the wounds of a few men, things which he preferred not to watch. When she finished, he said, 'This is a terrible place.'

That amused her, slightly. 'That what you came to tell me? This place is terrible? You never were too bright.'

'Forgive me. Stupid remark. But ... How do you come to be here?'

'Yeah. Good question. Plain dumb stupidity. I got no doctorin' skills, I ain't a nurse, I can't help these poor black sons-a-bitches. But nobody else has come near them. You're the first white man through that door. They been lyin' here, rottin' an' dyin' in their blood an' shit all week. I guess that makes you proud to be a Union officer. You fightin' to emancipate the niggers, right? You sure emancipated this lot.'

'I had no idea,' he said. 'I'm sure the general isn't aware – '

'Didn't come lookin', did he?'

'I'll get help at once. I promise you.'

She shook her head. 'Want to do these poor sufferin' niggers a favour, shoot 'em. They ain't goin' nowhere.'

Hudd was shocked. 'You need rest. You must rest.'

'If you won't shoot 'em, then I'll shoot you. Plenty guns lyin' around here. Armies are good at shootin' people. You Yankees shot George. I got word a month ago. Shot George dead.'

'I'm sorry.'

'Not much of a man, George, but he was the only big brother I ever had. Yankees shot him dead, on some ugly useless hill in Kentucky nobody wanted much anyway.'

Tears were beginning to flood her eyes. He had never seen her cry before. He felt a flicker of panic. 'I'll fetch help,' he said. 'You stay here. Then we'll see.'

He got out as fast as he could without treading on bodies that were already damaged enough, and he rode into Nashville. He sought out a senior medical officer, and as he was telling him about a barn full of wounded blacks, he knew he must sit down or he would fall down. While the doctor was taking his pulse, Hudd fainted. 'Malaria,' the doctor said.

It was ten days before Hudd could get out of bed. Three days later he was strong enough to ride to the battlefield. The sun shone on a fatigue party, digging graves next to the ashes of the barn. It had been burned down once the bodies were removed. Nobody knew anything about a white woman.

~

Hudd got discharged on medical grounds. Went back to Rock Springs. What was left of it.

He walked his horse down Main Street. That was a joke, calling it Main Street. Looked like a twister hit it. No hotel, no bank, no schoolroom. The sheriff's office had gone, so had the gunshop, the schoolhouse, bathhouse, all the stores bar one, the barbershop, lawyer's, rooming-house, all gone. Other gaps in the street were just burned-out frames; he couldn't remember what used to be there.

Maggie's tavern survived. She was sitting in the doorway, peeling potatoes.

'I never thought to come back to this, Maggie,' he said. 'What in God's name happened?'

'You're the expert,' she said. He was still in uniform. 'You tell me.' She tossed a potato into a bucket.

He went home to the farm and found it falling apart. 'Like the rest of Kentucky,' Mary said. She called her boys to help him up the stairs and into bed. The malaria was still sucking on his strength.

She nursed him back to health. He was on his feet when the South surrendered, and he was up and about on the day that Congress passed the Thirteenth Amendment.

The news took a long time to make its way up the Cameron. Most white people who heard it didn't want to believe it, said it was just rumour. In the war, a lot of news had turned out to be rumour, and wrong. By the time the report reached Rock Springs and was proved to be accurate, definite and true, 1865 was long gone.

Mary said, 'Well, this is what you were fighting for.'

'We fought to win,' he said. 'We didn't give a damn about the reasons.'

FREE TO WHAT?

Y ou're free to go,' Charles Hudd said.

Jacob waited. 'That all?'

'Enough, ain't it?' Charles kept walking up and down, in a hurry going nowhere. *If he wants to piss*, Jacob thought, *why don't he piss? Ain't nobody but me an' the hogs to see.*

'If you say,' Jacob said.

'I do say. Now stop doin' that.'

'I already stopped.' Jacob rested on his sledgehammer. 'I stopped when you hollered.'

'I mean stop for good.' Master Charles delivered a great kick at a clump of weeds. 'What in hell's name you doin', anyway?'

'Fixin' this fence so these hogs don't git out.'

'Well … forget it. Let the goddamn hogs go free. You're free, Zach's free, Josh is free, Lonzo's free, every last one of you darkies is free, understand? Men and women both. Children too. All free! You got any nigger hounds or nigger fish or nigger birds? They're free. All free! Understand?'

They stood a yard apart, staring. Jacob Hudd had to look up, for Master Charles was a foot taller. Jacob wore homespun shirt and trousers, sun-bleached and baggy, and cast-off shoes with the uppers cut to let his toes sprawl. His face looked as hard as iron, and just as blank. He'd never known exactly how old he was, but he knew he was a few years older than his owner, and Charles Hudd was thirty-five. Just thirty-five, and his shoulders slumped like a grandfather. Jacob remembered Master Charles when he was eighteen. Half the age but twice the man. Ah well.

'All free, Massah Charles,' Jacob said. 'Good. I understan'. You want me to tell the others? Fine, I tell the others. But these hogs, now. You don't want these hogs runnin' free, Massah Charles. So I'm gonna git on here and fix this fence.'

As he turned, Charles snatched the sledge from him, stepped away and swung it full circle, two-handed, time and again, until Jacob heard the rush of air and then a grunt, and the hammer flew high. Charles was gasping, and slightly giddy, when he turned back. 'You don't work for me any more, Jacob!' he cried. 'You and everyone like you – you're free! Now take your goddamn freedom and go, or else I'll kick your black ass from here to Washington DC!'

'You say free,' Jacob said. 'Free to what?' He had never seen Master Charles like this, never in his whole life.

'That,' Charles said, 'is your goddamn problem.'

$\sim$

Five miles downriver (or two miles as the buzzard flew, over the Ridge), the Killicks took less time to implement the Thirteenth Amendment, because they had fewer slaves to free.

During the war they'd lost some, either through sickness or through runaways, and what with markets being so bad and everybody else in the same predicament and no fresh stock coming up from the South, they couldn't get replacements. Soon the Killicks had to get twelve slaves' work out of six niggers. They kept pushing, kept driving, didn't spare themselves, never let up the pressure, sunup to sundown, seven days a week – but in the end they had to admit failure. By the time the war finished, the farm wasn't doing half as well as when it began, not that it had ever done well at the best of times, but now there were more mouths to feed: loud, large, fast-growing children who ate everything in sight and wanted more. Everybody grumbled; and dissatisfaction being catching, the slaves complained too. (They were down to four: one died of the flux and another vanished in the night.) It had already been proven that kicking niggers was bad for the feet and not good for much else, but the Killicks being poor learners they kept bitching and kicking and their farm kept on getting poorer, until they were forced into something shameful and degrading. They had to do nigger-work: chopping weeds, drilling crops, making harvest, fetching and carrying. The Killicks never forgave Lincoln for that. Now he'd stolen their last four slaves. And not a nickel in compensation. The man was a crook.

BUZZARD BAIT

It was a Tuesday when Hudd told his slaves to go, and they went. On Wednesday they came back. Nowhere to stay, they said. Nothing to do with me, he said, and ordered them off the farm. They went. It rained. After dark they came back.

On Thursday morning Jacob tried to get Hudd to hire them. 'I got no damn money, you old fool,' he said.

'You just pay us what you figure you can,' Jacob said.

'Nothin'!' Hudd roared. 'I've done my figurin' and there's nothin' left over for pay. Nothin'!'

Jacob was worried by Hudd's complexion. His cheeks were blotchy, his lips tinged with purple. 'Summon's gotta see to the crops,' Jacob said. 'Crops don't – '

'Get! Get away from here! You don't belong!'

Nobody wanted them in Rock Springs. On Friday they drifted back to the farm. Hudd saw them coming and went out with cans of rock oil and set fire to their cabins.

'Even the Yankees never done that to us,' Josh said.

The flames ate through the roofs and burst out, dancing.

'Yankees burned all Georgia an' half Tennessee,' Lonzo said. 'Lotta niggers in them states.'

'Tennessee's fulla harlots an' moonshiners,' said Josh. He had got religion during the war. 'Burnin's best thing for them.'

Everyone, including Hudd, watched the last cabin roof crash. 'Where you expect us to go now?' Jacob asked Hudd.

'Anywhere. Go north. Go to Chicago.'

'North's cold,' Lonzo said. 'People wears furs in Chicago. I read it in that newspaper you give me. Can't grow corn in Chicago, too goddamn cold, how can we – '

'I don't know! You can't stay here, that's all.'

The wind gusted ashes and made them turn their backs on the fires.

'Ain't no farm needs us,' Jacob said. 'Rock Springs don't want a bunch of niggers messin' up the street. Further south you go, more bust-up everythin' is. Great to be free, ain't it?'

'Well, it wasn't my idea,' Hudd said gloomily. His stepsons were watching from a distance, young men now, with minds of their own. Waiting to inherit, no doubt. He felt a chill shiver. Malaria again? He groaned at the thought.

'Yeah, I heard, we're goin',' Jacob said. Those who had anything to pick up, picked it up and began to drift away. 'Dunno where, but we're goin'.'

'Could go up there,' Lonzo said. He was pointing at the Ridge.

'Nothin' up there but rattlers an' dead Induns,' Nat said.

'Tree snakes,' Josh said. 'Black bear, jumpin' spiders, cotton-mouths, bats as big as buzzards, coupla panther. More Indum ghosts than you can count.'

'You seen 'em?' Lonzo asked.

'Didn't stay to meet the ghosts.'

'You're fulla muleshit, Josh. You ain't never been up there. Fact is, nobody ain't never been up there. Good. We can live up there.'

Charles Hudd laughed in astonishment. 'You niggers aim to live on Hudd Ridge? Buzzard bait, that's what you'll be. Hudd Ridge gonna live on *you*.'

'That bother you any, Mistah Charles?' Lonzo said; and Hudd had no reply: for the first time, he had been put in his place by a nigger. 'Seems like the Ridge the only place left for folks like us,' Lonzo said. 'We won't bother nobody, if nobody fusses us.'

Jacob had come back to listen. The others stopped where they were. Flakes of bright grey ash flew past, as light as spring blossom.

'You're serious about this,' Hudd said.

'Findin' somewhere to live ain't no joke to me,' Lonzo said. He looked at the farmhouse, neglected and in need of paint but still a big, extravagant building. Again, Hudd felt the sting of rebuke. His instinct was to retaliate. 'You see,' he said, 'the thing is, boy, I hadn't thought of sellin' any of that land up there.'

'Uh,' Lonzo said. His expression did not change. Too much Cherokee blood in him for that.

'No sir,' Hudd said. 'Sellin' hadn't crossed my mind.'

'Jake,' Lonzo said. He and Jacob went aside and talked softly. Zeke came back. 'How much an acre?' he asked.

'How much an acre what?' Hudd knew what Lonzo meant; he just wasn't ready to believe it, that's all. Niggers owning land: the world was turned upside-down: black was white.

'Top of the ridge, Mistah Charles. You ready to sell?'

'Look ... I ain't takin' Confederate paper money. All those hundred-dollar bills Andrew Jackson printed ain't worth wallpaper, so ...' He stopped because he could see Lonzo was waiting for him to stop.

'U.S. dollars, Mistah Charles.'

'Oh.' The thought of having his own darkies owning his own land gave Hudd a pain, a real actual pain somewhere between his belly and his lungs. On the other hand he needed money. But to sell the Ridge was a sort of defeat. And not to sell was a selfish folly. He pounded his chest, seeking to subdue the pain, and without thinking too much about it, he announced, 'Five dollars an acre.'

Jacob heard. 'Which way Chicago?' he said, and walked off.

Lonzo's face might have been cast in bronze. 'Onliest way that jungle up there could fetch five dollars an acre is it got a big old Indum silver mine up every creek bed.'

'Stop joshin' me, boy. I ain't in the mood. Seein' as you niggers are family almost, I'll make it a dollar. How many acres you want?'

'How many you got?'

Hudd didn't know, exactly. The Ridge twisted and plunged and sprawled. A thousand acres? Two? 'Plenty,' he said.

'Yup,' Lonzo said. 'We could take a hundred acres an' you wouldn't know it had gone. Pay you dollar an acre. Hundred dollar. Cash on the barrel.'

Hudd turned and looked up at the crest line. A tangled mass of green was edged a ragged black by the glaring sun. Twenty acres at five, or a hundred at a buck apiece, what was the difference? It was all worthless. 'Done,' he said.

They shook hands. Lonzo wanted title to the land in writing. 'We just shook on it,' Hudd said. 'Yeah, then one day you die,' Lonzo said. 'Paper don't die.'

'I should never have given you a pencil,' Hudd said.

'First spare nickel I get, I'll pay you for the pencil.'

His stepsons joined Hudd as he walked back to the house. Curtis, the elder, said, 'Did you just sell land to them niggers?' Charles nodded. Now Curtis was too disgusted to speak.

'But they ain't got no money,' said his brother, Floyd. 'They must of stole it.'

'They saved it,' Charles said. 'Made baskets an' sold 'em. Mended chairs. I always let 'em raise chickens, so they sold eggs. Caught fish an' sold.'

'That's pennies an' nickels,' Curtis sneered. 'Takes a year to save a dollar.'

'Time is what slaves got plenty of.'

'So we got niggers for neighbours now,' Floyd said.

'Not for long. That Ridge ain't made for livin' on. Hell, it ain't made for starvin' on. Those niggers bought themselves a graveyard. First thing they should do is dig a big hole so's the last man got somewhere to die in.'

DON'T THINK, JUST DO

The panther was old but the rabbit had been even older, in rabbit-years. Also the rabbit had got fat and lazy, while the panther was still lean and mean, even if one eye was clouded and the hip-joints suffered from the rain. He couldn't win a female any more. He lived alone, so he had the rabbit all to himself. He had eaten the meat and he was sprawling on his side, one paw trapping the carcass while he sucked at the rib-cage, when he heard the first faint whisper of voices. Then the trees shimmered in the wind, and that noise washed the whisper away. The panther's head was high and its neat, triangular ears were pricked.

The strange sounds came again, still distant but clearer. The panther fixed them: they were moving uphill, not fast. He got up and yawned. He sniffed the remains of the rabbit and decided they weren't worth taking. He loped up the hillside, using a tracery of tracks that were mostly tunnels in the undergrowth. When a gulley or a landslip crossed his path he jumped it without pause, front legs reaching and hind legs thrusting. He was old and grey about the muzzle but he could still make jumping look like flying. He was idly chasing a couple of small deer, just for fun because he could see them, when he caught a whiff of an extraordinary scent and he stopped.

Not the deer. Deer had a sweet, soft smell. Not wild pig, which smelled fruity; not black bear, which smelled sour; in fact not like any animal the panther had ever met. This smell teased his nostrils. At the top of the slope he hid among rocks and watched as the smell and the voices became stronger.

He had seen men before but always at a great distance. They had been slow and slight and no threat to anything. Now a whole bunch of them was trudging up a half-dried-out streambed, splashing and slipping and calling to each other. The panther saw that some were small. After the plump rabbit he was not hungry, but one day he might be. He slipped away. There was ample wilderness for all. And he was too old to go looking for a fight.

~

They rested at the top of the stream, where it bubbled out of the rock.

'You spent all we saved on *this*?' Sarah said. She'd been a house slave; she didn't like the land even when it was flat. 'Dollar an acre? Know how long it took me to save that three dollar I give you?'

'We shoulda gone to Africa,' Josh said.

'Five years,' Sarah said. 'Maybe six, I don't even remember, it's been so long.'

'Gone to Africa!' Nat scoffed. 'What you gonna say, you get to Africa? Full of heathen niggers don't speak English. You speak their jibber-jabber?'

'Ruthie gone to the right place,' Martha said. She soaked the edge of her skirt and wiped sweat from her face. 'Ruthie got took by the Lord cus the Lord knew she didn't deserve to suffer in this place, no sir. This ain't no Promised Land.'

'Hallelujah!' Josh cried. Martha threw a rock at him.

'We gonna live here?' one of the children asked. Outside the streambed they were surrounded by a tangle of brier, thousand of strands, millions of thorns.

'Ask Jake,' Bettsy said. 'He had the money.'

'Ask Lonzo,' Jacob said. 'He did the buyin'.'

'Hey!' Lonzo said. 'You agreed.'

'Didn't agree to no jungle. You said, look at that Ridge, no people up there, gotta be overflowin' milk an' honey you said.'

'Praise the Lord!' Josh said.

'I never said no milk an' honey. I said, if the bears an' the buzzards can live up there, we ain't gonna starve in a hurry.'

'Ain't gonna eat too good neither,' Buck said in his whispery lisp, 'seein' as how bears live off frogs an' snakes.' He peered at the blazing sky. 'What them buzzards live off is poor fools like us.'

'You're so big an' all, go catch us a bear,' Bettsy said.

'Don't you think I can't.' Buck lay back, with a rounded rock for a pillow. 'Speak kindly, maybe I might.'

'We gonna sit here an' listen to this foolishness all day?' Martha demanded. 'Or until the crack o'doom?'

'Mighty an' merciful God!' Josh cried.

'You go on like that and maybe I'll just strangle you,' Nat told him. 'You be first nigger martyr to die for his faith.' Josh did not know whether to be frightened or flattered.

'I never seen no bear eat no snake,' Bettsy said.

'Bears is fast,' Nat said. 'I seen a bear eat a big old moccasin snake so fast the head was comin' out the bear's ass before he swallowed its tail.'

Lonzo left them arguing and went back down the stream. He found a track, explored it, mostly on his hands and knees, and came out at the crest. It was all rock, curved and polished like a giant mushroom, with a fringe of pines. Far below, the fields that had been his life were scraps of patchwork. The Hudd farmhouse was so tiny he could reach out and cover it twice over with one thumb. He turned and looked behind him. Nothing but forest that way. For the first time the future scared him. They were just a bunch of has-been slaves, chop the weeds, make the butter, clean the harness, cook the Master's meals. Do this, do that, don't think, just do. Now they had a hundred acres of bad land, land so useless even the Shawnee and the Cherokee turned their backs on it. And the leaves were starting to change colour. Soon it would be winter.

He went back down the track and up the stream and fetched everybody.

They were mostly so tired when they reached the great mushroom-rock that they wanted to sleep there. Martha would have nothing of it.

'Ain't no wild beasts gonna bother us here,' Jacob pointed out.

'Too open. Ain't you got no brains, Jake? Weather blows up in the night, this the *worst* place to be. I want *shelter*. Lonzo, get up that tree, look around. Find us some place where the wind can't blow us into Virginia.'

That night they slept under a pair of cedar trees so old that the ground beneath them was soft with the gatherings of fallen needles. There was also a stream nearby but that was no miracle: Hudd Ridge was slashed all over with streams.

When the sun came up the air was cold and dank. Everyone was hungry. The children were silent and miserable. The fire had gone out. 'Get some wood,' Jacob said to Nat.

'Get it yourself, old feller,' Nat growled.

'You don't work, you don't eat.'

'What's there to eat?'

They had enough cornmeal to make a little porridge. Jacob saw Lonzo stretching and yawning and went over to him. 'Where you brought us to?' he asked. Age and despair had thinned his voice. 'Got no food, no shelter, you spent our money, children gonna be dead in a week, ain't even got a spade to bury 'em.'

Early in the day, his belly empty, Lonzo had no patience for anyone, least of all old Jake with his blaming and whimpering. Jake's eyes were sticky with sleep and snot had dried on his lip. 'I'll get you food,' Lonzo said without thinking. He just wanted to get rid of Jake.

'Need it now.' Jake didn't believe him.

'I'll get it now!' Lonzo shouted. They all watched him go. He enjoyed the feeling, even though he knew neither where he was going nor what he would do when he got there.

SOLID GOLD MIRACLE

Wild turkey lived on the Ridge. At night they roosted on the hardwoods and by day they fed on fallen beechnuts and acorns and the like. Sometimes they flew down into the valley for a change of diet. The Killicks' crops, for instance. The birds enjoyed them and made plenty of noise as they fed. Nobody at the farm heard this. They were all indoors, shouting at each other.

'So now we're equal, is that it?' Ma Killick shouted at her husband. 'Any nigger's as good as me! I might as well be black. Is that it?'

'Go ask Lincoln! I didn't do it.'

'Lincoln's dead, Pa,' Stanton said woodenly.

'Shut up! You got no rights in this conversation,' Dan told him. 'You sat out the goddamn war while we – '

'You?' Stanton, suddenly enraged, pounded the table with his remaining fist. 'You had yourself a high old time with Morgan's Raiders, gettin' drunk an' stealin' chickens!'

'No boy of mine stole any chicken!' Ma Killick snapped. 'This is a holy Christian household, this is!'

'Who gives a damn about chickens?' Joe demanded. He had been drinking ever since breakfast, and his good eye was tinged an angry pink. 'Them Yankee Republican sons-a-bitches in Washington just stole all my niggers, an' you fools argue about chickens!'

'Well, I ain't shovellin' no hog-shit,' said his son Devereux, a terrible name for a boy. 'That's nigger-work, that is. Shovellin' hog-shit.'

'You, boy! Go wash your mouth out!' his mother ordered. He ignored her. He was seventeen, faster and bigger than she was. He sprawled in his chair and picked at a stain on his pants.

'Well, this is just wonderful, ain't it?' Joe said. 'Washington robs us blind an' nobody ain't gonna lift a finger? I raised a bunch of quitters, is that right?'

'What d'you want, Pa?' Stanton demanded. 'Lee quit! Lee quit at Appomattox! The South got beat! The entire South quit! We *lost* the *fuckin' war,* Pa!'

'Oh, oh!' His mother threw up her arms. 'Wash your – '

'I never quit!' Dan said. 'Not me! I maybe ran a few times, but nobody made *me* surrender. No sir!'

'You go git those niggers an' tell 'em from me,' his father said vigorously.

'Yeah? Tell 'em what?'

In the silence that followed, Jessica (who was sixteen) said, 'Someone's gotta shovel hog-shit or we'll all get eaten up by the flies.'

'If only George was here,' Ma Killick said. 'He'd know what to do.'

'Well, George ain't never gonna be here again,' Dan said. 'We lost George, and now we lost the niggers. I reckon I'll go to Texas.'

'Charles Hudd started this tragedy,' his mother said. 'Hudd started it when he did that terrible damage to poor Stanton. Stanton was the first casualty of that war. The Bible says – '

'If I see Hudd,' Joe said, 'it'll be sudden death, you watch.'

'If you see anythin' beyond the drink in your fist,' Dan told him, 'it'll be a solid gold miracle.'

'I ain't shovellin' no hog-shit,' Devereux said.

WHIP AND SPUR

If Curtis Hudd hadn't looked down as he was dressing, and seen a dime in the crack between the floorboards, life might have been tolerable. Shabby but tolerable. As it was, he picked out the dime with his knife and it raised his savings to over the dollar. Now he had a dollar five. He knew that Lucy would have let him poke her for a dollar even. Too late.

Lucy was no older than he was, but her body was ripe as honeydew and just as round. One day, working in the fields, she had come up to him to ask about something, and she had stood close so that he could look right down her front, which made his pulse gallop like it was under whip and spur. Lucy knew what he wanted. 'Dollar an' a half,' she said softly, and went away. But he knew she'd do it for a dollar, and right then he would have killed for a dollar. Instead he walked uncomfortably to the river and swam until he was in a state to get back into his pants without busting any buttons.

From that moment, he concentrated on saving every cent. It was hard. His stepfather gave him nothing: the farm was losing money, he said. After four months, Curtis had ninety-five cents and he knew he was on the verge of exploding into manhood when, abruptly, all the niggers left. Lucy went up the hill with them. Went and left him clutching a dollar five and his virginity.

Curtis was too mad to speak. First they wouldn't let him fight (his mother had hidden the boys whenever the recruiting officer came by) and now there was no-one to fuck. He was throwing stones at the hogs when his mother came out and told him to go and empty the outhouse. He stared. 'I ain't never done that,' he said.

'We got no niggers to do it, and I don't intend to let it overflow.'

'Yeah, but – '

'You helped fill it. Now go and empty it.'

It was a two-holer, so there were two buckets, and they were so full that he had to walk slowly, arms bent at the elbows. He saw Lonzo come out of a barn carrying a big sack of cornmeal and he stopped so sharply that a bucket slopped over onto his foot. 'Hey!' he shouted. Lonzo didn't even turn or look, he just ran, sack and all. By the time Curtis had put down the buckets Lonzo was out of sight behind some sheds.

'Get my horse,' Curtis barked, and looked around for a nigger to obey the order. Some hens stopped pecking and watched. 'Shit,' he muttered. He sprinted to the field, caught his horse, didn't bother with saddle or bridle, just used knees and heels to ride hard towards the highest part of the farm, where a strip of steep pasture led to the woods of the Ridge. Lonzo had to cross that strip. Curtis sat his horse and waited. When Lonzo came out of a crop of beans, he was half-running, the sack balanced on one shoulder. Curtis caught up with him easily. 'Now you brought it up here,' he called out, 'you just take it back down there.' Lonzo kept going. Curtis rode square in front of him and stopped. 'Hear me, boy? Take it back.'

Lonzo stood and looked up. He had no breath to speak. Sweat had washed salt into his eyes until they stung. His heart was trying to fight its way out of his chest. The figure above him was calm and unmoving, giving him that white-man-boss look, the look that said if it wasn't so damned hot I'd kick your black ass so hard you'd bounce.

Curtis looked down and saw a captured animal. His stepfather had tried to teach him that slaves were third-rate human beings who deserved decent treatment, but only an animal would have the brute strength and dumb determination to carry a load like this so far and so fast. *Jesus,* Curtis thought, *they're worse than brown bears for raiding.*

'We need food,' Lonzo said. His lungs had recovered a little. 'We got nothin', up there.'

'You got Lucy.' The words came out before Curtis could stop them. 'Ain't you?'

Lonzo shrugged the sack to a more comfortable position. 'Yeah, she's up there.'

'I'll take care of this sack of cornmeal. You go send Lucy down.' Curtis slipped a hand inside his pants and eased his crotch. 'Don't like to think of you folks hungry. Gives me a real pain in the nuts.'

'Lucy can't carry no sack of meal.'

'We'll put it on my horse.' Curtis began to get angry: what was he doing, arguing with a nigger? 'Now you git, an' fast, before I whip you, boy.'

Lonzo took one pace and kicked the horse in the stomach and made it bolt.

The horse had no bridle; Curtis grabbed handfuls of its mane and struggled to force its head uphill. He was lying rather than sitting, and his testicles banged so hard as he plunged on its jolting spine that he roared with pain and he thought of falling off before he really damaged himself. Then a boulder loomed and the horse swerved into a dry streambed that was such hard work, it gave up and clattered to a trembling halt.

Lonzo was a hundred yards away, running for the trees. The hill got steeper, with more and bigger rocks for him to avoid. There was still a long way to go when Curtis caught up with him again. Words would be wasted. Curtis opened his pocketknife, rode alongside Lonzo, leaned down and slashed. The sacking was taut as a balloon, the blade like a razor. Cornmeal gushed. Lonzo saw nothing of this but he quickly knew the difference. The load was suddenly light and he felt like he was flying. He stopped and twisted and looked back. The stuff was pouring down his legs. The top of the sack was soft under his finger, a river of cornmeal was washing downhill. He ran on. When he reached the tree line he was holding maybe only a couple of pounds. Curtis was sitting on his horse, watching. 'Next time you try that, I'll blow your black head off,' he called. He dismounted and began kicking the fallen cornmeal into the scrub so that no-one could collect it.

～

An hour later, Lonzo was standing outside Stackmesser's store. In his fist was the bottom half of the stolen cornmeal sack. In the sack was a dozen small rocks.

Frank Stackmesser had set up first as a wheelwright, failed at that, then failed as the town's undertaker. Plenty of business during the war, as people brought their sons or husbands home from some nearby skirmish and buried them, but too many failed to pay. He started a newspaper, the *Rock Springs Bugle*. It failed when its principal advertiser, the general store, went bankrupt because the military of either side bought fast but paid slow. Too often they paid with chits against some distant commissary that denied all knowledge of the pieces of paper and in any case was striking its tents and preparing to move on, God knew where. Stackmesser took the store in final settlement of debt.

All the way down the Ridge, Lonzo had been sweating his brains to think of a better way to get food, a lot of food. He could beg a couple of stale loaves and a few bruised apples, but that wouldn't feed a whole colony. For the past hour he'd been standing like a statue, waiting for Stackmesser to come back from Maggie's, and all the time hunting for a better idea. Nothing came. All he had was a little sack of rocks and a story so thin he was ashamed to tell it.

Stackmesser came at last, walking slow and scuffing his boots and staring at the sidewalk ahead of him, which was nothing but warped planks. 'Hey, boy,' he said amiably, when Lonzo stepped forward. 'What you got there, goose eggs? Give you a nickel.'

At once, Lonzo knew that all his half-assed made-up stories about finding the body of a dead white miner were junk, and so he junked them. Instinct told him to say nothing. After that, say as little as possible. Thanks to Dr Fox, he had hard clear eyes, sharp lips, nose like an axehead, a sheen of copper in the smooth black skin. He could put on a stony face without even trying. He gazed at Stackmesser until Stackmesser blinked, and then Lonzo said, 'Not for sale.'

'Huh.' Stackmesser took a pencil from behind his ear and scratched his head. 'What you want, then?' Free niggers were a puzzle. How did you handle them?

Lonzo gave the sack a shake. Its contents chinked.

'Sure as hell ain't goose eggs. Open her up, boy. Lemme see.'

Lonzo walked away. Stackmesser was so surprised that he stabbed himself in the scalp and bust the pencil point. Then he saw that Lonzo was standing, looking sideways at a passing couple, waiting for them to get out of earshot.

'Reckon you better come inside, boy,' he said.

His store was quiet. A customer was looking at sandpaper, trying to decide whether to buy one sheet or none. They went into Stackmesser's office. 'Fess up, boy,' he said. 'What you stole? Crown jewels of England?'

Lonzo opened the neck of the sack. The rocks were small, no

bigger than walnuts. Thin veins made a dull glitter in the dark stone. There was a faint whiff of sulphur and a soft smell of cornmeal.

'Where you find this?'

Lonzo was silent for a moment. 'Want you keep,' he said.

'Sure. Easy. I'll keep.' Got to move slow with niggers. One step at a time. 'Now then. Where you – '

'Ridge,' Lonzo said.

The office was stuffy. Stackmesser's belly was full of beer and his mind was tired. He went to the window and looked up at Hudd Ridge. Its eastern end was a mile away, smoky blue in the thumping heat of the afternoon. Beyond that was a wilderness that ran all the way to Indiana, maybe. Just the thought of climbing into that godawful jungle made his legs weary. Different for niggers, of course. Their home was the jungle.

Stackmesser's brain fumbled and stumbled and finally got somewhere. It remembered a fragment of conversation he had overhead, customers talking about Hudd's niggers buying a stretch of the Ridge. Crazy thing to do, they'd said; but then who could figure a nigger brain?

'Got it up the Ridge, huh?' Stackmesser said. A sudden kick of excitement made the blood buzz in his ears. Ever since he came to Rock Springs he'd heard talk about Indian silver mines in the hills. The old pioneers had worked them, hid the silver, never came back for it. A fortune was waiting to be picked up, everyone said so. Now look at Lonzo: more Indian than nigger. Not so crazy, buying that patch, if he knew exactly where to buy. 'More like this up there?'

Lonzo grunted.

'Bring it on down. You did a right smart thing, comin' to me. You see, boy, the law says, you want to mine up there, you got to have a partner down here, that's what the law says. Got to have a white partner. For protection, see. Make sure you get a fair deal. That's the law.' Stackmesser knew as much about mining law as he knew about silver ore, which was nothing. But if he was lying, he knew it was a Christian lie because the white man had a duty to protect niggers from their own ignorance. Besides, if he didn't move fast and grab his share, some other bastard would. 'Partners, huh?'

They shook hands. Stackmesser winced and had to free his fingers from each other. It was the first time he had gripped a nigger's hand. It felt different, it felt *black*. He wiped his hand on his pants. 'Guess you want to get back to the mine,' he said. 'I'll get these rocks over to Bowling Green, they got an assay office there.'

'Chicago.'

Stackmesser tried to smile. 'Bowling Green's just as good. Honest.'

'All us niggers goin' to Chicago tomorrow. Got no food. Walkin' to Chicago. Tomorrow.'

'Well … let the others go. You stay an' work the mine. Make some money.'

'All us niggers goin' to Chicago.'

'Sure. What I'm sayin' is, they go an' you stay. I'll stake you to some grub.'

'All us niggers goin' to Chicago.'

'That's crazy. You got yourself a mine and – '

'All us niggers – '

'Listen! Listen to me. We're partners, right?'

'Chicago,' Lonzo said.

'Sweet Jesus Goddamn *Christ*!' Stackmesser picked up the bag of rocks and flung it at the wall.

'No food on the Ridge,' Lonzo said.

'Give you a sack of cornmeal.' Stackmesser forced his voice to stay sane and level, and the words emerged hoarse and flattened. 'Not sell. Give.'

'Two sacks.'

Stackmesser kicked the fallen rocks into a heap. 'Two sacks. You'll need a mule. I'll lend you one. *Lend*.'

'Want pork belly, molasses, coffee, salt an' lard.' Stackmesser's eyes widened with shock. 'We pay,' Lonzo said. 'Real soon.'

'How soon?'

'How far Chicago?'

'This town is killin' me,' Stackmesser said. 'Now I'm givin' credit to niggers. It's killin' me.'

FOOLISHNESS

The Hudds took the wagon to town to do a little buying and selling. The boys came along.

'Stay out of trouble,' Charles warned.

'Got no choice,' Curtis said, and turned his pockets out. 'Trouble ain't free.'

'That's where you're wrong,' Charles said. His stepson either didn't hear or didn't care. He slouched away with his thumbs hooked in his belt, looking like a bad man to cross. His brother Floyd followed, looking like a bad youth to cross.

'When I was his age, I called my father "sir",' Charles said.

'He has no father,' Mary said. 'His father died of diphtheria when he was seven.'

'I know.'

'I know you know. You just need reminding. Curtis is old enough to be a father himself.'

Charles gave an amused snort. 'He better not try. We can't afford such luxuries.'

'That is not a thought powerful enough to keep Curtis's pants buttoned.' Her words startled Charles. 'Well,' she said, reasonably, 'it didn't work for you at that age, dear, did it? And you have so much more self-control than Curtis.'

'Coffee,' Hudd said. 'I want coffee.'

~

Stanton and Devereux Killick rode to town to escape the perpetual nagging and bitching at home. Rock Springs was not a big improvement. Somehow it seemed drabber and dustier than ever. People looked dirtier, more work-worn. The day dragged.

125

They were sitting on a rail outside the ruins of the old bank, squirting tobacco juice at any passing animal, and Stanton was bragging about what a wild pair he and George had been until the war came along and the whole world went to hell and took his left arm with it. Devereux was bored because he had heard all this bunkum before and he never believed it to start with, on account of his only big memory of George was of being promised a dime if he kept watch in case their mother came by while George fucked a nigger-girl behind the polkberry bushes; and Devereux never got that dime. George just laughed when he asked for it. Then, when Devereux got mad, George gave it to the nigger-girl and laughed twice as much. She was surprised to get the dime. Ran like hell before Devereux could grab it off her.

Everyone else in the Killick family had wept when they heard George had been killed in some battle, but not Devereux. While they wept he went off and got the big old bullwhip, and practised laying it on so that it would cut. He practised in the smokehouse, on the big sides of pork that hung from hooks, getting the lash to split the skin. He wanted to be ready to do a man's job when he was old enough. Now the goddamn war had bust up everything and there were no goddamn niggers to whip. Life had done nothing but cheat Devereux from the goddamn start.

'Look,' Stanton said. 'Hudd boys.'

Curtis and Floyd strolled along the sidewalk, kicking splinters and saying nothing.

'See them two?' Stanton said loudly. 'Terrible bad luck. Could of bin my nephews. Now look. No breedin'.' He spat between his legs.

'You talkin' about me?' Curtis said.

Stanton yawned, and ignored him. 'Thing was, Dev, their daddy had his chance to wed your lovely sister JoBeth.'

'Watch your big mouth,' Curtis said.

'JoBeth dumped their daddy. Sad, ain't it? Otherwise you'd be their uncle! Me too.'

'Who cares?' Devereux said. He was hungry, as usual.

Stanton frowned. 'Well, they do, naturally.'

'Hey, stumpy!' Curtis shouted. 'You lose your guts when you lost your arm? Lookin' for a fight, or just givin' your brains a rest?'

Stanton got down off the rail and raised his right fist. He was four inches shorter than Curtis and little more than half his weight. Curtis waved him away in disgust. 'I don't fight cripples,' he said.

Stanton let his arm fall. 'This here is a matter of family honour,' he said. 'Devereux will fight you.'

'Like hell I will.'

'Don't fight children neither,' Curtis said.

'Plain fact is you Hudds don't fight,' Stanton said.

'Plain fact is we ain't Hudds. He's our stepfather.'

'That nigger-lover?'

'Hey!' Floyd said. 'You with the mouth!' He was tired of standing outside the argument.

'Nigger-lover, an' a traitor to the South,' Stanton said.

'Fight you one-handed,' Floyd challenged.

Stanton turned away. 'Don't fight children,' he said.

'Leave me out of it,' Devereux said to him. 'You started this foolishness. I don't care if they beat the holy shit out of you.'

They watched him walk away.

'That's real unmannerly,' Curtis said. 'A brother shouldn't talk like that.'

'He's feelin' mean today,' Stanton said.

'One-handed,' Floyd said again, loudly. 'I ain't a child.'

'Yes you are,' Curtis said. 'So shut up.'

'Losin' our slaves, see,' Stanton said. 'Dev took it bad. Made him mean.'

'Goddamn niggers,' Curtis said. 'If anyone deserves a beatin' it's them.'

'Amen to that.'

Curtis and Floyd walked back to the wagon. 'Was their sister really good-lookin'?' Floyd asked. 'I don't remember her.'

'She was trash,' Curtis said. 'All them Killicks are trash.'

NO JOKE

All their lives, Charles Hudd or his father had made every decision for their slaves. Decided when they worked, what they ate, where they lived, how they spoke, who their God was, why they existed and what they were worth. A slave could live and die without troubling his brain. Why think? Thinking changed nothing. Life happened. No reason for it.

Now the Hudd niggers had been on the Ridge for twenty-four hours with no Master to give orders and give food, and they were bewildered and hungry. A few berries did nothing. Scrappy arguments got nowhere. Nobody had any ideas except to go back to the farm, and they'd done that twice and been thrown out twice. They sat about, grumbled, blamed Jacob until he went off and climbed a boulder, blamed Lonzo for running off, and got hungrier and gloomier.

The mule was Stackmesser's worst, old and lame, and Lonzo had to carry one of the sacks of cornmeal. Even so, the mule refused the steeper, rockier stretches of the track. Lonzo had to find a chunk of wood and smash another path through barriers of bramble and tangles of creeper. By the time they reached the campsite he was stumbling with fatigue.

Everyone got up and hurried to him, whooping and clapping, the children squealing and bug-eyed at the sight of the food. Josh fell on his knees and made loud hallelujahs. Nat said, 'I knew you could do it, boy.' Buck, still the biggest and strongest of them all, had his hands on the sack, lifting the weight, when Lonzo tightened his grip and backed away. 'Get off me!' he shouted. 'Leave that mule! Leave it!' He lashed out with his foot. A woman jumped back, tripped, fell.

Shocked silence.

'Where's old Jake?' Lonzo demanded. 'Where's the fire?'

'Went out,' Martha said.

Lonzo dropped the sack and put a foot on it. 'Went out why?'

'I told 'em to get wood, but ...' She sniffed. That sniff told the whole story.

'I been to Rock Springs an' back,' he said. 'I got this grub. I kicked this no-good goddamn mule up the Ridge. What you niggers done?'

'Bellyached,' Jacob called. He was still sitting on his boulder.

'What you expect?' Buck said. His broken teeth turned the words to mush. 'Empty bellies ain't no joke. Folks here is sufferin'. Give us – '

'Nothin',' Lonzo said. 'Don't work, don't eat.'

'Hey, hey,' Josh said. 'The Lord Almighty wants us to have that grub.' Shouts of approval encouraged him. 'Lonzo is the messenger of the Lord! This here grub is a sign! Praise the Lord! A sign!'

'This here rifle is another sign,' Lonzo said. He slid it out of the bundle on the saddle. Buck was standing only a pace away. Lonzo aimed at Buck's crotch, looked him in the eyes, swung the gun to the vertical and fired at the sky. Everyone jumped. Before they could recover from the blast, he had reloaded.

Buck turned and walked away. 'Crazy,' he said.

'You had all day!' Lonzo shouted. 'Could have built cabins. Got an axe, ain't we? Don't work, don't eat!' His words struck like blows. 'Where's the damn fire? Where's your woodpile?' He was the overseer, he was the Master, he was weary and aching, scratched and bruised, but he enjoyed doing this. 'Don't work, don't eat!'

'A little grub,' Nat pleaded. 'To give us the strength. To work.'

He refused. They hated him, and he didn't care. They feared him, and he liked that. He held the gun with its butt on his thigh, the barrel aimed over their heads, and his fingers played around the trigger-guard: just the way he'd seen the overseer do it in the field. It wasn't much of a gun (only reason Stackmesser loaned it was because Lonzo said he could kill game and feed himself for free) but it was the only gun on the Ridge. That made Lonzo king. Or tyrant. 'Don't work, don't eat,' he said harshly. They went to work. That felt good. It was worth carrying a sack of cornmeal up a mountain to have such a feeling.

The sun was down before he left his stack of food to inspect their work.

Jake held a blazing pine knot and showed him the frame of a cabin and the start of two more. There was a great heap of fern leaves to make beds. A long stone oven was hot and ready to bake cornmeal bread. The woodpile was taller than Buck.

'Where's the kindlin'?' Lonzo asked. Jake showed him. 'Get more,' he said. 'Lot more.' Jake pointed at the fire, big and hot. 'Burn till sun up, that will,' he said. 'Could rain,' Lonzo said. 'Get a storm up here, that fire *drown*. I want kindlin', lots of kindlin', under a rock or somethin'.'

Everyone blundered about in the woods, collecting kindling. Nobody spoke. The pile grew.

'Stop now,' he said. He fetched the food.

'Milk an' honey,' said Nat. 'This must be the Promised Land.' Nobody laughed.

～

Food is just fuel until you're stumbling hungry. Then the sharp smell of it swamps your mouth with saliva. The first mouthful tastes as if touched by the hand of God. Suddenly, your stomach forgives you everything. Life has a future again.

Everyone on Hudd Ridge went to sleep with a full belly. The women and children were in the cabins (roofless, but a promise of better things) while the men lay down in the open. The night was full of the moan of winds searching through the trees, and out there animals were hunting and killing, you could hear the panicky gibber and sometimes a scream of terror: but the people on the Ridge slept well. They felt good. Tomorrow was a year away. Nobody even thought about it. Except old Jake and young Lonzo.

Jake fed the fire with hardwood logs that would burn long and slow. 'Never thought you'd get that grub,' he said.

'Stackmesser staked us,' Lonzo said. 'Thinks I'm workin' an old Indian silver mine up here.' The story astonished Jake, and Lonzo told it proudly, with all the colourful detail he could drum up. 'See, I was the dumb stupid nigger,' he said, 'an' old Stackmesser just had to do the rest.'

Jake was staring into the golden glow. 'That's a hard man,' he said, and heaved a huge deep breath. 'He ain't givin' you no charity. Stackmesser gonna want paid.'

'Well, he got half a silver mine.' Lonzo spat in the flames.

'You sold him a pig in a poke.'

'Didn't sell nobody nothin'. Stackmesser did the talkin'. I was the dumb stupid nigger.' Firelight flickered on Lonzo's grin.

'You think Stackmesser gonna see the joke?' Jake sat on his haunches. He did it slowly. His joints creaked and his muscles ached. Lonzo looked down and realized Jake was getting smaller and thinner. He might not live much longer. Maybe he had given up the fight already. It was a startling idea. 'Stackmesser gonna want paid,' Jake said again.

Lonzo yawned. 'You stole from Stackmesser.' Jake delivered the words flat, like he was dealing cards. 'No white man gonna let you get away with his money. You know that.'

'You just ate your share.'

'You fetched us trouble,' Jake said.

'No other way,' Lonzo told him. 'Eat or die. Which you want?' He walked off, scuffing dried leaves underfoot, and found somewhere to sleep, hot with anger at Jake because he knew the old bastard was right. Trouble would follow that grub as sure as buzzards brought little black babies.

POWER IS GOOD MEDICINE

Charles Hudd took some of the hundred dollars he got from selling part of the Ridge and hired a couple of white field-hands. They were ex-soldiers, released from the Union Army in Mississippi, walking home to Ohio, took a wrong turning when they hit Kentucky. Hudd gave them new boots and a big meal and set them to do what his blacks used to do. This made him feel uncomfortable. 'Wish I could give you men better work,' he said.

'Beats diggin' graves,' one of them said. 'Seems like all I did for the army is dig. Three feet down, hit water. Mississippi, you'd best be dead when they bury you, cus if you ain't, you're gonna drown.'

'I'll remember that.'

They were hollow-cheeked and bony: too much grave-digging on not enough food. Hudd made sure they got plenty to eat, plus a nip of whiskey every night. Curtis and Floyd resented this privilege. They were of an age to resent almost everything.

Charles Hudd was up a ladder, fixing a barn roof, when he saw one of the ex-soldiers leading a very tall, white-haired man towards the farmhouse. Sometimes the man stumbled and had to be helped. In his free hand the ex-soldier carried a revolver with a barrel long enough to stir a dixie of hot stew.

Charles met them halfway. The man's face was covered with blood, dried black as molasses. Streaks of blood marked his coat and shirt.

'Found him leanin' on a fence,' the hired hand said. 'He was wearin' this cannon, so I took it off him. Big, ain't he?'

The man was a good three inches taller than Hudd. He was swaying like ripe corn in a breeze, and the hired hand kept a firm grip on his coat. 'Charlie Hudd,' the man said.

132

'Judge Potter.'

'So the label says.' His voice faded to a whisper.

'What in the name of mercy happened to you?'

'Horse died. Just like ...' He tried to click his fingers and he almost fell over. They each took an arm and walked him to the house.

Curtis fetched Doc Brightsides. Mary had washed the black blood away and found a deep cut in the judge's scalp, an inch above the hairline. Brightsides scissored off enough hair to let him sew up the cut. The judge's pulse was down to fifty and his lips were ash-grey at the edges. He fell asleep as Brightsides was knotting the final stitch.

Next day he was still weak but able to eat and talk.

'Comin' back from New Jericho,' he said. 'Went there for a damn-fool trial. Prayer meetin' got to arguin' about humility, who's got the most of it. Led to gunplay, one preacher shot dead, two citizens blew holes in each other.'

'I heard about that,' Charles said. 'Pity the poor preacher.'

'He drew first. I hanged the other two. Charged the town fifty bucks for my services and their foolishness. Set off for home. Downeysville. Would've got there, too, except my horse upped an' died on me.'

'No reason?'

'She must of had a fit. Convulsions. Reared up an' threw me. Long way down. Hit my head on a rock. Came to, she was dead as the preacher in New Jericho an' I was gushin' blood faster'n I could drink it.'

'Well, horses die, I guess.'

'Everythin' dies. Think I'll sleep some more.'

Charles took the hired hand and found the judge's mare lying on a trail near the river. Already it had been much chewed up by vermin. Clouds of flies had joined the feast. Charles didn't want to leave it there. It was too heavy to be dragged to the river. 'I ain't diggin' no grave,' the hired hand said. The riverbank was littered with drift-wood. They made a funeral pyre. 'Judge said she was a good old horse,' Charles remarked. 'She deserves a good old send-off.' The flames roared, straining for the sky. The hired hand sat on his haunches and watched. He'd seen too many corpses to get excited over a dead horse. Still, he was getting paid, whatever happened.

~

Charles had always thought of Judge Potter as a tall, black-haired old man. Now he was a tall, white-haired old man. Older than his father had been, so he must be knocking on seventy.

They were sitting under a shade tree, drinking lemonade, when Charles asked him if he ever considered retiring from such a strenuous job, riding around the county in all weathers.

'Never. I like the law. Enjoy disentanglin' other folks' lives. Power is good medicine, Charlie. It keeps a man young. You should try it.'

Hudd laughed. 'Rock Springs would vote for a bucket of cold spit before it would vote for me. It's full of Rebs, judge.'

'Full of ruins, too.'

'Got raided by all three sides: us, them and a few wild men on the spree. So I'm told.'

'Now everyone's too tired to scratch their ass, an' you can't see the ruins for weeds.'

Charles poured more lemonade. 'I miss that old barbershop. Mary does her best, but ...'

'Run for mayor, Charlie.'

Hudd was too startled to speak.

'Think about it. You bin in the army, you held rank, you seen how a good officer can turn around a rabble of men. Rock Springs needs someone to shake it up, make it stop feelin' so damn sorry for itself.'

'I've got my hands full here.'

'Grant didn't load the guns. I don't do the hangin's. Get in power, Charlie, then give the orders. Make the other poor bastards work.' Judge Potter's eyes slowly closed.

'Mayor,' Hudd said. Why not? He'd taken on much bigger tasks for Grant and Sherman, and done them well. 'Can't deny the place needs a shake-up.'

'Help you with your speech.' Judge Potter drifted into sleep. Hudd wondered whether or not to call himself major. Probably not.

When he told his wife that he aimed to put himself forward as mayor of Rock Springs, all she said was: 'I hope you don't expect to get paid.'

'A nominal salary. And the costs of office, of course.'

'Town's flat broke. Do it as a public service, or not at all.'

Charles sucked in his gut and stared over her head. 'The labourer is worthy of his hire,' he said, and sounded like his father. 'It's a matter of principle.'

'Indeed! That changes everything. You should pay me for house-keeping, on principle.'

Charles had no answer. He smiled down at her, and that turned out to be a lot worse than no answer.

CROWS IS
AMERICAN TOO

Male slaves woke in the dark, went to work in the fields in the dark, came home in the dark. That was the routine. It was how it had always been on Hudd's farm and it was considered normal, by both sides. Slaves accepted it because toil was their only reason for being. Work all the hours of the daylight and then sleep, so you can get up and do it all over again tomorrow.

The habit was too hard to shake. On the Ridge, people were up and about long before the curve of the sun nicked the skyline. That was a luxury, hauling water and lighting fires not in blackness but in the pearly grey of pre-dawn. It had rained in the night: the forest was drenched. Because Lonzo had bullied every family into gathering kindling, fires glowed quickly and everyone felt good at the sight. Nobody thanked Lonzo.

He was the boss. He owned the food, told them what to do. Don't work, don't eat.

All day, axes bit and trees toppled. Soon each family had its cabin. Wind found gaps in the walls but the logs were nine inches thick, twelve inches, sometimes more. No panther would find a way in. Rain dripped through the roof, but trimmings like that could wait. Meanwhile, more food had to be found.

The day after Lonzo came back from Rock Springs with Stackmesser's grubstake, he saw Josh on his knees, praying.

'You puttin' in an order for loaves an' fishes?' he asked. 'Cus we could use some coffee too.'

'Just merely givin' thanks to the Lord,' Josh said. 'For His lovin' kindness, on account He gave us that cornmeal an' stuff.'

Sarah was passing. 'Give us all these snakes an' storms an' stuff, too,' she said. She had been a house slave, used to big comfortable rooms, everything clean, good food on the table. For her the Ridge was all ugly discomfort. 'Someone done a lot of sinnin' for God to hand out such punishment,' she said grimly.

'Us,' Josh said.

'We been sinnin', you reckon,' Lonzo said.

'The Lord sends these tribulations, it's cus we all poor wretched sinners.'

'Sinnin' supposed to be fun,' Lonzo said. 'Wish I'd knowed I was havin' such a good time before this. Someone shoulda told me.'

'When the Lord runs out of tribulations,' Sarah said to Josh, 'you tell Him, send us some more of that lovin' kindness, cus if all we got is cornmeal it ain't gonna last the week.' She stumped off to wash her children in the stream.

When everyone stopped work at midday, Lonzo climbed on a big rock and shouted for them to assemble. He stood in the posture he liked: one leg straight, one bent, with the butt of his rifle on his thigh.

All came, but some came slowly and grudgingly. They were hot and tired from cutting and hauling logs, and they wanted to eat.

'I'm gonna tell y'all somethin',' he announced. 'Yesterday was the first, last and onliest time I go to Rock Springs an' carry grub up this mountain for you.'

The ring of upturned faces waited to hear more. Lonzo was stuck. He wanted to say: *You got to help me*, but their dumb passivity angered him. 'I ain't gonna starve,' he told them. 'You can lie down an' die, who cares? Think anyone out there gonna *know*, even?' He swung an arm to indicate the whole of Dundee County. 'What you think? Huh?' They had been tired; now he made them weary. 'Ain't got no brain for thinkin'?' he shouted. 'That it?' Their silence fuelled his anger. 'Go eat,' he said. 'Eat the goddamn grub.'

As they trudged away, Martha called out: 'You bought this piece a jungle, you an' Jake. Didn't ask us folks. What you 'spect is waitin' up here? Paradise?'

Old Jake stayed. A couple of his fingers had been scraped by the sudden twist of a log; he rubbed spit into the skin. Lonzo got down off the rock.

'They think I'm gonna feed 'em, they're crazy,' he said.

'You got the gun.'

'Huh?'

'You got the gun, you talk mean, jus' like white folks. All my life, mean-talkin' man with a gun, that man fed me, regular. He wanted me to live.'

'Hey,' Lonzo said, 'you take the gun.' But Jake fended it off.

That afternoon, four ex-slaves from the Killick farm arrived, led by Moses. He was the biggest nigger Lonzo had ever seen. He was carrying a little old man on his back. 'Aaron here got busted legs,' Moses said, 'but the rest of us can work.'

Lonzo was trying to build a food store raised high on rock pyramids so the vermin couldn't get in. Nobody had offered to help and Lonzo wouldn't unbend enough to ask. Already the frame looked wrong, looked lopsided. 'Don't work, don't eat,' he growled.

'Hey, Aaron don't eat much,' Moses said. 'Besides, I can work enough for two. Ask anyone.'

'Look around. See any barns? Corn cribs? Smokehouse? Sheep? Chickens? Hogs?' Moses shook his head. 'All the grub we got, I bought in Rock Springs,' Lonzo said. 'Got a dollar?' This time they all shook their heads. 'Chicago's that way,' Lonzo told them, and turned back to his crooked structure.

'You-all ain't short of grub,' Aaron announced. He was still on Moses's back. His voice was cracked and thin but confident.

'Ain't short of fools neither,' Lonzo said. 'Take your foolishness an' go.'

'Lend me your rifle for an hour an' I bet you a dollar I'll bring back more'n everyone here can eat tonight.'

Lonzo looked up at him. Aaron resembled a white-haired monkey clinging to Moses's back, and because of that, Lonzo felt the group was mocking him. 'Countin' you four, that's twenty mouths to feed,' he said. 'You ain't got no legs, an' you ain't got no dollar.'

'Ain't gonna lose.'

Lonzo was tired of making decisions, of telling people they were wrong. He gave Aaron the rifle and a handful of shells. Aaron pointed, and Moses carried him towards the trees. The other two niggers stayed. 'You puttin' this thing up or knockin' it down?' one of them asked Lonzo.

~

Martha had a daughter, Bonny, ten years old, no front teeth, a bit bow-legged from walking too soon when her legs weren't ready, slight squint in her left eye, but quick as the wind. Bonny ran up to Lonzo and wanted to show him something. He waved her away. He had too much on his mind. Cornmeal was running out fast. Stackmesser was going to be a problem. Three Corrigan niggers climbed the Ridge yesterday. Every time he heard a distant shot he knew he'd been crazy to let that little old crippled fool waste his shells. 'Git!' he said.

Bonny was too excited. She made him see what she had. Blunt old axe-head and five bent needles. All black with fire.

'Goddamn it,' he said. His voice was as hard as his face. 'Don't waste my time, child.' Didn't know his own strength. Meant to discourage her and knocked her spirit down flat.

Slave children grew up knowing it did no good to cry. They endured pain, bloodshed, sometimes even the lash, without tears. Bonny was hurt but she did not cry; she turned away, hiding the objects in her hands in case they attracted more ridicule.

Buck stopped work and came over.

The war years had changed Buck. He was big and strong but too much heavy work on not enough food had left him bent in the shoulders and gaunt in the face. His hair was white as wood ash. Some of his jumbled-up teeth had fallen out, so his whispery lisp was worse than ever. Buck would never marry, would never amount to anything more than he was, a big slow nigger valued by nobody unless they had something heavy to be shifted. This was a sadness to Buck, but he had learned to live with it.

Buck scooped up Bonny and sat her on his shoulder. 'What you got for ol' uncle Buck?' he asked. She showed him. 'Holy molokey!' he said. 'Christmas come early.' He took the axe-head, spat on it and rubbed. Grey steel showed. 'You found *this?*' Admiration made his voice squeak; the squeak made her grin. 'Tell, honey,' he said.

She told how she had gone down to the Hudd farm and poked around in the ashes of the slave cabins. She had found more stuff – a skillet, spoons, a bowl – but it was too much to carry. Mister Curtis saw her but paid no heed; too busy chasing hogs that didn't want to be caught, she said.

'Clever girl,' Buck said. 'Pretty as a flower an' smart as the President's wife too. Tell your mammy I said so.'

He put her down and she scampered off.

Buck tossed the axe-head high in the air and caught it.

'Ain't no damn use without a handle,' Lonzo sneered.

Buck looked at him through the hole where the handle should be.

'She ain't pretty neither,' Lonzo said. 'Not with that squinty eye.'

'Hey, don't fret,' Buck said. 'She ain't plannin' on marryin' you.' That amused the two men from Killick's farm. Buck walked off, whistling badly. Nobody could hope to whistle with teeth like his.

About an hour later, Moses came back with a dead deer draped around his shoulders where Aaron had been. He let it fall in front of Lonzo and eased his muscles.

'Won't feed twenty,' Lonzo said.

'Get your dollar ready.' Moses strode away.

When he came back he carried the carcass of a wild turkey in each hand. He dropped one and tossed the other to Lonzo, who staggered as he caught it. The bird weighed sixteen or seventeen pounds.

'Get pluckin',' Moses said. And set off again.

When he returned, Aaron was clinging to his back and three fat cottontail rabbits hung from Aaron's belt. Moses was carrying a pair of woodpigeons in one hand and a bundle of bulrushes in the other. Inside his shirt was a load of mushrooms as big as plates.

All work stopped. Everyone came to see. 'Hey, Moses!' one of the Killick niggers called. 'Can't you stay out of them bulrushes?' It got a laugh: people sensed that the day was going to end well.

Moses brandished his bundle. 'These is good eatin'!' he declared. 'Old Aaron say so!'

'Old Aaron gets first bite then,' Lonzo said gloomily. 'First bite an' last breath, same time. That's swamp poison.'

'Hush, boy,' Aaron said, as if Lonzo were a mere chattering child, and they enjoyed that; this whole thing was getting better and better. 'See that root?' he shouted, shaking the muddy end of a bulrush. 'Tastes better'n corn. Wash it an' dry it an' pound it to pieces, what you got is better'n the finest cornmeal!' His high, cracked voice gave his words extra excitement, and won a cheer. Moses's shirt popped open and mushrooms tumbled out like a magician's act gone comically wrong. More laughter. 'See this part?' Aaron peeled some skin off the stem of the bulrush; it showed up as white as a candle. 'Cook it in water, tastes like turnip got into bed with a sugarcane!' Whoops of glee. 'An' that ain't all!' Aaron promised. 'But I guess it'll do until I get my dollar.' He clicked his fingers at Lonzo.

That was a mistake. Lonzo was gloomy and resentful and jealous, but he would have paid up if this pygmy monarch had not turned the wager into a test of strength. Lonzo would not hop to any nigger's clicking finger. 'Too late,' he said.

'What?' Aaron screwed up his face and cupped a hand to his ear. 'Too *what*?'

'Too goddamn late. We said an hour. You been gone a hell of a lot longer.'

'Took time for Moses to bring it in, is all. I got it. I win the dollar.'

Lonzo shook his head. 'My dollar,' he said. 'You ain't got a dollar, you better borrow. Ain't no room around here for – '

'Pick it up, Moses,' Aaron ordered. 'Just pick it all up.' Moses carried him over to the turkey, lying half-plucked, and seized them by the feet.

'Hey!' Sarah cried. Troubled sounds came from all around. Glee had slumped to gloom. 'Hey!'

'Your boss-man reckons this grub ain't worth a dollar,' Aaron said, 'so me an' Moses'll just put it all back where we found it. Reckon some old panther or bear might like it.' They were heading for the trees. 'Just leave that deer where we can find it,' he called.

'Here's your dollar,' old Jake said. They stopped. Jake spun the coin, high. 'Lonzo asked me to keep it,' he said. 'Stake-holder. You win.' They came back.

'You want some wild onions?' Aaron asked Lonzo. 'Brings out the flavour of the meat. I know where.' But Lonzo could not take defeat. He walked away. 'Big ol' plum tree, too,' Aaron said.

'Show me,' Nat asked. 'Onions is better'n apples to me.'

'You like apples?' Aaron said. 'I can find you apples.'

~

Supper was a feast.

'How come you did it?' Martha asked Aaron. 'None of these niggers catched a squirrel. An' you got no-good legs too.'

'Gimme a pint of whiskey an' I'll tell,' Aaron said.

Martha shrugged. 'Ain't got none.' Charles Hudd had never allowed his slaves any alcohol.

'I got some.' It was one of Mrs Maud Corrigan's niggers from

141

up river, Luke Corrigan, a man whose face was wrinkled like corduroy. 'Got half a bottle I'm keepin' for Christmas. He can have a little swallow.'

Aaron took the bottle and drank the lot, sucking like a baby, swigging hard and fast till it was all gone.

'That ain't nice,' Luke said.

Aaron giggled and tried to throw the bottle in the fire but it slipped from his fingers. Already he was falling asleep.

'People bust up your legs,' Moses explained, 'it don't make you nice.'

'Might of said thanks.'

'He ain't the thankin' sort.' Moses searched Aaron's pockets and gave Luke the dollar. Luke grunted: he would sooner have had the whiskey. 'See?' Moses said. 'You ain't the thankin' sort neither.'

'Nobody never gave me nothin' I didn't have to work for it,' Luke muttered.

Next morning, Aaron was hugely hungover. When people spoke, he spat, or he flailed his arms at them. His innards were still stewed in a syrup of bad booze.

About noon, Jake brewed up some coffee and took it and sat beside him. The aroma wandered with the breeze. Aaron's head came up, slowly, as if weights were being removed from it. 'Hooo,' he said softly. 'Feels like I been kicked to death by hornets.'

He drank. The coffee trickled down his gullet, a missionary expedition bringing salvation to the heathen.

All around them, men and women were felling timber, hauling logs, making homes.

'We get the land cleared,' Jake said, 'we can start plantin'.'

Aaron blew his nose with his fingers and flung the snot away. 'Won't grow nothin',' he said. 'Soil's thin.'

'You been here before.'

Aaron dragged himself into a patch of shade. Already, the coffee had worked with the hangover to bring drops of sweat to his brow. 'This here is my backyard,' he said. 'I lived near two year up here. Knew every tree, plant, stream, animal. Damn, I was an animal myself! First deer I killed was with a rock. Ate the meat raw, I was so hungry.'

Jake gave him more coffee, and waited. Just being free to wait was a pleasure. Sometimes he caught himself in a fit of worry in case

Mister Hudd caught him not working. Freedom was hard: you had to keep thinking at it.

'Ran away,' Aaron said. 'Ran away from old man Jim Crowley of Dawson County, Carolina.'

'Ran a long way, then. I never heard of Dawson County.'

'Oh, I ran. That Jim Crowley was the devil. He worked us niggers to death, an' that's the truth, I mean to *death*. Jim Crowley see somethin' he didn't like, one of his niggers takin' a little breath, he'd beat on him! Hit him, kick. Mostly he whipped. I seen him whip a nigger down to the dust, an' blood? You couldn't see the skin for blood. I *hated* Mister Jim Crowley. We all hated him. Bad food, bad clothes, work till we couldn't see, it was so dark. And always that whip. I seen a nigger couldn't get up after Jim Crowley whipped him. Dead next day. Then it happened. One time, he told two of us, me an' another field hand, 'Hold this nigger down,' he said, an' we had to do it while he laid on his whip, head to heels, blood jumpin' off that whip until I could taste it in my mouth. That night I ran.'

'He put out a reward?'

'Five hundred dollar.'

Jake looked at him. Aaron was so shrunk-up he wasn't worth two bits.

'I was a big, stout nigger,' Aaron said. 'I could lift my own weight, them days. No-one didn't fool with Aaron, no sir.'

'Jim Crowley did.'

'Oh, he had his hounds after me. Two whole weeks he hunted me. I killed one hound that found me, choked it with these hands, whomped its head on a rock, held it under till it drowned. Big hound. *Big* hound.'

Jake sighed. 'Animal ain't to blame,' he said.

'See? Squirrel,' Aaron said; but when Jake looked where he pointed there was only a swaying branch. 'Two good years I had here. Indians saved me. Showed me where the food is, how to trap. Nuts, berries. Where I saw trees, they saw grub. Eggs, honey, wild stuff. Two best years of my life. Help me up.'

Jake lifted him. Aaron clung to a tree and emptied his bladder against it. 'Damn coffee,' he said weakly. Jake carried him back. 'Old man Jim Crowley used to piss in our grub pails,' Aaron said. 'Come noontime, we'd go to eat, he'd come riding' up, tell the overseer to get the pails lined up, an' he'd piss in every one. Sometimes kick 'em over, let his dogs eat. Us niggers got sent back to the fields, work till sundown, no grub in us.'

Jake had heard too many stories of bad slavemasters. It was like complaining about the weather, it got you nowhere and it changed nothing. 'You get caught?' he asked.

'Got drunk.' Aaron almost laughed but it hurt his head. 'Came off the Ridge an' stole some whiskey. Old man Joe Killick found me. Found me drunk in his corn, figured I was a runaway. Got a hammer, whopped me on the legs, made sure I couldn't run no further. I woke, my legs was all bust.'

'Guess he wanted the reward.'

'Wanted brains. Jim Crowley wouldn't pay a bent penny for a slave couldn't walk.'

'Mister Killick keep you?'

'Yep. Bird scarer. Sat in a field an' shot crows. Twenty years. That's all I done. Shot crows. Twenty years.'

'Ever miss?'

'Once. Fourth July, 1858. Figured the black bastards deserved a holiday.'

'Crows is American too.'

Now Aaron was ready to talk about food on the Ridge. He talked of the herds of deer, of massive elk, of many kinds of wild duck, partridge, pigeon, turkey, of squirrels in abundance, colonies of rabbits, groundhogs so heavy that one would feed a family, raccoons, opossum, wild hogs that had escaped from the valley bottom and now roamed in scores. 'No such thing as a poisonous bird,' he said. 'You can eat any bird you can catch.' He talked of wild plants which the Indians cooked and ate: nettle, silverweed, pignuts, wintergreen, iron blood, juniper. He talked of plants to avoid, hemlock and yew-berries and curly dock. He knew everything for five miles around. It looked like dense wilderness but there were ways through it, and it was a well-stocked larder provided you looked in the right places.

Noon. No need to blow a horn. Years of toil made an invisible clock that sounded noon in everybody's head. Time to eat.

'Didn't anyone ever try to kill old man Jim Crowley?' Jake asked.

'Only once,' Aaron said. 'Mrs Crowley put a pistol in his ear while he was sleepin' an' blew his rotten brains out.'

'Good woman.'

'Yeah.' He let Jake raise him. 'I heard they hanged her.'

That afternoon, and for the next two days, Moses carried Aaron on his back, up and down and across the Ridge, with three or four niggers following, while Aaron showed them where to find food, how to trap, which way the game animals travelled. He rarely shot without killing something to eat.

Lonzo broke his promise and got more provisions from Stackmesser. He was jealous of Aaron but he said nothing: just gave the stuff to Martha and Sarah and went away. The camp was starting to look good. Bonny and other kids had sneaked down and salvaged a lot of household things from the burned cabins. For the first time, it occurred to Lonzo that maybe nobody needed him.

WORSE THAN APACHES

Charles Hudd saw no point in waiting. He mentioned it in Maggie's and word soon got around Rock Springs that he wanted to be mayor. After a couple of days, he rode into town and held a public meeting on the landing stage, which got a pleasantly cool breeze off the river. Most people came. Rock Springs was thin on entertainment.

Charles stood on a barrel, courtesy of Stackmesser's store. He was in shirtsleeves and workpants, clean but not new. No hat.

'You all know me,' he said, 'so you know this ain't the kinda thing I bin raised to do. I'm just a farmer. That means I feel the way any farmer does when he sees a crop that's failed, or a herd that's sick, or ...' He blinked a bit, and looked helpless. 'I had another example, an' now look, I went an' forgot it.' They liked that. They laughed at that. 'Guess I'm trying to say, when I see *nothin'* where I know there oughta be *somethin'*, well, I get an itch. That itch tells me: better roll up your sleeves an' spit on your hands, cus *nothin'* never turns into *somethin'* without work. I see you agree. A man gets back what he puts in. Ain't that the truth? Sure it is. Now I ain't stood here to say our town, Rock Springs, is nothin'. I'm proud to be here. Proud to be a neighbour. All the same ... Rock Springs ain't half what Rock Springs was. Ain't even a quarter what it was. Question is, what next? I got a hound back home, old old hound, tries to chase the young hounds, he can't win! So what happens? Young hounds chase *him*! An' he quits! Lays on his back, waves his tired old legs in the air!' Hudd did a bit of pantomime and made them laugh. His arms dropped to his side and he waited for total silence. 'I'm askin' you, cus that's what I'm here to do, not *tell* you, *ask* you. Is that what Rock Springs is gonna do? Quit? All lie down, wave our legs in the air, let the young hounds grow big an' take all our business? You know the hounds I mean. Placket's Ferry. Downeysville. Knuckle Creek. New Jericho, even.' All these towns were less than fifty miles from Rock Springs. He let them think about that for a moment.

'Now, I don't reckon to have all the answers,' he said. 'Maybe I got a few of the questions. Like law an' order. People tell me there's too much fightin' in this town, too much dukin' it out, even shootin' it out.' That brought a rumble of support. 'Makes me want to ask: that the best way to get a bank interested in Rock Springs? Or would a bank prefer some peace an' quiet? Just askin', y'understand. Just wonderin' aloud, if I was mayor of this town, what would *you* want? F'rinstance, would you want Main Street cleaned up? I remember when ... well, no point goin' into that. See from here, it ain't no thing of beauty ...'

Hudd quickly ran through his list of improvements. Repair to the sidewalk. Build a schoolhouse. Bring back the steamboat service. Hire a sheriff. Hold a barn dance. Finally he searched his pockets and found a scrap of paper. 'Some feller told me the best words in any speech, so I wrote 'em down.' He held up the paper and read: 'That's the end.' The crowd applauded. 'Any questions,' he said, 'I'll try an' answer.'

'Here's one,' Joe Killick said. 'How about lettin' me get up there? I'm runnin' for mayor too.'

It had been a bad day for Joe. All afternoon his wife had either ranted or whined. Without house slaves to cook and clean, wash and iron, scrub and brush and fetch and pump and carry, she had to work. She had never worked. The only housework she knew was watching to make sure the nigger did things right. Now the grim prospect of actually handling raw food and soiled linen and dirty dishes stretched ahead like a cruel punishment. Her husband got the blame. Finally he took refuge in the cellar. That was when he discovered that a keg of whiskey was missing.

None of the family knew anything except Stanton.

'Reckon Moses took it, Pa,' he said. 'I seen him hangin' around the cellar, before he got made free.'

'Little barrel, Moses could tuck it under his arm,' Devereux said. 'Took it to spite you, I bet.'

'Go get the bastard,' their father ordered. 'Where is he? Take your rifles. Jesus! Get him! Get my whiskey! Get – '

'Moses is on the Ridge, Pa,' Stanton said. After that they chucked words around, but there was nothing more to say.

Joe Killick was sick with loss. He went out to the porch. He wished someone would ride up and offer to buy the farm. The flies were bad. Nobody rode up. He got tired of knocking flies off his face and neck. He went to the paddock and caught his horse. That wasn't easy: the damned animal kept shying, and Killick couldn't run. They were both wet with sweat by the time he got the horse saddled.

There was a crowd at the far end of Main Street. Joe Killick's brain could manage only one thing at a time, and drink came first. Maggie's was empty but for the cook. He gave Joe two shots of whiskey and a beer chaser. The booze began to burn his stomach but he didn't care. He knew it would settle down to a hot, growling nag. He ordered another whiskey and eventually his brain took another cautious step. 'Place is quiet,' he said.

'Town meeting,' the cook said. 'Charlie Hudd's runnin' for mayor.'

'Mayor, huh?' Killick said.

~

Hudd had no choice but to give Killick his place on the barrel. The crowd grinned and nudged each other. Everyone knew there was bad blood between these two. Most could see Killick was well liquored-up. This could be fun.

'Never thought to get anywhere near politics,' Joe began, 'on account of my daddy told me all politicians are fakers, con artists an' syrupy-talkin' thieves.' The roar of laughter took him by surprise. He stumbled and nearly fell off the barrel. When he recovered, he saw grinning faces, realized he'd scored, wasn't sure how, but he liked the feeling. He stretched his suspenders and let them snap shut. The crowd clapped and whistled at this trick, so he did it again.

Someone shouted, 'What's your party, Joe?'

'I represent the Scallywag Party,' he said. The name just popped out of his head and into his mouth. 'Politicians say they want your vote. What they really want is your money.' Nobody laughed. Money was no laughing matter, not in Rock Springs, not in 1866. 'Now, us in the Scallywag Party ain't as smart as this other feller here … uh …' He screwed up his face and waved his forefinger vaguely in Hudd's direction. 'I'll get to his name right soon … Feller lives around here somewhere ... Wait, now, I got it wrote down on a little piece a paper here ...' He was making hard work of searching his pockets, and the crowd was enjoying it. 'Hey!' He brandished a scrap of paper. Shouts of encouragement. He peered at it. 'Yeah, that's him,' he said. '*Honourable Major Charles T. Hudd*. Hudds ain't the poorest family in the county. He got a middle name! That's one thing we're dead against in the Scallywag Party, can't afford middle names, ain't rich enough! Now just what you reckon that T stands for? *Taxation*!' he shouted. 'All that stuff Mr Charles T. Hudd wants to do when he's mayor – hirin' a sheriff, knockin' down this an' cleanin' up that, buildin' who knows what, maybe a free five-holer privy painted Union blue –' Raucous laughter frightened some passing crows and they swerved away. 'Who's gonna pay?' Joe demanded. 'You elect Mr Charles T. Hudd mayor, he don't come free.' He turned on Hudd. 'How much all this gonna cost? How much *you* gonna take?'

'A nominal salary. Purely nominal.' Too late, Hudd realized nobody there knew what *nominal* meant.

'Hah!' Joe Killick was triumphant. '*He* wants paid! Me, I'll be your mayor for nothin'! Do it for the honour! Done it before, do it again!'

'Last time, you got kicked out,' Hudd said, but it was lost in the cheering. His opponent got lifted down. The crowd carried him toward Maggie's.

Hudd walked over to his wagon. Judge Potter was sitting in it. 'Last thing I expected,' Hudd said. 'Killick made a monkey out of me.'

'You made an excellent speech.'

'Killick's more popular. By a mile.'

'He's a drunk. A bag of wind. The mob wanted someone to laugh at. Are you going to Maggie's?'

Hudd shook his head. 'Killick's buyin' drinks. I won't compete with that sort of politics.'

'A wise decision.' They headed home.

Joe Killick wasn't buying drinks; he was working hard on the drinks being given him. Briefly, he was the toast of Rock Springs.

'I never heard of no Scallywag Party,' Stackmesser said to him.

'Ain't my fault you never heard,' Joe said. 'I sure spoke up loud as I could.'

That was found to be highly witty by everyone except Sims. 'What do the Scallywags stand for?' he demanded. 'Can't tell me they founded a party just so you could run against Chuck Hudd. You got a platform, or what?' There was challenge in his voice.

'Sure I got a platform. I'm agin the niggers.' Joe took a big long drink and wondered whether or not he'd made a joke.

Nobody laughed. No joke.

When he looked up, men were nodding and scowling. Good. Said the right thing again! Turning into a hell of a day. Made Hudd look stupid. Stupid as hell! Worth another drink. Deserved it! He took a drink and raised a hand and they all shut up. 'That goddamn Lincoln stole my slave,' he said.

Nobody supported him. They just looked away, or shrugged. Bastards. Selfish greedy bastards. He decided not to tell them any more.

'Slaves ain't comin' back,' Hoke Cleghorn said. 'It's our women I'm thinkin' about. Who's gonna look out for the women?'

'Girls, too,' Job Sims said. 'You got daughters, Ryan.'

'Fact is,' Ryan Kidder said, 'niggers got it in their blood, see. Can't educate it out of them.'

'Kit Carson taught me. "Hoke," he said, "it's instinct for the Apache. Makes 'em come down from the hills an' kill, kill, kill." Carson knew.'

'Apache?' Dan Killick sneered. 'Ain't an Apache this side of Kansas.'

Hoke Cleghorn took out his Bowie knife and aimed it at the roof. 'We got nigger-Indians which is worse than Apaches! Up there on the Ridge!'

'They'll breed,' Morgan Watson said. 'Worse'n rabbits.' Watson was the least successful farmer in those parts.

'Nigger stud farm up there,' Ryan Kidder said. His blisters burned. That was niggers' fault. 'I got daughters.'

'Long as nigger-Indians on that Ridge,' Sims said, 'ain't nobody safe down here.'

'Burn 'em out, shoot 'em down,' Hoke Cleghorn said. 'Kit Carson told me ...' He stopped because Joe Killick was standing, one arm raised, struggling to get his eyes in focus. 'Niggers stole barrel of whiskey out my cellar,' he said. 'You get it back, give you fifty dollars.'

'Fifty dollars,' Ryan Kidder said.

'An' fifty more if you bring me the black sonabitch stole it.' The joy of bribery began to excite Killick. 'Another hundred if you get every last nigger off that Ridge!'

Two hundred bucks. Kidder would be lucky to get that much out of his farm in a year.

It didn't take long to recruit a dozen young men. Everyone was more or less drunk. When they finally helped each other lurch into the street, rain was falling and the wind was getting up. 'Ain't goin' nowhere in this,' Dan Killick said.

'Tomorrow night,' Ryan Kidder said. 'Bring ... Hell, you know what to bring.' They went back inside.

BLISTERS BIG AS SILVER DOLLARS

The rain didn't last. Next day Lonzo came down to Rock Springs and told Stackmesser that part of the old Indian silver mine had collapsed, so they would have to cut timber and prop the roof up. 'Take time,' he said. 'Need grub.'

'Uh-huh.' Stackmesser weighed a pound of nails from a barrel and thought about the talk in Maggie's, the fears, the threats. That had been whiskey talking. He knew so because his head throbbed and his mouth felt dry as a bucket of dust.

This nigger was real. Silver was real, too, and it could be the key to a better, richer life, with decent whiskey, not Maggie's hooch. 'Where exactly is this mine, boy?' he asked.

'Under big rock. Next coupla old pine trees.'

'Hundred of rocks on that Ridge. Hundred of pines.'

'Not like these.'

Stackmesser didn't like it, but either he agreed or he lost everything he'd staked. The assay results wouldn't be back from Bowling Green for a week. Maybe two. Lonzo got a sack of cornmeal and a mule-load of other stuff: axe, sledgehammer, wood plane, rope.

'Keep them darkies workin', boy. I'll make you rich.' Lonzo grunted. 'You could send the women an' kids to Chicago. Save on the grub.' Another grunt. 'Heard tell might be a bunch of hunters on the Ridge soon,' Stackmesser added. 'Wouldn't want any of our miners gettin' hurt.' Now Lonzo's grunt was a semitone higher.

Job Sims watched Lonzo lead the mule out of town, a sack of meal on its back and the sledge on his shoulder. Sims left his smithy, his hands black with charcoal and the tang of beaten iron around him, and asked Stackmesser what in hell was going on.

'Just another customer, Job. I don't enquire into people's business.'

This was such a lie that Sims felt insulted. He went back to work.

Later, Ryan Kidder stopped at the smithy, his muscles aching from doing slavework. 'That right, Hudd's uppity nigger's been in town, buyin' up Stackmesser's store?' He picked at blisters as big as silver dollars. 'You see him?'

'Walked down this street like he owned it.'

Elias Dunbar joined them. He was a cooper and a cobbler, and he cut hair and corns and embalmed the dead, using the same instruments for each job. He took photographs to order and several came out. Dunbar was short and had a squeaky voice. Now the niggers had gone, he wasn't equal to anyone in Rock Springs except Maggie's cook. 'All that stuff Charlie Hudd was sayin' last night, I kinda liked it,' he said. 'This town needs more business. I sure do.'

Ryan Kidder poked him in the chest. 'This town ain't goin' nowhere as long as any raggedy-assed nigger can walk his mule down the sidewalk like he owned it, an' you better hustle out his way or he's liable to tramp all over you, my friend.'

'I never saw no nigger mule on no sidewalk,' Elias Dunbar said.

'Nigger stud farm,' Sims said. 'Breedin' night an' day.'

'You want to be massacred in your bed?' Kidder demanded.

'Put it like that,' Dunbar said, 'I guess not.'

⁓

Ryan Kidder fired first. It was the signal for a barrage of gunshots. Sixteen men walked through the Hudd Camp in line abreast, slowly because the night was black and made blacker by the red-yellow flames streaking from revolvers, and also because nobody cared to step out of line and get himself shot; and as they walked they battered holy hell out of the night. The racket came bouncing back off the forest and drowned out the screech of birds. It was a truly murderous attack. It went on and on.

Kidder had planned it.

Everyone knew where the niggers were: by day you could see their smoke climbing out of the Ridge, thin as pencil lines against the sky. Getting there in the dark had been a long hard stumbling sweat. Kidder had a lantern, which helped, but he put it out as soon as he smelled wood-smoke from the dying fires. It was two in the morning.

153

First he got everyone lined up. They were going to flush these niggers out with a hail of lead, and then kick them down the hill.

No niggers to kick.

Kidder's men stopped when they reached the last cabin.

'Fuckers ain't runnin', Ryan,' Dan Killick said.

This was true. The cabins were full of niggers, and the niggers were full of fear, but they could not run because each cabin door was blocked solid with logs that had been slotted in place at night to guard against panthers. These logs kept the bullets out and kept the niggers in. But Kidder did not know that.

'Hell,' he said. 'Re-load, godammit.'

The line turned and walked back, banging away, and stopped again, ears buzzing, nostrils twitching from gunsmoke, wrists tired from the constant kick-back.

Still no niggers.

'Shit,' Kidder said. 'Get me the damn lantern, I'll kick 'em out. An' I want to find that whiskey they stole.'

'You took the damn lantern,' said Andy Cleghorn, Hoke Cleghorn's son.

'I gave it you to hold.'

'Fuckin' liar.'

'Well, where is it, then? Ain't goin' in no nigger cabin without a goddamn lantern.'

The lantern was lost. Everyone began cursing. That was when rocks started to whirr past their heads.

Lonzo did not believe in panthers; his cabin door had no barrier. When the shooting woke him he ran for the trees. Now he could hear strangers' voices. He crept closer and lobbed rocks at them. The Ridge had plenty of rocks, and in the blackness there was no telling where they were being thrown from. He heard furious shouts, and occasional screams of pain. He threw more rocks. For a while there was some wild, aimless shooting. Then Kidder's raiders withdrew. It was a hard journey down the Ridge without the lantern, a journey full of stumbling and falling into raking thorns, a journey of blood and bruises.

~

Came sunup, most of the colony were still shaking with fright. Half were for quitting the Ridge, now. One little boy wept hysterically; he saw panthers everywhere.

Jake called them all together. 'Anyone hurt?' he asked. It was hard to hear the answers for the little boy's howling. His mother shook him, and made the howls go up and down. 'Gimme,' Moses said. He sat the boy on his shoulders, a mile high. The amazing view quietened the boy. Moses tickled his toes and made him laugh.

No-one was hurt.

'The Lord has delivered us,' Josh said. 'Praise be the Lord.'

'Who were they, anyway?' Luke Corrigan asked. Even in the war, he had never heard such gunfire.

'Just a bunch of crackers from Rock Springs,' Aaron said. 'I recognized a few voices.'

'That bunch of crackers wants to kill us,' Nat said. Usually he was the first to make a joke of anything; now his face was dragged down with misery.

Moses tickled the other foot, but the boy's chuckling only strengthened the silence.

'Ain't waitin' here to get my head shot off,' Nat said glumly.

'We bought this land,' Jake argued. 'We got a right to live here.'

'You bought a graveyard, is what you bought,' Nat said. 'They ain't gonna let you live. You want to get killed, you stay. Not me.' He walked away.

'Nat, where you goin'?' Martha called. Nat kept going, heading downhill. 'Crazy,' she said. But a lot of people were watching Nat and were not listening.

Jake felt the whole colony about to break apart and drift away. He looked to Lonzo for help, and could not find him. 'We bought ...' he began. And didn't have the strength to finish.

A black woodpecker flew into the clearing, veered sharply and fled into the trees.

'Hey,' Lonzo said, not raising his voice. 'Want to see white folks' blood?' He was sitting on his haunches, a long way off.

They trailed over. Lonzo had found some fresh red splatters. He rubbed one with a finger and tasted it. 'Mm – *mmm*,' he said. 'Real white blood. Got that *rich* taste. Yes, sir.' He stood, and they saw that he was holding a revolver in his other hand. 'Lotta noise last night,' he said. 'Sorry if I spoiled your sleep any.'

'You was shootin' back?' Sarah said. The idea of a nigger firing at white men thinned her voice to a whisper.

'Weren't more'n twenty. Come up to have a little fun, I guess.' Lonzo rubbed the bloodstain with his foot. He stuffed the gun in the top of his pants and strolled away.

'Where you goin'?' Jake asked.

'Goin' to town,' Lonzo answered. 'Goin' to have a little fun also.'

Several people bent and touched and tasted the blood, including Lucy. She licked her lips. 'Hmmmm,' she said. 'Don't taste like no white man I know.' Her father swung a heavy hand, but she dodged it.

'You'll burn in hell,' Josh warned her. She shrugged. 'Might's well have some fun on the way,' she said.

A TEN-DOLLAR GRIN

The irregular rattle of distant gunfire disturbed the sleep of Charles Hudd and Judge Potter. Next morning they decided that Hudd should take the opportunity to campaign for law and order. They drove the wagon to town and had a second breakfast at Maggie's and asked her what the skirmishing had been all about.

'That fool Kidder took a bunch of jackasses up the mountain to scare the niggers,' Maggie said.

'Oh.' Charles Hudd forked butter onto his pancakes. 'They hurt anyone?'

'Hoke Cleghorn's boy got a hole in his head. Dan Killick fell down a gully, bust his nose. Little Billy Dunbar ran into a big old pine tree so hard, his poor little *cojones* swelled up an' now every time he coughs, everythin' goes dark an' he sees skyrockets shootin' through his head.'

'Goodness,' Judge Potter said.

'Plus he hears "The Star-Spangled Banner".'

'I don't believe that,' Hudd said.

'Me neither, but Brightsides said it, an' you know how he gets bored with just plain doctorin'.'

Morgan Watson's sow nosed the door open and looked around but the floor was freshly swept and there were no tobacco wads to eat. She slumped onto her side and went to sleep.

'Joe Killick was right about one thing,' Maggie said. 'What this town needs is a free outhouse. After market day, the bushes round here are a disgrace. Barber's Landing's got a four-holer. We could be the first town in Dundee County with an eight-holer.'

'Young man!' the judge called. A small boy stopped tugging on the sow's tail. 'Go tell Mr Kidder that Judge Potter wants him, pronto,

157

an' you'll get a piece of candy.' The boy vanished.

'That's Flub Phillips's youngest, little Arnie,' Maggie said. 'Ain't the fastest messenger you could have picked. Ten years old and can't do up his buttons.'

After breakfast, Hudd and the judge went for a stroll. The town was quiet. As they reached the end of one sidewalk, something stirred in the ruins of the old bank building, and the pedlar climbed out of the weeds. 'Good morning,' he said. His clothes were wrinkled like a squeeze-box and his face was still asleep. 'Please do not think I live here,' he said. 'My God, what a splendid night that must have been, although personally I remember little of it.' He was still a bit drunk.

'Maggie's place is open,' Hudd said. 'Don't step on the sow.'

They watched him walk away, stiff in every joint. 'Every town has one,' the judge said. The pedlar tried to step over the sow and trod on it. It screeched and chased him down the street. 'Never two,' the judge said. 'Only one.'

That was when Lonzo rode into town on the old mule.

'You all that's left?' the judge asked him.

Lonzo had never seen such a tall man with such thick white hair. 'Huh!' he said.

Hudd saw the gun in his pants. 'You come here lookin' for blood, boy?' he asked.

'Nossir. Lookin' for molasses.' When they laughed, Lonzo relaxed. He could play the dumb nigger better than anyone. 'Yessir, molasses,' he said. Now he sounded dumber than dumb.

It was two hours before Kidder got off his horse and limped into Maggie's tavern, bramble cuts all over his face. The place was moderately busy. 'Jesus, Ryan,' Job Sims said. 'Your wife throw you through the window?'

'Gimme a beer,' Kidder said. He would have hit Sims if Sims had been a lot smaller.

Hudd let him drink some beer, and then asked, 'You up on the Ridge last night?'

'What's it to you? You got no authority in this town.'

'Sure, sure. Still, if you weren't on the Ridge, blazin' away an' makin' life miserable for the owls an' raccoons an' bobcats an' similar respectable critters tryin' to get a decent night's sleep, then I guess you couldn't have left a gun up there.'

They had a brief battle to see who blinked first, and Kidder lost. 'What goddamn gun?' he growled.

'Lonzo, get in here,' Hudd called. By now everyone else had stopped talking.

Lonzo finished peeling a potato, tossed it in the pot and came in from the kitchen. He was holding a Colt .38 with a very long barrel. Nobody watching had ever seen a nigger with a handgun in Rock Springs or anywhere else. The silence was painful.

'Ain't loaded,' he said. 'Reckon belongs some hunter. Probably tripped on a rock, dropped it. Come to think, maybe I heard a shot.' There was no expression in his voice or face. He spun the gun on his trigger finger. People began to titter.

'Never seen it before,' Kidder said, angry at the laughter.

'I'll take that weapon,' Hoke Cleghorn declared in a voice like slowly tearing sandpaper.

'Hey, not so fast,' Charles Hudd said. 'This thing could be valuable. How do we know – '

'Look under the butt. Got my initials. Also five notches on top.'

Hudd took the revolver and examined it. 'Correct. Mighty unusual weapon.'

'Kit Carson gave it me.'

'Guess you'd hate to lose it.'

Cleghorn had no choice. He nodded.

'Worth a reward, then.'

'Five dollars.'

Hudd looked at the circle of faces. 'Here's this poor nigger's honest enough to come down the mountain, which means he lost a day's work, and – '

'Ten,' Cleghorn said.

'On top of which,' Hudd said, 'his night's sleep got badly disturbed ... You say you went huntin' up there last night, Mr Cleghorn?'

'I did not.' Cleghorn's face was red as rare steak. 'My son – '

'Oh! Your son. Well, he too would surely wish to help with the reward money also.'

'Twenty-five dollars,' Cleghorn said.

'Thirty,' Judge Potter said. Several onlookers gasped. 'Thirty dollars, or this honest nigger boy gets to keep what he found.' Nobody wanted that. Cleghorn had to borrow the money from Maggie. He took his gun and left, kicking the batwing doors as if they were the cheeks of his son's ass.

'Get back to them taters now, boy,' the judge said. Lonzo returned to the kitchen. 'I want to hear from someone ain't entirely stupid what all that foolishness on the Ridge was about,' he said.

'One them niggers stole ol' man Joe Killick's whiskey,' Kidder told him. 'We went to get it back, is all. Five-gallon keg, special premium best old mature whiskey, stole from Joe Killick's cellar by that big buck nigger of his, Moses.'

'That's right,' the pedlar agreed, now almost drunk again.

'Too much thievin' in this town,' said Morgan Watson. 'I just had a shoat took. Real good shoat.'

'Man's got a right to protect his own property,' Stackmesser said virtuously. 'Someone stole a hat from my store yesterday. Walked right out with it on his head!'

'I seen 'em,' the pedlar said. 'Seen all three. Big nigger wearin' a new hat an' carryin' a fat shoat an' a keg of whiskey. Name of Moses. That nigger ran so fast ...' Stackmesser punched him in the ear and he fell off his chair. 'Ain't no joke,' Stackmesser grunted.

'Whole damn nigger camp ain't no joke,' Sims said.

'They can't control theirselves,' Kidder said. 'We let 'em get lickered up, every man here is like to get his throat cut an' all the womenfolk raped like cattle!' Kidder was hoarse with indignation.

'Cattle don't rape,' the pedlar corrected. He was back on his chair. Stackmesser's backhand swing knocked him off.

'Reckon we was doin' your job,' Kidder informed the judge. 'Helpin' keep this town safe from whiskey-thievin' niggers.'

'Moses didn't steal no whiskey,' Maggie said.

Kidder stared. His arm slackened until beer began to dribble from his mug. 'Joe Killick told me – '

'Stanton Killick stole it,' Maggie said. She found an old cigar-stub on the bar and tossed it to the sow, which was back inside and browsing under a table. 'Stanton Killick sold me a five-gallon keg of whiskey, only it didn't have no five gallons in it, more like four, Stanton must of kept some back for himself, an' it wasn't no smooth old five-star liquor neither. Handy for removin' warts, maybe. Good enough for trappers or Irish or piano-players or suchlike.'

'Ain't no liquor bad enough for piano-players,' Sims muttered. His first wife ran off with a musician.

'I'm real surprised at you,' Watson said to Maggie, 'sellin' bad whiskey.'

'You drunk plenty of it last night,' she said. 'Didn't complain.'

Kidder had been brooding. Suddenly he came alive. 'You're lyin',' he said to Maggie, jabbing with a finger. 'Ain't so.'

Maggie reached under the bar and picked up an empty keg. 'See here,' she said, and threw it. Kidder caught it, but not before it banged into his ribs.

'First piano-player I see in here,' Sims said grimly, 'I'll break his neck.'

'Not in this town, you won't,' Judge Potter said. 'That there's a threat to commit violence. Fined one dollar. Payable now.'

'Don't push your luck, judge,' Sims growled. 'We put you up, we'll knock you down.'

'Tryin' to intimidate an elected official. Fined two dollars, makin' three in all.' It was no joke.

'Hey …' Sims turned to the others. 'Hear that? A man can't open his mouth! Jesus! Is this the sort of law we want?' Nobody answered. Sims was not as popular as he thought.

'Sound to me like attempted conspiracy there,' the judge said. 'Three dollars fine.'

'Makes six,' the pedlar said softly. Someone sniggered, and set off his friends.

'Ain't payin',' Sims grunted. 'You can go to hell.' He shoved his beer mug across the bar.

'Ain't servin' no criminals,' Maggie said.

Sims was trapped. Maggie's was the only tavern in Rock Springs. Barber's Landing had a bar but that was six miles downstream, ten if you rode, which meant a round trip of twenty miles every time he wanted a goddamn beer. He slammed six dollars on the bar and walked out. Kidder followed him, carrying the empty keg.

Judge Potter called out, 'Come in here, boy.'

Lonzo appeared, wiping his wet hands.

'There's twenty-four dollars,' the judge said. 'Reward money. I took out twenty per cent. That's my fee.'

'Huh.'

'You find any more guns, you bring 'em here.'

Lonzo nodded and walked out.

'Notice he didn't say thanks,' Watson complained.

'Notice we didn't neither,' Maggie said.

In the street, Kidder and Sims were taking turns to sniff the bung-hole of the keg. 'Horse-piss,' Sims said.

'Them Killicks never could make good whiskey,' Kidder said.

'Seems to me you been made a right fool of, Ryan.'

'We'll see about that. I made a deal. Just because that sonofabitch Stanton – '

'Yeah, sure.' Sims tossed the keg to him. 'You been made a right goddamn fool.'

'Well, at least I had sense enough to look foolish in the dark. Five minutes ago, everyone saw *you* actin' like a horse's ass in clear day-light.' Kidder strode away and left Sims glowering, searching furi-ously for an answer. By the time he found one, Kidder was nearly out of sight. Sims quit. Better never than late. All the same, someone was going to have to pay.

Joe Killick refused to pay Kidder for the empty whiskey keg. Why hadn't Kidder brought the nigger who stole it? Kidder said Stanton stole it. Killick rejected that, flat. His brain was in no shape for any sort of complication. His brain was permanently stunned by pain and usually flogged by booze. He cursed Kidder out of the house, lashing at him with his stick.

'I scared them niggers like you wanted,' Kidder insisted. 'Now you owe me. We had a deal ...' He stopped because Stanton Killick had appeared in the doorway.

'You take my brother Daniel up on that Ridge again, an' I'll smash *your* nose,' Stanton promised.

'Niggers did that,' Kidder said, so fast he surprised himself. 'We got split up in the dark, niggers cornered your Dan, I chased 'em away, he was liable to get killed.' He found that he was nodding like a donkey, so he shut up.

'You sure scared 'em.' Stanton had shaded his eyes and was looking at the Ridge. 'You sure put them niggers off their grub, yes sir.' Grey threads of smoke from cooking fires could just be seen on the remote skyline, bending in the wind.

Kidder mounted his horse and rode away.

'A thing needs doin',' Stanton said, 'you got to do it your

goddamn self. Ain't that right, Pa?' Joe Killick didn't answer; couldn't answer. Throwing out Kidder had left him as weak as a baby and shivering like a man in a fever.

~

Stackmesser found Lonzo in his store, trying on hats. 'Anythin' this nigger wears, he buys,' he told his assistant. 'Now wash all them hats, inside an' out. *Especially* inside.' He took Lonzo into his office. 'How's our mine comin'?' he asked. 'You got the cave dug out yet?'

'Cave done gone,' Lonzo said. Stackmesser flinched. 'Ain't where we done left it,' Lonzo said woodenly. 'Reckon we done got robbed last night.' He was grave as an undertaker.

'Robbed.' Stackmesser looked out of the window, as if the cave might be lying there.

'Bushwackers come,' Lonzo said. 'Us niggers got nothin' worth takin'. Guess them bushwackers done stole the cave. Mighty heavy. Heard 'em all groanin' an' cussin'.'

'Yeah, yeah.' So it was a joke. Stackmesser bared his teeth.

'Mean sonsabitches.'

'I had nothin' to do with last night, Lonzo. You know that. We're partners, for Christ's sake! You got the mine dug out yet?'

'Dug out, sure. Roof done fell in again.'

'Oh, shit.'

'Worse'n ever now,' Lonzo said gloomily.

He bought pork, salt, coffee, molasses, eggs, shoes and a newspaper, and paid for it out of his reward money.

The mule was old but not stupid, and it knew the way up the mountain by now. Lonzo ambled behind. Sometimes he whistled, sometimes he sang: *Polk an' Clay went to war, Polk came back wid a broken jaw.* Who the hell were Polk and Clay? Who cared? It was a good tune and it made him feel free. Damn, he *was* free! Free to sing what he liked, as loud as he liked! He filled his lungs and sang,

> *Run, nigger, run, de patroller ketch you,*
> *Run, nigger, run, it's almos' day;*
> *Dat nigger run, dat nigger flew,*
> *Dat nigger tore his shirt in two …*

It was colossally funny, so funny that he had to stop and laugh. The forest didn't like his noise: a red squirrel chattered angrily, jays and crows spread the alarm, for a quarter of a mile all around there was no peace. Lonzo enjoyed the attention. These animals didn't know what it was like to be outside a farm at night, dodging patrollers or paterollers, call them what you like, they'd whip any nigger they caught without a pass. But first they had to catch him!

> Over de hill and down de holler,
> Patroller ketch nigger by de collar;
> Dat nigger run, dat nigger flew,
> Dat nigger tore his pants in two!

He knew he should be scared: there might be a white man with a gun behind any tree; but the intoxication of liberty drove out fear and he sang with a full-blooded swagger that he had not known was in him.

Then he stopped. It wouldn't do to stroll into camp sounding carefree, he might lose respect. He made himself serious.

Nobody was working.

All around the clearing, men and women were sprawling or lying. It was long past dinner time. He led the mule to old Jake and asked him what the hell was going on.

'Lucy,' Jake said.

'What about Lucy?'

'Hey …' Jake waved a tired hand; too tired to argue. 'Trouble. You know how.'

'Oh.' Lonzo thought of Lucy. Tits that pointed at your two ears. A walk like an overloaded coffeegrinder. 'Oh, oh.'

'Yeah, oh, oh. Middle of the mornin', everyone's cuttin' timber, draggin' out stumps, suchlike. Lucy comes over with a pail of water to drink. One them Corrigan niggers takes her in the woods. They're walkin' side-by-side, he's squeezin' her ass, if she's screamin', ain't no-one can hear it.'

'I ain't screamin' neither. She's trash.'

'Uh-huh. Hour later, ain't come back. Someone says, if that nigger ain't workin', I ain't workin'. Throws down his axe. Next man says, you 'speck me to work for the both of you? Then – '

Lonzo stopped him. 'Then everyone sit on their brains an' wait to die. That it?'

'Josh, he done some prayin'.' Jake peered across the clearing. His eyes were weak but he made out two fuzzy figures. 'Ain't that her comin' now?' he said. 'Ain't that Lucy?'

Lonzo left the mule and strode towards them. 'Hey, you boy!' he shouted. He wanted everyone to see this. His head was up and his shoulders were back. He manufactured a hard stare and a frown.

They came to meet him. The Corrigan nigger had Lucy by the arm. 'No harm done,' he said, and smiled. It was a big, easy smile on a smooth, happy face. Lonzo's temper jumped several cogs. He hit the man square in the smile, hit him so hard that the man's knees turned outwards like a bad curtsy and he collapsed, dragging Lucy down with him. Lonzo's fist raged with pain but he ignored it and stripped the belt from his pants.

'Whites ain't gonna gun us out!' he bawled, and lashed at both their bodies. 'An' you ain't gonna fornicate us out!' The belt slashed cloth and it scored weals on flesh. 'This is our home!' Lucy was howling and struggling to break free but the man's elbow was locked onto her arm and Lonzo was flailing, left and right. 'Home!' he shouted, in time with his blows. 'Home! Home! Home!' Then Moses arrived at a run and barged him over.

Jake got there as they were picking themselves up, some weeping, some cursing. 'You got the wrong man,' Jake said. 'This ain't the nigger took her in the woods.'

'You said a Corrigan nigger.' But Lonzo remembered: three Corrigans had climbed the Ridge. Three. He didn't want to look at anyone. Something in his gut felt like a lump of frozen rock. He walked to his cabin and sat on his bed. Eventually he heard the distant sounds of work going on, but he was flattened by failure and he could not move; just sat and looked. Hungry. Empty. Couldn't eat.

～

Aaron took someone different each day to learn how to hunt. This day it was Gabe Killick, a clever, clumsy nigger who could fix anything that was bust but couldn't put a foot in the forest without snapping sticks. Game fled like ripples in a pool. The hunters hid, and after a long wait, Gabe missed a big hind from under thirty yards. Aaron stopped him reloading. 'Them deer are in Virginia,' he said. 'An' you couldn't hit Virginia if you were standin' on the border.'

On the way home they checked his snares and found three rabbits.

Martha thanked him for the rabbits and told him about the trouble with Lucy. Gabe carried him to Lonzo's cabin and went away.

For a while, the strong young man and the shrunken old cripple sat and looked at each other.

'Reckon it's time I quit.'

'Yeah.' Aaron nodded. 'You go, boy.'

'Leave for good.'

'Why stay? Everyone here hates you.'

Not what Lonzo expected. 'Would of starved without me.'

'Ain't you the hero? Hell, I ate that grub an' I hate you too.'

Lonzo sucked his knuckles, which still ached. 'Don't give a damn,' he mumbled.

'You give a big damn,' Aaron said, 'or you wouldn't be skulkin' in here. You want these good niggers to love you? Huh? So why work so hard at kickin' their black asses?'

'Ain't no other way.'

'Uh-huh.'

'You got a better way?'

'Yeah, but I ain't gonna tell, on account of you're a mean, miserable, nasty, bad-tempered nigger who ain't gonna love nobody cus nobody loves him.' Aaron crawled to the door and shouted. 'Gabe! Now where's the smartest, strongest, handsomest man I know? Come an' carry me.' Gabe arrived, grinning. Lonzo would have given ten dollars for someone to grin at him like that.

Gabe carried Aaron to old Jake. 'Ain't his fault,' Aaron said.

'Hit the wrong man,' Jake said. 'Near to bust his jaw.'

'Long as Lonzo can remember, white folks been hittin' the wrong man.'

'He ain't white folks.'

'That's what he got to learn,' Aaron said. 'Before someone here come up behind him an' knock his black brains out.'

NEVER QUIT

Joe Killick didn't want to debate the issues. 'I'm a Scallywag an' that's all anyone needs to know,' he said. Charles Hudd tried to hold another public meeting but only Flub Phillips came, and that was out of curiosity at the sight of a lonely man standing on a barrel.

'Might as well hold this election now,' Judge Potter said, 'while I'm still here to see fair play.'

Most of the town voted. Joe Killick got elected by a landslide.

'That business with Hoke Cleghorn's gun spoiled your chances,' the judge said. 'I could smell it in the air, when they saw your niggerboy holdin' a thirty-eight. Not a welcome sight.'

'Lonzo ain't my boy any longer. And Cleghorn got what he deserved.'

'Doesn't work that way. Only one rule of politics in this town. Anythin' goes wrong, blame the niggers.'

Next day, Judge Potter rode home.

'I'm glad you lost,' Mary Hudd told her husband. 'I ran this farm all through the war. Now you do it.'

~

That was the afternoon when Mrs Hudd sent Floyd to buy some necessities at Stackmesser's, and made him wear the goddamn hat. He blamed the goddamn hat for everything. Made him look like a goddamn girl.

Floyd was seventeen, too tall, too thin. Hair like yellow silk and big feet, getting bigger. Kept tripping over things or kicking them because he wasn't sure where his feet should be. The war meant he hadn't eaten enough to keep pace with his growth and now he sometimes fainted. Maybe the heat had nothing to do with it, but his mother made him wear the hat. It was apple-green and the brim turned up all the way round like a small sombrero. Floyd took it off as soon as the buggy was out of sight of the house, rolled it up, stuck it in the back of his belt.

Stackmesser's was busy. Floyd was hanging about, waiting, bent at the knees and round at the shoulders, trying to look less lanky, when he felt a tug on his belt. He turned, and Devereux Killick was picking the hat off the floor. 'This yours?' Dev said. He opened it and made it spin, slowly, on his finger. Everyone looked.

Floyd grabbed but Dev dodged and Floyd missed and stumbled.

'Hey!' Stackmesser warned.

'What?' Dev said. He put the hat on. Floyd grabbed again, just as Dev whipped the hat off. Floyd's nails raked his neck and drew blood. Dev gasped and kicked. He was off-balance and he staggered into a stack of coffee-pots and sent them clattering. 'Out, out, out!' Stackmesser roared.

The boys fought in the street for about five minutes, the usual sweaty, gasping mix of wrestling, punching and hacking. Quite soon, both of them were filthy and weary. Maggie sent out the cook with a couple of buckets of washing-up water, foul and greasy. He dumped one load on each head. 'Now go home,' she shouted.

If Floyd had had any brains he would have gone to the river, stripped off, soaked his head, washed his clothes. He could have invented some excuse – the horse bolted, or he fell out the buggy, anything. He had no brains. When his stepfather saw the fat lip, the bent nose, the scraped ear, the lumps on the head, and when he heard Floyd's account, much of it true, Charles Hudd saddled his horse.

'Only a fight,' his wife said.

'So was Fort Sumter. Give these Killicks an inch, they think you're a pushover.'

He found Joe Killick sitting in a rocker on his porch, holding his stomach. Everyone else was out in the fields, even the girls, even Ma Killick. 'Get off my land, nigger-lover,' Joe said. The words came feebly, and left him wheezing for breath. 'I'm the mayor, not you.'

'You will apologize before I leave,' Hudd said.

'You stinkin' cheatin' robbin' Yankee bastard.' Killick stood up, at the second attempt. Immediately his heart had a tiny tantrum, kicking and stamping. His legs felt as if they had been secretly emptied of muscle. He clung to a post while his strength dissolved and slowly returned. He knew that Hudd was making a long speech, but only the last few words penetrated the roaring silence in his head. '... and I do not look for trouble,' Hudd said, 'but when trouble comes looking for me, be warned, I am dressed in the armour of righteousness.'

'Goddamn Lincoln,' Killick said weakly. 'Stole my slaves.'

'That is beside the point.'

'Fought for the North.' Each word was an effort. 'Yankee son-ofabitch traitor.'

'Your boy brutally and without cause attacked my son. I demand – '

'You ain't got no son!' Killick found a spurt of energy. 'Ain't got the balls! Get away from me.' Pain flared. His eyes watered. 'I'm the mayor. You lost. Remember?'

Hudd saw Killick's face start to crumple, and he followed the example he had learned from Grant on the battlefield: be adamant in the face of suffering. 'By God, you will apologize,' he growled, 'if it's the last thing you do.'

Killick shuffled indoors. 'Need a drink,' he whispered.

Hudd followed him. *Never give up*, he told himself. *When the enemy retreats, pursue him, better him!* 'Where is your murderous son?' he demanded. 'Fetch him out!'

'Drink,' Killick whispered. He almost tripped on a rip in the carpet. The whole house seemed to be slowly rocking, like a big boat. He reached for a chair to steady himself and his hand missed it by a mile. Hudd's footsteps were huge and heavy. 'Get out,' Killick pleaded.

'You know what you must do,' Hudd boomed. *Never quit. Fight till you win. Nothing else matters.* 'You must apologize.'

Killick tried to climb the stairs. He knew he could never reach the top; he was simply trying to escape Hudd and escape this demon of pain before its talons ripped him apart. On the fifth step, the demon won. Charles Hudd, still shouting, suddenly found himself catching Killick's limp body.

At the top of the stairs, Devereux Killick, badly cut and bruised, saw it all. 'Leave my daddy alone, you bastard!' he cried, and split his lip again. Blood dribbled down his chin.

~

Joe Killick's funeral was reckoned the best since the Latimer family hanged themselves in the barn, husband, wife, four children and the hired hand, all buried together in the biggest single grave ever known in Dundee County.

The Reverend J. Hubert Hunkin took the Killick service.

Some said Flub Phillips was out-preaching him nowadays, said that good old Flub was the kind of preacher you went to because he made you forget what a mess this world was in by making you real terrified of the world to come, and there was nobody like an old-time leather-lunged Baptist to make you believe you deserved the both of them, foul wretch that you were. A man didn't know what a bestial sinner he was until Flub had told him about it for two or three hours.

So The Reverend J. Hubert Hunkin took this chance to get back by preaching a double sermon, using two texts, back-to-back.

The first was Ephesians, five, three and four: 'Fornication, and all uncleanness, or covetousness, let it not once be named among you, as becometh saints; Neither filthiness, nor foolish talking, nor jesting, which are not convenient.' He hammered the congregation hot and strong on that one. Was it, he demanded, worth satisfying the lusts of the flesh if the price was eternal damnation? He could see that his message hurt. Take away fornication and foolish talk, and Rock Springs would be a ghost town; that's what a lot of folk were thinking. 'The devil wants you to fornicate!' Hunkin roared. 'He's urgin' you on! Every time you sin, the devil sees more company in hell! He looks at you fornicatin' and he sees barbecue meat!' They laughed. He didn't mind because now he could catch them on the rebound. 'The devil can smell you sizzlin'!' he said. They stopped laughing. Everyone cooked barbecue in Kentucky. They knew exactly what hell looked like. 'How many here are lookin' forward to gettin' turned over on that red-hot grill by the devil's barbecue fork?' Hunkin worked that image for the next ten minutes.

Meanwhile, the coffin sat on trestles in the aisle, waiting for its final journey. Devereux Killick sat near it. He had suffered pangs of guilt because maybe the fight with Floyd Hudd had led to his father's death. Now the sermon made his anxiety worse. Dev had done a little fornicating recently, and he wanted to do a lot more, but he had burned his hand on a barbecue not long ago and he knew how it hurt. He whimpered. People glanced. He hid his face in his hands. Grief-stricken, they thought.

170

Hunkin's second text was Job sixteen, eleven to thirteen: 'God hath delivered me to the ungodly, and turned me over into the hands of the wicked. I was at ease, but He hath broken me asunder; He hath also taken me by my neck, and shaken me to pieces, and set me up for His mark. His archers compass me round about, He cleaveth my reins asunder, and doth not spare; He poureth out my gall upon the ground.'

Hunkin slammed his big black Bible so hard that the noise echoed. 'God did all that to Job,' he said, 'and Job was a good man! Now then: what you reckon God is goin' to do to *you*?' Devereux gave a quavering moan that grew into hysterical weeping. Hunkin preached over the top of it. At the end, Dev had to be helped out of the church. Hunkin was gratified. One in the eye for Flub Phillips.

That was when everyone heard the steam-whistle blow. It was faint, and they knew they had ample time to put Joe Killick in the ground before the excitement began. This was turning into one hell of a good day.

~

Not many riverboats came up the Cameron during the war. Too dangerous, and anyway there was scant trade with Rock Springs while soldiers were protecting that piece of country. If you had a hock of ham they protected it by eating it; that way it was warranted one hundred per cent safe. So a real sign of peace arrived when a scarred and paint-flaking old side-wheeler called *The Hon. Colonel Ralph Q. Chauncey* churned her way up the snaking river, sounding a string of blasts on her steam whistle.

Thirty minutes later, the *Chauncey's* whistle blew off steam, pure white against the pumping black smoke from her funnel, as she paraded past the landing stage. The pilot took her another hundred yards, ordered the starboard paddle-wheel into reverse, and she revolved with a mighty thrashing of brown water. Tree branches brushed her stern. He let her straighten up and drift until she kissed the shore with a mighty groaning of timbers. The population of Rock Springs applauded. The pilot touched his hat. Gangplanks thudded. Passengers and cargo began coming ashore.

Stackmesser was there, taking delivery of merchandise.

'Prices up again,' he said. 'Used to be a good razor cost a quarter. Now look: dollar each.'

'Crazy,' said Job Sims, searching for a keg of horseshoe nails. He had a beard; what did he care about the price of razors?

'Gettin' so a feller can't afford to cut his own throat,' Ryan Kidder said. He was still bruised and bitter from falling down the Ridge.

'I got a genuine Italian stiletto I'm sellin' cheap,' the pedlar said.

'Hey!' Sims said. 'Just look at *that*.'

Making her way through the crowd was a woman, about half a head taller than most men, with hair so deep red it shone black where the sun caught it. Her cheekbones were high and her skin was milk-white. She had a small nose and a broad upper lip. She wore black; black from bonnet to side-button boots. From the waist down she was slim as a cowboy. She stopped near the blacksmith. 'Where do I find the mayor of this town?' she asked.

'Dig deep,' Sims said.

'Oh. Town clerk?'

'Never had one.'

'Can I get a job in your courthouse? I can keep records and – '

'No courthouse,' Sims said. 'Raiders from Tennessee burned it down.'

'I can teach piano. And dancing.'

'Piano was in the courthouse. So was the dancin'.'

'Got a newspaper? I can write.'

'Went bust,' Stackmesser said.

She sat on a barrel of pickles. 'This must be the saddest, sorriest excuse for a town outside of Desolation, Texas.'

'Nobody asked you here,' Kidder snarled. 'Git on back to Texas.'

'Maggie's tavern could use a real cook,' Sims said. 'Man there knows a dozen different ways to ruin a good steak.'

'Done enough cookin' for two lifetimes,' she said. 'Don't care if I never see another stove.'

The clamour and hustle of unloading went on around them as they considered her situation.

'Guess you wouldn't jump at takin' in other people's washin',' the pedlar said. She narrowed her eyes. 'Guessed right,' he said. 'Don't sell much soap here anyway.'

What happened next was over so fast that later there were a dozen different versions of it.

Two men, expensively dressed in broadcloth, one in a dark blue cutaway coat, the other in a pea-green suit, and both wearing

172

starched white shirts with black four-in-hand neckties, stepped up to the Texas woman. The blue cutaway said, pleasantly, as he took her arm, 'Time to return to the boat, my dear. Doctor's orders.'

'My sister needs rest,' the pea-green suit explained to Sims and Stackmesser and anyone listening. 'The poor creature is not herself.' He took her other arm.

As they helped her up from the barrel, she took her hands out of the pockets of her skirt. Her right fist, wrapped in a brass knuckle-duster, cracked against the blue cutaway's kneecap with a noise like a pencil snapping. He howled, and the leg folded under him. The other man grabbed her right arm and he never saw the derringer in her left hand. She shot him in the chest. By the time the bang had echoed, her hands were back in her pockets and he was knocked flat and staring at the sky. It was done, finished. Ryan Kidder had been watching two dogs fornicating and he missed it all. He looked around and saw one man sitting and cursing, another man lying and bleeding, the Texas woman watching expressionless, no gun in sight, and everyone else totally amazed.

'He ain't your brother,' Sims said to her.

'I'll explain it all to your sheriff,' she said, but Sims shook his head.

'Out of town,' Stackmesser said. 'Ain't got no deputy.'

'You want one? I'll do the job,' she said. 'I'll be your deputy sheriff, starting now. Do it free.'

'Jesus!' the pedlar exclaimed. 'Is everyone in Texas always in such a hurry?'

'Now just hold it right there,' the blue cutaway said. His voice had turned thin and husky. 'Happens that I'm Sheriff William Fletcher, from Pine Bluff, Arkansas, and this woman is a fugue ... fu ... fugitive from j ... justice.' Ryan Kidder helped him up, and he leaned one-legged on Kidder's shoulder. A crowd had gathered. 'She's wanted for grand fraud, an' larceny, an' ...' Now pain reduced him to a whisper. ' ... An' now for the shootin' of my deputy, Stanley Greenway.' He staggered. The crowd gasped.

The Texan woman laughed. The crowd disliked that. 'This man's the biggest liar between here and Mexico,' she said.

'Got proof?' Sims asked Fletcher.

Fletcher felt in a vest pocket, and showed a dull gold star, slightly bent and missing one point.

'Two bits at any store in St Louis,' she sneered. The crowd disliked that too: sneering at a wounded lawman.

'She's dangerous,' Fletcher said. 'You all saw. Lock her up.'

'Jail burned down,' Sims said.

That was when Doc Brightsides arrived. He glanced at Fletcher's blood-soaked pants, and at the body in the pea-green suit. 'What happened here?' he asked.

'My deputy's hurt bad,' Fletcher said. 'Can't you see?'

'I can see you are strangers to me,' Brightsides said, 'and therefore by the sacred code of my profession I require ten dollars now.'

Fletcher grumbled but gave him the ten.

Brightsides checked the pulse of the body in the pea-green suit, and gave Fletcher three dollars change. 'Burial's only seven,' he said.

'Make it murder,' Fletcher said. 'Hope you people can afford a rope.'

Nothing as dramatic as this had happened in Rock Springs since Main Street got burned. The corpse was put on a wagon and everyone set off to the blacksmith's shop, where Job Sims kept a stock of coffins.

'She ain't a bad shot,' the pedlar murmured as he walked alongside Sims. 'Says she can write good. We could have ourselves a free sheriff.'

'Might have to hang her first.'

'Seems a waste.'

'Well, that was a waste of a good deputy, back there.'

The pedlar sniffed. 'Poor sort of deputy, if he let a woman shoot him. Also, he got gold teeth. Anyone wears gold in his mouth, ought to get a better job than manhandlin' a big strong Texas woman. Heat of the day, too.'

'No reason to kill him.'

'Guess not.'

'Women start shootin' every dumb useless sonofabitch they see, ain't nobody safe. Especially you.'

The body was placed on the blacksmith's workbench. Dan Killick and Hoke Cleghorn came over from Maggie's tavern to join Sims and the pedlar and Stackmesser and Kidder. Fletcher and the Texas woman stood on opposite sides of the room. The crowd watched from the street. 'You got a judge?' Fletcher asked.

'Over at Downeysville,' Sims said. 'That's a day's ride.'

'He was here all last week,' the pedlar said. 'You should of got here sooner.'

'Don't need old man Potter,' Cleghorn growled.

'What I hear, the facts are simple,' Dan Killick said. 'A jury is all we need.'

'You fellows won't mind if I prepare the deceased for interment,' Brightsides said, rolling up his sleeves.

'He's dead,' Fletcher said. 'Just put him in his box.'

'No post mortem? Unthinkable. The bullet could have missed. Maybe the man had a heart attack.' Brightsides was undoing buttons. The deceased was about his height and build.

'Please,' Fletcher said. 'Have some respect for the dead.' Brightsides merely smiled.

'Don't need no judge,' Stackmesser said, 'so what's the point of a jury?'

'Ain't none,' Sims said. 'Rest of this town are too stupid to scratch their ass without someone draws a picture of it first. We know best what's needed. Let's get on and do it.'

'That woman is still armed,' Fletcher reminded them.

'Only a derringer,' Cleghorn scoffed. 'I can spit further'n it can shoot.'

Fletcher shook his head. 'This is some hell of a trial.'

'Jesus!' Cleghorn said. 'All you do is bitch. You want her disarmed, you do it. You're the sheriff.' Fletcher turned away and looked out at the bleached glare of the street.

'First witness,' Dan Killick said loudly. He was feeling left out.

'Don't need no witnesses,' Stackmesser told him. 'We saw her do it.' Killick glared. 'Anyone got a question?' Stackmesser asked.

'Yeah,' Kidder said. 'What did she do, that she's on the run from?'

'Uh ... Swindled the bank in Pine Bluff,' Fletcher said. They wanted more. Who gave a damn for the damn bank? 'Seduced the minister an' stole all the funds from the church orphanage,' he said. 'And that ain't all.' They looked at her with new respect. She looked back at them as if their noses needed wiping.

'What else you done?' Kidder asked her.

'Sometimes I cheat at checkers,' she said.

'Found anything yet, doc?' said Stackmesser.

'Death by gunshot.' Brightsides took a cigar from the dead man's vest pocket and tucked it behind his ear.

'Guilty!' Killick said. 'Someone get a rope.'

'Why shoot him, lady?' Sims asked.

'They wanted my poker winnings,' she said. That got a big laugh. She shrugged. 'They lost, and they didn't like it.' From the back of the crowd a rope was flung into the room. It had a noose tied in the end. The knot was clumsy and unprofessional. 'What you waitin' for?' a man called, and won a roar of support. The crowd had a carnival atmosphere. After the funeral, it was greedy for entertainment.

'Hey, hey,' Stackmesser said. He hadn't expected things to get so serious, so fast. All he wanted was to make it clear the town disapproved of casual shooting.

'This is Kentucky,' Sims said. 'We can't hang a woman.'

'Give her to us!' the man shouted. 'We'll do it, right smart!'

'I got an idea,' Kidder said. 'Let's give her to Sheriff Fletcher here, he can take her back to Pine Bluff, an' *they* can hang her.'

The crowd, still growing in numbers, howled its disapproval.

'Killin' a deputy,' Cleghorn said. He sucked his teeth. 'You got to set an example. When I was ridin' with Kit Carson we hanged a boy, couldn't have been more than – '

'What d'you want?' Sims asked Fletcher. 'She's your prisoner.'

'Well, I'll tell you,' Fletcher began, and never finished. Doc Brightsides had unbuttoned all the dead man's clothes and now he began to remove the boots so that he could ease the pants off. He tugged on the heel of the right boot and pushed the toes the opposite way, and a card flicked out of the man's right sleeve. 'Hullo!' Brightsides said. He picked it up: ace of spades.

'Watch,' he said, and tugged on the heel again. Out of the sleeve came the ace of clubs. Another tug, another ace: diamonds. Another tug: hearts. 'You are witnessing a haemorrhage of luck,' he said. He fanned out the four aces. The crowd was silenced.

'What in damnation's goin' on here?' Sims growled.

'Get down to his long johns,' the Texas woman said. 'Then you'll see.'

They pulled the dead man's clothes off. Strapped to his right foot and leg was a series of thin metal rods, hinged at the ankle and knee and hips. More rods went up his torso and down his right arm, where they led to a small flat box a few inches above the wrist. When the foot was arched, the movement went along the rods until it worked a spring in the box, and out shot a card.

176

'That's Culpepper's Patented Make Good,' she said. 'Takes all the risk out of poker. Fifty dollars by mail order from Philadelphia. Money back if not fully satisfied.'

'He ain't a deputy, then,' Stackmesser said.

'He ain't Stanley Greenway neither. He's Smokey Slade. That over there is Eugene Q. Logan, known as Lucky Logan. I've been playin' poker against them all the way from Vicksburg, and winnin', despite all that fancy ironmongery Smokey wore to improve his hand.'

'I got to get back to the boat,' Logan said, but the crowd refused to let him through. Sims grabbed the man's arms and examined his hands, rubbing a leathery thumb across the fingers.

'Soft as silk,' he said. The crowd gasped. 'First sheriff I met with hands like the Queen of England.'

'You never met the Queen of England,' the pedlar objected, but nobody cared what he said.

'Logan sandpapers his fingertips,' the Texas woman said. 'Helps him find the marked cards. He's a cheat.' She strolled over to the corpse and worked its foot a few times. 'They're both cheats.' The pedlar gathered up the cards that she had pumped out. 'King flush,' he announced.

'String the bastard up!' someone shouted. The crowd noisily agreed.

'Card sharpin' ain't a hangin' offence,' Sims ruled.

'Impersonatin' a lawman?' Kidder suggested.

Stackmesser was confused by the rapid change of events. 'Look: I got a store to run,' he said to the woman. 'What you reckon we ought to do?'

'Toss him in the river,' she said. 'What else?'

The crowd carried Lucky Logan down the street and tossed him in the river. Small boys threw rocks at him and prevented his coming ashore. He clung to a log and drifted five or six miles with the current, to Barber's Landing, where he claimed to have fallen overboard from the *Chauncey*. Eventually he joined a wagon train and got knifed in a fight over a whore in Abilene, Kansas. Logan was never, in fact, especially lucky. Nor was Abilene, come to that. Still, who said luck would be evenly spread?

Sims, Stackmesser and the rest were escorting the Texas woman to Maggie's tavern when Dan Killick stopped them. 'If you're the new deputy,' he said, 'Ma wants Hudd charged with murder.'

'That's the widow Killick,' Hoke Cleghorn explained. He pointed to a group of figures in the graveyard. 'Killicks an' Hudds aren't friendly.'

'Lead on,' she told Dan.

Ma Killick was at the graveside, planting sunflowers in the fresh earth. 'It was a horrible crime,' she said. 'Poor Devereux, he saw it all.' Dev was sitting on a nearby headstone, looking with reddened eyes over at where Ryan Kidder's daughter, Amie, was talking with friends. No more Amie for him. Tits like rosebuds. He might as well shoot himself. He groaned. 'Poor Dev,' his mother said. 'Saw his Pa slaughtered before his very eyes.' She turned away. She was beginning to get the hang of this widow thing.

'Slaughtered, huh?' the deputy said to Devereux.

'Them Hudds are murderin' sonsabitches. Ask anyone.'

'What happened? Exactly.'

'My eyes was all banged-up by that bastard Floyd Hudd. But I heard his pa shoutin' like a madman.' Dev felt that his evidence sounded thin. 'Hope he rots in hell,' he said. 'Sooner he gets sent there, the better.'

'Uh-huh,' she said. 'If it happens real soon, I'll know to come lookin' for you.' That made him forget about Amie Kidder's tits for a while.

Hoke Cleghorn had been watching and listening. Now he came forward. He had dressed up for the funeral: captain's coat, alligator-skin boots, four-in-hand red silk necktie whose ends blew in the breeze, walking cane. He was not at ease with a female deputy, but in this rig he felt confident enough to establish himself as an authority. 'Hudd killed old Joe, that's for sure,' he said.

'You saw it?'

Cleghorn laughed. 'Live here long as I have, you can feel these things in your water.'

'Guess he had a reason. You feel that too?'

'Take your pick. See Stanton Killick over there? Hudd bush-whacked him not a mile from here an' shot his arm clean off at the shoulder. Miracle the boy didn't die.'

'Guess there was a reason behind that, too.'

'Certainly was. Hudd promised to marry JoBeth Killick. Prettiest thing in the county. Had his evil way with her an' then threw her out!'

'She still around?'

'Went south. Couldn't tolerate the dishonour to the family.'

'That matters to the Killicks, does it? Honour?'

'Whole entire family volunteered to fight for the South. Hudd's a damn Yankee. Lower than spit.'

'Seems a good reason for him not to go visitin'.'

'War ain't ended for Hudd. He can't stop killin' Rebs.'

She saw people shaking hands goodbye with the preacher, and went over and introduced herself. 'Were you here when Stanton Killick lost his arm?'

'A scandalous affair,' Hunkin said. 'And a scathing indictment of the sin of fornication.'

Elias Dunbar was listening. 'Damn right!' he said.

'Seventy-three separate acts of fornication!' Hunkin declared. 'Some folk think they can do it once or twice and stop, but I tell you the monster of lust never lets go once it has sunk its claws in your flesh! George Killick was overseer at Mr Charles Hudd's farm. He betrayed that position of trust by indulging in seventy-three acts of fornication with female slaves when they should have been toiling in the fields.'

'Who counted?' she asked, but Hunkin was in full flow

'And what's more, his brother Stanton fornicated alongside him sixty-eight times, making a total of one hundred and forty-one acts of fornication!'

'Did it in the hay barn,' Dunbar said. 'Ruined the goddamn hay.'

'Hudd hounded them like the wrath of God,' Hunkin said. 'Shots were fired. Stanton paid for all their orgies with his left arm.'

'George survived?'

'Killed at Vicksburg.'

'Powerful fornicators, both men,' Dunbar said 'Must have been a real sturdy barn.' The minister gave him a cold stare. 'Just a little joke,' Dunbar said. 'Fornication is not a laughing matter unto the Lord,' Hunkin told him. He breathed so deeply that his nostrils flared. He touched his hat, and left.

'He forgot the best bit,' Dunbar said. ''Tweren't Hudd shot Stanton's arm off. 'Twas George. Them Killicks never could shoot worth a damn.'

'Is that why the South lost?' she asked.

'You might say.'

'I need a beer,' she said. He escorted her to Maggie's tavern. 'This here is our new deputy sheriff,' he told Maggie. 'Says she'll do it for nothin'.'

'I got a room you can have,' Maggie said. She drew a beer, blew a dead wasp off the suds, and slid the mug down the bar to a drunk who was trying to pick a fight with his reflection in the mirror. 'Drink that and shut up!' she bawled. 'What's your name, honey?' she asked.

'Frances Fluck,' the Texas woman announced. There was a silence like a balloon waiting for the pin. 'First man who laughs, I'll break his jaw,' she said mildly.

'Deputy Fluck,' Cleghorn said, trying the name on for size.

'I like it,' Ryan Kidder said. Nobody cared. 'Gimme a beer,' he demanded. Maggie ignored him.

'Born Francesca Moloney, if that's any help,' the Texas woman said.

'Hell, no,' Stackmesser said. 'Sounds like macaroni. We don't need no wops here.'

'It's Irish, for the love of God.'

Sims shook his head. 'Even worse. Nobody wants the Micks, either. Change your name. Call yourself ...' But he couldn't think what.

'In Illinois, we had a sheriff called Prendergast,' Stackmesser said. Nobody liked that. 'Lousy sheriff, anyway,' he muttered.

Doc Brightsides breezed in, very dapper in a pea-green suit, slightly muddy. 'Turns out his real name wasn't Slade, or Greenway,' he told them. 'It was Nickel. Hubert D. Nickel.' He took a card from a pocket.

'Well, he don't need it now,' Mrs Fluck said. 'I'll take it. Frances Nickel. Suit everyone?'

'Frank Nickel sounds better,' Cleghorn said.

'Deputy sheriff Frankie Nickel,' Sims said. Nobody objected.

'Since that's official,' Doc Brightsides said, 'I can tell you what killed Joe Killick. Sour pickles and bad booze. Fought a duel to the death in his stomach.'

'Not murder, then,' Frankie said.

'When I laid him out I put a light to his mouth and another to his asshole and the gas burned for an hour and ten minutes at each end with a clean blue flame and not so much as a flicker.'

'Goddamn world's fallin' apart,' Dan Killick said in disgust. 'First they steal our niggers, an' now we got a sheriff in skirts.' He kicked the bar.

'Deputy,' she corrected. 'And I intend to wear pants, if nobody objects.'

Nobody did. 'Give you a special price on Levi's,' Stackmesser offered. 'Fit like a glove.'

'Got any that fit like pants?' she asked.

'You'll never last,' Killick scoffed. 'You ain't even got a revolver.'

'You ain't even got a brain,' she said, 'and look at you, lived to be over ninety.' The pedlar thought that was so funny, he slipped off his bar stool. Killick turned away. 'What you starin' at?' he barked at the drunk.

'Leave him be,' Sims said, but the drunk swayed towards them, pointing at Killick. 'Hey, I know you,' he said. Maggie's whisky was running out of his eyes and his breath stank like poisoned bait. 'You were with goddamn Sherman at Gettysburg, you Yankee bastard.' His fists came up, wavering like spring blossom in a soft breeze.

'You're in business, honey,' said Maggie.

Mrs Frances Fluck, now Deputy Frankie Nickel, took Hoke Cleghorn's cane from his surprised hands, stepped behind the drunk and whopped him hard, one-two, on the hamstrings. He fell to his knees so hard that the crash frightened the sawdust. She put a boot between his shoulder blades, and the floorboards came up and stunned his face. 'Take a foot,' she told Sims. Together they towed him to the door and rolled him into the street.

'You learn to do that in Desolation, Texas?' Sims asked. She nodded. 'You probably guessed,' he said. 'We ain't got no sheriff.'

'Does this town have a hot bath?'

'Yeah. Ask Maggie.'

'Well, that's one up on Desolation.' The drunk sat up and groaned. 'War's finished,' she told him. 'They made peace. It's all over, son.'

Sims scratched his beard. 'That just might be your first mistake, Frankie,' he said. 'Just might.'

BEAR WALLOW

No matter how much he cheated on the figures, Stackmesser still couldn't get his damn accounts to show the damn store making a damn profit.

Even without cheating, he was never strong at adding up and taking away. The columns of figures irritated him, then angered, and finally infuriated. Someone must be swindling him. It had to be the niggers. The niggers were to blame.

Well then, godammit, he'd make the niggers pay.

He saddled up and left Rock Springs, scowling hard, but during the long, bad ride up to the Ridge (he had to walk his horse most of the time) he began thinking about what he was doing, which made him nervous, and when he finally came out of the trees and saw the cabins, he knew this trip was a big mistake. He blamed the niggers for that, got angry all over again, and became loud and truculent. 'Where's that sonofabitch Lonzo?' he demanded. He rode so hard at the nearest group that he scattered them. 'Fetch the black bastard out so I can rip his ears off.'

'Ain't here, boss,' Luke Corrigan said.

'*What*?' Stackmesser made the horse turn in a tight circle, and people dodged its stamping feet. 'You lie to me, boy, I'll cut your evil heart out.'

'It's the truth,' Moses said. 'I swear.'

'So get him!' Stackmesser roared. He was carrying a pair of pistols and there was a rifle in the saddle scabbard, but what if they rushed him and knocked him off his horse? Fear drove him to action, and he rode wildly up and down the camp, cursing and slashing with his reins at anyone who was slow to move. He got the same frightened answer everywhere: Lonzo wasn't there. 'Fetch him!' he ordered. 'Fetch the bastard!' Women and small children hid. Once, twice, he

182

thought he saw Lonzo and galloped in pursuit, only to discover he was wrong, and he whirled about, suspecting that they were making a fool of him. It was hot; his throat was raw from shouting. The clearing was small. The only place left to look was inside the cabins. He was afraid to do that. He saw food cooking on a fire and charged his horse through it, scattering pots and skillets.

What now?

The horse stood, lathered, fighting against the bit, harassed by flies. Stackmesser's cracked voice chanted the same old curse-words but they were empty from overuse. He cocked a pistol and fired a shot at the sky. Its echoes faded. The sky did not fall.

After a while, old Jake limped up to him. 'Lonzo's huntin' with Aaron, Mr Stackmesser,' he said. 'Back in a while, maybe.' No reply. 'This about that old Indum silver mine?' Jake asked. Stackmesser nodded. 'Get you some coffee, if you like,' Jake said. 'Could've had fresh cornbread too, only ...' He gestured at the destroyed cooking fire.

A boy went and found Lonzo and Aaron.

'Assay must've come in,' Aaron said. 'Man wants his grubstake money back.'

'Damned if I'll pay.'

'Maybe damned if you don't.'

Stackmesser sat in the shade, watching the camp go about its business. It was a long wait before Lonzo appeared, Aaron on his shoulders and a wild turkey hung from his waist.

'That silver mine of yours is one hundred per cent muleshit,' Stackmesser said. 'You knew so all along, you sonofabitch. Now you gonna buy back my share and have the whole heap of nothin' for yourself, which is what a cheatin' nigger deserves, seein' as the North says I can't whup you, and that's the stupidest thing, even stupider than *you*, if you ever thought I was good for a free handout.' He ran out of breath.

'Uh-huh,' Lonzo said. From a distance, the whole camp was watching.

'Thirty dollars, I want.' That was double what Lonzo owed but Stackmesser knew niggers couldn't count. 'Thirty.'

'Ain't payin'. Mine ain't worth thirty cents. Roof done fall in.'

'Oh, you're payin', boy.' Stackmesser was breathing too fast for a man doing nothing. 'You ain't payin' money? Fine an' dandy. You're payin' blood.'

Lonzo had both hands on the barrel of the rifle. Its butt rested on the ground. Stackmesser's right hand was touching a pistol. The same question was in both their minds: could Lonzo swing the rifle before Stackmesser fired the pistol? 'Which silver mine you talkin' about?' Aaron asked.

Stackmesser blinked. He had thought Lonzo was carrying an unusually ugly child. 'How many you got?' he said.

'Black Stump mine, Twisty Creek mine, or Bear Wallow mine?' Aaron said. 'Which?'

'What's the difference?'

'Bear Wallow got big Indum ghosts guardin' it. Got old wood boxes inside it. Got big locks on 'em.'

'You seen these boxes?'

'Heard tell.'

'Who told?'

'Coupla Shawnee. Said Indum ghosts – '

'Yeah, yeah.' Stackmesser thought about it. Everyone said Indian silver had been found near Rock Springs. Not much, but maybe that meant a whole lot more was just lying somewhere, waiting. 'How far?'

'Far 'nuff. Good walk.'

'You walk. I'll ride.'

'Horse no damn good,' Aaron said.

Stackmesser didn't believe him. After ten minutes the trail went through a crack between two towering boulders, a crack so narrow he had to dismount and suck in his gut and wriggle sideways. After that the going got worse. Huge fallen trees. Washouts that left scarcely a foothold. Streambeds, steep and rocky. Wild vines and brambles. Boulders as big as houses. More fallen trees. When they got to Bear Wallow, Stackmesser's shirt was black with sweat, his face coloured patchy, dried spit outlining his mouth, his feet swollen and sore in the wrong boots.

Lonzo was waiting, sweating a little. He swung Aaron down from his shoulders.

'This it,' Aaron said.

The mine was a dark split in the hillside, so low it could be entered only on the hands and knees.

Stackmesser squatted and he got his breath back.

There was nothing to say. He couldn't trust Lonzo to go in there and fetch the stuff; the nigger would lie. He had to go in himself. He never wondered why Aaron had told him about this hoard of Indian silver – niggers were stupid, they did what the white man boss wanted, always had, always would. Stackmesser saw no contradiction in those views.

What he did see was the need for light inside the mine. He had no lantern. 'Hey,' he said, and stopped because Aaron was offering him a couple of stubs of candle. 'Huh,' he said.

About twenty feet into the cave he found bones. By then the space was bigger: he could almost stand. He saw half a skull and picked it up and it crumbled in his hand. Dust rose and he sneezed and almost blew the candle out. Brief panic.

He shuffled forward, breathing through his mouth. The cave made a slow bend. Still no wooden boxes. The candle guttered, spilling hot wax down his thumb. He could see something lying ahead. He was startled to find a leafy bit of branch, clustered with red berries. 'Some bastard brought this here,' he said aloud, and as if in answer there came a tired groan. He gasped, and noticed the smell: an acid stink that seemed to strengthen as he breathed it. Then the groan was a growl and Stackmesser was running.

Lonzo and Aaron were eating nuts when he squirmed out of the cave. 'There's a fucking bear in there!' he cried. Lonzo grabbed Aaron and they fled. A bear could rush like thunder and open a man with one slash.

Stackmesser ran until his chest felt like it had red-hot barrel hoops binding it, and he tottered to a halt. The others went back and waited for him.

'Bear fuckin' Wallow, huh?' he said, weakly. 'You shitty black assholes. That the best you can do?'

'That was *nearest*, boss.' Aaron scratched the white fuzz on his scalp. 'You want the *best* ... Well, best is Fast Rattlesnake mine.' He looked at the sun. 'We got time.'

'Fast Rattlesnake.' Stackmesser sucked in a deep breath and held it until he could hear the blood squealing in his ears: then he let it out in a rush. 'Home,' he said.

His whole body was weary. About a mile from the camp he tried to cross a creek on a fallen tree. The bark was loose. His boot skidded. He fell. The creek was almost dry. Lonzo was thirty yards away and he heard the crack of the leg bone.

There was never any question of carrying him down the Ridge. He would have to stay in the camp until he was fit to be moved. A month at least. Maybe two. Jake sent a child to Rock Springs to tell Mrs Stackmesser. The child came back and said Mrs Stackmesser hadn't seemed upset; not upset at all.

~

Martha had mended broken legs on dogs, cows, even horses. She knew what to do with Stackmesser.

He howled a lot when she straightened the bone. Lonzo found a flask of whiskey in the saddlebags. He poured a couple of fat slugs into a cup of Aaron's willowbark tea. Stackmesser drank it down and quietened. Martha tied splints from ankle to knee and encased the leg in yellow clay that dried as hard as plaster. She slapped on more clay until Stackmesser felt like his leg was stuck in a cannon. 'You get my wagon up here pronto,' he demanded. Lonzo gave him another slug of whiskey. 'Ain't boss here,' he said.

'Who is?'

'Nobody. Everybody.'

Stackmesser couldn't get his mind around that. 'I'll pay,' he said. The words tasted sour. A month ago he might have bought Lonzo for a thousand dollars. Now the world was turned upside down. 'You owe me,' he said. Why was he apologizing to a damned field hand? He flinched as Lonzo reached out, but all he did was touch the bulge of Stackmesser's paunch.

'Never see a fat nigger,' Lonzo said.

Stackmesser had to spend five weeks on the Ridge before Doc Brightsides visited and said the leg was strong enough for the ride to Rock Springs. Stackmesser went down by a longer, easier trail that only Aaron knew of. Jake was sorry to see him go. A large, slow-moving white man about the place was the best guarantee against having bullets fired at you. Worth the grub.

First thing Stackmesser did was hobble into Maggie's for a beer. 'Look at you,' the pedlar said, 'I got some purple Indian snake oil would cure that rheumatism in a day.'

'Bust my leg fightin' a mountain bear,' Stackmesser said gruffly. 'Anythin' happen while I was gone?'

'Flub Phillips's chapel fell down again,' Maggie said. 'That man can't build worth a damn. Your store's been busy. Everythin' two for the price of one. Tornado hit up Louisville way. That's about all.' He had swallowed his drink and was hurrying out. 'Off to do some bear-wrestlin', I expect,' the pedlar said.

Stackmesser saw signs on his store that said *everthin ¹/₂ prise* and went in and sacked his assistant. 'People kept comin' here with bills for stuff you bought,' the man said. 'I had to raise the money somehow.' Stackmesser told him he was a fool. He stumped about the store, ripping down the signs. The man took what he was owed from the cash box, and got his hat and coat. 'You must've liked livin' up there with them Hudd niggers,' he said. 'You startin' to look like them, you know that?'

He went. Stackmesser locked the doors and found a mirror. Six weeks on the Ridge had burned his face a dull chestnut colour. He scrubbed it with soap and water. Now he looked a shiny chestnut colour. Somewhat like Lonzo.

For the rest of the day he checked the stock, the sales record, the cash. Disaster. He couldn't even blame his assistant for everything. Bills had to be paid, or suppliers stopped supplying.

He saw Cleghorn talking to Sims and went across the street to them. 'The war was bad,' he said, 'but this goddamn peace is killing me.'

'You got it easy,' Hoke Cleghorn said. 'Since their damned Emancipation I can't even work my land.' He spat tobacco juice.

'What's happenin' up there?' Sims asked Stackmesser. 'What they doin'? Waitin' for us to go broke, so they can come down here an' grab everythin'?'

They turned and looked at the Ridge. It was a smoky blue in the late afternoon sunlight.

'Fuckin' niggers,' Stackmesser said. 'Them and their fuckin' freedom. They're to blame for everythin'.'

'What are we doing'? We're standin' around here like tomb-stones,' Sims said. 'You plan on wakin' up every day the rest of your life starin' at a bunch of uppity niggers all lookin' down, watchin' you sweat? I don't.'

'Got an answer?' Stackmesser demanded.

'I got a keg of blasting powder. That loud enough for you?'

~

Everyone soon knew that the Hudd Colony was to be blasted off the Ridge. A town that small couldn't keep a secret that big, especially when Job Sims discovered he only had half a barrel of gunpowder and it was too damp to light, so he had to send to Bowling Green for more.

Deputy Frankie Nickel went to see Sims. 'This picnic you-all are plannin', up there on the Ridge,' she said. 'I want your word nobody's gonna get hurt.'

Sims went on with shoeing a horse. He had too many nails gripped between his teeth for him to speak. The air stank with burned hoof and singed hair.

'Way I see it,' said the horse's owner, a sharecropper called Hutton, 'you can't damage a darky, on account of darkies ain't worth nothin' no more, ain't that right, Job?'

'Besides, what you exercisin' yourself about?' asked Morgan Watson, who had come in to get warm: there was a wet wind howling down the street. 'The Ridge ain't any part of your job.'

'I'll remember that,' she said, 'next time you're out huntin' an' some desperado whops you a good un'.'

'All we're doin' is holdin' a meetin' of the Scallywag Party,' Sims told her. 'Picnic, like you said. Might let off a few firecrackers.'

'I still want your word.'

'Hey, us Scallywags are decent Christian folk!' Hutton said. 'We're only goin' up the Ridge to pray that every last one of them poor niggers goes to Kingdom Come … Say what, Job: just look at her other feet too. Might need a nail.'

'They all get to Kingdom Come,' Watson said, 'they can tell God how he got the Bible wrong. Tell him personal.'

'Hey there, God!' Hutton said in a squeaky nigger-type voice. 'We been wastin' our time down there! Ain't no slaves in America! You done sold us the wrong ticket!' They both began to chuckle.

'That nice Mr Job Sims showed us the way to go home!' Watson said. 'He's a true Christian gentleman. A-men!' Now they were cackling with mirth. Even Sims nearly smiled.

Frankie let them laugh themselves out.

'Look,' she said. 'You go up there an' kill a nigger, next day the U.S. Army will send ten regiments into Dundee County, declare martial law, I'll be out of a job an' you'll be hangin' from that oak tree yonder.'

Sims took a rasp and rounded off a ragged hoof.

'Well,' Hutton said, 'they're just campin' anyway. Bears an' bobcats, that's all the Ridge is fit for.'

Sims dropped the horse's leg. 'Dollar fifty,' he said.

'Hell, Job,' Hutton said. 'You know I'm good for it.'

Sims flung the rasp at his anvil. It bounced high, ringing like a bell. 'Jesus Christ!' he roared.

MIGHTY FINE BANG

Two years on the run had taught Aaron something the others never had a chance to learn. It had taught him to look ahead and plan his life.

It was hard. He was a slave, and a slave never planned his future any more than a mule did, or a plough. Sure, a slave might dream. Did no harm to dream about, say, heaven. Lord God ran heaven. Down here, the Master was boss.

Then Aaron had run off and found himself alone and having to think ahead. In those two runaway years he learned to see trouble coming and to survive it.

This was a skill that none of the others on the Ridge possessed. After a while, when all the cabins were built and there was a good month's food in store, they began to take it easy. Slept late, sat in the sun, talked a lot. Did some work if they felt like it. Didn't if they didn't. Freedom took getting used to, but Jesus, it was *good*.

Especially now Lonzo had quit his shouting and cursing. Anything needed decided, Lonzo said go ask old Jake. Then Jake said, ask Aaron.

Aaron never stopped work. He couldn't do a damn thing unless someone carried him. Sometimes he got two, even three people to go with him and collect meat or nuts or fruit or some kind of eatable plants.

Then one day nobody wanted to go. Too damn hot. No breeze, air full of bugs, sky full of thunder. Not so long ago on a day like this they would have been watering the white man's fields with their sweat. Now they sprawled in the shade and were glad. Aaron nagged, joked, flattered. Nobody moved. Not even Lonzo. 'They ain't gonna work, I ain't gonna do it for 'em,' Lonzo said. 'Get no thanks, get no pay. No sir.'

'Then take me over to Jake. As a favour.'

Jake was drowsing. 'Hot, huh?' he said, and yawned. 'Where them little 'uns get the energy to run?'

'Want to know where they're runnin'?' Aaron asked. Lonzo put him down in the angle made by two big tree-roots. 'Runnin' to the grave, is where.'

'Ain't nothin' new. You an' me doin' the same.'

'Difference is,' Aaron said, 'they gonna be dead an' buried, this time next year. No, that's a lie. Takes strength to dig a grave. Ain't got that strength if you're starvin'. I reckon vermin gonna get the little 'uns. Yeah. Red fox, bobcat, skunk, coon, eagle, even a goddamn whitefoot *mouse*. I seen 'em strip a carcass to the bone in a day. Every time somethin' dies, somethin' else licks its chops. Looks like good chop-lickin' times ahead.'

'We got grub,' Jake said. 'Ain't nobody here gonna starve.'

'See these happy niggers?' Aaron said to Lonzo. 'All takin' their rest. All laid out ready for the grave.'

'They *earned* that rest,' Jake said. 'They worked – '

'I worked five times harder an' I near to died, my first winter on this Ridge! Near to starved. Grub we got now might last to Thanksgivin'. That means dead by Christmas. So you got to work *now*, sunup to sundown, every day. You ain't sleepin', you better be workin'. Work now or die soon.'

'They ain't gonna listen to me tellin' 'em that,' Jake said wearily.

'Nor me,' Aaron said. 'Hell, they can't hardly *see* me unless I wave a flag.'

'I ain't tellin' these people nothin',' Lonzo said sourly. 'Last time I went an' busted the wrong fella's jaw.'

'You slowed down his eatin',' Jake said. 'That's somethin'.'

'Didn't get no thanks.'

'You want to be liked?' Aaron asked. 'Make 'em hate you. They'll love you for it next year. Damn, they'll make you King of the Ridge.'

Lonzo picked his teeth with a grass stem. But he did nothing.

~

Curtis Hudd was out looking for a strayed calf when he saw Lucy on the hillside picking berries. At once he ran to the house and got his dollar savings. He also took a ham from the smoke-house, and forced his legs to hurry back to the edge of the Ridge, desperate for fear she had gone. But she was still there, and his gasping, stumbling eagerness amused her. 'Never seen such a sweat on a white boy,' she said.

She took him to a trickle of a stream and washed him. When she was done she took his clothes off. It seemed the right time to give her the dollar. And the ham. All she was wearing was a ragged no-sleeve shift; it fell off when she shrugged her shoulders. Apart from breasts and hips she was as lithe as a boy. 'That ain't much,' she said. 'Ain't hardly enough.'

'It's all I got.' Panic fluttered.

'Yeah, I can see it is.' She wasn't talking about the money. Panic turned to shame. Curtis could feel his face going a hot red. Lucy laughed at that. 'Poor white folks ain't got enough to stir their tea with,' she said.

'Ain't here to take tea.' Empty words, but he had to say something. He couldn't breathe deeply. His left eye kept blinking. His whole entire body was betraying him.

She found a grassy patch and they got down to business, or he tried. He was much taller than Lucy, so nothing matched, nothing fitted, nothing worked. He despaired. 'You couldn't piss into a ten-gallon hat,' she said. She gripped him with her legs and arms, and expertly rolled them both over. 'Now don't fuss,' she said, and took charge. Curtis shut his eyes against the dazzle. Red and yellow and green fireworks splashed and shimmered and spun.

'You wash your own self this time,' Lucy said.

They walked back to the stream. 'I ain't so small,' he said. Now it was over, he felt great self-confidence. 'Floyd ain't near half as big as me.' That sounded disloyal. 'He ain't small neither,' he added.

Lucy wasn't interested. 'You steal this ham?' she asked.

'I worked for it. Hudd, he don't scarcely pay no wages at all.'

'That's *bad*.' She clicked her tongue. 'You get yourself emancipated, boy.'

Curtis watched her put on her shift. As her arms rose, so did her breasts. 'Hey,' he said. 'Let's do it again.'

'Got another dollar?'

'Tell you somethin' worth more'n a dollar. Supposed to be secret. Them Scallywags in Rock Springs are plannin' on takin' gunpowder an' blowin' you niggers off the Ridge.'

'Sure,' she said. 'Everyone knows *that*.' She took her ham and her berries and climbed the hill.

She had lied; but when she told Lonzo he just nodded. 'You knew already,' she said.

'I got a friend in town.' He went on whittling.

'We gone get blowed up?'

'Probly.' He waited for her to turn sad and weepy, but she took the knife from his hand, cut two slices of ham and gave him one. 'Might's well enjoy while us can,' she said. Lonzo ate, and grunted. 'Stop right there,' she said. 'That's as much fun as a gal can take from you at one time.' She walked away and left him wondering.

～

The first explosion was pretty good.

All four walls of the cabin were flung outwards. The logs separated and spun and tumbled. The roof went up like a hat tossed in the air but as it twisted it fell to pieces. The bang was a mighty fine bang, too. Must have been heard in Barber's Landing. Maybe even Slade's Crossing.

'Not enough powder,' Hoke Cleghorn said.

He and Sims had picked five men from the dozen or so volunteers. All were armed. Stackmesser had decided not to come. Leg still hurt, he said.

The colony was deserted when they rode in, which was no surprise. Cleghorn said that the blacks would've had young 'uns in the trees all down the mountainside, watching out; and besides, the damn hounds made enough noise for a deaf man. They were the Killicks' hounds. Dan hadn't fed them for a couple of days and now they were baying and lunging, ready to kill for food. The bang silenced them, but only briefly.

'Start lookin',' Cleghorn told him, 'before they pull your arms off.'

Dan set off at a slow run across the clearing.

A mile or more away, the Hudd colony sat under a giant beech and waited. The dogs' excitement reached them as a string of high-pitched yaps. 'Never thought I'd hear *that* again,' Aaron said.

'Lord save us.' Josh got down on his knees.

'Last time I heard that, I was in a swamp with my head under water.'

'Those hounds catch us,' Sarah said, 'I ain't runnin', no sir, I'm goin' with the white man, the patroller, I'm goin' back.'

Lonzo looked at her, and saw she was still a slave. 'Goin' back *where*?' he asked. She shook her head.

'Maybe they're coon-huntin',' Lucy said.

'Hunt coons at *night*,' Gabe Killick said. 'Anyway, I know them hounds.' Another explosion boomed. 'That don't sound like coon-huntin', neither.'

'Lord, forgive us miserable sinners!' Josh appealed.

'What we done wrong?' Sarah said. 'Ain't done nothin' wrong. Why they persecutin' us?'

'Hey,' Gabe said to Aaron, 'you couldn't hear no hounds with your head under no swamp water.' He was indignant. 'You *lied*.'

'You ain't tried it,' Aaron argued.

'Ain't tried milkin' a bull neither.'

Another distant *crack-boom* shook Martha out of her silent despair. 'You said this was gonna be like the Promised Land,' she accused Lonzo. 'Listen! We're bein' hunted worse'n the Israelites!'

'Have trust in the Lord,' Josh urged.

The noise of the hounds was louder now.

'Ain't comin' for us,' Lonzo said. 'That'd be crazy. They got no place to take us to.'

'Sold south,' somebody muttered. The threat still made many of them shudder. Bad slaves got sold south.

'Must be a reason,' Moses said. 'Hounds ain't here for no reason.'

Lonzo was pretty sure of the reason, but he kept silent. Maybe he was wrong.

The hounds found a cabin full of food tucked away in the woods and went frantic. Dan had to use all his strength to drag them away from the smells. He tied them to a tree, and went back and removed the logs that blocked the doorway. The cabin was stacked with smoked meat and dried fruits. He took a piece of venison and threw it to the hounds; it was gone in seconds. He fired a single shot in the air and sat down to wait for Cleghorn or Sims or someone to arrive with the powder.

It took most of the rest of the day, but they blew five food stores and eleven cabins and half a chapel that Josh had started building. Some cabins were so sturdy they had to be blown twice. 'Comanche camps was easier,' Cleghorn said. 'We could flatten a Comanche camp before breakfast so's you wouldn't know it ever been there. These damn logs ...'

Some of the party grumbled because they had no chance to drive the niggers away, firing crackling volleys above their panicking heads. 'Where in hell are they?' one man asked.

'Walkin' to Chicago,' Sims said.

They blew up a stone oven with the last handful of powder. They rewarded themselves with a jug of whiskey and set off for town.

'Now they really got their goddamn freedom,' Dan Killick said. 'Free to go to hell, with my compliments.'

~

After an hour of silence, Lonzo scouted the site and went back and fetched the others.

The harsh smell of gunpowder was everywhere, like a stain in the air. Fragments of food were dotted on the ground or hanging in branches. Birds and squirrels and chipmunks and shrews were gorging themselves, unable to believe their luck.

A tall rock stood in the middle of the place. People called it The Altar. Lonzo climbed on it and waited. Eventually everyone wandered over. Nobody spoke. Some wept a little, but nobody spoke. He looked up and saw that it was early fall: the first reds and golds had tinged the more exposed trees. The setting sun made the colours burn. For the first time in his short life he saw how beautiful Kentucky could be, doubly beautiful when he knew that this stretch was home, because they owned it. The sky was a well-scrubbed blue. It would soon be night, and a cold one. They could not warm themselves at the moon. Empty bellies would hurt no less in the glory of a sunrise. Everyone was looking at him: he had to say something. Words would be feeble against the message of explosives, but words were all he had. 'They want us to go,' he said. 'Ain't goin'. Stayin'.' He spoke softly, so softly that those on the outside of the group edged forward.

'That all?' Sarah said. Her voice was sullen.

'Enough.'

'Ain't enough. We *needed* that grub, all that grub. You-all stayin'? Stay, then. Comes winter, ain't nobody leavin' this Ridge cus ain't nobody got the strength to crawl out of here.'

'Ain't goin', Sarah.'

'Look around. They had a battle an' we lost.'

'Ain't goin'.'

'Crazy fools.' Sarah grabbed her husband's arm and shouted at her children. People made room for them to pass.

'Who else wants to go?' Lonzo said. Bad move. He scared himself: he could end up alone on the Altar. 'You got nothin' to say?' he asked Jake. Now Sarah was leading her family away.

'Oh … I don't know any more.' The old man tried to spit and had to wipe the dribble from his chin. 'This is livin', I'm about ready to die.'

'So die in your own home.' Still Lonzo had not raised his voice. 'Them white crackers with the gunpowder … they don't give a damn about Hudd Ridge. They had their sport, now they gone back home. But we got no place else to go. Nobody wants us down there, nobody wants us no place else. But *here*, we got a right to be *here*. They wants us off Hudd Ridge, they got to kill us first.' He saw Moses and Buck and Luke Corrigan walk away and his voice failed. Lose the three strongest buck niggers and the rest would surely give up.

The three men started picking up scattered logs, starting stacking them.

'Move your black ass,' Aaron told him. 'You ain't told us nothin' we didn't already know.'

The children took baskets and collected fragments of food. Aaron built a fire. They ate. Tasted sort of salty in parts but it was better than hungry.

'Tomorrow …' Lonzo began; and then knew it was a waste of breath.

One day at a time.

NOTHIN' AIN'T NATURAL

Sarah led her family down the mountain, back to the Hudd farm. There was just enough light left in the day to show her Charles Hudd digging potatoes. His fork broke the soil, his fingers sifted and searched, found the crop and tossed it into a basket. When he caught a glimpse of the arrivals he didn't straighten up. That would hurt too much. He gave a grunt that was half a groan. 'Back again,' he muttered.

'Master Charles,' she said. They were amazed to see him so stained by toil, dirt to the elbows, shirt torn, hair a mess. 'Hopin' maybe give us some work.'

'Work.' He forked up another plant and added the potatoes to his basket. 'Work. Got more damn work than I can count. Got no money, though.' Now he straightened up, grimacing in anticipation of the pain. He kicked the fork, knocking clods of dirt off his boots. Riding boots, Sarah saw. 'Goddamn war took all my money,' he said. 'Prices went sky-high an' crops went to hell. Only good thing is I don't have any Confederate money either, cus it ain't worth blowin' your nose on.'

She had no reply. He sounded too weary to be bitter: he was simply telling her how it was, as if they were equals. When she was a house-slave she'd felt free to speak her mind. (Up to a point.) But not as an equal.

Charles emptied the basket into a sack, and heaved the sack onto his shoulder. They set off in the gloom. Charles carrying the load and the fork while she and her husband took nothing made her uncomfortable. It was almost sinful. Trouble was, her husband couldn't have carried the taters even if Charles told him to. William was twice her age, small and thin and creaky with rheumatism, good for nothing but bird-scaring and not too good at that. She hadn't wanted to marry him. Henry Hudd had made her. William was such a runt that he'd never be a field hand. For the same reason Henry couldn't sell him; couldn't give him away. Henry made them jump over the broomstick; now they were married. 'Go forth and multiply,' Henry said, 'or the Lord will be exceeding wrath.' In four years she bore three healthy boys. Henry smiled: three thousand dollars, as good as in the bank; except of course he died before his property grew big enough to sell.

'We got food you can have,' Charles said. He dumped the sack at the kitchen door. 'Sleep in the hay barn tonight.'

Floyd and Curtis came to see who he was talking to.

'We heard boomin',' Floyd said. 'You niggers had a private war up there?'

'They came an' blew up our cabins,' William said. 'Mr Dan Killick, Mr Sims, Mr Cleghorn, few others.'

'Got nowhere to live,' Sarah said.

'Can't live here,' Charles said bleakly. He dragged off his boots and padded into the house.

'Anyone hurt?' Curtis asked.

'Not as I saw,' Sarah said. She could smell food cooking. The boys kept edging forward. She shoved them back. 'We all hid, see. Jake, Buck, Martha, her little 'uns. Lonzo. Them Killick niggers, an' the Corrigans.'

'Anyone else up there?' Curtis asked.

'Aaron,' William said.

Curtis didn't care about Aaron. 'No more womenfolk?'

Sarah shrugged. Curtis's stare would not release her. 'Wasn't countin' heads,' she said.

'Lucy?'

'Yeah. Forgot Lucy.'

'She ain't hurt?'

Sarah shook her head. The cooking smell was all that mattered.

Later, after Sarah and her family had eaten and gone to the barn, the Hudds sat down to supper. Floyd had his question ready. Charles said grace, and then Floyd looked at his brother and said, 'Some reason you're concerned about one particular little nigger-girl?'

Curtis had his mouth full of bread, which gave him time to think. He shrugged.

'Who's that?' his mother asked.

'Lucy,' Floyd said. 'All that bangin', that was the Killicks blowin' up their cabins.'

'Killicks are thieving scoundrels,' Charles said. His wife looked at his hands and arms. His fists were clenched. She reached out and uncoiled the fingers of one hand. 'Stop working,' she said. 'The day's over, dear.' The tension shifted from his hands to his face. 'The days are over too soon,' he said. 'And never enough done.'

'Guess we're all pleased Lucy ain't hurt,' Floyd said. 'Yes sir.' It wasn't often he had a chance to make his brother squirm. 'You been worryin'?' he asked.

This time Curtis was ready. He could feel a flush of guilt heating the back of his neck, but he didn't let it disturb him. 'Worryin' about mother,' he said. That was enough to surprise everybody. 'This big old house, meals, mendin' clothes, so on. She works too hard. Ought to have help.'

'Well, Sarah's lookin',' Floyd said.

'No,' Charles declared. 'We take Sarah, we get William too and three hungry boys. One works and five eat. No.'

'I can manage the housework,' Mary said.

'Manage twice as well with Lucy doin' the heavy stuff,' Curtis said, and Mary didn't argue. 'Could maybe pay her in eggs or taters or somethin'. Word is they're short of grub on the Ridge. Want me to ask?'

It was less effort for Charles to nod his head than to shake it, so he nodded. Curtis gave Floyd a sidelong glance that said: *Don't mess with me, little brother*. Floyd was amused. At last, the prospect of some entertainment in this drab life.

In the morning, Charles asked Sarah if she had any friends anywhere. 'Got a sister was sold to a man in Lexington,' she said. 'Ain't seen her in twenty year.' Charles advised them to go there. They went.

~

Maggie's tavern was busy. Stackmesser had supplied a banner to go over the bar. It said: *Huzzah! For Cleghorn's Scallywags!* This irritated Sims, who'd had the idea and provided the gunpowder, but so many customers bought him drinks and wanted to hear his story that he was willing to seem generous. 'Just a job had to be done,' he said, 'an' I guess we went up an' did it.' He liked the sound of that. Modest. Manly. Mature.

Deputy Nickel said, 'Nobody got hurt, then?' Sims put a silver dollar in his eye socket and pretended to look at her. Got a big laugh. 'You know what I mean,' she said. 'Was there any trouble?'

Sims turned to Killick. 'They trouble you any, Dan?'

'Well ... Didn't say goodbye. That kind of hurt me.' Laughter from all around encouraged more of the same. 'My hounds, they was *real* upset.' Drinks flowed.

Much later, Cleghorn said, 'I got nothin' against niggers.' This brought a surprised but respectful silence. He stood on tiptoe and peered over the heads of the drinkers as if searching for someone. *Jackass*, Sims thought. Cleghorn relaxed his legs. 'Like Kit told me once,' he said. 'On the trail of that Apache scoundrel Broken Eagle and his no-good braves, an' Kit turned in his saddle an' he said to me, "Hoke," he said, "I got nothin' against these Indians. I got nothin' against a mean, hungry, grizzly bear neither. I just don't want either one within five hundred miles of me." An' I agreed.' He smiled benignly at the great whoop of support.

'That's the good thing about gunpowder,' Sims said. 'Shift anythin' with gunpowder. Uppity niggers, big old tree stump, anythin'. Hell, I bet I could throw an anvil clean over old Stackmesser's store with the right amount of gunpowder.'

'Bet you couldn't,' said Ryan Kidder. He was pissed off because he hadn't been included in the Ridge party.

Sims shrugged. 'Got no powder.'

'I got some,' the pedlar offered. 'Bought it off a feller went bust minin' for gold up Bittersalt Creek.'

Sims looked at him as if he had produced a three-week-old dead rat by the tail.

'Bet you five dollars,' Kidder challenged. He saw how Sims's face twisted, and said, 'Make it ten.'

The entire tavern emptied and surged down the street. It took four big men with a thick rope to wrestle the anvil out of the blacksmith shop. At the sight of this, the betting moved to very long odds.

'Need a volcano to lift that sonofabitch,' Elias Dunbar said, and for once nobody sneered, so he added: 'Ain't no volcano this side of Mexico.'

'Saw a twister in Tennessee, picked up a grocery store, put it down half a mile away, not so much as a can fell off a shelf,' Dan Killick said.

'What in hell's that got to do with anvils?' Kidder asked.

'Twister can pick up anythin', anvil included, is what I'm sayin'.'

'This ain't about twisters, for God's sake. The goddamn bet ain't about your stupid Tennessee twisters.'

'You callin' Tennessee stupid? Listen friends, I saw plenty good Tennessee soldiers killed flat dead for the sake of the South while *you* ...' Killick's forefinger was prodding Kidder in the chest. Kidder batted it aside. 'Don't you slap me, mister,' Killick warned. Kidder gaped at this arrogance. 'Don't *you* slap *me*, mister,' he said. Friends nudged each man forward. Sims had gone, vanished. Might as well have a good fight.

'Get back!' Sims roared. 'Comin' through!' He came staggering fast, legs splayed under the weight of another anvil, far smaller than the first. Everyone fell back.

Kidder said: 'That ain't ...' But it obviously was.

'U.S. Cavalry-type anvil,' Cleghorn said. 'Made small so it can travel in a wagon.'

'Gimme that powder,' Sims demanded. His chest was heaving like his own bellows: the little anvil weighed as much as he did.

With a rag he wiped clean the bowl-shaped hollow in the top of the big anvil. He poured in gunpowder until the top of the heap stood an inch proud. He poked a length of fuse into the powder and let the end hang over the side. Then he rolled the small anvil until it was upside down. He wrapped his arms around it, straightened up (groaning like a tree in a gale) and gently placed the small anvil on top of the big one, so that its hollow exactly cupped the heap of powder. He stood back. Lantern light showed sweat popping out of his face like fat raindrops. 'Here's where it gets to be real entertainin',' he said, 'so step up close, folks, an' get a good view.' He struck a match on the seat of his pants.

Everyone scattered.

Sims lit the fuse and made for his shop at a fast lumber.

The bang was like a collision between two locomotives full of church bells. It had a massive wallop, but it also had a reverberant ring of steel that left the air quivering. Some said the big anvil bounced and glowed orange. Some said it actually disappeared for an instant. Some said nothing because the shock knocked them on their backs. But all those who saw, were agreed. The little anvil went straight up in the air, fifty feet at least, maybe sixty; hung – slowly turning – at the apex; came down and landed with a thud that made hard men wince, while the glass from Stackmesser's windows was still falling.

'I win,' Kidder claimed.

'Just a practice,' Sims said. 'Ain't got properly started yet.'

He played with his flying anvil until the powder ran out, at two-thirty in the morning. The bangs reached the Ridge, and the colonists slept badly, if at all.

~

Sarah's going hit the colony hard. Five familiar faces lost: that was a heavy blow. Nobody had much to say next day. They gathered wreckage and collected scraps, but Aaron could see them thinking: what's the good? Might's well quit too.

He shouted to Lonzo and Jake. They sat and talked for an hour.

Aaron took the rifle and fired a shot in the air. The colony came running. 'Lonzo got somethin' to say,' he said.

'This don't take brains,' Lonzo said. 'Summer's runnin' out. Winter's hard, up here. You go lookin' for food, only thing you'll find is black bear an' *he's* lookin' for *you*.'

'It's the truth,' Jake said.

'Thing is,' Lonzo said, and paused to look around. 'Here's Aaron, he's the best shot we got. Here's all our good grub, all blown to blazes. Suppose Josh does some real good prayin' here. Suppose we *find* all them bits of grub, every last little bit. Aaron, you bin up here all through the winters. How much grub would that be? What I'm askin' is: enough for how many?'

'Maybe one in four.'

'Uh-huh. Leaves the other three with nothin' to eat, come winter? What happens?'

'Starve.'

Lonzo waited, but that was all. 'Hell of a way to die.'

'Ain't pretty.'

'Huh.' Nobody moved. 'Course, no reason to wait for that,' he said. 'We can choose now, three out of four, an' Aaron can just shoot 'em now, him bein' the best shot we got. Ain't that right?'

Most were too shocked to speak. Martha's face was stretched in disbelief. 'That ain't right,' she said.

'Watch,' Aaron said. He raised the rifle, slowly, Some people fell back. Little Bonny ran and hid. Aaron kept raising the rifle, turned, shut one eye and fired at a tree. A bunch of leaves jumped. A pigeon fell. It raised a spurt of dust where it hit the ground. 'Best damn shot you got,' he said.

'Good time to dig graves,' Jake said. 'Ground still soft.'

'You got to say which die,' Aaron said. 'I ain't decidin' that.'

'Big fellers eat most,' Lonzo suggested, and looked at Buck.

Buck laughed. 'Ain't nobody gonna get shot,' he said. But he sounded less than certain.

'Who you reckon gonna starve first, then?' Lonzo got no answer from Buck, so he looked at Moses, and Martha, and Luke Corrigan, and Bettsy. Still no answer. 'Reckon children should oughta starve first,' he said. 'Children an' old folk.' He glanced at Jake.

'I'm ready to go,' Jake said. 'My time's just about done anyway.' He went to Aaron and took hold of the muzzle of the rifle and put it in his ear. 'Do it quick,' he said.

'Hey,' Martha said miserably. 'Don't be that way.'

'Someone gotta decide,' Aaron said. 'Don't wait until the hunger makes you crazy in the head. Liable to kill anyone, then. I know, I been there.' He shivered.

For a moment the only sound was the high rustle of leaves: an answering shiver. Then Buck said, 'Plenty grub for the takin'. Just gotta work, is all.'

'Shootin's easier,' Lonzo said. He sounded disappointed.

Aaron took the rifle away from Jake's head.

After that, everyone worked until told to stop. If someone slackened, two words revived him: *Shootin's easier.*

'Nigger ain't gonna kill another nigger,' Buck told Lonzo. 'Ain't natural.'

'Livin' ain't natural, neither. Not for us niggers. Livin' up here is *war*. Us agin the Ridge, us agin Rock Springs, us agin the winter. That ain't natural.'

Buck wasn't sure whether this was some sort of cockeyed joke. Lonzo had a face as blank as a wet pebble. 'So nothin' ain't natural,' he said. 'That right?'

'Slavery, now *that* was natural,' Lonzo said. 'We was good at bein' slaves. *Damn* good.' He strolled away. Buck was more confused than ever. You could never tell with Lonzo. Too educated. Big mistake to educate a nigger. Wasn't natural.

~

Sims asked Stackmesser for a few dollars towards the cost of the gunpowder, and Stackmesser said if Sims could find a dollar in the store, he could have it.

Sims went to Cleghorn and failed there too. 'You got my leadership an' military savvy for free, didn't you?' Cleghorn said huffily. Sims went back to work, but so many people kept coming in to tell him what he already knew that he quit, and rode over to the Killicks' place.

Jessica had to get Dan out of bed. He stumbled downstairs in his long johns. 'Bring any drink?' he asked. 'Damn niggers stole all our whiskey.' His feet fumbled for a step that wasn't there, and Sims had to catch him.

'Best thing for you's coffee.' Sims was genial; it felt awkward, but he'd had time to think, and geniality seemed like a smart move. 'Jeez, Dan, you were king of Rock Springs up there on the Ridge.' They went into the kitchen.

'My head got bad lumps,' Dan said. His breath kept Sims at arm's length and Sims was used to working with horses that broke wind when he picked up their hind leg. 'See? Lumps. Bad lumps.' He felt his head, and winced. The lumps were on the inside. That was wrong. 'Shit,' he said. 'How'd that happen?'

Sims found hot coffee. He stirred in four spoons of sugar. 'King of the Springs, you were,' he said. His smile was exhausting him. 'Everyone said so … Hell of a picnic, eh? Stackmesser reckoned it was worth every penny of his ten dollars. Wanted to give me more, I said no. Hoke was the exact same, but I told him, I said with you an' Stack an' Dan Killick all good for ten – me, I'll only be twenty dollars out of pocket an' shucks, I can stand that.' He gave Dan the coffee. 'Hoke told me, why not ride out, see Dan, get this whole thing squared off, that's what Dan would want, Hoke said.'

Dan drank, both hands on the mug, spilling coffee down his chest and stomach. He did not seem to notice. 'Bad lumps,' he mumbled.

'Hoke said we could've sold tickets for ten dollars!' Sims laughed.

Dan frowned. 'Ain't it the truth?' Sims said.

'Ten dollars for what?' Dan looked into the mug as if maybe Sims had sold him the coffee. 'What for ten dollars?'

'For the gunpowder,' Sims said. Dan discovered the coffee was soaking into his long johns. 'To pay for the gunpowder,' Sims explained.

'Got to piss,' Dan said glumly.

He went out. Time passed, and he did not come back into the house. 'Hey!' he called. 'Ain't that smoke?'

Sims went onto the porch. It was a pure, clear morning. Even Dan's scummy eyes could see those grey streaks against the blue. 'Maybe,' Sims said.

'Them fuckin' niggers are still up there!' Dan cried. 'All that work, an' they ain't gone! Jesus!' He collapsed into a cane chair. 'Goddamn niggers've ruined everythin'. They killed George. Damn near killed me too. That nigger-lover went an' murdered my daddy, right here in this house! All my life, if I tell a nigger, you shift, boy! you can bet he shifts or I whup him, that's the law. Now he don't shift for bullets or gunpowder! This country ain't fit for white Christian folk no more ...' By now Dan was in tears. 'Everythin's contrary, black's better'n white, an' white's worse'n black, and them fuckin' niggers is to blame ...' He was talking to himself. Job was in the saddle, heading back to town, hungrier than ever for his lost money.

If at first you don't succeed, send for more blasting powder.

FLYING ANVILS

F rankie Nickel helped Sims with the words. Flub Phillips had an old printing press. Together, they picked out the kind of fancy typeface beloved of circuses and balloon ascents:

A CHALLENGE TO ALL SPORTSMEN!

A TEST OF PLUCK AND POWER!

FLYING ANVIILS

$500 FIRST PRIZE

TO WHOMEVER, BY THE MEANS OF GUNPOWDER ALONE,

FLIES HIS ANVIL HIGHEST ON THE DAY –

And so on. Sims was quietly proud of that 'whomever'. He rode all over Dundee County, tacking posters to trees and barns, storefronts and tavern doors. Often a small crowd gathered. When he left, they thought flying anvils were the eighth wonder of the world.

The posters brought Rock Springs to the attention of people who had never heard of it. Strangers drifted into town. Some were hoping for work. Some were ex-soldiers who found it hard to settle. One small group were Rebels let go by a Union prisoner-of-war camp and now making their way back south. They camped near the landing stage and waited for the next steamboat. They were ragged, gaunt, dark with dirt. Town folk felt an unhappy mixture of pity and guilt and brought them food and old clothes. The Rebs kept to themselves, talked quietly, never smiled. Then some fool of a farmer gave them a jug of whiskey, and they drank it so fast that he gave them another. A bearded Reb lobbed the empty jug at a passer-by who reminded him slightly of an evil-tempered prison guard and it smashed on his head. Knocked him cold. Blood all over.

'Hey, fellah,' the farmer said, husky with fright, 'you ought to be more careful.'

The bearded Reb found that amusing. 'Ain't short of jugs, are you?' he said happily. His friends found that even funnier.

'No.' The farmer was backing off. 'Ain't short of a deputy in this town, neither.'

'Like to meet him,' the Reb said. 'Got this other jug here. Like to smash it on his head just as soon as we got it empty.'

The farmer fetched Frankie Nickel. When the Rebs saw her star, that was the funniest thing yet in what was turning out to be a highly entertaining day.

'You did this?' she asked.

'Daddy, I cannot tell a lie,' the bearded Reb said. Hilarious. One of his friends laughed so hard he sprung a rib and had to sit down.

'This man do anythin' to you?' she asked. The victim was stirring.

'Hit my jug with his head.' The laughter was attracting a crowd.

'That's a finin' offence in this town. You ain't got no money, am I right?'

'Waitin' for our back pay, ma'm. Thousand dollars each.' Now *that* was the best joke of all.

'Here's the deal,' she said. 'Take this man to Doc Brightsides, get him fixed up. Then move on. I want you all gone from here within the hour.'

They stood and looked at each other. Even in jeans and a rawhide vest, she was so neatly dressed that by contrast he was as shaggy as a black bear.

'Look, lady,' he said. 'You get the sheriff, an' me an' him'll have a drink, an' you can – '

'No sheriff. You do business with me.'

Everyone was so quiet they could hear him scratch his beard. 'Well now, no,' he said. 'Matter of fact, I don't think I do.'

'Then we'll have to fight a duel.' She walked over to Stackmesser's and took two pickaxe hafts from a basketful on display. 'This has become an affair of honour, right?' she said as she walked back. 'Needs to be settled one way or the other? Agreed?' She tossed a haft to him.

'Don't want to hurt you, lady.' The haft was like a walking cane in his fists.

'Ain't no lady. I'm town deputy. Now: which end you want to hold?' As he made up his mind, she swung the haft and the thick end came up between his legs and whacked his sexual organs and he went down screaming. 'What they call *touché*,' she told Job Sims. 'In France.'

'Jesus, Frankie,' he said. 'You didn't give him scarcely no chance at all.'

'Didn't want to damage the stock.' She collected the other haft and gave them both back to Stackmesser.

'*His* stock ain't been improved none, though,' Sims said.

'Well, the man's a damn fool if he thought I was going to stand an' let him get his licks in first. Whole trick to fightin' a duel is to find out exactly where the good Lord Almighty placed a man's Achilles heel. Most times it's where the trail forks. Hit that real hard, an' I'm told the agony is so painful it *hurts*.' The Reb had stopped screaming and lay moaning, curled up, knees to chest. 'You could ask him, in a while,' she said.

'You should have hit his head,' Stackmesser said. 'That ain't fair on the next generation, what you did.'

'Next generation never did me no favours.'

Friends of the casualty had got over their shock and were gathered around him. One man was crying with rage or despair or both. He was small, and wore an eye-patch tied over a lopsided, filthy head-bandage. Several of his teeth were missing. He did not look much like a soldier. To the crowd, he shouted, 'This man saved my life! Shed his blood for your honour! Now look what you done to him … You people … You goddamn civilians …' He advanced on Frankie Nickel. 'You call us heroes an' then you kick us in the balls.'

'Didn't kick him,' she said evenly. 'I whopped him.'

At that the small man lost control. He drew a knife and waved it, maybe as a mere gesture, maybe not. She took back a pickaxe haft from Stackmesser. 'Guard your nuts,' she told the small man. His hands dropped and she swung the haft one-handed. It clipped his head. Everything about him slackened. The head fell sideways. The knife dropped. The body collapsed.

'Aw, Jesus *Christ*, Frankie,' Sims said. 'Can't you give these men a break?'

'Stack here said to hit them in the head,' she told him. 'I done what he said, an' now you're bellyachin'. Ain't no pleasin' you people.'

Brightsides patched up the injured. Later, the doctor and the deputy watched the Rebel group trudge out of town.

'Understand one thing,' Brightsides said. 'I'm not in this noble profession for the good of mankind. I want the money. You keep making charity cases for me. I wish you'd stop.'

Frankie sniffed. 'Some bum arrives, sees this star pinned to my buzoom, thinks he'll have himself a bit of fun. Never expects a lady to whop him first.'

'Must you break their noses?'

'That's the nearest bit.'

'Three in two days.'

'Law got to be respected.'

'You'll end up having to kill somebody,' he said.

'One less charity case. You can have his clothes. I'll shoot him through a buttonhole.'

The last of the Rebel soldiers turned a corner and was lost to sight. The sun had gone down, and Rock Springs looked old and dilapidated, every building leaning away from the winter winds that would soon bluster down the street as if they owned it. The doctor and the deputy walked back to the tavern.

'One of those men grew up in Texas,' he said. 'Told me he knew Desolation pretty well.'

'Hunh.'

'Well-named town, he said. Even the river's undrinkable.'

'Sure. Desolation River's poison.'

'Actually I lied. He said there is no river in Desolation.'

'Yeah? Well, I lied too.' She was quite bland.

'Why would you do that?'

'Why would you?'

That was the end of their conversation. The tavern was busy that night. Harvest was just about finished and people were drifting into town, attracted by news of the Anvil Flying. There was a fight over cards and Frankie had to bust another nose. 'Ten dollars,' Brightsides told the sufferer, and when the man protested, he snapped shut his bag. 'Breathe through your ears,' he told him.

HOLY MOSES

People thought there was money in religion. Flub Phillips could have told them different. The most Flub had ever earned from his calling was ten dollars and thirty-five cents after preaching nearly two hours. That was before the war. Now some people wouldn't give him a nickel for a glimpse of Eternity. Too many friends and family had gone to see the real thing, suddenly, free of charge.

So Flub did other things: a little horse-trading; some auctioneering as needed; maybe animal-doctoring or even water-divining. When he got word that Ma Killick wanted him, he figured it must be a sick horse and he mixed up a fresh bottle of his Universal Colic, Staggers and Thrush Cure, composed of equal parts of swamp-maple tea, sassafras and corn whiskey. Flub himself took it whenever he felt a bout of fever coming on. If the stuff didn't get a horse back on its feet, the beast was fit to die anyway.

It wasn't a sick horse. Ma Killick wanted to sell the farm. Fields, barns, house, crops, everything. Flub was so astonished that he choked on his own saliva. She didn't notice. Had too much to say.

'My poor late husband Joseph's wish, Reverend Phillips. Taken from me so cruelly, so quickly.' She opened a box of black handkerchiefs and took a fresh one. 'His dying words ... his final wish ... I should live out my days in modest comfort. Do not let this place break your heart as it has broken mine, he said. Go, he said, leave here, he said, you have earned your rest.' She had more to say on that theme.

Flub sat and nodded and mentally worked out a price.

She talked about her children and the sleepless nights they caused her. 'But ain't this best for them too, Reverend Phillips? The mother bird knows her darlin' chicks must fly the nest, though it breaks her heart to see them go ...'

Anyway, she said, golden opportunities awaited them out West. There were Killicks in Nebraska, in Montana, even in California. 'Blood is thicker than water, Reverend Phillips,' she said, and quoted several examples of family loyalty.

Flub kept nodding. She didn't want her brats under her feet. He could understand that.

Then came God. 'I asked the Lord, was I doin' the right thing? I asked Him an' I asked Him. Should I sell the farm? Is that what You really want me to do, Lord? Know what He told me?' Flub didn't stop nodding. He was one hundred per cent sure he knew what God told her.

Eventually she finished with God, and fell silent.

'Well,' Flub said. 'If that ain't the most inspiring thing I ever heard.' He blew his nose.

'The perfect husband.' She hid her face in her handkerchief. 'Never once raised his hand or his voice to me.'

Flub reckoned he had done his pastoral duty. He was not a great listener, especially to somebody else's conversations with the Almighty, which got near to poaching on Flub's own property. 'Big place like this,' he said. 'Ain't gonna be easy to find a buyer.'

Ma Killick handed him a folded piece of paper. He opened it and held it at arm's length.

'Charles Hudd,' he said. 'You want to sell to Charles Hudd?'

'Joseph's wish. He wrote that name with his dyin' breath.'

Flub thought fast. Doc Brightsides said Joe died lying head-down on the stairs, stinking of booze. 'Well, Hudd's the biggest landowner in these parts,' he said. 'Who knows, if the price is right ...'

She handed him another piece of paper. He looked at the figures on it.

'Holy Moses,' he said. 'That much?'

'It's what Joseph wrote. He didn't want me to be cheated of my inheritance.' A tremble was creeping into her voice.

He waited, and watched her, cautiously. 'Is that all he wrote?' She nodded. 'An' you want me to go an' see Mr Hudd?' Another nod. 'That's a big barrel of money,' he said. 'Shall we bow our heads in prayer?'

As he was leaving the farm he met Stanton. 'What you doin' here, preacherman?' Stanton demanded. Ever since he lost his arm he had been aggressively atheist.

'Came to doctor a horse,' Flub said, and pointed to a grazing mare.

'She don't look sick.' Now Stanton was suspicious.

'Of course she don't look sick,' Flub said blithely. 'I just doctored her. Want a swig? You're lookin' sorta peaky yourself.' He offered the bottle, Stanton said no. Flub took a drink. 'You look more'n more like your pa every day,' he said, and smiled and rode on. Long preaching taught a man how to draw blood.

An hour later he found Hudd and his family in the fields, bringing in the last of the corn. The wagon was full. Mary had the reins. The boys went ahead. Charles walked behind. Flub noticed that he had a limp. Flub walked with him, the horse ambling alongside.

'The widow Killick wants to sell you her farm,' he said. 'I'm the honest broker, if you can believe that.'

'Last month she wanted to hang me. Next month she'll want to marry me. Why didn't she come here herself?'

Flub made a vague gesture. 'Poor woman's in a delicate condition.'

'She may be poor, but she ain't delicate. You know that, Flub. She's a hard, selfish, stupid woman. That whole Killick family is a blight on this valley, always has been.'

'So buy her out. Get rid of them.'

'Attractive idea.'

'You've got first refusal.'

The wagon went through the gateway, swaying as it hit ruts. Hudd pulled the gate shut and stood resting his arms on the top bar. 'Strange how things work out,' he said. 'I have cousins in Georgia. Good-sized plantation. Sherman's army burned it. All the wells poisoned, all the stock dead. Nothing left but their silver. Got hid in a wood. Silver's not worth a hell of a lot now the war's over and Dixie's just one big pawnshop, but they'll raise enough to get here. Two families. Thirteen Hudds, four of them children. We'll work this farm together.'

'Families grow, Charles. Look ahead.'

'You haven't said the price.'

Flub gave him the piece of paper.

'She's crazy,' Hudd said, and gave it back.

Flub was not surprised, and not discouraged. The advantage of using paper was you didn't have to say the amount out loud. Once you spoke a figure, it was hard to un-speak it, whereas Flub could screw up this piece of paper and pretend it meant nothing serious; and so he did.

'Supposin' I had another piece of paper, blank,' he said. 'what figure might you be interested in writing on it?' He felt in his pockets as he spoke. 'Praise the Lord, here is such a piece! And a pencil, too.' He offered them. Hudd did not move.

'A dollar. I'll give her a dollar for the farm.'

Flub waited, but nothing followed. If it was a joke, Charles hid it behind a tired face, and Flub couldn't see the humour. 'Well,' he said mildly, 'that's a start. Leaves some way to go, but it's a start.'

'The farm isn't hers to sell, Flub,' Charles said. 'She'll never understand that. She's one of those women who think, because they say a thing, it must be so. South's full of them. Emancipation kicked 'em flat on their ass and they want the world to kiss it better. Nobody's gonna kiss Mrs Killick's ass again.'

'I can say you're interested?' Flub asked. 'In principle, that is?' He whistled for his horse.

Supper was a quiet meal in the Hudd house: they were tired, they'd seen enough of each other for one day. Charles said even less than usual until Lucy (now hired full-time) took the dishes out. He cleared his throat, fiddled with some cutlery, finally glanced at Curtis. 'Ever wished you had a farm of your own?' he asked. It was not a real question; the boy never owned five dollars in his whole life. Curtis just stared. 'Think I'll buy the Killick farm,' Charles said. 'Yes ... Why not?' He stood up. 'Long day,' he said. 'Time for bed.' And left the room.

They looked at their mother. 'Don't ask me,' she said. 'I know nothing about it.'

She checked all the doors were locked, and Lucy had left the kitchen ready for breakfast, and the laundry had been put to soak. It gave her time to think. When she went upstairs her husband was in bed. 'That's what Flub Phillips came to see you about,' she said. He nodded. 'I ask because the boys believe it's some kind of joke.'

'I'm not surprised. Your boys think *I'm* some kind of joke. Everything's a joke at their age.'

She thought: *He's gone too far. They're stepsons, he'll always be a stranger, but not a joke. Doesn't he understand them at all? After all these years?*

213

'So this is going to teach them a lesson, is it?' she said.

'Might open their eyes some.' His own eyes were half-shut.

'Whole Killick farm. You want it all.'

'It's all on offer.'

She sat on the bed and eased off her shoes. 'I bought these three years ago. Last pair I ever bought. Look: patches on the patches. Floyd's wearing Curtis's cast-offs. Curtis is wearing yours. I still cut their hair. You got Floyd straightening bent old nails, to use again. Now you're going to buy a farm.'

'That's my intention.'

'When we have no money.'

'I can buy the Killick place,' Charles said, and raised one finger, 'for a single, shining dollar.'

'It's too late to play games, Charles.'

'Not a game. That farm has been mortgaged three times. Joe Killick borrowed so much, he ended up not owning the bed he slept in. The Killicks don't just owe the bank interest. They owe interest on the interest.'

'So do other of our neighbours. That's what banks are for.'

'This bank is sick of the Killicks. It would have called in their mortgages long ago if the war hadn't murdered the price of land. But if I buy the mortgages, the bank will give me the land for nothing, because ...' And here he spread his hands and smiled at the wonderful simplicity of it all, '... the bank trusts me to make the payments on time.'

'*Buy* the mortgages?' She held up her patched shoes.

'The bank will lend us the money. Happy to oblige. No cash changes hands. Bank gets rid of a bad debt and acquires a good one. Simple switch. All done on paper.'

She stood up and began to undress. 'You're saying we have to borrow money? That means putting up security, doesn't it?'

'This land is good, and in the long run, good land is still the best security there is.'

She stepped out of her skirt, and sat on a stool by the dressing table. She was too tired to think straight, and he was not helping her to understand. 'We borrow money on our land. Is that right?' She started unbuttoning her shirt. 'That's the same as ...' She heaved a sigh: her eyes were refusing to focus on the buttons. 'Same as ... as a mortgage. It means we mortgage the farm. Doesn't it?' She looked at him, her brow bunched.

'Not all. Only part.'

'How much?'

'Half, probably.'

'Half.' She went back to her buttons. 'What's that in dollars?'

'Half. Dollar's not worth what it was. Say … Seventy-five thousand.'

A buttonhole had frayed and the threads trapped the button. 'Your father owed nobody a nickel. You inherited free and clear. We've never been in debt. Never. Now you want to … to mortgage this farm so you can own the Killick farm and be mortgaged up to the neck in both places. *God damn and blast it all to hell!*' She ripped the shirt wide open, sending buttons pinging against the mirror.

Charles came awake with a jerk. He was shocked: she had never spoken or acted like that before. Now she was weeping. Mary didn't weep. He felt bewildered and betrayed. It was as if the bed had collapsed and dumped him on the floor. 'Look, no need for that,' he said.

'All I do is work.' She wept as she spoke, and her tears gave the words an anguish that swamped their meaning. 'Sunup to sundown, and then some more. Work and worry, work and worry.' Now the torrent overflowed and left no room for words. Her lungs could not labour hard enough to keep up with the weeping.

'Same for us all,' he said. Part of him urged: *Get up and comfort her.* Another part said: *Let her cry if she damn well wants to.* The second part won. 'Anyway, what the hell's that got to do with buying the Killicks' farm? I'll handle the deal. You just forget about it.'

She flung a shoe. It missed his head, narrowly. He could not have been more astonished if she had fired a pistol. The awful thought struck him: she's insane, a lunatic. 'Forget about it?' she shouted. 'What else d'you want me to forget? The war, when you left me alone? And the raiders came, and the recruiters? This farm, and the mess it's in because you won't hire enough help?' Suddenly she had stopped crying. 'Your cousins, should I forget them? Thirteen more Hudds on the way, all poor, all hungry?'

'With them here, I shan't need to hire any help.'

'You could hire an army of help. Money's no problem. Ask the bank.'

'You don't understand – '

'One thing I never had to worry about was debt. Sometimes it seemed like the only thing. Whatever else, we never owed. Not one penny.'

'It's my goddamn money,' he said grimly.

'Oh, sure. And here's how you don't spend it.' She tossed the other shoe onto the bed. 'Like pulling teeth.'

'And it's my farm.' *Never give in. Never give up.*

'One isn't enough? You must have two?'

'For your boys.'

'I don't think so. This second farm is for your pride and vanity. You'll mortgage everything, just to get the Killicks thrown out. That's a mean, miserable action.'

'They're a mean, miserable family.'

'I see.' She put on her skirt and picked up her shoes. 'They are shits, so you must be a shit too.' She left the room. Never before had she used that word in his presence. His face was flushed as if she had slapped it.

WRONG, WRONG, WRONG

This time they hid the food where Killick's hounds might hunt for a week and still not find it. Maybe.

Some they buried: stocks of roots and bulbs, thickly wrapped in layers of fern to keep insects out. Other stuff went into caves, some into hollow trees, some into little shacks built by children who crawled along rabbit runs to get to the heart of tangles of thorn and bramble where no dog would go. Some was hidden in piles of rocks that looked exactly like piles of rocks.

Forest vermin would steal their share, everyone knew. Nothing to be done about that except collect even more.

They worked all the hours they could see to look. It was like being a slave again. Work till you couldn't, then sleep till you could: they'd done it all their lives, could do it again. Do it a lot easier than any white man.

A couple of days after the gunpowder attack, Lonzo rode down to town. People looked at him strangely. He still had some of his reward money; with it he bought 200 burlap bags. Stackmesser served him silently, until Lonzo asked, 'Comin' up to see Fast Rattlesnake mine?'

'I wouldn't climb that stinkin' Ridge to see the Second Coming,' Stackmesser said. 'Not if you served striped ice cream. And I want my goddamn mule back.'

'Need goddamn mule to carry goddamn bags. No mule, no bags.'

Stackmesser sniffed, and looked away. 'Anythin' else? Stomach powders?'

'What for I want stomach powders?'

'Powerful loud fartin' been goin' on up there.'

To Stackmesser's surprise Lonzo laughed. This made a noise like

217

splitting bad wood with a dull axe. Stackmesser grinned. The expression made him look guilty of murder while insane. They made a strange coupling.

As he left town, Lonzo met Frankie Nickel. 'You didn't get blowed away, then,' she said.

'Li'l earthquake, was all. Gave the chillun a scare.' He kept going.

'Earthquake,' she said to Morgan Watson's sow. 'Ain't that interesting?' The sow grunted, and waited, expecting food. None came. People usually let you down, that was the sow's experience. It took a lot of hope to be a sow. Hope and tits.

~

Flub waited a day before he went back to the Killick farm, and when he got there nearly all the family was in the kitchen, playing poker. Dried red kidney beans for money. Nobody saying much. Stanton saw him standing in the doorway and pointed upstairs.

Ma Killick was in the room Joe had used as an office, and she was tearing pages out of his accounts books. 'Wrong, wrong, wrong,' she said. The floorboards were snowed under.

'Mornin', ma'm,' Flub said. 'I was over to the Hudd place, like you asked.'

She went on tearing. 'Figures don't add up,' she said. 'Just look.' She stirred a few pages with her foot. 'If I believed any of that, we'd be bankrupt!' Her laughter was scornful. 'That price I gave you ...' she ripped a book in half. 'Wrong. Big mistake. Joe's book-keeping was ...' She shook her head, and her black veil tumbled over her face. 'Seventy-five thousand is ridiculous! I bet Mr Hudd was mightily amused.'

'It took him aback some,' Flub said.

'My poor late husband wasn't altogether right in the head, towards the end. His side of the family ...' Now she was ripping the torn pages into strips. 'You understand. Charles Hudd is no better. Since my late daughter refused to marry him ... Poor man became unbalanced. Needs help. I'm only sellin' to him as an act of charity. He is almost kin, after all.'

'*Late* daughter,' Flub said carefully.

'My JoBeth is with the angels, Mr Phillips.'

'I hadn't heard that JoBeth passed away.' Flub was shocked. How could the family have kept such a secret? 'I'm truly sorry, ma'am.'

'Consumption. That horrible climate down there in Louisiana. I begged her not to go. Well, a hundred and fifty thousand dollars is my new final price, and if Mr Hudd chooses to live here, I have two daughters every bit as pretty, he can take his pick, and you can have the other.'

'I have a wife, ma'am. So has Mr Hudd.'

'She might die. What then? Man like Hudd needs a wife. Don't he?' Even through her veil, her scowl was powerful. 'Whose side you on, anyway?'

He let that pass. Ma Killick only had one other daughter, Jessica. He let that pass, too. 'One hundred and fifty thousand dollars, you say.'

'Not enough. I can read it in your face. Of course it's not enough! If I choose to be charitable, then so I shall. What is money, when I have suffered a loss that cannot be counted in rubies?' She scooped up torn strips and let them flutter through her fingers. 'All that's left of my husband,' she said, getting the widow's throb into her voice, 'and it's wrong, wrong, wrong.'

Flub decided to go. The family was in the parlour, playing poker for beans; the mother was upstairs, practising to be a loony; nobody was outside, working the farm.

She followed him downstairs. 'Take someone with you,' she said. They stopped and looked at the card game. 'Stanton's all mouth and no brain. Dan's probably drunk, usually is this time of day. Not Jessica, she can't keep her knickers on. Take Devereux. He's smart.' She turned and clumped upstairs. 'Wrong, wrong, wrong,' she sang. 'Wrong wronger wrongest.'

Devereux demanded to know what was going on. Flub said he might be needed to witness a signing. That satisfied him.

Charles Hudd was slaughtering a pair of hogs when they arrived. They watched him drain the blood into pails, then helped him hang the carcasses on hooks and catch the guts in wooden tubs. Water was nearby, boiling; Charles scalded the skins and scraped off the bristles. The others cut free the offal and put it under cheesecloth to keep the flies off.

It was fast, hard work, and they were all bloodied to the elbows. Charles saw Curtis nearby, leading a wagon, and shouted to him, 'Take Mr Killick here to the house. Let him clean up, get some refreshment.' Devereux went.

'Fine-lookin' boy, your stepson,' Flub said.

'Hates my guts. Never said a thank-you to me in his life.'

They washed in what was left of the hot water.

'You ever said thanks to him?' Flub asked.

'For hating my guts? No, I never thought to thank him for that. He can go run the Killick place and find what real work's like. So: what did she say?'

'Hard to tell. She was kind of fevered.'

'Entire family's fevered.'

'I been wrong before, but I'm pretty sure she ain't gonna take your offer, Mr Hudd, an' before you say anythin', sir, I want you to consider what's best. Best all round, that is.'

'Don't start preaching,' Hudd warned. 'I get a bellyful of preaching indoors without you adding more.'

'Well, sometimes Christian charity is good business sense too,' Flub said. 'Now, certain things we agree on. F'rinstance, you an' the bank can evict the Killicks tomorrow. Say you do. Where they gonna go? Gonna hang around. How they gonna feel? Feel bad. Bad and mad. Mad at you. Shootin' mad, maybe. You sure you want that arrangement?'

'I got a dozen Hudds coming to live here. We got guns, too.'

'Sounds like the makin's of a war. Talkin' of which, here's a widow lost a son fightin' for the South, had another son wounded, she's gonna be made homeless by a rich Yankee major. No offence, sir, but that's how folks'll see it.'

'Her farm's bust. I didn't bust it. Joe Killick did.'

'Joe's gone on to a Greater Reckoning.'

'Tell the bank that.' Hudd took a sour pleasure in the thought.

'You're a man of principle, sir,' Flub said mildly, 'but you ain't gonna go lookin' for a reason to make everyone hate you. Excuse me.' He strolled over to his horse and loosened a girth that was perfectly loose already, and looked at the animal's teeth, and counted its legs and divided by four, and felt satisfied, and finally strolled back. 'I don't hardly know why I even mentioned that,' he said. 'You're a clever man, Mr Hudd. My trouble is, I just run off at the mouth. My wife says – '

'Ma Killick can stay,' Hudd said. 'We'll build her a little house somewhere.'

Flub clicked his fingers. 'Why didn't I think of that?'

'The girl can stay on as hired help. I don't want the sons. They can go west. I'll pay them travelling money.'

'Just leaves the price. Now, one dollar – '

'Is what it's worth.'

Flub picked up a splinter and cleaned the dried blood from under his fingernails. 'My opinion, sir, one small dollar could buy you a load of grief.'

'Uh-huh.' Charles picked up a pig's head and held it at arm's length. Its half-shut eyes made it look sly. 'Late in the day to mention grief. Those Killicks already caused me more grief than ...' He shrugged. 'Than I can measure.'

'Think about it, is all I'm sayin'.'

'Think? I've done nothin' else but think, ever since JoBeth let herself get taken, God knows why.' He flung the pig's head at a wandering chicken, which squawked and fled. 'A black mystery,' he said heavily. 'Beyond my comprehension.'

'When Gabriel blows his horn, we all got to go,' Flub said. Charles stared. 'I was told consumption,' Flub said. 'You know Louisiana air. Wet as dishrags.'

'JoBeth died? You say she died?'

She got taken, you said it yourself, Flub thought. Then he realized Charles meant taken away by *someone,* not taken by God. That explained why he was looking like he walked into a tree. All these years, JoBeth had been at the back of Charles's mind, the ghost of his lost love, a name he couldn't speak to anyone until now. The first time he takes a chance and says it, and she's dead. Flub felt sick. *This Killick deal is cursed,* he told himself. Briefly, he considered mentioning Ma Killick's confused state of mind. No. Enough confusion already.

Curtis pumped water so Devereux could wash, and then took him into the house. He poured lemonade for them both.

'Sure is a big house,' Devereux said. 'Ain't never been in a house this big.'

'We got high standards in our family.' There was an aloofness in his voice that impressed even Curtis. 'Come on up, I'll show you.'

The view from the belvedere silenced Devereux. 'That's my brother Floyd out there, mendin' fences,' Curtis said. He had brought a walking cane and used it as a pointer. 'Yonder's my mother, pickin' plums, I guess.' He turned to another direction.

'Must be Lucy.' She was hanging out bedsheets.

'Wish we had a nigger,' Devereux said.

'They got you emptyin' the outhouse?' It was a lucky shot, and Curtis was pleased to see it strike home. 'Huh,' he said. 'Fuckin' Lincoln.'

'What all does she do?'

'Lucy does … Lemme see … Lucy does what we say. Lucy makes us happy. She sure gives *me* pleasure.' That was enough. Dev's eyes were big with envy. Curtis cupped his hands and shouted: 'Hey Lucy! Make us some more lemonade!'

They went down and waited in the kitchen. Curtis was afraid his stepfather would come in and order him back to work. Devereux was a tall, good-looking boy, and Curtis enjoyed boasting about how he ran the farm, what changes he planned to make.

Lucy came in with a fresh jug. 'Give Mr Devereux some,' Curtis said. He talked as if she were still a slave. She didn't answer like a slave. 'You one of them redhead Killicks, huh?' she said.

'That's right.' Devereux looked her full in the face as she filled his glass. 'You take care of Mr Curtis's needs, I believe.'

'I surely do.'

Dev nodded. His pulse was suddenly pounding. He didn't know where these words came from; they surprised him. 'Shame you can't take care of my needs too.'

'I surely can.'

'That's all, Lucy,' Curtis said, grimly. 'You can go.'

'Yeah.' She topped up their glasses. 'Got a dollar?'

'I do too,' Dev said.

'Ain't worth a cent on this farm,' Curtis told him, very angry now. He opened the door and shoved Lucy out, spilling lemonade.

They sat in bleak silence until Flub came in and said he and Dev were leaving. 'Mr Hudd's had a piece of bad news,' Flub told Curtis. 'He ain't feeling too great. I thought you ought to know.'

'Sure,' Curtis said. Maybe the news would kill the old bastard right off.

At that moment, Charles Hudd was sitting halfway up the staircase. He'd been heading for his room, making hard work of the climb, hauling on the banister, when his heart began kicking like a cat in a sack, and his knees started to wobble, so he sat down.

It hurt that she was dead, hurt as if he'd been shot with an icicle, frozen. But what hurt even more was nobody had told him. Finding out by accident, that doubled the pain. Why hadn't someone told him?

As he sat and tasted bile, and kept swallowing hard to drive it away, he worked out the answer.

Everybody in Rock Springs believed he knew. Even if they weren't totally sure he knew, who was going to be the first to mention it? Knowing how he'd felt about her. Why revive his grief? Let it pass. Let it fade. Of course.

Mary Hudd found him on the stairs, hunched-up like it was mid-winter. 'Have you been taken sick?' she asked.

'Life ain't fair,' he muttered. 'Just ain't fair.'

That was when she knew the Killick deal had fallen through. For a few seconds she despaired. Not getting elected mayor had made him sour and silent for the best part of a week. This failure looked even worse. She sat on the lower step and held his hands, felt a steady tremor and squeezed hard to check it. 'No, it ain't fair,' she said. 'But life goes on, and we must go on with it.'

'Missed my chance,' he whispered.

'Look around. This is next best, and it isn't so bad.' It was the worst thing she could have said.

She helped him up to his room. He sat at his desk. She got him a glass of whiskey but he didn't touch it. Just sat and cleaned dried pig's-blood from under his fingernails. Said nothing, wouldn't look. She went away.

After a long time he opened a deep desk drawer and took out his scarred, scuffed telescope case. Drank half the whiskey. Took out the portrait. Tried to tear it in half but the canvas was strong and his fingers feeble. He caused a little damage. Not much.

Mary was in the kitchen, asking herself why Charles had to be such a wretch. She told herself what she'd told him, that life must go on, and got no satisfaction from the question or the answer. She did what she always did when times were bad: made a good meal. Food helped.

She sent Curtis to collect mushrooms.

～

Devereux was seventeen and he knew how to pleasure a woman. He had watched the boar being put to the sow, the stallion covering the mare, the ram serving the ewe; and he himself had been briskly deflowered by Amie Kidder in her shift behind a bramble bush near the swimming hole while she was waiting her turn to be baptized by Flub Phillips; so he knew all there was to know. In less than a minute and a half he had pleasured Lucy. A minute later he had buttoned his pants, brushed off the bits of straw and left the barn.

It was dusk, and he went home the long way, by the fields, avoiding the road, and it was just bad luck that he met Curtis, who was out collecting mushrooms. They stopped and looked.

'Somethin' we can do for you?' Curtis said.

'You already did. Best dollar I ever spent.'

You cannot kill a man with a bag of mushrooms; otherwise Curtis would have knocked him to the ground and bashed his brains in. Since their first coupling, Curtis had been lusting after Lucy until his loins ached. No dollar, no deal. Now this goddamn Killick pretty-boy blew in with the breeze and stole the pleasuring that Curtis rightly deserved ten times over! There were no words, no sounds, to express his rage. And before he could find any, Dev grinned like an idiot and shrugged and moved on.

It ain't fair, Curtis told himself, *it ain't right, an' somethin's got to be damn well done.* He didn't want Lucy now: Lucy had been spoiled. He wanted Dev Killick cut down and butchered like the hog he was.

While this adolescent frenzy was exhausting itself, Lucy was still sitting in the straw, wondering. *They get their enjoyments,* she thought. *All I get is their squirts. And a dollar. Why can't I enjoy too? How come I get the chore side of it? Tell me that, God. I really want to know.*

TROUBLE AIN'T FUNNY

Two days before anvil-flying was due, Elias Dunbar saw bunches of strangers arriving in town. He left his coopering work and built a lean-to shack from scavenged timbers on the old bank site. There he sold chili con carne. Mrs Dunbar cooked it by the tubful at home and Billy Dunbar hustled it over to the shack on their buggy. Very peppery. Very popular.

Morgan Watson saw Dunbar's success and he opened a burgoo stand at the other end of the street. His stew simmered day and night in a twelve-gallon cast-iron pot. Watson slept beside it, to protect the recipe from thieves. 'Kentucky's prize dish,' he told Ryan Kidder. Ryan asked what went into it. He said ten squirrels, hind leg of a cow, five big birds (any kind), vegetables in season, and the other ingredients were a secret handed down from Watson generation to generation like best china, except he could reveal a double handful of cayenne pepper went in there, along with two bottles of bourbon and a quart of oysters. Ryan tasted the burgoo. It made his eyeballs sweat. 'Keep that sow of yours away from it,' he warned. 'She'll fart fireballs. Where is she, anyway? Ain't seen her lately.' Watson shrugged. 'Oh,' Ryan said.

The Dunkerley woman came down from her scrubby sharecropping farm, and she fried chicken at the roadside all day long. The pedlar set up a tent where he sold bunion-vanishing cream, toothache cure, and one-size-fits-all eyeglasses. Hoke Cleghorn announced a horse race on Anvil-Flying Day: twice round his Forty-Acre meadow and the finish line to be outside Maggie's tavern. Maggie took on two extra bar-keeps. A man who called himself Colonel Daniel G. Noble rented her barn as a dancehall. Hunkin was scandalized, but overnight Colonel Noble had the barn painted red and converted the loft into a dozen bedrooms. He hung a sign saying

Noble's Academy of Terpsichore. Sporting Gentlemen Catered For. Sheets Changed Weekly. He did good business.

Job Sims had stumbled on something: with the war over, people were eager to catch up on pleasure. Flying anvils were just crazy enough to excite their imagination. As the entertainments attracted more people, so the people attracted more entertainments, until Rock Springs had doubled in numbers. Doc Brightsides was right about one thing: having a lady deputy was part of the attraction.

Word of her showdown with the homegoing Rebs had spread. It improved in the telling. Some disbelieved the story.

She was ambling down Main Street, hands in pockets, comfortably doing nothing like the rest of the crowd, when a large young man blocked her way. 'You ain't no deputy,' he said, amiably. Black hair poked out the top of his shirt like a bust sofa. 'My old aunt Maud was tougher'n you, an' she got kicked to death by baby cottontails.' It was plainly a rehearsed speech.

'You ain't from these parts.' She thrust her hands deeper in her pockets, and rocked a little on her heels. 'Ask around, they'll tell you who's deputy. You're in my way, sonny.'

'If you're the deputy, where's the sheriff?' He mimicked her stance: hands in pockets, rocking on heels.

'No sheriff. Just me.'

'Yeah? Don't seem hardly legal. Ain't nobody to give you orders. Little old lady like you needs a feller to hold her hand when it thunders.' Snickers and chortles were breaking out nearby.

Frankie felt small kicks of angry excitement rushing the blood in and out of her heart. She felt it prickling her fingers, heating her cheeks. 'Blockin' my way is obstructin' the course of justice, sonny,' she said. 'That's a ten-dollar fine in this town.'

He acted out a gape of astonishment. 'Ten dollars! An' here I come out without my purse!' Loud laughter made him smirk. 'Lend me ten dollars, lady.'

'These your friends?' she asked, and pointed. He turned his head. Her hand came from her pocket and threw white pepper into his eyes. It had been ground fine and it blinded him instantly. He staggered. She kicked an ankle, not hard, just enough to make him trip himself. He could not see the dirt rushing up to hit his face. He was yelping with fright: everything had happened so fast: blindness, pain. Frankie took a looped cord from her other pocket and slipped it over his head and tightened it. 'Hold that,' she said, and gave the end to the nearest person, who happened to be little Arnie Phillips, 'and pull when I say.' The man on the ground was choking, writhing, panicking. 'Twenty dollars,' Frankie told his friends. 'I want it now.'

'Ben ain't got no twenty dollars!' one of them protested.

'Pull, Arnie,' she said. The boy pulled and the man frothed and gargled, so he pulled harder. This was more fun than killing chickens. He wrapped the cord around his little hands and braced his bare feet and hauled. The man's face went a funny colour. 'Enough, Arnie,' Frankie said. 'They gave me the twenty. Let go now. Quit, Arnie, will you? Stop pulling! Jesus ... Listen: run and tell Maggie to give you some candy!' Arnie dropped the cord and ran.

After that the fame of the lady deputy spread. There was still trouble, but it usually ended as soon as she gave the troublemakers a long, cool look. She levied fines, on the spot. 'Sixty-two dollars total,' she told Maggie. 'Best day yet.'

It was late, and they were in the tavern kitchen, grilling a couple of steaks. Maggie's cook had gone down with food poisoning.

'You're the first person I ever met came from Texas,' Maggie said. 'Around here it's the other way. See an empty farmhouse, it's got 'Gone To Texas' chalked on it.' Maggie forked the steaks and turned them over. 'Wish I'd seen some place except Kentucky.'

'You wouldn't like Desolation. I sure didn't.'

'Well, Rock Springs ain't no Paris, France.'

Doc Brightsides came in, his hands bloody. 'My personal belief is that no such place as Desolation exists,' he said. Frankie looked hard at his hands. 'Accident,' he said, and poured water into a bowl. 'Idiot chopped a side of beef and chopped himself instead. By the time they found me he'd bled to death. Know what his wife said?'

'It's the Lord's will,' Maggie said.

'Correct. A truly desolate thought. Desolation lies between a true believer's ears.' He dried his hands. 'If there's another steak, I'd be grateful.'

'Dunno,' Maggie said. 'Maybe it's the Lord's will for you to go hungry tonight.'

'And if Desolation doesn't exist,' he said to Frankie, 'perhaps you don't even come from Texas.'

'Mind your manners, Doc,' Maggie told him. 'Where people come from is their business.'

'I apologize.'

'Have my steak,' Frankie said. 'I'm too tired to eat. Goodnight.' She went out.

'See what you just did?' Maggie said. They heard her footsteps climbing the stairs, fading to nothing.

'Why would a slick gambler give up the riverboats just as business is getting back to normal?' he asked. 'Why would a smart woman change her name and move to a two-bit town?'

'Who cares?' Maggie forked the steaks onto plates.

'She doesn't fit here. She stands out like a jay-bird in a flock of crows and sooner or later someone's going to blast her tail feathers off, because that's how people act around here.' He sat down and began eating. 'Brains scare them. If it thinks, shoot it. That's their motto.'

Maggie had been tossing wood into the firebox of the stove, but she stopped. 'Now look at that,' she said bleakly. 'Look what I did.' She held up a blackened log. 'This wood has been lightning-struck. I just went and put a piece of it in the goddamn fire.'

'Well?'

'That's bad luck. Now somethin' really bad's gonna happen around here, soon.'

He waved his fork, dismissively. 'It's already happened,' he said. 'It's lying on your plate. Sit down and take your punishment.'

'Ain't funny,' Maggie said. 'Trouble ain't funny.'

ALL SPORTING TRIUMPH
VANISHED

The day before the contest, the pedlar sold Stanton Killick a bottle of Dr Bentley Overstreet's Patent Gargle and Voice Linctus, as supplied to the New Orleans Opera Company. His mother had a sore throat, caused by standing at an upstairs window and shouting at the slaves. The family tried telling her the slaves had left, there were no slaves now. 'Sure, they're smart,' she said, hoarsely. 'Always got an excuse.' She went back to the window. 'I want every last nigger here and be slippery about it!' she bawled. 'You don't whup 'em enough,' she told her family. 'Watch out an' get that old bullwhip ready.'

Sometimes she shouted for Flub Phillips to bring her the money Hudd owed. Once or twice she ordered Joseph to stop hiding. In the end they found it easier to tell her Flub was on his way, or father was out in the fields, giving orders to the slaves. 'He's a good man,' she said, and forgot him for an hour.

Next day, all the Killicks rode on the wagon to Rock Springs to see the fun. The medicine had done Ma Killick's voice so much good, she sent Stanton to buy another bottle. On his way back, he met Doc Brightsides in the crowd. 'This feller Overstreet,' he said. 'Gonna put you out of business soon.'

'May I?' Brightsides pulled the cork and sniffed. 'I wouldn't give that to a sick buffalo.'

'Did Ma a power of good.'

Brightsides raised one eyebrow. He returned the bottle. 'This kind of stuff keeps me *in* business.'

Now Stanton was worried. 'Six bits, that cost me. What's in it?'

'Bad booze, mainly. Apple jelly to thicken it up. Little aniseed to disguise the taste. Most expensive thing you're holding is the glass bottle.'

Ma Killick was eager to continue the treatment. 'Take it easy, Ma,' Stanton warned. 'One spoonful an hour, the pedlar said.'

'Pedlar's a damn fool.' She took a good long pull.

Meanwhile, anvils began flying.

Job Sims had set up the official competition site on a platform of natural rock that blocked the end of the Main Street furthest from the river. Nothing of any value nearby except the graveyard, largely empty. Judge Potter had come over from Downeysville to act as judge of height. He sat in the shade of a chestnut, with a telescope in one hand and a glass in the other. He was not there for sport. An election was coming up, and now half of Dundee County seemed to be in Rock Springs. 'Done a fine job, Job,' he said. 'Is that burgoo I smell?' He aimed his telescope at Amie Kidder, who was holding Devereux's hand. 'Pretty little town,' he said. Sims sent a boy to fetch a bowl of burgoo.

'First contestant ready to fly his anvil, judge,' he said.

'Fly away!' Potter replied. Personally he considered the whole damnfool nonsense to be extremely childish, but if he could sit all day in a comfortable cane chair and shake hands, it was a fine way to do politics. 'Let's see them anvils fly!'

The first explosion turned every head. It began as a dull boom that suddenly and brilliantly expanded into a harsh crack as the top anvil separated and climbed. The climb itself was a marvel: to watch a hulking lump of metal leave the ground, slowly it seemed, almost thoughtfully, turning slightly as if finding its way upwards: there seemed no reason why it should stop: the law of gravity had been reversed in this one special case. For an instant it hung, balanced between push and pull. When it fell, you felt sorry for the ground it was going to hit. Nothing should be hit with an anvil.

Main Street was awash with people; all were still; then the hubbub and the hustling resumed.

'Some bang!' Amie Kidder said. 'They gonna be doin' that all day?'

'Yeah,' Dev said, and spat. 'Ain't much. I heard worse'n that.' He scuffed the spit, and looked around, everywhere except at her, which irritated her.

'You better be nice to me,' she said.

'Or what?'

'Or I won't be nice to you ever again.'

'That so?' He pretended to be slightly amused. 'Well, there's nice, an' ... What comes after nice? *Real* nice, maybe.'

'Maybe. Except I know every person in an' around Rock Springs. Ain't no secrets between us gals. Don't tell me you got another sweetheart, Devereux Killick. Just don't tell me no lies.'

'Rock Springs ain't the whole world.'

'What's that mean?'

'What's it mean?' He looked down at her, and saw with surprise the hurt in her face. 'Why, I guess it means ... uh ... it means you'll have to guess what it means.' He walked off, feeling triumphant, and left her feeling angry and betrayed.

Everybody at the Hudd place wanted to go to town, except Charles. He wanted to clear more land, burn the brush, fell the trees, cut the logs, draw the stumps. He could do it all without help, except for two big horses which heaved on a stump while he chopped its roots. Such work satisfied him, wearied him, helped him sleep. It didn't improve the farm. They already had more land than they could handle.

'Take a holiday,' Mary urged. 'Come with us.'

'Stumps to be pulled.'

'Still be there tomorrow.'

'Might rain tomorrow.'

'You'll miss the fun.'

'Fun?' He rubbed the calluses of one hand with the thumb of the other. That was the most fun he allowed himself, these days.

'Oh well,' she said. 'Get you anything, in town?'

'Axe handles. Get two. Better get three. Not the ordinary kind. I want ...' He clenched his teeth. It would take too long to describe the kind he wanted. Then she'd get it wrong. 'Never mind. Get 'em myself. The wagon ready? I'll lock up.'

'No need for that. Lucy's staying, she'll look after – '

'No! You crazy? Think I'm gonna leave a nigger all alone in my house? She comes with us.'

That was the last word he said until they neared Rock Springs.

Mary and her sons talked easily. Lucy put in her two cents' worth, now and then. Charles drove the rig, boot-faced as a baboon. Half a mile from town, with the bangs getting louder and more startling, Lonzo Hudd came out of the trees and trotted alongside.

'Hey, Lonzo.'

'Hey, Luce.'

'How come you ain't carryin' no anvil, boy?'

'Must of forgot.'

'Where you goin', then?'

'Stackmesser's. Need rifle shells.'

'God speed the plow!' Charles shouted. 'You two gonna yap all the way, you might's well jump up!' Another explosion cracked the morning and made the horses flatten their ears.

~

An anvil climbed high, like a spurt from a geyser; toppled and fell. Its thud reached Maggie and Frankie a half-second later. They were strolling with the crowd, sidestepping potholes and horsedung.

'That foolishness ain't gonna keep these hicks entertained,' Maggie said. 'See one flyin' anvil, you seen 'em all.'

Maggie was right. The crowd wanted more than the spectacle of hunks of iron going up, only to come down. Already there had been several fist-fights, and a couple of minor knifings, and some horse-play with rifles in which The Reverend Hunkin's church bell rang to the hammer of bullets.

'Couple things about you I don't get,' Maggie said. 'You been married.'

'Twice.'

'*Twice.* I ain't never been married once, an' there ain't a whole lot of women west of the Appalachians can say *that*. I seen men chasin' women so ugly they could put the fire out just by lookin'.'

'Nature's way. We're here to breed.'

'What for? So's the next brood can breed some more? Look at all these sorry people. Can't lace their boots without gettin' a headache.'

They turned and strolled back. Frankie said, 'Women make the best friends, I've found, but they ain't dangerous like men, and I get itchy for risk. Know what I mean?'

'No,' Maggie said. 'Why d'you kill that gambler got off the boat with you? You could've shot him in the leg.'

'He grabbed me. I don't like bein' grabbed.'

Maggie laughed. 'Man gets too near you he ends up wed or dead. Dangerous either way.'

Shouts and cheers came from behind the blacksmith shop. The women followed the noise and found a makeshift arena. Reuben Skinner was charging fifty cents for a ride on the back of a large black bull. First man to stay on for twenty seconds wins twenty dollars. The last contestant was being carried away by his friends.

'Internal injuries,' Doc Brightsides said. 'Nothing I can do. I'm waiting for a multiple fracture, that's where the money is.'

'Laze an' gemmen!' Skinner bawled. 'Ay-nuther test of true Ay-merrican grit an' skill!'

The bull was standing, head down, dribbling thoughtfully over a half-chewed turnip, when a horseman cantered into the arena. The contestant stood behind the saddle, holding the rider's shoulders. As they passed the bull, he jumped onto its back. It was neatly done. The bull bucked: a ton of convulsive muscle. The man clung on. The bull put its massive head down and charged, its stocky little legs working hard, and rammed the fence. The man somersaulted out of the ring.

'Five seconds!' Skinner announced. 'Next!'

'I need a drink. Stupidity makes me thirsty,' the doc said.

'That young feller broke his head,' Maggie told him.

'A wise decision.'

What happened next was Cleghorn's horse race. He agreed with Sims on a pause in the anvil-flying and they moved Judge Potter to the finish-line outside Maggie's tavern. Ryan Kidder led six men on horseback down Main Street. They cracked whips and waved hats until the crowd fell back. The race had already started: twenty-seven riders were making two laps of Cleghorn's biggest field.

This took longer than the crowd had patience for, and they edged forward. Boys dared to sprint across the street. Kidder's men hollered and threatened. Still no sign or sound of the race. A drunk came out and tried to dance, and he got picked up and flung back, which was unpopular.

At last the first riders came in view, half-a-dozen, bunched up. It had already been a long race; the horses were heaving and weaving. They took the bend near the anvil platform, and the crowd started to roar, a great gust of primitive noise that startled both horses and riders: it was by far the loudest human sound they had ever heard, and it inspired in them a final, painful effort. Four horses broke free from the bunch but one stumbled and shouldered another and both lost pace. The other two were left to battle stride for stride, each gaining then losing a lead of inches, until all sporting triumph vanished in an instant of human frailty. The crowd surged. A mother's hand was torn from the hand of her small child. The child ran in panic from one stampede of feet and ran straight into another. The horses were too tired to swerve. The child got trampled.

'Hell of a race,' Judge Potter said.

'Hell of a mess,' Cleghorn muttered.

'Yes sir.' Potter was slightly deaf in that ear. He was a good race judge: he had kept his eyes unblinkingly on the horses' heads. 'I got the winner. Never fear.'

Word spread slowly through the crowd. They saw Ryan Kidder standing his horse next to the small body, protecting it as other riders pounded by. *Kid got hurt. Ain't that a shame?* The real shame was it spoiled a good race. Kids act foolish all the time, get themselves hurt, some get killed, that's why the Lord sends big families. Horses are dangerous, everyone knows that. Except kids. Well, here's how they learn, I guess. You see it happen? Me neither. I was watching the winner. Hell of a horse, huh?

The rest of the riders came in, not knowing what had happened, all determined to finish well, what with their friends watching and all. So Main Street still had a big clear space down the middle when the Hudd family arrived. A couple of back markers cantered past their wagon, too blown to gallop. There was nowhere for Charles to pull in, so he kept going, right as far as the landing stage. When he stopped he found himself looking at Ma Killick, sitting in her wagon.

'You owe me big money, Charles Hudd,' she announced. Dr Overstreet would have been proud: her voice could have won a hog-calling contest. 'And you ain't gonna swindle me like you cheated my poor innocent daughter.' Now the hog-calling rasp had got some widow's throb in it. She began to draw a crowd.

'Shut up, Ma,' Stanton said, and reached for the bottle as she raised it. She whacked him in the ribs with her elbow. He had no other arm to grab the wagon and he fell out. The crowd loved it.

She rewarded herself with a swig. 'What is the value of a maiden's honour?' she cried. 'Tell me that, Mr Charles Hudd. You should know. You stole it! And never paid!' The crowd cheered. 'Not a single red cent!' she added.

Hudd and his family were stuck, surrounded by a crowd ten deep, greedy for entertainment. He couldn't respond: any reply would provoke more indignation. What he denied, she would redouble. So he and Mary and the boys sat and suffered. Behind them, Lucy enjoyed watching while folks' troubles. Made a change from scrubbing their sheets. Lonzo enjoyed sitting beside Lucy.

'Well, you had your pleasure, Mr Charles Hudd,' Ma Killick shouted, 'and then you broke my poor daughter's heart.' The crowd booed and whistled. 'Not ...' she began, but they were ahead of her. 'Not a single red cent!' they chanted.

They did it for fun; but still it was a grim experience, to be jeered by a hundred strangers, and Mary Hudd was shaken. She gripped Charles's hand. 'The woman's raving,' he muttered. 'Ignore her.' But his hand was trembling.

'The value of a maiden's honour!' Forget the throat linctus: now Ma Killick was intoxicated by the raw pleasure of public speaking. 'And what is the value of a son's honour, Mr Charles Hudd?' The crowd was silent. Nobody gave a damn for her sons. They preferred the betrayed-maiden stuff. 'A son who saved you from fire, and thieves, and drowning!' Hey, that was better. 'Yet you spurned my son, Mr Charles Hudd! Spurned him too! Where is the reward he earned, the reward you never paid?'

'Not a single red cent!' the crowd roared, and felt pleased with themselves. This was fun.

Lucy was bored. She couldn't join in, and she didn't understand what was going on. Just words, and that damnfool woman waving her arms. Lucy noticed Devereux standing beside the Killick wagon. She gave him a quick little smile, just to say she'd seen him.

Dev had a dollar. He was ready, if she was. He tried to move fast and trod on feet, and got himself kicked.

'Not one red cent! That is how Mr Charles Hudd valued the honour of my son George, who fought and died for the South!' That raised a patriotic cheer, and the cheer brought Ma Killick leaping to her feet. Big mistake. Too much linctus, too much excitement, too much air sucked down the gullet. She got the hiccups. She kept going, aiming her arm and shouting: 'George got killed by Yankees!

Ain't that the truth, Mr Yankee Major Charles Hudd?' Hiccup. Laughter. For a moment she doubted herself. Why weren't they cheering? She blinked, hiccuped, stared, and amazingly she saw exactly what she needed. She saw Lonzo. 'Nigger-lover!' she screamed. 'And there's the nigger-boy he loved, right there!' She pointed at Lonzo. And hiccuped.

Charles Hudd was trying and failing to get his horses moving. Men dodged the hooves and cannoned into other men. Fights started and lurched against the horses, which backed off. Behind the wagons, Devereux was still thrusting towards Lucy. He knew this was not wise but his brains were in his loins and they could think of only one thing and it was black and ripe and just ten feet away.

Ma Killick took some linctus for her hiccups. 'He murdered my Joe,' she announced. 'What's a dead husband worth? Huh?'

But the crowd refused to play her game. Some shouted insults, obscenities. Ma Killick was a sad, sick spectacle, not even a bad joke any more. The melodrama had flopped. Tomatoes whizzed past her head. She hiccuped painfully, looked for Devereux to protect her.

Devereux got his elbows and knees jabbing and punching and he reached the side of the Hudd wagon. He put his hands around his mouth and called: 'I got a dollar! Let's go someplace!' A wildly dangerous thing to do, but Lucy looked like a little black goddess.

'What you say?' she asked.

'Got a dollar!' The wagon was shaking, the crowd was roaring, he got kicked on the knee and nearly fell. 'Dollar! Want my dollar?' Curtis heard that. He turned and saw Dev grinning up at her, and he punched him in the mouth with one fist and on the ear with the other.

Now the air was streaked with tomatoes, a nickel a bushel at that time of year, everyone was sick of them, tomatoes were exploding on both wagons, turning Lucy's white dress into a battlefield. Curtis got his share, standing beside her, aiming to kick Dev in the head, missing and roaring, 'Bastard, bastard, bastard!' Up front, Charles Hudd was using his whip on the crowd, clearing a way out for the frightened horses. His wife, splattered scarlet, was cursing Ma Killick with words that made Floyd gape.

Ma Killick was hiccuping a jerky stream when Dan forced his way onto the seat. 'I won the race, ma! What in hell's name's goin' on? I won the goddamn race! Sit down, for Christ's sake!' A tomato plastered itself over his left ear.

That was when someone bawled, 'Get them niggers!' and the idea was like a breath of fresh air in a dying furnace. Sure, why not? Why bring a bunch of white folks together on such a fine fall day if not to kick the bejesus out of a couple of darkies? 'Get the goddamn niggers!'

It was Stanton shouting, poor one-armed Stanton, couldn't go to the war, got elbowed out the wagon by his ma so people laughed, been bitten in the ear by Hudd's pretty-boy slave, bit so hard he could feel the agony yet. 'Fuckin' niggers!' he told the crowd. The crowd liked that, the crowd got its tongue around that and chanted. Lucy and Lonzo felt hands grabbing, punching, and it scared them. Why had everyone turned on them? Who cared? Wrong colour. Wrong place. Lonzo tried to fend off the blows and failed. Lucy hid behind him, but got hit all the same. No place to hide. Then Charles Hudd's whip finally cracked a hole in the mob and the wagon jumped. The jolt flung Curtis out. He fell on top of Devereux and brought him down. They lay in each other's arms, both half-winded. The wagon bucketed up Main Street, pelted with tomatoes. A little farewell gunfire trimmed leaves from the trees. Ma Killick watched, and hiccuped helplessly. 'For Christ's sake, Ma,' Dan said.

Curtis wheezed until he felt strong enough to drag Dev's knee out of his stomach. 'She ain't worth this,' he said. 'I ain't fightin'.'

'Look, I got two dollars,' Dev said. 'You want one?'

Dan leaned out of the wagon and threw the empty linctus bottle at them. 'Nigger girl's gone!' he said.

'Keep your goddamn money.' Curtis lay on his back in the dirt. 'I can get her for a dozen eggs, any time I want. And eggs are free.'

When Job Sims saw that he had lost much of the crowd to an obscure counter-attraction down by the riverboat landing, he called on the next contestant to fly his anvil, and he crammed an extra handful of gunpowder into the hollow. A big handful. The charge exploded with a *whump* that tossed the anvil clean over the tree Judge Potter was sitting under. The noise spooked Hudd's horses and they nearly ran off the road. He had to stop the wagon and get down and calm them.

'What's the excitement back there?' the deputy asked. She was standing nearby with one foot on the head of a drunk who had been demanding a ride on the next anvil.

'Ma Killick's got the hysterics,' Charles said. 'We're goin' home.'

'They tried to hang these niggers,' Floyd said. 'Killicks did.'

'I heard shots.'

'They were only firin' tomatoes,' Floyd explained. Now it was over, he wanted to go back for more. He liked excitement.

'What these niggers do?' Frankie asked.

'Here come Curtis,' Mary Hudd said. 'Lost his hat.'

'Niggers did what niggers do,' Charles said. 'Say the same about Killicks. They make trouble.'

Another stunning bang, another soaring anvil.

'Sometimes this job ain't worth the money it don't pay,' Frankie said. The drunk squirmed and groaned. 'Shut up or I'll give you what you want,' she told him.

~

The Reverend Hunkin wanted the anvil-flying abandoned before it led to riot and tumult; but as the doctor pointed out, the only casualties had been accidental. Two mule-skinners got into an argument about religion, whether Rome was in France or Spain, and shot each other dead. Judge Potter thought the deceased pair looked familiar, probably wanted for murder or similar, so Rock Springs was now a safer place.

Furthermore, Mrs Dunbar was boiling up a fresh batch of chili, and there was a long string of contestants who had paid their money and if they didn't get a chance to win the anvil-flying prize they would stuff Job Sims with the remaining gunpowder and scatter his parts throughout the county. So the contest went on, and the deputy found the atmosphere relaxed. 'A good hangin' would have settled everyone down nicely,' Maggie told her, 'but they got a picayune shoot-out so they ain't complainin'.'

'Two men dead,' Frankie said.

'Strangers, an' they didn't owe money. Never shoot a man who owes money. That's the golden rule,' Maggie said.

The Anvil-Flying Contest made a profit of thirty-eight dollars and twenty cents for Job Sims.

Morgan Watson made such a heap of money selling burgoo that

he was tempted to quit farming. Elias Dunbar, too, made a killing out of chili. Mrs Dunkerley's fried chicken was so popular that she ran away with a retired horse-doctor passing through on his way to New Orleans, who said she was wasted in this two-bit town. (He bought her a restaurant in the French Quarter; she died, very old and very rich, in the influenza epidemic of 1919.)

Deputy Nickel made good money, over a hundred dollars, from fines. Stackmesser did non-stop business until he wearied of it and shut up shop. Maggie's tavern never closed, of course. Doc Brightsides scarcely had time to wash his hands, and no time at all to wash the blood off the money he collected.

Flub Phillips buried the two mule-skinners, free; but he preached a hell of a sermon over their graves and the crowd passed the hat and he got nearly eleven dollars.

A QUILT MADE BY
AN IDIOT

Old Jake had got a big conch shell from somewhere. He blew a long, grey, mournful sound at odds with the crisp sunshine, and everyone gathered. Conch blows, slaves gather.

Aaron was perched on Moses's shoulder. 'Today we get nuts!' he announced. 'This is the fall, see? Nuts fall! We get 'em before them sonofabitch squirrels.'

He knew the best trees; spreads of sweet chestnut; single walnuts standing huge; ranks of beech; a few hazel; plenty of oak. The walking was long and hard, the pickings were good. Everyone came home with a heavy sack. 'Acorns?' Martha said. 'We got no hogs.'

'Acorn coffee,' Starr Killick said. She was a handsome woman, whipped too much when she was a young field hand and she couldn't hoe her row fast enough; then whipped some more for begging the whipping to stop. Now she rarely spoke. 'Ain't bad coffee,' she said, and ducked her head.

Martha gave a sack of acorns a soft kick. 'Got coffee forevermore here.'

Aaron heard. 'Makes a good porridge too!' he said. 'You soak out the bitterness, you grind up the nuts, you got an acorn-meal you can cook up stuff with, keep out the cold better'n anythin'.'

It rained hard overnight. Next day Aaron was delighted. 'Soft dirt!' he said. 'We go for roots, roots! Before it dries out.'

Luke Corrigan, eating breakfast close to the fire, looked at the mist climbing halfway up the forest and knew it was cold as charity out there. 'Can't see nothin' in that mess,' he grumbled. 'Best wait.'

Aaron was indignant. 'Ain't you never pulled roots? They *slides*

240

out easy after a good rain! Dry roots is got a hold on underneath like a dead man.'

Bonny, the little girl, was impressed. 'That true, Aaron?' she asked. Briefly she forgot to eat.

'Sure it's true. Then when it rains, like now,' Aaron explained patiently, 'that dead man down there gets hisself *drowned*, an' he lets go the roots. You ever seen a drowned person, Bonny?'

'Saw one, in the river.'

'He holdin' anythin'?'

'Just water.'

Aaron led the colony through a couple of miles of dripping woodland to a chalky spur that was mainly grass and thistle, brightened by patches of a yellow flower growing knee-high.

'This here famous plant, called the Sugar-Cake Plant,' Aaron said. 'Parsnippy sort of thing, only better. Ain't gonna take 'em now, 'cus when the frosts nip 'em they tastes right sweet. Look around, remember where to dig. Ain't gonna be no yallery flowers to help.'

Next he led them to a clearing dense with dandelions. 'You lookin' at another real famous plant,' he announced. 'This the Piss-a-Bed plant.'

'Them's fairy clocks,' a child objected.

'Roots go down so far they don't never want to get up,' he said. 'Kinda like Moses in the mornin'.' That got a laugh. 'But now, dirt's kinda slimy, you poke a sharp stick down aside the root, win yourself a yard of Piss-a-Bed every minute.'

They dug sacks of fat white dandelion roots, and moved on to a place where grew what Aaron called Black Bear's Meat, a kind of wild turnip. 'Once you tasted bread made from these beauties, you ain't never goin' back to cornmeal,' he promised. 'Very famous plant.'

'Black bear don't make bread,' Buck lisped.

'Never knew such uppity niggers,' Aaron said.

'Just observin'.'

'Quit observin'. Dig.'

The mist had long since burned off and the ground was drying. On their way home they paused to pick a few wild peas. 'Famous plant called Comanche Gut Glue,' Aaron said. 'Don't eat too many.'

It was a long and heavy trudge. They ate dinner. In the afternoon they went out to pick nuts. That work lasted until sundown.

'How we doin'?' Lonzo asked.

'Not enough.' Aaron said. 'But you knew that.'

～

The visitors left. Rock Springs returned to normal, plus a few anvil-shaped dents. Lonzo went down and bought shells for the rifle. Nobody bothered him.

But the memory of that other day had a gloomy effect on the Hudd Ridge colony. The image of two blacks cornered by a roaring mob was all the more vivid because the others saw it only in their imagination, and their imagination said: saved by a miracle. You couldn't expect two miracles. Josh's nightly prayer meeting grew bigger, lasted longer. Lonzo and Aaron watched from a distance. 'Keep 'em workin',' Aaron said. 'They start thinkin', they'll go stupid in the head. Keep 'em workin'.'

That was the day before Luke Corrigan shot a small stag, and that was the end of old Jake too.

These days, Jake did what he could, which wasn't much. Carrying loads, bending down, any effort made him giddy, made him gasp, made his chest hurt. His eyes were still good. He wandered the woods and looked for stuff that someone else could get: wild honey, ripe fruit, fungus up a tree. Trouble was, his memory. He found stuff, then forgot where. That annoyed him.

He was walking home, trying to remember what he had forgotten, or even *whether* he had forgotten, and getting angrier with himself by the minute, when his path was blocked by a half-fallen tree, and that really maddened him. The goddamn tree hadn't been there an hour ago. He gave it a push, and it wobbled. One hard shove and it would crash flat and he'd step over it. As he shoved he tasted something strange, like iron, only bitter. A rifle fired. Pigeons exploded out of nearby trees and startled Jake so much that he stumbled and tripped and fell on his face.

Little Bonny saw it all. She ran to Martha and told her someone shot Jake. Martha sent Buck to get Lonzo, and she sent Josh to round up everyone else before they got shot too. That way, the whole colony was running up and down, grabbing children and belongings, make enough noise for a hundred, when Lonzo carried the body into the camp and said it didn't have a bullethole in it.

They didn't like that. Made them look foolish. Started a big argument.

'They *scared* old Jake to death,' Bettsy said. 'Shot an' missed an' frightened the life outa him.'

'Who?' Lonzo asked.

'You know who!' Martha said.

'They been here twice already,' Gabe Killick said.

'Tried to gunpowder us out,' Martha said. 'Now they gonna shoot us down, each separate, on his own.'

'Ain't no way we can stop that,' Moses said. 'They got the guns.'

'We got the right,' Lonzo said.

'Old Jake had the right, too,' Bettsy said, 'an' look at him.'

'Jesus!' Lonzo shouted. 'Nobody shot him! Ain't no bullethole! He died natural!'

'Bonny saw. What you see, Bonny?'

'Gun went bang,' Bonny said. 'Jake fell down.'

Nothing is more convincing than the simple words of an innocent child, especially one with no front teeth and a slight squint. Lonzo gave up.

Aaron was nearby, sitting on the Altar. Its bulk made him look even tinier. 'We done all this work, got all this grub,' he shouted at them. 'You just gonna walk out on it?'

'Ain't gonna stay here an' get killed,' Martha said. 'Grub ain't no good when you're shot fulla holes.'

'Ain't no hole in old Jake,' Lonzo said, but he knew they weren't listening; in their minds they were already halfway down the mountain, heading for another Promised Land, they didn't know where, that was tomorrow's problem. He looked up and saw a tall nigger dressed in rags limp so slowly out of the trees that for a moment he didn't recognize Nat. 'Jesus Christ Almighty,' Lonzo said, and went to meet him.

Nat was bad to see. His face was both gaunt and swollen: gaunt from hunger, swollen from blows. There seemed to be damage to every part of his body. Certainly his nose was broken, a couple of fingers too, one eye was milky, scars and scabs and fresh cuts on his legs and arms. He had been a strong, big-built man when he left. Now he couldn't raise his head.

Everyone wanted to know. Nobody wanted to ask.

Aaron sent for hot water and his bags of herbs. Nat sat on a stump. Martha fetched a spare shirt, but Nat didn't want it. Aaron ignored his wish. A couple of tugs, and the rags fell away and Nat's back was revealed. He shut his eyes when he heard the gasps, the sobs. His skin was rumpled and plaited. In some places the furrows were regular as giant corduroy; in others they criss-crossed and bulged and overlaid each other as if scraps of the same giant corduroy had been jumbled together in a quilt made by an idiot.

Gabe Killick was the only one brave enough, apart from Aaron, to come forward and look. 'Salt,' he said.

'Right,' Aaron said, and sighed in pity. 'Even old Jim Crowley never done that to his slaves. First the whip, then salt rubbed in the cuts.' He pushed down the top of Nat's pants. The weals went all the way down to the buttocks. 'Boy,' he said, 'you got a real warm welcome down there, didn't you?' His voice ended croakily. Lonzo looked, surprised. Aaron was crying.

It was many days before Nat spoke; and he never spoke of what had been done to him, or who by, or why. No need to speak: they all knew. Freedom might be the law now, but Hudd Ridge was something else again. Nat's back was a message. Niggers weren't meant to be *that* free.

After that, nobody talked of leaving.

~

'Dan Killick won Hoke's horse race,' Flub said.

'So I heard,' Charles said.

'Of course. You were there. Foolish of me.' They were strolling through the little orchard, collecting windfalls for Flub to put in a sack. 'He won five hundred dollars.'

'Not possible.'

'Had some bets placed. Backed himself to win. And there was prize money.'

'Five hundred.' Hudd spoke as if he had lost the money, rather than Killick won it.

'That ain't all.' Flub hadn't wanted to make this visit, there was no satisfaction to be gained by anyone; but he had a tidy mind. 'I'm told you didn't stay for the end of that anvil-flyin' contest.'

'No, we had to …' Hudd picked up an apple but wasps buzzed out of it so he tossed it aside. 'Now hold hard,' he said. 'You didn't come out here to tell me *that*.'

'Killicks won that prize too,' Flub said. 'Judge Potter said they flung their anvil higher'n anyone, so Dan took the money.'

'And how much did Judge Potter take back?'

'Now, Mr Hudd,' Flub said gently. 'You ain't bein' fair. Judge Potter couldn't take a bribe if his life depended on it. That man's as straight as a dozen arrows.'

'I've seen bent arrows.'

But Flub shook his head. 'Plain simple fact is, there's an election comin' up, and there's Killicks all over this county, hot to vote, so Judge Potter did the decent an' honourable thing. Pure politics. Besides ...'

'There's more?'

'The judge ordered Dan to pay his winnin's into the bank,' Flub said. 'Secured the mortgage. For a while, anyway ...' He stopped because Hudd looked ill: grey about the chops, drained about the eyes.

'That mad old bitch never intended to sell, did she? She put me through all this play-actin' just for her fun, just so she can pull out, make me look stupid. Everyone knows, don't they? Everyone in town knows.'

'Probly. If they don't, they surely will.'

Hudd took a running kick at a half-rotten apple, and it exploded off his boot. 'I blew the arm off her thievin' son, an' I frightened her useless husband to death,' he said, 'and still she hasn't learned. Next Killick tries to fool with the Hudds, I'll shoot him in the cockeyed head, an' that's a promise.'

Flub thought, while Hudd stood and scraped rotten apple off his boot, and finally decided *Ah, the hell with it,* and said, 'That's more or less what Dan Killick wanted me to tell you, Mr Hudd. Only the other way round, naturally.'

He rode home with a sack of apples and a cheese. Not a big commission, but it was more than he'd got from the other party; so he didn't complain.

BEWARE OF FAKE
PROPHETS

Where there is hunger there is no beauty. On a fine afternoon, crisp yet bright, the panther was very hungry. Twice that day he had hunted and lost: first when he chased a muskrat into a patch of fallen timber whose branches were too thick and tangled for the panther to penetrate; and then when he cornered a deer in a blind gulley but the deer leaped the dead end, flew easily onto a rocky place and stood there, trembling, looking down at the panther failing to reach it with jump after jump.

The sad fact was that panthers have strong legs but small lungs. Chasing the deer had left this animal breathless. His lungs were not only small but old, and age was the worst enemy a panther could face. It meant working twice as hard, just to stay alive.

So now he lay in the forked branch of a tree, a big oak, so big that he was lost in the sprawl of its hefty branches. The oak hung over a game trail. Something must use this trail. No more chases. The panther would simply drop. Even his ageing lungs could manage to fall thirteen feet.

He lay in wait so long that the birds forgot him. The forest was full of whistling and cackling and hooting, as usual, so the red fox that finally came padding down the trail heard nothing to alarm it, such as silence.

Only the panther's eyes moved. Less than a meal but more than a snack. The fox was loping along, moving fast. The panther tensed his legs, hooked his claws against the bark, gauged the instant of sudden and massive violence. The fox was only a dozen paces away when a gun went bang, a mile off, and long before its echo answered, the fox was into the undergrowth and gone. The panther retracted his claws and licked his lips. If these new noises went on, he would have to find somewhere else to hunt. This was home and he hated to leave it; but he hated hunger, too.

~

The foliage was brilliant in the fall, but then so it should be. Nobody went around Rock Springs congratulating Mother Nature.

Instead, some people began worrying about their wells. The previous winter had been unusually dry. An occasional rainstorm in spring and summer wasn't enough. The Cameron looked good, but it was fed by streams way up in the mountains, and anyway you couldn't drink the Cameron. On a few farms the wells had begun to bring up brown water.

When the Reverend J. Hubert Hunkin celebrated Michaelmas, he spoke of an impartial God who heard prayers for better weather even as he condemned fornication. 'He maketh his sun to rise on the evil and on the good,' Hunkin said, 'and sendeth rain on the just and on the unjust; Matthew, five, forty-five', and that got a lot of loud Amens. It rained heavily next day. Hunkin was suddenly popular.

Flub Phillips waited until the sun came out, and he preached a corker, standing in the open air with the hot fog reaching his knees.

'Canst thou lift up thy voice to the clouds,' Flub cried, 'that abundance of waters may cover thee?' He aimed his Bible at Hunkin's church. 'Canst thou send lightnings,' he shouted, 'that they may go, and say unto thee, Here we are? Job, thirty-eight, verses thirty-four an' five!' Job was in bad trouble with God again. You couldn't go wrong with the Book of Job. Flub hammered the gathering for a good hour on the sin of pride. 'A living dog is better than a dead lion,' he warned them finally. 'Ecclesiastes, nine, four.' He slammed his Bible and went off to supper, content that he had cut Hunkin down to size.

But it rained hard again that night. The general opinion in Maggie's was that Hunkin's religion was more reliable.

'Easy for Flub to badmouth Hunkin,' Morgan Watson said. 'Flub's well ain't hurtin' like mine is.'

'Dig a deeper well,' Doc Brightsides suggested.

'Ain't got the niggers. No job for a white man, well-diggin'.'

'Maybe, we give old Hunkin five bucks,' Ryan Kidder said, 'he can get God to abolish the goddamn Emancipation too.' Nobody laughed. Ryan sulked.

'Rev. Hunkin told me somethin',' Frankie Nickel said. She was playing ten-cent poker with Stackmesser and Maggie and Dan Killick. 'Told me Stanton got his arm shot off tryin' to save his little sister from old Charlie Hudd. That true, Dan?'

'Sounds true.'

'Ain't,' Job Sims said.

'You callin' Reverend Hunkin a liar?' Elias Dunbar demanded. 'With this rain comin' down straight from heaven?'

'Dan's sister weren't so little,' the pedlar said, 'an' if Chuck Hudd was chasin' her it must've bin to get his pants back.'

Everyone looked at Dan. 'JoBeth was an angel of purity an' innocence,' he said, shuffling the deck. 'Only reason she had Hudd's pants was she was sewin' a button on his fly. Ask Flub. He saw the whole thing through a pair of spy-glasses.' Dan began to deal. 'Red deuces, black queens an' the fourteen of spades wild,' he said. He was a little drunk, but then Dan had inherited the ability to be a little drunk all day.

'Yeah, I'm callin' Hunkin a liar,' Job Sims said. 'Just got to look at him.' He spat a stream of tobacco juice into the open stove, a good ten feet, never touched the sides, created a small convulsion in the fire that caused Hoke Cleghorn, who was dozing, to slide off his stool. 'Look at Hunkin's piggy eyes,' Job Sims said. 'Man ain't natural, you ask me.'

'I knew a feller kept a pet hog,' Ryan Kidder said, loudly. He felt left out: people never asked his opinion like they ought to. 'Right smart, too.'

'What cards did I say was wild?' Dan asked. 'I misremember.'

'That hog was so smart,' Ryan persisted, 'the feller had its picture painted.'

'Last week everyone was bitchin' about the drought,' Elias said. 'Now look. You ought to show more respect.'

'Will someone shut that damn door?' Frankie said. The wind was blowing rain in. Stackmesser kicked it shut.

The talk about a pet hog had stirred Morgan Watson and made him sentimental. 'I miss that old sow of mine,' he said. His voice broke up and he had to wipe his nose on his sleeve. 'She was a real true friend.'

'She bit you, for Chrissake!' Maggie said.

'Affection. She liked me.'

'Hey, Morg,' Ryan said. 'When you gonna cook up some more burgoo?'

Morgan did a strange thing. He took a lot of money from his pocket and spilled it on the bar. 'Drinks all round,' he said, in a thin voice like an old man's. 'Except him.' He pointed at Ryan. Then he picked up the wrong hat and went out.

Maggie scooped the money into a beermug and put it behind the bar. 'You left your brains in your other pants,' she told Ryan. The pedlar cackled. Ryan growled at him, 'You think you're so smart but you ain't. Fact is, I ain't got no other pants.' Everyone laughed. Ryan gave up.

'I been thinkin' about it, and in my experience it just ain't possible,' Hoke said. 'All the years I rode with Kit, I never once saw a man's arm shot clean off.' He looked around to enjoy their appreciation of this. 'Seen a sword do it. Big old axe. Butcher's cleaver. Never a bullet. Bullet drills a hole, that hole ain't enough to dismember the entire limb. So ... Anyone said that boy Stanton's arm got shot off's a liar. Kit would tell you if he was here.'

The door banged, and Reuben Skinner trudged in, well drenched. 'Blacker'n a nigger's armpit out there,' he said. He had fallen in the mud. His hands looked like gloves.

'Wet, huh?' Frankie said.

'Like stickin' your head in the Mississippi.' He shook like a dog, and water sizzled on the stove.

'Reverend Hunkin always gives good measure,' Elias Dunbar said. 'Flub Phillips can't pray hard enough to lay the dust.' But a week later it was still raining as hard as ever, the Cameron was rising, everyone was sick of feeling damp day and night, and always hearing the sluice of water from roofs, and sleeping in clammy beds, and watching food grow mouldy; and the feeling in Maggie's was it was high time to hold another prayer-meeting, and this time Flub Phillips got the vote.

~

Open-air preaching was impossible. Maggie let Flub use the barn that had served as Colonel Noble's Academy of Terpsichore. The

249

place was full. The air was thick with the smell of wet wool, and dull with the drumming of rain.

Flub opened with Jeremiah, eight, twenty: *The harvest is past, the summer is ended, and we are not saved.* ('Hell, that ain't news,' the pedlar muttered.) Later he moved on to Matthew, seven, fifteen: *Beware of fake prophets, which come to you in sheep's clothing, but inwardly they are ravening wolves.* That got a chorus of amens. Finally he got down to serious business with First Samuel, seventeen, twenty-eight: *I know thy pride, and the naughtiness of thine heart.* Flub was hot on pride, and he could name a dozen different kinds of naughtiness before he got you into bed. When he wound up with Romans, twelve, nineteen: *Vengeance is mine, saith the Lord*, and released them, they knew they deserved all they got, and probably more. They had sinned. They admitted their guilt. Now maybe the Lord would see fit to ease up on the goddamn weather.

That night the Cameron flooded its banks. By dawn, it was halfway up Main Street. Briefly, the rain turned to hail. Then it went back to rain again.

It was too wet to get into trouble. Only place to go was Maggie's. Only thing to do was drink, play poker, talk. Talk was cheapest, so a lot of it got done, until just about everyone had said just about all they knew to say, and said it so often the others knew what was coming and knew not to listen because it hadn't been worth the wax in your ears last time around and nothing had happened to improve it since.

The doctor and the deputy were sitting in Maggie's kitchen one night, when the bar had shut. Maggie was making chili; she didn't trust the cook to burn it properly. Frankie was shuffling a deck of cards, cutting the deck, looking at the new top card. Shuffling, cutting, looking. Shuffling, cutting, looking. Endlessly.

'What you looking for?' he asked.

'Life, liberty an' the pursuit of happiness.'

'Interesting.' He didn't sound interested. 'And you left Texas to find them here.' No answer. 'Should we assume,' he said, 'that Texas was a disappointment for you in that respect?'

Still no answer; but she had stopped shuffling the deck.

'Illinois let me down,' he said. 'Should I try my luck in Desolation, Texas?'

'That's a strange word, comin' from you, doc. You ain't in the luck business. Ain't a gambler.'

'Dear lady ...' Brightsides almost laughed. 'You have a very sunny view of medicine. Doctors gamble all the time. We pretend we always win. The truth is, the patient who loses is in no condition to complain, which is just as well, or there would be no brave doctors to do the gambling.'

'Brave?' Frankie said. 'You're in it for the money. Just like I was, on the riverboats.'

'Not enough money in Texas for you?'

Frankie got up and tasted the chili. 'You ain't never gonna be happy until you get my life story, are you?'

'I don't give a damn whose story it is,' Brightsides said. 'Just make it fresh and keep it lively. We got a long winter ahead of us.'

'Tell you one thing about Texas,' Maggie said. 'They put beans in their chili. *Beans*. That's a crime.'

'Born in Baltimore,' Frankie said. 'Over a butcher shop. Not a smart way to start, and it got worse.'

'Wouldn't mind livin' in Baltimore,' Maggie said.

'Fine an' dandy. You tell the damn story.' But Maggie waved her big iron spoon, signalled no, no; and Frankie took a run at it.

Frances Stott Fluck was her born name. She always hated it. The Fluck part was her father's fault and he was no damn good at anything else either, being a poor butcher who didn't understand meat. When she was six he ran off with a circus acrobat, female. Mrs Fluck sold the shop, paid the debts and had enough for fares to Galveston, Texas, where she had a sister. Once. No longer. The sister had moved away.

For the next ten years Mrs Fluck washed other people's clothes. As soon as she was big enough to handle the heavy flatirons, Frances did the ironing, hour after hour, every day, all year round. The leathery slap of wet laundry, the heavy smell of soap, the perpetually clammy air: years of confinement at hard labour, punishment for the crime of poverty. At seventeen she was tall and strong, thanks to years of slamming flatirons about, and she escaped. She married a cheerful bricklayer and moved out. When she was nineteen he fell off a ladder, smashed a leg, and died of clumsy surgery. A year later she married Douglas van Orman, changed her first name to Charlotte for good measure, and went to live in San Antonio.

He was a lawyer. He was addicted to the law, couldn't get enough of it. Successful lawyers know enough law to win and they stop there. Douglas made such long and detailed presentations to the court that he bored the backside off everyone, especially the jury. His career, and the marriage, were going to hell when his father came to the rescue. He died.

Old man van Orman left them a dry-goods store a hundred miles away, in Desolation, Texas. They went to look at it. Desolation wasn't much of a town. It had no law business to speak of. The store was no more exciting than the town. Douglas quickly decided to sell up, sell out, get back to San Antonio. He cut every price by half. A land boom was going on in that part of Texas and it was a seller's market even before he cut the prices. Very quickly, half the stock sold out. This pleased Douglas. While he was wondering how to get rid of the other half, he left his wife in charge of book-keeping and all the tedious paperwork. Secretly, she re-ordered all the stuff that was in hot demand.

When this new stock began to arrive, he was so enraged that she locked herself in her office. He smashed open a crate of pistols, loaded one and fired four shots at the door. A customer who was waiting to buy rope asked him the price of the gun. 'Twenty bucks!' Douglas shouted.

'Give you thirty bucks for two.'

'Done!'

'Forty for three.'

'Sold.'

Charlotte escaped through a window and went for a walk. When she came back she showed him their accounts. The store had made more in a week than he earned from the law in two months. What's more, they could sell the pistols for only thirteen dollars each and still show a profit. 'Do it again,' she said. 'Good advertising. And cheap.' Next day, Douglas lost his temper, and accused his wife of giving away goods at insane prices. She fled into the office. He grabbed a gun and fired shots into the door. 'Bankrupt!' he roared. 'You'll make us bankrupt!'

It was an act. Or was it? Douglas always sounded furious. Anyway, it spiced up the shopping and maybe there really were great bargains to be had at Mad Doug's, which was what people called it. He opened branch stores in nearby towns. Mad Doug's became Mad Dog's. Occasionally he would burst into a branch, interrupt a sale and denounce the manager. 'These prices are killing me!' he would cry. 'If I go, you go!' He would force the manager at gunpoint into his office. Shots would be heard. Douglas always came out, apologized to the customer and gave him the goods free. It was crazy but it was good for business. In twenty years he built up Mad Dog's Dry-Goods Stores until they monopolized that whole stretch of Texas. He was good at running a hardware empire, and he enjoyed it. Liked the fame, success, wealth.

The van Ormans stayed in Desolation. Built a big house, raised a family. Could have moved to Austin or Houston; but Douglas was smart enough to stay close to his customers. Besides, nobody challenged him in Desolation. It might be a heap of nothing but he was king of the heap. And he travelled a lot. Speculated in land. In women, too.

Charlotte knew. One month he had a pecker like a policeman's truncheon, the next it was worn down to a corrugated stub. Business worries, he said. But she still kept the books, she knew the profits. The war was over, not that it ever troubled south Texas a whole lot. Trade was good. 'Business worries my ass,' she said at long last, one night when she was angry because he hadn't made the effort to think up a new excuse. 'Listen to me, Doug. I know the score. Now you know I know the score. Just make damn sure everyone in Desolation don't know it too. Now goodnight.'

The bare fact of that statement left her sleepless and miserable. Next day he was gone again, another business trip, and the house was empty, the children away at various schools, and her loneliness became unbearable. She went to see her new neighbour, not long arrived from Nashville. Name of JoBeth Killick.

'God stone the crows!' Doc Brightsides cried out. 'As my dear old drunken daddy used to say.'

'This before or after she died in Louisiana?' Maggie asked.

'Ma Killick has a knack of spicin' up the conversation with a new death in the family,' Frankie said. 'Could be true, could be ramblings. Ain't for me to say. You want to hear more?'

The Nashville Killicks had left Tennessee about two years ago, to get away from the fighting. JoBeth didn't go with them, said she reckoned Tennessee was as safe as anywhere, stayed in the farm. They took everything, cattle, carts, horses, farm equipment, bedding, guns, slaves; and they walked all the way to Texas. They bought the farm next to the van Orman place. Big mistake. Everything was different in Texas: crops, climate, cattle, methods, market. The farm never made a nickel.

Then the war ended and JoBeth appeared. She'd been wrong about Tennessee being safe. The farm there was a battlefield. She'd ridden from Nashville, arrived just in time to see them sell the equipment and the slaves – the Union said slavery was finished, but it took a long time for news to reach Desolation, and even longer for people to believe it. Nobody wanted the farm. They gave it to JoBeth and moved to Baton Rouge, Louisiana. If she sold it, she could keep half.

She couldn't sell it, so now she had half of nothing to live on.

Charlotte van Orman didn't believe in charity, but she didn't enjoy solitude either, so she rented a few fields from JoBeth. They both knew what was happening. It was just money. No big deal.

They became good friends. She liked JoBeth's spark and candour. Her own children were affectionate but dull, doomed to wed and breed and age and die in bed, and she wished she'd had JoBeth as a daughter. 'Doug's cattin' around all over south Texas,' she said.

'Leave him,' JoBeth said.

'Way I feel, either I'm the housekeeper or he's the lodger, I don't know which. Maybe both.'

'You heard me. Leave him.'

'Ain't as easy as that. This is Texas. A woman can't get divorced unless her man rapes the governor's daughter inside the Alamo.'

They kicked it around, but she knew she wasn't ready to leave Doug, not with more than half her life invested in the marriage. Maybe all this catting-about would pass. A man turns forty, suddenly discovers he's mortal, gets desperate to prove something, as if the grim reaper was around the corner waiting to cut off his thing with the scythe. 'Don't know why I fret,' she said. 'Most days I'd as soon have a good rump steak.'

'It ain't what you're *not* havin',' JoBeth said, 'it's what somebody else *is* havin'. That's what hurts.'

Charlotte worried, on and off, during the following weeks and months. Some days she disliked going into Desolation in case she caught the tail-end of a pitying glance or heard a conversation cut short as she passed. At home, Doug acted much the same but looked older. Suspicion was corroding: sometimes she shook with fury at the thought that he might be making a fool of her. Trouble was, she could prove nothing. Then she got a letter. All it said was *Redondo*.

Standish Hotel. Room 10. Today's date. No signature.

Redondo was twelve miles away. On a clear day you could almost see the Standish from Desolation. That's what made it insulting.

She took a pistol and a horse and she was in Redondo within an hour. She was not thinking; done too much thinking already. Desk clerk said good afternoon. Two old men playing checkers, slamming and cursing as if they were both losing. She pounded along the corridor and kicked open the door to room ten and saw Doug's bare ass and part of his head while the rest of him was covered in a tangle of bedsheets and she shot him and he shuddered and rolled over. Who was under him she didn't know or care, she kept shooting bullets until the gun was empty and the room stank of fumes. 'You knew the score,' she said. That was when JoBeth came out of the bathroom, wearing nothing and carrying a glass of water and a pillbox. 'Ain't gonna shoot me, are you?' she asked. Much of the water was getting spilled.

'I killed *him*,' Charlotte said. 'Why not *you*?'

'He was dead. You didn't kill him. His heart quit on him. He felt bad an' asked for his pills an' before I could get outa bed, he went an' died on me.' They stared at each other, one dripping water, the other raising smoke. 'There wasn't no pulse left at all. No breath. Nothin'.'

'That bastard.' Charlotte felt as if she were high above her body, watching this whole impossible scene. 'He cheated me right to the end.'

'He was pumpin' too hard,' JoBeth said. 'I told him to slow down, take it easy, he wouldn't listen.' Already the sheets were more red than white.

'Why fetch his pills?'

'Dunno.' She sipped what was left of the water. 'Had to do *somethin'*, an' ...' There was noise in the corridor, shouts and banging on doors. 'Hey, you're in trouble! Get out. Bathroom window.'

Charlotte got out and got away. She did not hurry home. There was no telegraph between Redondo and Desolation, the desk clerk probably hadn't recognized her, and in any case her horse was leg-heavy, couldn't make more than a trot. This gave her time to think.

She hadn't killed Douglas but she had murdered him. In her mind she had murdered him. The law would call it murder, unless the law believed JoBeth. Charlotte didn't know how much she believed

255

JoBeth herself. It could happen: her doctor had told her he'd been called more than once to prise the stiffening corpse of a husband from on top of his wife, and sometimes she wasn't his wife. Doug had always been the runaway-locomotive type of lover. No surprise if his boiler exploded on the up-grade.

No remorse. No pity, either. Doug knew what sort of woman she was. Had he really expected her to get on with her quilting while he made a public fool of her? He thought he was such a stud, when he was just a stiff prick on legs. As to JoBeth … She felt betrayed but it didn't matter because the woman was already in the past, like every-one else she'd known. The instant she pulled that trigger, Charlotte knew she'd blown away the first half of her life and started on the second.

It was dark when she got home. They had no live-in servants and the children were elsewhere. She packed only what she could carry in one bag and she collected all the money in the house. She turned loose all the animals and saddled the best horse and went down to the original Mad Dog's store and emptied the safe. She went back home, set fire to the house and rode away. An hour later she could still see the blaze, pulsing red and yellow on the horizon.

'So that was goodbye Desolation,' Doc Brightsides said. 'What an interesting case … On the face of it, you as next-of-kin stand to inherit everything. Assuming you survive the trial, of course. But a smart lawyer –'

'Yeah, sure. All the smart lawyers in Texas are men, and nine out of ten of them are cheatin' on their wives. They ain't anxious to see a miserable precedent like mine interfere with their horny lives.'

'Two husbands gone,' Maggie said. 'I can't find 'em, you can't keep 'em. Jeez.' She went back to chopping onions.

'JoBeth?' Doc asked. Frankie just looked at him as if he were a small boy who had broken wind. 'Sorry,' he said. 'I guess we can deal her out of the game. Not your concern. Probably in Mexico.'

'You set the house on fire,' Maggie said. 'Big house, right? Texas Rangers, or whatever the hell passes as law down there, maybe they thought you got all burned up inside it.'

'Empty safe.'

'Oh. Forgot that.'

'So now you're on the run,' Brightsides said. This was turning into an entertaining story.

'I moved fast,' she said. 'Rode to the Gulf, took a ship to New Orleans, but that was still too close to Texas for my likin'. Mississippi seemed like a good place to hide. Thousand miles of river and then some. Add in all the other rivers feedin' into it, big enough to take a steamboat, must be twenty or thirty of them.'

'More,' Brightsides said.

'Nobody owns the Mississippi. Good place to hide. I went on the riverboats. Had to make a livin', so I found an old retired gambler to teach me poker. Figured I could get good enough to pay my way. Figured wrong. Lost my stake. That's when I got real serious about poker, when I knew if I didn't win I didn't eat. *Then* I got good.'

'Good enough to cheat?' he said.

'Good enough to know who else was cheatin', and how. I never went hungry. Stayed good for a few months, every day dealin' cards, dealin' cards, dealin' cards. In the end, trapped on a boat, might as well be in jail. Then I remembered Rock Springs. The way JoBeth used to talk about it, nobody was gonna find me there. Rock Springs sounded like Desolation with extra mildew.'

'We ain't got mildew,' Maggie said. 'That's a damn lie.'

'Remarkable story,' Brightsides said.

'Some of it's true,' she said.

'We got tobacco blight,' Maggie said. 'That ain't mildew.'

'I don't suppose you remember the name of the pills?'

'Magic exploding gunpowder pills,' Frankie said. 'Made double-strength for Texas.'

'Anyway, you can't help but get mildew here,' Maggie said, 'way it rains.'

'Which bits are true?' he asked.

'Well, probably none of it,' Frankie said, 'except Galveston. Stay away from Galveston. It makes Desolation look like Paris, France.'

'I bet they got mildew in Paris, too,' Maggie said. It annoyed her when people looked for bad things to say about Rock Springs.

REPUBLICAN WEATHER

Canada had more winter than it could handle that year. The Canadian blizzards swung south and crossed the Great Lakes and buried Minnesota and Wisconsin, Michigan and Ohio, New York and Pennsylvania. Nothing new about that. Then the storms surged again, and left Illinois and Indiana all white, even great stretches of Virginia. Well, people expected that kind of thing. But Kentucky? Kentucky was the gateway to the South. Kentucky didn't deserve that brutal, frigid, *Republican* weather. Nevertheless, its people smelled the raw edge of incoming bleak air that had travelled a thousand miles from Ontario and Quebec, and they looked out their extra blankets. Those without thick underwear got warm by sawing logs for burning. Most didn't saw near enough. Kentucky shivered from Thanksgiving to Easter.

Up on the Ridge, the panther hunted through the whine and groan of naked trees. His eyes watered until the fluid formed a yellow crust. This had nothing to do with the cold wind. The panther was diseased.

That's why he went hungry. When he found something worth the chase – and that was not often, with every animal hiding against the cold – his legs did their best but at the instant of kill his eyes betrayed him. At close range they couldn't focus on the racing zigzag of a rabbit, and the panther's jaws snapped on air. If he was lucky he ate mice and squirrels. If he was really lucky he found the remains of something another predator had killed, a part of a bird perhaps. Once he blundered against a tree so rotten that it fell, and he feasted on the insects in its core. That was a rare luxury. In two months he lost thirty pounds, and he was gaunt and stiff when he saw the elk.

Snow was falling. Six or seven elk were scraping and snuffling, searching for good grass. In a freeze like this, elk meat would stay eatable for a month. A fat month might just help him live through the winter.

He circled downwind and stalked them. Belly-down, and moving by slow inches, he was coated with snow everywhere except his amber eyes.

He chose one of the small elk. It was still five or six times heavier than he was, which promised plenty of food. The trick was to rush it, hit it with such speed and force that it fell, and then get the teeth in its throat. So he dug his claws in the snow and bunched his muscles and charged, and the elk turned out to be a young bull with fine eyesight and instant reflexes. It glimpsed the attacker, whirled, shoved its antlers forward.

The panther swerved. As the elk magnified, the panther's eyes lost focus and his target blurred. The point on an antler hooked his shoulder and ripped out six inches of skin and muscle. He skidded, spraying blood, and came straight back for a second attack. The damaged shoulder made him lopsided, and he missed, and the young bull got in a couple of good raking slashes on the neck and right foreleg. The rest of the herd had gone. The bull followed them. The panther chased it and ran smack into a snow-covered rock, invisible to his sorry eyes. His lower jaw was broken; teeth were hanging loose.

He dragged himself back to a cave. Clumsy, agonizing scraping and tugging with his claws got rid of the dangling teeth, but he couldn't hunt and he couldn't eat. Five starving weeks later, still in the cave, he died.

Some miles away, the Hudd colony had their own ways of keeping warm and staying alive. These didn't all work too well. Some didn't work at all.

'Got to keep 'em movin',' Aaron said to Lonzo.

'It's this damn wind. They ain't got the clothes.'

'They could of made clothes. Warned 'em, didn't I?' Aaron sat with two entire buckskins wrapped around him, and sipped foxglove tea to strengthen his hiccuppy heart.

'One or two pretty well give up already,' Lonzo said. 'Starr Killick there. Just lies in her cabin, don't speak, don't cook, can't keep a fire goin'. She think Santa Claus gonna come along, save her?'

There were others like Starr: a Corrigan called Charlie, slow as cold molasses in body and mind; Martha Hudd's aunt Jenny, twisted in the legs so it hurt to walk; others. Lonzo patrolled their cabins and urged everyone to move, collect wood, hunt, get out, do *somethin'*. They said yes, sure, when the sun comes up. The wind whistled low through big cracks in the cabin walls like it had bad news to deliver, which in several cases it did.

The first to die were an old man and woman called West and Matty. Never said much: did their share, took their needs and went off to their little cabin to sleep. Next morning their panther door was still in place. Moses and Buck used an axe to smash their way in. A thin, grey smoke wandered out. West and Matty were in their bed and everything was coated with sticky black smuts: walls, floor, bed-clothes, faces.

Gabe Killick found the killer inside the stone-built chimney. A rock had fallen and blocked the air-space. Smoke had filled the room, filled the lungs.

They buried the couple at noon, alongside old Jake's grave, every-one watching.

'Make it short, Josh,' Lonzo said. 'The Lord ain't gonna thank you for keepin' Him waitin' in this cold.'

'Our friends have crossed over the river Jordan an' entered the Promised Land, that's God's truth, bless their souls, amen.' Josh took a shovel and dropped dirt in the grave. 'I was gonna say a piece about sinners an' the roarin' lakes of brimstone in hellfire, but I reckon I'll save that for summer.'

As the grave filled, Martha said, 'Somebody ought at least say a thing about poor West an' Matty.' Everyone looked at Lonzo. 'Last chance,' Martha said.

'Well, they never did nobody no harm, least not as I heard,' Lonzo said. 'Only ever stole from white folks. Never got drunk 'cept Christmas time. Matty made good griddle cakes, until she got the rheumatiz bad in her fingers. West ... ' Lonzo scratched his head. 'West used to have an old banjo, got bust somehow. Never could play it. Guess it's in the cabin.'

Aaron nagged them into digging more graves before the ground froze rock-hard. He wanted six but all he got was three. They went back to the camp and set fire to West and Matty's cabin. The blaze was wonderful, but there was no comfort in being roasted on one side and chilled on the other. People drifted off to their cabins. By the middle of the afternoon it was snowing again. 'Shit,' Aaron said.

'Wrong colour,' Lonzo said. Another day, Aaron might at least have smiled. Not this day.

West and Matty had had their time. Little Katie Killick, Starr's daughter, was not yet three years old.

One day, mid-December, dazzling sunshine and a sky like blue heaven got everybody outdoors, all busy, meeting, gossiping. Little Katie toddled off, singing slave songs she didn't understand the words of, toddled a good mile and found a frozen pond. By now Starr was searching the camp. Ice looked pretty, but it was thin. Katie splashed and cried so hard that within two minutes she was exhausted; within four minutes, unconscious. After ten minutes, only the shattered ice told a story. The search widened, and widened. Gabe came by, saw the ragged hole and waded in. The shock of the cold made his head buck and his heart pound, but he smashed the ice with his fists and found the body.

Starr Killick never spoke a dozen words in a week. So people listened when she went to Josh and said, 'You ask the Lord why He done this to my Katie. You ask. He don't talk to folks like me.' Josh nodded. He knew when he and God were beat, both.

And Starr was beat, too. It seemed nothing she ever did was good enough. She didn't weep: all the tears had been whipped out of her, long ago. She sat in her cabin. Didn't go to the burial. Just quit.

'Them fuckin' Killicks done that,' Aaron said. 'Killed her with the fuckin' bullwhip.'

'Ain't no reason to *die*,' Lonzo said. Aaron looked at him with deep contempt. 'Don't know one goddamned thing, do you, sonny?' he said. 'Don't know, an' can't learn.' Aaron was feeling bad. He had a flighty fever. From time to time a brutal pain flared in the gut, a pain that would have crippled him if Joe Killick hadn't already done that with a hammer, one of the rare occasions Joe Killick had used a hammer in his whole life. 'Know what's wrong with these niggers?' Aaron demanded.

'Nothin' wrong,' Lonzo grunted. 'Need small piece a luck is all.'

'Luck?' Aaron spat. There was blood in the spit, so he did it again to show he didn't care. 'Black bastards wouldn't know piece a luck if it was rainin' silver dollars. What's wrong is they got fancy ideas what they're worth. Look at that Charlie Corrigan, there.'

Lonzo looked. Charlie was sharpening an axe with a stone, gently, in case he wore them both out, and stopping often to hitch his pants up.

'That fool was worth maybe a thousand bucks to old Mrs Maud Corrigan,' Aaron said. 'Thinks he still is. Look, there.' Charlie hitched his pants up. Aaron scoffed. 'Ain't worth a nickel now, Charlie ain't. Can't keep his pants up. Know why? Charlie's waitin' for some white-man boss to get mad an' say *Charlie! Go get some goddamn twine an' tie them dumb nigger pants up afore I whop you!* These niggers carry their brains in their pants ... Look! Look! He done it again!'

'You ain't worth no thousand bucks yourself,' Lonzo said. 'Sittin' an' bitchin' an' countin' the number a times Charlie Corrigan hitches his pants. Reckon that's worth a nickel? Ain't worth mine.'

'Difference between Charlie an' me is, come spring I aim to be here an' bitchin' still, if there's anyone left to bitch to.'

'Well, I aim to be here, too.'

'Yeah.' Aaron blinked as the sweat of fever trickled into his eyes. 'You, you're part-Indian. Take a lightnin' strike to kill *you*. Charlie ain't got the brains to live, you ain't got the brains to die.' Lonzo was flattered, and Aaron could see it. 'Stinkin' murderin' Pawnee,' he growled. 'I'd swap the entire heathen Pawnee tribe for one swaller of good corn liquor.'

'Sweet Jesus, Aaron, I ain't no Pawnee!' Now Lonzo was insulted. 'My daddy was a full-blood Cherokee warrior!'

'Yeah? Go an' kill Charlie, then. Go scalp the sonabitch. Look, he's hitchin' his pants *again*!'

'Seems to me, you're hotter on killin' than anyone.'

'I got wolverine blood in me. Wolverines eat coupla Cherokee for breakfast.' Aaron threw a rock at Charlie, but his arm was weak and Charlie didn't even notice. 'Bastard,' Aaron said. Sweat ran down his face and neck like a spring shower, but the air was wintry and his head and shoulders were shuddering with cold. He reached in his bag of herbs and took a handful of dried wild rose-hips. 'Grind 'em down, make a tea thick as paint. If that don't cure me I deserve to die.'

Aaron didn't die, although he couldn't speak for weeks on end and all his hair fell out. Jake's widow died, an old frail creature who had always been his shadow and now she couldn't even be that, so she gave up. A little boy called Tom probably got the consumption. He coughed his life away. Martha's aunt Jenny slipped in the mud, bust her arm, poisoned it and the swelling just spread and spread, two days and she was gone.

Who else? Charlie Corrigan had malaria and went strange in the head, climbed on the Altar, said the angel Gabriel was coming with a ladder reaching up and down from heaven. Josh stood in the pelting rain and told Charlie it was Jacob had the ladder, not Gabriel, and anyway why not come inside and wait in the dry? Charlie squatted on the Altar, shirt so wet you could count his ribs, and explained all over again about Gabriel. Josh said there was food inside. Charlie said Gabriel was bringing fried chicken and cornmeal dumplings with snap beans. Josh gave up. Buck and Moses and Lonzo dragged Charlie down, but he went back in the night, and he was dead by breakfast.

The young, the old and the sick: winter on the Ridge reaped its harvest.

A bad winter drove wild beasts down off the mountain. Well-known fact.

Elias Dunbar saw a panther, ten feet long, skulking around his place when he came home one night, and it sobered him up so fast he went back to Maggie's tavern and told them. Next morning he found bear tracks near his outhouse. Panther *and* bear! Elias was so scared he nearly went to church. Instead he went to Stackmesser's store and nearly bought a big steel bolt to lock the outhouse door. 'What you afraid of?' Stackmesser wanted to know. 'Ain't nobody stole a bucket of shit in Rock Springs since eighteen twelve.'

Elias put his money back in his jeans. 'Four bits is too much,' he said. 'Reckon I'll ride to Barber's Landing and get it cheaper. Them peanuts look kinda cheesy,' he added.

'Some folk like 'em cheesy.' But Stackmesser knew he'd lost. Elias went home and whittled a bolt from hickory wood. His son, Billy, asked him what it was for. 'Keep bears out of the outhouse,' Elias told him.

'You aim to put it on the outside or the inside?' Billy asked. His father, forced to think, couldn't decide. 'Only a fool like you'd ask a stupid question like that,' he said. 'Go chop some logs.' Billy went. Elias brooded on the problem, and eventually threw away the piece of hickory. He got his rifle and went bear-hunting. Saw no bear, shot a raccoon near the river instead. Raccoon looked kind of like a bear cub anyway.

THE PENNSYLVANIA
RIFLES

In December the skies turned to blue, frost struck, and mud turned to iron.

By day the sun smiled as if life was wonderful, but the sun could afford to smile, it didn't have to live in Rock Springs. By night the freezing air bit deeper into the ground.

In January, Ryan Kidder had to use a big felling axe to chop turnips out of the ground, to help feed his cows. He loaded a wagon with turnips, which took him all afternoon, and it was dusk when he drove home across a ploughed field that was so hard, the wheels didn't even dent the furrows. The horses' nostrils pumped steam like locomotives.

He opened the big barn doors, worrying about how to thaw these turnips, they were like cannonballs, and the horses backed the wagon into the gloom without waiting to be told; they knew, they'd done it a thousand times. He unharnessed them and they walked away to their stable, firefly-sparks coming off the steel shoes.

Ryan threw the tack across an old sawhorse and turned to go out and shut the doors, and saw two men do it for him. Now they were inside the barn and it was dark as tar. Ryan was too amazed to be afraid. 'Open them doors!' he said, but nobody moved or spoke, and he knew it was a stupid thing to have said: they weren't going to open a door they'd just closed, for God's sake! *Now* he felt fear. He held his breath and heard men breathing. Still nobody spoke. Ryan wanted to shout, and clenched his jaws till the muscles ached. He tried to think. Didn't know *what* to think. Longer he stood, less he could move.

This lasted for a bad minute. Then his daughter Amie said, 'Open up the smokehouse, Pa.' That was the first he knew she was there.

Ryan always kept the smokehouse locked. He fetched the keys. Six men were waiting, all in hats and long coats, with scarves to the nose and ears. Well, it was freezing; but when they lit a lantern, Ryan got a glimpse of black hands. Nobody spoke. They filled burlap bags with hams, venison, mutton legs, cheeses, dried fish, pork bellies, a couple of small beef joints. Ryan folded his arms and shivered and watched his year's work being carried into the night. He didn't hear the last man come up behind him and knock him cold. He didn't know he'd been knocked cold until he woke up with his mouth in the dirt, and tried to stand, and he vomited over his hands.

Amie was unharmed. She was waiting in the barn, as the raiders had told her to do. Mrs Kidder was in the house, sewing, unaware that her winter larder had gone.

Ryan took a drink of corn liquor and his stomach sent it straight back, along with the rest of his dinner. He felt better now he was quite empty. Shaky but better.

He locked the women in the house and rode into town.

'You ain't the first,' the deputy told him. 'There's Reuben Skinner, farms way out beyond Cleghorn, he's along with Doc Brightsides now, gettin' his head mended. Took him all day to get out of the barn they locked him in. How many you reckon they was?'

'Ten, maybe a dozen. I fought 'em but – '

'Big niggers? Tall?'

'Yeah. Big *and* tall.' Ryan was angry because they were sitting calmly in the tavern, eating supper, while his head throbbed like Indian war drums. Ryan had never heard war drums but Hoke Cleghorn had said plenty about them, and Hoke knew. 'Hate to spoil your steak,' he said, real hard, which made her eyes widen, 'but them black heathen savages is *out* there, raidin' an' rampagin'.'

'Rampagin',' Frankie said, as if it was a brand new word. 'Rampagin', huh?'

Ryan looked at the steak, and his stomach made a noise like a distant avalanche. 'You ain't gonna raise a posse,' he said.

'To hunt a bunch of niggers in the night? Hell, no. You can't say which way they went, an' the ground's so hard a herd of buffalo wouldn't leave a trail. I'll think again in the mornin'.'

The usual crowd of drinkers had been listening with interest.

'Don't need no stinkin' trail,' Stanton Killick said. 'We know where them thievin' niggers come from. I say we go up an' smoke 'em out!'

It had to be ten degrees colder on top of the Ridge, maybe more. Someone had reported seeing wolves. Ryan said he'd been robbed by a dozen big niggers, but Ryan had been whacked on the skull. Maybe there were twenty. And now Stanton was drunk, so drunk that when Elias Dunbar suggested Stanton go ahead and light a fire on the Ridge for the rest to aim at, Stanton lurched towards the door and had to be tripped by the pedlar, who got into a fight with Dunbar. Maggie threw them both into the street. 'Gettin' too old for this,' she grumbled. 'Next time anyone sees a bunch of big bad niggers, send 'em here. They can do the chuckin' for me.'

'Ain't funny,' Ryan said.

'Neither are you. Nothin's funny today.' Maggie's knees were on fire. Rheumatism was real. Nigger bandits were just shadows in the night.

~

Next morning the deputy tried to raise a posse.

Reuben Skinner said his farm had been attacked by a swarm of blacks, at least forty, maybe fifty; but Reuben was still seeing double and jumping at loud noises, both feet clear off the ground. If the raiders were as strong as Ryan Kidder said, she would need at least twenty men. By noon, twelve had gathered at the landing stage. Soon it was nine: Sims, Dunbar and Stackmesser disappeared. Dan Killick went looking for them. After a while, someone offered to go and look for Dan. Little Arnie Phillips came by with a jug. Dan had sent him to get beer at Maggie's. Dan was eating dinner with Frank Stackmesser.

The remains of the posse trailed back to the tavern. 'All I got is eggs an' fried taters,' Maggie said. 'You want ham an' sausage, go up the Ridge, I hear they got the best.'

'Get our fool heads blown off,' Elias Dunbar said.

'It seems highly unlikely the raiding party is on the Ridge,' Doc Brightsides said. 'They must know it's the first place you'd look.'

That annoyed and confused them. Hutton the sharecropper said he was ready to risk his life but who would take care of his family if he got killed? Ryan said he wasn't scared and Elias Dunbar said hell, no, none of them was scared, but all the same why not send to Barber's Landing for extra men? Hoke Cleghorn wanted to say something about using Indian tracking scouts but it got lost in the uproar. 'Let's vote on it,' Ryan said, just as Stackmesser came in. 'Vote on what?' he said. 'You ain't part of this,' Reuben Skinner told him. 'You're too damn busy feedin' your face.' Stackmesser was full of beer and he hit Reuben, hard. The bandages fell off and blood ran like spilled wine. Maggie and Frankie grabbed Stackmesser and hustled him back outside, and met Job and Dan. 'Where's the posse?' Dan asked. 'We been waitin' along at Frank's place.'

'Go back to Texas, honey,' Maggie said to the deputy. 'Let the damn niggers kill these dumb crackers if they want.'

'Listen,' Job said. 'Dan reckons we ought to get paid.'

'I got a nickel,' Frankie said. 'You got change?' They didn't understand her. 'What for?' Job asked. That was when Maggie said, 'Jesus ... Here comes the U.S. Cavalry.'

A troop of mounted soldiers had appeared at the end of the street. The frozen mud was covered by a thawed skin that made it slick, and the horses picked their way carefully, until a sergeant called a halt about twenty yards away. He dismounted and walked forward, a neat and stocky man in a uniform whose blue was weather-faded and spotted with dried mud. He looked about forty, and he looked tired; but he had shaved recently and all his buttons were done up. When he saw the star on Frankie's buckskin coat he was surprised, but she was accustomed to that, and he looked her in the eyes as he saluted, which was more than some men could do. 'Sergeant Bennett W. Payne, ma'am,' he said. 'Fourteenth Pennsylvania Rifles.'

'Deputy Frank Nickel. Sheriff's out of town.' They shook hands. 'Glad to see you. *Damn* glad. I'm tryin' to raise a posse, but ...' She shrugged.

'Niggers been troublin' you?' Sergeant Payne said. 'Stealin' food, an' such?'

'Yeah, an' whackin' farmers too. Who told you?'

'Oh, we been chasin' these black bastards all over three counties afore we got here,' Payne said wearily. 'This is only half my troop. I got another ten men up near Slade's Crossing. Apologize for my language, ma'am.'

'Bastards?' Maggie said. 'That passes for flattery in Rock Springs.'

'Wastin' your time at Slade's Crossin',' Dan said, bright with drink. '*Here* is where them savages are runnin' wild.'

'Cracked Ryan Kidder's skull like a boiled egg, just last night,' Stackmesser confirmed.

Sergeant Payne squared his shoulders. 'They can't cross that river, not easily,' he said. 'If they're trapped on this side, maybe we've had a piece a luck at last … I'll need all the information you can give me.'

'Bring your men inside,' Maggie suggested. 'Coffee an' eats. On the house.'

'Cracked like a boiled egg,' Stackmesser said again. Sometimes he impressed himself, he was so damn smart.

The posse was pleased to see the riflemen; now they could leave the hunt to the army, who got paid for being killed. The soldiers were polite but reserved. They sat together at one long table, answered questions briefly, said little else. 'You boys been a long time on the trail,' Hoke said.

'Yes sir,' a corporal agreed.

'Know the feelin'. Rode with Kit Carson.'

The troop had nothing to add to that. Hoke went over to Job Sims. 'Don't run off at the mouth, do they?' he murmured.

'Pennsylvania, that's the deep North,' Sims said. 'Kentucky's got one foot in the South, the way they see it.'

'Should of been both feet.' Hoke felt himself get excited. 'Could of blown fuckin' Lincoln on his ass,' he said, and moved away quickly before he lost all self-control.

Sims was impressed by the discipline of the troop. These were white Northern troops who had won a war against slavery, and now here they were, hunting down blacks and defending whites who a year ago might have been fighting for the South and for its peculiar institution. No wonder the soldiers had little to say.

Sergeant Payne listened patiently to Reuben Skinner, but Ryan kept interrupting and saying Reuben was getting it all wrong, so the sergeant heard Ryan's story, which Reuben interrupted just to get his own back; until the whole childish business grew so tedious that Frankie took the sergeant away.

'Those two couldn't piss straight *before* they got whacked,' she said.

The sergeant awarded himself a wry smile from his weekly allowance.

'Fact is,' she said, 'nobody knows for sure how many of these niggers are raidin'. They come when it's dark. Could be four, could be forty. An' we don't know which way they went.'

'Mr Kidder mentioned a nearby colony.'

Frankie explained about Hudd Ridge. Sergeant Payne made a note. 'Think I'll take my men up your Ridge and see what's for dinner.'

'Could be you gets eaten,' said Stackmesser, who had been listening. 'They got black bears bigger'n me, an' I know cus I fought one there last summer.'

'Niggers are worse'n bears,' Sims said. 'This whole town's been up there twice, tried to clear 'em out.'

'Bullets ain't no good against 'em,' Hoke added. 'Nor gunpowder neither. I rode with Kit Carson, an' I never – '

'They got Indian blood in 'em,' Dan Killick said. 'Makes 'em real mean.'

'I'll send for reinforcements,' Payne decided.

'Cherokee blood.'

'Artillery, too.'

That brightened up the afternoon. The U.S. Army was going to blast the Hudd colony into Indiana! Hell of a thing. Beat anvil-tossing. Meanwhile, Frankie told Sergeant Payne about some of the farms that might be at risk, and he went off with his troop on a local patrol. 'If we can't catch the rascals,' he said, 'maybe we can scare 'em a little.' The posse cheered. 'Hooray for Dixie!' shouted Reuben Skinner. For the first time, some of the soldiers laughed.

THE DEVIL'S WORK

When the 14th Pennsylvania Rifles rode into Rock Springs, Charles Hudd's cousins and their families had been living at his farm for two months.

They were fundamentalists. They believed the Devil existed, was in America, and might be encountered at any time. When they left their burned-out plantation in Georgia and headed for Kentucky, the senior cousin, Marcus Hudd, took proper precautions. He found an army quartermaster who sold him a dozen rusty revolvers for ten dollars, and threw in a box of bullets. 'Be sober, be vigilant,' warned First Peter five, eight, 'because your adversary the devil, as a roaring lion, walketh about, seeking whom he may devour.' Marcus gave a gun to every man, woman and child.

There were four women, two men, six children and a newborn infant in the party. They reached Kentucky intact except for one accidental wound: a boy shot off two of his brother's toes. This was reassuring proof that the weapons worked.

Within a week, Charles was sorry he had ever invited his kin. 'Got no manners,' he grumbled as he got ready for bed. 'Treat this place like they own it.'

'They work hard. I like them,' Mary said.

'There's such a thing as gratitude.'

'You want them to call you "sir", don't you? *Yeah suh, Colonel Hudd suh, you the boss, suh.*'

'I deserve respect.' He threw his boots at the wall. 'I fought at – '

'Nobody cares. They lost two brothers and a nephew killed, and a farm burned. Don't you have any respect for that?'

'For dead Rebs? For losers? No.'

They went silently to their separate beds. Charles felt cold in bed alone; he huddled and stared at the darkness. Mary listened to his breathing and wondered why he had become so difficult to love. She desperately wanted someone to love. Her first man had died young, her second was growing sour with selfishness. She worried; she seemed to be a curse on husbands. Charles worried too, but refused to admit it to himself. *Never give in. Never give up.*

It was still his house. He could live where he liked in it. As the late fall gave way to a harsh and crackling winter, he moved away from his relatives, moved symbolically upwards to a room that he converted into his study. While the others worked the farm, Charles planned to go into politics. The war had shown him how to lead men. All it took was total confidence in the right ideas. He had the confidence. Now he needed a few ideas. Lucy saw to the fire in the study, and brought him his meals. He read the *Louisville Courier* and the *Lexington Gazette* and the *Bowling Green Bugle,* and wrote to men of influence he had met in the army.

Occasionally he thought of the Killicks, having to tend their own fires because they didn't have a bright little nigger like Lucy to do it.

Sometimes he thought of them still shackled to a mortgage, while he would soon be county commissioner. Or state senator. Governor, even, one day.

He was up in his study, shutters closed against the fast-falling, freezing dusk. His stepsons were in their mother's room, being taught elementary book-keeping. The rest of the family were in the kitchen. Nelson Hudd came in with a pail of milk. Nelson was the son of Marcus: a young fifteen; skinny because of the skinny war diet; but a good milker. 'Feller in the barn just told me to get the keys to the smokehouse an' the cellar,' he said. 'Told me not to tell no-one.' He shrugged, and spilled a little milk. 'Thing is, Pa, dunno where them keys is kept.'

Total silence. His mother took the pail from his hand.

'What kind of a feller?' Marcus asked.

'Big, an' dark.' Nelson swallowed, loudly. 'Said he'd cut Nancy's throat if I told.' All the adults stood up.

A bench tipped and crashed. Now Nelson was very frightened. 'Had a funny sorta smell,' he said, voice cracking. 'Sorta sulphury smell.'

'It's Satan!' Marcus roared. 'Fetch your guns, everyone!' Part of his brain said Satan was supernatural, didn't need keys to get into the smokehouse; but Nancy was his daughter, just sixteen, thin as a buttercup, and the thought of a knife at her throat turned him a little crazy.

He was the first out of the house. The blackness swamped his senses as he rushed to the barn, blindly thumbing the revolver to know whether the hammer was cocked or not. He thumped into the barn door, fumbled for the handle, flung the door open, and stood staring and gasping. He should have brought a lantern. There might be a dozen murdering devils in this darkness. Or none. He heard a cow cough. 'You there, Nancy?' he called.

Silence.

This was torture. He held the gun out, far in front, and stepped inside, sniffing. Something smelled. It might be cowshit. Might be sulphur. 'Nancy?' he said. The blackness flowered brilliantly and briefly and Marcus felt all his strength draining out of his legs, and into his boots, and into the ground, and he tried to grab something but his hand found nothing to grab. Then his brain quit while he was still falling.

The rest of the family were less impetuous. They brought lanterns. Marcus's wife, Ruth, was scared but sensible. The barn door was open, and the barn had taken her husband and daughter. Nobody answered her call. Foolish to send another victim into that black silence. The family held back, and watched and waited. For what, nobody knew.

The last one out of the house was a boy called Lewis, nine years old. He was last because two of his toes had been shot off, and his foot still hurt. He was afraid of his gun. He carried it in both hands. He didn't want to go to the barn: all those revolvers being waved about: he might get shot again. Faintly, a horse snorted. The night was still, and sound carried. Just one faint snort, but Lewis heard it.

Well, it was a farm; there were many horses. But not where that snort came from, up the hill behind the house. He knew all the Hudd horses were in stables, out of the cold.

Lewis went to see.

Nobody missed him at the barn. Ruth was convinced something terrible had happened to Marcus and Nancy. She'd heard a troop of Yankee soldiers was based in Rock Springs. She told Nelson to go saddle up, ride hard and fetch them. Also the deputy and anyone else who might help.

The horse up the hill didn't snort again, but it stamped a foot when Lewis was fifty yards away from it and he stopped. For a full minute he listened to the frosty tingle in the air. Then he heard a blurred murmur of men's voices and he eased towards them, flattening his breathing. He thought he could make out a black something that might be men or horses or both, and then everything suddenly changed. Nelson rode his horse out of the stables and – overwhelmed by excitement – let out a shrill whoop to force it into a gallop. The clatter of hooves was like a nervous drumbeat.

Before Lewis could escape, he heard men cursing and running downhill. All he wanted was to keep them off, stop them hurting him. He held the revolver as far away as he could and shut his eyes and squeezed hard and shot a big black-coated man in the stomach, knocked him up the hillside and made him scream with pain. After that Lewis was out of control: he shot and shot and shot, the booming smash of noise battering his ears, the heavy gun making his thin arms jump. He missed the other men, but he hit two horses and stampeded them all.

The family stampeded too. The bangs and screams sent them running into the night, leaving the lanterns burning in front of the barn. They crouched and hid and waited. For what? Indians? Cherokee, lusting for blood? Niggers, drunk on homebrew grog, crazy for white women? Ruth was shaking with fear and cold but she knew one thing: nobody was going into that barn until her Nancy came out.

Nobody appeared. Nothing happened. The screams stopped. *How long to fetch the troopers?* Ruth wondered. *An hour at least ...* She couldn't wait half that long. Already the children's bodies were shuddering, and the night would get colder.

A stone skipped between the lanterns, then another. A third bounced over the top. Ruth's brain was too cold to comprehend. 'They're tryin' to smash the lamps,' someone said. A near-miss sprayed dirt over a lantern. The next rock smashed it. For a second the light was less; then abruptly it was more; far more; the lamp-oil spread and caught fire and made a leaping pool of flames that lit up a group of men with rocks in their hands. Ruth's hands were faster than her brain. She fired, and that one shot created a broadside. Everyone fired. The night was full of stupendous explosions and badly aimed bullets.

The range was crazy: a revolver was little good outside of a room, and these men were thirty or forty yards away. But when nine revolvers are fired wildly, a lucky hit is as possible as a lucky miss. Two bullets found targets: one in the head, the other in the thigh. Both men fell. The rest ran off, vanished in the blackness. Smoke drifted above the flames and got scattered by their heat. The echoes died.

Nancy appeared in the doorway. 'Don't shoot,' she said. 'He's gone. Bust a plank an' got out the back.'

Mary Hudd and her sons ran from the house. Charles followed at a fast trot, still in his carpet slippers, waving the pair of horse pistols he blew off Stanton's arm with, or so folk believed. There was a lot of hollering and questioning and dashing about. One man lay dead, the other wasn't going anywhere. Marcus got helped out of the barn, dazed and wobbling like a new-born foal.

'It's Satan all right,' he said, even though that hurt to say. 'Look at his evil face.'

Charles got hold of the dead man's head and turned it towards the light. The face was black, a kind of streaky black. He looked at his own fingers: they too were black. He sniffed them.

'Sulphur,' Marcus said.

'Lamp black, probably. Got sulphur in it, maybe.'

'Gotta be sulphur,' Marcus insisted. His head was roaring and lurching like a carousel. 'These are devils from hell. Ain't they?'

Charles went to the other man, who was sitting on the ground, holding his shot leg tight where the bullet went in. Blood was seeping all over his black hands. Charles dipped a finger in the blood and rubbed the man's face. It made a pale streak. He removed the man's hat. Wavy blond hair.

'Where you from?' he asked.

'Well, it ain't Pennsylvania,' the man said.

~

When Frankie Nickel arrived, along with Doc Brightsides, Job Sims, Ryan Kidder and Dan Killick, all heavily armed, there were three corpses laid out in the barn.

'My boy Lewis shot this one, up behind the house,' Marcus said. 'Womenfolk killed the next. Got him through the head from forty yards with a rusty old Reb revolver.' He was sitting on an oak stump, holding his head in one hand and a hot toddy in the other.

Brightsides looked at the third body. One pants leg was stiff with blood. 'This one bled to death?' he said.

'Would of done, only we hanged him first,' Marcus said.

'Shouldn't have done that,' Frankie said.

'Well, he shouldn't have grabbed my Nancy.'

'You told me some other feller grabbed her.'

'The other feller got away.'

'I had nothing to do with the hanging,' Charles Hudd said. 'I was in my study, drafting a report on this shocking affair.'

Dan Killick held a lamp close to the hanged man's face, and then moved back. 'Sergeant Bennett Payne,' he said. Frankie grunted. 'That's a shame,' Dan said. 'Maggie was kinda struck on him. She liked his manners.'

'White niggers,' Charles said stiffly. 'Cowardly scum. Any man who covers his crime in a black man's skin is doing the devil's work.'

'Told you that,' Marcus said. 'Stunk of sulphur all over. Didn't I say so?'

~

With three of the white-nigger raiders dead, Frankie had no difficulty raising a posse but all they caught were two horses. These did not carry a Union Army brand. Back at Maggie's it was agreed they must have been stolen.

'Why?' Frankie Nickel demanded. 'These are bushwhackers, not soldiers. We ain't dealing with any Pennsylvania Rifles here! They ain't ridin' army mounts!' No-one was interested. 'Goddamn horse-thieves,' Hoke said. 'That's worse'n murder. Hudds did right to hang 'em.'

'They only hanged one,' Doc Brightsides said. The nights were long; he was grateful for any argument.

'An' when they hanged him, it wasn't for a horse-thief,' Frankie said, 'which was just as well, considerin' that he wasn't.'

Now Hoke was confused. 'So why the heck did they hang him?' he demanded.

'He was shortest,' Dan Killick said. 'Damn tree-limb was too low. The others was all too tall to be hanged. Also too dead. Understand, Hoke?'

Maggie went into the kitchen, snuffling into her apron.

'Now see what you done,' Frankie reproached him. 'Maggie was fond of that sergeant. They might've married.'

'No life for a woman,' Hoke said, 'married to a trooper.'

'He wasn't a damn trooper,' Doc Brightsides said impatiently. 'He wasn't a damn sergeant.'

'That's right an' proper,' Dan said. 'Ain't a nigger born that's fit to be a sergeant in any man's army, an' I should know.'

'One good thing come out of it,' Stackmesser said. 'That uppity bunch on the Ridge knows what we do to nigger robbers.'

'The robbers were not niggers,' Frankie said, an edge in her voice like cracked glass. 'An' the niggers weren't robbers.'

Stackmesser glared. He felt offended but he had no answer. Ryan Kidder saved him. 'Hudds didn't know that when they hanged 'em, did they?' he said. 'Thought they was hangin' three blacks for bein' uppity.' Ryan smirked. He had outwitted the great deputy sheriff.

'If Kit was here now,' Hoke said, 'him an' me, we'd hunt 'em down till there wasn't a single Sioux left in all Dakota.'

'Cherokee,' Dan said. 'Lonzo's part-Cherokee.'

Hoke bridled. 'Don't contradict me, boy. I rode with Kit Carson in Dakota before you – '

'This is Kentucky.'

'You tryin' to be smart?' Hoke took out a Bowie knife big enough to cut cane with. 'This here's evidence!' It trembled in his elderly hand. He had forgotten what they were arguing about.

'That's all beside the point,' Doc Brightsides said. 'The point is – '

'Forget it, sweetheart,' Frankie said. She took the knife from Hoke while he was still blinking at Dan. 'Reckon I'll go cut some ham.'

Maggie was eating a little burnt chili to calm her nerves. 'There goes my first, last an' only chance to get out of Nowheresburg.' She had been crying. 'An' don't tell me about Desolation, Texas.'

That left Frankie with nothing to say, so she looked around and saw a rat and threw Hoke's knife and scared it down a hole. Maggie didn't even move her head. 'Sonofabitch,' Frankie sighed.

'Well, all men are sonsabitches,' Maggie said. Her voice was so flat she might have been talking to herself. 'I just wanted one sonofabitch man to myself before I die. Otherwise what's the point? Someone to love. Just one day, even. Way it's goin', I'll be dead an' I won't know what this love means that everyone talks so much about. Ain't that kind of a waste?'

The answer is yes, Frankie thought, *but I can't say that.* 'There's always tomorrow,' she said.

'No, you're wrong,' Maggie said. 'There's always yesterday.'

'If you say.' Frankie went and picked up Hoke's knife. She came back and stood behind Maggie's chair. On impulse, she put her arms around Maggie's shoulders.

'You gonna cut my throat?' Maggie said, still eating.

'Jesus, I'd need a goddamn scythe for that.' Frankie dipped the knife in the chili and ate a little from the point. 'This stuff gets worse. Why burn it so much?'

'Well-known aphrodisiac. You know what that word means?'

'Yeah. How much you got to eat before it works?'

'Coupla tons. Need strong arms.'

Frankie looked down. Maggie wasn't tall but she was wide. Almost as wide as Job Sims. And twice as hairy.

During the war each side turned its guerrillas loose on the other. The Jayhawkers killed and looted for the Union, the Bushwhackers looted and killed for the Confederacy; and both did what they liked for themselves too. After Lee surrendered, many went on raiding and raping and robbing. It was quick and easy and it paid better than work. Deserters, guerrillas, renegades, common outlaws – they were all called bushwhackers now. Kentucky had its full share, but most bushwhackers avoided Rock Springs. Word spread concerning the Massacre at Hudd's Farm, where four women and six children gunned down and hanged an entire gang of ex-army raiders in less than half an hour, a clear warning to all who felt inclined to covet their neighbour's ass.

Dan Killick warned his family next morning, at breakfast.

'Want to get your head blowed off,' he said, 'just take a walk out to Chuck Hudd's place an' fart.'

'Profanity,' his mother said. She took a knife from the kitchen table and tried to stab him but couldn't reach.

'Hudd murdered someone?' Stanton asked. He still nursed hopes of revenge.

'Not him. His kin from Georgia do it for him,' Dan said. 'Every little 'un's got an army Colt as big as a turkey drumstick.'

'That Hudd's a murderer!' his mother shrieked. Nobody paid her any attention. She advanced, stabbing the air. Dan moved around the table, putting chairs in her way.

'You see 'em do this killin'?' Devereux asked. He disbelieved three-quarters of anything Dan said and he wasn't too persuaded about the rest.

'It was night. Eat your grits, Ma, for Chrissake.'

'Blasphemer.' She lunged with the knife and fell over a chair. Jessica kicked the knife from her hand. Ma Killick grabbed her daughter's leg and bit it. Jessica watched. There were so few teeth in the mouth that it didn't hurt. 'How many they kill?' she asked.

'The children? Five, maybe six. Hudd's womenfolk did most of the shootin', they got the rest.'

'You sayin' they hit all these desperadoes,' Devereux said, 'in a night as black as a nigger's nuts? With *revolvers?*'

'I saw the bodies, little brother.' There had been only three, but since Dev was so sceptical, Dan was prepared to make it six, or nine, or a baker's dozen. 'Those kin of Hudd's can shoot straighter than Daniel Boone. Leave Jessy's leg alone, Ma. Eat your grits.'

'Your father an' me came through Boone's Trace,' Ma Killick announced. 'Wilderness Road. Boone found it.'

They ignored her. Heard it all before.

'Ain't scared of no Hudds,' Stanton said.

'Me neither,' Devereux said.

'You got barn litter for brains,' Dan told them. 'How you plan on handlin' a six-year-old boy with a Colt? Gonna shout at him, make him cry? Do that, his little sister'll put a bullet through your head from forty yards.'

'Cumberland Gap,' Ma Killick remembered suddenly. 'Boone's Trace goes through the Cumberland Gap. That's a fact.'

Stanton turned on her. 'Ma, will you for fuck's sake shut up an' eat your goddamn grits?' he bawled. She shook her head, defiantly. 'Listen!' he shouted. 'I cooked 'em, so you're gonna damn well eat 'em! If we have to sit here all day!'

She got to her feet, a quivering, frightened, furious old woman, and clung to a chair because her heart couldn't cope with the change. 'Not one red cent!' she whimpered. 'I made my will and that's what you get! Not one red cent!' She sat down and ate her grits, fearfully, spilling most.

A myth grew up. Everyone knew that most of the so-called 14th Pennsylvania Rifles had escaped. Everyone knew the raiders hadn't been genuine troopers. So maybe the ones that got away were real niggers. Maybe they were hiding, up there on the Ridge. Secretly, that idea appealed to a lot of folk. It explained why they hadn't been able to knock the colony off the Ridge, not with bullets, not with powder.

'They ain't your ordinary coons,' Stackmesser said. 'I seen 'em close up! Showed 'em how to hunt bear. Let me tell you, I'd sooner wrestle a black bear than some of those coloured gentlemen.'

'Ain't no wonder the U.S. Cavalry quit when they heard,' Reuben Skinner said.

'U.S. Cavalry never came here,' Frankie Nickel said.

'Easy for you to say. You never got whomped on the head.' That was the biggest thing ever happened to Reuben, and he wasn't going to let the town forget it.

'Indian blood,' Hoke said. 'When I – '

'Hudd got sense,' Ryan declared. 'He's closest. Brought in all them guns, keep the nigs away.'

'He never did that,' Doc Brightsides said. 'Listen – '

'Know what I reckon?' Stackmesser said. Nobody waited for anyone in Maggie's. 'I reckon we got the meanest, coldest, fiercest, baddest bunch of sonabitch niggers up there in all Kentucky.' It was a good reason for leaving them alone. For a little while, anyway.

GOTTSCHALK'S
FORMULA

The more died, the more survived. That was the story of the Hudd Ridge colony's first winter. Aaron was right. There wasn't enough food for everybody, so it was just as well that West and Matty and little Katie and Starr and Charlie and some others moved on and left room for the rest.

Even so, come spring, everyone was sick of eating nuts and dried roots and tough old smoked wild turkey, and drinking Aaron's herb tea that tasted like hot wet hay. Lucy worked down at the Hudds', five or six days a week. When she visited the camp, she said nothing of the fresh cornbread and fried pork belly and red cabbage they knew she was getting, and only Luke Corrigan was fool enough to ask. The second time he asked, Lonzo steered him behind a cabin and punched his face so hard that he couldn't chew for a week. Luke still didn't know what he'd done wrong. If Lucy was Lonzo's woman, why didn't they jump the broomstick, so everyone knew? But he shut up about farm grub, and everyone chewed the same old tasteless stringy stuff and tried not to think of what couldn't be.

Aaron thought of what *must* be.

He had dozed through the winter, cocooned in buckskins, a fire always smouldering in his cabin. A little malaria came and went, draining his strength. He lived on spoonfuls of a porridge made from a bitter red-black root, shredded and boiled, and a yellow syrup so thick he had to suck it off the spoon. His cabin stank. People thought he was dead, but if anyone touched him his eyelids flickered and he growled like a hound.

A morning came when Lonzo saw, for the first time, a shimmer of fresh green growth on the trees. Aaron was perched on the Altar.

Somebody must have lifted him up there.

'Earth's gettin' warm,' Aaron called. 'Time to put the seed taters in.'

It wasn't yet noon and already Lonzo had done a day's work, shouting at people to mend their sagging roof or fill their empty logpile or wash their stained clothes, when all they wanted to do was sit in the sun. 'Ain't got none,' he snapped.

'Need a milkin' cow too,' Aaron said. 'Brood sow. Some chickens.'

'Uh-huh. Want ice cream? Peach pie?'

Aaron clicked his fingers. 'Fish hooks. Children can catch us some catfish.'

'Got no money.'

'Mule of yours looks about ready for mule heaven. Get us a good animal. Not big. Thick in the legs.'

'Where from? Stackmesser? That door's shut, Aaron.' Lonzo ran out of the energy to be angry. He sat against the Altar and watched a buzzard soar and circle until some crows chased it away. Everywhere you looked, something was bothering something else. 'Got no goddamn money,' he said again.

'Need real grub. Sick of eatin' this wilderness shit.'

'Don't you never listen, you old fool? I got seventeen cents. Seventeen.'

'Ain't enough,' Aaron said. 'Get more. Lot more.'

Lonzo went up and down the camp, asking. Nobody had money, nobody had ideas for raising money. They looked around, helpless, at trees and rocks, and they shrugged. Lonzo went back to Aaron. 'Seventeen cents,' he said.

'Gimme.'

Lonzo hesitated, but he was tired of bearing responsibility and he wanted to see what Aaron could achieve with so little. He fetched the money: a dime, a nickel, two pennies. Aaron took them and swallowed them. They were all inside his shrunken, meagre body before Lonzo could grab. 'Now stop dreamin' you can magic seventeen cents into a bag of gold,' Aaron said. A tiny belch shook him. 'Children need milk, eggs, bread, or this camp gonna *die*.'

Lonzo was still staring up, his face twisted by sun-dazzle and astonishment. 'You sonofabitch!' he said.

'Easy, boy. Your savin's are safe. Fact is, you'll get 'em back soon as I get a good meal.' Aaron cackled. 'Big plate of pork an' beans'd make a difference.' His cackle drove Lonzo away.

He worried. The colony wouldn't survive on what it found in the forest. He daren't go back to Stackmesser without money. The colony had nothing to sell except the Ridge. Nobody wanted *that*. Lonzo worried, and worried, until his head hurt. *That* hadn't happened since he was ten and he got bullwhipped by Master Henry Hudd for dropping his hoe.

He was washing his shirt in a stream, thinking it would fall apart if he rubbed any harder, when Martha sat on the next boulder. 'Gimme that,' she said. 'Go an' see Luce.'

'What for?'

'Just *go*.'

He found her in her cabin, resting. 'Martha said ...' he began, and stopped. Martha hadn't said anything. Lonzo was no good at making conversation with a young woman whose looks left a catch in his throat and a lump in his loins.

'I got fifty-eight bucks you can have,' Lucy said. 'But you got to give me a real good reason.'

Fifty-eight bucks would solve all their problems, so Lonzo – being Lonzo – scowled. Lucy laughed at him, which he found hurtful.

'Ain't stole,' she said. 'Ain't Confederate paper, either. You want it or not?'

'Damn right we do. We *need* it for – '

'Sure, sure, sure.' She took a canvas bag from under her pillow, held the bag high and made its contents chink. 'Ask friendly, boy.'

Now Lonzo was confused. He grunted. She grunted back, mockingly, like a happy hog. 'If you don't ...' he began, and couldn't finish.

'Hey!' she said. The canvas bag went back under the pillow. 'Sounds like a *threat*. Now you *scared* me, you bein' so big an' strong an' all.'

'Want me to whop you?' Lonzo asked. He had heard of women who liked being whopped.

'Want me to rip your throat out?' she said pleasantly.

He went back to Martha. 'She talks crazy,' he said.

'You never was a good listener,' Martha said. 'You need a new shirt.' She held it up: split to the collar, front and back. 'An' I ain't even got the price of a button, so don't ask again.'

Winter quit. One week it was so cold, nobody could remember what summer felt like; next week, winter shrank northwards and hot spring weather moved in like a last-minute reprieve from the Governor. Main Street got baked dry. Grass began to grow. Some people even unbuttoned their coats.

Maggie and Frankie were sitting under a big old sycamore behind the tavern, drinking coffee and eating ham sandwiches. 'What's it like, bein' married?' Maggie asked.

'Easy as fallin' off a rock, and just about as stupid.'

'You're sayin' that, because you had bad luck.'

'Men are all the same. Carry their brains in their pants. Got very small brains. They look around, see somethin' don't move, they fornicate with it. If that don't work, they bust it. Does move, they shoot it. All you need to know about men.'

'In Texas, maybe,' Maggie said. 'Kentucky's different.'

'Sure. Couple months ago, this town was all set to hang me.'

'Nothin' personal.' Maggie stood and exercised her right leg. The knee ticked like an old metronome. 'Just lookin' for some excitement, was all. Ain't had a hangin' since '59, an' he was a disappointment, seein' as he only had one leg an' one arm.'

'What he do?'

'Tried to rob the bank. Had his gun in his hand, but could be he was tryin' to sell it an' he went though the wrong door. Gun store was right next to the bank in them days.' Maggie sat down and carved more ham. 'Got burned down by Morgan's Raiders. Bank and gun store both.'

Frankie grunted. 'Progress goes backwards at one hell of a lick around here.'

'Damn war.' The bang of a revolver shot sent pigeons fluttering from the tavern roof. 'That's a forty-five,' Maggie said. 'Nobody in this town owns a forty-five.'

Frankie took her coffee. As she walked away, another bang cracked the silence. A third exploded when she reached the street. A crowd was watching a man in blue uniform writing in a notebook. He tucked the pencil behind his ear and took ten long paces down the centre of the street. He knelt, fitted a stethoscope to his ears, and placed its end to the ground. Then he produced a revolver and fired a shot, vertically, down into the dirt, and listened for about ten seconds. The gun was holstered, the pencil came out, more notes were taken. He stood, his head cocked, looking at the bullethole.

'What in thunder's goin' on here?' Stackmesser demanded. He had been sleeping off his lunch.

'Not now, sir, if you please.' The officer had a fine chestnut moustache and a deep, resonant voice. He waved Stackmesser aside and measured a further ten long paces down the street.

'Know anythin' about this?' Sims asked Frankie. She shrugged. The officer went through his routine with the gun and the stethoscope again.

'Why don't you stop him?' Dan Killick asked.

'He ain't harmed anythin',' Frankie said. 'So far.'

'You seem an intelligent man, sir,' the officer said to Stackmesser. 'Kindly take this.' He gave him the end of a tape measure. 'And this.' He gave him a hand-compass. 'Proceed twenty-five yards north-west and mark the spot.' Obediently, Stackmesser strode away. The crowd watched him scrape a cross with his heel. 'I'm vastly obliged to you, sir,' the officer said. He walked along the line, winding in the tape, and stood astride the cross. 'It's as I thought,' he said, 'but I'll make quite sure, all the same.'

'Sure of what?' Stackmesser asked.

The officer took two small glass bottles from his tunic pocket, one red, one green. He tipped a little liquid from the green bottle onto the centre of the cross, added a few drops from the red bottle, and quickly stood aside. There was a hissing flash and a gush of brilliant yellow smoke. The crowd gasped. 'Yep,' the officer said. 'It's as I thought. Right here is the heart of the earthquake zone.' He stamped hard on the burned stain, and the crowd jumped back. 'My task is done. Where can I get a hot meal and a clean bed?'

Inside Maggie's tavern, he introduced himself as Major de Glanville, United States Army, Brigade of Engineers. He ordered a steak. Frankie Nickel told him who she was and asked if he planned to waste any more bullets on the only real street that Rock Springs had. Major de Glanville assured her that his business in Rock Springs was complete.

'What business?' Job Sims asked.

'Secret and confidential,' de Glanville said. 'As you can see from my orders.' He showed them a letter.

'This ain't English,' Frankie said.

'Indeed it is not. That is Latin. At the highest level, the army commits its instructions to the Latin tongue as a double measure of security. But only at the highest level.' He took the letter back. A circle of faces stared, wanting more. 'I assure you,' he said, 'my investigations here will make no difference to your town.' It was not what they wanted to hear.

'You said somethin' about an earthquake zone?' Ryan Kidder asked.

'A mere technicality, sir. Ignore it.'

'Look,' Cleghorn said, 'I rode with Kit Carson, so I know a little bit about the military, and this is one hell of a long way for the U.S. Army to send a major and then it makes no difference.'

'Quite correct, sir.' Major de Glanville buffed up his moustache with his knuckles. 'No difference to your town is what I believe I said. However ...' He paused, briefly. 'However, I can reveal that I have been seconded to the Department of the Treasury. It is to them that I report.' His steak arrived. He sawed off a corner. They watched him eat it as if it were the first, last and only steak in Kentucky.

'Treasury,' Sims said.

De Glanville, still eating, took out his letter of appointment again, opened it one-handed, waved it, folded it, put it away.

'U.S. Treasury don't know we exist,' Stackmesser said. 'Washington D.C. couldn't find Rock Springs with a pack of coon-huntin' dogs.'

De Glanville looked at him sharply, and briefly stopped eating. 'Hmmm,' he said.

'You sayin' the Treasury's interested in us?' Kidder asked.

'Treasury's only interested in collectin' taxes,' Maggie said. She came over from the bar.

'You want my taxes?' Dan said to de Glanville. 'Washington already took my niggers. Sell 'em, keep the money.'

'Long before the war ended,' de Glanville said, 'the U.S. Treasury made plans for a prosperous peace. Those plans reach into every corner of every state, but *especially* ...' He turned his head and looked out of a window. 'Especially those places that found themselves, during the recent conflict, between a rock and a hard place.'

'That's us,' Stackmesser said.

'We got hurt *bad*,' Maggie said.

'I got hurt worst,' Kidder said.

'Communications,' de Glanville said. 'When I was in Washington, all I seemed to hear was that word, communications.'

'We could use a post office,' Sims said.

'The Rebs was the worst,' Kidder said. 'Never had no trouble with none of your Union boys.'

'Glad to hear it. Of course, I was in the Engineers, not the infantry.'

Cleghorn twitched his nose. 'What exactly did you do, sir?' he asked.

'Bridges,' de Glanville said, and frowned at his food.

'Now Washington wants to build a bridge over the Cameron,' Cleghorn said.

De Glanville cut a potato in half and did not eat either piece.

'Bridge,' Kidder said. 'We talkin' about a real bridge?'

'My lips are sealed,' de Glanville said.

'A bridge would be the makin' of this town,' Stackmesser said. 'Hot damn! A real bridge!' He grinned. The sight jolted the others: it was like seeing a horse smile. 'When they gonna start?' he asked.

'My hands are tied,' de Glanville said. 'Heaven forgive me, I shouldn't even be *discussing* the project. Please, let us change the subject. What of your crops? Are they – '

'Same as ever,' Dan said.

'You said earthquakes, out there,' Sims said. 'That was some kinda joke, right?'

'Firin' bullets into the street,' Cleghorn complained. 'What in hell's the point of that? Ain't nothin' to hit.'

'Let the man explain,' Frankie said.

'A matter of simple geology,' de Glanville told them. 'The explosive detonates and sends concentric vibrations shooting down deep into the ancient rock formations, from where echoes return which, to the trained ear, describe conditions underground as clear as day. I apply Gottschalk's Formula: twice the impact ratio plus the square root of the speed of sound divided by the age of the rock in millions of years gives you its percentage liability to fracture or not, as the case may be. It's so simple a child could do it,' he told Cleghorn. 'You probably used the same formula when you were campaigning with Carson.'

'Oh … similar,' Cleghorn said. 'Somethin' similar.'

'We ain't gonna get a bridge, are we?' Frankie asked. The others glanced angrily at her. 'Man here says he found earthquake signs,' she told them. 'You think Washington's gonna build a bridge that might get shook down, you're crazy.'

'You been testin' anyplace else?' Sims asked.

'Barber's Landing,' de Glanville said. 'Knuckle Creek. Placket's Ferry. Downeysville. Yellow Bottom.'

'One of them gets a bridge, that's goodbye to Rock Springs,' Stackmesser said. 'All the trade in the county will go there, an' we'll be dead.'

'Earthquake hits, we're dead anyway,' Kidder said.

'That may never happen, of course,' de Glanville said. 'Nothing is certain in this world. Not even Gottschalk's Formula. If I had my way, I would never use it. I much prefer to use Stamford's Principle. Far more reliable.'

There was a pause while they took that in and he mopped up gravy with a piece of bread.

'Why not use this Stamford's thing?' Maggie asked.

'Expense,' de Glanville said. 'To test by Stamford's Principle costs an extra two hundred dollars in rare chemicals. A great pity, in my opinion. Now, if you will excuse me, I shall retire and write my report.'

They watched him climb the stairs.

'Two hundred,' Stackmesser said.

'Cheap for a bridge,' Sims said.

'I don't know,' the pedlar said. He had been silent for so long that they all listened. 'This bridge idea ... I seen nice quiet towns like this one get all ambitious an' before you can turn round there's gamblin' joints an' sportin' houses an' rotgut bars an' you can't see across the street for half-naked floozies shakin' their ass an' bouncin' their tits. Is that what we want?'

'I'm good for five dollars,' Stackmesser said.

CAN THE FRUIT

Josh tried religion on Lucy. 'The Lord wants us to buy a cow an' a breedin' sow with that money,' he said. 'That's why the Lord give it you.'

'Lord ain't give me nothin'. I *worked*.'

'I'm gonna pray for you.'

'Go ahead. Long as it don't cost me.'

Later, Luke Corrigan came and pointed out to her that, whatever they bought, she would own; so for instance she'd soon have a whole mess of hogs. Lucy said the ugliest, smelliest and most disgusting thing in the world was a whole mess of hogs. Luke went away.

Gabe Killick, probably the cleverest nigger in the camp – Lonzo had already taught him to write his name – Gabe had a clever idea. He took Luce and showed her Nat's bullwhipped back. Nat was washing at the stream. Luce had never seen such ravaged skin. Nat ran and hid while he got his shirt on. 'Ain't them cuts worth somethin'?' Gabe asked her. 'A dollar a cut?'

'You got a mind like an overseer,' Lucy said, and threw rocks at him until he backed off, bewildered.

Next day, Buck came and asked her if there was anyone she wanted smashed. For money. He would do it. 'Smash his legs. Arms. Head. Anywhere,' he offered. The lisp made it sound worse. Lucy laughed so hard that Buck turned away, tears in his eyes. Women were a big mystery.

When Lucy set off for the Hudd farm, Bettsy walked with her. Bettsy was the kindest, gentlest of nigger women, now that Starr Killick was gone. 'Luce, if I had that money, I'd give it to these people,' she said. 'They need it bad.'

'Everyone needs my dollars,' Lucy said. 'Nobody needs me.' Bettsy had no answer to that.

Doc Brightsides rode into town, his pea-green suit bloodied by an unusually bad childbirth – both twins damaged and dying, the mother unconscious from pain, the father drunk in a corner of the room – and he saw what looked like the entire population crowded together near the landing stage. He walked his horse to the edge of the crowd, hoping it wasn't going to be more work for him. 'What's happening?' he asked.

'Please!' Major de Glanville called. 'I must have complete and utter silence. This is a very delicate test.'

The crowd had formed a wide ring around him. He was tinkering with five small wooden boxes, arranged in a line. 'Utter silence,' he said. 'The slightest noise …'

Brightsides moved next to Job Sims, who was standing on a saw-horse for a better view. 'Army officer,' the blacksmith whispered. 'Surveyin' for a bridge. This might be earthquake country. Way he finds out, he makes a little earthquake. Them boxes give a light. Bad foundations, red light. Good foundations, green. Ain't that the cleverest – '

'Unless I have total, utter and absolute silence,' de Glanville announced, 'I cannot possibly proceed. My scientific instruments are extremely delicate. They will react to the slightest vibration.'

Everyone shut up.

Across the river, a mockingbird called. A late-afternoon breeze washed softly through the leaves of a giant willow. Everyone heard these sounds; everyone was alert, attentive. This was better than a hanging. Nobody knew how it was going to turn out.

De Glanville struck a match, lit a fuse, and walked to the edge of the crowd. He folded his arms. 'I have played my part,' he said quietly. 'Now we are in the arms of Science.'

They were ready for a bang. It was loud and crisp and it made them jump. While they were grinning at each other a second bang, even heavier, staggered them and a third bang, twice the size, knocked a few off their feet. It was gratifying, this sequence: like whacking a stake into the ground: smack-bang-wallop: very scientific. They approved. Then the real bang erupted. The first three sounds had just been stepping-stones to this final explosion, a thunderous crump that spoke through the soles of everybody's feet and seemed to blow a great hole in the afternoon.

'Holy shit,' the pedlar whispered.

'Utter silence, *please*,' de Glanville said.

A silvery flame sparkled back and forth in the gaps between the five boxes. One box began to smoke. The crowd, still half-stunned, gasped and pointed. Now all the boxes were pouring out purple smoke, so dense it looked liquid. Abruptly the colour changed to red and turned to flame: five raging red blossoms. 'Goddamn science,' Sims muttered. People were booing. But slowly the red turned to green. What's more, the flame pulsed higher and spread wider, a throbbing, healthy, positive green. The display went on burning for a good minute. 'Thank God for science!' Sims was shouting. 'Hooray for science and the U.S. Treasury!' People were cheering, and even de Glanville allowed himself to look mildly pleased.

~

Maggie did good business that night. There was plenty to talk about. For one thing, Flub Phillips had reminded everybody that the land across the river was marsh. How could you build a bridge on a marsh? At length Job Sims was elected to put the question to de Glanville, once he'd finished eating. 'Simplicity itself,' the major told him. 'The army knows how to tackle a marsh. After all, what is it but good land in need of proper drainage? The marsh is the least of our problems, I assure you.'

Sims went back to the waiting citizens. 'Simple,' he said. 'That marsh is the least of our problems.'

'We got bigger problems?' Ryan Kidder said. 'What bigger problems?'

'Squeezin' money out of Washington,' Maggie said. 'Take more blastin' than we saw out there today to get a dollar out of that ratsnest.'

'Got to fight,' Hoke Cleghorn said. 'This is a fightin' matter.'

More talk. Louder talk. Argument, dispute, challenge, proposal, ridicule. After a while, de Granville strolled over and listened.

'Got to fight,' Cleghorn said. 'Ain't that right, major?'

'Nothing of value is won without effort,' de Glanville said. He spread his arms. '*He which hath no stomach to this fight*,' he declared, '*let him depart; his passport shall be made …*' It wasn't just the words; the grand style, the steely clarity, the royal richness of delivery earned everybody's silence. *'And crowns for convoy put into his purse …'* Now de Glanville gestured bravely. *'We would not die in that man's company,'* he cried, *'that fears his fellowship to die with us! This day is called the feast of Crispian …'* He looked at his spell-bound audience; coughed, smiled, sat down. 'My apologies,' he murmured. 'I allowed myself to be carried away.' When nobody spoke, he added: 'Shakespeare used to be a little hobby of mine.'

The conversation resumed, but de Glanville was silent; and soon he stood up and said goodnight. Frank Nickel stood up too. 'That tunic of yours, major,' she said. 'Looks to me like it needs a good brushing.'

'I wouldn't dream of imposing.'

'All included in the service. Maggie's an expert. Only take a minute. Besides, I have a question about … uh … Shakespeare.'

She led him into the kitchen. Maggie wasn't there. 'This isn't necessary,' he said. 'An army engineer – '

'Who d'you serve under? Sherman?' He nodded. She peeled his tunic off. 'Build a lot of bridges?'

'Yes. Dozens.'

'Which was the hardest? Most dangerous?' She had found a brush and was beating dust out of the cloth.

'Oh … Difficult to say. Place in Georgia called Spartanburg, probably.'

'How about Fiddler's Bend?' He was silent, so she added: 'Only reason I ask, I met a couple of Rebs who fought in Georgia, an' they reckoned Sherman's engineers deserved a basketful of medals for the bridge they threw over the river at Fiddler's Bend.'

He nodded, with a slight smile of professional appreciation.

'Shot an' shell fallin' like hailstones, they told me, but those Union engineers didn't blink. After that, the Rebs had a sayin': Brave as Fiddler's Bend. You never heard of that sayin'?'

'Ah, yes. Fiddler's Bend,' he said. 'A truly heroic achievement.'

'You were somewhat brave yourself.' She had turned his tunic inside out and was holding it close to the lamplight. She fingered three holes in the back and three in the front. They more or less lined up. They couldn't be seen from the outside: someone had stitched panels of similar material over the damage. 'That's surely worth a medal,' she said. 'Here you got shot bad enough to kill three ordinary men, but yet … Hey!'

'Aren't you getting a little carried away?' he asked. 'It's only a uniform.'

'See this.'

Deep inside a pocket she had found a name. It had been written on the lining with a hard black pencil whose markings had penetrated the white fabric and survived soakings by sweat and rain.

'Had an uncle Bill in Baltimore was a tailor,' she said. 'Used to watch him work. Every garment he finished, he wrote the customer's name inside a pocket. Doesn't show and never gets lost. Look here: you ain't Major de Glanville at all. Captain Eugene Q. Verrier, that's you.'

'Eugene fell in battle at Spartanburg. His dying bequest to me was his uniform. My own had been cut to shreds.'

'Real friendly of him.'

'We were like brothers,' he said simply. 'It's not something a woman can understand.' A slight huskiness tinged his voice. 'There is love on the battlefield that transcends the lust and longing of romantic passion. We soldiers know – '

'You won't take offence if I ask to see that letter of appointment just one more time,' she said.

'It's in Latin. You won't understand it.'

'No,' she said, 'but Doc Brightsides will.'

He took his time over answering. 'It's a prescription for treating neuralgia or sciatica,' he said. 'The physician who wrote it wasn't sure which. He was a little drunk at the time.'

She gave him a thoughtful stare. 'And who the hell are you?'

'I?' he said, balancing on his toes. 'I am J. Benton Greatorix, actor extraordinary, one-time soldier, and now – in a sense – restored to the stage, since all the world's a stage and ...' He stopped when she raised a hand.

'Just can the fruit. The show's over, right?' She tossed his tunic back to him. 'Soldier, you say. Which side?'

'The South, naturally. The side of chivalry, colour, dash – '

'Just hold your water. This has been a long day.' He nodded agreement and ate a piece of ham. 'If you were a Reb,' she said, 'how come the blue uniform?'

'Looted on the field of battle ... Is there, perhaps, some mustard? Ah ... Too kind ... The Confederacy did win occasionally. I was at the battle of New Windsor, in '64. After the slaughter I came across

292

the corpse of Captain Verrier, riddled by our brave Southern bullets, poor fellow, and exactly my height and build, so I removed his uniform and put it somewhere safe. The rest is history.'

'The rest is crime.'

'Well, most of history is crime.'

'How much money did you make?'

'Today? A hundred and sixty-three dollars, all Mr Sims could raise from his fellow citizens. I had sundry costs to cover. Explosives and pyrotechnics are not cheap. I cleared about a hundred and thirty dollars.'

'You swindled those folk.'

He looked pained. 'Surely not. They enjoyed a stunning perform-ance that will live – '

'They ain't gonna get no bridge.'

'Probably not. But ultimately they will get a valuable lesson in ethics: that you can't bribe Uncle Sam. As the Bible tells us: a pure heart is worth more than bridges.'

'Hogwash. I ought to throw you in jail. If this town *had* a jail.'

He waited. She was half-perched on a table, studying his lean and handsome face. 'Alternatively,' he said, 'you want your share.'

'Yeah,' she said. 'Put it like that, I think I do.'

KING SOLOMON LOVED
MANY STRANGE WOMEN

Curtis Hudd grew to full manhood very quickly. At nineteen, he was strong enough to do any job on the farm all day without slacking. He could take responsibility for other men; take risks and not hesitate; judge crops and weather and livestock at a glance. About the only thing he didn't understand was women. He had been isolated from them. Apart from his mother, and the slave women, the only females he saw were in Rock Springs; and he went there rarely. He was lucky to lose his virginity to Amie Kidder, but he had learned little from this brief eruption of raw pleasure. He begged her to do it again; however, Amie had to go and get baptized.

He learned nothing of courtship from Lucy. She handled him like a cow to be milked, expertly and indifferently. Hudd's female cousins were polite but distant. No point in talking about girls to Floyd. Floyd had discovered books. All he did was read. Curtis despised him. He despised almost everyone except Amie Kidder. He thought a lot about Amie.

On a bright spring day, he drove a wagon into Rock Springs with his mother. She went to the store to buy stuff; he took a couple of bust wheels over to Elias Dunbar's to get new spokes and rims. 'Your grand-daddy must've brung these from Virginia,' Dunbar grumbled. 'Why don't your pa buy new wheels 'stead of always patchin'?'

'Either do it or don't,' Curtis said. 'Just don't bitch. An' it wasn't my grand-daddy, an' he's not my pa.'

Thus he left feeling well peppered, and by the greatest of good luck met Amie Kidder. She was wearing a long green coat with a hood. He hadn't seen her for months. She looked a bit older and a whole lot prettier. 'Hey, there!' he said.

'Hey yourself.' Perhaps she smiled; it was hard to say.

'I been thinkin' about you.' No answer. He remembered he had his hat on, took it off, and felt awkward, as if he was in church. 'Dreamin', too,' he said boldly.

She looked at him, and then at a passing mule, with equal interest.

'I better not tell you what I was dreamin',' he said.

'I'd prefer you didn't,' she said. 'Goodbye.' And walked on. He followed. After all these empty months, it was impossible that their meeting should be so brief. 'Look, Amie, we was good friends,' he said. 'Can't we ...' But his brain was in a panic.

'No we can't,' she said flatly. 'That was then and now is now, an' I learned a lot about men in between, none of it to the good.'

'Dev Killick? You been seein' Dev Killick?'

'Go home, Curtis.'

'You're crazy.' Curtis put his hat on. 'Dev's got nigger blood! All them Killicks used to bed their slaves, regular. Everyone knows that. Killicks are trash.'

She stopped so suddenly that he stumbled, and felt foolish. 'You get your dollar's worth from little Miss Lucy?' she asked him.

Dev told her, he thought. *I'll kill him.* 'That's a lie,' he said, but when her eyebrows went up and her mouth twisted, he realized she thought he meant he hadn't got his dollar's worth, and he was furious. 'I don't mess with nigger women,' he muttered.

'Maybe they already messed with you. You catch a disease?'

Curtis was shocked. He knew men got sex diseases, but for a woman to speak of them was a profanity. 'I'm clean,' he said, 'but now I ain't so sure about you.' He could hear his voice trembling. 'Word is, you passed an awful long time in the barn with that nigger bushwhacker. Hope you got *your* dollar.' They parted.

Mary Hudd had been watching from outside Stackmesser's. She crossed the street. Amie was a strong, courageous young woman: her nerve had been strengthened by the bushwackers' raid; nevertheless, she was now on the edge of tears. 'Curtis really likes you,' Mary said. 'It's just he can't always find the words.'

'Oh, he found the words, all right,' Amie said. Her shoulders were hunched, her arms tightly folded. Mary Hudd was smart enough to know when she had said the wrong thing, and she shut up. They walked together.

'Why is God so hot on marriage,' Amie said, 'when every man that you know – every white man – prefers to enjoy himself on a black woman?'

'Not every man. Some husbands are faithful.'

'Yeah? I heard different.' Amie was making it up as she went along. 'Still, we don't want to pay no heed to silly old gossip, do we, Mrs Hudd?' The tears had gone now; this was straightforward revenge. 'That little nigger maid you got? Lucy? Pretty enough to make any man bust his buttons.'

'That's enough, Amie.'

'Young or old. Dollar a time, I hear.'

'Enough, I said.'

'You know best, Mrs Hudd. Leastways, I hope you do.' They parted.

Mother and son drove home in silence.

Charles Hudd was in his study, thumbing through his Bible, when she came in without knocking.

That annoyed him. He was looking for references in support of polygamy, which might be an exciting new idea in his political programme. The West needed people and it worked for the Mormons, and hullo hullo, look here, First Kings, eleven, one: *King Solomon loved many strange women.* 'I'm busy,' Charles said.

'Folk in Rock Springs say Lucy's selling her body for a dollar a time.'

'That offend you?'

'It's wrong.'

'The gossip, or the sellin'?'

'You're very casual about it.'

'Look: if she offends you, get rid of her. Now, as I said, I'm busy.' Mary did not move. 'You have *another* problem?' he said.

'Perhaps.' She peeled off her gloves, slowly. 'Do *you* have another problem? With our marriage bed?'

'What bed? You left mine. I guess you're more comfortable alone.'

'I'd be more comfortable if I knew when I should look the other way.'

Charles was losing patience. 'You want to know am I satisfying my carnal lusts with Lucy. Well, I am not. But think what you like, if it gives you some lunatic cockeyed satisfaction. Now – '

'If that's how you see me, as some cockeyed lunatic, it's little wonder I have my doubts about you.'

'Doubts? I thought they were cast-iron certainties.'

'And I thought you wanted to be elected.'

'I do.'

'Then think what other people might say.'

'What do you want of me?' he roared. 'A banner over Main Street saying Charles Hudd does not fuck his niggers?'

'Anger and guilt.' She picked up her gloves. 'They go together like lust and deceit.'

'You never give in, do you?' he said. 'Never give in. Never give up.' The words were familiar, but he was too angry to remember where they came from. Mary went out. A gusty draft slammed the door. She paused, still holding the handle, wondering whether to go back and tell him the slam was not intended. No. Let him think what he pleases.

Charles lit a cigar, and was surprised to see the flame shaking. *So everyone thinks I'm poking little Lucy.* The Bible was still open at First Kings. King Solomon still loved many strange women. Very many: seven hundred wives, it said, and princesses, and three hundred concubines. 'Well now, boy,' he told himself, aloud, 'you're gettin' all the blame, you might's well get some of the pleasure.' That sounded oddly familiar, too.

When Lucy brought him his supper on a tray, he gave her a dollar. 'What's that for?' she said. 'Piece a chocolate,' he said. They both laughed.

THE RICH TAPESTRY
OF LIFE

First thing Maggie did when she went into the shack where Brightsides had delivered the dying twins was to open the windows. The air was as thick as old armpits.

Second thing she did was bawl at the kids (two girls, one boy, none over the age of six) to light the stove and get more wood. Maggie had a face like an old boot and a voice like a rusty pump. The kids ran.

Third thing was to kick the drunken husband. She was wearing her riding boots. She kicked him out of his chair, across the room and through the door, cursing him and his private parts every foot of the way, until he did what she said and went to fetch water. 'Keep fetchin' till I say stop,' she warned.

That was the hard work done.

'You poor dumb bitch,' she said kindly. 'Shift your sorry ass out of that stinkin' pit.'

The wife, her face the colour of old porridge, had to be helped out of bed. The elder daughter dropped a load of wood and held her mother up, while Maggie flung the fouled bedclothes into a corner. The wife had on a worn-out man's shirt, crusty with dried blood, sticky with fresh blood. 'Hey, you!' Maggie snapped at a four-year-old. 'Get some rags. *Clean*!' She pulled off the shirt. The woman's arms were so thin that the sleeves felt empty. The husband came in with two buckets of water. 'Boil 'em,' Maggie snarled. The woman's loins were a mass of puffy blue bruises and streaks of clotted blood. 'See what you done, you asshole?'

'That ain't fair, Maggie,' he protested. 'If the Lord sends – '

'Oh, sure. God gotta be a man. Only a man would think of somethin' as stupid as this.'

298

She cleaned up the woman, put fresh blankets on the bed, fed everybody with whatever had come to her hand in the Tavern kitchen – fried chicken, bean soup, cold rice – and set the fouled bed-clothes to boil. 'Come here,' she said to the husband. He came. She seized him, one-handed, by the throat. He was a head taller than she was. She looked up and said, 'If she dies I'm comin' back to break your dirty ugly neck.' Her fingers had found an artery and he felt himself growing faint. He managed a high-pitched grunt.

She rode back to town, wishing that all the white trash in Kentucky would return to the slums of New York or Boston or Baltimore and get themselves wiped out in one big epidemic of cholera, and do it quietly, so as to stop bothering people with their smelly misery. Brightsides was running the bar when she walked in. 'You sure left that Dunkerley woman hip-deep in shit,' she told him.

'I sewed her up. That's not enough for you?'

'I seen hogs take better care of theirselves.'

'All them Dunkerleys got spokes out their wheels,' Hoke Cleghorn said. 'Comes from marryin' their cousins.'

'Bad stock,' Ryan Kidder said wisely. 'Their kids got hair growin' on the palms of their hands. I seen it.'

'If Dunkerley was a stallion I'd pay to have him shot,' Maggie said.

'God Almighty, Maggie,' Brightsides said, 'you're in a terrible temper. Take a drink.'

She cleared her throat, spat at a cockroach and swamped it. 'I need a bowl of chili.'

'Shot an Apache once, enough hair on his ass to stuff a sofa,' Cleghorn said.

'Ask me if I got paid,' Brightsides said, as Maggie went past him.

'Kill an Apache, his hair keeps growin',' Kidder said. 'Well-known fact.'

'Not a dime,' Brightsides called. 'Not a nickel. Expect me to dust and polish? For nothing?'

Frankie Nickel was in the kitchen, cleaning her Derringer. 'Do any good?' she asked.

'I couldn't improve that family with a sack of soap and a wagon-load of bibles. She'll live to do it all over again. Ain't life monoto-nous?' Maggie shoved a pot of chili onto the stove. 'Anythin' happen while I was out?'

'Not a damn thing. Got to do somethin' about your cook before he gets hit with one of his own steaks and killed dead. You need eggs. Damn rat's back again. I got engaged to be married to Major de Glanville.'

Maggie got a chair and sat and looked at her.

'Your chili's burnin',' Frankie said.

'How I like it. Why marry that slick, smooth, connivin' sonofabitch?'

'Cus I love him.'

Maggie thought about that until her eyes went out of focus. 'Always seemed the worst possible reason to me,' she said. 'Still does.'

~

At the end of the week, Lucy walked back up the mountain. Lonzo had been waiting, but he didn't go to meet her. He sat and watched her, until the day shrank and dusk wandered in from the east, soft and silent as a field hand finishing work. When he saw the first stars he knew he had to act or she would soon be invisible to him, black on black.

He got up and walked, and a painful thudding made his chest ache. He thought he was ill. He felt slightly sick in the throat and very light-headed. In a moment he would have to speak, and he had no words.

'Well, Lonzo,' she said.

'Say why.' For some reason he was whispering. He never whispered. Something to be said, let the whole world know. Now he was whispering. 'You don't care if we eat or starve. If this place, which we bought, goes back to wilderness, an' we go to ... I don't know where we go to. You don't care, so why come back up here? Why?'

'Sixty-one bucks.' She sounded wistful. 'That's what this is all about. Not me. Sixty-one bucks.'

'You said fifty-eight.'

'I whored some more. You all know I whored this money, everyone knows that. You ain't shocked, so don't say you is.'

'Ain't pleased, neither.'

'Why not? I give good value, I *worked* my black ass, this is honest money. Might take me to Louisville. Chicago, even.'

'Do what, then? More whorin'?' That was no whisper. 'You gonna go to your grave on your black ass? Workin' for a lousy dollar under some sweaty boozed-up whitey?' He was too angry to stop until he heard the rage in his voice. 'Oh, goddamn,' he said. 'Sorry, Luce, I'm sorry.'

'Well, don't be,' she said. 'Cus there ain't no sixty-one dollars. I lied. Ain't no sixty-one bucks. I just said there was, to make people treat me different.'

Lonzo was slow to understand her; but when he did, he laughed: more of a cautious chuckle. 'You ain't goin' to Louisville, then,' he said. 'Praise the Lord.'

'Jesus wept!' she said. 'I ain't got forever, Lonzo. You want me? I want you, but I gotta go back an' bake for the Hudds tomorrow. We gonna stand here all night?'

Lonzo had to wake up Aaron to tell him. 'Her an' me, gonna jump the broomstick tomorrow.'

Aaron groaned, and spat, and groaned again. 'Go to hell,' he said. 'Dyin'. Can't you see I'm dyin'?'

Next day Lonzo and Lucy got married by holding hands and hopping over a broomstick, while the whole colony watched. There was a feast of roast rabbit with nuts and dried fruit and herb tea, if you can call that a feast.

When Lucy had to leave, Lonzo walked with her. Where the track zig zagged down through the forest, she stopped at a rotten stump and reached inside and took out a canvas bag. 'Seventy-five dollars,' she said, and gave it to him. 'I lied when I lied.'

'You got any more surprises?'

'I got a few moles in places you ain't seen yet.' She hugged him. 'You want milk an' pork an' stuff, you gotta have a whore for a wife. Get used to it.'

He watched her until she was lost in the trees. He had never expected to get married: too definite, too nailed-down. Now he was sharing her with every horny whitey who had a dollar in his pants. Forever. It grated. Forever was a lot of grating.

MONEY AIN'T IT

I married you for better or worse,' JoBeth said, 'but not for Kansas.'

Her husband thought that was so funny, he had to stop and lean against a wall. Well, one reason why she'd married him was because he laughed easily. She needed some fun, after the way her life had gone. The law in Redondo had told her to vanish before her story spoiled the reputation of the town, so she'd abandoned the farm and ridden to San Antonio, which was big enough to hide in, and a sight better to live in than Desolation, being Spanish, and pretty, and not the kind of place where people got shot in their beds, dead or alive. She stayed away from newspapers, so she never read any reports about Douglas van Orman. Or Charlotte van Orman, either. Found work in a flower shop, making bouquets and wreaths. On a whim, called herself JoBeth Hudd, but not for long. Met a cowboy called Jack Chisholm. Married in a month.

He was tall and lanky, thin even, with yellow hair and grey eyes that many women envied. Wasted on a man, they thought. The rest of his face seemed worn fine by long days of work in the endless Texan winds. He was just eighteen. Eighteen and one month. She was surprised. 'That makes me kind of *old*,' she said.

'I'll catch you up, don't worry.'

'How d'you reckon that?'

'See a thirty-year-old cowboy, he looks forty or more. Truth is, the feller's only twenty-five.' He was laughing before he finished speaking. Jack Chisholm found life thoroughly entertaining.

'Is it the food, or what?'

'It's the life, I guess. Why d'you think people call us cowboys? Cus that's what we are, most of us, boys. Dollar a day, that ain't a man's pay. Thing is, we still got young bones. Got grease in our joints.

Bounce like a rubber ball. I seen old-timers, end of the day, hangin'
by their arms from a tree, stretchin', gettin' the knots out their spine.'
He laughed at the memory. 'Hard way to earn a dollar.'

'Why do it?'

He had no answer to that; only a smile.

They lived happily for a few months, all the more happily because
they were often apart for days at a time. Jack Chisholm worked for
a ranch just outside San Antonio. The rancher had no time for
cowboys' wives; no room, either. She kept her rented rooms, and
whenever the couple were reunited they coupled until the sweat
made their skin squeak. It was a good time. Texas was picking itself
up and grudgingly admitting to itself the South had lost, while never
conceding victory to the Northerners who came down to enforce the
Union. But there was trade again, and more money. Jack Chisholm
was happy being a cowboy and a husband. JoBeth was happy being
Mrs Chisholm, and fooling around with flowers, and looking
forward to seeing Jack again, and idly wandering what might come
next in her patchwork life. What came next was what didn't come
next. Idle wondering ceased.

'I've been regular as the moon, ever since I was thirteen,' she said.
He was sitting in the tub. She was washing five days' dust out of his
hair. It gleamed like fresh straw between her fingers. 'Now I missed
a month. Nothin' wrong with the calendar, so it must be me.'

'Must be us. Don't I get some credit?'

'Big joke. Well, this ain't no joke. You understand what I'm
sayin'?' She poured a bucket of water over his head and then, in a fit
of impatience, placed the upturned bucket on his head.
'Understand?' She rapped the bucket with her knuckles.
'Understand, cowboy?'

'You're carryin'!' he said, loud and muffled at once. 'That's wonderful! Ain't it?'

'I guess so.'

He stood up, skin gleaming like moonlight, and reached blindly
for her. 'Never thought I'd say this, but I think you're nicer'n my
horse.'

'That's just flattery. Never thought I'd ask this, but are all your
family hung like you?'

'Only the men.' After that the bucket came off and the talking
ended.

They went out later, had as good a time as a couple could have in San Antonio on five bucks, came away with two dollars forty-five in change, and were walking home when he told her he was leaving in two days, going on a cattle drive to Kansas. Take two months, maybe three. He'd be back long before the baby came. That was when she said she married him for better or worse, but not for Kansas. And he laughed.

'We don't need the money,' she said.

'Money ain't it. I get the same, dollar a day. It's the name, Chisholm. My uncle was Jesse Chisholm, he found the Chisholm Trail, north out of Texas, up through Indian Territory, right into Kansas. Chisholm Trail. Named after him.'

'Yeah, I worked that out. Don't explain why you have to go.'

'I know some of the trail. Uncle Jesse showed me. Now I can help find the way. Ain't a big herd, thousand head, but they fetch big prices in the North. If we get these cows through the Chisholm Trail, we can take two-three thousand next time. How 'bout that?'

It was an adventure. She didn't try to stop him.

Two days later, they went together to watch the herd move off. He tossed his bedroll and a bag of spare clothes into the chuck wagon, and introduced her to the cook, an old man called Chinky Jones because he had slanty eyes. Husband and wife embraced, and kissed goodbye.

The herd was sluggish and mulish. It made only ten miles that day. Next day was better: fourteen miles. Even so, the cows took their own sweet time settling on the bed ground. The sun was melting into the horizon by the time the men turned hungrily towards the chuck wagon.

No Chinky Jones. JoBeth Chisholm was cooking.

The boss foreman was a gruff Scotsman called Mabon. 'What the devil's this?' he demanded.

'Chinky took sick,' she said. 'Went home.'

'And you just happened to be here.'

'On my way to visit a sick aunt. She ain't so sick as Chinky, so she can wait. I made this here stew.'

Mabon didn't like surprises, hated losing control, especially disliked seeing women within a mile of his camp. One thing he couldn't control was his mouth, which was salivating gently. He had a plate of stew. They all did. Most came back for seconds.

Mabon said, 'Thank you, ma'am.' His tongue had trouble with the strange words. Tomorrow he would get another cook.

～

J. Hubert Hunkin was a Presbyterian ex-navy chaplain who shaved in cold water and brushed his hair so severely that at times his scalp bled. As a preacher he was less popular than Flub Phillips, but Flub had no church and there was rain in the air. The pews were full. It was the first time Rock Springs had seen a bridegroom with a French name wearing a sword in a scabbard, found by Maggie in a trunk. The wedding cost twenty dollars, including harmonium and bell-ringing. It was cheaper to die in Rock Springs.

Hunkin married the couple briskly, and started his address. 'Guilt and sin are the burden we each inherit when we come into this world,' he said, his voice harsh from years of shouting into the wind of human ignorance and folly, 'and you can be sure that matrimony does not lessen that burden. Some say it doubles it.' That was meant to be a joke. Nobody laughed. *Rot in hell, the lot of you*, Hunkin thought. 'With guilt comes retribution,' he said, 'just as surely as with sin comes eternal damnation. The Bible warns us: Abstain from fleshly lusts, which war against the soul ...' Hunkin was hot on fleshly lusts. If you didn't have any when he began, you were certainly well informed before he finished, which was not soon.

～

The wedding celebrations were loud and happy. Maggie hired a small band from Barber's Landing for dancing. There was a pig roast, courtesy Hoke Cleghorn, and a tub of fruit punch that gave off a curious shimmering blue haze. Dusk had fallen, and crows, scandalized by the noise, were circling over the town, when Ryan Kidder saw an empty chair beside Sims and Stackmesser, and he slumped into it. He had a good view of the dance. The happy couple were going strong. 'Where we gonna find ourselves a deputy tomorrow?' Kidder asked.

'Upstairs,' Sims said. Stackmesser grunted laughter.

'He's in the goddamn army. He can't live here.'

'He quit,' Stackmesser said. 'Resigned his commission. Gonna be the deputy's wife now.'

'Ain't love wonderful?' Sims said, sourly. His first and only wife had run off with a consumptive Polish piano-player, a choice that baffled him on all three counts.

'What about our bridge?' Kidder asked.

'Oh, he sent in his report to Washington. Last thing he did before he resigned. We'll get our bridge.'

THE YEAR OF JUBALO!

Lucy's seventy-five bucks got the colony out of a hole, got it eating better, got it busy planting corn (the earth was thin but any fool could grow corn) and hooking catfish down on the Cameron, and selling buckskins to the pedlar, who sold them on, down river. Then two pieces of luck came along and made a big difference.

The first was when Aaron bribed a passing trapper to teach the men how to trap. Later they found a beaver pond deep in the wilderness, so deep that nobody had trapped there before. A good beaver pelt was worth three dollars; if nobody in Rock Springs would pay, someone in Barber's Landing or Slade's Crossing certainly would. The other piece of luck was Martha's brother, T. Speed Hudd.

He didn't look lucky when he arrived. He looked like what he was: a man who had walked from Jackson County, Alabama, living on little more than fresh air and hope. His body was so worn-down that when he shuffled into the Hudd colony, Lonzo was surprised he had enough face left to smile with. 'Ain't no dogs here?' T. Speed asked softly. Lonzo said no, just hogs, no dogs. 'Dogs dislike me,' T. Speed said, and made that amazing smile like a candle in a pumpkin, except even the emptiest pumpkin is never that hollow.

Many of Martha's family had been sold south by Henry Hudd, including her mother, cried off on the auction block in Rock Springs. (Hudd had kept Martha as a playmate for his little niece, who was visiting.) Whisperin' Jim Metcalfe, a part-time preacher with a voice that rattled windows, was the auctioneer. That day he sold twenty-eight slaves in under an hour, all stark naked so customers could recognize any mean niggers from their bullwhip scars. Whisperin' Jim was famous for his honesty. He even provided white gloves, free, to those who wished to feel teeth for evidence of cup worms, or prod loins for signs of hernia. 'This here is a fine wench,' he shouted when Martha's mother climbed on the block. 'Thirty years old, strong as an ox.' He cracked his whip, just for effect; he never cut the stock. 'See them legs? All muscle! Trot for the gentlemen. Trot, trot!' Martha's mother jogged on the block, arms crossed to keep her breasts from flopping. 'She can do that all day. How much for this field hand?' He got only eight hundred dollars because she had a wall-eye, product of a stone that flew up from a buggy wheel. 'A fair sale,' Whisperin' Jim boomed. 'Let all things be done decently and in order. First Corinthians, fourteen, forty.' People trusted a Christian auctioneer. A plantation owner's agent from Crawfordville, Georgia, bought her and her two boys, Jeff and T. Speed. Jeff was small, never grew big, couldn't keep up with the others working in the fields, got thrashed with a leather strap by the owner's son so often that it killed him. The strap bled him again and again until finally he walked away from a thrashing and fell on his face. No time off the working day was allowed for a nigger funeral. At sundown they dug a hole in the corner of a field and put Jeff in it. That field never did make a good crop again. The slaves said it was cursed, Jeff was underground cursing the roots and making them shrivel. The plantation owner got so disgusted, he sold Jeff's mother and brother to Mr Dewey Simpson of Jackson County, Alabama. That was where they stayed until Emancipation. Somehow, word of the Hudd colony reached them. Martha had done a lot of walking around Dundee County, looking for Hudd niggers, and this news got all the way down into Alabama. Slave grapevine. The old lady was too frail to leave Jackson County, so T. Speed set off alone. It was a long walk from Alabama to Kentucky, made longer by the many dogs that disliked him.

Martha didn't recognize her brother. She fed him and gave him a bed. For a week he did little but eat and sleep, eat and sleep. He put on weight like soft fruit in the sun. His creases smoothed out, his back straightened, he got shoulders again. And that smile grew stronger: the candle never flickered. It bothered Lonzo a little.

'Good thing you didn't come here coupla months back,' he said. 'Was livin' on roots. *Wild* roots.'

'Them days is past,' Martha said. She was permanently pleased: she'd found her brother! Even if she didn't recognize him. T. Speed smiled, and ate more cornbread and honey.

'Maybe,' Lonzo said. It was Thursday, or was it only Wednesday? Easy to lose track. Might have to wait two days before Lucy came up the Ridge. Or three. He was twitchy and itchy with wanting her. 'Ain't never heard a name like yours,' he said to T. Speed. If he couldn't have Lucy, he grudged everybody everything.

'Got two names. Speed comes second, after the T part. Master Henry Hudd give me them names, when I was born. Said I looked special, give me a special name.'

'The T mean anythin'?' Lonzo asked.

'Never knew. Got sold south before I was big enough to ask.'

'T. Speed,' Lonzo said. He envied the mystery, and he scowled to hide his envy. 'Could mean trouble. T for trouble.' Martha scoffed.

'One thing I ain't is trouble,' T. Speed said softly. 'Do what folks want, give 'em what they need. Make 'em happy.' Now that his face was filling out, his nose looked narrower, his lips thinner and curling. He looked at Martha, and the sunlight glanced differently from his skin. Lonzo saw a copper sheen blended into the black. He turned and left.

'Master Charles made Lonzo read stuff,' Martha explained to T. Speed. 'Now he got a brain so full of readin' there ain't no room left for sense, sometimes.'

~

Judge Potter died.

He had been in the woods with his hounds, chasing a coon, when they got all excited and so did he. His feet blundered into some brambles which snared his ankles and he banged his head on a rock. When the hounds got tired of baying at the coon up a tree, and came back, Potter was cold as last night's candlewax, and about the same colour.

Charles Hudd went to Downeysville for the funeral. In church, the tributes made Potter sound like Pericles with good taste in cigars. Later, when the body was buried, and the great and the good of Dundee County were eating fried chicken and drinking up the judge's stock of whiskey, he was remembered differently. 'Worst lawyer this side the Mississippi,' a retired state senator said affectionately. 'Maybe this side the Rockies.'

'Potter never actually finished law school, you know,' another man said. 'Hated writing. Fact is, he wasn't too comfortable at reading, neither.'

'Smartest thing he ever did was give up the law and run for judge.'

'All you need is a gavel.'

'A gavel, and a gut like a goat.'

'Sure. Sam had both. Who gives a damn about statutes an' such?'

Charles Hudd overheard this, and many similar remarks. A month later, he went to the auction and bought Potter's gavel and law books, both of them: *Rules of Evidence*, and *The Trial of King Charles the First*. He read them inside a week. When he campaigned, he called himself the Honourable Colonel Charles Hudd, wore a big hat, smoked long cigars, and made short speeches full of folksy jokes, like the story of the city slicker who asked a Kentucky farmer the selling price of his beef, and told him he could get ten times that in New York, so the farmer pointed at his duck pond and said he could get a dollar a drop – in hell. People like that sort of stuff. Not the Killicks, who naturally voted against him. Still, Hudd won the election without breaking sweat. Judge Hudd. Sounded good.

~

When Flub Phillips told Lonzo he would pay five dollars a skin, for one hundred full-grown beaver skins, Lonzo said yes, didn't stop to think twice, five bucks was one hell of a price. Flub was unusually happy-looking: pink in the cheek and bright in the eye. Lonzo went back up the Ridge like it was a piece of prairie, and got the men and boys out trapping. Five hundred dollars! Maybe Josh had been right: maybe milk and honey was going to be theirs. He had Luce. The corn and taters were looking good. No white man had tried to kill a Ridge nigger since last summer. Optimism oozed like pine pitch.

A hundred good skins took nearly a month to get. Trapping beaver was hard work: finding a beaver dam was just the start, it didn't tell you where the entrance was to the lodge that a family lived in, because the tunnel began underwater and it might be ten, twenty, forty feet long. And if a beaver swam out to feed and got half a glimpse of something strange in the woods, it went straight to the bottom. Big lungs, slow heart. Ten, fifteen minutes later it might be thinking of coming up but by then it could be at the other end of its lake, climbing a tunnel which no stranger could see because that tunnel began underwater.

One day, they brought home only three skins. Luke Corrigan wanted to smash the dams, drain the lakes, get on with the job.

'Kill 'em all, huh?' Aaron said. He was perched on the Altar, more than ever looking like a wizened infant.

'Yessir.' It had been a long three-hour walk to the beaver pond and a longer three hours back.

'I had a blind mule could see further'n you,' Aaron told Luke. 'What you gonna trap when you killed the last beaver?'

Luke rubbed spit on his scratched arms. 'Um,' he said.

'Um?' Aaron said. 'Um ain't fetchin' good prices lately. You fill a wagon with um, you be lucky you get one thin dime for it. Um is right out a style, boy.'

'Now you had your fun,' Lonzo said, 'you got anythin' to say might help?'

'Start thinkin' like a beaver, stop thinkin' like a nigger,' Aaron said. 'An' leave enough of the critturs alive to fuck each other. Got no right to mess with Creation.'

'Amen!' said Josh. 'Praise the work of the Lord!'

'The Lord done made my guts all twisted,' Aaron told him. 'He did a bad day's work on my guts. I got pains – '

'Bad whiskey ain't the Lord's fault,' Josh said, so sternly that he surprised Aaron into silence. 'Ain't nowhere in the Bible says you got to drink bad whiskey.'

'Grub time,' Lonzo decided. 'What we got to eat?'

'Um,' Luke said, just like that. It was a joke, the first joke Luke had ever been known to make. 'Fried um.'

'Hallelujah!' Josh said.

They cut tracks deeper into the wilderness. It was all concertina country: you were either going up or down. They explored the streams, jumping from boulder to boulder, an exhausting way to travel which usually led to nothing but a hole in a hillside. One stream in twenty might have a beaver dam, and sometimes that dam was collapsed and abandoned. But Lonzo's enthusiasm never failed. 'Five bucks a skin!' he kept reminding them, and on the fifth day of the fourth week they trapped their hundredth beaver. As they marched back to the Colony they carried it like a flag on a pole, and sang a slave song that had spread up from the

311

south at Emancipation. It ended:

De massa run, ha ha!
De darkie stay, ho ho!
Must be now dat de Kingdom am a-comin',
In de year ob jubalo!

It was Saturday. Lucy came up the Ridge that evening. She brought a small roast duck, a bunch of turnip greens and half a peach pie, all stolen from the Hudds' kitchen. They ate in their cabin, by the light of a pitch-pine torch stuck in the doorway. Lonzo had sat under a small waterfall and let the creek wash away the sweat and grime of the wilderness. Now he wore only a pair of clean pants, and the torchlight wandered across his upper body as if happy at the play of coppery skin on muscle. She wore a soft cotton dress that Mrs Hudd have given her, buttermilk yellow, and because her shoulders were much broader than Mrs Hudd's she had made a deep cut down the front. She watched Lonzo watching the swing and sway of her breasts, and enjoyed being enjoyed.

'Gonna be sweet to me tonight?' she asked. They were sitting face to face, her legs tucked inside his, their toes nudging each other's buttocks.

'No.' He was chewing a duck-leg. 'Gonna crawl off an' read the newspaper.'

'Aaaaw …' She twitched her toes and made him squirm.

'Listen, I ain't so young any more. I got to be … I dunno …' This was an old routine between them. He slumped his shoulders, and she looked aslant, brows squashed together. 'Mebbe twenny-three,' he said. 'My sweetness gettin' kinda scarce.'

'I can pay.'

'Don't need your dollar. Got me a hundred beavers.'

'You ain't never seen a beaver like my beaver.' She said it so briskly that she made him laugh.

'You keep on doin' that with your toes,' he said, 'I'm liable to go off bang like a big old cannon an' then I ain't gonna finish eatin' this juicy old duck.'

She licked her fingers, and eased the dress over her head and carefully laid it aside. Lonzo's eyelids were heavy with hunger; he felt swamped by sexual greed; he could taste it crowding the back of his throat. He was helpless, yet he was trembling with a surplus of power. 'Jesus, Luce,' he said. 'You ain't ugly.'

'You ain't old, neither. Ain't we the lucky couple?'

Breakfast was cold blueberry pancakes and syrup, also stolen. Lonzo felt as if he had been taken to pieces, oiled, cleaned and polished, and put together again. Lucy was drowsy as a well-fed cat. 'Tell you who's old,' she said. 'Old man Hudd's old. His nuts've dried up. Now all I do is hold his hand. Still get a dollar.' She gave Lonzo some money.

'Eight dollars an' a quarter,' he said. 'A *quarter?*'

'Little Nelson Hudd. Boy got excited an' creamed his britches tryin' to get his little dingus out.'

Lonzo sniffed. 'White folks ain't got no damn control *at all*.'

'Ain't all bad, you get to know 'em.'

'Animals,' Lonzo said. 'They can't help theirselves. It's in their blood.' He could afford to be generous.

PANCAKE-WRANGLER

Mabon was as much fun as a boil on the backside but he was a good foreman. He knew cattle. It rained during the night, suddenly and violently, a cold, stabbing rain that needled the cows until they got to their feet. Lightning flickered. Mabon woke four men and sent them to ride guard on the herd, extra to the two cowboys already on duty. But the rain closed in like shutters, and when dawn came, and the storm drifted off to bother someone else, Mabon knew that cattle were missing.

It took most of the day to get them all back. Some strays were found grazing a mile away, others had wandered for three or four miles and were scattered, hidden by brush. An evil-tempered steer that never liked the herd in the first place had led a bunch of young animals halfway to San Antonio.

Mabon got the herd on the move for a couple of hours, just to remind them of the habit. No time to go searching for a new cook. Everyone was hungry.

'This beef's bloody,' Mabon said, not looking at JoBeth. 'I don't eat bloody beef.'

She forked his steak and tossed it back on the grill. She hooked another steak, black as charcoal, and dropped it on his plate. Mabon took a bite and it crunched like overdone bacon. He grunted approval and moved away.

The food was eaten in ten minutes. JoBeth was amused by their speed. 'I'll take it as a compliment,' she said.

'Don't pay to linger,' said a cowboy called Elliott.

'Trouble happens fast,' Jack Chisholm told his wife. 'No sadder sight than the meal you had no time to eat.'

She looked around. It was twilight, mild and calm. The herd had settled and was quiet. The sky was clear. 'What trouble?' she said.

'This is the most peaceful place in Texas.'

Nobody had the bad manners to laugh, but everyone was amused. A hand called Brogan told her, 'Cus some cows misbehaved last night, don't mean it can't happen again tonight. Takes a herd a while to learn its manners.'

'Same goes for the *remuda*,' the wrangler said. His name was Huckaby. 'Just the smell of a wolf worries a horse. One runs, they all run.'

'*Remuda*,' JoBeth said. 'That's a word I keep hearing.'

'Trail horses.' Jack pointed to the rope corral attached to the chuck wagon. 'There's your *remuda*.'

'You ain't never heard of a *remuda* before?' Huckaby was amazed and a little disgusted.

'She's from Kentucky,' Jack said.

'Oh, Kentucky.' Huckaby forgave her ignorance. All he knew about Kentucky was it wasn't cattle country, so the hell with it. 'No *remuda*, no trail herd. No wrangler, no *remuda*. Each man here has a string of ten horses. That's an exact one hundred in total, plus two extra for the foreman, and I know each horse by name, smell, an' stride.'

'Horse has a bigger brain than a cow,' Elliott said. 'Things'll spook a horse that a cow never sees. Wind makes a tree creak. Owl kills a rabbit. Shootin' stars in the sky. But I never heard of no wolves south of Austin. Horse can't smell what ain't there.'

'Heard of Indians?' Huckaby said. 'There's Indians can sound like a wolf, an' smell like a wolf. They're more'n halfway to bein' animals themselves.'

'I was told all them tribes were gone out of Texas,' JoBeth said. 'Sent north into Indian Territory.'

'All got sent,' Huckaby said. 'All didn't go.'

'There's renegade Comanche hidin' out over towards the Louisiana border,' Brogan told her. 'Some in Piney Woods.'

'Big as Delaware,' Elliott said. 'So I'm told.'

'Most are in Big Thicket,' Brogan said. 'Nothin' lives in Big Thicket 'cept Comanche, horse thieves, red wolves an' black bear. Comanche get tired of the company, they sneak out an' raise a little hell.'

'Louisiana's two hundred miles from here,' JoBeth said.

'That it is,' Huckaby said. 'And a Comanche could be hidin'

315

behind a blade of grass, listenin' to every word we say.'

Mabon had been silent throughout all this. Now he stood up and said to JoBeth: 'There's two other things about the *remuda* that our wrangler didn't say. First, no man rides a horse from another man's string. Second, there's never a mare in a *remuda*. I don't need to explain why. Aside from cows, anythin' female is bad luck in a cattle drive. Normally I'd require you to sleep a good mile from this camp. Since your husband is here, you two can bunk in the wagon together. Tomorrow we pass New Braunfels. I intend to hire a new cook there. Goodnight.'

Jack got into the blankets fully dressed, but JoBeth took exception to the spurs, so he took his boots off. He fell asleep almost immediately. She lay awake, thinking about Comanche and their dreadful habits. Next thing she knew, Jack was being shaken awake, getting up, dragging his boots on. 'Third night-guard,' he said, and clumped away. It was more than two hours before he came back.

'Was that you singin'?' she said. 'Awful faint, but it sounded like you.'

'Keeps the cows happy. They don't like strangers.' He took his boots off without being told. 'Don't like anyone ridin' too close, either. Night guard keeps twenty, thirty feet away. Cows know the singin', know it's us.'

'What do you sing?'

'Oh, old Spanish stuff. Longhorns come from Mexico, they like Mexican songs. I been thinkin': bet you paid old Chinky to vamoose.'

'Ten bucks. You smell of horse.'

'And a damn fine horse he is. Chinky would've gone for five. Hates cookin'.'

She snuggled close to him. 'Think your foreman would object if we indulged our lusts a little?' But by then he was asleep again. He had the cowboy's knack of grabbing every minute of sleep on offer. 'Guess I'll have to get used to that,' she said.

～

The hardest part about being cook was driving the chuck wagon. It had no springs. The trail was all lumps and dips. JoBeth sat on a pair of bedrolls but that didn't save her sweet butt from a day-long hammering.

She cooked breakfast at dawn: pancakes and bacon for ten. The herd was already awake and noisy, restless, impatient. 'Ain't great sleepers, are they?' she said as she went around with fresh coffee.

'You don't know *nothin'* about cattle, do you?' Huckaby said. With a stomach full of chuck better than Chinky ever cooked, he was prepared to be generous.

'Never studied the animal, no.'

'They want breakfast, just like us. Can't eat where they are now, that's old dead grass, what we call bed ground, good for cows to rest on. Now they want to eat, so we give 'em what they want.'

'Always give a herd what it wants,' Mabon said. 'That's the trick. I never liked that word cattle *drive*. You can't *drive* a thousand head for two thousand miles, and there's no need to try. Texas Longhorns like to walk. Outwalk a horse, some of them. Just point 'em north and let 'em think you're followin' 'em. After a few days, after a herd gets trail-broke, this can be a very boring job. Walkin' to Kansas. Dull.' He stopped abruptly. It had been a long speech, for Mabon.

Already the men were on the move, tossing their bedrolls into the wagon, swigging the last of the coffee, heaving their saddles onto the mounts that Huckaby had ready and waiting. Soon only Jack Chisholm and Brogan were left. Brogan was short and wide, with a heavy moustache going grey at the end. 'Mabon just told us a whole bunch we all knew anyway,' Jack said.

'Wasn't talkin' to us,' Brogan said.

'Who to, then?'

Brogan nodded at JoBeth.

'Me?' She was scrubbing the big cast-iron griddle with ash from the fire. 'I'm just the pancake-wrangler.'

'You found the foreman's weakness,' Brogan said. 'He can't say thanks, ain't in his nature. Can't say sorry, same reason. So he goes the other route. Tells you it's one long, dull walk to Kansas, no place for a lady. What he really means is, damn, them pancakes was a little feast, wish I could get chuck like that every breakfast.'

'Chinky made pancakes you could shingle a roof with,' Jack said.

'Sooner eat shingles than Chinky's pancakes,' Brogan said.

'They'd make damn fine shingles,' Jack said. 'Take a big storm to get past Chinky's pancakes.' Both men laughed, and went to their horses.

She was left to load her cooking gear, fetch the mules, harness and hitch them, and drive past the herd, which was stretching out like an army on the march.

She had learned that it was best to be in front, beyond the dust-cloud raised by a thousand animals. Jack was riding swing, watching the flank, checking any cow that might have a mind to stray, chasing off any range cattle that might like to join the herd. He waved his hat, and she waved her whip. It was not yet six o'clock. Apart from the midday meal, he would be in the saddle until near sundown. Same tomorrow, same all week, all month. Mabon was right. Walking to Kansas was not exciting.

The herd forded the Guadeloupe easily. It was fast but shallow, except in midstream, when the wagon threatened to float; but by then the lead mules were on stony ground. She drove them hard, and the wagon charged up the bank, bucking and jolting like a live thing.

The grass was good. They nooned there. While they were eating pork and beans, Mabon rode back from New Braunfels. Smoke from its chimneys was obvious, a mile or so away. 'Smallpox,' he said. 'They put a sign up. I went no nearer.' He took his food and ate standing. The herd was on the move fifteen minutes later.

'Looks like you still got the job,' Jack said.

'How could those poor people get the smallpox?' she asked. 'In the middle of nowhere?'

'New Braunfels is all Germans,' he said. 'Maybe they brung it from Germany.'

RICH AS CREOSOTE

hundred beaver skins made a big parcel. Lonzo decided to take someone along to help carry. 'You,' he said to T. Speed. 'You ain't done nothin' lately.' Niggers who didn't work made Lonzo restless. Don't work don't eat; and here T. Speed was starting to look smooth as brown silk.

'Can't,' T. Speed said. 'Promised Mistress Hudd I would go tune her pianner.' And he smiled like a sunflower opening its face. All generosity and innocence.

At first Lonzo was too startled to speak. 'Huh,' he said. 'Huh ... You ain't never met Mrs Hudd.' When T. Speed shrugged, modestly, Lonzo said: 'How come she wants you to ...' He couldn't say the words.

'Guess Lucy told her I could do it. It's a gift,' T. Speed told him. 'Like hog-slaughterin'.'

'Ain't a bit like hog-slaughterin'. How much she gonna pay?'

'Depends. Every pianner's tuned different.'

There was a golden tranquillity about T. Speed that defeated Lonzo. He turned to Luke Corrigan. 'You come,' he said.

'Down to town?' Niggers got run out of Rock Springs.

'Safe with me,' Lonzo grunted, and looked around for any argument. Nobody argued. He liked that. 'Safe with me, boy,' he said.

It was a pleasant stroll down the mountain. Flub Phillips's boy Arnie was sitting outside the house. 'Pa's awful sick,' he said, flat and unfussed, like he might say *Pa's diggin' taters.*

'Watch these skins,' Lonzo told Luke. He went inside and found Flub in bed, sweating like old cheese. His hair was so stuck to his scalp you'd think he'd come in from the rain. Lonzo had never seen a nose so sharp, nor a white man look so white.

After a while Flub began shaking and slowly woke himself up. He saw Lonzo, and recognized him, and cracked a smile, and said: 'Hey.' That was a week's work, right there.

'Brought your beaver skins, Mr Phillips,' Lonzo said, but Flub was asleep again, still shivering.

Lonzo went out. 'He eat anythin'?' he asked.

Arnie shrugged. Lonzo knew there was no woman: she died of the lockjaw or some such after she stepped on a big old rusty nail. Little Arnie was slower than tar. 'Make a fire,' he said.

In the kitchen he found food stuff with different colours of fuzz growing on it, and a cupboard half-full of jars and pots. He sniffed them all. One pot held some old, grey, crumbling strips that might have been willow bark; he took that, along with a handful of dried rose-hips and something that smelled like powdered-up foxglove leaf. He was gambling, but it was a risk against a certainty, because old man Phillips wasn't going to live long unless he got medicine.

Luke had got water boiling; done it without being told. 'Smart nigger,' Lonzo said, and Luke grinned. They brewed a gallon of willow-bark tea, and cooked it hard. 'Make him drink a cup every time he wakes,' Lonzo said. 'It's – '

'Good for the fevers. I know that,' Arnie said, bored already. 'Everybody knows *that*.'

'Notice you didn't *make* none.'

'He didn't ask.'

'*You* could of asked *him*.'

'He been sleepin'.'

Lonzo gave up on that.

Luke picked up the skins and they went and found Doc Brightsides in a shed in the back of his house, laying out a body for burial: white man, about forty, short and fat. 'Name of Sewell,' Brightsides said. 'Kin of Job Sims. Here on a visit.'

'Huh.' Lonzo saw a sturdy pair of boots on the floor, hardly worn. 'You ain't throwin' them out?'

The doc looked at him. 'You come here to bid?'

'Nossir. Came to say, Mr Flub Phillips, he's sick. Got the shakes bad.' The doc nodded. 'We cooked up a mess a tea,' Lonzo said. Those were ten-dollar boots. 'Told Arnie, but ...' Another nod. Lonzo's toes curled, imagining the luxury of ten-dollar boots.

'What he die of?' Luke asked the doc.

'Well, it wasn't his appendix. Just proved *that*. So maybe kidney stones. Or gall bladder. Or plain old-fashioned calendar. Maybe the man ran out of days. A disease which afflicts us all.' He completed sewing up the stomach.

'Ain't buryin' his boots too?' Lonzo asked. 'Bible says, give to the poor cus – '

'Take your chattering head out of here,' Brightsides said, 'before I emancipate it from your greedy body with this small, shiny scalpel.' He knew Sims wouldn't pay him, and Sewell couldn't, so those boots were his, in lieu of fee.

Stackmesser was leaning on the rail outside his store, trying to squirt tobacco juice at a dead cat. Just out of range. Nothing went right, nowadays. War. Niggers. Bad winter, worse flood. Bushwhackers. He spat, and missed, and winced. Cramps in the stomach. He'd eaten Job Sims's fried pork belly and turnip, same as Job's visiting cousin, Sewell. Now look: too weak in the wind to hit a dead cat.

Two niggers came into his line of sight and stopped. 'Got us some real fine beaver,' Lonzo said.

'Got me the guts-ache,' Stackmesser said. 'Think if I blew your black head off I might feel better?'

'Nossir.' There was a rifle within Stackmesser's reach. Lonzo and Luke moved away, not fast enough to avoid the stream of brown juice that hit Lonzo's right foot. 'Ain't dead yet,' Stackmesser muttered with gloomy satisfaction.

Nobody in Rock Spring wanted the beavers, not at five dollars a skin. Doc Brightsides came back from attending Flub. 'Malaria,' he said. 'Thinks he's flying. He liked that tea you made. Highly stimulating. Asked me to get him a woman. I advised against it. Still, if you see a flying woman who might be available ... Good day to you.'

There was nothing to stay for but Lonzo hated to go, hated to trudge to Barber's Landing or, worse yet, back up the Ridge. Luke was drooping under the load. Lonzo bought a stale wheat loaf, cheap: a rare luxury after so much cornbread. They went to the landing stage, and sat on the edge and ate. Little fish showed flashes of white belly as they fought for crumbs.

'Rain comin',' Luke said.

The day was hot, hot enough to boil up huge clouds as crisp as new cotton cloth, tall as mountains, carved at the tops into castles, three-cornered hats, lamb chops, anvils. Especially anvils. Thunder was grumbling on the horizon.

There had been a day long ago, when Luke was a boy and working in the fields. Gathering taters. Head down, back bent, fingers groping deep in the dirt, not seeing the clouds turn black, not hearing the thunder creep closer, until a couple of crack-bangs made him jump. And the others. They looked across the field to where Mrs Corrigan and the overseer were sitting their horses. No sign, no word. Back to work. Rain was no reason to stop: rain that hammered so hard the children couldn't stand, had to kneel and scrabble in the mud. Lightning hit a field hand called Joel, kicked him in the air, fried him stone dead, blackened his black skin, burned his eyes out. The men carried Joel's body to the edge of the field, everyone following, and Mrs Corrigan and the overseer whipped them all back to work. Harsh man, that overseer. Mrs Corrigan was worse. A little blood improved next year's crop, she said. Wouldn't let her slaves pray but they prayed anyway, secretly. Prayed for a special sort of hell that she would go to, soon. Since that day, Luke had a good nose for rain.

Lonzo was thinking of Lucy, and babies, which meant schooling, so money would have to be found: another task. A skiff came downstream with a white man in it. They knew his face. Mungers. Ansel Mungers. Farmed somewhere over the Cameron. Or used to, before he lost his slaves. 'Lookin' for work?' he asked.

'Lookin' to sell beaver pelts,' Lonzo said.

Mungers beached the skiff and waded ashore. He wore a dirty white linen suit with the pants legs rolled up and a too-big hat that sat on his ears. He had jaw enough for two men, and a nose fit for a boy. Lonzo thought all white folks were ugly, but Ansel Mungers could win ugly prizes at the county fair. 'Lookin' in the wrong place, boy,' Mungers said. The voice went with the nose, not the jaw: thin and squeaky. He tore a big piece off the loaf in Luke's hand and fed it into his mouth, bite by bite, like a log into a stove.

'Flub Phillips would of bought,' Lonzo said.

Mungers said: 'Heh-heh-heh.' It was his way of laughing. Sounded like a bust hinge. 'Forget Flub. He's bad luck. Me, I'm good luck.'

Luke hid the rest of the loaf inside his shirt.

'Flub would of sold your skins in Nashville and got double,' Mungers said. 'I got a raft *goin'* to Nashville! Heh-heh-heh … You gonna be rich as creosote, boy.'

'What raft where?' Lonzo asked. The river was empty. Low, too.

'I got her ready an' waitin' in Candle Creek.' He gestured upstream. 'Next good tide, off she goes.'

'Rain comin',' Luke said.

'Real smart nigger! I *need* a real smart nigger for a piker on my raft. Fifty cents a day, an' you can take them skins free to Nashville.'

'Piker,' Luke said, tasting the word, unsure.

'Piker is a man has a pole,' Mungers said. 'Keeps the raft goin' good. Easy work. Free grub too, heh-heh-heh.'

'Ain't never been on no raft,' Luke said, worried. 'Ain't never been nowhere 'cept Rock Springs. Want me to go raftin' to *Nashville?*' he asked Lonzo.

Lonzo didn't, but it was the only way he could figure to sell the beavers. Probably take a week, Mungers said. What could go wrong in a week?

THIS MIGHTY BEHEMOTH

When Major de Glanville told Frankie he got one hundred and thirty dollars for using Stamford's Principle to test for earthquake tendency, and then recommending to Washington that Rock Springs should get a bridge, he lied. He only got ninety-three dollars.

He lied not from vanity, but just to keep in practice. Still the townsfolk had to dig deep to find ninety-three dollars, and now they were getting impatient.

The main contributors met de Glanville one night in Maggie's. 'Money well spent,' Job Sims told him. 'Nobody ain't disputin' that. But how long does Washington take to make up its fool mind?'

'There's been a slight hitch,' de Glanville told them. 'The plan to build bridges all over the nation was conceived by the late President Lincoln. Now that Andrew Johnson is President, I'm informed that he is personally reviewing every aspect of his predecessor's plans. Inevitably, that takes time, so – '

'How long?'

'My information is that three months – ' A harsh rumble of discontent stopped him. ' – which of course is completely unacceptable,' he said, 'and I have urged Washington to act on my recommendation *immediately.*' They did not look happy. 'If you'll excuse me,' he said, 'I'd like to get an early night.'

Frankie went upstairs with him. As she was getting out of her clothes, she said, 'My opinion, you should've left town the minute you cleaned it out. You were treadin' water down there, an' you're wearin' heavy boots.'

'I'll think of something.'

'Better be good.'

After a moment he kissed her on the lips. 'I thought of something very good.'

'What? Oh ... *That*. Well, we could try it out an' see if it works.'

'Not only does it work magnificently,' he said, 'it also sounds bugle calls, sets off red rockets and gives free candy to blind children.' That last bit made her laugh.

Downstairs, Maggie was trying to get rid of the last drinkers while Doc Brightsides was describing a hatter in Granite City, Illinois, in whom he had diagnosed the potato blight, first case of its kind ever known outside Ireland, when the pedlar interrupted him. 'Old Boney found somethin' to laugh at,' he said. 'A dollar says four minutes.'

He was looking at a human skull, very old and stained brown with tobacco smoke. It hung by a cord from the ceiling. Thick cobwebs hid the fact that the cord went through the ceiling. It continued up through a hole in the floorboards. It was tied to the centre of the frame of the bed. Bouncing on the bed made the jaws open and shut.

'I'm gonna chuck that stupid thing in the river,' Maggie growled.

'You can't,' Stanton Killick said. 'It's the only honest gamblin' game in town.' The jaws began to clack. 'Two minutes an' a half.'

Hoke Cleghorn won with five minutes. 'Speed ain't everythin',' he told Stanton. 'You young fellers ought to learn that.'

~

A week passed. Rock Springs was starting to hate Washington. Half the town gathered in the tavern. They wanted a real final definite answer, once and for all.

'President Andrew Johnson has signed his approval of the Rock Springs Bridge,' Major de Glanville announced.

'Hot spit!' Ryan Kidder said. That was the new fashionable exclamation; nobody said 'Holy Moly!' any more.

'We are seventh in line for construction,' de Glanville said, consulting an out-of-date riverboat schedule, 'after Natchez, Vicksburg, Greenville, Clarksdale, Memphis and Oak Bluff.'

'Oak Bluff?' Sims said. 'I ain't never heard of that. How did Oak Bluff get in ahead of us?'

'Politics,' de Glanville said. 'The vice-president's wife has a cousin lives in Oak Bluff. Need I say more?' That got a big laugh.

'When they gonna start?' Cleghorn demanded.

'Next fall.' Nearly everyone cheered.

'Provided …' The cheering died. 'Provided you agree on the type of bridge to be built.' They were silenced. What the hell was this? A bridge was a bridge, wasn't it? 'Do you want a conventional low-level platform bridge,' he said, 'bank-to-bank, one wagon wide; or a cantilevered suspension bridge, high enough to let the steamboats pass under?'

Silence; then a rumble of comment grew to a roar of talk, which stopped when Stackmesser pounded a table. 'You sayin' the *Chauncey* won't go under a platform bridge?'

'Too low,' de Glanville told him. 'And in any case, with a bridge at the end of Main Street, your actual landing stage will have to be rebuilt somewhere downstream.'

'Ain't no place there,' the pedlar said. 'Ground's all soft an' swampy downstream, for a mile or more.'

'That's why the goddamn stage is where it is,' Maggie pointed out. 'That's why this place is called Rock Springs, for Christ's sake.'

'Settles it, then,' Cleghorn said. 'We go for the high bridge. Who in hell cares? Government's payin'.'

'They got new riverboats now,' Kidder said. 'Shallow draught. Might go all the way up to Judd's Creek, maybe Pottsville, even.'

'Talk of the railroad comin' through Pottsville,' Sims added.

Suddenly Rock Springs seemed a lot closer to the big outside world. The meeting brightened.

'Being cantilevered,' de Glanville said, 'a suspension bridge requires extensive support. The cables must be anchored a long way from the river. There are only two suitable sites for such anchorages on this side.' He took out what looked like a plan, consulted it, tucked it away. 'One site is occupied by Mr Sims's blacksmithing establishment,' he said, 'the other by Mr Stackmesser's emporium. The question is – '

'Ain't shiftin',' Sims growled.

'What?' Stackmesser shouted. '*What?* Tear down my store just for your shitty bridge? No sir. Never!'

That was when the debate became loud. Soon de Glanville slipped away. His wife was waiting in their bedroom.

'Pretty slick,' she said. 'I guess you're proud of yourself.'

'It was a good Second Act closing scene, even if I say so myself. My performance gave the audience plenty to think about.'

'Bully for them.' She was stepping out of her jeans. 'I been thinkin' about your performances all day long.'

He kicked off his boots as he threw off his coat. 'This one is going to make Antony and Cleopatra look like a Shaker funeral,' he said.

~

North of San Antonio was what everyone called the Hill Country. JoBeth didn't think it was hilly, certainly not compared to Kentucky. Away to the left of the trail the land rose to form a long escarpment that gleamed white. 'Them's the Balcones,' Jack told her. 'That's Spanish for balconies, on account they look kinda like balconies.' He had come to the *remuda* to get a fresh horse, and now he was riding alongside the wagon.

'Strange,' she said. 'They look to me like three old ladies drinkin' gin.'

He whooped with laughter and loped away. Sometimes she wondered about Jack. Nearly everything was funny to him. He hadn't had much education, she knew that, and cowboy humour was usually restricted to practical jokes, such as filling a man's boots with fresh horseshit. That was a real thigh-slapper, that was. So her maverick remarks usually caught him on the wrong foot, and that made him laugh. It was as easy as tickling a puppy. He was tremendously proud of her, and she spent all day looking forward to the night, and the warmth of his wonderful body. She didn't care that he smelled of horse. She smelled of mule by now.

The land below the Balcones was easy on the herd, plenty of pasture, drained by clean, green streams. They made a steady twenty miles a day. Texas Longhorns gained weight on the trail; even JoBeth could see they were fatter and happier. 'Five bucks a head in San Antone,' Brogan told her. 'Fifty bucks a head in Abilene, Kansas. Good, huh?' She thought about that, as she went through the routine of another day, just like the last: feed ten men, spend the morning looking at four mules in front and hearing a thousand cattle behind, stop where Mabon decided to noon, feed ten men, watch the same mules and hear the same cows all afternoon. Stop when Mabon found a bed ground. Feed ten men. Talk some. The routine of night-watches was unchanging. First watch from eight to ten-thirty. Second from ten-thirty to one. Third from one to three-thirty. Last from then till daybreak. Jack always had third watch. It got so she woke a minute before he got called, and woke again a minute before he climbed into the wagon and slid into their blankets.

Five dollars a head in Texas, fifty in Kansas. The simple arithmetic of it encouraged her to go to Mabon. The herd had just forded the Colorado, the biggest and fastest river they'd met so far, and all the hands were wet to the skin after swimming their horses across and back and across again, channelling the cows into the ford, never allowing the procession to slacken. A sharp wind was blowing, and there was no sun.

'We need stores,' she told Mabon. 'And there's Austin, only ten miles away.'

'Got enough to take us to Waco.'

'Waco? That's a hundred miles. I know what we have. Long before Waco, you'll be eatin' your own cows, an' I'll be fryin' 'em in axle-grease, cus that's all we'll have left.'

'A cattle drive's hard livin'. These men expect it.'

'Sure. My daddy taught me that hard livin's easy. All you do, is do without. Anyone can do that. Takes no great skill to eat bad chuck. The real trick is eatin' as good as you can, for as long as you can. Still, it's your decision.'

Mabon turned away and stood rock-still, as if frozen. JoBeth got on with her work. Elliott came by, to get more coffee, and said softly, 'Smart feller, your daddy.'

'He never taught me nothin',' she said. 'Stupidest man I knew. Don't tell Mabon.'

When it was time to move, Mabon put Brogan in charge of the herd and drove the wagon into Austin with JoBeth beside him. He didn't speak a word, going in or coming back. She bought what she needed, and several items she liked the look of.

'Eggs?' Jack said that evening. 'Chinky never gave us eggs.'

'Ain't a crime,' she said. They spoke normally. Mabon was half a mile away, riding slowly around the herd. 'I thought for sure he was goin' to hire a new cook in Austin. Instead of which I bought a sack of Irish taters, two sides of real good bacon, yards of blood puddin', two gallons of genuine Canadian maple syrup, and a box of cigars. As well as the usual staples.'

'Mabon ain't stupid,' Jack said. 'It's just, he can't think an' talk at the same time.'

'Most men can't. What d'you reckon Mabon was thinkin' when he wasn't talkin'?'

'Thinkin', hey, that Jack Chisholm's a lucky dog. Why can't I get a girl like his?'

'Tell him, two reasons. First, by the time he quits thinkin' and gets round to askin', she's probably moved to Colorado. Second, he's in love with his ugly Longhorns. Want me to tell him?'

'No. You're givin' him eggs for supper, that's more than any cowboy's brain can handle.' He poked his finger through a long tear in her skirt. 'You should of bought new duds in Austin. These ain't goin' to last till Waco, let alone Abilene.' He was right. They were torn and stained, scorched from the cookfire, blackened with smoke. 'I got some things are spare. Might fit.'

They threw a tarp over the wagon. Everyone knew by now that meant: keep away. They got in and she took everything off. 'I know what would fit,' she said. 'Perfect fit, an' you can have it back afterwards.'

He raised the tarp and looked out. Most of the men were washing at a little creek. Mabon had left the herd and was walking his horse back to the camp. 'Two minutes, at most,' Jack said. Already his belt was unbuckled.

'Two? Kinda long-winded, for us, ain't it?' she said. 'Don't wake the baby, that's all.'

When she made the meal, there were admiring remarks about her man's shirt and Levi's.

'Feel a bit tight,' she said.

'They'll give, soon enough,' Huckaby told her. 'But you don't want 'em loose. Flappy trousers catch themselves on thorns an' stuff. We wear our trousers tight, there's a reason. Everythin' I wear, there's a reason.' He took off his hat. 'Jack Stetson made that. Man deserves a medal. You can bucket water with it, you can wave it at cattle, make 'em move, if you get a fever you can fill it with hot rocks, put it in your bedroll, help you sweat it out.'

'Hell, you can even put it on your head,' Brogan said. 'Ain't a bad hat.'

Nobody else spoke. They were all eating too fast.

'Got a big tin of peaches,' she said. They grunted. Ten men grunting made a big grunt. 'Next time,' she said, 'just wave your Stetsons.' They did, all ten of them; even Mabon. 'Serves me right,' she said. 'This ain't no academy of elocution.'

Later, there were the usual campfire yarns. Jack and JoBeth soon went to bed. 'Call of nature,' she told him, and took a spade.

She was crouched behind a bush, enjoying the pleasure of relief, wondering why she bothered to hide, it was dark night and nobody was likely to come this way; when a creature did just that. Something blacker than the night walked towards her and stopped about twenty feet away. She heard it sniffing, then snorting: a deep and angry noise that frightened her so much, she couldn't move. Now there were two of these things. Or maybe it had moved closer. She pulled up her Levi's and flung the spade at it or them and ran to the chuck wagon.

Jack wanted to go and look, but she refused to let him leave her. She was shaking. 'It could of jumped me, could of killed me. What was it?'

'Weren't rustlers. They keep good an' quiet. Probly coyote. Maybe wild pig. I'd say coyote, but they usually turn an' run. Coyote won't attack. Leastways, I never heard of it. Sometimes, vermin get that mad-dog thing, you know, where they foam at the mouth? Liable to do anythin', then. You see any foamy mouth on this one?' That was when she punched him, half from fear and half from anger. He laughed. 'Hey, I didn't do nothin',' he said.

It was a long time before she fell asleep. She kept thinking what might have happened, and what might have followed. Just suppose the beast, or those beasts, had attacked and savaged her. Austin was near. But what if she got sick or hurt two or three days from now? Where would the nearest doctor be? Waco? It had a loud reputation as an outpost of the Texas Rangers. Not famous for their doctoring. Then it would be seventy miles to Fort Worth, with nowhere in between worth stopping at. After that, a couple of hundred miles across Indian Territory ...

For the first time she realized how empty this part of America was. If disaster struck, it was a long haul to the nearest aid; and a long haul would almost certainly kill anyone struck by disaster. She tried to forget about it. Fear kept creeping back.

~

The deadlock over the site for the bridge anchorages lasted more than a week, until one day Frank Stackmesser got a ladder and climbed onto the roof of his store. The stovepipe was loose. Trade was slow, day was hot, might's well fix the goddamn stovepipe. So

330

hc did. It was pleasant up there, nobody to hassle him. He cut his toenails with a nine-inch clasp knife. Down on Main Street, a couple of dogs were flopping about in the dirt, snapping at each other. It was too hot to fight. They quit and went to sleep. He thought: some towns had a dog-catcher. What sort of place would Rock City become after Uncle Sam built a bridge? Full-time dog-catcher, probably. What else? Courthouse, bank, sheriff's office, jail, newspaper building, post office, every kind of store, churches, theatre, cathouse, dentist, lawyer ...

He shouted until Job Sims came out of his blacksmith's shop. 'Come up here,' he said. Sims climbed the ladder. 'We got to quit fightin' over where the footin's go for the bridge, Job,' he said. 'Look around here. Once the damn bridge is in, everythin' you can see is gonna be worth a buck an inch.'

Sims looked. 'Rock Springs could be as big as Nashville.'

'Bigger. Could be big as St Louis.' Stackmesser flung his hammer at the dogs, and missed, but at least it gave them something to think about. 'Let's find the big bridge man.'

Major de Glanville received them courteously. He was in the tavern, sitting at a table, building a model theatre out of cardboard and bent wire.

'Me an' Job ain't fussed where you anchor this bridge,' Stackmesser said. 'Just so long as it happens.'

'Soon,' Sims said.

'Even as we speak,' de Glanville said, 'wheels are turning in Washington. Not only wheels, but wheels within wheels. The giant cogs of government interlock.' He demonstrated this with his fingers. 'And so its massive machinery clanks and lurches into action. Once begun, this mighty behemoth cannot be deflected from its proud purpose, for that, my friends, is the duty of democracy, just as democracy is the anvil of America.'

'Uncle Sam tell you that?' Sims asked.

'In a sense, yes.'

'Well, you tell Uncle Sam we already got two anvils. We need a goddamn bridge.'

'Otherwise how is Rock Springs ever gonna be big as St Louis?' Stackmesser asked.

'That sonabitch river is a knife at our goddamn throat,' Sims said.

'I shall take horse today,' de Glanville promised, 'and telegraph

Washington with our most urgent instructions.' He picked up his model and headed for the stairs.

'See, if we had a bridge,' Stackmesser called, 'we'd have a telegraph office too, an' then you wouldn't have to go noplace.' The major waved acknowledgment.

'I ain't so sure about this whole notion,' said the pedlar, who had been listening from a safe distance. 'You build a bridge, this entire town's liable to cross it an' never come back. Only reason Rock Springs is here is *because* of that big river. Look around. You see any reason for stayin'?'

'We're stayin' so as to get the goddamn bridge,' Sims said, with huge contempt. 'If we don't stay, we can't go. You jackass.'

Frankie was in the bedroom when her husband came in and told her why he was leaving. 'Well, you ain't gonna find no bridge,' she said.

'I might. Something must be done. I'll be back in a few days.'

'Bring some money, honey. Ain't been no crime in these parts lately. Times is hard.'

~

Aaron liked to sit on the Altar rock. It caught a nice breeze, and it put him out of reach of some young hogs that Lonzo had bought. They liked to sniff him or chew his feet. He nearly fell off the Altar when Lonzo told him Luke was with Ansel Mungers, and would soon be rafting the skins to Nashville.

'That heap of black crap?' he screamed: a weak, rattling croak; Aaron's lungs were no longer taking orders. 'He couldn't sell cold beer on a hot day in hell.'

'That's how it's gotta be.'

'God damn Flub Phillips.'

'Flub can't help gettin' sick.'

'Shouldn't be a preacher if he don't get no special treatment.' Lonzo laughed at that, which made Aaron angrier. 'Look what you done! You wasted half summer trappin' beaver you ain't gonna make a dollar from!'

'Listen,' Lonzo said. 'Nobody in Rock Springs had money for them skins. When Luke gets 'em to Nashville – '

'Sure. Go tell it to the goddamn mule. Got more brains'n the both of you.' Aaron turned his back on him.

'Plenty more furs waitin' to be trapped.'

No reply. Lonzo left him, and got Nat and Gabe, and they set traps until sundown. Not for beaver: too far away; but red fox, raccoon, even bobcat and muskrat and opossum were worth catching. Those were one hundred fine beaver pelts, the best, even Luke should have no difficulty getting a better price in Nashville than Flub would have paid. Meanwhile, no harm in keeping working. That's what Lonzo told Aaron. 'Gallstones are killin' me,' Aaron said, all gloom and doom. No pleasing some people.

~

Twenty miles a day, some days more, some less. Nothing much changed. Same dust, same smell, same dull rumble of hooves. From dawn to dusk, cows bellowed. There was no escape. JoBeth's body had toughened; now nothing bruised her; she'd learned to relax on the wagon seat and let the jolts pass through. Sometimes she even slept for a few minutes. The mules kept going, they knew they had to do their twenty miles. No point in stopping.

Accidents were interesting. Horse didn't see a gopher hole, broke its leg, cowboy shot it dead and was waiting, sitting on his saddle, when Huckaby brought him another mount. A man fell asleep too near the fire and burned the toe off his boot. There was a broken finger. Mabon used cord to lash it to the next finger, neat as needlework. That was interesting. But generally nothing happened except the same as what happened yesterday.

They reached the Brazos near Waco. This was bigger than the Colorado, and the leading Longhorns jibbed when they saw how wide and fast it was.

Immediately, Mabon turned the herd and had it walked a good seven or eight miles back the way it had come. For the rest of that day and half the next, the herd was not allowed to drink. It could smell the Brazos, and when Mabon set it on the trail again, thirst did the rest. The first cows rushed the river but men were waiting to drive them on, stop them drinking, get them swimming. When one cow climbed the far bank, there was no doubting that the rest would follow.

Mabon left his men to finish the job, and drove into Waco with JoBeth. He had refused permission for anyone else to go, on the grounds that their only purpose would be drinking, whoring and fighting. This was true. Nobody argued.

Waco was an ambitious trading post with hopes to be much more. Somebody had laid out a site for a town, with lines for streets, but there were few houses. Mabon went straight to a row of log-built warehouses that doubled as general stores. He stood aside while JoBeth bought what she needed. They loaded the wagon and forded the river. 'Goodbye, Waco,' she said. 'The boys didn't miss much.'

'Grew a lot of cotton around here, one time. War killed that trade stone dead. Tornado came through.'

'Not a lucky burgh.'

'There's more.' He stopped the wagon. 'The Brazos floods, regular.' He pointed to layers of silt, high up the bank. 'We're gettin' into north Texas now. It rains here. But that ain't it. Over there to the west, hundred miles from here and more, is the Staked Plains. That's stormy country. Lots of streams have their headwaters back west. Storms up there, floods down here. Big, fast rivers. Cold, too. We've got to cross those rivers. No choice. Can't turn back.'

'You're sayin' this is my last chance to quit.'

'Stay in Waco. We'll find you on the way back.'

'No.'

He shook the reins, and the mules got the wagon rolling again. After a mile, he took a wide-brimmed canvas hat from his pocket and gave it to her. 'Keeps the sun out your eyes,' he said. It was new. She put it on, and turned to show him. He nodded approval. He would have smiled, but it was too big a risk. A man can get the face-cramps that way.

STARK NEWS INDEED

When Lucy took T. Speed to meet Mrs Hudd, he did not smell like a nigger. This was because he had first bathed in a tub in a corner of the laundry, lavishing the suds and the hot water, while Lucy pressed his clothes. He wore an old white linen shirt that Charles Hudd had thrown out. It was too big for T. Speed. It hung in such generous folds that it made his body look slender from the waist down. T. Speed had a dapper build; he was no taller than Mary Hudd. His eyes were a clear, unblinking grey: very unusual for a negro. Most things about him surprised Mary. Naturally she hid her feelings. Lesson number one: keep the nigger in his place.

She sent Lucy away, and took T. Speed up to what she called the music room. It was next to her bedroom. She kept it locked. She didn't want the children fooling around with the piano, banging the keys. 'Can you tune it?' she asked.

T. Speed sat down and played a few soft, simple chords. His hands were small and showed no signs of toil: not so much as a callus. That, too, surprised her.

'This is a good piano,' he said. 'But it has been neglected. Piano's like a beautiful person, Mrs Hudd. Needs regular attention to bring out the best.'

'Uh-huh. Well, I've never been beautiful, mister.' She surprised herself: nobody called a nigger *mister*. 'I'll leave you to get on.'

The upper part of the house was empty. Charles was off doing politics somewhere, the others were working the farm. Mary sat in a window seat, enjoying the sun, patching a quilt, listening to T. Speed's fingers testing the octaves. His touch was soft and persuasive, hunting for something good that wanted to be found.

After an hour he stopped. She put down the quilt. The silence seemed to gather weight.

He was polishing the piano with a duster.

'Have you finished?' she asked.

'For now. I don't want to work this piano too hard, all at once. She needs to get used to her new self.' He folded the duster.

'I never saw such fine hands on a nigger,' she said. 'Your hands make mine look like an old washerwoman's.'

T. Speed held his hands out, palms up, and smiled at them as if they were gifts he had just opened. Mary Hudd put her hands beside them. Fingers touched. 'What did you do when you were a slave?' she asked.

'Just whatever my Master told me to do.'

She felt his hands: smooth as silk, not a crack, not a lump. This was wrong. She held his face by the jaw, and studied it. Neat, clean, regular features; no scars; skin like bone china. She touched his lower lip with a forefinger, and exposed neat and glistening teeth. Normally you could tell a nigger's age by his teeth. She knew T. Speed was over thirty; he looked like he was eighteen. Must have dodged work. 'I bet you were an upity darkie,' she said. 'Take off your shirt.'

No scars on his chest. She turned him, and looked at his back. It tapered from shoulders to waist, and the spine curved inwards just where the pants hung on the hips. His back had never been whipped; she could see that, but she ran her hand over it, top to bottom and side to side, just for proof. At her first touch, his skin made one small flinch; after that it was calm and untroubled. She had almost forgotten how good it was to touch a man.

'Some slaves got whipped lower down,' she said. 'That way, the marks don't show. Kept the price high.'

T. Speed was silent. He placed his hands on top of his head, the fingers linked. It was an invitation.

Mary dragged his pants down. This was madness, and the blood was pounding in her temples. If anyone came in her reputation would be destroyed: all for the sake of one rash, crass act. *Then make the most of it,* she told herself; and her hands stroked and squeezed his buttocks.

'No marks down there either.' She could scarcely speak: excitement swamped her throat. 'Better get dressed.' She reached the window seat just in time. Her head was thumping like a steamboat engine.

'I'll be back tomorrow.' The door opened; the door closed. Mary Hudd saw a red cardinal fly from a green tree, against a blue sky. Wondrous colours. Truly wondrous.

~

After de Glanville had been gone a week, Sims and Stackmesser began asking the deputy if she had any news. This annoyed her. She missed him. Waking up alone in bed was a small heartbreak; there was not an hour in the day when she did not think of him. She was glad when Hutton the sharecropper ran into the tavern, shouting that the sky on the other side of the Cameron river was full of Indian smoke signals, and the town got all excited and distracted and forgot de Glanville.

'Send for the cavalry,' Reuben Skinner said.

'Send for your brains,' Maggie told him.

'Easy for you to say. You didn't get bushwhacked by – '

'Hey!' said Elias Dunbar. 'Smoke signals is a message.' They all looked at him. 'Means there's a whole tribe over there. Sendin' messages.'

Doc Brightsides cleared his throat. 'To whom?' he said.

Devereux Killick burst through the batwing doors. 'Indian smoke signals!' he cried.

'Yeah, we know,' Frankie said. 'Go and get Hoke, will you, boy? We need someone can read Cherokee.'

Everyone trooped down to the landing stage and watched the puffs of white smoke rise beyond the trees and float away, fraying at the edges until they came to bits as if dissolved by the sun.

Hoke arrived at a hard gallop.

'Hot damn! Never thought I'd live to see that devil spoor again,' he said. 'My advice, get the military here an' do it fast.'

'Told you,' Reuben said.

'I heard there weren't no Cherokee left in Kentucky, nor Shawnee neither,' Frankie said. 'All got sent to Indian Territory, didn't they?'

'Some must have hid,' Dunbar said. 'Hid in the woods.'

'That's where my ducks went!' Hutton exclaimed. 'Cherokee came down out of the goddamn woods, stole my goddamn ducks!'

'Not Cherokee,' Hoke corrected. 'Apache, maybe. See, your duck is a sacred animal to the Cherokee nation.'

'Well, some bastard stole 'em, cus they're gone.'

'Dan Killick tried to sell me some ducks, yesterday,' Sims said.

'Those were geese,' Devereux said.

'So why did he say they was ducks?' Sims asked. He and Dev stared at each other, mutually baffled.

'My geese got stolen too,' Hutton said gloomily.

'Maybe I misremembered,' Hoke said. 'Maybe it weren't ducks. Now, if Kit was here – '

'What does that say?' The deputy pointed at the signals. Hoke took a long time squinting. 'Could be one thing,' he decided. 'Could be another.'

'Somebody get a rowboat,' she said.

They crossed the Cameron. The wood was mainly swamp, but there were animal trails; and sprawling tree-roots made a kind of walkway. They searched, and found the ashes of a fire; beside it was an old blanket with a hole burned in the middle. Hoke sucked his teeth. 'Looks bad,' he said. 'Fightin' talk.'

Stuck into a nearby tree was an arrow with long red ribbons dangling from it. 'Jesus!' Stackmesser said. 'What's *that?*'

'That there's a sycamore,' Hoke said confidently.

'Let's go home,' Frankie said.

The Indian scare kept the town jumpy for a couple of days. Someone said the widow Corrigan, who farmed upriver, had shot dead a Cherokee brave as he climbed in her bedroom window. Dan Killick said he'd heard war drums at night. The pedlar said he'd heard drums and bugles playing *My Old Kentucky Home*, by Beethoven. The remark was considered to be in poor taste and it got him thrown out of Maggie's. Next day a genuine Cherokee in a feathered bonnet was seen in the distance, on the opposite bank of the river. He danced around a tree, briefly, and went away. That night, an armed guard patrolled the town.

'Why in blazes have they come here?' Ryan Kidder demanded. 'We ain't important. Why don't they go an' frighten New Jericho?'

'That's easy,' Hoke said. 'They always knock off the weakest places first so they can steal their guns. Me an' Kit, we saw the Comanche do it a hundred times.'

'Cowards,' Reuben Skinner scowled. 'That ain't the American way.'

'Sure ain't,' Dan said. 'When me an' George was fightin' the

Yankees, General Braxton Bragg used to look where the enemy was the *strongest*, an' that's where we'd make our goddamn attack, no foolin'.'

'Brave fellers,' Hoke said. 'There's Dixie spunk for you!'

'Bragg never won, though, did he?' Doc Brightsides said.

'Ain't you got no gall bladders to chop out?' Dan asked.

'That's right, Bragg lost,' the pedlar said. 'It was in the newspaper.'

'Of course he lost,' Ryan Kidder said. 'The whole damn South lost. Weren't Bragg's fault.'

'Weren't nobody's fault,' Reuben said. With redskins across the river, he was anxious to maintain unity. 'Just bad luck.'

'Fuckin' Lincoln,' Hoke said, brooding. 'Any man acts like Lincoln did, ought to be shot.'

'Book a theatre,' the pedlar said. 'Sell tickets.' That remark was reckoned to be in bad taste, and he was thrown out of Maggie's again.

Next day, a Sunday, the Reverend J. Hubert Hunkin preached on the text of Jeremiah, five, eight: *They were as fed horses in the morning: every one neighed after his neighbour's wife.* It was reassuring to hear the same old familiar condemnations, and the men in the congregation came away from church making cheerful horse noises at each other, until the glimpse of another Indian, flickering through the trees beyond the river, brought their spirits down with a thud. A heavily armed party rowed across and found three small piles of stones, forming a triangle. 'Apache sign-language,' Hoke said sombrely. 'Means blood will flow before the next moon.'

'What if it's Cherokee?' Frankie asked.

'Why, that'd be different. Could mean "Sharpen a thousand tomahawks", or it could mean 'This is where we buried our grandmother'. Never know, with your Cherokee.'

'Treacherous,' Ryan said.

They went home. In the evening Flub Phillips preached on the text of Matthew, three, seven: *O generation of vipers, who hath warned you to flee from the wrath to come?* This was generally considered to be unhelpful, and the collection raised only two dollars and sixty cents. The night patrol was doubled. When Major de Glanville rode into town next day, he found the same old crowd in Maggie's but they were unusually thoughtful. He climbed onto a table and waved his cap.

'Work on the bridge foundations is scheduled to begin in four weeks,' he announced. 'The U.S. Army Corps of Engineers will be responsible.' He was grimy from travel and he needed a shave, but his manner was blithe.

'They can build a goddamn stockade, too,' Sims growled. 'We got Indians across the Cameron.' The major got off the table.

'This is stark news indeed,' he said. He walked to the door and stared across the river. 'Indisputably Indians, you say?'

'Maud Corrigan shot one off her windowsill,' Hutton the share-cropper said. 'Scalp-knife in his teeth.'

'Shot one, winged another,' Ryan said.

'Trail of blood,' Skinner added. 'Dogs lost him in the swamps.'

'I must admit I am shocked,' de Glanville said.

'Us too,' his wife said. She was sitting on the stairs, playing check-ers with little Arnie Phillips. 'Renegade Cherokee. Been hidin' in the woods. Come out to massacre us in our beds.'

'We fooled 'em,' the pedlar said. 'Didn't go to bed.' Nobody laughed.

'When Washington referred to an encampment,' de Glanville said, 'I naturally assumed they meant some kind of refuge for travellers, not a reservation, but from what you say ...' His voice was drowned by the grate of chair-legs and the snarl of protest. Every man was on his feet. Stackmesser was loudest. 'Reservation?' he bellowed. 'Government's gonna make a stinkin' Cherokee reservation right across our river?'

The uproar intensified: everyone was shouting, nobody was lis-tening. The major walked to the bar and sipped Dan Killick's beer until the racket died down.

'No damned reservation!' Cleghorn said. 'No murdering Indians in Rock Springs!'

'You asked me to get you a bridge,' de Glanville said. 'Well, the plans are drawn, the engineers are engaged. The other matter is not my charge.' He spread his arms in a gesture of simplicity.

'We don't want no lousy bridge bringin' no stinkin' Cherokee killers in here,' Sims said. There was a harsh rumble of agreement.

'That, alas, may be impossible. Washington – '

'Fuck Washington! You tell 'em – '

'My dear Mr Sims,' de Glanville said, 'I have been working night and day, on your instructions. I do not expect thanks, but your contumely is ill-placed, sir. Now, if you will excuse me, it's time I took a bath.' He climbed the stairs. Frankie went with him.

'I won,' little Arnie told everyone proudly.

'First we lose the niggers,' Ryan said heavily, 'then we get the Bushwhackers. Now we got the Indians. What next? Fuckin' Mormons?'

'I won,' little Arnie said. 'I fuckin' won.' It didn't happen often. He wanted everyone to know.

~

After Waco, the herd moved into the Blackland Prairie. The soil was rich, and the grazing was better than ever. There was always water within reach, either creeks or lakes. The only thing that was miserable was the weather. Every day it rained; sometimes just for an hour, sometimes without stop; and always, it seemed, it rained at dawn. Breakfast was wet, and the slickers were on. Everyone started the day feeling chilled. No amount of hot coffee could overcome that grey cold start.

The cattle didn't mind. They were putting on weight, and when they settled on a bed ground they generated such body heat that a steamy mist formed over the herd. JoBeth did mind. At the end of a day her joints ached from the damp. A big, roaring camp fire baked her back to normal again. But rain was never far away.

She was tired of cooking, tired of travelling, and just plain tired. Fatigue made her careless: her hand brushed a hot griddle and it got burned. Elliott saw it happen, moved fast, grabbed a big jar of beef dripping and slathered the stuff on the damage. 'Got to keep the air off it,' he said. She felt faint, and sat on the wet ground while someone tied a bandage. Jack finished making the pancakes. They weren't right, too big and over-cooked, but nobody said anything.

That night, in bed, she told Jack she was tired.

'Hell, we're all tired.' His eyes were almost closed.

'I think it's the baby.'

That woke him. 'Baby, huh? Show me.'

'What good you think that's gonna do?'

'Well, if you can feel it, you should be showin' it.'

His simplicity irritated her. 'That's a stupid thing to say.' But she showed him her naked belly. 'An' it ain't an it, it's a she.'

He stroked her skin. 'Don't seem no different, to me. Anyway, you can't tell what it is.'

'I know. It's mine, and I know.'

'I did my share. Fifty-fifty it's a boy. Bet you a buck, even stakes, it's a boy called Jack.'

That was when she hit him, a backhander on the face. He didn't know why, he didn't know what to say. He lay back and looked away. Within two minutes he was asleep.

It took her longer to find sleep. This was the first time they had not kissed each other goodnight. She felt miserable about that. On the other hand, why did he have to be so dumb?

~

Next day he acted as if it never happened, and soon there were more important things to worry about. A cowboy called Villiers was cantering back to collect a stray, when his horse saw something nasty in its path, locked all four legs, and tossed Villiers like a sheaf of wheat. There was only one rock in his path, so it was bad luck that his head hit it. Knocked him cold. The horse waited, sniffed his body, then trotted off to join the *remuda*.

Huckaby found Villiers, now sitting and groaning and bleeding freely, and took him to Mabon, who looked at the cut and took him to the wagon. 'It's straight and clean,' he told JoBeth. 'Blood washed the dirt out of it. But it's long and deep, almost to the bone.' He gave her a strong needle and a spool of waxed thread, normally used for mending bridles and saddles and such.

'Why me?' she asked.

'Any woman's got a neater stitch than any of us.' He saw her shoulders slump. 'An' he'd sooner be lookin' at your face while it's bein' done than one of ours.'

Mabon had a flask of bourbon that JoBeth didn't know about. Villiers took three swigs of it, fast. He sat on a barrel and gripped his thighs just above the knees. She told herself she was sewing up a rip in a piece of canvas, done it before, could do it again. She whetted the needle on a wagon wheel to get a sharp point. Even so, the skin was surprisingly tough.

It took fifteen separate stitches to close the cut. Villiers blinked a lot. Other than that, he never moved. When she had knotted and scissored the last stitch, she reached for Mabon's flask and rewarded herself. Her hands were slippery with Villiers's blood; she almost dropped the flask.

While all this was happening, the herd had been walking past. Now Villiers thanked her, put his hat on, got on his horse and went back to work. Of course. What else was there to do?

NULLIFICATION

For two days, de Glanville rested in his room, recovering from his journey to the nearest telegraph office, and from the strain of badgering Washington.

That was two days nearer the arrival of the Army Corps of Engineers and a bridge into hell, as Hoke Cleghorn put it. 'Kit Carson told me he'd sooner be blown to smithereens by cannon than captured by Cherokee. They got ways of choppin' up a man's giblets, makin' garlic meatballs, an' feedin' them back to him while he's still alive. What they do to a woman,' he added, 'you wouldn't believe. Women got bigger giblets than men.'

'That true?' the pedlar asked Doc Brightsides.

'Utterly,' Brightsides said. 'In Berlin, Ohio, I removed a woman's kidneys that were big enough to stun a buffalo.' The listening drinkers were impressed. 'I have somewhere a photograph of the buffalo,' Brightsides said. 'Clearly concussed.'

'Don't depend on Uncle Sam to protect you from Cherokee,' Hoke warned.

'Fourteenth Pennsylvania Rifles,' Reuben Skinner said bitterly. 'Got here too damn late. I should know.'

'That was different,' Maggie said.

'Easy for you. You wasn't bushwhacked.'

'Morgan Watson is leavin',' Stackmesser said. 'Goin' to Oregon. Reckons it's safer.'

'No loss,' Ryan said. 'He scarcely ever comes to town, not since we made them jokes about his sow.'

But it was indeed a loss, and it made Rock Springs even more uneasy.

When at last de Glanville appeared, looking fresh as a bridegroom, he took a stroll around town with Frankie. They met Job Sims, standing on a barrel, searching the woods beyond the river through a broken telescope that wouldn't focus. 'Somethin' movin' over there,' Sims muttered. Pigeons clattered out of the trees. The telescope twitched. 'Was that an arrow?' he said. 'I could of swore I seen an arrow.'

'Just birds,' Frankie said.

'Tranquil, isn't it?' de Glanville said. 'After my brutal battle with bureaucracy, this is balm to the Christian soul.'

'Them savages are watchin' me, I know it,' Sims said.

'You got customers waitin',' Frankie reminded him.

'They're watchin' me watchin' them.' Sims didn't care about customers. 'I can smell Cherokee.'

'What they smell like?' Frankie asked.

'Like old blackcurrants,' Sims said, which astonished her; but he was serious. 'Can't you smell 'em?'

Little Arnie Phillips challenged de Glanville to play him at checkers for the world championship, and they were into their third game when the leading citizens of Rock Springs marched into the tavern.

'Seems like we got no choice left,' Stackmesser said. 'We're gonna invite in some guns from Barber's Landing an' Slade's Crossing, an' we're goin' over there an' puttin' an end to this Cherokee foolishness. Hoke here's in command.'

Cleghorn said: 'Kit an' me – '

'Wait just a goddamn minute,' Ryan Kidder said. 'How many Indians are livin' in that wood?'

De Glanville moved a checker. 'I believe I was told there's room for five thousand.' Little Arnie took his piece and two more, bang-bang-bang. 'Of course, I wasn't paying close attention,' de Glanville said.

'Five fuckin' thousand,' Ryan said stonily.

'Impossible,' Dan Killick said. 'We'd have heard 'em. Five thousand, that's an *army*.'

'These are early days,' de Glanville said. 'It may be only a scouting party over there. Fifty, a hundred. My advice is, cross the river and scour the wilderness. Search every inch of the swamps, canebrakes, laurel thickets. It's where they like to hide.'

'Wise move,' Doc Brightsides said. He was tending bar for Maggie until someone fell sick. 'Search the impenetrable areas first, and the rest is easy.'

'You'll need brush knives,' de Glanville said. 'Axes, too. Might take a month, but you'll track down the rascals.'

'A month?' Hoke cried. 'My corn's sproutin'! I can't – '

'Don't believe what I'm hearin',' Elias Dunbar said. 'Fifty Cherokee? Only fifty? Where's the rest? What in hell's name is goin' on here?' Elias had a small brain; it overheated quickly.

'Well, the bridge must come first,' de Glanville said. 'Don't cheat,' he told little Arnie, who blushed from ear to ear.

'What you mean?' Elias demanded.

'At present the Cherokee are deep in their Appalachian hideouts.' De Glanville gestured eastward. 'The U.S. Army will escort them here as soon as the bridge is complete. Surely you didn't believe,' he said brusquely, 'that the army is building this bridge entirely for *your* benefit?'

There was a silence lasting one minute and seven seconds. Doc Brightsides timed it. It was the longest silence in the history of Maggie's Tavern. The record was to be broken in 1882, when Maggie herself died of a heart attack while working a beer pump, and all present stood in silence for a minute which actually lasted nearly two, because Brightsides's eyes were full of tears and he couldn't properly see his watch.

'You sayin' the reservation opens when the bridge is up?' Stackmesser asked.

'That is my understanding.'

'No bridge, no reservation,' Sims said.

De Glanville looked up so sharply that his knee knocked the checkers board. 'I hope you are not suggesting a *volte-face*?' he said. 'In effect, a nullification?'

'Hell, no,' Elias said. 'We don't want them. And we don't want no fuckin' bridge, neither.' There was a rumble of approval.

'Gentlemen ...' De Glanville's shoulders slumped. His head seemed too heavy: he had to prop it up. 'First you ask me to make an omelette. Now you want me to put the eggs back in their shells.' He sighed. 'I don't think you realize how many officials will have to be persuaded. The U.S. Army is not a generous employer. These engineers have been willing to build your bridge out of duty and patriotism. They are overworked and underpaid, and now, I fear, an appeal to their patriotism will not be enough.'

'How much?' Sims asked.

'All you can raise,' de Glanville said. 'I assure you, it takes a lot of money not to build a bridge.'

An hour later, Frankie sat and watched him pack. 'You're good,' she said. 'You're real good.'

'Nearly two hundred dollars. I had expenses. Feathers and arrows and such.' He gave her fifty dollars, and kissed her.

'If they ever find you out,' she said, 'they'll kill you.'

He shrugged, and smiled, and left. In fact he had raised nearly three hundred. He was a professional. He was always in practice.

～

So far they had been making a trail. Now they were following one, grass-grown but still obvious. Jack said it was the Shawnee Trail, used by Indians to bring cattle north, back in the days, twenty-thirty years ago, when there still were Indians in Texas.

It took them through Waxahachie, another trading post trying to be a town. Mabon didn't pause. The herd entered one end of Main Street, if that's what they called it, and left by the other end, all in twenty minutes. Fort Worth was less than two days' drive away. He bypassed that, too, and crossed the West Fork Trinity with no more than the usual loud, strenuous, soaked-to-the-skin persuasion.

This was rich farming country. Often the herd had to cross fields, and it left wide gaps smashed in the fences. Nobody tried to stop them. Many of the farmhouses they saw had been abandoned; the war had knocked the bottom out of the market. But somebody was still there. Distant horsemen were seen, watching the herd. Mabon set extra guards at night. Yet when it happened he couldn't stop the stampede, any more than he could stop the rain.

JoBeth was dragged out of a deep sleep by Jack shouting at someone. He was hauling on his boots, grabbing his gunbelt. 'What is it?' she said.

'Shots. Didn't you hear?'

'No.' Then he was gone. She had slept through gunshots. Now she worried about Jack. More shots, very distant, and the rumble of the running herd, then silence. She was so tired that within minutes she was asleep again.

She cooked breakfast all next morning, as men came in, driving parts of the herd. By noon all but twenty Longhorns had been found. Mabon asked the night guard which of them had fired the first shots, and why. None of us fired those shots, they said. That's what made the herd run: somebody got among them, loosed off a revolver. In that rain, easy to sneak in. And that's why the cows ran every which way. Got spooked from the middle.

Mabon nodded. He was not surprised. 'Rustlers. All these home-steaders, half have gone bust. Those twenty cows we're missing, I guarantee they'll be in somebody's barn by now. Well, let's eat, an' move on.'

'I hate bein' made a fool of,' Brogan said. 'Here we brought these beeves all the way from San Antone, just so some sodbuster can steal them.'

'Rode all yesterday, rode half the night, an' today ain't half done,' Jack grumbled. 'I'm ready to hang any cattle-thief I find.'

'We can't search every barn we see,' Mabon said.

They pushed the herd another ten miles north before he called a halt. A calf had been crushed in the stampede; supper was beef stew. Nobody had much to say: too tired. They were sprawled beside the fire, picking their teeth, scratching, belching, the usual after-dinner entertainments, when Mabon said, 'They'll be back again tonight.' The men looked at him, expecting more. 'Sure they'll be back,' he said. 'The herd's still jumpy, we're all dog-tired; if you were them, you'd come back for more. Worked once, it'll work again. That's how they think.'

He kept the extra night guards, three men always circling the herd, and Mabon himself never slept. When dawn came up the herd was intact. Huckaby had bad news. 'We lost six horses,' he said. 'Rustled 'em from right under my nose.' He was too ashamed to eat.

The herd moved on. 'I hate north Texas,' Jack told JoBeth. 'Sooner we cross the Red River the better. Then it's nothin' but fuckin' Indians in their fuckin' Territory. If they trouble us, we can sic the army on 'em.'

She took his hand. 'Been thinkin'. If it is a boy, we call him Jack.'

He was enormously pleased. He was trying desperately hard to think of something to say when Mabon shouted, and he had to go.

~

Last chance to buy stores before the Red River was at Gainesville. 'Solid little town,' JoBeth said to Mabon, 'considerin' it's in the middle of nowhere.'

'Oh, the forty-niners came through here. You're standin' on the trail to California.' He gestured to the west. 'Couple thousand miles.'

'Gold fever did that?'

'That an' a lot more. Not for me. Long as I can get into the saddle, I ain't gonna shovel dirt. That ain't a job for a man, shovellin' dirt all day.'

'Might strike gold.'

'What use is gold?'

She said the only thing she could think of. 'Make jewelry out of it.'

Briefly, he raised his eyes to heaven.

They bought what they needed, drove out of Gainesville, and caught up with the herd as it neared the Red River. Brogan had ridden ahead, and now he returned to report that the river was high but not impossible. He had swum his horse across and back, and he needed a fresh horse; the current had swept him a hundred yards, each time.

'The near bank is soft,' he said, 'I reckon the Red's flooded lately. I found a little narrow piece of shingle for my horse, an' we nearly got stuck in *that*. These cows ain't gonna like it.'

Mabon left half the men to hold the herd, and took the rest to the river. Herds had crossed there in the past, and that was half the trouble. The ground had been smashed and mashed, and flood and rain had made it into a bog.

This was the only crossing for miles. Mabon and Jack Chisholm knew the trail well. Upstream, thick forest grew alongside the river. Downstream, the bank was both steep and high. Other crossings existed, but they were a day's ride away. By then, the Red might be in flood again.

They got axes from the wagon and cut brush and trampled it into the mud, cut more brush and laid it crosswise and trampled again, and cut and trampled one final layer. The causeway looked and felt sound and reliable. They cut out ten young Longhorns and ran them to the river. When he saw them coming, Jack Chisholm swam his horse into the stream, to set an example. The cows disliked the causeway. They milled about and drank, but they refused to cross. Jack reached the far bank, waved his hat, shouted. No good. Mabon returned the cows to the herd. Jack swam his horse back, hanging onto its tail. He had stripped to his long johns, and when he got out he was shuddering.

They repaired the causeway and tried again, with different animals. They roped a young steer. Jack rode ahead, taking the rope, and when they reached the causeway he charged his horse into the river and tried to drag the steer after him. The splash made it panic and turn away. The rope tightened and the steer tumbled onto its back. The load was too great for the horse. Jack let the rope go. When he looked back, the cows were standing, looking at him.

Mabon sent for the wagon, for hot coffee and cold cornbread.

Everyone was cold, dirty, weary. Two days on the trail, two nights of extra guard, a stampede, horse-thieves, and now this. JoBeth had never seen such exhaustion, or such despair.

'All we need is one steer over there,' Mabon said. 'Rest see one, they'll follow.'

'Build one of them Roman catapults,' Huckaby said. 'Throw the bastard over.' Nobody laughed.

Brogan said, 'Ain't we got a calf back there? Born a couple weeks ago?'

'Got two or three,' Mabon said.

'Mother-cow won't leave her calf, not for any reason. We take the calf, the mother's going to follow.'

'Ah,' Mabon said.

'Mother-love,' Jack said. He looked at JoBeth. 'Nothin' so powerful in the universe.'

'Don't you forget it,' she said.

'It's either that, or wait until the Red freezes over,' Mabon said.

This time they brought the whole herd forward. It was led by a roped calf, with the mother close behind. Jack Chisholm had the rope, and as the calf stepped onto the causeway he tightened the rope until the calf began to choke, and it bellowed. The cow became frantic. He dragged the calf to the river and the cow hurried after it. Behind her came a dozen steers, excited by the noise. She charged at the water, and so did they. Jack's horse towed the calf, the rope holding its head up. Behind them, the whole herd was on the move.

It took half an hour to complete the crossing. Nobody knew why Jack Chisholm decided to swim his horse back over the river. Probably it was tired, and he wanted a fresh mount from the *remuda*. And maybe he was concerned about how the wagon and JoBeth were to be floated across, roped over, with men on both banks working the ropes. The reason no longer matters. The light was fading when he set off. He was heard to shout, and someone saw his arm raised. Then it went under, and he was gone.

They searched for two miles downstream. It was moonlight when they found him, snagged by a fallen tree.

'Cramp, probably,' Mabon told JoBeth. 'That river's cold as charity. Maybe the horse had cramp too.' There was nothing she could say to that.

They buried him beside the river next morning, with plenty of rocks to keep the vermin away. Mabon read from a pocket prayer-book. Man was full of surprises.

'I can't go on now,' she told him.

He paid her what she was due, plus what Jack would have got. 'Huckaby will give you a horse,' he said. 'Go back to Gainesville. The Butterfield Stage Line passes through. West to California, east to Little Rock, Arkansas, or on to the Mississippi, if that's what you want.'

'That's what I want.'

They shook hands. He went north, she went south. 'Damn,' she said aloud. 'I never wanted to be a widow.' Tears would have been good, but she was too shocked to cry.

DAMAGED GOODS

Lewis Hudd turned ten that summer. He was a small, serious boy with a thin face like a sad rabbit. He was lonely because he referred it, and quiet because he was lonely. His mother, Ruth, had the sense to see that he was not unhappy, just different, and she let him be different. Marcus, his father, was not so sure. He suspected the devil's hand in anything odd. Still, he hadn't the time to fuss over a ten-year-old, especially one who usually wasn't in sight.

Down by the river was where Lewis liked to be. He found an exciting and mysterious life-force in the Cameron. It had its changing moods and tempers, like people, but it made no demands on him. He went wading in the shallows, knee-deep, where the water throbbed past his legs. He sat on polished rocks that rose from the river, sat so long without moving that fish swam past him and herons sailed by, so close he saw the ruffle of leg-feathers. One day a raft floated past.

It wasn't much of a raft: half a dozen logs held together by twisted vines. The thing was so loose and rotten it would come apart if it snagged a rock. Yet it carried a passenger, a mallard duck, sitting in the middle, travelling in style. The duck stopped grooming its lovely blue-green breast and looked at Lewis. Its head kept turning as the raft passed. 'Hullo, duck,' he said. It took a long time to think about that; so long that it drifted out of sight, still looking back.

The next day he had to work, helping bring in the third crop of hay. The day after that, he went to the river and began collecting timber, towing dead branches and trunks to a patch of sand. He cut vines and lashed his collection into a rough square: very rough. But it was strong and he was sure it would float. When he tried to drag it into the water he couldn't move it, not one inch. Too heavy. He might as well try to move the big barn.

He sat and chewed his knuckles and stared at his raft and failed to find an answer. He went home for supper.

That night it rained. Not on the farm, but somewhere upstream; and not much, but enough to raise the Cameron by eight or nine inches. Next morning the raft had gone. Lewis wondered what people at Rock Springs would think when they saw it go by. Then he realized that nobody saw it, probably. It went by in the night. He began to feel proud. A little bit of little Lewis was on its way to who knew where? Nashville, maybe.

He built a better raft and this time he did it in a backwater. He used straighter, smoother bits of timber and lashed them into a flat and tidy platform. He was glad the old raft had vanished. He moored the new one to a tree and went home.

Next morning he stowed some apples and a hunk of cheese inside his shirt. An old dog called Bess followed him all the way to the river. Maybe she smelled the cheese. If so, it wasn't strong enough to persuade her to get on the raft.

Once, and only briefly, Lewis had been allowed to drive a buggy; that had been pretty exciting, but nothing like the thrill he got from rafting on the Cameron. As soon as he had poled it laboriously out of the backwater and he felt the current draw it into midstream, he knew that a great natural force had taken charge of his raft and therefore of his life, slowly spinning it and showing it strange and unexpected views. 'Hey, Bess!' he shouted. 'This is fun!' He spread his legs and threw his weight and made the raft rock. Water squirted up between two logs and soaked his pants. He laughed and Bess barked a couple of times, just to be friendly, but she soon got bored and went home.

He was lying on his side, head propped on an elbow, and eating an apple, when he floated past Rock Springs. Job Sims saw him. 'Hey there!' he called. 'Where you goin'?'

'Don't know, sir.' Lewis had been taught to stand when spoken to, but this stranger couldn't touch him, so why move? 'Don't much care, either,' he added. His boldness amazed him.

Sims was greatly amused. 'You get to Nashville,' he called, 'you get me a newspaper.'

Nashville ... Lewis felt like Columbus. Never in his life had he gone so far from home, all alone. A fish rose, and he threw the apple-core at it. Nearly hit. Today nothing was impossible.

One hour and five big bends later, an island split the Cameron, and the raft chose a narrow channel studded with black rocks and bubbling with white water. It bounced and rushed so exhilaratingly that Lewis had to lie flat, grasping stubby bits of branch. Spray siphoned up through holes. This was better and better. Then his raft swung broadside and trapped itself against two boulders. The Cameron couldn't wait. It swarmed and sloshed and tried to wash him away. Lewis scrambled to the highest log, suddenly afraid. He couldn't swim, and he knew he couldn't stay where he was. He looked around for help. On the island a man with a fishing pole was watching him. It was Devereux Killick, although he didn't know that.

Devereux waded out and rescued the boy and took him to shore on his shoulders. 'Who the blue blazes are you, boy?' he asked.

'I'm Lewis Hudd, sir.'

'Lewis Hudd,' Dev said. 'Hudd. Now where've I heard that name before?'

~

'Look what I caught, Ma,' Dev said. 'Got me a Hudd child.'

Ma Killick was rocking on the porch. She had her good days and her bad days; sometimes both on the same day. Yesterday she had been Martha Washington, which was easy, all she had to do was nod and smile a lot; but it got boring. Nobody paid her any heed. This morning she woke early and read her Bible. Now she was Delilah. Delilah had fun. 'Speak up, boy!' she ordered.

'Yes, ma'am,' Lewis said. This ramshackle farm, with its patchy crops and untidy people: it was strange to him. This old woman with no teeth was very strange, and she kept staring with a peculiar intensity. 'I'm Lewis Hudd, ma'am,' he said. What else was there to say?

'Huh.' She used a walnut walking stick to lever herself out of the rocker. 'What's that you got in your shirt, boy?' She tickled it with the end of her stick. 'Jawbone of an ass, ain't it?'

'No, ma'am. That's an apple.'

'Don't lie to me, boy.' She hobbled around him. 'Charlie Hudd sent you here with that jawbone of an ass so's you could make sport with us Philistines!'

Her voice brought Stanton out of the house, chewing on a drumstick.

'Look what I caught,' Dev told him. 'Caught me a Hudd tad.'

'He can empty the outhouse,' Stanton said. 'Seein' as how you an' Dan keep forgettin'.'

'Shut up,' their mother ordered. She had been sleeping in the rocker, and her drool had dried and made a yellow crust at the corners of her mouth. 'They call me Delilah,' she told Lewis. 'Think I'm pretty, don't you?'

'No, ma'am.'

Dev laughed loud enough to startle the chickens under the porch, but Stanton went and kicked Lewis: an amiable kick up the ass, but it sent the boy sprawling. 'Where's your goddamn manners?' Stanton demanded. 'Where in hell you think you are?'

Lewis had been raised to tell the truth. 'Nashville, sir,' he said. That was the funniest thing Dev had ever heard. He stamped, and sent the chickens running for their lives. 'Nashville!' he bawled. 'Naaash-viiiille!' Now Jessica poked her head out of her bedroom window and wanted to know what the ruckus was about. She saw a strange child being prodded by her mother as if he were a shoat at market. 'What's happenin'?' she called.

'Nothin',' Stanton said. 'Interrogatin' a spy, is all.'

'Ain't this Nashville?' Lewis asked. There were splinters in his hands. The palms burned.

'You come to the right place, boy,' Ma Killick said. 'This is Gaza, an' these here are Philistines, an' I'm Delilah. Judges, sixteen, four. Dev, get some shears, I'm gonna shave his head, cut the strength out of him.'

'You can't do that, Ma,' Dan told her.

'It's written. Judges, sixteen, nineteen.'

'He ain't got no hair. Just a cowlick.' It was true. Like most youngsters, Lewis had his head cropped short, all but a curl at the front and not much of that.

'It's written,' she insisted, and tried to swagger into the house, but her knees were stiff with rust. Jessica caught her. 'Jesus, Ma,' she said. 'Stop dancin'.' Ma Killick fended her off and lurched through the doorway.

'Look what I caught, Jess,' Dev said. 'Caught me this piece a Hudd property. Gonna empty the outhouse for us.'

'Kinda flat in the face, ain't he?' Jessica was sixteen now, pushing seventeen, nearly as tall as her brothers, twice as handsome and very critical of men. Or boys.

'Nobody ain't askin' you to marry him,' Dan said, because he knew that would annoy her. Dan and Dev talked a lot about finding a good husband for Jessica. It passed the time. People had to make their own fun now there weren't any slaves to fuck or flog. Besides, the farm needed money and the easiest way was to marry into it.

'Maybe there's a reward out for him,' Dev said. 'What you reckon he's worth?'

'Ten bucks,' Jessica said. 'Use your eyes. This here is damaged goods.'

'Where?' said Ma Killick. She came shuffling out, sharpening a carving knife on a steel.

'Right foot. Half his toes is missing.'

Lewis hid the foot behind his other leg. The swish-swish of blade on steel hurt his ears. He wanted to pee.

'Ain't nothin',' Devereux said. 'Don't matter.' He'd caught the boy, and he resented criticism.

'Does too. Makes him all lopsided.' Jessica stood on tiptoe, just to demonstrate her perfect balance.

'Lopsided?' Ma Killick said. 'Can't have that.' She stopped sharpening. 'Nothin' but the best is good enough for Delilah. It's written!' She lunged, and elbowed her daughter out of the way, and hacked at Lewis's left foot with the carving knife, and missed because he jumped. 'For Chrissake, Ma!' Dan shouted. The knife stuck in a plank, buzzing softly. 'I was gonna even him up!' she shouted back. 'If thy feet offend thee, cut them off and cast them from thee! Matthew, eighteen, eight! The Bible says!'

'I swear it, you old bitch, I'm gonna strangle you one of these days,' Dan said.

'Heathen.' She tried to spit at him but her mouth was dry. 'Get the whiskey,' she ordered Jessica.

'It's under your bed, same place you always hide it,' Jessica said.

'You ever emptied an outhouse, Mr Lewis Hudd?' Devereux asked. Lewis shook his head. 'You're gonna have to learn, then, ain'tcha?' Lewis walked where Dev pointed. Dev ambled after, throwing little stones at him.

It took Ma Killick ten minutes to find her bedroom, and five minutes to remember why she was there, and another five minutes to get on her knees and use her stick to hook the bottle from its hiding-place. She had a long swig, and then another, and went to the window so she could spit on her son. Dan had gone. They had all gone. She spat anyway. Tomorrow might be too late.

EVERYONE PAYS

By the early afternoon, most of the family were out looking for Lewis. He had a ten-year-old's appetite, and now he'd missed a meal, so something was wrong. They searched the riverbank, the fields, the slopes that fringed the Ridge. Then his father set off and rode briskly to Rock Springs.

Reuben Skinner, Hoke Cleghorn and Dan Killick were sitting on the landing stage, sharing a pitcher of beer while they watched the sun go down, the finest free entertainment to be had, short of sexual congress with a willing partner, which could sometimes turn out to be costly in the long run, as Reuben was remarking. 'That Kidder girl,' he said. 'Amie.' He shook his head. 'Scandal.'

'She don't charge,' Dan said. 'Not so I hear.'

'Wouldn't have time to make change,' Reuben said. 'Not so *I* hear.'

'Nothin's free,' Hoke said. 'Everyone pays. Sooner or later.'

Reuben broke wind at both ends. 'No charge for *that*,' he said proudly.

'You ain't sittin' where I'm sittin',' Dan said.

That was when Marcus arrived and dismounted and said he was looking for his son, aged ten, name of Lewis.

'Job said he saw a young 'un raftin' down the river,' Hoke said. 'When?'

'Oh ... noon.' That was safe. In Rock Springs, noon covered three or four hours.

'Raftin',' Marcus said. Worry had twisted his face. 'Why would Lewis go raftin'? What's down there, anyway?'

'Mississippi,' Dan said. 'Course, he wouldn't never get that far. On account of the rapids.'

That was when the sun finally dropped out of the sky. The last orange slice had been hanging on, but now it lost its grip and got swallowed by the horizon.

'He's a smart boy. He'll get off the water,' Marcus said, and wished it were true.

'Better to stay *on* the goddamn water,' Reuben said. 'Bushwhackers everywhere. I should know.'

'Kit an' me spent five weeks on a raft, once,' Hoke said. 'Worst thing was the watersnakes.'

'Want some beer?' Reuben asked Marcus, but the pitcher was empty. 'Shit,' he said.

'Bastards could jump six feet straight up out the water.'

'I got to find a boat,' Marcus said.

'What you say his name is?' Dan asked.

'Lewis.'

'Saw one jump six feet an' take a man by the throat,' Hoke said. 'Dead before he could speak.'

'Boy about so high?' Dan said.

'Speakin' wouldn't of helped the poor sonabitch,' Reuben told Hoke. 'I mean, what could he say? Say goodbye, but that ain't no help, is it?'

'Yeah,' Marcus said to Dan. 'About that high. Why?'

'You got a brain as big as a bobcat's balls,' Hoke growled. Reuben couldn't figure whether that was praise or not, so he shut up.

'My brother Devereux said he fished a boy out the Cameron today,' Dan said. Marcus's head jerked as if mosquito-bit. 'Said the boy got your looks, too. Squashed-in sorta face, like an elk stepped on it or somethin'.'

'Ain't hurt, is he? Why'n't you send him home?'

'Dev was plannin' to. Just as soon as you paid us what you owe.'

'Exactly who the hell are you?' Marcus asked.

'Dan Killick. George was my brother. He worked for your cousin Charlie. We got back-pay comin'.'

'I never thought I'd ask this question of a white Christian man in the state of Kentucky,' Marcus said. 'How much d'you want for my boy Lewis?'

'Don't want nothin' for that skinny brat. Fact is, he's so little an' skinny, he'd be hard to find. You pay Dev what you owe, which is one thousand dollars includin' interest, an' maybe we can afford some lamp-oil, go lookin' for your boy again.'

359

That was it. Hard words were spoken on both sides. Reuben and Hoke took part and confused things, not fully understanding the quarrel, but that made no difference. It was black night, and Dan Killick got on his horse and rode off into it. Marcus got onto his and rode home. Marcus would have shot Dan dead if that could bring his son back. The more he thought, the readier to kill he became. He had met evil, and its name was Killick.

Charles was back from doing politics. He and all the other adult Hudds heard Marcus's story. Their general opinion (Mary excepted) was to take arms and ride out to the Killicks' and keep shooting until someone produced Lewis.

'Impossible,' Charles said. 'You forget that I am an elected judge. I cannot condone wild gunplay.'

'Never bothered no judge in Virginia,' muttered Ernie Hudd, younger brother to Marcus.

'Killicks never voted for you,' Ernie's wife, Celinda, said to Charles. 'Ain't like you're losin' nothin'.'

'Not the point,' Charles snapped. Judging wasn't as much fun as he'd expected. 'Killicks haven't committed any crime, not that you can prove. If you go over there blastin' bullets left an' right, *you'll* be the criminals. Just hold your damn water an' *think*. I know it hurts.'

They stood in a circle and hated him.

Mary came to the rescue. 'What about habeas corpus?' she asked.

'Just what I was wondering. Yes. Habeas corpus. If they're holding the boy, I have powers to make them produce him.' He sat down and scribbled a note, sealed it, handed it to Marcus. 'Go now,' he said.

'Ain't gonna work,' Celinda said bleakly. 'Not unless you poke it up Dan Killick's ass an' set fire to it.'

'I got matches,' Marcus growled. He left.

'That true, George Killick worked for you once?' Ernie asked. Charles grunted yes. 'You should of paid him,' Ernie said.

Charles stared. It had been a long day, doing politics, riding, talking, working on people, getting nowhere. Now his cousin was looking accusingly at him, through eyes that bulged like small boiled eggs. 'What I should do,' Charles said, 'I should break your foolish face.' He felt Mary grab his arm.

Ernie took a pace back. 'Violence don't prove nothin',' he said reprovingly. 'Thousand dollars, that's a lot of pay.'

'I'm going to bed,' Charles said.

'Ain't sayin' they're right,' Ernie told everyone. 'Feller back east still owes me thirty bucks from ten years ago. I take that hard, real hard. No hope of seein' it. Feller got thrown by his horse, broke his neck an' died.'

'George Killick was killed by the war,' Mary said.

'That so?' Ernie said. 'Well, I know just how he felt. Bet you he took it hard, real hard.'

~

The Killick place looked like it had died in the night. Moonlight washed it stark and cold. Everything was locked up solid. Marcus Hudd stood his horse, while three dogs made a wide circle and barked at him until his ears ached. Still the house was dead.

He had been working since dawn, and worrying since afternoon, and now he was weary and afraid. Partly for Lewis but mainly for himself. A Killick with a rifle could kill him now, dump the body in the wilderness, be back in bed by dawn. Could happen any second. His loins curled as if he were on the rim of a deep gorge. And still the dogs barked.

He took out the piece of paper and it looked sillier than ever. He got furious with Charles, with Lewis, with God. Fury drove him to the door. He pounded on it, kicked it, shouted. No response. He took out his pistol and hammered with the butt until splinters flew. Even the dogs were impressed, and fell silent. Still nobody came. Marcus began to realize how helpless he was. He quit hammering before he broke the gun. 'Oh ... *fuck*,' he said.

'You must be Mr O. Fuck,' Dan Killick said. He was leaning on the sill of an upstairs window. 'Guess you're kin to I. Fuck an' U. Fuck.'

'You got my boy in there.' Marcus sounded empty and breathless; he filled his lungs. 'You got my boy Lewis! This here's a writ for ...' He forgot the words, and panicked, and then remembered. 'For habeas corpus! Now hand him over!'

Dan yawned, and scratched his jaw. 'Who told you we had your boy?'

'You did.'

'I'm a terrible liar. You bring any money?'

Marcus's neck began to ache. 'Give me my boy, Killick, or I'll put a bullet through every goddamn window.'

'Can't stop you doin' that, Mr O. Fuck. Course, your boy might be inside. Just guessin'.'

They stared each other out for a long minute. Dan won. Marcus had no more threats to make. He got back on his horse and rode away. The dogs saw him off the property.

~

Lewis heard the dogs, faintly, and the pounding on the door, less faintly. He heard none of the talk. He was locked in the cellar.

It had taken him five hours to empty the Killicks' outhouse.

In fact they had three. When one got full, they moved to the next and left the door of the old one open in the hope that someone would come in the night and steal the contents. The Killicks believed in miracles; it saved doing a lot of work. And now, Glory be! Here was a small, ten-year-old miracle! Dan gave the boy a bucket, showed him where to dump the stuff, and told him not to damn well stop until all three outhouses were empty.

It was clumsy, stinking, exhausting toil. The bucket had to be carried a very long way each time, and it leaked. Lewis soon quit trying to stop it slopping onto him. He was stumbling with fatigue and choking on the stench when the task was only half-done. His arms ached like fire, and the wire bucket-handle raised blisters that burst. All this should be remembered, for it altered not only Lewis's small body but also his way of thinking.

At the end, he was foul-smelling, trembling with fatigue, his hands unable to relax from being a pair of burning hooks.

Devereux sniffed him from a distance. 'You ain't fit company for man nor hog,' he said. He got the bullwhip and drove Lewis to the river. The whipcracks were near enough to keep the boy moving at a steady trot, although he fell twice.

'Get in,' Dev said. 'We ain't here to fish.'

It was twilight. The water looked steely and deep. 'Can't swim,' Lewis said. That made Dev laugh. 'Well, get on an' drown, then,' he said amiably. He put the sole of his boot against the boy's back and shoved. The splash was gratifyingly big. 'Ain't as if you'll be much of a loss to anyone.'

Lewis thrashed about, and swallowed a lot of water, and got

washed by the current down to some shallows. Dev flicked the whip, and wrapped it around Lewis's wrist. 'You're lucky I'm the best man with a bullwhip in Dundee County, boy,' he said. He dragged him out, and led him back to the first place, and kicked him in. Then he did it all again. Then he told Lewis to take his clothes off and wash them. All this should be remembered, too.

Jessica gave him some food: a mug of cold soup, the heel of a loaf, a bruised apple. He was too tired to eat the apple.

'Trust you to bring home the crit of the litter,' she said to Dev.

'Best I could find. Say what: if you don't like the way this little bastard worked, I'll make him put it all back. Every last piece a shit. Then you can go squat in the woods.' Lewis gaped, dribbling soup. Dev laughed so hard he hurt his ribs.

He was still holding his side when he put Lewis down in the cellar. It smelled of sour potatoes. Dev pointed at a pile of old potato sacks and Lewis understood: that was his bed. Dev went out, and his lantern glinted through a barred hole in the door. Bolts slid. Dev went away, and the last glint went with him.

The cellar had a stony chill. Lewis's clothes were still wet from the river. He wrapped himself in sacks, and shivered and cried, but not for long. Sleep came and rescued him before he knew it had happened.

The dogs' barking disturbed him; then the hammering on the door brought him awake. It had stopped before his brain became alert enough to figure that probably someone was up there looking for him. He thought about shouting. The silence was total; he could hear his own heartbeat. He was afraid to shout.

He got up and walked a few steps. His body was as sore as if it had been beaten. He had done nothing to deserve a beating, nothing to deserve being kicked into the river, or mocked, or sneered at. Even at ten years old, Lewis knew his own worth. He felt wretched and lonely and despairing. He also felt angry. A whiff of fresh air reached his nostrils.

The grill in the door was just above his head. Standing on tiptoe he could, he guessed, see through the hole, except that there was nothing to see but more blackness. He thought about it for several minutes. Then he set off and explored the cellar with his hands. He found a lot of bad potatoes and his bed of sacks, and that was all.

Think.

All the sacks had holes in them. Big holes. So big, he could put his hands through the holes.

Think, think.

He fitted one sack inside another, to give it an inner skin. Still there were holes on holes. He put them both inside a third sack, and tasted triumph. He scrabbled potatoes into the bag and dumped it hard, scrabbled and dumped, scrabbled and dumped, then screwed the neck tight. There were enough sacks to make two more bags. There was no lack of potatoes.

He dragged the bags to the door and stacked them against it, one on top of the other, and when he climbed on the pile, potatoes poured out because the necks weren't tied and the whole thing collapsed.

Lewis refilled the bags, and thought. He had nothing to tie the necks with. He wasn't strong enough to tear strips from the sacks. He wasn't even strong enough to tear his own shirt. How to keep the potatoes in the bags?

Use the door. This was so brilliant that he spoke it aloud: 'Use the door.' His voice sounded so thin and childish that he added: 'Stupid.'

He made the bags only about two-thirds full. He rammed one, neck-first, against the door, at right angles to it, and tucked the neck underneath. He built the second on top of the first, then added the third. He climbed. The stack held. Potatoes wobbled and slid under the sacking beneath his toes, but the stack held. He put his head between the bars.

He had a face like a rabbit and a head like a ferret. His mother had once told him why cats have long whiskers: 'If his whiskers go through a hole without touching, the cat knows the rest of him can do it too.' Lewis had been impressed by this animal cunning. Now he flattened his ears, and his whole head slipped between the bars. Would the rest of him go through, too?

He twisted his body sideways and got most of his shoulders to follow his head. That was a start but also the end. No matter how much he kicked, he knew that most of his weight was inside, and inside was where it wanted to stay. He wriggled free and fell off the stack and banged his elbow so flowers of pain bloomed behind his eyes. It was the first un-black thing he had seen since Dev left him. He rubbed the elbow and enjoyed the view, until it faded.

He got back up, put an arm through the hole, groped about, found nothing to grip. But it made him wonder: where would his body balance? Suppose he got his head and an arm and most of his shoulders through ...

The right hand and arm went first: easy. He put his chin on his right shoulder and heaved his head through, losing bits of skin off his ears as they went. Now his left shoulder was jammed and his left arm was waving helplessly inside the cellar. He was on tiptoe, so he couldn't do much with his legs. His shirt was bunched against the bars like a snake shedding its skin.

He painfully reversed the whole process and fell off the stack. This time he saved his elbow. He was learning. 'Bastard!' he said. The word was forbidden at home, and he felt he might as well make the most of where he was. 'Bastard, bastard, *bastard!*'

He took off his shirt. He felt a lot lighter and thinner.

Without the extra layer of cloth, his right arm and head and shoulder went out at least a couple of inches more. The other arm was still trapped inside. His right hand searched around for the bolts to open the door and didn't find them. What it did find, low down, was an iron ring. His hand gripped the ring and at last he had leverage. It was a struggle to drag his left shoulder through the hole but after that a quick wriggle got his left arm free and he slid through the bars. He fell onto his forearms and lay gasping. 'Sonofabitch,' he said, another forbidden word. Well, he'd earned it.

He fumbled his way up some stairs, through a door, across a room, into the moonlit kitchen. He found half a ham, a cooked beetroot, a few tomatoes, some boiled potatoes, and a .44-calibre revolver hanging from a nail. Everything went into a basket. He drank from a pitcher of milk.

There was a door. Its bolt slid easily, so easily that Lewis was surprised. Nothing else had been easy. The door swung open and three dogs were looking at him. They seemed unafraid, but they stood in his way and he was definitely afraid of them. He was so tired he could scarcely carry the basket, and his brain felt stunned with struggle. Then he noticed that the dogs were reaching forward, sniffing. They wanted what was in his basket.

He tore chunks off the ham, three big chunks, and tossed them inside the house. The dogs went past him like shaggy shadows. He went out and shut the door, and the latch clicked. He walked away. 'Fuckin' smart,' he murmured. He was entitled, even if he did burn in hell forever.

Ten minutes later his brain made one last effort and told him he was lost. A barn stood handy. It was half-full of hay that felt as warm and welcoming as a feather bed. For the second time that night, sleep pulled the plug and all Lewis's troubles drained away.

BELLS IN MY HEAD

When Major de Glanville promised Rock Springs he would put an end to the Indians skulking about in the woods beyond the Cameron, some people doubted he could do it. But he was as good as his word. The threat vanished. When he returned he was welcomed as a man who knew how to pull strings in Washington. The town could rest easy again.

He was eating breakfast with his wife when Charles Hudd rode into town with his cousins Marcus and Ernie, and stepsons Curtis and Floyd, plus Marcus's son Nelson. All were armed. They clumped into Maggie's so heavily that they sprung a floorboard.

'You're lookin' for your lost boy,' Frankie said.

'I am.' Since elected judge, Charles had allowed his hair to grow thick and long. He wore a black tailcoat, a grey cravat, and his officer's sword in a scabbard. 'Habeas corpus has been defied. I call on you to lend force to the cause of justice.'

Frankie was eating a stack of pancakes. 'You men had any breakfast?' she asked.

'Coffee,' Marcus said.

'Sit down an' eat,' Frankie invited.

'You ain't much fussed,' Ernie said. His legs were spread so wide you could drive a sheep between them. 'Where we come from, kidnappin's a hangin' offence.'

'Boy ran away from home,' Job Sims said from the doorway. He had seen the Hudds arrive, and left his smithy. He was bored already with hammering horseshoes, and a whole day of it stretched ahead. 'I saw the boy. I know.'

'I shall establish the facts when we recover the child,' Charles said. 'Talk will not accomplish such a recovery. Are you ready to move out?'

367

'No,' Frankie said. 'Got coffee to drink. An' when I *am* ready, you-all ain't goin' along. We already had the South against the North. Killicks see you comin', all gunned up like the Texas Rangers, it'll be war again.'

Charles cleared his throat. 'I suspect the boy is hidden.'

'We'll see about that. You Hudds stay here. I'll go an' talk to the Killicks.'

'And I shall come with you,' her husband said. 'Why should a man, whose blood is warm within, sit like his grandsire cut in alabaster?'

'Don't even try to answer,' Frankie told the Hudds. 'He's full of that kinda horseshit.'

She had to listen to a short lecture on habeas corpus, which Charles had just read up on and damn well wasn't going to waste. 'By defying my writ,' he told her, 'the Killicks commit a second offence.'

'Maybe the boy fell down a well,' Maggie said. 'Got bit by a cottonmouth. Killed by a bear. Drowned himself.' Charles wasn't pleased with any of them.

'Well, I ain't arrestin' Dan Killick on the strength of his own say-so,' Frankie said. 'Dan's noise ain't evidence. If I believed what Dan said, I'd have to arrest you too.' He had no answer to that except to crank out a glare. 'Go an' eat breakfast, for Chrissake,' she said. 'You're thinkin' with your belly, an' it's empty.'

As they rode out of town, Major de Glanville said to her, 'Dearest, you really must not call "The Merchant of Venice" horseshit. "Pericles", yes. "Two Gentlemen of Verona"', possibly. Large portions of "Lear", undoubtedly. But not "The Merchant". Not that.'

'Sure. What you doin' here?'

'Merely keeping you company.'

'First time. You plannin' on workin' some con?'

'No.' He laughed at the idea, but she did not laugh with him. She said, 'You got it in mind to sell shares in the Eternal Gold Brick Company, you better hurry your sweet ass back to Rock Springs.' He shook his head. 'Killicks got no manners,' she said, 'no morals, more to the point no money. I don't want you blowin' smoke in their ears an' tellin' 'em you're the king of Egypt an' this is their last chance to buy a Pyramid, only ten dollars down. I got enough trouble findin' this boy.'

For a while, they rode in silence. 'I had a premonition,' he said.

'When all those Hudds came into Maggie's, I had a feeling something was going to go badly wrong. And I never have premonitions.'

'Hell, I have 'em all the time.'

'Yes? How often do they come true?'

'Never.'

It was a pleasant morning: fresh, bright, warm: birds swooping and singing.

'I've reached a decision,' he said. 'I'm going to give up conning people out of their money. It's wrong, it's hard work, and I nearly got caught a couple of weeks ago.'

'Well, two cheers for you.'

'Thought you'd be pleased.'

'Yeah, I'm delighted.' But she was poker-faced. 'We still got to eat.'

'I've been thinking about that. If Rock Springs had a theatre, I could double as actor-manager. That cuts the costs and raises the profit. Where's the nearest theatre? Bowling Green? Folk would travel thirty, forty miles to see a drama in Rock Springs. Not just plays. Opera. Ballet.'

'Anvil-tossin'?'

'You're making fun.'

'You're dreamin'.'

'Am I? Memphis has an opera house, so why – '

'Why not go to Memphis, then?'

'I would, if you'd come.' That silenced her. 'It's really very simple. I care for you. Want me to say it backwards? You are the one I care for. Curtain. Roars of applause.'

'There you go. Back into the theeyater.' Something had softened her Texas twang. She stopped her horse, stopped it so abruptly that he had to turn and come back. He reined in, alongside her, knee to knee, and touched her chin with a forefinger. 'You all right?' he said.

'No. I hear bells in my head. You serious about Memphis?'

'I'll go if you'll go.'

'Now?'

'Sure. Why not?' They looked into each other's eyes until she laughed. She had a pleasing, brief laugh; it hadn't been much used in her life, it was still fresh. The laughter brightened his face. 'Nothing keeps us here,' he said.

'Only little Lewis Hudd.'

'Then let's find him, fast.'

The Hudds stayed in town, waiting to hear what the deputy got out of the Killicks.

They saw a small crowd by the landing stage, and walked down Main Street to see what was happening.

Somewhere, far away, the sky had dumped rain and now the Cameron was suddenly in flood, surging up its banks, washing away the summer's weeds and seeds, wind-torn branches, bugs and rubbish, and the occasional drowning lamb.

Ryan Kidder sidled up to Charles. 'Hear one of your cousins went visitin' the Killicks,' he said. 'Some tide, huh?' A small tree swept past, roots first. 'You need a jury, I'm your man.'

Charles said nothing. What interested him was a hundred-foot raft being rushed downstream. People cheered it. Charles cupped his hands. 'If you come across a boy, name of Lewis Hudd,' he bawled; but he could not think what to add. Luke Corrigan waved, and then got back to his piking. That raft was hell-bent for Nashville.

~

When Ma Killick came down for breakfast, the rest of the family was arguing so loudly about ham and about dogs that she had to shout, and then nobody listened, so she went looking for her walking cane.

'Look, the fuckin' ham's *gone*,' Stanton shouted at Jessica. 'Ain't *here!* Jesus, a one-armed man can see *that*.'

'Leave your stupid arm out of it, for once,' she snapped. When she got mad, especially early in the day, you could see what Jessica would be like in twenty or thirty years: like her ma, who had now found her cane but forgotten why she wanted it. Their mouths were each a grim thin slash. Hard frowns dragged their eyebrows down. No point in looking at people. Nothing good to be seen.

'If you just put the goddamn food away at night, this wouldn't happen,' Devereux told Jessica.

'Do it yourself. Ain't your slave.'

'Hey!' Stanton said. 'Half them taters've gone! Who's been – '

'Shut your damned row,' Dan said. He had gone out to get a fresh jug of milk, and now he was back. 'Hounds ate that grub. I just kicked 'em out the house. Some fool let 'em in last night. Ain't you idiots got no brains at all?'

Hunger made the argument worse. The fire had gone out and nobody was willing to take on the messy chore of re-lighting it as long as everyone was being accused, or abused, or both. So: no coffee, no eggs, nothing hot. Ma Killick shuffled around the kitchen, searching for something, couldn't remember what, when accidentally her fingers found it in the pocket of her dress, and she turned and lashed the table with her cane. 'Shut your nonsense!' she rasped. A china jug spun off the edge and smashed. They were silenced.

'I got news.' She unfolded a letter. 'It's from your cousin Jimmy-Sam Wiggins.'

'Jimmy-Sam died,' Dan said.

'Wife died,' his mother corrected. 'Last year, she died. Says so, here.' She rattled the pages.

'Well, I heard Jimmy-Sam died,' Dan grumbled.

'Won't be long,' Devereux said. 'Jimmy-Sam's older'n pa was. Seventy, eighty maybe.'

'That's lies!' Ma Killick said. 'Jimmy-Sam ain't no more'n fifty, an' I should know.' He was a cousin on her side of the family. 'That man's in the prime of life.'

'Jimmy-Sam,' Stanton said. 'Two of the nicest fellers you could wish to meet.' He blew out his cheeks and made his eyes pop. His mother missed the act.

'Nicest an' richest,' she said. 'Perfect husband for Jessica.'

'Ain't marryin' that fat old bastard.'

'Are too. I wrote an' said yes.'

'Now I know you're crazy.'

'Not many gals get a chance to wed a big man,' Stanton said. 'Jimmy-Sam must be three hundred pounds stark naked, not countin' the hair.'

'Got more hair'n a brown bear,' Dan said. 'His wife had to curry him like a horse.'

'Hell, you could do that easy, Jess,' Devereux said. 'You're good with horses.'

'Ain't marryin' that fat hairy old bastard.'

Her mother lashed the table again. 'You'll do as you're damn well told!' Another blow broke a plate.

'For Chrissake, Ma,' Stanton said. 'Hit somethin' else. We ain't got enough plates already as it is. Hit Dev, he don't feel no pain.'

Dev, hungriest of all, had thrown kindling into the stove and was striking match after match, failure after failure. Stanton was sitting in a corner, watching him. Jessica was leaning in a doorway, chewing a curl and dreaming of living in New York. Dan was staring at an empty hook on the wall. 'My forty-four was hangin' there,' he said.

'Aw, shit,' Dev said. The day had scarcely begun and everything was wrong. He went to check the cellar.

~

Frankie and de Glanville rode into the farm and found Stanton splitting logs for the stove. Long ago he had learned how to swing a felling-axe one-handed, and he worked while he talked.

Stanton was outwardly bland but inwardly twitchy. If the Hudd child had gone home, there was no telling what he might have said. The Hudds were easily riled: look what they'd done to those bushwhackers. They were riled already. Look at Marcus Hudd, last night. 'Smart thing to do,' Ma Killick had said, in a rare fit of common sense, 'is find the boy, take him home. Act neighbourly, let everyone see it.' You go find him, Dan had told her, kid's got my forty-four, I ain't going near the little bastard. Me neither, Devereux had said. Got baking to do, Jessica had said. Ma Killick had turned to Stanton. 'I ain't lookin' to get the other arm shot off too,' Stanton had said. Jessica had said: 'Bet you the little sonofabitch is already home, and whatever he tells his folks, he's lying.' They had stood around and worried about that.

Now Stanton split logs and said his piece. 'Sure,' he said, 'the Hudd boy was hangin' around here. We fed him, he did a few chores, wandered off. Went home, so we all thought. Boy didn't steal nothin', if that's why you're here.' Frankie said her piece about alleged kidnapping and extortion. Stanton said, if he had the time to go stealing fool Hudd children, which he didn't, he wouldn't pick the crit of the litter. Also it was a well-known fact that Judge Hudd owed money, ask anyone; and he went into a rambling account of how he lost his arm while trying to persuade Hudd to honour the debt, and Hudd's nigger Lonzo led him into an ambush and …

De Glanville lost patience. They'd never get to Memphis this way. 'So the Hudd boy isn't here?' he said.

'You see him anywhere?'

'You won't mind if I look around.'

'You're the law. You do what's legal.'

Frankie went to talk to the rest of the family. Major de Glanville rode about the farm, checking outbuildings. He knew he was wasting his time, merely going through the motions, and he didn't care. He hadn't felt so happy since the war ended and left him, amazingly, alive and intact. Now he was setting out on another new life. Goodbye to Rock Springs, a nothing town going nowhere. Hullo to Memphis! The city bustled in his imagination: the Paris of Tennessee. He imagined Frankie on his arm, walking through Memphis as if she owned it. As if they didn't give a damn *who* owned it. As far as he could tell, she loved him. He loved her. Some people didn't even *like* her. Their stupidity astonished him. He was eager to get back to her, and he dismounted and strode to the next barn and dragged the door open.

That woke Lewis.

What he saw was the silhouette of a big man, black as sin against the dazzle of sunlight. The man said: 'Are you in there, boy? I've come to take you back.' It was a terrifying threat. Lewis knew how to save himself; he had done it before. He took the forty-four out of the basket and shot the man. The flash hurt his eyes and the kick knocked him into the hay. He got up and the doorway was empty. He grabbed the basket and ran. The man was lying on his back. Lewis didn't look at him. It was late summer and the grass was tall. He was soon chest-deep in it. Then he saw woods. He ran for the woods.

When T. Speed tapped on her bedroom door and Mary Hudd told him to enter, she had been lying on her bed for an hour, not reading a book.

'I have been listening to you at work,' she said. 'I cannot remember when last a man gave me so much pleasure, simply doing what nature fitted him for.'

T. Speed smiled. Gently.

'Mr Hudd is in town on business,' she said. 'They are all in town on business.'

He shifted his weight from one foot to the other. 'The house is quiet,' he said.

She swung her legs off the bed.

'I suppose I must reward you,' she said. 'Now that your task is done.' She looked at the title of the book.

'My task ain't never done,' T. Speed said, 'not till I have given all the satisfaction in my capacity.'

'You may have noticed ...' She looked around as if she herself had only just noticed it. 'Mr Hudd does not sleep here. He has his own bedroom.'

He nodded. 'So he don't get disturbed, when you ... uh ... feels like playin'. The piano.'

She tossed the book at him, and he caught it easily, one-handed. 'Come see,' she said. 'Come finish your task.' She stroked his buttocks as she went past him. 'And if you give me satisfaction I shall be properly grateful.'

'Same here,' T. Speed said, with complete sincerity.

～

Doc Brightsides met the wagon almost exactly halfway between Main Street and the Killick farmhouse. Major de Glanville was lying on it, on the barn door used as a stretcher. He was dead.

Brightsides knew that, as soon as he saw the wagon's walking-pace. He stopped and waited. He had been in the middle of a late breakfast when Devereux had arrived, shouting, his horse's neck and chest white with foaming sweat, and Brightsides had stuffed bacon into his mouth and put a small steak into a side pocket. Now he got off his horse and he ate the steak. Hunger never improved a doctor, or his patient.

Dan stopped the wagon when it reached Brightsides. The deputy was on the seat, beside him. Two horses were tethered to the tailgate. Neither person had anything to say. Dan looked ill. He was all hunched-up, like an old man feeling the cold. Frankie's eyes were squinting hard into the glare of the sun, except that there was no glare.

The doc found the bullethole, just south of the ribcage. Blood had soaked up as far as the shoulders and down as far as the thighs. Already it had begun to dry in the sunlight. The shirt was stiff as canvas. Major de Glanville's eyes were closed but his mouth was open. Brightsides took a length of bandage and tied the mouth shut. If he couldn't do anything for the man's life, at least he could stop him looking foolish in death.

Brightsides climbed down. He had to make some kind of comment. 'Not one hell of a lot to be said at times like this,' he said. Frankie nodded. 'Move on,' he told Dan.

POKER IN THE CELLAR

Gabe Killick came back from checking the traps, and he carried one old red fox, in bad condition. He had been gone a long time. He draped the fox on top of the Altar, and looked around for food.

'Ain't much,' Buck Hudd said. He meant the fox. His lisp made it sound even less.

'Well, ain't you smart?' Hunger lit a fire under Gabe's anger. 'Damned if you ain't the smartest nigger in Kentucky.'

'Well, it ain't much.' Buck got confused by sarcasm. 'You get lost?'

'No. We all got found, is what.'

'Huh.' Buck made no sense of that. 'This sorry-lookin' thing ain't worth a dime.' Gabe hit him: a punch on the ear. Buck lurched sideways, and came back swinging both arms. Martha walked over and threw a bucket of water at them. They glared, staggering and dripping. 'You quit, now!' she commanded. 'Or I'll sic my little Bonny on you both!' Bonny went up and kicked Gabe on the leg and ran away. The camp all laughed. Gabe and Buck did some more glaring.

Lonzo had arrived, carrying Aaron on his shoulders, as light as a child. Aaron picked the fox off the Altar. 'This the best you can do?' His voice was a shrill, nasal sneer.

'I can do better,' Gabe shouted. 'I can whomp you, old midget!'

'Try it!' Aaron flung the fox in his face. 'I'm waitin'!'

'Hey, hey, hey,' Lonzo said. He dumped Aaron on top of the Altar. 'Bastard,' Aaron said. 'Now tell me,' Lonzo said to Gabe.

'Traps were empty, all but one. Sprung an' empty. Some sonabitch got there first.'

Gloomy news brought silence. Bonny saw long faces and stopped her cackling. Gabe trudged off to eat.

'Wanna see them traps,' Aaron said.

'Empty,' Lonzo said. 'Ain't nothin to see in 'em.'

'Remains to be seen,' Aaron said. He thought that was a pretty good joke, and he sniggered whenever he remembered it, while Lonzo carried him into the wilderness. 'You sound real proud of that noseful of snot,' Lonzo said. 'How many years you had it?' Aaron tried to bite his ear but his teeth were too loose. 'I could give you lessons in ear-bitin',' Lonzo said. 'I et Mr Stanton Killick's whole ear for dinner once, with sweet pertaters an' snap beans.'

'I heard different.'

At each of the first five traps they found splashes of blood, or scraps of fur, or bits of guts. These were deadfall traps, made so as not to damage the pelt. Two were bust. 'Panther,' Aaron said at last. 'Smell 'im? Panther piss smells like bad moonshine.'

'He got a lot of free meals from us.'

'She-panther. Feedin' cubs. That's why she took everythin'. Go get the gun, shoot 'er dead.'

'Hell, no. Me hunt panther? I ain't that smart.'

'You're learnin', boy. Never thought to see the day.'

Lonzo grunted. 'Learnin' ain't eatin'.' They left the traps. Furs were finished, and winter was that much nearer.

~

The funeral was in the afternoon. Maggie asked the deputy if she was up to it, and Frankie told her she had already been widowed twice, and she wasn't the swooning sort. But Maggie could see her left hand twitching and jerking, like a child trying to attract its mother's attention.

Flub being sick, there was no question but that the job would go to the Reverend J. Hubert Hunkin. He charged only five dollars, seeing as it was almost an official occasion, and he preached on a text from Second Timothy, four, fourteen: 'Alexander the coppersmith did me much evil: the Lord reward him according to his works.' Nobody understood. Rock Springs didn't have a coppersmith, nor anyone called Alexander. Hunkin got the wrong man. Certainly wasn't worth five bucks.

They sang a hymn, and carried the coffin out. When it had been put on the planks across the grave, Doc Brightsides stepped forward with his hand up. This had been a poor funeral. A death deserved better, this one especially. For a few seconds he was short of breath, couldn't speak; and wondered wildly: *If I die now – heart attack, collapse – what a spectacle!* He filled his lungs, oxygenated his blood supply, felt his heart thud, and said:

'We're here to bury a good man. He brightened up this town whatever he did, whether he was playing checkers with young Arnie Phillips, or talking about Shakespeare with anyone at all. I was always glad to see him. I'm sorry he's gone.' Everyone said *Amen.* 'I'm sure he would have made a better job of what I'm trying to say,' Brightsides said, and stood back.

Soon the burying was done, and Hunkin had said his ritual words, and dirt had been shovelled into the hole, and people were leaving. Judge Charles Hudd drifted over to Frankie Nickel. 'This is a bad time, I know,' he said, 'but we've got unfinished business, if you can stand it.'

It took her a long moment to remember somebody else's problem. 'You mean young Lewis ain't turned up.'

'His mother would have sent word if he had.'

The sky was as grey as slate, and as flat. 'Look at that,' she said. 'Sun in the mornin', gloom in the afternoon. They say the Lord loves a sinner. He sure rubs it in.'

'It's only weather. Signifies nothing.'

'Yeah.' She took one last look at the grave, and turned away. 'Nothing. That's exactly what it does signify. Not a damn thing. Not a damn, blessed thing.'

They walked towards Main Street. 'I intend to hold an inquest soon,' he said. 'Tomorrow, probably. Meanwhile, my people will continue to search for the boy, while there's still light.'

She nodded. 'Signifies nothing,' she said, and walked away.

～

The panther was downwind of Lewis Hudd and she smelled him a quarter of a mile away. There were two reasons why she went no closer: one, she wasn't hungry, thanks to all the food from the traps; and two, he stank of the Killicks' outhouses. Even after getting dumped in the river, he still had enough human filth on him to offend a panther's nose. She left Lewis to his stench.

Her two cubs were some miles away, up a gorge, in a cave. She had moved into this area last spring, found it free of competition, and mated almost at once with an old, scarred tom who turned up from God knew where and went back there before she gave birth, in late July. The cubs fed and grew, fed and grew. She could never keep up with their hunger. Deer were what she liked to hunt, but deer were scarce. So when she followed the trail of human scent and found fresh food for the taking, she took it all. The trapped animals were small; she carried three or four home at the same time. The rest she hid and covered with the litter of the forest.

Lewis, too, was in a cave, but he was almost out of food and he did not know where to go next.

What he did know was that he had shot a man, and he was very much afraid that that was a mortal sin and he would burn in the eternal lakes of fire in hell because of it. The person who knew about such things was his father, which was why Lewis was definitely not going home.

~

After the funeral, the Killicks went straight back to the farm, rammed the bolts shut and slammed up the shutters. When the Hudds got there they found a house that was a solid cube of wood. They rode all around it and ended up looking at each other. Dusk was fast becoming night.

'Why they hidin',' Ernie asked, 'if they got nothin' to hide?'

'Bet you Lewis is bound an' gagged an' locked in some stinkin' rat-hole,' Curtis said.

Marcus was short on sleep and he took the idea badly. 'That's crazy,' he said. 'Why would anyone do that to a boy?'

'You don't know the Killicks like we do,' Floyd said. 'They *are* crazy.'

'Ain't no lights showin',' Ernie said.

'Want me to knock on the door, pa?' Nelson asked.

'No!' Marcus was shocked. 'They already killed the deputy's husband, didn't they?'

'Well,' Ernie said doubtfully.

'He came here lookin' for Lewis. He got killed. You sayin' some *stranger* shot him?' Desperation was stretching Marcus's voice till it cracked.

'If they ain't done nothin' bad,' Curtis said, 'they oughta have the guts to come out an' say so.'

'I'll wake 'em up,' Floyd said. He was tired of being the younger brother. He took out his pistol and aimed at a weathervane on the roof, black wood against grey sky, and fired and fired and fired, until the gun was empty and the sky was saturated with echoes. 'Beats knockin' on doors,' he said.

'You asshole,' his brother said.

A shutter banged open. Stanton put his hand out and fired six shots, he knew not where, because his head was tucked back behind the wall. The Hudds scattered and hid and shot at the house. Its timbers were three feet thick. They absorbed the bullets with only a tremor.

But the noise was considerable. Ma Killick thought it was her late husband hammering to be let in. She wanted to open the shutters so that she could spit on him. It took Dan and Jessica and Devereux to wheedle and shove her down into the cellar. If one of them tried to leave, she kicked the others. 'Hell, Ma!' Dan shouted. 'I'm only gettin' you some corn liquor!' That worked.

He came back with the bottle, and chairs and a lantern and a pack of cards. Upstairs, Stanton went on shooting holes in the grey evening, at minimum risk to himself. Downstairs, Ma Killick took sips, and watched them play poker.

'These taters stink enough to choke a person,' Jessica said.

'Goddamn Hudds got no right to behave like this,' Dan said.

Devereux scowled. 'Soon's I can, I'm goin' over an' shootin' a couple hundred holes in *their* pretty little house, see how they like it.'

'What they want, anyway?' Dan said. 'We ain't got their little Two-Toes.'

'Maybe they think you killed that feller,' Jessica said. 'Mr Deputy.'

'Maybe they do. Ain't no call to put us in jail. Jesus, this is *worse'n* jail.'

'Trespassin',' Ma Killick said suddenly. 'We don't allow no strangers on Killick land. You done right, Dan.'

'Taters stink enough to choke a *mule*,' Jessica said.

'No, I didn't, Ma,' Dan said. 'So just forget it.'

Outside, the gunshots banged erratically.

'What burns my gut,' Dev said, 'is I save the crit from drownin', an' this is their thank-you.' He sneezed. 'Cold as the goddamn tomb in here.'

'Don't ever say you never done right,' his mother told Dan. 'That's for the court to decide. You had your reasons.'

'Ain't gonna be no court, Ma.'

'You were nearest to that barn,' Dev said. 'You see any fellers runnin' away?'

'No. I was ...' Dan threw down his cards. 'Jesus wept. *You* think I shot the bastard.'

'Someone sure did,' Jessica said.

'Just as well Jimmy-Sam Wiggins comin' to marry you,' Ma Killick said. 'He's a real big lawyer.'

'He's a real big fart, an' he ain't touchin' me.'

'Look, it's obvious,' Dan said. 'The Hudd boy took my forty-four. *He* shot that feller.'

Dev shivered. He draped a potato sack around his shoulders. He took the bottle and had a swig and gave it back.

'We playin' poker or what?' Jessica asked.

'Everythin' be all right once Jimmy-Sam gets here,' Ma Killick said.

They sat, hunched against the cold, breathing through the mouth to avoid the stink, until Stanton came down. 'They went,' he said. 'Rainin' like a bitch out there.'

The rain had crept across the Hudds as a fine drizzle. Then it worked itself up to a hard, pelting downpour, and finally it took on the serious task of dumping water on this corner of Kentucky as if it were delivering some bleak, severe punishment. Marcus saw rain bouncing knee-high and knew there was no point in waiting. A dying cow lay screeching, the sole victim of all that gunfire. He rode over and killed it. Then he took his people home.

~

'Goin' to bed,' Frankie said.

'Too early,' Maggie said. 'Have a drink. On the house. Play some cards.'

'Stop being so goddamn pleasant. Everyone keeps treatin' me nice, like I got the consumption or somethin'. It's a burden. I'm goin' to bed.'

The tavern was full, because for once there was something to talk about, only nobody wanted to talk loudly, not with Frankie standing there; and if you couldn't talk loud in a tavern you might's well go outside and howl at the moon. Not that there was a moon. So everyone was glad to see Frankie go upstairs to her room, where a widow-woman belonged, and let them wash the memory of the deceased in rivers of beer, as was proper.

Frankie sat on the bed and the first thing she saw was a pair of his boots standing in a corner, the wrong way round. Right boot on the left, left on the right. That troubled her so much that she was about to get up and rearrange them, when the pointlessness of doing so, of doing *anything*, hit her and actually made her gasp. Part of her had been waiting for him to come home.

The boots were a bad joke. Out of the corner of her eye she saw the shape which his foot had made, the folds and the creases. Nobody else's foot would ever make or fit that shape. So now the boot was wasted, useless, with no purpose except to cause her pain. She turned violently away and saw the unmade bed. He always slept on the left. There was still a dent in the pillow. 'Oh, go away!' she cried. She reached out and knocked the pillow to the floor. But by speaking she had turned an emotional key that released grief, and the sobs began. She went to the window and pressed her forehead against the black glass: tears and rain separated by next to nothing.

She was thinking, for no reason, of a cat her family had owned when she was very small, a cat that would jump on her bed and lie on her chest and stare into her eyes. There was a knock on the door and Mary Hudd walked in. 'Charles told me,' she said. 'I'm sorry I missed the funeral.'

'We bury 'em quick in Rock Springs,' Frankie said.

'Just as well, I suppose. This rain.'

'Yeah. The wake is downstairs. Had to leave. Too much compassion. Stinks worse than stogeys.' She wiped her eyes.

'I know,' Mary said. 'I was a widow myself.'

'People can't handle it, they treat you like it was *you* that died, maybe it's catchin', they get too close they'll catch it too.'

Mary took off her bonnet and cape. She was very wet. 'I don't normally drink,' she said. 'Can you suggest something?' Frankie went to the stairs and hollered at Maggie to send up the makings for hot toddies.

They drank and talked, drank and talked.

Before this, they had met only briefly; now, it was as if they were sisters who had been parted for a few years. They talked about their experiences during the war, the friends who had been killed, the damage and the waste, and the shock of Emancipation, which was painful but also satisfying because it meant the war had made a lasting difference after all. 'If you're gonna lose, lose big,' Frankie said.

'Where was Major de Glanville from?' Mary asked. 'Somebody should inform his next-of-kin. I'll do it, if you ...'

'He said Charleston, South Carolina, but that ain't true. He lied, you see. Lied about everythin'.'

'Not everything, surely.'

'Well ...' Frankie hoisted her left shoulder until she could rub her ear on it, then let it slump. 'Said he loved me, an' he couldn't of been actin' *all* the time. But the rest ... Nah.'

'No marriage is perfect. We all cheat a little.'

'Uh-huh.' Frankie set about making more toddies. 'You tryin' to make *me* feel better, or *you*?'

Mary surprised her with a big, cheerful laugh, and Frankie made the toddies a bit weaker. 'Between you and me,' Mary said, 'someone has already made me feel better. I never knew fornication could be such fun.'

'Anyone I know?'

Mary shook her head. 'This man is an artist.'

Frankie grunted, and waited, but Mary had heard her own words and knew she'd said far too much.

'That's one thing I'll miss,' Frankie said. 'The major an' me, we gave this old bed no rest. I'll miss his lies, too.'

'I don't understand. How could you like a man for lying to you?'

'Well, it meant I never had to fret about the truth. Half the stuff gets told to a deputy is lies. Folks do wrong, they cover up. That's work an' worry, for me. With de Glanville, I never had to worry, I *knew* he was lyin', he knew I knew, we neither of us cared. Fact is, I enjoyed it. He was good.'

Mary Hudd was uncomfortable. The idea of a happy liar bothered her. Nothing in her code of conduct and manners had prepared her for *that*.

'Them boots have got to go,' Frankie said, and her voice cracked on the last word. Mary Hudd abruptly stopped being bothered. 'You're right,' she said. 'In fact, why not ...' She spread her arms.

'Yeah,' Frankie said. 'Burn 'em.' She was smiling and crying at the same time. 'Let's have a fire. Everythin' on the fire.'

'If you're gonna lose, lose big.' That made them both laugh.

They collected his clothes, belongings, army uniform, even razor and shaving brush, and dumped it all on the bed. Frankie tied it in a blanket. Then she untied the blanket, unbuttoned the breast pocket of a tunic and took out a piece of paper with Latin writing on it. 'Keepsake,' she said. She tossed the tunic back and money spilled from an inside pocket. 'Jesus,' she said.

'Let us not rush into any burning,' Mary said.

They counted just under two thousand dollars. It was a very deep pocket.

'He never said nothin' about this,' Frankie said.

Mary finished her toddy. It had been an extraordinary day. She had already broken so many rules of polite behaviour that another wouldn't matter. 'Two thousand bucks would buy an awful lot of first-class fornication,' she said.

'That ain't how he made it,' Frankie told her. 'He made it the way came most natural to him, and that was operatin' some smooth-talkin' swindle.'

'A swindler married to a deputy.' Mary was amused.

'He gave good value. Most times, the folk enjoyed havin' their money took. Anyway ... we can afford a coupla gallons of lamp oil now.'

Stackmesser sold them the oil. The rain hadn't stopped, so they made a fire inside Maggie's barn. She brought over a jug of toddies for comfort. They sipped, and watched the flames reduce the heap to red ashes. Maggie was beginning to feel the loss.

'Times like this, I just can't see the point of nothin',' she said.

'Mrs Hudd here rates fornication very high,' Frankie said.

'Before now, I never knew it was meant to be so enjoyable,' Mary said. 'Excuse me, ladies. Nature calls.' She went outside.

'What was all that about?' Maggie asked.

'I hope I never find out,' Frankie said.

GOINGS AND
COMINGS BACK

L uke Corrigan not only could not swim, he did not understand a
river. Why should he? He had never before been on a raft or
any kind of boat. To him, a river was where cattle drank and
little children played at the edge and catfish lived somewhere deep.
Now the raft was twisting and groaning in the grip of the hurrying
floodwater, and he marvelled that catfish could live down in that wet
brown hell, and prayed that he would not fall in and join them.

After Rock Springs, the Cameron swirled through a series of fast
bends. Luke got soaked. Not by spray: there were no waves; but
every time he dragged his pole free and raised it, water ran down his
arms, his whole body. The other pikers laughed at him. Nap, the
steersman, never laughed. Nap cursed and hurled chunks of bark
when Luke was slow or clumsy. He rarely hit, Luke being forty feet
away and Nap always having to keep one hand on the long oar that
stuck out over the aft-end.

Luke was scared of Nap. When Ansel Mungers first took him to
the raft, waiting in Candle Creek, he'd said Nap was boss. Luke was
big but when he looked at Nap he felt small. 'I ain't boss,' Nap had
growled. 'I'm king an' god an' the devil! I can drown you, boy, any
time I like.' Mungers had said: 'He's right. Steersman just has to
sneeze an' you all drown! Heh-heh-heh.' Mungers could afford to
laugh. He wasn't going.

By the last of the fast bends, Luke had learned something about
piking. He'd learned you had to start turning the raft *before* it was
in the bend. Look ahead, think ahead. You had to stick your pole in
the water far out and *in front*, because by the time you struck bottom
and began heaving, the river would have rushed the raft onwards

and you'd be shoving straight out sideways. The pole was long and heavy, Luke was anxious, he used the wrong muscles, he wasted effort. Hunger didn't help. Then the rain came.

It fell so hard that it raised a thick spray on the surface. Dusk arrived early. Luke was not sorry: it meant they would stop for the night that much sooner. The Cameron widened and slowed; Nap fell silent. Even Luke saw places where they could easily drift ashore and tie up. At last Nap gave his oar to a piker and came forward, splay-legged for balance. 'We're goin' on through Slippery Falls. This river ain't done risin'. Tomorrow, them Falls'll be runnin' wild.' To Luke, he said, 'You see white water comin', you better get to work, boy, cus that's rocks. Don't wait for me.'

Luke had never before seen rapids. He saw precious little of these. He heard a roar that swelled and began to boom, and then the raft dipped its nose and he was staggering. Before he knew it, they were racing downhill on a torrent of leaping waves, and travelling faster than he thought possible. A boulder skimmed by, outlined in froth, and he remembered his task, and stabbed the pole at a patch of white water, missed, dragged back, stabbed again, jarred his arms and shoulders against solid rock, nearly lost the pole as the river snatched it, stumbled and fell and got up. Noise and spray and shuddering thuds were everywhere. The raft took a sudden swing and he almost went the opposite way, ended up clinging to the edge, one leg awash. But he never let go of his pole, he got back to his feet, he put in a couple of good, hard shoves. The raft emerged.

Nap kept dry kindling in a bag. They made a fire. Coffee, flapjacks, a swig of corn liquor. 'Smoother'n I thought,' Nap said. 'Last time I brung a raft through them Slippery Falls, it was real unpleasant.'

～

The rain was so heavy next day that Judge Hudd postponed the inquest. Even Marcus gave up looking for his son. He half-believed the boy was still somewhere near the Killick farm, but the mud brought horses down to a slow, exhausting trudge and nobody could see much through the downpour, so he quit. He wouldn't have found Lewis, anyway.

Bonny did.

Rain never bothered her. You couldn't get wetter than wet. Martha had plaited every bit of Bonny's hair and the rain made the plaits cling to her head like a black helmet. She like to stand with her face to the sky and let the raindrops splash into her mouth. She liked the way they tapped at her eyelids and drummed on her ears. Rain was as natural and friendly as sunshine, and if you ran now and then it made you just as warm.

Bonny had set some rabbit snares in a secret corner of the Ridge. She walked carefully, checking the runs, and found a good fat buck with its neck broken. The rainstorm had knocked most of the other traps flat. She stopped to eat some berries: fat, blue, deliciously sharp. She squeezed them for the pleasure of seeing the juice squirt and stain her fingers, and up ahead was a crash and a cry. Then silence.

Panther, maybe. Hunting. She'd never seen a panther. She moved cautiously, peering around rocks, and saw Lewis Hudd, face-down in the dirt, his legs uphill. His left ankle was in a snare.

She freed him. He stood, but his ankle burned like it had been whipped, so he sat down. He was almost in tears. It was a day and a night since he'd seen anyone, he was cold and soaked and weak with hunger, and now he'd been trapped by this small black heathen. God was punishing him. Now and forever. God is a *sonofabitch*, he thought, and felt better at once. *Sonafabitch God. Fuckin' sonabitch God.*

'You live round here?' Bonny asked.

Lewis thought about that. He pointed.

The cave interested her. It was deep and dry, and smelled faintly of sulphur. 'Ain't got no fire,' she said. 'Got no grub. Ain't you got nothin'?' Lewis showed her the forty-four and she laughed, so he sat in a corner and sulked.

She made a fire. Even in heavy rain you can get a fire going, provided you know where to look for tinder and kindling: dead ivy, thin as straw; old twigs blown beneath an overhang; pine cones, and fragments of resinous bark on the dry underside of a tree-limb. Aaron had taught her how, one damp afternoon. The gun was steel, she found flint. It took patience and perseverance but it worked. The flames turned dark gloom into a happy warmth. Lewis stopped sulking.

Later, they ate roast rabbit. When Bonny left, he still had not spoken. He seemed to have lost the need.

Next day the rain eased off and T. Speed came home. He had tuned another piano. He gave Lonzo twenty dollars, which was a fortune for a couple of days' work. Lonzo was glad of it. The Hudd Colony could live for a month on twenty bucks.

'How many pyanners you reckon there are, T. Speed?' Aaron asked. 'Say, in a day's walk?'

'Fifteen, twenty.' He was wearing Charles's old clothes and he smelled of perfumed soap. The Colony was impressed. 'What happened, Mizz Hudd gave me a letter to show Mizz Amelia Benson, on account she knew her pyanner needed a mess of tunin'.'

'Mizz Benson,' Martha said. 'Wasn't she that sweet child, went an' married ol' man Benson when his first wife got took?'

'Uh-huh.'

'He bought my daddy,' Gabe Killick said. 'Bought him from Mr Joe Killick. Got him cheap cus he was old. That Mr Benson, he ain't still livin'?'

T. Speed nodded. 'Moves awful slow. Don't see too well.'

They stood around him and thought about the big old house, halfway to Black's Landing, which only T. Speed had seen.

'She treat you good?' Martha asked. 'Give you plenty of grub?' He nodded, and smiled his sunflower smile.

'Tunin' pyanners can't be so damn hard,' Lonzo said. 'How 'bout you teachin' me?'

T. Speed stroked his perfectly shaven chin. 'Folks come in two sorts,' he said. 'There is pyanner-tuners an' there is pyanner-shifters. Lonzo, you is a pyanner-shifter.'

'Huh,' Lonzo said. He went off and chopped a big pile of logs. Winter was coming. Try playin' *that* tune on your pyanner an' see how cold you get.

~

Marcus and Ruth brooded over the loss of their son. They could not sleep, and they gave Charles no rest either. It got so he even asked Mary what he should do. You're the judge, she told him; go and hang somebody. And she went off the play the piano. He was getting sick of its jubilant sound.

He rode into town, feeling maybe he shouldn't have run for judge. He'd expected to get kudos and esteem, and that hadn't happened. He hadn't expected to be chivvied by his cousins, and made to decide the law, and then to enforce it. A man was entitled to the respect and admiration of his neighbours, and there had to be an easier way of getting it that *this*.

Steam was rising from Main Street as the clouds broke and let the sun attack the mud. He passed Mrs Ryan Kidder. 'We never had none of this trouble before them darkies of yourn went an' hid up the Ridge,' she said accusingly.

'You'd prefer they were down here?' he said. 'Where you could see them?' She didn't like that either. He rode on.

Charles went into the tavern, and found Frankie in her office: a back room that Maggie used for private poker sessions. A thousand bad cigars had lived and died here and their ghosts were in the air to prove it. 'Anything new?' he asked.

'Nothin'.'

'The boy's father ...' That was when he saw how weary she was. Her eyelids were heavy, and their weight seemed to drag lines of stress across her face. He said, 'A murder and a kidnapping, same place, same time, there's got to be a point to it. Aren't there any rumours? Gossip?'

'Ask Maggie.'

'The weather's cleared. Surely ...' He wanted to say: *You must hunt down your husband's killer*, but he couldn't. He was in the wrong job.

~

That was more or less when a man in a black corduroy suit rode down Main Street. He wore a light, biscuity Stetson and cowboy boots. He had shaved so closely that his face looked polished. He had the cleanest fingernails in Dundee County.

He stopped and looked at all there was to see. This took little time. He dismounted and went into the tavern.

'Sheriff?' he said.

'Out of town,' Maggie said. 'You married?'

'No. Why?'

'Well, you an' me, we're about of an age. Never ask, you never get.

Ain't that the truth?'

He was taken aback. 'I'm sure a lady such as yourself ...' But he couldn't think of a way to finish.

'No call to get embarrassed.' Maggie knew she needed a shave, and here comes this smooth bastard who looked like he already shaved twice that day and rubbed his chin with pumice stone too. 'You must be real desperate to come to this town if you don't want a wife.'

'Have you coffee?'

The only other customers were Stanton Killick, who was slumped in a corner, slightly drunk, and the pedlar, who was hungover. They succeeded in making the place seem emptier, not fuller.

'Maggie's a princess,' the pedlar said. 'Got royal blood in her.' He could see the stranger wasn't listening. 'Ever play poker?' he said. 'I hear tell it's an interestin' pastime.'

'James L. Boston,' the man said. He placed a card on the bar. 'Employed by the Pinkerton Detective Agency. We're searching for this woman.' He put a small sepia photograph beside the card. It had been taken in a studio, very formal, very stiff. 'Charlotte van Orman.'

Maggie looked. It was Frankie Nickel, several years ago. 'Nobody around here called that,' she said. 'Never saw this woman, either.'

The pedlar came over. 'Kind of like Maud Corrigan's daughter that married an' went to Canada, only Jessy was short an' fat an' she had that wall-eye ...'

'What you want her for?' Maggie asked.

'A serious matter,' Boston said.

'Reward out?' the pedlar asked.

Boston thought about that. 'Could be.'

'You don't sound like Kentucky, nor yet even Tennessee,' Maggie said. 'You from Texas?'

'Us Pinkertons are everywhere.' He sipped his coffee. 'Keep the picture,' he said. 'You never know.'

'That was just a joke about us gettin' married,' Maggie said. 'We make our own fun around here.' Boston raised a finger in acknowledgment.

～

'Maybe we should bring in another law officer to investigate,' Charles said. Frankie picked at the splintered table top and said nothing. She'd been doing a lot of that.

Charles despaired. Bringing in a law officer meant a telegram to Bowling Green, which meant a day's ride. Two days for the man to get here. Meanwhile, nothing happens. That would look bad to people. Unforgivable. He turned away, searching the blank room for a solution, and one kicked the door open and walked in. It was Ma Killick.

'Needed a pound of nails,' she said. 'Roof leaks bad. That Stackmesser's an idiot.'

'This is a private meeting.' Charles flapped his hand at the door.

'Beg pardon.' She kicked the door shut. 'See, we don't allow no strangers on Killick land. Dan had every right. Anyway, that's for the court to decide.'

'Decide what?' Charles demanded.

She recoiled, and clutched her bag of nails to her breast. 'Wilderness Road goes through the Cumberland Gap,' she said defiantly. 'Us Killicks took the Wilderness Road.'

'Sure you did,' Frankie said. 'Now tell us about Dan an' the stranger.'

Ma Killick shuffled sideways until the table was between her and Charles. 'He was trespassin'. We don't allow no trespassers. The Bible says forgive us our trespassers, an' we do forgive 'em, but we gun 'em down first, so they won't argue. That's in the Bible, too. Let us do evil, that good may come. Romans, three, eight, look it up. So there.'

'Your son shot a man?' Charles asked.

'His late father Joseph would've done the same, only he got murdered by a stranger in his own house.' She squinted at Charles. 'Very well-known stranger. That's the worst kind. Our family suffered once, but never again. Dan had every right. You look like you swallered a plum-stone.'

'I see no need for an inquest,' he said to Frankie. 'Bring him in for trial.'

'Not me. I'll never go there again.'

'He murdered your husband.'

'Damn right you did,' Ma Killick said. 'Pushed him down the stairs. I saw it.'

'Be silent, madam!' Charles roared. He frightened her so much she dropped the bag. Nails spilled everywhere. She tried to stoop but her legs sent messages of pain. When Maggie came in, the deputy and the judge were on their knees, collecting nails. 'Stackmesser is an idiot,' Ma Killick explained.

'Prayer ain't gonna change that. Frankie, come out of there. Somethin' you gotta see.'

She led the deputy through a side door into the kitchen, and shut the door. 'I got a Pinkerton man in the bar. Wants the sheriff. Says he's lookin' for Charlotte van Orman.'

Frankie let out a long, weak groan: a sound that Maggie had never heard her make before. 'What d'you tell him?'

'The sheriff ain't in town, nobody knows when he'll be back. Ain't no lie.'

'Keep him here for half an hour, can you?'

Charles was putting the last few nails into the bag. 'I'll go,' Frankie said. 'I'll go now. But not alone. You find me two more deputies. I'll be out back, waitin'.' She left before he could argue.

Ma Killick weighed the bag in her hand. It went *chunk-chunk*. 'I know how many was in here,' she warned. 'You cheat me, you'll suffer.'

'How many?' he demanded. 'Exactly how many?'

'Ain't tellin',' she said. He went out. She stood for a while, face squashed-up in thought. Suddenly she dumped the nails on the table and began counting. 'Can't fool me,' she said.

Charles recruited the first two men he saw, Reuben Skinner and Hoke Cleghorn, and ten minutes later they left town with Frankie. Maggie was on the sidewalk, washing her windows in such a way as to smear the dirt. She saw them go and went inside.

'Yeah, I could of bin a Pinkerton,' Stanton was saying.

James L. Boston glanced at him and looked away.

'You ever catch any real big criminals?' the pedlar asked.

'Bein' shy of an arm ain't no problem,' Stanton said.

'Used to be lotsa bad outlaws around here,' the pedlar said. 'We shot 'em. You shot anyone?'

'Pinkerton's got a secret handshake,' Stanton announced. 'I know it.' He showed them his hand.

'Yeah?' Boston said.

'Course, I ain't showed no-one. Wouldn't be a secret if I did.' Stanton smirked.

'Uh-huh.'

'I'm gonna write a book,' the pedlar said. 'Soon's I get the time. Gonna be real interestin'. Maybe me an' you could write it together.'

'No,' Boston said.

'Yes sir,' Stanton said. 'Mr Pinkerton wanted me to join real bad. *Real* bad.'

After another twenty minutes of this, Maggie felt almost sorry for Boston, and more than sorry for herself.

'I'd appreciate some more coffee, ma'am,' Boston said.

'None left. We run out of beans.'

'Steak?'

'Kitchen's shut. Cook quit. In fact, tavern's shut. Everybody out.'

Boston stared. 'You can't shut a tavern.'

'Stocktaking,' Maggie snapped. 'You got a horse. Next tavern's downriver, at Barber's Landin'. Ten miles. Real friendly folk.'

'Flub Phillips used to take in boarders,' the pedlar said helpfully, 'but he got a case of the galloping convulsions. You could come back next year.' He followed Boston out, and waved goodbye. It was something to do on a dull day.

~

Nap reckoned it took five days to run a raft to Nashville. Five long days, dawn to dusk. Luke already knew what tired him the most: it was balancing hour after hour on wet and slippery logs. Ansel Mungers had given him an old pair of boots, which helped; but when the raft was skidding and lurching and shuddering and running wet, Luke's feet often lost their grip.

A little cabin was built into the raft, just in front of the steersman. It held Luke's beaver skins, a mooring rope, various pieces of logging gear, a frying-pan big enough to take twenty eggs, and an axe. Luke noticed that the other pikers stood more easily than he. Later he saw why. Notches had been cut in the wood. Later still, he thought of the axe.

The Cameron sucked the raft into a boiling narrows; Nap steered it down the centre of see-sawing waves, and the Cameron spat it out into a broad tranquillity. Nap ordered grub-time. Luke got the axe and began chopping. One notch was all he cut. Nap barged him flat and snatched the axe and threatened to split him from asshole to gizzard. Luke lay, head singing from a bang on the logs, elbow skinned, brain trying to make sense of the curses. Nap stalked off.

Mud on the elbow kept flies away from the blood. It took longer for Luke to recover his wits. Being hit by Nap was like running slap into a tree at night: the shock was as bad as the blow.

One of the other pikers, Wes, brought him some grub. Wes traced the notch with the edge of his boot. 'Spoils the wood,' he said softly. 'Nap wants top price at Nashville.'

Luke got to his feet and looked at the piker's notches cut at places further up the raft.

'We cut ours before Nap come,' Wes said. 'You shoulda done yours too.'

'Didn't know.'

Wes clicked his tongue. '*Gotta* know, boy. Gotta.'

That was unfair; but Luke had been raised not to expect fair treatment; not to expect anything at all, simply to take what came. Overseer whopped you, you didn't feel bad. Didn't whop you, you didn't feel good. Feelings were a white man's luxury.

Luke ate his grub. Nap ate very little. The man worked harder than any piker yet he ate almost nothing. Luke wondered.

The raft made good time that afternoon. They met hazards. A huge poplar had fallen across the river and it forced the pikers to lie flat, but Nap squeezed the raft under it, and only the cabin got knocked crooked. The worst falls went downhill in steps like a staircase, but they were short and straight. The raft nosed and reared, bucked and kicked, and survived intact. Nap tied up before sundown, near a one-storey house. 'Go up an' eat,' he said.

As they climbed the bank, Luke said to Wes, 'Don't he eat none?'

'Man's got the toothache. Food makes it hurt worse.'

The woman of the house had seen them coming. They ate fried pork belly, hot cornbread, gravy, and came again for more, with jugs of black coffee sweetened almost to a syrup.

It was twilight when Luke went out and searched for a pine tree. He scraped off a handful of the yellow pitch that oozed from the bark, and took it to the raft. Nap was squatting, his back to the cabin.

'Poke this here pine-pitch in your tooth,' Luke said. 'Soaks up the pain.' Or so Aaron had said.

Nap shook his head. He couldn't speak. The ache raged throughout his jaws like hot coals being raked from a fire. Only one thing could overcome such pain: a greater pain.

He stood up. He took Luke's right hand and shaped a fist of it. He let go of the fist and pressed his forefinger against his jaw where the rotten tooth was. He braced his legs. Luke swung a punch so hard that, if he had missed, it would have spun him into the Cameron. Nap landed on his backside with a thud that shook the raft. He put his head between his knees and did a lot of spitting. Luke sat on his haunches beside him. 'That what you wanted?' he asked. Nap looked up and showed him his gaping mouth. Luke put his fingers in and searched around and plucked out the bloody stub.

After a while he plugged the hole with pine-pitch. Later still they went to the house and Nap ate a big meal with half his mouth.

They slept at the house, ate breakfast there, went down to the raft. A row of notches had been cut in the logs where Luke stood. He figured that Nap got up in the night and did it. Nobody said anything. Big river ahead.

~

Maggie told Doc Brightsides about the visit of James L. Boston.

'You did right to send him to Barber's Landing,' he said. 'This town's got more excitement than it can handle.'

'Reckon I'll go up an' rest. You take care of the bar.'

A couple of hours later, Brightsides was leaning against the doorway, watching two flies circle and fight, wondering what could be so important to a fly that it had to fight over it, when an unfamiliar rider appeared, moving slowly. 'Two strangers in one day!' he told the flies. 'Sometimes it gets so's a person just can't take it all in.'

The stranger walked the horse down Main Street. He saw it was a woman, riding like a man, not sidesaddle, which was unusual for Kentucky in 1867. She stopped beside him and it was JoBeth, though he had to look hard to be certain. She seemed fifteen years older. Her face used to be milk-white, guarded by bonnets and parasols; now it was tanned like saddle-leather and creased like paper fans at the corners of the eyes. Those eyes had been as clear as London gin. Nobody in Rock Springs drank gin; Maggie had one bottle she kept the IOUs under; but he had seen gin in Chicago and the next clearest thing to gin had been JoBeth's eyes. Now they appeared to be filmed with dust, which he knew was anatomically impossible but they carried that sense of dullness.

She wore buckskin trousers and a man's red check coat and an old, tired canvas hat with her hair tucked up inside it.

'Well, you took your time about coming home,' he said.

'Well, it was a long way to come,' she said.

That was just noise to break the silence, and they knew it. Still, the sound of a familiar voice was reassuring, even if his was a little thinner and hers a little harsher than the last time.

'You look like you could use a meal,' he said.

'I surely could. I been sick every mornin' for the past week.'

'In that case I'd better cook you two meals.' He saw young Billy Dunbar watching, and shouted at him to tend to the horse.

He fired up the stove and put on water to boil for coffee. She sat in a rocker and fell asleep. He shook her awake. 'D'you want me to look at you?'

She got up and took off all her clothes. They just tumbled off: boots, pants, coat, shirt: naked in twenty seconds.

After five minutes the water was boiling and he told her to get dressed. 'Two things wrong,' he said. 'You're thin, and you smell like a horse.'

'The horse never complained, an' we bin partners a long time. What about the little lodger downstairs?'

'You said you reckon three months.'

'Give or take, yeah.'

'My opinion is you're right. It's not my business but ...'

'You want to know who the father was.'

'You're going to need help.'

'Forget him. He's dead. Cowboy called Chisholm. Got drowned in a river.'

'Perhaps his parents – '

'Chisholm never had no parents. He was too poor.'

Brightsides cooked ham and eggs and fried potatoes, and watched her eat. If he used all his imagination he could still see the vivacious girl under the leathery tan. Well, he'd given her a free examination; that was worth one question. 'Where've you been?' he asked.

'Everywhere. Anywhere. Nowhere worth goin' back to.'

'We understood you first went to Tennessee.'

'George made me. I heard George got killed in the war. That right?'

'Right. Rumour had you dead and buried in Louisiana.' That amused her, but not much. He said, 'I guess you've been out of touch. With your family.' She nodded, concentrating on shovelling down the grub. 'Your father died, too,' he said. She didn't even blink. 'His heart,' he said. 'Very sudden.' She put more salt on her eggs.

She refused his offer of a bath, but borrowed a horse. As she rode away, he realized that he had not told her of Hudd's marriage. He thought of running after her; then decided she had taken all the news she needed in one day. Like most men, Brightsides had been somewhat in love with her in the old days. How pleasant it would be if she came and lived with him now, shared his bed. It was a dream; all right, so it was a dream. What was wrong with dreaming?

He watched her diminish to a dot. The town drowsed.

AIN'T THAT THE TRUTH?

Lonzo called a meeting of the colony. Aaron sat on the Altar, wrapped in his smelly furs. 'What it comes to, you niggers've over-trapped,' he said.

'Could be the panther, too,' Gabe Killick said.

'Or buzzards, eagles,' Martha said. 'See 'em flyin' all the time. Big old owls, even.'

'Who gives a damn why?' Lonzo said. 'Traps are empty. No more skins this year.'

'Let us pray to the Almighty to help us,' Josh said.

'Later,' Aaron told him.

'Luke got them hundred beavers,' Buck lisped. 'Big money there.'

'Beaver don't enjoy bein' trapped,' Aaron said. 'Beaver probly up an' moved to Oregon. I would.'

Buck didn't understand. 'We already trapped them beavers. Luke sellin' 'em now.'

'Aaron means next year,' T. Speed said gently. 'How we to live next year?'

'Oh, somethin' gonna turn up,' Moses rumbled.

'Your toes gonna turn up,' Aaron said sourly.

'Don't want no more roots,' Bettsy said. 'Et so many roots I got pointy feet.' Much nodding of heads. 'Wanna eat *real* grub.'

'Takes real dollars,' Nat said. He rarely spoke. Aaron approved. He clicked his fingers and pointed. 'Only nigger here talkin' sense,' he said. Nat turned away, confused by praise.

'Well, what we got to sell?' Martha asked. 'Ain't no silver mines, you tried that. Ain't no furs. What we got? Dirt? Rocks?'

'Trees?' Lonzo said. 'Trees.'

'Hallelujah,' Josh said thoughtfully. But then nobody spoke for such a long time that Bonny grew bored and slipped away. She was

398

more interested in her secret playmate. She had already given Lewis an old half-bust stewpot and a tattered blanket her mother wouldn't miss until winter came. She'd stolen scraps of food and trapped three squirrels and a chipmunk. Bonny never had a doll, though she'd seen white children with dolls. Lewis was her doll.

He was pleased to see her. He had killed two pigeons with a sling-shot; they would have a feast. He stacked a great supply of firewood in the cave, seasoned hardwood that burned hot and made little smoke. She noticed how brown his skin had become. Sun, dirt, char-coal and grease from food had worked to make him dark all over. She thought he looked good.

~

The ride out to the Killick farm was hard on Frankie. Every turn in the road, every change of view, was a stabbing reminder of the way fate gave happiness and snatched it away. Reuben and Hoke knew this and didn't bother her with a lot of talk. But they needed to know what they were meant to do when they got there. Ask some questions, she said, poke around, sniff around. After that? Depends on what we find.

She didn't reckon on finding a Killick cousin, big as a bear and twice as shaggy, who practised law upstate. Name of Jimmy-Sam Wiggins. He gave her his card. She gave it back. 'I can remember,' she said. 'Gettin' widowed don't damage your memory.'

'Of course.' He smiled at each of them in turn. Only Reuben smiled back; Jimmy-Sam's snow-white suit impressed him enor-mously. It was like meeting a 300-pound angel with a cavalry mous-tache.

'You representin' the family?' Frankie asked. They were in the kitchen; Dan and Devereux were leaning against the wall, hands in pockets, looking at the floor.

'Why should I do that?'

'You heard what happened out here?'

'As to that,' Jimmy-Sam said. He had a rich, deep voice, like whiskey barrels rolling over flagstones. 'As to that, I doubt whether anyone here knows exactly what happened. Do you?'

'Their mother just told me – '

'Ma's not right in the head,' Dan said. 'Gets these wild ideas.

Thinks the war ain't over.'

'She's right there,' Hoke said grimly.

'Anyways, she's still in town, with Stanton,' Dev said.

'I talked to her,' Frankie said. 'Now I want your story.'

'None of this is evidence,' Jimmy-Sam announced. 'No proper record of statements is being kept. The law – '

'Hey, hey!' She beat on the kitchen table with a rolling pin. Grey, stale flour popped from the cracks. 'The only man I don't wanna hear from is *you*. Where's your sister?' she asked Dan.

'Upstairs. Ain't well.'

'Go fetch her,' Frankie told Hoke.

'Harassing a witness,' Jimmy-Sam murmured.

'What you want *me* to do?' Reuben asked her. All this fast talk was over his head. He preferred action.

'Oh, hell. Go an' look around the house. Anybody here object to that?'

'Shut up, Jimmy-Sam,' Dan said. 'We got nothin' to hide.' Jimmy-Sam shrugged and smiled. He enjoyed confrontation. It made his fingers tingle.

She asked Dev to go outside while she questioned Dan. Dan had nothing much to say: sure, he'd seen the Hudd boy about the place, paid him no heed, too busy working. Same with the major's death: heard the shot, left his work, found the body, sent Dev for Doc Brightsides, fast. Not fast enough, and that was a great shame.

Dev came in. He rattled off the sequence of events: raft capsized, boy fished out of river, brought here, fed, did some chores, must have wandered off, never said goodbye. Strange boy. Didn't talk. As for the shooting: Dev was mending fences, out of sight of that barn. Came running, but ...

Jessica appeared, yawning, hair a mess, no shoes. She had scarcely anything to add. Remembered seeing the boy, all wet. Didn't remember seeing the man. Now she had a fever. Ma went to town to get a powder, wasn't back yet. Probably forgot. Jessica gave the deputy a bad-tempered stare, the one she had been practising recently.

Jimmy-Sam Wiggins had retired to the end of the table and was playing solitaire.

'Well, now you heard everythin',' Frankie said to him. 'You got any observations to make?'

He placed a red jack on a black queen so firmly that the card smacked. He thrust his head forward and frowned at the jack as if he had caught it cheating. 'Hey, Wiggins!' she barked. He moved his eyes but not his head. 'I understood that you did not wish to hear from me,' he said. Devereux laughed. Jessica yawned.

Now Frankie lost her temper with all of them. 'This is murder I'm askin' about! For the love of Jesus, someone killed that man in *your* barn, shot him dead, same time a young boy came onto *your* land an' was never seen leavin' it! You jackasses think that's funny! I tell you, them Hudds ain't the forgivin' kind! You folk gonna be lookin' behind you for the rest of your life, ever thought of that?' She grabbed Dev, pulled him to his feet, spun him around. He fell over his feet. 'When you're lyin' on a barn door, wonderin' who shot you, don't send for me, boy. Seems I don't speak your language.'

The only sound in the kitchen was her panting for breath.

'Alas,' Jimmy-Sam said, 'my kin cannot tell you what they do not know.' He groomed his moustache with his fingers. 'And if this comes to court, I shall point out the biased and highly prejudicial nature of your recent words.'

That was when Reuben Skinner came in, waving a small and filthy garment. 'Found this in their cellar,' he said. 'Looks to me like a young 'un's shirt. You got any young 'uns here?'

Devereux turned away; he did not want to see. Dan glanced at the shirt, then at Wiggins, then at the ceiling. Only Jessica spoke.

'Saw a nigger over near that barn, after the shootin',' she said. 'Seemed to me he had a gun. Could of bin a forty-four. Takin' a white boy away, too. Mighty big hurry.'

Frankie threw her arms in the air.

'You just remembered all this?' she asked. Her voice rose until it cracked with disbelief.

'Been sick,' Jessica said. 'Got a fever.'

~

We all want to go back home, but the home we want to go back to never existed, and that's a sad disappointment.

JoBeth had been away seven years. She knew everything must have changed; she was ready for that. The surprise was there was no surprise. The road to the farm was still as ordinary as mud, and plenty of it. She let the horse make its own pace; after a thousand miles she

401

was in no hurry to face her family. No George, of course. Not much of a loss. As for the others, maybe they'd improved through the years. Her horse walked around a bend, and up ahead was a buggy skewed across the track, one end of its axle dug into the dirt, the wheel lying where it had run off and bogged itself in a piece of swamp.

Stanton was trying to unharness the horse. He was just drunk enough so that his fingers wouldn't work. His mother was cursing and kicking him. Her legs were unsteady and she sometimes kicked the horse. 'Bible says,' she ranted, 'look not upon the wine when it is red, you one-armed heap of muleshit! Proverbs, twenty-three, thirty-one!'

Stanton mumbled: 'Get the fuckin' hell outa my fuckin way, Ma.'

She took careful aim at Stanton's knee and kicked the right fetlock joint. The horse screamed and shied. Stanton's fingers got trapped and he was dragged a full quarter-circle, the buggy skidding and screeching.

JoBeth calmed the animal, got Stanton's fingers out, released the harness, led the horse clear. ' 'Twern't nothin' to do with me,' her mother said, piteously. 'I was mindin' my manners, same as always.'

The pain had sobered Stanton considerably. 'Damn me to hell,' he said. 'It's my little sister. They told me you were dead.'

'Give me a hand here.'

'One hand is all I got.' That joke always worked. Her mouth gave a twitch, and he felt encouraged. They heaved the buggy onto its side. She went and dragged the wheel out of the muck.

Ma Killick sat on a fallen tree and pretended to watch the horse while squinnying sideways at JoBeth.

'You ain't marryin' Jessica,' she said at last, 'so don't go gettin' your hopes up. Jessica's spoke for.'

They hoisted the wheel and fitted it back on the axle. Stanton rested, blowing hard. Liquor-sweat popped out of his forehead. 'Them buckskin pants,' he wheezed, 'an' you ridin' straddle. Confuses her ...' He took a deep breath. 'JoBeth, Ma!' he shouted.

'Bless her soul.' Suddenly she made the connection. 'Was you at the deathbed, sonny?' she asked her. 'Did she say anythin' nice about me?'

JoBeth took off the big old canvas hat and shook her hair loose. She walked over to her mother. 'Take a good long look.'

Ma Killick recognized her and went into a mild flustery panic. 'None of this ain't nothin' to do with me,' she said. 'Jimmy-Sam Wiggins is gonna see to everythin'. Every last nail.'

JoBeth whittled a hickory pin and whacked it in the axle slot. 'Horse must of got spooked,' Stanton said. They heaved the buggy onto its wheels, and put the horse in the shafts.

'Just keep your damn-fool wheels out the damn-fool ditch,' JoBeth told him. They loaded their mother and set off.

~

Mary Hudd hadn't realized how trapped she felt in that house until T. Speed came along and the door got thrown open and sunlight streamed in.

It wasn't just the sex, although the raw rush of pleasure created a memory she could live on for a month, or three. It was also the freedom, the sense that she had a life of her own again, that she made the rules. She wasn't a Hudd, never had been, never would be. When Ruth Hudd – Lewis's mother – came to see her, Mary observed the blinking eyes, the hollow cheeks, the eternally restless fingers, and felt nothing but impatience. Grief was an unattractive business.

'I'm at my wits' end,' Ruth said.

'Well, you won't find your boy there.'

'I wonder sometimes: are we being punished?'

'Lord knows.'

'Ernie thinks that we are being tested.'

'If the Almighty is communicating through Ernie, He's really desperate.'

Ruth was hearing without listening. 'Marcus thinks he can hire a pack of bloodhounds. The kind that tracked runaways? And a woman in Barber's Landing has the second sight. For a few dollars – '

'Sure, Abigail Hockaday, I taught her children, she'll invent what she thinks you want to hear. Hounds? After this rain, hounds couldn't track a French perfume salesman.'

Now Ruth was listening. 'What am I to do?' she cried.

'Listen: I taught school long enough to know: boys run away. Maybe your Lewis will come back. Maybe he won't. Maybe he's in Nashville. Nature is prodigal, Ruth. And – '

'The Killicks have him.' Abruptly, Ruth had become stern, grim, vengeful. 'I know it. The Killicks have him hidden away. Somewhere secret.'

'That beats Abigail Hockaday,' Mary said. 'And you just saved a dollar.'

'They took one of mine,' Ruth said. 'I'll take one of theirs. Then we'll see.' She turned and strode out.

They all tramped down into the cellar. The light was dim, and the stink of potatoes was thick. Reuben held up the shirt as continuing proof of his detective skills.

Jessica said she thought it looked like the kind of thing her little nephew Tommy might have worn when he visited last year, and Devereux agreed, sure, Tommy was about that age, and Dan said yup, and Frankie said Lewis's mother would have to see it. That shut them up.

'This here is where I found it,' Reuben said. 'I found it here.'

'Coldest room in the house,' Frankie said. 'Strange place for a little boy to take off his shirt.' Nobody had any opinion about that. 'You, Dev,' she said, 'show me exactly where on the Cameron you say you found him.'

'River's flooded. Ain't nothin' to see.'

'Let's go.' The truth was she couldn't think of anything else to look at.

Dev left with the three deputies. Dan was set to go up the stairs too when Jimmy-Sam checked him. 'That deputy's right. Cold down here. Damp, too. If this thing goes to court,' Jimmy-Sam said, 'three questions in the jury's mind. Was little Lewis here? If he was, why? And did he leave alive?'

'Jess said she seen him, next day,' Dan said.

'Where were you?' Jimmy-Sam asked her. 'And where was he?'

She ignored him. She had not looked at him or spoken to him since Hoke had brought her downstairs. She put herself as far as possible from him and she never faced him. 'Said I saw the boy,' she told Dan. 'Saw the nigger, saw the gun, saw the boy, now can we get out of this stinkin' hole?'

'Not yet,' Jimmy-Sam said. 'I came a long way to ask Jessica to be my wife, and I hoped to get a fair hearing, at the least. If I stand up for Dan in court, my job would be to get *him* a fair hearing, at the least. But I ask myself: if I don't get a fair hearing here, why should I care about fair hearing there?'

'For Chrissake, Jess,' Dan said. 'Here's a fella can buy Rock Springs at one end of Main Street an' sell it at the other! Why in hell won't you marry him?'

'I don't like him,' she said.

'She's got a fever,' Dan said. 'It'll pass.'

'Times like this,' Jimmy-Sam said, 'I begin to doubt my own judgment.'

'No, no!' Dan said. 'Don't do that. Jesus.'

'Even lawyers are human.'

'Listen, I know Jess. She's a tease.'

'If you even try to make me marry him,' she said, 'I'll blow your balls off. His too.'

Hooves and wheels sounded, and Stanton shouting. It was a welcome excuse to get out.

Stanton was loud with the power of knowledge.

'See here! Gather round! Got a big surprise. This here's our own little sister, JoBeth, back from Down South, been away ... Jesus ... how long?'

'Good while.'

'Don't be fooled by them buckskin pants, it's JoBeth, sure enough! There's brother Dan, look, gone awful grey, ain't he? Ugly bastard, not like me ... This here's big cousin Jimmy-Sam Wiggins from upstate, three real nice fellas, heh-heh-heh, that's a joke, an' there's your sister Jessy, looks better when she brushes her hair, she's gonna marry Jimmy-Sam.'

'Ain't.'

Nobody missed Devereux. That was normal.

Ma Killick insisted everybody go into the parlour. The room had not been used since the laying-out of her husband. Dead flies littered the windowsills, and the stubs of black candles recorded the outline of the corpse on the table: his widow's idea. She had thought it stylish. The air smelled faintly of horse liniment. It always had; nobody knew why.

'This warms the heart,' Jimmy-Sam said. 'A family reunion. My great good luck. Won't you sit down?'

'I bin sittin' for the last thousand miles,' JoBeth said. 'It ain't no luxury.'

'Look, Ma,' Dan said, 'you got us all in here. Now what?'

'Parlour's for visitors. Sit, talk, drink some tea.' She was starting to recognize her daughter, who had died long since in Louisiana, which explained why she looked different.

'You get my fever powder?' Jessica said.

'You never asked. Anyway, Stackmesser sold out. Besides, you need a good purge is what.'

'Shit,' Jessica said wearily.

'Tell me,' Jimmy-Sam said, more and more impressed by JoBeth's looks, 'where have you been living all these years?'

'Long story. Some other time.'

'And … and do you see many changes here?'

'Changes.' That amused her slightly. 'No, I don't see a whole lotta changes. Everythin's just the way it always was. Dan here's gone and killed a major for no reason, Dev went an' kidnapped a little 'un from the Hudds, kicked its little ass so hard he bounced it clear out of sight, Ma's wearin' her brain back to front, an' Jess ain't marryin' nobody, especially you.'

Dan turned on Stanton. 'You got a mouth like a horse's ass.'

'Now hold on there – '

'An' Stanton's drunk,' JoBeth said. 'Nearly forgot that.'

'Got your roof nails,' Ma Killick said. She offered the bag to Jessica. 'See? Pound a nails.'

'Fever powder, I said. Not nails. *Fe-ver pow-der*.'

'Can't mend a roof with fever powder,' her mother said, and when nobody argued, she knew she'd won that trick. 'Now get up there an' start hammerin'!' Jessica ignored her. 'Don't worry,' Ma Killick told Jimmy-Sam. 'She'll see reason when the rain starts comin' in.'

BIG DOLLAR

One thing the Ridge had plenty of was trees. And if Ansel Mungers could make money by rafting timber down the river, then so could the colony.

Lonzo and Buck went down to Stackmesser's and spent some of T. Speed's dollars on four heavy felling axes. When they got back, Aaron had picked out a couple of dozen mature and valuable trees: sycamore, white and red oak, maple, massive black walnut, tulip poplar, buck-eye. 'Start choppin',' he said. 'Best done when it ain't rainin'.'

The men had gathered around a red oak. It was so tall that its upper branches were hidden by the tops of neighbouring trees. When you looked up, its trunk seemed slim and handsome. When you looked at the base, a man with outstretched arms could stand behind it and not be seen.

'We gonna cut through *that?*' someone said.

'This is one damn good tree,' Aaron said.

'This is *ten* damn good trees,' Buck said. 'Take a month. More.'

'Look over there,' Nat said. 'Ain't that another red oak? Cut that thing down in one hour. Less.'

'You got a nigger brain,' Aaron said. 'Always lookin' for the easy row to hoe. Gotta think like whitey! White man in Nashville don't want no spindly little sorry red oak like that. Wants this.' He spat at the big tree. 'Big tree, big dollar.'

'Yeah,' Gabe said. 'After this 'un gone through the mill, got planks six feet wide, easy.'

'Easy?' Buck gave him an axe. 'Easy, this darky says. Show us, easy.'

Gabe made a start. That was at noon. Lonzo carried Aaron back to camp for rabbit stew and hot biscuits with T. Speed and Martha.

T. Speed was off to tune another piano. 'How about fellin' a couple black walnuts first?' Lonzo said. 'Work the cramps out your fingers?' T. Speed smiled like a pastor refusing a second slice of cake, and stroked one smooth hand with the other. 'Gotta be able to feel the music,' he said.

'It's a gift,' Martha added.

'It's ten bucks,' Aaron said.

When T. Speed left, Lonzo asked Martha how come he ever learned this piano-tuning thing in Jackson County, Alabama, a place where a slave who looked clever must be getting uppity and needed the whip.

'He told me Mr Dewey Simpson, the Master, he made him learn it,' Martha said. 'On account T. Speed had so much time, nothin' to do.'

This made no sense. 'Always weeds to chop,' Lonzo said.

'Weren't that kinda farm,' Martha mumbled.

'What kind, then?' Aaron demanded.

'You see Bonny around? That child … Never to hand when I got chores to be done … Bonny!' She went away, shouting.

'Nigger slave got nothin' to do?' Aaron said in his whispery croak. 'Ain't what I heard 'bout Alabam.'

They went back to the big red oak. Men were taking turns to hack at the trunk. Sometimes a chunk went whizzing; sometimes the axehead buried itself and the impact shivered the shaft and jolted the hands and arms. The men were shining with sweat. From a short distance, the cut they had made looked more like a scar.

'Doin' it wrong!' Aaron cried. They stopped. 'Gotta be flat across the butt. Way you're choppin', gonna end up with a point on her! Nobody gonna want – '

They threw jagged chunks of tree at him. Lonzo scooped him up and ran. 'Assholes,' Aaron wheezed. 'Gonna be sorry,' he told Lonzo. He was right, as it turned out; but for the wrong reason.

~

All the pikers were big and strong, so Luke was surprised when Nap fetched an oilskin bag from the cabin and gave each man a pair of revolvers. It was the first time ever that Luke had touched a gun. Now he had two.

The others were not surprised, just took the weapons and kept on eating, so Luke did the same. This was the noon break. One good thing about rafting with Nap was the grub. He took plenty out of a man but he put plenty back.

They drank coffee and talked. Luke listened. Two of the pikers were from way down South: Mississippi, Louisiana. From plantations where slaves rose at three in the morning, walked to the fields, worked until sundown. Worked in a row. Each man kept up with the next and if somebody didn't, overseer rode up and bullwhipped him. If he still went wrong, overseer got off his horse. Then you knew bad times were coming. Overseer got off, two other slaves held that nigger down, so he could whip him real hard. And he did.

Luke found himself nodding with the rest. Nobody showed anger. In fact they were laughing.

'You hear of the nigger ring?' said someone. Any slave did wrong, he got put in a ring of niggers, each with a stick. Had to run round and around while they hit him. Nigger didn't hit hard enough, *he* got put in the ring too. That way, niggers did all the work. More laughter.

They talked about stupid, crazy beatings. One man's young brother, just a boy, tied to a log and beaten bloody with a cowhide strap, and died, because he wasn't strong enough to work. 'That day I turned to the Lord for my salvation,' the piker said. 'Prayed every night. Prayed that white man gonna roast in hell for all eternity.' Nobody laughed now. Laugh at a whipping, not at a killing. Each one knew of a slave beaten to death for some small offence: sassing the Master, stealing a yam, learning to read, breaking a hoe. Or no offence at all. Master was drunk, or got a bad price for a crop, or just plain woke up feeling mean.

Nap stood, so they all stood. Wes helped Luke strap on his revolvers. Thongs passed through holes in the butts and got tied around the waist. Nap tested the knots. 'Them forty-fours are worth more'n you, boy,' he said. 'They ain't tied to you. You tied to them.'

The Cameron ran straight and smooth for a couple of miles. Luke could enjoy the richness of the rolling hills: maples that seemed to glow red or yellow; oak and hickory he knew to be hard as iron yet looked soft as cloth; blue ash so blue it could hardly be a tree; others whose names he did not know, all fine, gentle colours. Briefly, he took pleasure in the richness of nature. Probably some whitey owned it, but Luke was free to like it. Then the hills crowded in and became cliffs. The cliffs became a gorge. Luke was working again.

The roar of the falls was louder than ever before. The gorge boxed it in and bounced it from wall to wall until the air seemed to shudder. Luke kept telling himself that Nap and Wes and the rest had done this before. He said it even when the raft skidded around a bend, the pikers stabbing hard to keep it in mid-stream, and ahead he saw grey mist boiling up. This was new. The roar became a thunder. The mist was made by the river pounding itself to nothing. Luke looked back at the steersman. Nap was singing. The sound was blotted out, but he was singing. The bastard was happy. Luke looked forward. The front end was into the falls and riding ten feet in the air, fifteen feet. Then the raft's weight told and it tilted and the stern came up and everything was bouncing and shaking so fast that it knocked Luke to his knees.

Every other falls had dropped like a flight of steps, making the raft pitch and toss. This was different. The current swerved from side to side in one long diving corkscrew, and the raft swung with it, bucking Luke high and then sucking him low, time and again, until he was so giddy his eyes were useless. But he could hear. The corkscrewing was twisting the raft's spine: it screeched and groaned. If it snapped, the halves would capsize. Probably. Nothing was certain in this madhouse.

But the falls ran out of fury. The raft slid into tranquillity. Luke heard someone singing, and was too tired to turn his head. Anyway, he knew who the bastard was.

Later, as they were drifting under the sheer face of a palisade, rocks crashed onto the raft, big rocks, big as melons. Nap was the first to fire; Luke the last. The guns sprayed bullets at the rim of the palisade. Minutes later, more rocks fell. All but one missed: Wes's pole got smashed. The cursing was as furious as the gunfire.

'We ain't done them no harm,' Luke said.

'Oh … They just funnin',' Wes said. 'Ain't much to do these parts. Besides … they get lucky, kill us, they got a free raft.'

That night they ate at a farmhouse but slept on the raft. Luke dreamed about a gunfight and woke to the heavy crash of revolvers.

'Goddamn thief,' Nap said. 'Sneaked up in a canoe. Stealin' your beaver skins.' Luke checked: a dozen were missing. 'Bad piece of river,' Nap said.

'You hit him?' Luke asked.

'Maybe.'

After that, Luke couldn't sleep. A dozen skins gone meant sixty dollars lost. He couldn't eat breakfast, he felt so bad. They pushed away from shore in early dawn light, through a mist as soft and grey as a pigeon's breast, and found the canoe broadside-on to a little sandspit. The beaver skins were there, somewhat stained by the blood of a skinny blond boy, aged twelve or thirteen, shot twice, stomach and side. 'Soak them skins,' Nap said. 'They ain't spoiled.' He was right.

They left the body in the canoe. 'Ain't nobody's business but his folks',' Nap said.

~

Bonny stole a turnip and some Irish potatoes from a field. There was a rabbit in her traps. Lewis picked mushrooms. He found chestnuts. He also had the leg of a small wild turkey, dropped by a buzzard when he surprised it in the act of tearing the bird to bits. Bonny discovered a patch of wild onions. Altogether, they had the makings of a delicious stew.

Made sleepy by a full stomach and the throb of the fire, Lewis relaxed completely for the first time since he ran from the barn. Before he could stop himself, he said something. 'Killed a feller,' he said.

'Huh,' Bonny said. 'White feller?'

Lewis squeezed his eyes tight shut and tried to remember. Bonny watched. Woodsmoke had carried on the work of dirt and grease. There were niggers on the Ridge who were lighter than Lewis. He opened his eyes. 'Yeah. White.'

'White folks are trash,' she said. 'Ain't worth nothin'. You shoot him?' She had seen the forty-four.

'Yeah.'

'I shot two-three whiteys,' she said. ' 'Tain't nothin' special.'

~

Mary Hudd went downstairs to find out what all the noise was about. The rest of the family were out front, gathered around the judge and the deputy, watching them dismount. The chatter died away as Charles spoke. Mary heard the word *evidence*. Frankie

411

unfolded a boy's shirt, very dirty, and held it out for Ruth Hudd to take, but Ruth turned her head away. 'Has the tail been patched?' she asked. 'Red patch? Kind of square?'

'Yes, ma'am,' Frankie said. The way they looked at her, it was all her fault. Marcus grabbed the shirt and, briefly, Mary thought he was about to rip it in half. Instead, he rolled it up tight, and kept rolling it, as if something could be squeezed out of it.

'I need that,' Frankie said. 'Evidence.'

'Where was it found?'

'That will emerge at the trial,' Charles said.

'Killick place,' Ernie said, challenging him. 'Right?'

'Pure speculation.'

'Aw, hell,' Frankie said wearily. 'Reub Skinner's in Maggie's tavern now, tellin' everyone how he found this thing in the Killicks' cellar.'

Ruth Hudd gave a cry that was half a gasp.

'I swore Skinner to silence,' Charles said.

'Skinner's probably told them you did that, too,' Mary said.

'Stay out of this, madam.'

'Don't need no trial,' Ernie said. 'Need a posse. Tear that Killick place apart! They got the boy and – '

'No,' Charles said. 'Not as simple as that.'

'Kidnappin' ain't simple?'

'Hold your water,' Marcus said. 'More ways to skin a cat than feedin' it gunpowder.'

'Stay clear of the Killicks,' Frankie told Marcus.

'Ain't gonna skin no cat,' Ernie said. 'Makes no sense.'

'Least of all to the cat,' Mary said.

'Come with me,' Charles told her.

They went inside, to his study. 'You seem intent on making a joke of all this. I find that offensive.'

'Everything offends you. That's why you're a judge, isn't it? You need offenders. Without them, you'd be nothing, would you?'

He wasn't listening. He was walking up and down, cracking his knuckles. 'A son abducted. A husband murdered. Are those jokes to you?'

She took her time, and then said, 'Depends who's telling the jokes. I'll laugh at anything, if it's funny.'

He stopped and stared. 'Are you drunk? You talk like a woman not fit to be a wife or a mother.'

'That's always possible.'

She seemed amused, and that made him angrier. 'I'm glad I find you so ...' He searched for the word. '... so jaunty. I have an idea which may help to calm things. A simple exchange. One of the Killicks lives here, while a Hudd goes to live with the Killicks.'

'Hostages.'

'Yes. I had you in mind as our representative.'

She wasn't sure that he was serious. 'Impossible,' she said.

'I'm sure you can be spared.'

'Oh no. I must be here. My piano is to be tuned.'

'It was tuned last week.'

'This weather affects it.'

'That could be another joke,' he said, 'or it might not. I can't tell. But since your piano is so important, I suggest you go and play it, and leave me to attend to the trivial matters of abduction and murder.' She went out, feeling and looking uncomfortable. Which gratified him.

NO TIME TO HORSE
ABOUT

After Frankie and the other two deputies left the farm, about the only good thing that happened was Stanton found a bottle of corn liquor he had forgotten he had hid.

Jessica was out doing the evening milking. JoBeth was in her old room, asleep. Ma Killick was in the parlour, underlining the bits in the Bible that God had got right and crossing out the rest. The three brothers took the bottle up to the attic and talked about the trouble they were in.

Dan blamed Devereux. Everything had been fine and dandy until Dev decided to keep the Hudd kid for himself, worked him harder than any house-slave, nigh near worked him to death, for all anyone knew. Damnfool thing to do.

'Kid was okay when I put him to bed,' Dev retorted. 'An' I didn't hear you complain none, I got them outhouses emptied.'

'Yeah, but where's the boy?' Stanton said. Dev said he didn't know, and Dan said a jury might not believe that, which led to a long loud argument about how juries think; until Stanton said the man to ask was Jimmy-Sam, because, hell, that's what they were paying him for, wasn't it? Dan said no, you bucketbrain, it wasn't, on account they weren't paying Jimmy-Sam a red cent, he was working for free.

'Better yet,' Stanton said. 'He's free, we can afford to work his ass off.' Stanton felt pleased. Finding this liquor had been a stroke of brilliance.

'Ain't here. Gone to see Hoke.' Unlike Stanton, Dan was not a happy drunk. His future was looking worse through the bottom of his glass. 'What worries me is Ma. She gets everythin' all turned-around. Remember in the cellar? Ma sayin' I done right? He was tres-

414

passin' an' all? Jesus wept. If she starts jabberin' on like that to folk …'

'Might even talk to the deputy,' Dev said.

'Did that already,' Stanton said. 'This mornin', I heard her hollerin'. She told the deputy you done right.'

Dan crumpled. He put his arms on his knees and his head in his hands.

Stanton moved his glass before it got spilled. 'Everyone knows she ain't playin' with a full deck,' he said. 'Besides, I told Maggie, you had a damn good reason for bein' at that barn.'

'Was nowhere near the fuckin' barn,' Dan said through his fingers.

'Yeah,' Stanton said thoughtfully. 'Well, we always got Jessica an' her big buck nigger to blame.'

Dan straightened up. There were white splotches on his face where his fingers had pressed. 'That's *all* we got. Face it, this farm's been a real unhealthy place lately. Jess'd better stay well. Gonna need her. Me an' you both.' He looked at Devereux.

'You were a damn fool to drop that young 'un's shirt in the cellar,' Stanton grumbled. 'You got some strange habits, boy.'

'Never took his stinkin' shirt! What the blue blazes would I want with – ' Dev was speechless with indignation.

While they killed the rest of the bottle, they decided to make sure Jessica's memory was still reliable. They were waiting in the kitchen when she came in, fingers aching from squeezing teats, her nostrils full of the smell of cow.

'That mornin',' Dan said. 'When the major got shot.'

'Ain't forgot what I saw.'

'Good. This family gotta stick together, Jess. We're all we got.'

'Yeah? Tell you what I got. Got too much milkin', too much churnin' butter, cookin' grub, washin' clothes. You do your share or I'm leavin'.'

'You can't leave,' Devereux said, carefully, as if his teeth were loose. 'This is home.'

'An' it stinks of booze.'

'Aw … be fair, Jess,' Stanton pleaded. 'We're just plain folks, we know this ain't no palace. Makes us feel bad, you bein' a princess an' all. You deserve better.' If he smiled any harder his lips would split. 'That's why we all think you'd be real happy if you became Mrs Jimmy-Sam Wiggins.' They nodded. Dev frowned to show his sincerity but it hurt his eyes, so he quit.

'Wiggins is a baboon. If I was gonna marry a baboon, which I ain't gonna, the least I'd want is for the baboon to do the proposin' himself, 'stead of gettin' three other monkeys to do it.'

'He ain't here. Went to see Hoke Cleghorn,' Dan said. 'On business.'

'Hoke ain't got no business. Hoke got debts.'

'Baboons ain't big,' Devereux said. 'I seen a picture once. Baboons is small. Jimmy-Sam's a lot bigger'n any old baboon,' Dev said. 'Must be twice as – ' Dan picked a cold boiled potato from a bowl and stuffed it into Dev's mouth. It was a good fit. Dev whined and waved his arms. Snot ran from his nostrils, and he turned a full circle, almost dancing, like a small boy who has to pee. 'Eat that,' Dan growled, 'I'll give you another.'

'See? Dan done that for *you*,' Stanton told Jessica. 'Dan an' me, we're lookin' out for your interests all a time.'

'What does Hoke want with a lawyer?' she asked. 'Must be crazy to hire a Bluegrass windbag.'

'None of your business,' Dan said. Stanton nudged him. 'Aw … What the hell … You'll find out soon anyway. *Will you for Chrissake shuddup?*' Devereux was choking and spluttering, stamping his feet, spitting bits of potato. 'We all want what's best for the family, right?' Dan said to her. 'For the fuckin' family. We all gotta make sacrifices. I mean, look at Stanton there. He did what he had to do. Lost his goddamn arm.'

'Yeah, big shame. So now I got to do all the milkin'. I milked so damn much, *both* my arms feel like they're coming off.'

'You don't have to lose an arm, Jess,' Stanton said reassuringly. The liquor had freshened his drunkenness and made him tearful. 'See, Jimmy-Sam wants your hand. Can't give him your hand if'n – ' That was when Dan lost all patience and grabbed Stanton and hurried him on wobbly legs out of the kitchen. When Dan came back Devereux was squatting in a corner, groaning. The potato felt like a goose egg stuck in his gullet. 'I swear I'll kill …' Dan said.

'Well, you know,' Jessica said. 'Family. What can you expect?'

'Listen. Jimmy-Sam an' Hoke. Thing is, Hoke owes the bank, so Jimmy-Sam went to see him. Bank business.'

'Banks are goddamn leeches. Pa said.'

'Yeah, well, times have changed.'

His dull tone made her suspicious. 'Don't we still owe the bank?'

'Yes an' no. See, Jimmy-Sam *is* the bank. Made so much money outa the war an' the law, he bought the bank, few months ago. It's his bank.'

'You're sayin' … we owe that gasbag? How much?'

'Enough so he can made our lives real uncomfortable.' Such honesty was painful to Dan. As he wandered about the kitchen, searching for drink, any kind of drink, liquor, beer, cider, and failed to find anything, a husky note of appeal entered his voice. 'Thing is, Jimmy-Sam has a problem too. Can't find himself a wife anyplace upstate, not to suit his taste. But you, Jess, you have stole his heart away. You are his ace-a-trumps sweetheart.' Dan paused. Never heard himself talk like that before. It was startling, disturbing. 'We got our problem. Problem with the bank. Jimmy-Sam got his. Harness them two problems together … you made yourself a solution.'

Devereux had got rid of the last remnant of potato. 'One good thing about Jimmy-Sam,' he croaked. 'For a big fella, he don't sweat hardly at all.'

'Must be fulla muleshit, then, cus he stinks to me,' she said, 'an' I ain't marryin' him, an' that's flat.' She went out.

Dan walked to the window and stared at the night. 'You marry the bastard, Dev,' he said. 'You're the stupidest fucker we got.'

Jessica was walking to the outhouse, her eyes not yet fully adjusted to the darkness but her feet knew the way, when three figures in white sheets and white hoods closed on her. 'You're comin' with us,' one said.

'I'm goin' to the outhouse first,' she said, 'an' you better stand aside real fast 'less you want your boots to get splashed.'

'Well … be quick. An' don't – '

'Hey! That there's Curtis Hudd, ain't it? Kinda early for Halloween, ain'tcha?'

'We're the Ku Klux Klan. We go around puttin' things right. You took our Lewis, so we're takin' you.'

She used the outhouse. They had a horse for her. 'Hope your food's better'n ours,' she said. 'At least I won't have to do the milkin'. You boys sure you know the way?' They set off.

'Ain't how I expected it,' Ernie muttered.

'Too late now,' Marcus said.

The wind changed during the night. Nothing that Moses, Buck, Nat and Gabe could do about that. After breakfast, they went back to the red oak, two men cutting while the other two put an edge back on their axes. They worked without halt for a couple of hours.

They had hacked deep into the heart of the tree, so deep that it was groaning like a wounded bull elk whenever the wind swayed the top branches. There was a lot of wind up there and it was gusting. Nat's ears were full of sweat; all he heard was the *chunk* of the axe sinking into hard wood. He hated this oak. It sucked the strength out of him, left his hands hot and aching. He didn't hear Moses shout. He swung the axe, felt it bite and jam, jerked it but couldn't work it loose, and he cursed. Then Moses had him by the shoulders and was dragging him away. Nat looked up and was terrified to see the red oak falling the wrong way, falling towards him, falling with an astonishing, silent speed. Faster than he could run, than anyone could run. Moses still had him by the shoulders but Nat's feet were pointing the wrong way and he tripped on a root and they both went down, Nat still looking up at an avalanche of timber blotting out the sky before it blotted out him.

It shuddered and stopped, so close he could touch it.

They crawled away and got up and looked. The oak had fallen into another tree, smashed it backwards and then been caught in the massive fork of a beech.

Lonzo and Aaron came to look.

'Way I see it,' Aaron said, 'you get up there an' you cut your oak free.'

Lonzo scrambled up the angled trunk. He was fifty feet high when the reached the beech. 'Ain't nothin' here to stand on,' he called, 'unless you figure standin' on this here oak.'

'Well then, cut down the whole damn beech.'

Lonzo scrambled down. They all went and looked at the beech. It was ten feet across.

'I been thinkin',' Gabe said. 'Where we gonna take this oak, when we got it down an' trimmed an' all?'

'Creek,' Aaron said. 'Drag it to the creek, float it down to the Cameron.'

'Creek's half a mile away.'

Moses and Buck and Nat sat down and looked at the length and width and weight of the oak. 'Sonofabitch,' Buck sighed.

'First thing my daddy told me,' Moses said. 'When you're tyin' up sacks a taters, don't never take the sacks to the string.'

After breakfast they went to the creek and found good trees growing on its banks. 'Now you can go straight to hell,' Buck told Aaron.

'Got bendy legs. Can't go nowhere straight.' He tittered so much that Lonzo picked him up and carried him away under his arm. 'Fuckin' fools,' Aaron said. 'Could of told 'em that red oak was in the wrong place.'

~

Heavy rain soaked the raft for most of the day. With the rain came bursts of stinging hail, always driven upriver by a punishing wind. Rain or hail, it attacked the pikers' eyes until peering into the weather became hard toil. When the rain stopped, the wind pierced their clothing and made them shudder with cold. This was the most miserable day by far. And although the Cameron was now wider and deeper, rafting was no easier, because around any bend might come a riverboat, paddles thrashing white, smokestacks pumping black, pilot tugging the siren-chain and sending harsh whoops of warning through the foul weather.

Then it was a test of nerve. The pilot hated to leave the deep, safe channel. The raft steersman hated to make a sudden change of course that might send him drifting broadside to the current, almost helpless. Normally there was time and space, and they avoided trouble. At mid-afternoon on this wretched, soaking day, the pilot of a three-stacker refused to give an inch, forced Nap to veer sharply away, and left the raft lurching on his wake. It drifted over a hidden mudbank and trapped itself against the bough of a waterlogged tree.

They found it hard to reach the boughs with the axe, harder still to swing the axe with any force without falling into the rain-pocked river. Light was fading when the last visible bit of the obstacle got chopped off. Still the raft was stuck. Nap fastened the rope, swam ashore with the end, passed it around a tree, swam back. Everyone hauled. The rope twanged, the raft squirmed and did not come free. Nap swam ashore and put the rope around another tree, at a different angle, swam back. They hauled. There was a muffled, muddy cracking and splitting, and the raft drifted away.

Nap got her pointing headfirst and they went on for a good hour, until they saw the lights of a farmhouse. Three other rafts were tied up. Luke had eaten nothing since dawn, but he hated leaving the beaver skins. The farmhouse was a wonderful, hot, dry, noisy cockpit of eating and drinking and singing and boasting. Luke ate fast and went back to the raft. He slept in the leaky cabin. The rain never stopped.

~

Stanton had another brilliant idea. While Ma Killick was busy in the parlour he raided her bedroom and found a bottle of hooch in a linen chest. The brothers killed it, and woke up next morning to find that the whiskey was taking revenge on their throbbing heads, on top of which there was no coffee. They shouted until it hurt. Jessica did not appear.

Dan searched the house, but he knew. Cows hadn't been milked, bed hadn't been slept in.

Jimmy-Sam was sitting on the porch, waiting for someone to bring him breakfast. Dan sat beside him. 'Guess you ought to know,' he said. 'Jessica left last night, dunno where. Might come back, might not.' He tucked his hands into his armpits to stop them trembling. 'She talked of leavin'.'

'I'm sixty-two,' Jimmy-Sam said. 'That's more than my daddy or my grandaddy lived to. We don't make old bones on my side of the family. Reckon I've got three good years left to me. You listenin'? You look like you won't last long enough to be hanged.'

'I'm listenin'.'

'How old am I?'

'Sixty-two.'

'Rule one in court: never ask a question you don't already know the answer to. Where exactly were you when this Major Somebody got himself shot?'

'Yonder. Fixin' a bust gate.'

'How far is that from the barn?'

'Couple hundred yards.'

'Can you hit a man with a revolver at that range?'

'Can't hit nothin'. Can't hit the goddamn barn.'

'Was the dead man shot with your revolver?'

'Yeah, I reckon. It was – '

'Wrong. Wrong answer. Correct answer: *I do not know*. Nobody knows. The bullet was a forty-four calibre. That proves nothing. Did you possess a forty-four calibre revolver on the morning of the shooting? Think carefully.'

'No, I didn't.'

The lawyer rocked a little, looked at the scenery, and let everything sink into Dan's thudding mind.

'I'm sixty-two, I've buried a pair of wives, now I'd like to enjoy what's left to me in the company of someone young and lively and nice to look upon. Nothing else matters. Does that sound selfish? Well, I am selfish. Haven't got time to horse about. Time's runnin' out.' He grabbed at a passing fly and caught it. 'Time's runnin' out for all of us.'

'You can't call in the mortgage.' It was a plea, not a statement.

'Which mortgage? You got three. I'll call in all of 'em, if I've a mind to.'

'We're kin, Jimmy-Sam.'

'And I'm sixty-two.' He opened his fist and released the fly. 'See how close life is to death? Why didn't I foreclose on that fly's mortgage? Truth is, I'm not sure myself. Next time, might be different.'

Dan got up, went inside, went upstairs and straight into JoBeth's room, without knocking. She was awake but drowsy. 'First time I slept good in a month,' she said. 'Looks like you slept with the hogs.' She yawned and stretched. 'An' the hogs got the worst part of the deal.'

'Listen,' he said. 'Yesterday, you took us kinda by surprise, an' then you was real tired an' all, we didn't get around to askin' … When you was Down South, you ever get married?'

'Yup.'

Dan sat on the bed. He squeezed his forehead between his hands to stop it splitting. JoBeth had been his last hope. Now the bitch was married. He could take a chance on bigamy with anybody but not with Jimmy-Sam. The man was a lawyer big enough to buy a bank. Dan knew deep in his bitter gut that he didn't have the brass gall to try to sell Jimmy-Sam another man's wife, not even to save the farm and maybe his own neck too. Besides, JoBeth couldn't be trusted to lie.

Then curiosity nudged him. 'Why d'you leave the sonabitch?' he asked.

'He was dead.'

Dan straightened up. 'Dead,' he said. That was good. 'That's bad,' he said.

'Well, it happens to people. You're not careful, might even happen to you, one day.' She combed her hair with her fingers.

Dan didn't even want to think about that. He wanted to steer the conversation towards re-marrying, but how to do it? *Did you like being married? What sort of guy was he? I guess that makes you a widow?* No. None of those worked. 'How long was you two together?' he asked. Harmless.

'Three months, about.'

'Jesus. What happened?'

'He got drowned in a flash-flood. It was kind of a flash-marriage. Barely got to know how he liked his eggs. Funeral didn't take more'n ten minutes, neither. Turns out the only thing that wasn't flash was the baby.'

'The baby.' Dan was running hard but he still couldn't keep up.

'Yeah. Baby. Cute little thing. Give it milk an' it pays you back in piss, shit an' screamin' tantrums. You must of seen 'em lyin' about the place.' She was growing impatient with his stunned expression.

'That's why you came home.' It hurt, but he smiled. 'To have the baby. Listen, I'm real glad.'

'Well, I'm real glad you're real glad.' She got out of bed. She was wearing a man's shirt. Dan tried to see her through Jimmy-Sam's eyes, and he was mightily encouraged. 'Remember how I left?' she said. 'Everyone was real glad to see me go, then.'

'George's doin'. He got killed.'

'I heard.' She turned away and began sorting her clothes. 'Gotta get dressed,' she said.

He knew he should go, maybe this wasn't the best moment; but he was no good at slow persuasion, no good at hints and nudges and waiting for the idea to sink in; he was worried *now* so he wanted action *now*. 'That baby,' he said. 'Gonna need a father, you reckon?'

'You mean like Pa was to us? All belt an' booze?'

'Just thinkin' ... Bound to be doctor's bills. We ain't rich, an' – '

'I'll manage.' She gripped the shirt, ready to peel it off. 'You plannin' on stayin' to watch?'

Stanton and Dev were in the kitchen, watching water come to the boil in the coffeepot. No sign of Jessica, they said. Dan told them of Jimmy-Sam's hopes and threats. All spoke in low voices.

'Jess ain't bein' reasonable,' Dev said. 'Who the fuck she expect to marry? King of England? Jeez, I'd let ol' Jimmy-Sam fuck me if I got – '

'Ain't no king of England,' Stanton said. 'King of England's a queen now.'

'That is the most ridiculous thing I ever heard.'

'Forget it,' Dan said. 'What matters is, Jess ain't here.'

'What happened to him? His pecker fell off?' Dev demanded of Stanton. 'Lost his royal nuts in the bath? Ridiculous.'

Stanton had lost interest. 'Jimmy-Sam's a hardnose bastard. Lawyers hate to lose. Bankers hate it even worse. Jimmy-Sam can't get Jess, he'll take the goddamn farm.' The water boiled. He tossed in a handful of coffee, stirred it, moved the pot to where it would simmer. 'Face it, we're fucked.'

'Not yet,' Dan said. 'JoBeth's waitin' upstairs. She's with child, an' she's without husband. She's tailormade for that bastard.'

'She gonna do it?' Dev asked.

'I just showed her what a good deal it is. She ain't crazy. Want to come back to the family, gotta go along with the family.'

'Women can be funny,' Stanton said.

'Not if you're firm. Look: *we* got no choice, *she* got no choice.'

'That's reasonable,' Dev said. 'Damn, that's very reasonable.'

JoBeth came in and they all turned and looked at her as if she might say something special, such as the South would rise again. 'Smell coffee,' she said.

'Coffee. Sure, we got coffee,' Dan said. 'We got the best. An' another thing, JoBeth. We got you the best husband, too.'

'Livin' right here,' Dev said.

'Mrs Jimmy-Sam Wiggins,' Stanton said.

'See, what's good for the family is good for you,' Dan said. 'Ain't that the truth? Course it is. No two ways about it, JoBeth: you get your ass down to the church with Jimmy-Sam, that's what's bin decided, hell, you ain't got no choice, lady, we already done your choosin' for you, an' the way I see it, all the luck's on your side, cus you need Jimmy-Sam more'n he needs you!' He ran out of words and breath at about the same time.

'Coffee?' she said.

'Oh. Yeah.'

Dan picked up the coffeepot and the handle snapped. The pot was old and heavy and the handle just broke off, and the pot fell and tipped all the coffee into the stove. There was an almighty gasp of steam as the fire went out. 'Fuck!' Dan shouted. He flung the handle across the room.

'You are a truly sorry bunch,' she said. 'You can't make fire, you can't make coffee, an' you sure as hell can't make me marry Jimmy-Sam.'

Dan hit her in the face, twice. The second blow knocked her stumbling backwards and she fell over a bench. Dan went after her, grunting curses, but Dev tripped him and he crashed to his knees. When JoBeth ran out of the room they were fighting each other with chairs while Stanton hid in a corner.

It took her three minutes to pack. Nobody tried to stop her leaving. In ten minutes she had saddled her horse and gone.

I SEEK BEELZEBUB

Charles Hudd talked easily with Lucy. He told her anything that happened to be on his mind. She learned a lot.

He tired easily nowadays. When he came home from riding, he climbed the stairs with a hand on each knee to heave himself up. Lucy knew to come and take off his boots. Also his coat, shirt, pants and long johns. She poured him a glass of red wine, rubbed him down with a hot wet towel, eased the pillows under his shoulders, smiling and talking cheerfully while saying nothing worth thinking about. She behaved like the good wife he thought he had never had. He told her so.

They both knew he couldn't make love more than once a month without risking cramp and palpitations, but she gave him great carnal pleasure simply by being as naked as he was and manipulating various parts of his slack white body with her strong black hands. The routine never changed. As she massaged his buttocks, she always said, 'Big ass. Take a big hammer to knock in a big nail.' And he always grinned.

He liked her to be sassy, it raised his spirits, he gave her an extra dollar or two. One day she said, in her sassy voice, 'You don't need me, you got a wife could do this free.' And knew at once: big mistake.

He pushed her away from him, got out of bed, drank some wine from the bottle.

'Money is no part of it. See, niggers don't understand white folks. I never went away from Mrs Hudd, always had a loving feeling for her, *she* turned *me* away. That's how white women are. Not warm, not natural. Want to be virgins even when it's too damn late. They turn … icy.' He drank again. 'White women are cold, they force white men to …' He made a vague gesture at Lucy. 'Niggers don't understand,' he muttered.

Lucy got no dollar that day. She understood *that*.

At the other side of the house, also behind locked doors, T. Speed sat in a rocking chair with Mary Hudd sitting on him, facing him, legs straddling him and poking through holes in the side of the chair. Both were naked. As they rocked, so they gently engaged and released, engaged and released. Cane creaked, and thigh slid against thigh. 'We can do this for ever,' she murmured.

'Well … until tomorrow. Tomorrow I have to tune the piano of Mrs Dyer at Chestnut Creek.'

Mary stopped rocking. 'Dear Lizzie,' she said. 'Her husband always began and ended the day with a female slave.'

'You know this from her?'

'Heavens, no. From Lucy.' She resumed rocking. He kept up a perfect rhythm.

Later, T. Speed had his supper downstairs with Lucy. She told him what Charles had said about his wife's coldness. Lucy said she must have heard the same thing a dozen times before, from other white men. She named a few. 'Ain't true,' T. Speed said, sopping up white gravy with cornbread. 'I tuned their wives' pyanners.'

'Yeah. An' one day someone's gonna catch you doin' it.' She gave him more fried chicken.

'It's my trade,' he said. 'Ain't nothin' else I can do.'

~

A man came through the doors of Maggie's tavern with a gun in his hands. It was Flub Phillips, legs wobbling, arms shaking, eyes flickering like candles approaching their end, spit all round his mouth. 'Blessed are the dead which die in the Lord from henceforth,' he said. He thumbed back the safety.

'Startin' tomorrow,' the pedlar said.

'Go home, Flub,' Maggie said. 'You're still sick.'

He had a piece of paper, which he consulted. 'I seek Beelzebub, Lord of Flies,' he said.

'He was in but he left,' Frankie said. She was eating breakfast: small steak, hash, fried tomatoes. 'Gimme that gun afore you drop it.'

'How about …' He searched the paper. 'How about the dragon, that old serpent, which is the Devil and Satan?'

426

'They waited for you. Couldn't stay.'

Flub was distressed. Tears ran into his food-stained, month-old beard. 'Is this not Babylon the Great?' he asked. 'Mother of Harlots and Abomination of the Earth?'

'Ten miles downriver from here,' the pedlar said.

Flub gaped at his bit of paper. Sweat trickled into his eyes. His arms shook more than ever. The shotgun went off and blew a hole in the floor. Dust rose in clouds. Before the echoes had died, Frankie had him by the collar and the seat and had run him out into the street. 'I seek Beelzebub,' he whimpered. 'Let go, you're bustin' my nuts ... I seek Beelzebub ...' She snatched the shotgun from him and whacked him on the backside with the butt until he ran. 'Ain't no devils here!' she bawled. 'Devils all gone to California! Compree?'

JoBeth got off her horse. 'Who the hell are you to knock that poor old man around?' she said. It was turning into a bad day for violence.

Frankie was scraping horseshit off her boots; she had trodden deeply in a steaming mound of the stuff. 'I'm the deputy here, an' that *poor old man* keeps comin' in, wantin' to preach with buckshot. Fever done boiled his brains.' She looked. 'Oohhh ...' It came out as a long groan.

'Never thought to see *you* again,' JoBeth said.

Frankie emptied the shotgun and hurled it high and far behind Flub. She took off her boots and tossed them to the nearest small boy. 'Candy,' she promised.

They went inside. Maggie was sweeping splinters into the hole. 'You need a piece a beef on that eye,' she said. JoBeth said, 'I need a pound a steak in my gut, is what I need.'

They ate in the kitchen, and talked.

'My side of the story's easy,' JoBeth said. 'Got a baby on the way, husband in the grave, decided to come home.'

They looked at her damaged face: an eye turning black, a bruise already so swollen that her jaws would not fully close.

'Stanton's too drunk, an' Dev's too lazy,' Maggie said. 'Had to be Dan.'

JoBeth nodded. 'I came home yesterday, an' left home today. Tomorrow?' She shrugged. 'So ... That's me told. Now you. Last place I ever expected to see you was here.'

'Yeah. That was the whole idea. You kept sayin' Rock Springs, Kentucky, couldn't scratch its ass without a compass and an Indian guide. Only place worse than Desolation, you said. So I figured, nobody would ever look for me in Rock Springs. Wrong. Pinkerton man's been sniffin' around.'

'Bastard,' JoBeth said. She was chewing, but gingerly.

'Maybe he followed you.'

'He got here first,' Maggie said. 'Couldn't be followin' her if he did that.' Frankie didn't look convinced. 'That day you told us why you left Desolation,' Maggie said, 'doc an' me, we wondered if maybe it could be the same JoBeth, decided not. Must be hundreds of women called JoBeth in Texas.'

'You turned up at a bad time,' Frankie told JoBeth. 'This town got troubles enough. Last thing I need is you to remind me of a hotel in Redondo.'

'I borrowed her man,' JoBeth explained. 'Privately.'

'I know,' Maggie said. 'You an' him, tryin' to make the upgrade, he bust his boiler, an' Frankie let off a little steam of her own. She told us.'

'Hey!' JoBeth put down her fork. 'No call for you to ruin my good name.'

'No call for you to come back.'

'My home town, ain't it?'

'Sure. An' you ain't been too welcome here, by the look of it.'

They each did their share of glaring. Stalemate.

'That Pinkerton man,' Maggie said. 'Why's he sniffin' around?'

Nobody liked the question. Nobody had an answer.

AIN'T THE DOG'S FAULT

Marcus hid Jessica in a barn. He was worried about Charles finding out they had her. Ruth wanted him to go straight back to the Killick place and tell them no Lewis, no Jessica, but Marcus remembered what had happened to Major de Glanville and he was in no tearing hurry to follow him. Anyway, Ernie and Curtis wanted to do it the Klan way. The Klan had only recently been formed, just over the border in Tennessee, and it thrilled them to ride about at night in their sheets, bringing justice to bad people and scaring evil-doers so much they wet their pants. There was a shortage of evil-doers. They had dressed up and ridden over to Flub Phillips's place and rebuked him for going into Maggie's tavern with a loaded shotgun and upsetting the customers, but Flub had been awful hard to rouse from sleep and when he finally woke he said he was always pleased to see the Horsemen of the Apocalypse but what had happened to the fourth feller? So that was not a success.

The only person completely sure of herself was Jessica. 'Told you *fried* taters, not boiled,' she said raspingly to Curtis. 'Take these back an' fry 'em. This steak's too bloody. I never eat onions. I want mushrooms an' black-eyed peas.' She thrust the tray at him. 'An' where's that dress? Washed *and* pressed.'

'Doin' our best,' he muttered.

'Ain't good enough.'

~

The Cameron joined the Cumberland and made it into a big, fast, busy waterway that hustled the raft to Nashville in a day and a half.

The river there was thick with vessels. Nashville was recovering from the war. It had more rafts and riverboats than the dockside could handle, and so they were moored five or six deep. Luke was bewildered by this floating city, attached to a real city, vastly bigger than anything he had known, the whole thing too big for his eyes to accept: wherever he looked there was always more, and more, waiting to be seen. It scared him.

They tied up and went ashore. Luke sat on his bundle of furs. Nap came back from somewhere and paid the pikers in silver coin: nine days at fifty cents a day, nothing taken off for grub; best pay Luke had ever had. When he looked up from counting it everyone had gone. He didn't know where to sell the skins. Nashville was full of men loading or unloading, shouting, pointing, driving wagons, cursing. There were signs everywhere, big signs on buildings. Luke couldn't read them.

He picked up his bundle and walked along the waterfront. He was searching for a friendly black face and quite soon he found one: a small man, nearly bald, wrinkled as a walnut, sitting on a barrel and smiling gently at the passing crowd as if everything he saw pleased him. 'Welcome to Nashville, son,' he said. He croaked like a parrot: a happy parrot. 'Business or pleasure?'

'Lookin' to sell these beaver skins, sir,' Luke said.

'How much a skin?'

'Hopin' for five dollars, sir.' He was ready to be laughed at.

'I can get you seven or eight. See that place?' He pointed further down the waterfront. 'Big yaller doors.'

Luke couldn't see them. The traffic was thick; maybe a wagon was in the way. 'No sir,' he said.

'Well … See that feller up that ladder.' Now the old man was standing on the barrel and pointing. Luke stood on tiptoe and saw no ladder. 'You ain't lookin' right, son,' the old man said, and put out his hand. 'Jump up here. Clear as day from up here.' Luke dumped the skins, took the hand, climbed onto the barrel. 'Now you see them yaller doors.' Luke did. 'Well, that ain't the place to go,' the old man said. 'That's a place sells rope an' such. Ain't no use to you. There's a street on that corner, you go up there …' Luke wasn't listening. Ten feet away a small boy was laughing so hard it hurt. Luke turned to see the joke and saw the beaver skins vanish into the crowd. He uttered a roar of rage that flattened the ears of nearby horses.

The thief was strong and fast and smart. As he ran he barged into people, knocked them spinning. Luke had to pick his way through this trail of angry bodies. Some of them thought he was to blame and lashed out. The chase crossed the waterfront, zigzagging between wagons, and up an alley. That was when the weight of the skins finally told. The man stopped, turned, flung the bundle at Luke. Luke caught it, staggered, didn't fall. He stood, gasping, chest heaving. Neither man could run. The thief grinned and walked away. 'I catch you, I kill you!' Luke called. The man waved goodbye without looking back.

Luke walked about Nashville until he saw a warehouse with furs in it. The rest was easy, so easy that it felt like a reward for the long struggle. The white man in charge of the warehouse wanted to know where the skins came from, smiled approvingly when Luke said Rock Springs, and agreed that five bucks a skin was a fair price. 'Five of these one-hundred-dollar bills, that suit you?' he said. Luke couldn't read but he knew what a hundred looked like. The man showed him how to fold the bills up small and stuff them in the toes of his boots. 'Don't take 'em off until you get home,' he advised.

～

All the way up the Ridge, Frankie Nickel asked herself why she did this stupid job. It didn't pay. She went around cleaning up other people's mess. It didn't pay. It had no future. Rock Springs was going nowhere. Maybe the bullet that killed de Glanville had been meant for her. Maybe next time Flub Phillips would shoot her first and call her Satan afterwards. Maybe the Hudds and the Killicks …

She heard shooting higher up.

The camp was deserted. Fires down to hot ashes. Washing spread on bushes. The shooting was further on, where the steady *chunk* of axes sounded. She found men squatting beside fallen trees. In a hollow, Moses and Buck had started to fell a white oak. 'Who's got the guns?' she asked.

'Killicks,' Bonny said.

The deputy hadn't noticed the little girl, looking over a tree-trunk so big that only her head showed.

'You seen 'em?'

'Follered 'em up.'

A bullet snapped through the air and cut some twigs off a nearby chestnut. The bang followed. Moses and Buck kept on cutting: the hollow protected them.

'You given 'em any cause?' Frankie asked.

'White folks,' Lonzo said. 'They need any cause?'

She walked towards the source of the shooting. The land was broken and tangled: wild vines, fallen trees, great slabs of rock. She kept shouting, 'Deputy Nickel. Hold your fire.' Three more shots ripped through foliage before she found Dan and Devereux Killick sitting in the branches of a giant hickory. 'What in hell's name are you doin'?' she asked.

'Aw, look here, Dev,' Dan said. 'That ain't no bull elk. Dev said he heard a bull elk crashin' an' roarin'. Wanted to shoot the critter. I said no. Elk meat gives me wind.'

'We're huntin'.' Dev fired at something, or perhaps nothing. 'See?'

'Get down outa there. Somethin' I want to show you.'

She led them to the timber-cutting. The colonists all stood; sitting in a white man's presence still made them uncomfortable. 'This is where you were shootin' at,' she said.

Dan was inspecting a felling axe set in a stump as if he'd never seen one before. 'How long this cuttin' bin goin' on?' he asked.

'Few days,' Gabe Killick said.

'Huh. You boys cut these trees down, now what you figure on doin' with 'em?'

'Sellin' 'em,' Lonzo said. 'Raft 'em to Nashville, make us some money.'

'That a fact?' Dan eased the axe free and carried it over to Lonzo. 'Ain't yours to sell, boy. Us Killicks own this piece a forest. You sell our timber ...' He raised the axe above him and flexed his knees as if about to split Lonzo's head open. '... You ... are ... committin' ... a ... *horrible* ...' His whole body tensed. Everywhere men were about to rush forward. '*Crime!*' he shouted, and let the axe slip down behind him. Devereux thought that was so funny he had to sit down.

Lonzo picked up the axe and whacked it back into the stump. If Dan had struck, Dan would have been nothing but raw steak and broken bones by now. The colonists would have battered him to his knees like driving home a big fencepost. Devereux too. It was almost worth dying to know two Killicks would go to hell before your body was cold. 'That true?' he asked the deputy. 'They own these trees?'

'God knows.'

'The Lord Almighty is bountiful,' Josh said. 'He made plenty for all. You don't need these trees, Mister Killick. We don't get some dollars, we ain't gonna last the winter, Mr Killick.'

'Say what,' Dan said. 'Sell you the timber. Twenty bucks a tree.'

'Ain't worth that much in Nashville,' Buck said.

'Worth it here, though. I love these trees. Love Nature. It's the way I am.'

'You've had your fun,' Frankie said. 'Now go home. Stop botherin' these people.'

'They bothered us first,' Dev said. 'Amen!' He hated nigger preachers. They had no right preaching in the white man's Bible. That was sacrilege or heresy or some damn thing.

'Some stinkin' nigger came on our land,' Dan said, 'stole the little Hudd boy, probably murdered him too. Now our sister Jessica, she disappeared too, ain't that a coincidence?'

'What makes you think they're up here?' Frankie asked.

'What makes *you* think it?' he said. She was silent. Who could figure the coloured mind except the coloured? Revenge, ransom, plain madness: anything was possible.

'Ain't no white child here,' Lonzo said.

'Funny thing,' Dev said. 'I never seen a nigger hanged. Bullwhipped, plenty. Shot, a few. None hanged. Ain't that funny?'

The Killick brothers left. The deputy stayed to ask questions. Nobody could tell her anything about anything. Women and children and Aaron came out of hiding. Cutting began again. 'See how it is?' Aaron said. 'We starve, or we break your goddamn laws. You gonna toss us all in jail?'

'Seems to me you're in jail now. You're trapped on this Ridge.'

'We bought the trap. We own the jail.'

Lonzo walked with her part of the way down the mountain.

'Why don't you go North?' she said. 'Plenty work up there.'

'Plenty room down here. Take a look. Ain't Kentucky pretty?'

'You see pretty, I see trouble. You niggers are kinda like the family dog. Anythin' goes wrong, kick the dog. Ain't the dog's fault, but … Listen, I'll do my best for you, but mostly you're on your own.'

'How it's always been,' Lonzo said. 'Woof-woof.'

⁓

Charles Hudd was in the orchard behind the house, taking the last apples from the trees and putting them carefully in a basket. He didn't know if the womenfolk wanted or needed apples and he didn't care. He enjoyed clearing the trees, and the orchard was one place he was fairly sure no-one else would be.

The sky was so blue that his eyes craved a blemish, and found one in a few faded scribbles of creamy cloud. *If heaven isn't up there,* he thought, *somebody blundered.* He looked about him and saw scarlets and golds that glowed more than any cathedral ever could. A flicker of happiness taunted him and was gone before he could seize it. That was always the way. He moved his ladder to another tree. His problems followed him. There must be a trial, soon, and he must judge it. His pigheaded cousins against his foul-mouthed, greedy enemies, with a jury of jackasses: it was going to be an ordeal. No support from his wife, who seemed to be losing her wits. No sheriff. A deputy widowed a week ago. Everything overshadowed by a colony of niggers, some half-Indian, some half-witted, none with any cause to like a white. Somebody came trudging up through the orchard, and he silently cursed his loss of privacy, until he felt a boot on the bottom rung and he had to look down.

'We had some good times right here, you an' me,' JoBeth said. She knew his look of shock. 'Thought I died in Louisiana. Dunno how that story started. Must've bin another JoBeth Killick of the same name. Takes more than gossip to kill me. You aimin' to live up that tree, or what?'

He climbed down, and stood and looked at what seven years and wartime food had done to her: made her thinner, harder-looking. That smile, those eyes still startled him, but she was no longer the vision of smooth-skinned desirability that used to make his loins lurch. Were those bruises? Yes, by God, they were. 'Well,' he said.

She kissed him on the mouth. He recoiled, and wiped his lips. 'Don't do that,' he said. 'I'm married now.'

'Don't brag about it, Chuck. I got married too.'

'Yes?' He polished an apple. 'He's a lucky man.' The relief he felt was almost as great as the shock had been. 'One day I'd like to meet him. Things are kind of hectic here. I got elected judge, you probably didn't know, it's a big responsibility, people expect ...' He looked around, frowning, as if people might be approaching with demands. 'Doesn't leave much time.' He checked his watch.

'Poor bastard died,' she said. 'I'm three months pregnant. That's why I left Texas.'

'Oh my Christ,' he said. 'Poor suffering sweet Jesus Christ.'

'Don't get so gloomy. Happened before, you know. *Your* ma was three months gone, once. Ain't the worst thing can happen.'

'No, of course.' He cranked out a sort of a smile. 'Are you on your way home? Your mother will be pleased. Take some apples.'

'They kicked me out. Dan did this.' She touched her face, harder than she intended, and winced. 'Damn. How's it look?'

'I'm shocked. His own sister? How could he?'

'Oh ... best I remember, he swung fast, I ducked slow, that's how. Look, can I stay here?'

'*Here?* No, no. Out of the question.'

'All I need's a bed.'

'The house is full. My cousins – '

'A bed in a barn. I'll work for my keep.'

'You don't understand. Everything's changed, I'm a married man, I got elected – '

'Yeah, you told me. Judge, congratulations. Ain't gonna interfere with that, or your wife, or *anythin'*, I got a baby to make.'

'Surely your friends – '

'Got none. Ain't goin' back to Texas. I'm in trouble, Charlie. Need help. Not much. You won't even know I'm here.'

'But everybody in the county will.' He spoke before he could stop himself.

She found a loose thread on his coat and picked it off. 'It's your damned reputation, isn't it?' she said. 'It's your goddamned standing in this wonderful community. You're afraid to lift your hand in friendship in case these assholes think you've got it up my skirt.'

'A judge cannot afford to risk the whiff of scandal.'

She took a running kick at the basket. Apples went running through the grass. 'I can't compete with that!' she cried. 'You keep your reputation! Take it to bed, take it to court, take it to the out-house, keep a good grip on it in case anyone steals it! I hope you'll be very happy together.'

She went down through the orchard to where her horse was tethered. Lucy was sitting there. 'Heard most of that, Mizz JoBeth,' she said. 'Seems like none of the white folks has any room for you.'

~

That night, when T. Speed came home, he gave Lonzo thirty dollars. 'I'm thankful,' Lonzo said. 'We're all of us thankful and obliged to you, T. Speed. Don't think we're not, cus we are.'

'But somethin's wrong.'

'Wait here. As a favour to me.'

Lonzo called together all the menfolk and took them to T. Speed. They sat on their haunches. He stood. In the jumping light of the fire, wearing tailored linens, handsome and shaven and self-confident, he looked imperial.

'Well, Martha told us,' Lonzo said.

'Well, I knew she would,' T. Speed said. 'She worries. Wish she wouldn't, but she does.'

'When you was owned by Mister Dewey Simpson,' Buck began, but his lisp was so bad he quit.

'That was Jackson County, Alabama?' Aaron said. He hadn't had his supper; he was impatient. 'Niggers made a good price down there, huh?'

'Slaves was a crop,' T. Speed said. 'Plantations in Mississippi, they always needed more slaves. Slaves kept dyin' on their owners. They died … well, you know how.'

'An' that was Mister Dewey Simpson's crop,' Gabe said. 'He bred slaves.'

'He did. Kept about two hundred nigger women, had to be good stock.'

'And you,' Lonzo said. 'You was the bull in the herd.'

T. Speed nodded.

'Two hundred,' Moses said. 'All for you.'

'That all you did?' Buck asked.

'No, I tuned the pyanners. They had two. But mostly, I hoed my row. You know.' They nodded. They didn't know, they could only try to imagine. 'Mister Dewey Simpson, he told me he wanted two hundred nigger babies every year, or he'd sell me on. I didn't want that. So I did my stuff. I made sure …' He chose his words. 'Every woman I pleasured, I made sure it was a real big pleasure for her. Happy. I made her happy. That was my skill, my trade.'

'You were a fucker,' Aaron said. 'Good. Why not? Some fucker has to do it. I'm starvin' of hunger here.'

'An' that's what you're still doin',' Lonzo said. 'This money ...' He held it up. 'Ain't just for doctorin' pyanners.'

'It's what I know how to do,' T. Speed said simply. 'Ain't nothin' else I'm good at.'

Nat spoke for the first time. He rarely spoke; they always listened. 'Them white crackers catch you, they'll kill you,' he said.

'We want you to stop,' Aaron said.

'It's what I do,' T. Speed said. 'And we need the money.' Nothing more to be said.

~

Frankie Nickel rode out to the Killick place and charged Dan with murder and Devereux with kidnapping and maybe murder too.

Charles had told her to do it. Time kept slipping by, Lewis hadn't turned up, folk were angry and noisy, Ruth Hudd the loudest of all. Someone's got to be charged, Charles said, or everyone will think the law is useless and toothless. Maybe it is, Frankie said, in this case. Maybe so, Charles said, but we can't let them think so.

'You gonna put us in the lock-up?' Dan asked.

'You plannin' on runnin' away?' she said.

He decided not to answer. The town had no jail, but they could put a lock on Stackmesser's cellar, use that. Flooded every winter, stank all through summer. Best say nothing.

'My clients will appear as required,' Jimmy-Sam said, 'have no fear of that.'

'You defendin'?'

'I am. You prosecutin'?'

'Me or nobody. Two o'clock this afternoon in Maggie's barn. Shouldn't take more'n coupla hours.'

'Don't bet on it,' Jimmy-Sam said.

'That barn got rats,' Stanton said.

'Reverend Hunkin wanted twenty-five dollars a day for his church. Barn's free.'

'A word in private,' Jimmy-Sam said. He went outside with the deputy. 'You have nothing,' he said. 'This trial is sheer folly. And if a rat bites a client of mine, I shall sue the county, the town, the judge and you until you're bogged down in debt to the end of the century.'

'First thing,' she said. 'Jury decides that. Second thing: if you kept Stanton off the hooch he wouldn't see rats in every room.'

When Jimmy-Sam smiled he seemed to grow a size larger all over. 'That's good. I like that. Can you prove a nigger didn't shoot your husband?'

'Can you prove a nigger did?'

'I don't need to. I will lift mine eyes ...' He looked at the Ridge. '... unto the hills, from whence cometh my help. Jury'll understand. See you in court.'

He watched her ride away. Dan came out and stood beside him. 'Do not delude yourself into thinking I am doing this for fun,' Jimmy-Sam said. 'Nothing has changed.'

'Ain't no fun for me an' Dev.'

'Self-pity. That is the biggest crime in law. Get my breakfast.'

In all her time as a law officer, Frankie Nickel had never galloped her horse. Crime was not so scarce that she needed to run about in search of it. If someone reported a shooting or a robbery or a riot, she thanked him, finished her conversation, told Maggie where she was going, walked to her horse and set off at an easy trot that was more of an amble. He was a good old horse. Frankie fitted him like an armchair. If she galloped him they might arrive half an hour earlier, but what was she going to do with that half-hour? The dead were dead, the goods stolen, the heads cracked. Or possibly not. There were false alarms. And so she did not hurry. After all, the law couldn't start without her.

About a mile outside Rock Springs, her horse began thinking of the bucket of water waiting and he eased into a lope just as a horseman spurred out from behind a stand of laurel and blocked her way.

It was a big black mare, and its rider had chosen either his horse or his suit to match; together they looked like the model for some expensive statue to a costly battle.

'Charlotte van Orman,' he said. He had a deep voice, almost gruff. 'I got enough warrants in my pocket to paper the parlour. You don't want me to read them.'

'James L. Boston,' she said. With all her work, she had actually forgotten about him. Now he was one burden too many. 'You come on a bad day.'

Their horses drifted alongside each other, so their tails could flick the flies from their eyes.

'You shot your husband. Nobody cares too much about that in Texas.'

She opened her mouth, then changed her mind. 'Oh, the hell with it.'

'But he bought land, him and some others. Worthless land, turned out, so they let him keep the deeds. Now it ain't so worthless. The railroad wants to go through that land. Big money. Trouble is, can't find the deeds.'

'I probably burned 'em. Burned down the whole damn house.'

'Mistake. Big mistake.'

'I was the widow, I inherited. I could burn anythin' I liked.'

'The late Mr van Orman's partners don't agree. Your existence puts the land transaction under what the attorneys call a legal cloud. Railroad don't like that. Easy way is, take you back to Texas, get you jailed for murder, have the court declare you unfit, release the land. You'll be out in five years.'

She reached out and scratched her horse between the ears. He liked that. 'I don't want any part of Texas. I'll write a letter, you can take it back.'

He shook his head, once. An economical man.

'You chose a real bad day,' she said. 'I got to lead off on a murder trial, coupla hours.'

'Captain Cleghorn will take your place.'

'*Hoke?* Hoke Cleghorn can't tell when little Arnie Phillips is cheatin' him at checkers. You expect him to prove *murder?*'

'The captain was confident enough when I spoke with him.'

'He's old, an' he was a bag a wind when he was young.' She thought of Jimmy-Sam Wiggins versus Hoke Cleghorn. It would be all over before the pedlar could start selling peanuts. 'Texas can wait. Ain't goin'.'

'Texas has waited too long.' James L. Boston sat his horse without moving a muscle. His expression never changed. 'This trial ...' He shrugged: at last a movement! 'There's no reason to believe the Killicks killed your husband.'

'Reason don't count for much in Rock Springs.' Her hands moved to her coat pockets.

'I know about the Derringer,' he said. 'That's not your style, is it? Not here. Not like this.'

'Style. First I knew I had one.'

'Accept it: I'm taking you to Texas, one way or another.'

'Only way you're taking me to Texas is bound hand an' foot. Accept it, I'll make your life a bloody misery every inch of the way. Somethin' else: this ain't no mail-order murder trial. Folk feel pretty strong about it, and not just because he was my husband. There's a kidnappin' involved. Young boy. Maybe worse than kidnappin'. Now I guess you can oblige me to go with you. How far they'd let you go before they put a bullet through that fine corduroy suit is another matter. These Kentucky long rifles, they can hit a squirrel in the eye from a hundred paces, eight times out of ten. So that would oblige me to hold *another* murder trial.' She shook her head. 'All these murder trials, it ain't my style. Not my style at all.'

Boston sat his horse and reviewed what she had told him. A patient man.

'I'll make you a sporting offer,' he said. 'You stay in Rock Springs and prosecute this trial. If you win, if you get a guilty verdict against these Killicks, then I'll leave and you won't hear from me again. If you lose, you come with me to Texas, no resistance.'

She nodded.

He moved aside, and let her ride on.

When she reached town, Doc Brightsides was waiting for her. 'Did you find them?' he asked.

'Found 'em. Charged 'em. Done my share.'

'Hoke Cleghorn's been telling everyone he's better qualified to do the prosecuting.' She rolled her eyes. 'I keep thinking,' the doc said. 'I saw Dan Killick just after the killing, and he didn't act like any murderer I've ever seen.'

'Yeah. I was there too.'

'Oh.' Brightsides felt foolish. 'That's right, I forgot.'

'Maybe Dan didn't do it. Maybe none of the Killicks did it. All I know is they got this fat freak who thinks he's twice the lawyer Abe Lincoln ever was, an' he's got the answer to every question, which is blame it on the niggers on the Ridge. You think Hoke Cleghorn can handle that?'

'Hoke can't button his fly without takin' his pants off first.'

'Well, that's one thing I can do. I hope it impresses the jury.'

~

The steady *tock-tock* of axes travelled into the wilderness. The occasional thud as several tons of tree fell to earth sent vibrations through the ground. The panther was warned and stayed away from the Ridge. In any case, she knew that hunting was bound to be poor near such disturbance. Deer, especially, would avoid it.

On the other hand, there was meat on the Ridge. Hogs. The panther could smell them when the wind was right, smell them a couple of miles away. A curious smell. Ripe and fruity. She had never eaten hog but it smelled as if it might be tasty. Definitely something to be remembered.

Meanwhile that *tock-tock*, like a woodpecker as big as an elk, sent the panther the opposite way. Her cubs grew fast, they were as big as wildcats now, and always hungry. She hunted ten, fifteen miles from the cave. When she brought down a deer she had to rip it, butcher it so she could carry home a hindquarter or a ribcage. It was wearying work.

One day she was dragging a great hunk of meat when she got a whiff of something odd and unpleasant and went up a tree with the meat in her jaws like a lizard up a cliff.

After a while Gabe Killick came by with the rifle, hunting wild turkey. He was clever and observant, and he saw splatters of blood on the trail, stooped to touch them, see if they were fresh, and got a big drop of blood on the back of his neck.

He looked up and saw nothing but branches. Took a pace back; still nothing. Two paces forward, he was looking at the panther's eyes. Blood trickled down his spine. His strength went with it.

He could shoot the panther, kill it, be a big hero. He might miss and be a dead fool. Then the panther'd be a big hero. Panther go home, all the other panthers say, what you do today, boy? Got me a nigger. Hey! Was he hard to catch? No. He was stupid. Slow and stupid.

Gabe walked on. It was half a mile before he breathed easy. When God made the wilderness he made plenty of room for all. Hallelujah!

441

THEY CAN UNDERSTAND
NOTHIN'

F lub Phillips wanted to take his shotgun into the courtroom so
that he could shoot the Devil.

'Can't allow that, Flub,' the deputy said.

'You agin shootin' the Devil?' Flub asked. Once he had been the
most balanced, sensible man in Rock Springs. Now he was permanently angry, always on the go, staring as if blinkered. He gripped his
shotgun with both hands and it shook because he shook. 'Ye are of
your father the devil,' he said, 'and the lusts of your father ye will do.
John, eight, forty-four.'

'My pa lusted after grand pianos an' red-headed women, an' I
wouldn't give a wooden nickel for either of 'em. Now, this here barn
is full of your friends an' mine. Your problem, Flub, you can't shoot
straight. The other day you came into Maggie's tavern to put a load
a shot into Satan an' you blew a hole in her floor.'

'Scared him though, didn't I?' Flub said defiantly.

'Show me which one here is Satan. Just point your finger.'

Flub's head was trembling and his eyes were milky. 'There,' he
said.

'That's the judge.' It wasn't; it was a Killick cousin, one of many
down from the hills; but Flub couldn't tell. 'Come outside. Let the
doc take a look at you.'

He let her hold the gun while Brightsides checked his pulse and
looked at his tonsils. 'You got a bad dose of miasma,' the doc said.
'Go to bed for a week.'

'My strength is made perfect in weakness. Second Corinthians,
twelve, nine.' Flub walked away, leaning into a wind that didn't exist.

'Malaria boiled his brains,' Brightsides said. 'He's what us doctors call cuckoo.' But the deputy still had the shotgun, which was what mattered.

The barn was full an hour before the trial was due to start. Many had come in from the surrounding countryside, bringing charcoal and barbecue. It was a holiday. The heat of bodies quickly built and all the doors had to be opened and kept open. Dogs and children ran in and out. There was singing, fiddle-playing, card-playing, even a little horse-trading. The barn smelled of sweat and overdone pork chops and the sour drift of cigar smoke and the sweet memory of ancient cow manure; Maggie had never had the floor properly cleaned. The noise was loud. It was one long fight to hear and be heard.

Charles Hudd arrived and was shocked. He had expected an atmosphere like church. 'What do they think this is? A circus?' he said. 'That's what they're hoping,' Frankie said.

She had borrowed three wagons. They filled one end of the barn. On the middle wagon there was a table and two chairs, for the judge and Doc Brightsides, who was to do any clerking thought necessary. The smallest wagon was the dock; the largest was for the jury.

By two o'clock the Killick brothers had climbed into the dock and the jury had somehow chosen itself: Sims, Stackmesser, Cleghorn, Skinner, Dunbar, Hutton, Kidder, Dunkerley, and four out-of-town nonentities who reckoned they would get a better view from up there. The judge and the clerk took their places. Nobody stood. The noise went on. Two boys were fighting; a bench crashed and six people fell; the noise grew worse. Charles Hudd pounded the table with Judge Potter's gavel. The gavel snapped. Not a good start.

Maggie fetched a bucket of water and a hammer, dumped the water on the fight and booted the boys out, gave the hammer to the judge. Ten minutes late, the trial began.

Dan pleaded not guilty to murdering Major de Glanville. Devereux pleaded not guilty to kidnapping Lewis Hudd and then murdering him. Dan never blinked. Devereux's left foot never stopped shaking.

Hudd beckoned to Frankie and Jimmy-Sam. 'This jury,' he said softly. 'How was it selected? I ask because I think I see a possible prosecution witness in the jury. That can't be right.'

'I have no objection,' Jimmy-Sam said. 'I think I spot a couple of defence witnesses in there too.'

'Either we go with this jury,' Frankie said, 'or we start over and pick a new one from these people.'

Hudd looked at the crowd. 'There aren't three men there I'd trust to decide a hog-callin' contest. We'll go with what we've got. Deputy, you say your piece first.'

Frankie turned. The delay had made the crowd restless, some were talking again. As she looked at them, it suddenly hit her: she was going to have to talk about her husband's murder, ask questions about it, probe it from every side. Until now she had not admitted to herself that he was dead. He was always going away, sometimes for weeks at a time; then he always came back. She had been waiting for him to come back, and now she knew it would never happen; never. That fact struck like an icy gust and left her, briefly, breathless. He wasn't lost; he wasn't late; he was dead. Someone had shot his life away. Dead. That's why all these people were here. And when they left this barn he would still be dead, and the hurt would be as great and maybe greater. They had loved each other. *Not worth it,* she thought. *Love isn't worth this pain. It should never have happened.*

The talking had stopped. She had no idea what to say, so she just stood and looked. Someone was whispering. That stopped. The coughing stopped. The shuffling stopped. Now the silence was absolute. Everyone was watching her. Words came from nowhere.

'I am a widow,' she said. 'I was widowed in one of these murders we're here to try. You all know that. I want to say it now so we can get it right out in the open and then forget it. Forget it because it don't matter. This trial ain't about me, it's about the two got murdered. Now listen, you in the jury. I aim to prove the crimes were joined together. Hey! Ryan Kidder, forget your cigar.' She scowled until he quit trying to light it. 'Here's what happened. Very simple. Little Lewis Hudd ran away from home. Ended up on the Killick farm, never seen again. Me an' Major de Glanville went out to investigate. He got shot, killed. Why? Only two men could ever say why. One's dead. The other's the murderer, an' that's Dan Killick here. All we can do is look at the facts. Lewis Hudd vanishes on the Killick farm. Next day Major de Glanville gets shot. Lookin' for Lewis. On the same Killick farm. That ain't coincidence. Had to be a link. Think about it.'

She sat down.

Jimmy-Sam Wiggins took his time standing up, straightening his clothes, ruffling his hair.

'Thank you, ma'am,' he said, and bowed his head in her direction. The courtesy was not wasted. Folk appreciated courtesy. Courtesy was as rare as royalty in Rock Springs, so it was memorable. 'That was pretty darn good stuff there.' His voice had changed. It was no longer deep, resonant, authoritative. He had lightened it, relaxed it, allowed his words to sprawl and drag. 'Fact is, I found myself agreein' with ... uh ... almost every word you just said.' He hooked a thumb in his suspenders; he had done without a vest today. '*Almost* every word,' he told the jury softly. The crowd exchanged knowing looks; they had worked out which words it was he didn't go along with. 'You see, the truth is – and that's the sole an' only reason I'm standin' here – them two Killick brothers didn't kill nobody. There's no evidence they did. Not a single blessed scrap of evidence. Now that may cause you to wonder. I know it did me.' He spread his arms: a simple man, searching for the honest truth. He might have been a farmer talking to friends about strayed cattle and his efforts to find them. 'Until I figured it out. Why ain't there no evidence? *Because they didn't do it.*' Jimmy-Sam didn't exactly smile, but his eyes widened, at the wonderful simplicity of justice. 'See, this is all kinda strange to me.' He gestured at the barn, the three wagons, the deputy, the townsfolk. 'Kinda law I usually do, I'm lucky if two men an' a dog come to watch.' A few soft chuckles could be heard. Jimmy-Sam twanged a suspender. 'An' sometimes the dog goes home early.' The chuckles were louder now. 'Cus, see, the sorta stuff I generally get asked to handle – that's if nobody else in the office can do it – is boundary dis-putes.' He made it two words: *dis putes*. Somewhere, somebody snorted. Jimmy-Sam glanced in that direction, looked down at his boots, looked up, said, 'You suffered too, friend, I guess. Boundary dis-putes.' He shook his head. 'Worst mistake I ever made – '

'Mr Wiggins,' Hudd said sharply.

'My apologies.' Jimmy-Sam squared his shoulders. 'Tell you later,' he whispered to the jury; and already, the deputy knew that the crowd liked him and it disliked the judge for spoiling his story. 'What I was gettin' around to,' Jimmy-Sam said, 'is murder an' kidnappin', they're a long way from boundary dis-putes, so I ask you to bear with me if I stumble now an' then. That's all I have to say for openers, your honour, except that when these two innocent young men have bin turned loose, if anyone here has a boundary dis-pute they want settled … I gone fishin'.'

He sat down. Devereux grumbled quietly, 'He made hisself sound like an asshole.'

Dan muttered: 'That's good. Jury's fulla farts. They love an asshole.'

'But he didn't say *nothin'*.'

'Yeah. They can understand nothin'. If they think real hard.'

Charles Hudd hammered for silence. 'Proceed with your evidence,' he told the deputy.

She got Job Sims out of the jury box and had him sworn by the doc. 'I'm Primitive Methodist,' Sims said. 'You sure you got the right book?'

'Nothing could be more primitive,' Brightsides said. 'That I guarantee.'

'All right. Turn her loose.' Sims took the oath.

'When was the last time you saw Lewis Hudd?' Frankie asked him.

'Well … I didn't know that's who it was, when I saw him.'

'But you know it now.'

'Objection,' Jimmy-Sam murmured, so soft that only the judge and the deputy heard.

'You mustn't tell the witness what to say,' Hudd said. 'Start again.'

She had to think. 'Okay,' she said 'I'm gonna have to leave Mr Sims an' call another witness. Mrs Ruth Hudd.'

'Do I get a chance to cross-examine?' Jimmy-Sam said.

'Cross-examine?' Hudd said. 'The witness hasn't said anything yet.'

'My point precisely, your honour.'

'Oh, well. If you must.'

'Mr Sims,' Jimmy-Sam said. 'How many white boys between the ages of ten and twelve live within walking distance of Rock Springs?'

'Jeez … I dunno. Plenty.'

'Thank you. I congratulate you on refusing to guess when asked for hard facts. That's all.'

As Sims stood down, he twanged a suspender. It was done without thought but the crowd enjoyed it. He grinned.

Ruth Hudd got sworn in. 'When did you last see your son Lewis?' Frankie asked.

'Last Tuesday. He ate breakfast, went out to play. Never came back.'

'What does he look like?'

'Oh … Thin for his age. Ten. Yaller hair. Face was kinda squashed-up. Some folk said it looked like a rabbit, I never saw it that way myself, but …' The barn was hushed. This was every mother's nightmare being re-lived. 'Coupla toes missin'. Accident, year ago. Didn't slow him down none. Brave boy. When them raiders came in the night he shot one. Shot the man dead.'

'No more'n them sonabitch bushwhackers deserved!' Reuben Skinner said. Hudd glared. 'Well, it's God's truth,' Skinner mumbled.

'Where did he go, when he left the house?' Frankie asked.

'River. To play. Took our dog, Beth, some apples, a chunk a cheese. Leastways, they were missin'. Beth came back.'

'Might he have built a raft?'

'Objection,' Jimmy-Sam murmured.

'Don't ask the witness to guess,' Hudd said.

'Sorry … Did Lewis have the strength an' the skill to make a raft?'

'Yes. He was a right smart little boy.'

The hush had to break; the strain was too great. A woman began sobbing. There was a general shuffling of feet and shifting of limbs. It was as if that one woman spoke for them all.

Jimmy-Sam had no questions. He helped Ruth Hudd from her chair. Frankie recalled Sims. 'Now we all know what the boy looked like. Did you see him last Tuesday?'

'Can't say for sure.'

'See a boy who looked like him, on a raft?'

'Yep.'

'When?'

'Tuesday.'

'This is like pullin' bear's teeth,' she said. 'Just tell us what time of day, an' where, an' anythin' else might help this court, like for instance was the boy eatin' apples?'

It was a lucky stroke. Sims had forgotten, but now he remembered. 'That's exactly what he was doin'. Floated past town about noon, eatin' a big red apple. Skinny yaller-haired kid. Said he didn't know where he was goin'. I said, you get to Nashville, get me a newspaper.' Nobody laughed. 'Jokin', see. He thought it was pretty funny.' Still nobody laughed. Sims gave up.

447

'Then what?'

'Nothin'. Floated away.'

Jimmy-Sam had some questions. Did Sims ask the boy's name? No. Ask where he came from? No. Count his toes? No. Could he swear the boy was Lewis Hudd? No. Was it possible the boy on the raft was a different skinny yaller-haired young'un altogether? Yes.

Then Sims saw an obstacle. 'Only thing is,' he said, 'ain't nobody else lost a son like that except Mrs Hudd here.'

'Who said the boy on the raft was lost? He floated away, you said. Who knows what he did then? Maybe he swam to the bank, walked home an' – '

'Objection,' Frankie said. 'He's makin' it up. That ain't evidence.'

'Withdrawn,' Jimmy-Sam said. 'Nothin' more.'

At the other end of the barn, a tethered sow had been quietly chewing through the rope. It broke the last few fibres and began butting people out of the way. Someone grabbed at its tail. The sow snorted and bolted. It left a trail of chaos that had the judge pounding with his hammer until he saw the animal standing looking up at him. For once in his life, Charles said the right thing. 'Is this your next witness?' he asked. Frankie shook her head. Laughter burst like a bomb and scared the sow; it turned and raced for daylight. 'Ten-minute break,' Charles said.

Frankie went to Ruth Hudd. 'Get some fresh air while you can,' she said.

'Look at 'em,' Ruth said. 'They think it's funny. Ain't funny to me.'

'Forget 'em. They're nothin'.'

'They're alive. That's everythin'.'

Jimmy-Sam went to his clients. 'You look bored to hell,' he told Dan. 'You look like you're bustin' to piss,' he told Devereux. 'Can't you both look natural?' They stared at him, Dan frowning, Devereux leering. 'Never mind,' Jimmy-Sam said.

The deputy's next witness was Marcus Hudd. She took him up to the point where he rode to town and met Skinner, Cleghorn and Dan Killick on the landing stage, at sundown. 'Killick asked me the boy's name an' how tall he was, an' then he said his brother Devereux found a boy looked just like him in the river, that afternoon.'

A soft *aaaahhh* rose from the crowd like mist made audible. At last: something tied a Killick to a victim. And out of a Killick's mouth, too.

'What did you do then?'

'Wanted my boy back, of course. Asked why the Killicks hadn't sent him home.'

'Dan Killick tell you why?'

'Said Dev planned on keepin' him until us Hudds paid the Killicks what we owe 'em. Said his brother George, killed in the war, George worked for my cousin Charles – that's him up there – an' he had back-pay comin', from them days before the war.'

'Say how much?'

'Thousand dollars, includin' interest.'

That produced a gasp and a buzz of comment and much pounding from the judge.

Frank Stackmesser stood up in the jury box and asked permission to say something. Charles Hudd nodded. Stackmesser said, 'Don't need no telescope to see how the judge here is soon gonna be smack in the middle of somethin' he should ought to be high above of where it ain't none of his business to be down there at all, especially now.' He sat down. There was applause. Sims nudged him. He stood and bowed. 'Just tryin' to help,' he said, flustered by the strange experience of popularity.

'It's a good point,' Charles said. 'I'll be as fair as I can, but I can't alter the circumstances. If the jury wants a new judge ...' He shrugged. 'So be it.'

'Where's the nearest?' Jimmy-Sam asked.

'Bowlin' Green,' Frankie said. 'You won't get him here, not with winter comin' on. This whole trial would have to go there.'

There was an angry rumble of protest. Just as they were sinking their teeth into this juicy steak, it was being snatched away.

'His honour has my total confidence,' Jimmy-Sam said. 'Me too,' Frankie said. 'Weren't my idea,' Stackmesser said. 'I mean, shit, Bowlin' Green ...'

'Carry on,' Charles said. He was already beginning to feel weary, and it wasn't three yet.

'After Dan Killick tried to get a thousand bucks for your boy,' Frankie said, 'what did you do?'

'Went home. Held a family meetin'. Got a writ of habeas corpus an' rode straight back to the Killick place. Had to wake 'em up. Dan Killick opened an upstairs window, wouldn't come down. Wanted the money. Wouldn't give me the boy. I was ... I couldn't ...' Marcus looked sick. 'Couldn't do nothin'. Had to leave.'

The silence was like glass. Frankie waited a long moment before she said, quietly, 'Thank you, Mr Hudd.'

Jimmy-Sam walked to the Killick brothers, and then turned and walked to the jury, all the time nodding his head. He stopped and rested his hands on the wagon, and said, 'Any father loses his son, only ten years old, that father's liable to be well an' truly steamed up. Ain't that so, Mr Marcus Hudd?'

'I was worried. Naturally.'

'*Very* worried?'

'Sure.'

'Night fallin', small child lost somewhere out in that blackness, you must of bin close to … uh … desperate.'

'I've said I was worried.'

'Not desperate?'

'Actin' desperate gets a man nowhere. Whoever took my Lewis must of bin desperate. An' crazy. I ain't crazy. So – '

'So let's move forward a day. Or I should say a night. Next night you an' your kin got yourselves all gunned-up an' rode over an' blasted my clients' residence an' terrified their womenfolk includin' a frail old widowlady. You carried out that desperate act, didn't you?'

'I never knew about the widow,' Marcus grunted. 'All we did was give back some of the grief they gave us. We didn't hurt nobody.'

'You shot a cow.' When Marcus looked away, Jimmy-Sam said, 'Ain't that kind of desperate? Twelve grown men runnin' amuck an' all they can hit is one cow never did a bad thing in all its short an' sorry life?'

''Tweren't twelve. Five was all.'

'Only five desperate gunmen. Well, I'm sure the cow feels better now we got that settled.'

'Mr Wiggins,' Charles said, 'nobody is charged with killing a cow.'

'It's relevant, your honour.'

'I hope so. I don't want any boundary dis-putes here.'

'Let's go back,' Jimmy-Sam said to Marcus. 'Back to the time you met Dan an' Reub Skinner an' Hoke Cleghorn on the landing stage. Now, we know you were halfway to bein' real desperate about – '

'Objection,' Frankie said. 'He doesn't know that.'

'You weren't there, Mr Wiggins,' Charles said. 'Start again.'

'Pleased to, your honour. I believe the jury is well able to decide how steamed-up the witness was.'

'Or not,' Charles said.

'A good father. Dutiful. Anxious. Very anxious. Only one thing on his mind. Little Lewis. Am I right?'

'Yes,' Marcus said.

'Now, these three other individuals on that landin' stage. What were they doin'?'

'Nothin'.' Marcus disapproved of idleness. 'Doin' nothin'. Drinkin'.'

'Drinkin'. Milk? Lemonade?'

'Beer. Pitcher of beer.'

'Uh-huh. They offer you a drink?'

Marcus scoffed, short and sour. 'Pitcher was empty.'

'Empty. Nothin' left. Every last drop drunk. Uh-huh. Now... the way Dan Killick behaved to you, would you say that was unreasonable? Unkind? Not nice?'

'Devilish.'

'Devilish, huh? You blame him for that? After all, the feller was drunk, he didn't know what he was – '

'Jesus!' Frankie said. 'Can't you ever stop inventin'?'

'Come on, Mr Wiggins,' Charles said. 'You know better than to embroider on the facts. You can't say Dan Killick was drunk.'

'Why not?' Hoke Cleghorn asked. 'He was drunk.'

'And *you* can't say it, either. You're on the jury. You're not on oath.'

'I can say it,' Job Sims said. 'I been sworn in legal. Dan Killick was drunker'n a fiddler's bitch, an' I should know cus I carried him – '

'Sit down! One witness at a time. Mr Sims, you weren't even *on* the landing stage at the time in question. Please stay out of it. Mr Wiggins: if you feel Dan Killick's sobriety or otherwise is important, you'll have to prove it.'

'Fine an' dandy,' Jimmy-Sam said. 'When my time comes I'll call Dan Killick.'

'Why wait?' Frankie said. 'I'll call him now.'

'I'm agreeable.' He was too agreeable. She wondered if she had made a bad mistake. But she wanted to get this thing over and done with, fast.

Dan was sworn. He seemed indifferent to the occasion. He noticed

451

a relative in the crowd. 'How you been?' he said. They might have been pitching horseshoes.

'You heard what Mr Marcus Hudd said about meetin' you an' Hoke an' Reuben at the landin' stage last Tuesday,' Frankie began. 'We can all move along right fast now if you agree. D'you agree?'

'I don't remember none of it,' Dan said. 'I was drunk.'

'I got other witnesses. They'll say you wanted a thousand dollars ransom for the boy Lewis. Did you or didn't you?'

'I was drunk. Last Tuesday, you say?' He stared up a sunbeam slanting through a hole in the roof. 'No, I don't remember Tuesday. No part of it.'

'Well, let me remind you. That was the day you made certain threats to Mr Marcus Hudd. You said your brother Devereux had his son Lewis, and you said the Hudds owed the Killicks a thousand dollars, and you said none of your family was goin' to help find the boy until you got paid. We got witnesses to all that. Now, how could you say all that, clear as a bell, if you was blind drunk?'

Dan made a small, baffled gesture. 'It's a goddamn mystery, ain't it?'

'Maybe you don't remember what you'd sooner forget. Ain't that the truth?'

'Hey ...' He raised a finger. 'I do remember one thing. Yeah ... This feller come over, was awful gloomy. *Aw*ful gloomy. Needed cheerin' up ... He was breakin' my poor heart, he was so ... *gloomy*. I told him a joke, funniest joke I knew, just to ... just to ...' He narrowed his eyes until half his face was wrinkled. 'Now why did I do that?'

'Cheer him up. What was the joke?'

'I forget. See, I was drunk.'

'Are you always drunk, Mr Killick?' He wanted to think about that, so she said, 'Are you drunk now?'

'No.'

'How about later that Tuesday night, when Marcus Hudd brought his habeas corpus to your house. Were you drunk then? Too drunk to remember what you said or did? Too drunk to control yourself? Don't look at Mr Wiggins, he don't know the answer. Look at me.'

Dan hunched his shoulders: a tiny, protective action. Even the stupidest listener knew he was in a bind. If he kept saying he'd been drunk morning, noon and night, well, maybe he did do these terrible things he was accused of. Did them when he was in the grip of booze. Or, if not, what really happened? Everywhere, heads craned and strained to get a better view. 'You ain't drunk now,' she said. 'You ain't forgot my question already.'

Dan scratched his chin and surprised himself: nothing there to scratch. Jimmy-Sam had made him shave twice. His face felt like a china jug. 'I remember,' he said. 'Trouble is, what I remember ain't same as what *he* remembers.' He nodded at Marcus.

A dog woke up, and yawned and stretched, and cocked its leg and pissed on a man's ankle. 'Shit!' he roared, and booted the dog a good seven feet. Briefly there was uproar. Charles hammered it down. 'I will not tolerate profanity in this court!' he warned. The man tried to hide. The crowd settled again.

'We're waitin',' Frankie said.

'Well, it was black night,' Dan said. 'I was asleep. Whole house was asleep. Next thing I know, some sonofa... some feller's hammerin' an' hollerin' fit to bust his britches. Now ... lotta bad men about. He ain't got no lantern. I ain't got no lantern. Ain't no moon, no stars. He's still hammerin' an' hollerin'. I open the window a crack, ask the stranger who he is. Hey you, I says, what's your name?' He sucked his teeth. 'Yes sir, that's what I did. Asked his name.'

'And what did he say?'

'Oh ...' Dan puffed out his cheeks. 'Said his name was O. Fuck.' There was a stunned silence. 'Mr O. Fuck. That's what he said.' The shock began to wear off. Slight tittering could be heard at the back. 'I didn't argue with the feller,' Dan said. 'He had a pistol. That's what he was hammerin' on the door with. Must of bin in a terrible temper, cus he bust his pistol. 'O. Fuck,' he says when I ask him ...' Dan had to stop. The titters had been the fuse that ignited a huge, raucous belly-laugh.

Charles Hudd folded his arms and waited for the racket to pass. At last it slackened to a buzz, with odd, occasional cackles. He felt helpless. If he told Dan to cut out the jokes, Dan would say he was just telling what happened. Not his fault if folk laughed. *Never give up, never give in,* Charles told himself. 'Proceed,' he ordered.

'Well, I knew straight away he wasn't from around these parts,' Dan said, and that released another great whoop of mirth. Dan sat still, hands linked, legs crossed at the ankle, face blank. 'Ma said she knew a feller in Barber's Landin' who was called Hans von Shit,' he said, 'but he – '

'Enough!' Charles said. 'Ten-minute break!' His words were swamped by laughter.

He took the deputy and Jimmy-Sam outside and walked with them. 'This is a disgrace to justice,' he said. 'I'm minded to declare a mis-trial and send it to Bowling Green.'

'Dan's throwin' dust in our eyes,' Frankie said. 'He won't tell jokes when we get to murder.'

'Mostly, that hoo-ha was just people blowing off steam,' Jimmy-Sam said. 'They needed an excuse. They'll be quieter now.'

When they went back, Charles reminded everyone that this was a trial for murder, and he lambasted the crowd for its selfishness, child-ishness and stupidity. He spoke with a controlled ferocity that sobered them, especially when he mentioned contempt of court and his powers to fine.

Frankie had few further questions for Dan. She expected to get little from him; she got almost nothing. He said he had seen a boy wandering around the farm, might have been a Hudd, might not, no concern of his, never saw him leave. First thing he knew about Major de Glanville's death was when he heard the shot. Took him about a minute to get to the barn. 'Fact is,' he said, 'I wasn't sure *where* to look, at first. Sound echoes round that field, pistol shot specially. I kept lookin' every which way, an' then I seen a body by the barn door. Lyin' on its back. He was dead when I got to him.'

Frankie shut her eyes and tried to remember the field, tried to picture Dan running into it, dodging, searching. She opened her eyes. 'That's a big field,' she said. 'You were lookin' every which way, wonderin' where the shot came from. You see anyone run away?'

'No,' Dan said sadly.

'Anywhere in that field a man can hide?'

'Only in the barn. Weren't nobody there.'

'No tracks by the barn? Horse, or mule?'

'No.'

'Here we got a big empty field, an' a man just bin shot, an' you. Did I miss anythin'?'

'No.'

'If you was Lewis's ma an' pa, where would you look for him?'

'He ain't,' Jimmy-Sam said, 'so he can't.' Charles nodded. Frankie gave up.

Jimmy-Sam walked to the doorway of the barn. Some people thought he was leaving. He borrowed a man's hat: high-crowned and dark green; and held it up. 'What's this, Dan?' he called. Dan leaned forward, squinting hard. 'Cabbage,' he said. 'Or a basket, maybe.'

'You got bad eyes, ain't that right?'

'I can see. Gets kinda fuzzy, is all.'

Jimmy-Sam pointed through the doorway. 'Who's that man out there under that big old maple tree?'

'Stranger, I guess.'

Jimmy-Sam walked back. The jury could see there was no-one under the maple. 'That'll do,' he said.

Dan went back to his place. He muttered, 'Now every bastard son-abitch piece a piss in Dundee County knows I'm blind as a bat.' Devereux was astonished. 'You rather be blind or hanged?' he said.

'Old ladies gonna be helpin' me along the sidewalk,' Dan said. Tears of rage ran down his polished cheeks. He said, 'Since George went, this family got no pride, I gotta have pride for you all. Now I'm goin' goddamn blind.' Devereux was silenced. That kind of pride he could not understand.

Charles was massaging his eyes. He felt drained of strength; he had to force his brain to work. He beckoned Jimmy-Sam and Frankie to approach him. 'We won't finish today,' he said quietly. 'This might be a good time to adjourn.'

'I want to call another witness while the jury's memory's fresh,' Frankie said.

He sighed. 'If you must ... Who is it?'

'Lonzo Hudd. Used to be your slave.'

Charles was jolted awake so sharply that he bit his tongue. 'Great God Almighty ... Can you do that?'

'Any law against it?'

Charles looked at Jimmy-Sam, who shrugged and smiled. 'Just had a war freed the niggers,' he said.

'I know, but ...' Charles looked at the jury, the crowd, the dock. He lowered his voice to a whisper: 'I can see three men I know of, and they each killed slaves, murdered them, in front of other slaves who never gave evidence, because it was illegal for them to do so.' He sucked his tongue and swallowed blood. 'I don't know how these

455

people are going to feel about putting a nigger up to testify against white men.'

'This ain't a case of a murdered nigger,' she said.

'True.' But Charles still looked wretched. 'And I hope it doesn't turn out that way.'

Frankie signalled to Maggie, who went out. A minute later she came back with Lonzo, and the tension in the place leaped as if she were leading a pack of panthers.

Lonzo took the oath. Frankie got him to say his name and age and the fact that Charles Hudd had owned him until Emancipation. Did Lonzo remember, before the war, an overseer called George Killick? Yes, ma'am. What did Lonzo remember about him?

'Stole,' Lonzo said. 'Got found out. Got kicked out.'

That caused a gasp which ended before Charles could reach for his hammer. Nobody wanted to miss a word.

'George Killick stole from the Hudd farm? That what you sayin'? Stole what?'

'I could write it out. Make a long list.'

This was badly received: uppity nigger showing off he could write.

'Just say the main things.'

'Cheeses, hams, sacks a cornmeal, candles, beef, eggs, chickens dead an' alive – '

'Enough. How did you know he stole this stuff?'

'I loaded it. All us niggers loaded the wagon when Master Charles was sellin' cheese an' ham an' stuff to town. Stuff got wrote down in a book, so much a this, so much a that. Only, Mister George took more. Book said two hams, he took three. I knew that, cus I knew how to read.'

'And George Killick didn't know you knew?'

'No, ma'am, he didn't.'

A lot of grumbling and head-shaking was going on in the crowd: see what you get when you educate a nigger? Bastard cheats on you. Charles crashed his hammer and beat the noise down.

'Sounds like your master trusted George Killick,' she said. 'Did he?'

'Yeah, ma'am.'

'Leavin' aside stealin' food an' such … did George Killick do anythin' else crooked?'

'Told lies.'

'What lies?'

'Said he saw coupla white men stealin' a slave called Old John, like they was Abolitionists. Said he fired his pistol, scared 'em off. Didn't never happen. Weren't no Abolitionists. Other time, said he saved the hay when it went on fire. Easy for him, he was the one set it on fire. Other time, went in the river, pulled out a cow got stuck, near to drownin'. What Master Charles never knew, Mister George put that poor cow in the river. Us niggers knew. Farm like that, niggers everywhere. See everythin'.'

Charles Hudd had his elbows on the table and his head in his hands. That way, they hid his expression.

'Killicks reckon the Hudds owe a thousand dollars for pay George never got,' she said. 'You surprised at that?'

'Maybe they reckon he shoulda bin paid for lyin' an' stealin',' Lonzo said. 'He was real good at that.'

Now there was no rumble of discontent from the crowd; only the frozen silence of hatred.

'I'm through here,' Frankie said to the judge.

'I couldn't do any better than you've done,' Jimmy-Sam said. 'No need for me to say another word.'

'Adjourned,' Charles said. 'Ten tomorrow morning.' Bang!

~

As the barn emptied, Brightsides went over to Wiggins and introduced himself. He knew perfectly well that the attorney knew he was the doctor, but there is a certain ceremony to be followed in these things. Brightsides said it was an interesting case, and Wiggins agreed, yes, it was interesting; not difficult, but (he spun a silver dollar and caught it without looking) the imponderables were perhaps a bit less ponderable than usual.

Brightsides enjoyed *imponderables*. He took Wiggins's arm and steered him to a corner, saying he himself had been doing a little pondering, during the trial, on the matter of life and death, which perhaps they should study further. Wiggins said, 'You know I can't discuss this case.' Brightsides said, 'But we can talk about your future.'

Wiggins wiped his neck and face with a handkerchief and looked at the sweat marks. 'I should have lost sixty pounds about fifteen years ago. I know that, so don't tell me to do it now.'

'I'm more interested in your heart than your weight.'

'Got a heart like an ox.'

'That's good, because it's been galloping like a racehorse. You have a very visible pulse in your neck, so visible that I could count your heartbeat from where I sat. Excuse me.' He touched the pulse with his fingertips. 'Still pumping hard.'

'You're wasted here.'

'You mean medicine is only for the rich? Let me hear your chest. Keep talking, wave your arms, nobody will notice.' He undid a few shirt buttons, slid his stethoscope over Wiggins's chest, listened, rolled up the stethoscope, put it away. 'You've seen other doctors? Yes, of course you have. And they say ...? No, don't tell me.' He scribbled a few words on a piece of paper. 'Am I right?'

'Well, ...' Wiggins glanced at the paper as he buttoned his shirt. 'That's something you're all going to have to wait a little while to find out. But ...' He struck a match and set fire to the paper in Brightsides's hand. 'Yes, the others think the way you do.'

Brightsides held the page, and they both watched the creeping flame eat the paper, until he dropped the last corner.

They strolled out into the late afternoon sunshine. 'I understand you're down here to marry Jessica,' Brightsides said.

'If she'll have me. The jury's still out on that question.'

'If she does ... and if you do ...' Brightsides stopped. Wiggins waited and watched, keenly interested, as if the doctor was a key witness about to betray himself. 'Well, you know it's a gamble,' Brightsides said, lamely.

'No, it's an ice-cold certainty,' Wiggins said. 'That's what I like about death: no ambiguity. I thank you for your kindness.' They shook hands, and Wiggins waved to the Killick buggy to come and take him home.

SECRETS

Jessica enjoyed being held captive. She liked being able to boss good-looking young men like Curtis and Floyd and Nelson, tell them to bring her different food or drink, and then feel their muscles and flatter them and make them blush. Being locked up in a barn was no hardship with visitors coming and going. Not having to cook and milk and wash for three surly brothers and a falling-down mother was a great pleasure. Yes, captivity was nice. Then the Hudds all hurried off without telling her. She missed the company and she missed the grub. Jessica was a girl who liked her grub. Hunger made her angry.

Shouting did no good. Throwing things at the wall did no good. Shaking the door and screaming did no good.

She was lying on her bed, quietly cursing, when she saw a rope, coiled and hanging from a peg. The other end disappeared in a confusion of rafters.

By standing on a broken barrel and reaching with a broken hoe, she dislodged the rope. She jerked it and a bell rang. It was the old slave bell. She rang it until Mary Hudd – the only person not interested in the trial – unlocked the barn door. Mary was surprised.

They went to the kitchen and made tea. Jessica explained her presence – retaliation for Lewis's disappearance – and Mary told her the trial had begun.

'Damn. I was supposed to be at that thing. You mind if I made toast? I got a cravin' for buttered toast.'

Mary sliced bread. They spoke of the pre-war times when she had taught Jessica at Rock Springs school. That was long ago. Not much to be said.

'I ought to be in that damn courthouse,' Jessica said. 'I'm a whatchamacallit. Witness.'

'Yes? What did you see?'

'What did I?' She thought about that as she ate toast. 'Witness. Yeah ... That's what it means, don't it, witness, sure. Well, I didn't witness nothin', but I told everyone I saw a big buck nigger run off with that little boy near where the feller got shot.' She spread jam, generously.

Mary hid her astonishment. 'And that's what you were going to tell the court?' Jessica nodded, jaws working. Mary said, 'Why would you say it, if it wasn't so?'

'Aw ... cus ...' She swallowed, and licked her lips. 'They was all so damn fussed about what happened, kept *arguin'* an' tellin' lies an' *arguin'* about the lies they told, I got sick an' tired of their noise, I just said what I reckoned would most likely stop their nonsense. It did, too.'

'And you plan to repeat it to the court?'

'Yeah. Nice an' simple, huh?'

'Well ... simple, maybe. Nice?' Mary poured more tea and hoped that Jessica was thinking. 'There's the boy's parents to remember. They're still looking for him. Is it fair to tell them a darkie took Lewis ...' She got up and put a log on the stove.

'Well, if a nigger didn't take him, where is he?' Jessica said crossly. 'Jesus ... More fuss an' horsefeathers. Can't anythin' be easy?'

'Let's talk about it.'

'Does it *matter* if a nigger gets the blame or not?'

'Have some more tea.'

'They're *our* niggers up there, half anyway. Stole from us by damn Lincoln. Pa always taught me, anythin' goes wrong on the farm, blame the slaves, they did it, an' Pa was right. You believe those coloured ladies an' gentlemen have changed into angels since they got theirselves emancipated? I don't.'

'You may be right,' Mary said. 'Let's talk about it.'

~

Despite the Killicks' threats, the axes went on swinging. From time to time there was a little silence, and then a tree fell and sent birds spiralling upwards. Soon the steady *tock, tock* of axes sounded again. The wood was hard: walnut, oak, cherry, beech. Each blow sent a shiver up the shaft and polished the callused hands a little more. The hands were tougher than the shafts, three of which split or snapped inside an hour. The remaining bits of wood needed to be burned out of the axe-heads. The cutters quit work and went back to camp and found Aaron squatting on the Altar, telling everyone that JoBeth couldn't stay. 'We came up here to get *away* from goddamn white folks!' he said. She sat on the ground, resting against her saddle, chewing smoked turkey that was as tough as plug tobacco. 'Ain't no use to us!' Aaron cried. 'Toss her out!'

'You ain't no use neither,' Martha said. 'How 'bout we toss you out first?'

'Who tossin' out who?' Gabe Killick demanded, and then he recognized this strange woman in buckskin pants. 'That's Mizz JoBeth,' he said, voice flattened by wonder.

'Ain't Dolly Madison,' she said. 'I feel her age, had to practically carry my horse up this Ridge.'

'Ain't dead, then.'

'Just stiff.' She levered herself up and shook hands. Gabe's fingers were limp as a glove. He had never shaken hands with a white woman before and he was afraid of damaging her. 'That's Moses, ain't it?' she said. 'An' them two big handsome niggers, I remember you from the Hudd place, don't I?'

'Hey!' Aaron shouted. 'Don't let her sweet-talk you! She ain't got nothin' to give! No money, nothin'!'

'You ain't come up to buy timber, then,' Buck said.

'Come to be a burden!' Aaron cried. 'We ain't got enough burdens, we need more? Ha!' He spat, and hit himself on the arm. 'See what you done?' he told Martha furiously.

'Cus we got plenty a good timber,' Buck told JoBeth. He flexed his fingers. Nowadays they constantly shaped themselves to fit an axe handle.

'You come up to sell stuff?' Gabe asked her. 'Lonzo takes care all that.'

'Got nothin' to sell.' She rested against the saddle again. 'Came up here to live, is what.'

'Big bad luck,' Aaron grumbled. 'She stays, white folks gonna give us hell, you see.'

'Live *here?*' Moses said to her. 'You got the whole Killick place to live on. Up here, we ain't got ...' He stopped, baffled by the task of listing what they hadn't got.

'I tried it, Moses. Can't live down there. They won't have me.'

'Trouble,' Aaron said. 'Didn't I say?'

'You're family,' Gabe said. 'Family got to ...'

She showed him her bruised and swollen jaw. 'Dan likes hittin' people. Didn't he hit you a few times? So I went to Mr Charles, an old friend, an' he backed off so fast when he saw me comin' he must be in Barber's Landin' by now. Seems nobody wants me.'

'Ain't fools,' Aaron said. 'Nor we ain't neither. Paid money for this Ridge so's to – '

'Trouble,' Buck said. 'You in trouble?'

'Man is born into trouble,' Josh said.

'Three months with child, if that's trouble.'

'As the sparks fly upwards,' Josh added.

'An' I've nowhere else to go.'

'Shit,' Aaron said, 'you got the white en-tire *world* to go to.'

'You're a fool,' Martha said. 'She ain't goin' nowhere.'

'Still workin' for whitey,' Aaron sneered. 'You gonna teach her little 'un to whop you?' But he had lost the argument; the others were drifting away. 'Trouble comin',' he said.

Martha made a bed for JoBeth in her cabin. Bonny helped. Bonny had been fascinated by the arrival of this pretty white lady, dressed like a man. Everyone except Aaron admired JoBeth and she liked everyone, even Aaron. Bonny wanted some of that affection, but she had nothing to buy it with. Yes, she did. Had a secret. She tugged JoBeth's sleeve. 'Got somethin' to show,' she whispered. They went outside. Now Bonny was embarrassed: she had nothing to show. Her secret was hidden in the woods. She squirmed her toes in the dirt and sucked her lower lip. JoBeth squatted on her haunches and looked at her. 'Secret,' Bonny said, almost cross-eyed with excitement.

'Hey,' JoBeth said lazily. 'Ain't had a good secret since I nearly got et by a black bear at Satan's Bathtub.' Bonny took her hand. 'Goin' for a walk,' JoBeth called to Martha. 'Gonna look for a lemonade tree.'

They walked through the woods, always drifting downhill. Bonny chattered nonstop, about panthers, and beavers and ghosts, and people who died last winter, and ghosts and how Moses carried whole trees, and Josh talked to God, and ghosts, and the way Aaron ate dimes to magic them into dollars. It wasn't lies but it wasn't truth either and anyway who cared? JoBeth chuckled a lot. She was lost, but Bonny trotted confidently. This wilderness was her backyard. Then they heard the rolling echoes of distant gunfire. Bonny stopped.

'Rifle,' JoBeth said. 'Anythin' worth huntin' down there?'

'He got a forty-four,' Bonny said. 'He ain't scared. Big old forty-four.' She was talking to herself. Her voice was squeaky with worry.

'Who ain't scared?'

'Secret,' Bonny said. 'Secret-secret-secret.'

They went on. Bonny said little, but she did a lot of listening and looking. After ten or fifteen minutes she stopped and sat on a rock. 'Lonzo comin',' she said. JoBeth heard nothing but birdsong. 'Where?' she asked. Bonny pointed. Then she hugged her legs and sucked her kneecap. 'This the secret?' JoBeth asked. Bonny shook her head without unsucking her kneecap. JoBeth sat beside her and wondered what childbirth would be like, aside from painful.

Lonzo saw her first. His skin blended into the shadows of trees.

'Hey,' he said. 'Mizz JoBeth.' Maggie had told him she was back, but still, this was a surprise, up here.

'Well, Lonzo.' After six or seven years, what was there to say? Nothing.

'Get shot at?' Bonny asked.

'Yeah … Just some crackers got fired up on account they didn't like what I said in court … Aimin' to miss, aimin' to scare me off, is all.' He told them about the trial: just the bare facts, Dan and Dev accused of this and that.

'Ain't made yourself any friends, Lonzo,' JoBeth said.

'Deputy asked me to speak.'

'Don't mean you got to do it.'

'Done now.'

'Yeah.'

That ended that.

'You come lookin' for me?' Lonzo said. 'Somethin' wrong?'

This day had gone on long enough. JoBeth wanted a wash, a meal, and a good sleep. 'Came lookin' for some kinda secret person with a forty-four,' she said. They both looked at Bonny. 'Ain't another ghost, is it, Bonny?'

She took them to the cave. Lewis was black with dirt. JoBeth and Lonzo knew the difference between nigger-black and dirt-black. Besides, the hair wasn't crinkly or fuzzy and the eyes were blue. 'You the little 'un ran off from the Hudds?' Lonzo asked. 'You Lewis?'

The boy flinched as if prodded with a stick.

'We got hot cornbread an' gravy waitin',' Lonzo said, 'an' milk an' peach pie an' …' He stopped. Lewis was already out of his cave.

Aaron was not pleased to see the boy, but by now everyone was tired of Aaron's bellyaching and bitching. And later that evening, JoBeth said to Lonzo, 'Let's keep him here. For a little while. It'll teach my sonofabitch brothers for whoppin' me.'

'Sure,' Lonzo said. Made a nice change to watch the white folks giving each other all sorts of grief.

NO BARN DANCE

James L. Boston was waiting for the deputy outside the barn next morning. 'If you win this case, you're a better lawman than I reckoned. After you called that cocky nigger to give evidence, you couldn't win if both brothers confessed right here in court. Trial's over. When you lose, you come with me. To Texas. That's the deal we made.'

'Yes.' Calling Lonzo had been a mistake. Brightsides said so. He had watched the jury when Lonzo gave his evidence. Looked like twelve cases of food poisoning, Brightsides said. And all the time, Jimmy-Sam Wiggins had been gently shaking his head, as if he just couldn't comprehend such folly.

'Hope your bag's packed,' Boston told her. 'I aim to leave right smartly.'

The crowd in the barn was smaller; cows had to be milked, stock fed, fences mended; but the sense of eagerness was just as great. Yesterday had been highly entertaining, and they hadn't even got to the meat of the trial yet.

Frankie got Reuben Skinner out of the jury and had him sworn in.

He agreed he had gone with her and Hoke Cleghorn to search the Killick place for Lewis Hudd, and he'd found a boy's shirt in the cellar. She showed it and he said yes, that was it.

'You found Lewis Hudd's shirt in the Killicks' cellar, two days after he disappeared.' She turned to the judge. 'Now, I can ask the boy's mother to swear she recognizes the shirt. We really going to put the poor woman through all that?'

'Defence accepts this is Lewis Hudd's shirt, your honour,' Jimmy-Sam said. 'I have some questions, however.'

'I'm done here,' Frankie said.

'When you found this shirt,' he said to Reub, 'was there anything else in that cellar to prove a boy – any boy – had been there?'

'No. I didn't look – '

'No. Nothing else in the cellar. Was the cellar door locked?'

'No. Wide open.'

'What's it like down there? Clean, dry, warm?'

'Hell, no. Miserable place. Stinkin' hole.'

'Can you think of any reason why a ten-year-old boy would take his shirt off in that cold, wet cellar?'

'No. Crazy thing to do.'

'So maybe he didn't. Maybe somebody else, *another* boy who'd *stolen* that shirt, *threw* it – '

'Not a question!' Frankie shouted. 'He's tellin' his fairy stories again!'

'Withdrawn.' Jimmy-Sam held his hands up in surrender. 'Nothin' more. Honestly.' He backed away from her.

'The jury must ignore what Mr Wiggins said there at the end,' Charles Hudd ordered. 'It's not evidence.'

'The sonofabitch keeps doin' it!' she rasped. 'He asks his questions, an' then his last question turns out it ain't no question at all, just a load of hogwash he's sellin' to the jury!' She stamped her foot. 'Sonofabitch ...'

'Watch your language,' the judge said.

'Apologize. But it makes me so goddamn *mad*.'

Several of the jury applauded, until Charles glowered at them. Frankie was surprised and pleased. Aggression paid. She had friends after all. 'Call Mrs Killick,' she said. That made the crowd buzz.

Ma Killick had bought a new hat at Stackmesser's for the trial: red, with a green feather. She wore Jessica's best coat, since the girl didn't seem to need it. She swore to tell the truth and all, smiled at Doc Brightsides, frowned at the judge. 'Not one red cent,' she snapped.

Frankie knew it wouldn't be easy to get the old lady to say anything useful. The trick was to steer her gently and hope she didn't turn stubborn. 'Remember that morning you came to town to buy some nails, Mrs Killick,' she said. 'From Stackmesser.'

'Stackmesser is an idiot.'

'An' you owe me six bucks,' Stackmesser said.

'Nails, Mrs Killick. Remember buyin' nails?'

'Headache powder. Nails ain't no good for headaches.'

'Sure. So you bought headache powders – '

'Ain't true,' Stackmesser said. 'I sold out of them powders last month.'

'Your chance will come, Mr Stackmesser,' Charles Hudd said. 'Until then, be silent.'

'After you bought supplies,' Frankie said patiently, 'you came to see me in the back room at Maggie's tavern. Remember?'

'I don't patronize saloons. Booze is the invention of the devil.'

Flub Phillips shoved his way out of the crowd. 'Where's the devil?' he demanded. 'Show me Beelzebub! Gimme my gun!'

'Someone get that buffoon out of here,' Charles Hudd said. The pedlar took Flub's arm and led him away. 'Ain't far off,' Flub said. 'We'll catch the rascal soon.' The pedlar had to hurry to keep pace with him.

'Try again, Mrs Killick,' Frankie said. 'Maggie's back room. You an' me, talkin'. Remember now?'

'What did I say?' Ma Killick asked.

'That's what I want you to tell me.'

'I don't repeat gossip.' She dismissed the deputy and turned to the jury. 'Us Killicks got more blue blood'n you-all tied together. Wilderness Road goes through the Cumberland Gap, an' us Killicks took the Wilderness Road.'

'Your honour,' Jimmy-Sam said. 'Please.'

'I'll give you one more chance here,' Charles Hudd told the deputy.

'Mrs Killick,' she said. 'You spoke to me about Dan. You remember that, don't you?'

Ma Killick seemed to shrink. It was a sign that she was thinking. Devereux nudged his brother. 'Here comes trouble,' he whispered.

'Daniel?' the old lady said. 'You want to know about Daniel?' Frankie nodded. 'Ain't no secret,' she said. 'Shadrach, Meshach and Abednego, ye servants of the most high God, come forth and come hither. Daniel, three, twenty-six. You want the writin' on the wall? Daniel, five, twenty-five. Mene, Mene, Tekel, Upharsin. I got more – ' Nobody heard more. A wall of laughter fell on her. She was shocked and bewildered: you didn't laugh at the Bible. She looked around for help and saw her sons laughing, falling about as if drunk. *God is not mocked. Galatians, six, seven.* She frowned but they would not stop. Meanwhile Charles Hudd was hammering the table as if he was trying to break it.

When the noise died down, he said, 'Next witness, I think.'

'We don't allow no strangers on our land,' Ma Killick said clearly. 'Dan had every right.' That killed off any lingering chuckles. Frankie had turned away. Now she went back.

'Crazy old bitch,' Dan said under his breath. 'Die, for Chrissake, die.'

'Dan had every right to do what?' Frankie asked her.

'Bible says forgive us our trespassers, an' so we do, but we gun 'em down first, in case they argue.'

'Mrs Killick. Did your son Dan shoot a man?'

'That's what he said an' I believe him. Dan always told truth.'

'Did you see it happen?'

The intense silence was beginning to bother Ma Killick. 'I might have,' she said. Her head was tired.

'How about your other son, Devereux? Did he kill the Hudd boy? Lewis?'

'Might have. We don't allow no strangers on our land.' By now she was mumbling. 'Stranger killed their father Joseph. They got every right.'

Frankie looked at the slumped, trembling figure, with the nodding green feather. 'That's all,' she said.

Jimmy-Sam was in no hurry. He stood beside Ma Killick, and waited for her to look up.

'Mrs Killick,' he said, and gestured softly at their surroundings, 'what's going on here? Why have all these people gathered together?' He smiled.

'Barn dance?' she said. Nobody laughed. 'Barn dance,' she said confidently.

'Thank you.' He helped her up.

Frankie looked at what was left. No point in calling Hoke Cleghorn: all he could say was Reuben came into the Killick kitchen with the shirt, which wasn't in doubt, and being Hoke, he'd probably confuse things. Stanton? He'd lie, and his missing arm would remind the jury of the feud with the Hudds: another piece of confusion. 'I got no more witnesses,' she said.

'Your turn,' Charles Hudd said.

'Dan Killick,' Jimmy-Sam said at once.

'We've already heard from him.'

'There's more to hear, your honour.'

'Oh ... very well.'

Jimmy-Sam asked a lot of questions. He took Dan through the day the Hudd boy went missing. Dan's answers were brief. Had he seen the boy? Didn't know. Had he seen *a* boy? Yes. Recognize him? No. Could have come from anywhere? Sure. Pay him much attention? No. Why not? Too busy. Work to do. And afterwards, when he went to town? Couldn't remember. Why not? Drunk. Next day, did he expect anyone to come looking for the boy? No. Why not? Didn't know he was lost. See the major go to the barn? No. Why not? Barn was out of sight. Hear the shot? Yes. Run to the barn? No. Why not? Didn't know that was where the shot came from. Why not? Echoes kind of bounce around there. You did run? Yes. And search? Yes. What did you find? Major's body, by the barn door. Face up or face down? Face up. Shot in the chest.

Jimmy-Sam took a little stroll. 'Did you shoot him, Dan?'

'No. I liked the man.'

'Someone killed him. An' that someone was waitin' inside the barn. I mean, ain't that how it looks? From where you found the body?'

'Yeah. Seems that way.'

'But no-one knew the major was even *goin'* to that barn. How could someone ambush – '

'He's doin' it again,' Frankie said.

'Cut it out, Mr Wiggins,' Charles Hudd said.

'He's yours,' Jimmy-Sam said.

'We all heard it,' Frankie said briskly. 'You told your ma you killed a man. We heard her say it, clear as daylight. I heard it first, cus she came to Maggie's back room, nobody asked her to, an' she said it then, an' she came here an' said it again today, for all to hear. Which one of you is lyin'?'

Dan was silent. He sat still, shoulders slumped, just like his mother.

'Afraid to speak in case you get caught lyin' again?' Frankie said. She found she enjoyed the taste of blood.

'Ain't no liar,' Dan mumbled.

'An' this ain't no barn dance.' The jury smiled. They liked the taste too. 'Finished.' Dan got down.

'I call Deputy Nickel,' Jimmy-Sam said.

She turned so fast that she stumbled and he grabbed her arm. The jury bounced on their seats. This was getting better and better.

'Explain yourself, Mr Wiggins,' the judge said.

'Crucial evidence, your honour.'

'And who's to cross-examine?'

'Let the jury do it, if they want,' Frankie said. 'I got nothin' to hide.' Charles shrugged. This whole trial was slipping through his fingers like fine sand.

The deputy got sworn. 'That time Reuben found the shirt,' Jimmy-Sam said, 'you sent for Mrs Killick's daughter. Jessica Killick. Why do that?'

'Find out if she knew a thing about the boy.'

'And did she?'

'Wait a minute,' the judge said. 'You want to know what the daughter said, ask her. Get it first-hand.'

'Daughter can't be found.' Charles stared in despair: young folk were disappearing right and left. 'We have complete faith in the witness's memory, your honour ... Now: what did Jessica tell you?'

'Three things,' Frankie said. The interruption had given her time to prepare her answer. 'First, she was sick. Said she was sick. Certainly looked sick. Next, said she remembered seein' a nigger with a forty-four an' a white boy runnin' near the barn. Third – '

'Nigger, huh? And did you search for – '

'Slow down, Mr Wiggins,' the judge said. 'We haven't heard the third thing.'

'Third, she had a fever,' Frankie said. 'A big hot burnin' fever, real bad, she said. Couldn't hardly see straight.'

'Like Flub got,' Ryan Kidder said at once.

'Flub got the conniption fits,' Hoke said.

'Enough!' the judge shouted.

'A *slight* fever,' Jimmy-Sam said. 'Isn't that what she said she had?'

'You were there,' Frankie said, careless now; she couldn't win, but she'd lose in style. 'Jessica was seein' double. Saw two of *you*, which didn't leave much room for the rest.'

'And enough of that, too,' Charles Hudd ordered.

'She said she saw a *nigger*, with a forty-four, near the *barn*, with a *white boy*,' Jimmy-Sam said, making the words boom. 'Is that right?'

'Jess was ramblin',' Reuben said. 'Fever-struck.'

'Them conniption fits hurt a small person worse'n a big,' Hoke said.

'That's a goddamn lie!' a woman shouted. The crowd turned to stare. Charles Hudd waved at Jimmy-Sam to continue, but half the jury were on their feet, gaping at the disturbance, which boiled out from the back of the barn to the front. It was Jessica Killick bouncing about like a fly in a thunderstorm. 'Ain't sick!' she shouted. 'Never had no fever! Never had no fits!'

'Madam!' Charles Hudd said, and gave up. She was beyond anyone's control.

'You sonofabitch horseshittin' bastards ...' She raged towards her brothers. 'Ain't bad enough you made me a liar! I gotta be crazy in the head too!' She strode to the jury, elbowing Jimmy-Sam aside, and climbed on the wagon. 'You see any conniption fits?' she demanded. Her face was inches from Hoke Cleghorn's; her spit was on his moustache. Ryan Kidder, next to him, leaned away as far as he could. 'You're so damn smart!' she told him. 'How many fingers I got here?' She thrust her hand at him.

'Uh ...' Ryan's eyes almost crossed. 'Five.'

'Wrong!' She made a fist and punched him in the face. He fell off the bench. 'Anybody else want to bad-mouth me?'

Frankie pulled her down from the wagon. 'You made your point, honey,' she said.

'Ten-minute recess,' the judge ordered.

He took Jimmy-Sam aside and asked him if there was any reason why Jessica Killick should not be his next witness. Jimmy-Sam suggested she was mentally confused. 'No,' Hudd said. 'She's mad. *I'm* confused. Let's get at the truth.'

Jimmy-Sam had only one question for Jessica. 'What can you tell the court about the killing of Major de Glanville?'

'Nothin'.'

The crowd sighed glumly. Things had been going so well.

Frankie asked: 'Where exactly were you, time of the shootin'?'

'In the house.'

'See the barn from the house?'

'No.'

Frankie rocked on her heels and tried to think of another question. Reuben Skinner muttered: 'I still reckon a nigger did it.' Frankie had her mouth open to say *I'm through here* when she suddenly remembered Devereux and Lewis. 'Rest of your family saw a boy on the farm. You see this boy?'

'Sure. We all did. Dev found him in the river, on a raft.'

'Huh. This boy have a name?'

'Said he was Lewis Hudd. Had some toes missin'. Ma wanted to chop his other foot, even him up.' The crowd gasped; some people hissed. 'She was just funnin', is all,' Jessica said, too late. Nobody believed her. Abruptly she ceased feeling mad at her brothers and started hating the crowd. 'Little bastard would've drowned without Dev,' she told them.

'What became of him?' Frankie asked.

'Did some chores, ate some grub. Then ... dunno.'

'I can put Devereux up here, if you want,' Jimmy-Sam said.

Frankie gave it five seconds' thought. 'He's like his brother,' she said. 'When he ain't drunk, he's blind. Let's move on.'

'No more witnesses.'

'You ready to say your piece, Mr Wiggins?' the judge said.

Jimmy-Sam did his talking as he strolled up and down, looking at each juryman in turn. 'Let's start with what we all agree on, both sides. The major got killed in the doorway of the barn. Shot by someone in the barn. And – '

'Wait there,' Elias Dunbar said. 'Might of bin shot somewheres else.' So far Elias had said nothing; this was his chance to score. 'Dragged to the barn, put by the door, to make us think ... See?'

'Would of left a bloody trail in the grass,' Frankie said. 'Weren't no trail.'

'Big buck nigger could've carried the body on his shoulder.'

'Forget the nigger, Mr Dunbar,' the judge said.

'Easy for you,' Reuben Skinner muttered. 'You ain't bin bush-whacked, like some.' Dunbar reached over and shook his hand.

'So we're agreed,' Jimmy-Sam said. 'The major got shot at the barn. Now, where was everyone when this terrible thing was done? Dan was fixin' a bust gate, so far away he couldn't even *see* the barn. No more could Devereux, mendin' fences, halfway to the river. Stanton was splittin' logs, back of the house. Jessica and her ma were inside the house. There wasn't a member of the whole Killick family could hit that barn with a rifle, an' we know it was a revolver killed the major, besides which, Dan here can't see further'n he can *throw* a forty-four, which I guess is ...' Jimmy-Sam turned in a slow circle, searching for some standard by which to measure Dan's throwing ability. 'Oh ... about three times the length of a good spit of tobacco.

If I was back home upstate I'd say four times the length, but I know, down here, you folk can spit good.'

'Mr Wiggins.'

'Movin' right along, your honour. What it comes down to, Dan Killick was nowhere near the shootin' an' nor was Dev, an' nobody's come forward to say different. That leaves the Hudd boy, Lewis. Where he's got to – well, on that I ain't any smarter than you. I just don't know. Wish I did. Maybe he was the tad Devereux saved from drownin', maybe he wasn't, we can't be sure. Why can't we be sure? Because nobody who *knew* Lewis saw him on the Killick farm. We can't even go by what the boy said. Ten-year-olds ain't like you an' me, they do strange an' peculiar things. This one tossed his shirt in the cellar. Why? We don't know. Crazy thing to do. Maybe it wasn't even Lewis, maybe Lewis swapped shirts with another boy, I used to do that when I was his age, swap clothes for a while: here, you wear my shirt, I'll wear your hat, it's fun, I be you, you be me. We don't know what happened with Lewis. Ain't no dead body, no evidence of murder, no witnesses. Nothin'. You know as well as me, young 'uns run away from home. I did. Ain't ashamed to say it, ran off an' joined a circus, got bit by a camel, ran home again. So … Let's face facts, this whole Lewis Hudd thing's a mystery. You can't convict a man because of a mystery, that ain't American justice. Justice demands proof, there ain't no proof, you can't convict *either* of these men, they're innocent.' Jimmy-Sam let his arms drop, in a gesture of helplessness. 'I can't think of anythin' else to say,' he said.

Everybody had a good cough and shuffle and stretch, and then settled down.

'You next,' the judge said to the deputy.

'For a man who can't think what to say, you sure found a lot of ways of sayin' it,' she told Jimmy-Sam. Several of the jury nodded. They had hoped for more attack, more cut and thrust.

'This whole thing is about the boy,' she said. 'It's got to be, cus nothin' else makes sense. Start at the beginning. Lewis Hudd, age ten, makes a raft, floats down the Cameron. We know cus Job Sims saw him go by. Dev Killick fishes him out of the water, takes him to the farm. Jessica Killick says the boy said he was Lewis. Got no reason to lie. Anyway, he's missin' some toes, an' we found his shirt in the cellar, so you can believe it: Dev had Lewis, all right. Then Lewis does chores, gets fed, vanishes. Nobody sees him after that day

473

– or that's what the Killicks claim. We know somethin' more. We know Dan comes to town an' gets drunk an' tries to sell the boy to his father for a thousand bucks that he claims is an old debt owed to his late brother George, 'cept *that* story turns out to be not true because the fact is George was stealin' off the Hudd place every chance he got. So that thousand bucks begins to look more like ransom money.'

Her legs ached. Her throat hurt. A vein in the side of her head was throbbing.

'Ransom money. Thousand bucks, Killicks want from the Hudds. So we got a crime right there: kidnapping an' extortion.'

'They didn't extort nothin',' Ryan Kidder pointed out.

'The crime's in the threat. Next: me an' the major ride out to the Killick place to search for the boy. Now, you heard Mrs Killick say they don't tolerate strangers on their land, trespassers. You heard her say they gun 'em down. Those were her words: gun 'em down. You heard her say Dan told her he shot a man. Ask yourself: why would anyone gun down the major? Well, what was the major doin'? He was lookin' for Lewis. The major found somethin' in that barn. Whoever shot the major had to be feelin' bad about Lewis, an' Lewis is the boy the Killicks kidnapped an' were tryin' to ransom for one thousand dollars. Figure it out for yourself. A boy disappears an' a man gets shot to death, both in a couple of days, both on the Killick farm, the place where they like gunnin' strangers down. If these two brothers didn't do it, then who in hell did? Apologize for the profanity, your honour. I feel strongly.'

'After what we've heard,' Charles Hudd said, 'your peccadillo is a mere bagatelle!' Maybe Wiggins understood that, nobody else did. Hudd didn't care. 'That just leaves my summing-up. First let me tell the jury what to ignore. This trial is not about who does or does not owe money to whom. Nor is it about who did or did not steal property from whom. So forget all that. Just think of the charges, which are murder and kidnapping, and think of the evidence you heard in here. Not the gossip and rumour you may have heard outside. Forget all that, too. Just think over what each side has *proved* happened. Hard facts. Nothing else. Some pretty fancy kite-flying has gone on in this court, people suggesting maybe this or that or the other thing might have happened. Forget it. Kite-flying isn't proof. Next, and this is important, so listen hard: Mr Wiggins doesn't have to prove these men innocent. It's the deputy's job to prove them guilty.'

He paused to let that sink in. The jury looked at him as if he were talking Choctaw.

'Murder and kidnapping, that's about as serious as we can get. If you say guilty, you'd better be sure. How sure is that? The law says: "beyond a reasonable doubt". What does "reasonable" mean? That's for you to decide. You got a tough job. These Killick brothers may be friends of yours, but the dead man had friends here too. Forget friendship. Forget vengeance. Forget trying to be fair.' Hudd felt the trickle of sweat down his ribs, the sting of sweat in his eyes. *Never give up; never give in* ... 'Study what each side offered as proof, decide what it's worth, and do your duty, even if it hurts. Now, everybody else, including me, is going to get up and go out and leave you in here. Anything you want to ask?'

'Can we send down to Maggie's for a pitcher of beer?' Reuben Skinner asked.

'Certainly not.' He banged the table once with the hammer and was about to stand when he saw Brightsides pointing at the doorway. Three figures stood, silhouetted against the sunlight. 'What hath God wrought?' Hudd asked weakly.

'Sorry we're late,' JoBeth said. 'Damn mule got spooked by a snake an' ran off. This the boy you're lookin' for?' Between her and Lonzo stood Lewis.

Ruth Hudd tried to shriek but she only managed a trembling gasp. She rushed towards her son and either tripped or swooned, or maybe swooned and tripped as she fell. Lewis made no move. His face, as he watched people help his mother, was as blank as a bored cat's.

Charles Hudd had been saving all his strength for his summing-up. Now he felt drained, useless. 'What does this mean?' he asked.

'Means I ain't guilty of nothin', for a start,' Devereux said. 'Can I go?'

'No. Remain. You are not acquitted until I say so.' Charles Hudd's brain was struggling to catch up with events. 'First of all ... First of all I want an explanation from the boy himself.'

'He ain't said a word to us,' JoBeth told Hudd, 'so don't get your hopes up.'

Lewis was brought forward and made to stand on a chair. He had been scrubbed and combed and put into clean cotton clothes. He appeared swarthy; slightly Indian. The judge stepped down and looked at his face and his right foot. 'This is Lewis Hudd,' he

475

informed the jury. 'Let's hear it, Lewis. Where've you been? What's been happening? What've you been up to?'

That last question was a mistake. Lewis knew he was in trouble. First he went rafting, without permission. Then he got trapped by Devereux Killick, who was over there now, squinting sideways at him. That day became a nightmare and the night was worse. Stole food, stole a gun, ran away, woke up, shot a man, ran away again. Lewis had done nothing but sin, sin, sin. If he confessed they would punish him, painfully, and God knew he was already going to burn in hell for all eternity when he died, so he kept silence now. Lewis would never tell Mr Charles Hudd what he'd been up to. He was sinful, but he wasn't stupid.

The judge tried a great variety of questions. Lewis stood with his hands locked behind him, his knees slightly bent, his toes turned in, his shoulders drooping so the suspenders kept threatening to slide off, his expression as grave as a rabbit's, and he made no sound. The judge began to wonder if the boy had lost his wits, or his hearing, or his voice. All three, maybe. He felt defeated. 'You want to try?' he said to the deputy. She shook her head. He looked at Jimmy-Sam. 'I'm just happy the tad's back in the arms of his lovin' family,' Jimmy-Sam said. 'I never thought there was any case to answer, an' this proves it.'

'It's still a matter for the jury. Let's clear this place so they can get to work.'

JOKERS AND JACKASSES

Frankie and Maggie walked down to the tavern for coffee. James L. Boston joined them. 'That horse of yours was too old,' he said. 'I traded it for a stronger animal.'

'Pity you couldn't trade me too. I feel like my granma looked when she was three days dead.'

'You were doing well in there, until the boy showed up. Might even have finished second. Now you won't make that. Trial's over.'

'Jeez, I'm glad I never married you,' Maggie said.

'Well, that's what us Pinkerton men are for,' Boston said affably. 'To bring gladness into people's lives.' He touched his hat and turned away.

'Slick bastard,' Maggie said. 'You goin' to Texas with him?'

'Looks like. He ain't givin' up, an' I'm sick of dodgin'.'

Boston found Doc Brightsides. 'No offence meant,' he said, 'but why are you living here?'

'It's not so bad.'

'Not so good, either. You've travelled, same as I have. America's full of nowhere towns like this. I meet these people all the time. 'Ain't stayin' here,' they say. 'Just catchin' our breath. Soon's we get two dollars to rub together, we're off to find Happy Valley.' Twenty years later they're wearin' the same overalls and they still haven't mended that hole in the fence.'

'Too much going on,' Brightsides explained. 'Busy, busy, busy.'

'What d'you do for entertainment?' Boston asked.

'Well, there's fornication. And whenever a thing goes wrong, folks go up and massacre the niggers on the Ridge.'

~

477

Lewis had been reclaimed by his family. The only time he opened his mouth was to eat cold fried chicken.

Jimmy-Sam was with the Killick brothers. 'You never asked about the forty-four I lost,' Dan said. 'You forget?'

'Do not judge me by the standards of Rock Springs. If nobody mentions your gun, the jury cannot connect you with it. Understand?'

'We gonna get off?' Dev asked.

'I never knew a jury that didn't argue,' Jimmy-Sam said. His cousins deserved to suffer a little.

Jessica saw JoBeth sitting on a mossy outcrop of rock, Lonzo beside her, and she went to them. 'You livin' up there now?' she said.

'Yeah. No decent white family wants me.'

'Ain't gonna be too popular myself, neither. Not after what I said in that barn.' JoBeth looked interested. 'Dan an' Dev was makin' out I had fever so bad it gave me the fits. I told 'em they were sonofabitch horseshittin' bastard liars.'

'Hell, everyone knows that,' Lonzo said.

'Sorry I missed it,' JoBeth said.

'Who whomped you?' Jessica asked.

'Dan. He gets mean when he ain't had his breakfast coffee. He would've whomped you, only you wasn't there. Where you goin' now? Back home?'

'So's Dan can whomp me? Hell, no.'

'Want to live on the Ridge?' Lonzo offered. 'We don't hardly ever whomp our womenfolk.'

'There's another way,' JoBeth said. 'Bein' married ain't so bad, I bin married an' I'd do it again, an' don't get that sour-pickle look on your face, Jess. You go on livin' with Dan an' Dev an' Stan, you'll turn into the biggest sour pickle this side the Rockies. Think on that. You reckon any man gonna marry a sour pickle, just to pleasure himself?'

'I sure wouldn't marry no sour pickle,' Lonzo said.

'Hey, I aim to get married,' Jessica said. 'Real soon.'

'Who to? Andy Cleghorn? Billy Dunbar? Wear flour-sack dresses the rest of your life? Barefoot an' always got a baby at the breast? That your idea of married bliss? Don't say nothin', Jess. Don't even *think*. Go to Doc Brightsides there. He's got somethin' to tell you. Go!' She shoved her sister.

When Jessica went away, Charles Hudd approached.

He had left the barn feeling greatly relieved, but it had been the relief of knowing that an ordeal was over. Things had gone badly: people told him so. 'You made a horse's ass of that,' Ernie Hudd said. Marcus was more scathing: 'Call that justice? You just let them bastards escape scot-free, is what you just done.' Ruth was still in tears. 'See them laughin'?' she said. 'See them laughin'?' Charles walked away and met Ansel Mungers. 'I never voted for you, Hudd,' he said. 'Smartest thing I never did.' There were other comments from other observers. One woman just looked at him, shook her head, and spat a stream of tobacco juice at his shadow. In the end he walked away from them all, leaned against a tree, cracked his knuckles one by one.

The attacks were unfair. He hadn't let the bastards escape. It wasn't up to him. The jury decided. Sure, the trial had opened badly but later he'd got a grip of it. Wasted. All wasted. That was the real kick in the stomach. For two days he had struggled to lead this band of brainless, thankless, foul-mouthed fools through a swamp of deception and dishonesty, and he had succeeded, and it was all for nothing. He had been made to look a fool. He saw JoBeth and Lonzo sitting together, and he was striding towards them before he knew he had made the decision.

'You did that deliberately,' he accused her. His fierceness made her recoil. 'I sweated blood in that courtroom. Two days, plowing a furrow for justice while all around me, jokers and jackasses were trampling it down! Finally, my last ounce of strength ... ' He felt tears trickling down his face. 'You just *wander* in and wait while I say my last word so you can pull the whole creation down around my ears. You did that to make me look a fool. You and your n-n-nigger f-f-f ...' The stammer infuriated him; he slapped his head to shake the word loose. 'Friend!'

'You got it wrong,' she said.

'You had that boy Lewis hid. You were waiting. Big joke.'

'Ain't no joke,' Lonzo said, thoroughly baffled.

'Ain't no joke *now*,' Charles sneered. 'I get the last laugh. You wait. You gonna suffer, boy. And you, Mrs ... I don't even know your damn name. I *never* knew your name.' He walked away.

'You wanted us to keep the kid on the Ridge?' JoBeth called. 'So you could hang my brothers?' Charles made no reply. He knew what he knew.

Before anyone could speak, Hoke Cleghorn said he reckoned he was elected foreman of the jury on account of his rank of captain awarded by Kit Carson. Nobody argued. Nobody cared. He said he aimed to move along right smartly by asking each man in turn what his verdict was. That was when Stackmesser noticed they were only eight. The four out-of-town jurors had slipped away with the crowd. 'Two of them fellers was real hungry,' Hutton said. 'Stomachs rumblin' like moose callin' to each other.'

'We don't need 'em,' Sims said.

'Wait a damn minute,' Hoke said. 'Eight-man jury? I never heard of – '

'Job's right,' Ryan Kidder said. 'They ain't needed, an' I'll tell you why. Them fellers gave me their votes. You vote for us, Ryan, they said. You know how we feel.'

'Now wait just another goddamn minute,' Hoke said. 'That don't sound constitutional to me.'

'Sure it is.' But Ryan saw a ring of suspicious looks. 'What the lawyers call proxy. Votin' by proxy. It's in the Constitution. Ask Jimmy-Sam.'

'Proxy,' Hoke said doubtfully.

'We ask Jimmy-Sam, we got to ask the deputy too,' Reuben argued. 'That's only fair.'

'Proxy,' Hoke said. 'That ain't an American word, is it?'

The debate widened and deepened. After ten minutes Stackmesser lost patience. 'Jesus Christ!' he said. 'Let's settle this damn thing one way or the other. Let's vote on it.'

'Hey!' Hoke said. 'I'm foreman. I decide what we vote on.'

'Then decide, for Chrissake.'

'I surely will decide, you give me just one second.' They glared at each other. 'My decision is: we vote on it.'

'Good. Now, who's in favour of this damnfool proxy thing?'

'I ain't,' Elias Dunbar said.

'I'm against,' Sims said.

'How many votes have I got?' Ryan demanded.

'One,' Hoke said.

'That ain't democratic. What we're decidin' is whether I got the right to use them four proxy votes when we vote on a verdict. Ain't that so?' Hoke nodded, glumly. 'Ain't nobody took them proxy votes away from me yet,' Ryan said. 'I got a right to use 'em, *plus* my own personal vote, makes five. There's only eight of us here, so I got the majority. Proxy wins.'

The silence was dense with resentment.

'That ain't right,' Hoke said. 'I mean, that don't sound democratic. Do it?'

'Look, there's a simple way around this,' Stackmesser said. 'Question is: can Ryan use his stinkin' proxy votes when we decide whether or not we're gonna let him ...' He sucked in a deep breath. '... let him use his same stinkin' proxy votes when we get down to hard business here, if we ever do. Agreed? Are Ryan's proxy votes gonna count when we decide if the fuckin' things are worth countin'?'

'You lost me in the middle,' Hoke said.

'It's simple!' Stackmesser cried. 'Are they gonna count or ain't they gonna count? Put it to the vote! Jesus! That's fair, ain't it?'

'It's only fair,' Ryan said, 'if I can use my proxy votes.' Sims threw his hat at him. 'I want my democratic rights, is all,' Ryan said. 'They're in the Constitution. Look it up, you don't believe me.'

~

'How long they gonna be in there? I need a drink. Got any money? Jesus ... I'm gonna strangle Ma when all this is over. Look at Chuck Hudd prowlin' about. He's a mean bastard, ain't he?'

'Shut up, Dev,' Dan said. 'Sit down.'

'I been thinkin'. That jury got to be disagreein' over something'. That's what's usin' up the time. Huh?'

Dan yawned.

'Jimmy-Sam said there weren't no case! So what the blue blazes is goin' on in there?'

'Playin' poker, maybe.'

'Hudd ought to go in, speed 'em up. Jeez, I need a big drink. They got to be arguin', right? Shit. What they arguin' *about*?'

'Does a flush beat a straight.' Dan settled back on his elbows.

'Way I see it, they're arguin', so that's good for us. Means some of the jury ain't buyin' what that sonabitch deputy was peddlin'. See what I mean?'

Dan squirted tobacco juice at a passing butterfly and made it swerve.

'Then again … maybe it ain't good. Can't be arguin' unless the others think different. Think the deputy's right. Jeez … How much longer?'

'They're waitin' for you to foul your britches,' Dan said. 'Shouldn't be long now.'

~

Hoke Cleghorn finally sent out for a dictionary, couldn't find *proxy* in it anywhere, told Ryan Kidder to go to hell. 'Ain't nothin' in here between *prolapse* an' *prussic acid*,' Hoke said. It was a medical dictionary, the only dictionary in Rock Springs, owned by Doc Brightsides, but Ryan didn't know that. He gave up. 'Let's get on,' Hoke said. 'I'm hungry.'

'I guess we can't nail Devereux for murderin' the boy,' Job Sims said. 'I keep lookin' at it every which way, but …'

'Snotty bastard,' Elias Dunbar said. 'Needs a fist in his face.'

'How about the kidnappin'?' Hoke asked. 'Anyone believe Dev did that?'

'Job saw the boy go by on a raft,' Hutton said. 'Looks to me like he went willing.'

'There is *evil* in Dev Killick,' Ryan said. 'We ought to do somethin' to stamp it out.'

'Been sniffin' around your Amie, ain't he?' Reuben said.

'Look,' Stackmesser said. 'We ain't here to stop people havin' a roll in the hay.'

'Amie is a pure an' innocent girl,' Ryan said with heat. 'I trust her absolutely. *He's* the nigger in the woodpile.'

'You ask me, the niggers must of done it,' Reuben said. 'One of them black bushwhackers came down off the Ridge, the major catched him doin' somethin' bad, an' … *boom*.'

'Doin' what bad?' Hutton asked.

'I can't watch her all the time,' Ryan said.

'Personally, I agree,' Hoke told Reuben. 'See a halfbreed, you see trouble. But, unfortunately, no nigger been charged here.'

'Should of bin.'

'I ever find Dev Killick shootin' his evil seed into my Amie, I'll kill him.'

'Dan's a born murderer,' Dunbar said. 'You noticed? He got eyes like old pennies.'

'Don't mean nothin'. That's bad hooch done that,' Sims said. 'Look at Reub there. He got eyes like belly-buttons. Ain't killed no-one, though.'

'Just wait,' Reuben said, offended. 'Next bushwhacker I see, shoot him dead.'

'Maybe Dan thought he was bein' bushwhacked,' Hutton suggested. 'Maybe the major came up behind him, an' ...'

'Major wouldn't bushwhack nobody,' Ryan said scornfully.

'I said Dan maybe *thought*.'

'Killicks ain't had a thought worth a damn in twenty years,' Stackmesser said.

'Them Hudds was pretty stupid too,' Hutton said. 'Took ten of 'em to shoot one of Killick's cows, didn't it? That ain't clever.'

'Ain't evidence, neither,' Hoke said. 'Don't prove nothin'.'

'I bin thinkin',' Elias Dunbar said. 'Everyone got all het up about how them Hudds lost a ten-year-old boy, only they didn't, an' they don't even *belong* these parts, I mean, Georgia for Chrissake, my pa-in-law was from Georgia, miserable cheatin' sonofabitch – '

'Hey!' Hoke shouted. Hunger pangs were biting him.

'What I mean is ... We let that uppity nigger badmouth George Killick when we all knew George was a genuine hero died for the South. Are we gonna hang his brother Dan, who also fought against the North, gallant officer an' gentleman, all on the say-so of a goddamn thievin' darky an' a buncha strangers don't even like us ...?' He saw Hoke blinking with boredom. 'If we find Dan guilty,' Elias said, 'ain't we sayin' George's sacrifice was all for nothin'?'

They looked at him. It had been a long speech, and some were not sure it was ended. 'Well, ain't we?' Elias said. Now they looked at each other.

'Don't that kinda depend upon certain things?' Job said.

'What things?' Elias asked.

'Shit, I don't know. Things in general. This was your dumb idea. Don't heap it on me.' Job turned his back on him. Elias gave the finger to his back. Reuben laughed. Job turned again. 'Who in hell you laughin' at?' he demanded.

'Free country,' Reuben said. 'I got a right to laugh.'

'I got a right to break your face.'

'No, you ain't,' Ryan said.

'We ain't afraid of you,' Hutton said. He was the smallest man there. 'Ha ha. Hear that? Hee hee.' Job kicked over a stool. 'Ho ho,' Hutton said.

'Now listen here,' Hoke said loudly. 'We talked enough. I want to hear a decision. Do we hang these Killicks or let 'em go? Speak up.'

'Hang 'em!' Job snapped.

'Damn right,' Stackmesser said.

'Wrong,' Elias said, and enjoyed saying it. 'Let 'em go.' Ryan and Reuben and Hutton said the same.

That left Hoke and a man called Dunkerley, thin, bald, poor, gloomy, who had so far spoken hardly a word. 'Maybe they done it. I dunno,' Dunkerley said. 'But them Killicks is all animals. They'll kill some poor bastard soon, sure as fate. Might as well hang 'em now.'

'That's four to three says innocent,' Hoke said. 'Ma Killick told us Dan said he done it, an' I believe her. Ain't enough respect for old folk nowadays. I say guilty.'

'Hung jury,' Ryan said. 'I got a pack of cards. You want to cut for it?'

～

Jessica came back and sat beside JoBeth but she didn't look at her. She looked at Jimmy-Sam Wiggins, who was strolling about, touching his hat, flattering and joking and befriending wherever he went. He was good at it.

'Well, now you know,' JoBeth said. 'Kinda makes a difference, don't it?'

'Hard to credit. Look at him, such a big feller, enjoyin' his life ... You don't suppose Doc Brightsides could be wrong? Forget I asked that. He wouldn't say unless he knew for sure ... Damn.'

'You gonna do it?'

'Dunno. I might.'

'What you got to lose? A year? Two at most.'

'Couple years livin' in style. I guess that couldn't hurt too much.' Jessica leaned against her sister. 'Can't work up no enthusiasm for the bed part, though.'

'Twenty minutes every month. Do it in the dark. Besides ... There's more to be wed than four legs in a bed.'

'I'll be a widow before I'm twenty-one.'

'Rich widow. Then you can marry some pretty boy with a pecker you can hang your bonnet on. Last piece of advice: when you an' Jimmy-Sam do your couplin', make sure you're on top an' he's underneath.'

'Ain't what ma taught.'

'Ma never had to crawl out from under a feller died of a heart attack. Takes muscle.' JoBeth kissed her on the forehead. 'You ain't as strong as I was, an' I wished I had a crowbar.'

'She ain't the romantic sort, is she?' Jessica said to Lonzo.

'Dunno,' Lonzo said. 'Us niggers don't know nothin' about that stuff. Got a crowbar you can lend the borrow of, though.'

~

Hoke sent word to the judge that the jury was ready.

It took ten minutes to get everyone back inside and settled. Milking was long since finished, the stock fed, chores done. The crowd was bigger than ever, and they felt comfortable in this setting: they knew the actors, they understood the plot; all that was left was to discover how it all came out. The smell of chewing tobacco sweetened the air like incense.

Charles Hudd hammered for silence and got it at once.

'I am informed that the jury has reached its verdicts,' he said.

Hoke stood. 'That's correct, your honour.'

'The accused men should stand.' They got to their feet. Dan had his hands in his pockets. Devereux's eyes were shut. 'We'll start with Devereux Killick,' Charles said. 'The charge is kidnapping Lewis Hudd and murder. What do you say?'

'Well, in the end, we decided to let him off on both,' Hoke said. Devereux's eyes popped open, wide and bright as a child's. *Aaaaaaah*, went the crowd, merely letting their breath out.

'You find him not guilty.'

'Yup. Dev's got the manners of a skunk, an' we reckon he was probly mixed up in somethin' crooked – '

Charles hammered hard. 'I don't want to hear it.' The crowd muttered: they did want to. He hammered again. 'Next charge! Dan Killick. Accused of murdering Major de Glanville. What do you say?'

'Well, this one wasn't so easy. Some of us – '

'Never mind that. Just state your verdict.'

Hoke got disgruntled. 'If you want to know who shot the major, if that *interests* you at all, or these good folk – ' He saw Charles reach for his hammer. 'Our verdict is, one them niggers done it.' He stared defiantly while Charles restored silence. 'Came down off the Ridge an' massacred the poor man!' Hoke declared.

'Only Dan Killick is charged with that crime,' Charles told him. 'Now: what is your verdict?'

'Them Killicks got terrible tempers, everyone knows – '

The hammer came into violent action. 'Mr Cleghorn! For the last time!'

Ryan Kidder said, 'Not guilty.' Hoke shook with fury. 'Not guilty!' he said. 'We found the bastard not guilty! Hope you're satisfied!'

'This trial's over,' Charles announced. 'Prisoners are free to go.' Nobody but Brightsides heard him: the crowd was surging out. He leaned back, looked at the barn roof, relaxed fully for the first time in a week. He had got through his first trial and no harm done. All it took was calm and honesty and determination. When he straightened up, Jimmy-Sam was standing, amiably waiting. 'I guess you counted the jury,' Jimmy-Sam said.

'Why should I do that?'

'Only eight in the jury. Must of lost four somewhere along the way.'

'You mean that's … not enough. It's …'

'Illegal, yeah. Or, look at it another way, two-thirds legal. Plenty enough for Rock Springs, wouldn't you say?' He fanned his face with his hat. Charles was silent. 'There is no victory,' Jimmy-Sam said. 'It's not like war. Not that there is any victory in war, either.'

~

Maggie's tavern soon filled up. The male Hudds were at one end, the male Killicks at the other. In between was a roaring, bumping, arguing, joking mob of drinkers. The eight jurymen were there, telling the inside stories of their verdicts in exchange for booze. Frankie Nickel was there, saying her goodbyes. James L. Boston was alongside her, nudging, interrupting the well-wishers, impatient to start the journey. Flub Phillips, a longtime enemy of alcohol, was searching restlessly for someone, he couldn't remember who, but in the confusion he got given a glass of beer and he drank it fast and found it refreshing. 'Hey!' he said. 'This ain't the devil's brew, is it?' Nobody answered. Flub was worried. Gaunt as an old greyhound, he hustled from group to group, borrowing drinks, tasting, testing. Nobody minded. It was only old Flub.

Lonzo was not in the tavern. Lonzo sat on the sidewalk and watched the flies fighting over the horsedung and waited for JoBeth to come out.

'Texas,' JoBeth said. 'Full of goddamn Texans.' She was drinking bourbon; Frankie, beer; Boston, coffee. 'Hurry it up,' he said.

'I'll say one thing for Texans,' JoBeth remarked. 'Ain't fussy where they live.'

The pedlar, drunk already, found that amusing, and went off to tell it to anyone who would listen.

'You ain't too fussy, neither,' Frankie said.

'Got somethin' against livin' with niggers?'

'Damn right. Ain't natural.'

'Well, charity never was your long suit.'

'Drink up,' Boston said.

'Jesus,' Frankie said. 'You gonna be like this for the next thousand miles?' She caught sight of the pedlar's happy face, and smiled back. Of all the citizens of Rock Springs, she would miss him the most. He had no respect for anyone, least of all himself. That was refreshing.

The pedlar allowed the crowd to jostle him wherever it pleased. This kept his conversations brief and interesting. Now he found himself facing Curtis Hudd. 'Just heard a joke about Texas,' he said. Curtis grunted encouragement. 'Damn, I forgot already,' the pedlar said, and he cackled so loudly that Curtis was embarrassed. 'Shut your damn noise,' he said. 'Hey: who's that woman talkin' to the deputy?' He knew who it was.

'That's Miss JoBeth Killick,' the pedlar said. 'Your daddy should of married her, only ... ' But then the crowd swirled and plucked him away.

Curtis felt bombarded by emotions. First, he was thunderously in love with JoBeth; had been ever since he saw her walk into Maggie's barn with young Lewis, prettiest thing in Kentucky, only woman he could ever marry, no contest. Then he had learned she was a Killick;

even worse, a nigger-lover, living on the Ridge: that astounded him. Now he was told she might have married his stepfather. For a moment, Curtis dreamed of winning the woman whom Charles Hudd had lost, and the raw power of love thumped his temples until they hurt. The moment passed. He couldn't have her, and it was her fault. He hated her. She had cheated him. Someone must pay.

At the other end of the bar, Dan Killick too had strong views on women. 'See, you gotta shout at 'em,' he told Devereux. 'They got picayune brains, takes twice as long for a woman to see sense than a man, scientific fact, ask Doc Brightsides.' He took a long sip of whiskey and washed it down with beer. 'Jessica finally got my message.'

'JoBeth sure didn't.'

Dan turned to Stanton and smiled. 'Hear that? Dev never had no patience, did he?'

'Hair-trigger pecker,' Stanton said.

'Only thing he ever could hit was the inside his long johns.'

'This Ridge thing, that's only female foolishness,' Stanton said.

'JoBeth be back in a week,' Dan said, 'bakin' an' cleanin' like Nature intended.'

'She better.' Dev was chewing his thumb. 'Ma can't cook worth a damn.'

'That trial shook you up, didn't it?' Stanton said. 'Never saw a man act so guilty. Hey! You ain't done nothin' to stain the family honour, have you, Dev?'

'Piss in your hat.'

'Talkin' of clothin',' Dan said. 'I never could figure out why you made the Hudd boy take his shirt off.'

Devereux was so offended that he could not speak. His silence did him no good. 'Maybe that's why little Lewis never said nothin',' Stanton suggested. 'Dev gave him coupla dollars keep his mouth shut.' Devereux turned and forced his way through the crowd. Laughter followed. He stumbled and kicked himself on the ankle and welcomed the pain. Pain was what he needed. Anybody's pain.

Ryan Kidder was annoying James L. Boston with the length of his goodbye. 'See, if you stayed,' he told Frankie, 'you could of hung a nigger.' Drink had made him hugely generous. 'Me an' Hoke, we'd guarantee you the verdict.' He shook her hand, then kissed it. 'Best damn lady deputy this town ever had,' he told Boston. 'You got no right …' He shook his head.

'Speed it up,' Boston said.

'Got to say goodbye to Maggie,' Frankie told him.

Maggie was behind the bar, pumping beer, pouring whiskey, taking money, dripping sweat. She said, 'You comin' back from Texas one day?'

'No.'

'Gonna live in Desolation?'

'Who the hell knows?' Frankie sounded breezy. She felt breezy. 'Maybe this Pinkerton dummy's done me a favour, Mag. First time in my life I got no plans. Nobody to fret over. I feel free.'

'Don't look free.' A noisy disturbance made Maggie reach across, grab Flub Phillips by the armpits, drag him over the bar, drop him, put a foot on him. 'Keeps stealin' drinks,' she explained. 'You an' me, we been good friends.'

'Yes. An' that's more'n some folk get in their whole lives.'

'Ain't complainin'.' They shook hands.

Devereux went out behind the tavern to empty his bladder. Curtis saw him go, followed and stood beside him. 'Sister of yours is shackin' up with that half-breed, huh?'

'Want a fight? I'll fight you.'

'I never hit a man with his thing in his hand.'

'Or without. Shootin' cows is more your style.'

'I'll fight you when I got time. Flatten you, too. Right now I'm here to say, JoBeth Killick is a disgrace to this Christian community.'

'That's family business.' Devereux wished his bladder would quit. He must have drunk a gallon of beer.

'Klan business, too. You heard of the Ku Klux Klan? We do good things to bad people.'

'You touch JoBeth, I'll kill you.'

'Keep her off the Ridge, or we might just kill the both of you.' He watched Dev finish. 'Everyone said you were full of piss, and by God they were right.' He walked away before Dev could think of an answer.

～

Frankie said goodbye to little Arnie Phillips and then it was time to go. Half the drinkers followed her and the Pinkerton man into the street. Maggie and Brightsides and JoBeth came out too.

Frankie got onto her horse and looked around. 'Ain't much,' she said, 'but I'll miss it.'

'Hadn't been for me, you'd never of come here,' JoBeth said.

'Hadn't been for you, I wouldn't be leavin'.'

'That's true. Life is peculiar, ain't it?'

Boston was ready and waiting. The sun was low. It made Rock Springs look comfortably shabby. A town that gave little, he thought, and demanded even less. JoBeth turned and walked towards Lonzo and never reached him. She was surrounded by Hudds: Marcus and Nelson, Ernie, Curtis, Floyd. 'You ain't goin' back up on the Ridge,' Marcus told her. 'The forces of Satan had their way once already, but they ain't gonna triumph over Christian decency an' righteousness.'

JoBeth started hacking at knees and shins and ankles. She was in riding boots and their pointed toes did much damage. Curtis grabbed her but she fought him furiously and he got an elbow in the eye. The shouting and cursing brought the Killicks in a rush and there was a fist-fight. A couple of Killick cousins joined in. Everyone was more or less drunk; the blows were swung wildly; often they hurt the knuckles more than the head; to those watching, the struggle was comic and they cheered it on. But the fighters were serious. Maggie looked at Frankie. Frankie shrugged. Not her job any more.

James Boston pointed.

Marcus Hudd had gripped JoBeth by the throat. He was shouting at Dan Killick, 'You stole my boy! You threw your sister to the forces of Satan! Time to call a halt!' Dan was trying to punch Marcus, whose fingers tightened the angrier he got. JoBeth was being choked. Lonzo was alongside Marcus, pleading. Curtis saw Lonzo put his hand on JoBeth and he hit him so hard he broke his hand. Marcus never noticed.

'I knew we should have left an hour ago,' Boston said bleakly. He dismounted and gave the reins to Arnie and walked towards Marcus. That was when Frankie noticed Flub Phillips, hobbling through the crowd, limping very badly. Boston shoved Dan aside and put his face close to Marcus's face and said, 'Let this woman go or I'll break both your arms.'

'Which one here is the Devil?' Flub asked someone.

'That feller there figures this feller is.' The man pointed at Dan, sprawling in the dirt.

'Fine.' Flub pulled Maggie's shotgun from inside his pants-leg and aimed at Dan and the man shouted in horror and knocked the gun up and Flub blew the back of James L. Boston's head off.

~

It was dark when JoBeth and Lonzo reached the Ridge. He got her a bowl of hot water and she cleaned herself up. There were splatters of dried blood and brain all over her head and shoulders.

Lonzo fetched Aaron. Martha came too. They sat around a fire and ate pork barbecue. The hogs were getting big.

'Lonzo says the fight was over you bein' here,' Martha said.

'Yeah.'

'Told you she was trouble,' Aaron said.

'I didn't start it,' JoBeth said. 'The Hudds an' the Killicks were spoilin' for war. Any excuse would of done. That trial got both sides heated up. You hear the verdict?'

'Don't matter to us,' Aaron said. 'White against white. Bet you five dollars, white won.'

'Yeah,' Lonzo said. 'White won an' Lonzo lost.' He laughed. 'Jury wanted to hang *me*.'

'Why did you do it?' JoBeth asked. 'Why give evidence? You didn't even get paid.'

'Well … deputy knew I knew what George got up to. An' I wanted to show all them white assholes I wasn't scared.'

'You scared now?' Martha said. 'You better be. Way I see it, you got everyone agin us 'cept the deputy.'

'An' the deputy wants us to go to hell or Chicago or some damn place,' Aaron said.

'Wish Luke would get back,' Lonzo said.

FALSE PROMISES

Rock Springs felt badly about the death of the Pinkerton man. Everyone blamed someone: the Hudds, or the Killicks, or Maggie for leaving Flub behind the bar where she kept her shotgun, or Frankie for not being the deputy when she was needed, or Flub, although it was hard to blame a man who was in a coma: someone had snatched the shotgun from him and cracked his skull with the butt, and now he was in Brightsides's house, scarcely breathing.

They buried James L. Boston next day. Hunkin did it free, and preached on Romans, seven, twenty-four: *O wretched man that I am! Who shall deliver me from the body of this death?* JoBeth came down from the Ridge and didn't try to hide the bruises on her throat. Marcus and Ernie Hudd got booed as they left the church. Maggie banned all Killicks from the tavern for a week. Frankie fined a couple of trappers, down from the hills, ten bucks each for excessive profanity in public, which bewildered them. After all that, the town felt slightly better.

Charles Hudd rode home from the burial. He had talked to no-one, avoided everyone, kept his eyes down. Memories of the trial still dogged him. He told himself it was all in the past and anyway justice had been done. Memories of certain episodes – the moment when he broke his gavel; Dan Killick saying *O. Fuck;* Ma Killick quoting the Book of Daniel – these kept surging back and he found himself frowning, shaking his head, feeling his cheeks turn hot. The sense of shame and defeat and public mockery would not go away. Only in Rock Springs could you have a murder trial where the victim turned up too late and then failed to give evidence. No wonder people had laughed.

He went up to his room and locked the door.

Fell into his armchair, looked at the wall, didn't move for an hour. Two hours. What difference? He knew he was a failure.

Failure in love. Lost the only woman that mattered. Failure in war. Not worth a damn as a fighting soldier. Failure as a husband. Wife didn't want him, need him, love him. Failure as a farmer. Cousins ran the farm. And now failure as a judge. No future in politics.

The nagging, tuneless repetition of a single piano note eventually tapped a hole in his brooding. That bloody nigger was tuning his wife's piano again. He put his fingers in his ears.

Much later he heard her playing the piano, a jaunty little waltz.

Still later, Lucy brought his meal. He had to get up to let her in.

'That nigger. What's his name?'

'T. Speed.'

'Huh.' Fancypants name for a mere nigger. 'He still here?'

'No, sir. Came downstairs ten minutes ago. Went away.'

'How many times has your Mr T. Speed tuned Mrs Hudd's piano?'

'Three times.' She waited. He looked to be awful tired, but he never stopped clicking his fingers. 'You want I should come back?' she asked.

'Why?'

That was a question he had never asked before. She shrugged. 'Earn a dollar.'

'That's all you black folk think of, isn't it? Earn a dollar. Earn a dollar. How many dollars do white men pay you each week?' She would have told him but he kept on going. 'The wages of sin,' he said.

'You an' me, we don't do nothing' in bed. That ain't sinnin', is it?'

'You poor misguided fool.' He wished beyond anything that Lucy would take her dress off right now, peel it off in one magical action. 'God has cursed you with the power to arouse lust. The sinning must stop. This house must be cleansed! I have been through the furnace and am emerged purified.' Charles felt suddenly light-hearted; his tongue seemed to be running away from him. 'Pray for me,' he said, and gave her a dollar.

'That all? Just pray?'

'Go now. Go away.'

He ate some of his meal and wondered why he had married. Women were a snare and a delusion. They trapped you with promises: false promises. And then they flaunted their falsehood, flaunted it shamelessly. Well, that must stop. He decided to stop it now, at once.

It was only when he knocked on the door of his wife's bedroom that he saw he was still carrying his knife. How odd.

'Who is it?' she called.

'Your husband. Charles Hudd.'

'Can't it wait? I'm resting.'

He tried the handle. Locked.

He fetched the poker from his room and smashed the lock with three crashing, splintering blows.

She was sitting on the edge of her bed, buttoning her dress. 'Well, that certainly ended my rest,' she said. She sounded calm enough, but the buttons refused to be fastened.

'This house must be cleansed,' he announced. 'I intend to start with your piano, madam.'

'My *piano*? What's wrong with my piano?'

'It is the cause of vice and sinning.' He went into the next room. The piano lid was open. He pounded the keys with his fist. 'A depraved and diabolical instrument! Did you ever hear such an evil noise?'

She stood in the doorway. 'You're drunk or you're crazy. Leave my piano alone. And get out.'

'Oh, I shall do that.' He began to drag the piano across the room.

At first she was too surprised to know what to do, but then she blocked the doorway. 'You shan't,' she said. 'It's mine, I brought it here …' He let go of the piano and charged at her shoulder-first, and the blow tore her hands from the doorframe and knocked her flat on her back. She lay winded, wondering if she were dying. Then, as her grudging lungs began to work again, she saw him haul the piano towards her.

He too was gasping for breath. The piano legs cut splinters from the floorboards, and the smooth soles of his boots slipped as he strained. Already his muscles ached. Before he reached the bedroom door his wife was on her feet, fighting him, trying to pull the piano back, punching his ribs, kicking his legs. With one hand he picked up a small chair and swung it at her, to beat her off. He misjudged his

494

swing and struck her head and shoulders. She fell again, shrieking with pain. He saw blood on her face. 'This house,' he shouted, feebly, his chest heaving, his mouth dry, 'must be cleansed!' The top of the staircase was thirty feet away.

She followed but she could not interfere. He heard her weeping, sometimes cursing. Once or twice he saw her bloody, damaged face. Nothing could stop him now. Sweating and staggering, mouthing his slogan, he got the piano where he wanted it, overhanging the top step. The noise had aroused the rest of the family: Marcus, Floyd and Celinda were coming up the stairs. 'Get back!' Charles shouted. 'Back or die!' He got his fingers underneath the piano, straightened his legs and heaved.

There was no bend in the staircase; it was just a long, straight, steep flight. The piano somersaulted twice, each impact fetching an angry discord from its strings. It wiped pictures off the wall and it might have killed Celinda, who had been slow to turn, if it hadn't smashed through the banisters and dropped fifteen feet onto a stone floor. Lewis Hudd was standing nearby. He thought the bang was louder than a forty-four.

Charles sat on the top stair. He had torn some part of his stomach. The family gathered and gazed up at him; him and his wrecked wife. 'This house is cleansed,' he whispered. 'Hallelujah.' It hurt to speak.

~

One thing the Ridge had plenty of was water. The mountain pumped streams out of its sides and some of these streams joined to make creeks. The colonists snaked their trimmed logs down a stream that led into Stumbling Creek, which zigged and zagged and finally poured into the Cameron. Nat, Buck and Gabe dammed the lowest of its pools. Their harvest of timber floated in this pool: black walnut, white oak, wild cherry, beech, sycamore, lime, enough to build a hundred fine houses, or ten thousand gleaming sideboards. When the next heavy rains flooded the creek, the men would raft their logs, spring the trigger that broke the dam, and ride the raft on a great gush into the Cameron. Stumbling Creek was upriver from Satan's Bathtub, it was in the wilderness. The dam troubled no-one. Probably no-one knew it existed.

The violence at the Hudd house changed everything there. Curtis took his mother to Doc Brightsides; their story was that she had fallen. 'From what?' he asked. First she was silent; then she wept. He asked no more questions. Men beat their wives; it happened all the time and it baffled him. He found all women beautiful, even when damaged, like this one.

Charles locked himself in his room. His cousins cleared up the wreckage. Everyone was angry and most were bewildered. Lucy hated the atmosphere and she quit without telling anyone; just came away.

T. Speed knew nothing of any of this. He was walking the fifteen miles to the Williamson place, a big farm where the eldest daughter, Sarah, was thirty-three and would dearly like someone to tune her piano. That was what Mary Hudd had told him. She and Sarah had met at market, in Rock Springs. 'Men think, cus I'm plain, I'm cold,' Sarah had said. 'I ain't cold! I'm ragin' hot. But I can't stand up an' say it, can I?'

When Lucy reached the Ridge, JoBeth left what she was doing and went over and embraced her. Everyone stopped work and watched. White lady huggin' a nigger woman, right out in the open! Surely the day of jubalo had come! Or maybe not. Some felt downright uncomfortable.

'Hadn't been for you, I'd be sleepin' in a cave,' JoBeth said.

'Might wish you were, way things are goin',' Lucy said. JoBeth's neck was ringed with bruises and her voice was rough.

'Just a scuffle.'

'Pinkerton man's head got scuffed clean off.'

'Yeah.'

'That ain't all. We had us a pyanner-throwin' contest down at the Hudds. Mister Charles won an' now he can't hardly pass water.' Lucy went to the stream to wash off the sweat of the climb. JoBeth went with her and heard the rest of the story. 'Ain't goin' back,' Lucy said. 'War ain't ended down there.'

'Up here's pretty. This is better.'

Lucy, sitting on a rock while the sun dried her skin, thought: *Not in winter. Rain, cold, and wind howling like a mad person until you felt you'd go mad too.* 'Reckon on stayin'?'

'If you folks'll have me.'

'This ain't no Garden of Eden. We got men here keep their brains between their legs.'

'Who needs 'em? I've had enough of men.'

'Maybe men ain't had enough of you.'

JoBeth made her fingers into a pistol. 'Pow! I got me a forty-four. Got it from little Lewis Hudd.'

That silenced Lucy. She thought: *Lewis? Boy's only ten. Ten-year-old carryin' a forty-four? Could be hanged for murder?* 'I don't believe what I'm hearin',' she said. 'He's too skinny.'

'I knew a couple in Texas got shotgunned by their little girl, age six. Did it while they slept. Had to rest the barrel on a chair. Said an angel told her to do it.'

'They hang her?'

'I don't want to talk about it,' JoBeth said. 'I don't want to *think* about it. Let's go eat. I ain't hungry, but the lodger sure is.'

Lucy found Lonzo looking gloomily at the last sack of cornmeal, only half-full. 'What you doin' here?' he said. 'Ain't Saturday.'

'I quit. Them Hudds ...' She wrinkled her nose. 'Worse'n animals. Besides, ain't no end to work. I always washin' a big heap of greasy pots. Milkin' ten cows. Carryin' coal upstairs. Plus all the whorin'.'

'You think you got it bad? Can't be bad as cuttin' down big trees all day every day.'

'Try it, Lonzo. You sell your sweet ass.'

'We need the dollars. You can't quit.'

Luce had a temper that turned like the flip of a coin. 'You *own* me, nigger?' She grabbed the top of his pants and jerked up so hard that the crotch bit into his fork and made him gasp. 'You the new over-seer up here?' she shouted. 'You want me off the Ridge so you can do some whorin' your own self?' She let go and turned away. JoBeth was watching. 'You touch my man I'll kill you both,' Lucy said.

'Take my gun,' JoBeth said. She walked away.

'You can quit, Luce,' Lonzo said, still blinking. 'Jeez, but that hurt.'

'You better be nice to me tonight, or I might kill you anyway.'

'My niceness just got a bad fright,' Lonzo said, easing his pants. 'It run off an' shrunk up an' hid behind itself. Can't find it nowhere. Ain't you sorry you treated me so bad?'

'No.' But she almost smiled.

~

497

After Nashville, Luke Corrigan took off his right boot only twice, and that was because he had to ford rivers and he wanted to keep the notes dry. He always slept with that foot tucked under a rock or down a rabbit hole, so no-one could steal the boot. He walked from dawn to dusk and spent fifteen cents a day on food, which made two meals, so he ate pretty well. When he limped up the Ridge he didn't look too thin but as soon as he sat down, he couldn't get up. Legs quit. Well, they had a right.

Everyone came running.

Luke had never been so popular. It flustered him. Martha said, 'What's Nashville like?' Luke thought hard. 'Big,' he said. 'An' loud.' Buck asked: 'Anyone get drowned?' Luke shook his head. 'See any gators?' Gabe asked. 'Couple,' Luke said. He felt overwhelmed. That was when Lonzo arrived, carrying Aaron.

'You sell them beaver skins?' Lonzo asked.

'Oh, yeah. Sure.' That raised a cheer. Luke felt tears on his cheeks, and ducked his head.

'How much they fetch?' Aaron asked.

'Same as Lonzo said. Five bucks a skin.' That brought a whoop of delight, and Luke risked looking up. He had never seen faces so happy.

'Five hundred bucks!' Martha said. 'We gonna be fat this winter. Fat! Pancakes an' molasses every day.'

'Honey-roast ham,' Moses said. 'Buckets a greens. Sweet taters forever.'

'You got the money there?' Aaron asked. Luke bullied his leg into bending so he could ease off the boot.

'You sell that raft?' Buck asked. 'We got a raft ready, almost. How much you reckon – '

'Here.' Luke poked about and fished out the paper money: squashed, stained, crushed. 'Five hundred.' He gave it to Lonzo. For the first time in a long time, he could relax. Rest easy. Lonzo smoothed out the notes. Aaron, sitting on his shoulders, reached down and took one, held it close to his eyes. Wet his finger, rubbed the paper. Spat on it, screwed it up, threw it away. 'Ain't worth shit,' he said.

Nobody spoke. Nobody moved, until Bonny darted out and snatched the bill.

'He gave me five hundred,' Luke said. He felt faint in the stomach.

'White man in Nashville gave me five bills, hundred dollar each. Easy to carry, he said.'

'These are one-dollar bills,' Lonzo said. 'You got five bucks.'

'No, no. He showed me ...' Different tears ran down Luke's face.

JoBeth had been at the edge of the crowd. She came forward and looked at the bills spread fan-like in Lonzo's hand. Someone had used a pen and written HUNDRED after ONE, and added two zeroes after the numeral 1. It hadn't even been carefully done. It didn't look at all like printing. 'Stinkin' cheatin' thievin' sonofabitch,' she said sadly.

'No pancakes?' Bonny asked. Nobody answered, so she knew what that meant.

~

Flub Phillips died and got buried. Hunkin did it. *The sleep of a labouring man is sweet*, Ecclesiastes, five, twelve. Nobody argued with that. Collection raised twelve dollars forty.

After the first rains it was a dry fall. Rock Springs threatened to become drier when word arrived that Dundee County had voted against the manufacture and sale of liquor, with effect first day of next month. When Charles Hudd went to the county seat and complained that Rock Springs had not been given a chance to vote, he was shown a box full of ballot papers. Electioneering in Kentucky was an art, not a science. Counting, not voting, was what mattered.

And dry counties were springing up all around Dundee, as a temperance crusade swept the state. Soon there were great swathes of Kentucky where bourbon was illegal. These temperance movements were as powerful and unpredictable as flood or drought. Bad booze helped. It made men sick and left families poor. Much of the booze made in Rock Springs was bad.

After the trial, Jessica had gone upstate with Jimmy-Sam Wiggins and married him. The Killicks stopped thinking about the triple mortgage, and hired a housekeeper. She quit after two days and they hired another, a big woman who had boxed bare-knuckle in a circus until she broke her hands. Her cooking was dull and monotonous. Nobody criticized it. In the afternoon, she and Ma Killick sang hymns. This drove the others out to work.

On the Ridge the colonists were living on fear, hope, and T. Speed's dollars.

Their constant fear was that some white cracker might arrive and cause trouble. Their hope was that the next rains would made a good tide for rafting. Their dollars were never enough: JoBeth was not the only newcomer. Hudd Ridge was beginning to attract homeless or helpless or hungry blacks. Nobody got turned away, but nobody got fat either. And T. Speed was running out of pianos to tune.

Day by day he had to walk further and further. The risk was greater, the earnings poorer. One day he was walking along a dusty lane when someone rode up behind him, slipped a sack over his head, tied it at the throat before he could get his hands up. He had to suck hard to force air through the fabric. It was thick and filthy, and often he choked on bits of dirt. He walked on the end of the rope, and then he was thrown onto a wagon. The effort of breathing exhausted him. Twice he passed out.

When the sack was removed, T. Speed was tied to a chair. He was in a barn. In front of him were a lot of men in bedsheets with eye-holes cut in them. They were talking and drinking and attending to firearms. One man made a short speech, full of mumbo-jumbo words he couldn't get his tongue around, so he said, 'Oh, fuck it.' The others laughed: an oddly muffled, distant noise. Then they all aimed their firearms and shot T. Speed. It was the first Klan murder in Dundee County, Kentucky.

The barn was remote. By the time someone found the corpse and brought it into town, it was stiff as a brick. The deputy spent her own money on a coffin. When T. Speed was forced into it, the sides creaked under the pressure of his splayed limbs. She lashed the coffin to a big mule and set off up the Ridge. She got lost twice and she was cursing a landslip that had destroyed her track, when little Bonny heard her and turned her around and led her to the top in fifteen minutes.

Somebody had to look at the body, say who it was. Martha insisted, Frankie resisted, Martha won. Took a quick look, went away and threw up. Lonzo looked too. He had a stronger stomach, but only just. He felt it lurch and he shut his eyes. Frankie slid the lid on the coffin and banged it shut.

'Don't ask who done it,' she said. 'Enough bullet-holes there to allow for every white man in Rock Springs.'

'Dig a grave,' Lonzo said to anyone; everyone. Four men went away.

Flies had got trapped in the coffin; Frankie could hear them buzzing. That was too much, and she left it and sat on one of the boulders as smooth as a giant mushroom. Bettsy brought her a bowl of tea. 'We knew it was comin',' Bettsy said. 'Man couldn't stop himself. T. Speed just couldn't stop.' Frankie nodded.

She stood behind the crowd when they buried T. Speed. The grave-yard was under the tremendous, protecting branches of a giant cedar. Already there was a scattering of headstones, flat lengths of natural stone with no inscription. Josh said some prayers. Lonzo looked at Aaron, but Aaron shook his head. Lonzo sighed. 'T. Speed never harmed no-one,' he said. 'That's all I got to say.'

As they went back to camp, JoBeth joined the deputy. 'Bet you ten bucks he was tied to a chair.'

Frankie stopped, and waited until the others had gone on and couldn't hear her. 'Any nigger jumps into bed with ten, twenty white women is gonna end up tied to a chair. You know that. He knew it. Nigger goes about askin' to be killed, ain't a damn thing I can do about it.'

'From what they tell me, his dollars been keepin' this place alive.'

'Worst thing he could of done. This place is trouble.'

'Not of our makin'.'

'Ain't the point. Every mornin', Rock Springs gets outa bed an' sees the Ridge, an' hates it all day.'

'Too bad.'

'Havin' you up here don't make it any better.'

'Ain't leavin'. Not now. Not after what they done to T. Speed. Not ever.'

~

Ansel Mungers, in his skiff, couldn't see up Stumbling Creek for trees and such, but he knew it wasn't right. The stream wasn't running into the Cameron with its usual energy. He went up and had a look. He sat on the dam and thought. Then he went to see Charles Hudd.

The house was quiet. 'I regret I cannot offer you refreshment,' Charles said, which was a lie: he disliked and despised Mungers. 'My wife has gone to live with a sister in Georgia.'

'You're lookin' well,' Mungers said, also a lie: Charles looked old, so old he made Mungers feel young.

They sat. Charles winced and pressed a fist hard against his stomach.

'Ain't you the sly fox,' Mungers said. 'Goin' into the timber business an' not a word to anyone, heh-heh-heh.'

Maybe Charles nodded, or maybe it was the pressure of his fist.

'Happened to be passin' Stumblin' Creek, saw the dam. Saw the timber. Some nice trees waitin' there. Real nice.'

Charles grunted, 'Mmm.'

'Tell the truth, I never knew your property reached that far.'

'Mmm.'

'Well, if you ever need a crew for your raft, I got the best. Heh-heh.'

Charles showed him out. 'Hey,' Mungers said, 'I never did congratulate you on makin' judge.'

'A nightmare. It has cost me every friend I thought I had.'

'Ain't that a shame.'

'The price of duty.' He shut the door.

He knew a man who made blasting powder. He sent Floyd to buy some. Ten days later, heavy rain woke Charles at four in the morning, and it was still dark when he blew the dam. He had tethered his horse, but the flash ripped the night and the crack-boom made the ground jump, and the animal took fright and snapped its tether. He had to walk home. In the drenched grey of dawn he could see the massive, neatly trimmed trunks of trees being hurried down the Cameron.

The final, faintest tremor of the explosion even reached the cave of the panther, and she half-opened her eyes. Nothing more happened, and her eyelids slowly closed. Her cubs were no longer cubs; they were big and clever enough to catch their own food. The heat made by three bodies kept the cave snug. The panther was content. They would get through the winter and next year her family would leave her. If they didn't, she would leave them. Either way, life would go on. She slept.

RAIN AND TREES

Losing the timber was just too much for some.

The beaver skins made five bucks: all that work, walking and trapping, week after week. Five miserable bucks. Lucy quit before a piano fell on her: nobody blamed her. Anyway they had felt bad about living off her dollars. Shabby way to live. Had to end sometime. T. Speed was different. Lonzo was right: he never harmed no-one, made his world a happier place, whitey couldn't tolerate that, now T. Speed was torn apart worse than a pack of hounds had done it. And after all that, the timber was gone. It had taken a river of sweat to cut and trim and haul those trunks, snake them down the creek. That had been winter's grub, lying in that pool, waiting to be rafted. One bang blew the dam to blazes and now some lucky, happy bastard twenty, thirty, forty miles downriver was hooking those logs out of the Cameron. Easy pickings. Walnut, oak, cherry, tulip poplar: all gone to feed some whites who weren't even hungry.

Well, that was too much for some. Moses left, and when he went, Gabe Killick left. Others thought about last winter, all that forest food, roots and nuts and stuff, and they left too. 'Can't beat whitey,' Gabe said to Lonzo. 'He don't want us here.'

'Don't want you *there*,' Lonzo said, pointing down the Ridge. Gabe shrugged and smiled and left.

That was a bad couple of weeks. The leaves were coming down in great brown showers, the wind was starting to whistle the sad, slack tune it would keep up until spring. Rainstorms pounded so hard that even T. Speed's grave was washed smooth and flat.

During one downpour, Lonzo and Lucy went to see Aaron in his smelly, leaky cabin. Water dripped and hissed into the open fire.

It was an old familiar conversation: how much food was left, how much needed. Not enough of one and too much of the other.

After a while Luke Corrigan ran and joined them. 'Wish we could eat rain,' he said. 'Wouldn't never go hungry then.'

'Rain an' trees,' Aaron said. 'That's all we got. All we're gonna get.' He felt too old and tired to think.

'Could of sold coupla these streams to old Mrs Corrigan,' Luke said. 'Always bitchin' she never had no good pure streams.'

Everyone was gloomy, beaten down by failure and a grim future. It was a whole day before Lucy repeated that conversation to JoBeth. They were watching the sun make the Ridge steam, getting it dry fast because another storm was coming soon. 'Why would Mrs Corrigan want a pure stream?' JoBeth asked. It didn't matter. Just something to say.

Lucy shouted, and Luke came over.

'Make corn liquor,' he said. 'Corrigan whiskey was worse'n lamp-oil. You need plenty a pure stream-water to make good corn liquor.'

'We got that,' Lucy said. 'We got streams.'

'Need other stuff. Cornmeal. Malt.'

'And a copper still,' JoBeth said. 'Us Killicks made our own whiskey. What killed Pa, you ask me.'

'Anybody here ever made corn liquor?' Lucy asked. They went around the camp and asked. Nobody had ever run a still. It had been illegal for slaves to make their own booze. Illegal for them to drink anybody's booze. Bullwhip law.

'If George an' Dan did it,' JoBeth said, 'it's got to be easy.'

By now it was raining again. They went to see Aaron. The idea was obviously crazy but it was different, and it made you forget your stomach.

'Niggers can't make corn whiskey,' Aaron said. 'Ain't got the brains.'

'Seem to remember, you said once, when you was a runaway, you made a still,' Lonzo said.

'I got white blood in me.' Aaron's voice was a squeaky whisper.

'Me too,' JoBeth said. 'You an' me, bet we could make the best damn moonshine in the county.'

Aaron sneered so hard he hurt his face. '*Moonshine* … You don't know *nothin'*. Ain't called moonshine. Called John Barleycorn, for Chrissake.'

They knew he was wrong, but Aaron's brain had a mind of its own nowadays, and there was no point in arguing. JoBeth smiled. 'Tan my hide,' she said gently.

'Well, don't make no never-mind,' Lucy said. 'We can't wait. Real sippin' whiskey, it takes four years to come good, don't it?'

'Hellfire … I made corn whiskey good enough for the governor's wife an' I made it in five days!'

'Must of had one damn good still,' Lonzo said.

'Copper still. Made special.'

'Who by?'

Aaron chewed his lip so hard he bit it. He cursed, and sucked his blood. 'Hungry,' he croaked. 'Gimme food.' He began throwing things. Everyone left.

Next day he sent for Lucy. His eyes were milky and his head kept nodding like a poppy in a breeze. He made her put her face close to his. 'You ain't Starr,' he said.

'Starr's dead.'

'I know that. Ain't stupid.' He thought about poor dead Starr and cried a little. Lucy wiped his tears away and that surprised him. He drew back and spent a long time looking at her, remembering. Finally he knew. 'You're the one's makin' the moonshine,' he said.

'Tryin' to. Ain't got no still, though.'

'Find the gypsies. Find Irish Paddy. He'll make you a still.'

'Where is he?'

'Copper still. Got to be copper. Poor Starr.' He began crying again.

It took Lonzo a week of searching to find the gypsies. Irish Paddy was long since dead; now his son Tom was gypsy chief. King of a dozen caravans and the best metalsmiths in Kentucky.

Tom was open-faced and friendly. He wore his hair to his collar, a mass of tight ringlets, and his eyes were black as ink, and he had absolutely no knowledge of pot stills. Lonzo was given tea. Tom said he was sorry that they had nothing stronger to offer. 'The law, you understand, the law. The same in Ireland, I'm told. A terrible thing, but there you have it. The law must be obeyed.'

Lonzo drank his tea and thought that these people had a fine life, able to stay or go as they pleased. 'What do you make?' he asked.

'Kettles. We make a powerful lot of kettles.' Tom was talkative. He talked about kettles, horses, the war, the weather, the price of salt bacon. He talked for an hour. Lonzo listened, and sometimes he said something about life on the Ridge. Once he mentioned Aaron.

'You don't mean old Aaron with the busted legs?' Tom said. 'I remember him. But the fellah can't still be living, surely.'

'Looks dead,' Lonzo said. 'Talks some.'

'Ask him, will he visit here. Promise him a dish of real Irish stew, with dumplings. He liked that.'

Lonzo walked home, knowing the Aaron wouldn't visit. Aaron never went anywhere. He was right. 'Think I'm crazy in the head?' Aaron growled. 'Irish Paddy can come here, he wants to see me. He got legs, ain't he? It's an insult.'

'Paddy's dead,' Lonzo said. 'I just told you.'

Aaron tried to kick him. 'Damn insult,' he said.

Next morning was sunny and pleasant. Aaron threw rocks in Lonzo's direction. 'You an' me, we're goin' visiting,' he croaked. His voice was worse than a frog's. 'Go see Irish Paddy.'

'Dead.'

'Yeah. Better hurry.'

Lonzo carried him on his shoulders. Aaron clung to his ears, which could be painful but Lonzo knew better than to say so. It was a long walk. When they reached the caravans his ears felt like barbecue beef. He dumped the old man on an anvil and was glad to be led away and fed.

Irish Tom took Aaron into his caravan. 'That fine upstanding nigger told me you want to make corn liquor up there on that terrible Ridge of yours,' he said.

'Yeah. We get us a good pot still, we'll do it.'

'I can sell you my best pot still for one hundred and fifty dollars.'

Aaron was startled by the price. 'How much is your second-best?'

'I only make the best.'

Aaron ordered one, and gave him four dollars, all the money he had. 'Get the rest later.'

'Good,' Tom said. 'Now we can talk about the old days. Will you take a little bourbon?'

The journey back to the Ridge was easier on Lonzo's ears. He borrowed some twine and tied Aaron's hands together, then looped the arms around his neck. Aaron was too drunk to notice. It wasn't until next morning that he told everyone they now owed Irish Tom one hundred and forty-six dollars, and he was offended when they laughed. But of course the bourbon was still in him.

~

Every day, since she came back to Rock Springs, Doc Brightsides had thought of JoBeth. He thought of her living in dirt and discomfort on the Ridge, with child, widowed. She needed a husband and he desired, more than anything, to marry her. Hopeless. He could tell from the way she had looked at him, or more often not looked at him, that he stood no chance. There was no-one else he wanted to marry. Life was lonely. Life was dull. So when she sidled through his door, leaning backwards to get some balance, and she waddled to a chair, Brightsides felt a rush of love.

'What you starin' at?' she said. 'Never seen a brood cow before?'

He'd had little confidence in his power to appeal to this woman. Now he had none. Anger filled the vacuum. If she wouldn't like him as a man, he would damn well make sure she respected him as a doctor. He went behind his desk and began sharpening an old scalpel on a whetstone.

'Last pregnancy I saw who was as mad as you,' he said, 'I diagnosed toxaemia. Been known to cause acute yellow atrophy of the liver, maybe pernicious vomiting, even convulsions. Comes from having albumin in the urine. Consequence of too much meat in the diet.'

'Well, that ain't me.'

'No doubt you have swollen feet? Cramps in the legs? What we doctors call perversion of appetite?'

'I could eat a bucket of strawberries. Nothin' perverted about that.'

'Painful breasts? Not uncommon. I recommend applying warm olive oil. Rub from the circumference towards the nipple. I'll show you how it's done, if you like.'

'No. This baby got big feet, and it keeps kickin' me, but I still got a month to go and I feel good.'

'A *month?*' Brightsides got up and went over and felt her belly. 'I think not.' He asked her to stand up, and he felt her again. 'Expect labour to begin soon. Within a week. Maybe two or three days.'

'Hey.' Her voice was faint and her face was shocked. 'Two or three, you say? But I ain't ready. Look, I *counted*. I counted back, then I counted forward, and ...' Brightsides shook his head. 'I *did*, damn you,' she said. 'I can count. I *counted*.'

'Oh, I believe you. But maybe your body played a trick. A woman can conceive, and still have a monthly flow *after* that conception. Then she'll miss the *next* month's flow, and that's when she starts counting. Four weeks too late.'

'Swindle.'

'No. Just Nature being natural.'

JoBeth linked her hands under her belly to ease the load. She stared into space until she was slightly cross-eyed. She was thinking about the next two or three days, maybe a week, and whether she'd be alive at the end of it. Plenty of mothers died of childbirth. Just Nature being natural.

But she hadn't come to town to see Doc Brightsides about the baby. 'I need a hundred and fifty dollars,' she said. 'Better yet, two hundred.'

'Now there's a coincidence,' he said, which made her look. 'So do I,' he told her. 'Some years, all the sick are poor, and some years all the poor are sick. This year it's both. I suggest you try Maggie.'

He escorted her to the door and watched her walk away. All his anger had gone. He was genuinely sorry he didn't have the money. There was no-one else in the world he would have given it to.

Maggie was in the tavern, on her knees, hammering nails into loose floorboards. She didn't get up while JoBeth said her piece. 'I got debts owed me worth twice as much that I can give you free,' she said. 'Try Frankie. All widows are rich. Everyone knows that.'

JoBeth climbed the stairs and knocked and went into the deputy's room.

She was sewing a patch on a shirt. 'You better not come here to say you found who done that T. Speed murder,' she said. 'I don't need that sort of foolishness.'

'I need two hundred dollars,' JoBeth said, 'an' if you don't give it me I'll marry Doc Brightsides.'

Frankie stitched, and thought, and knotted her last stitch, and bit through the thread, and dropped the needle in a bowl, and thought some more.

'The man is crazy enough to do it, too,' she said.

'He's in love with me. Half the goddamn world is in love with me.

What did I do to them? Ain't fair. Wish I was ordinary, like you.'

'Soon you will be.' Frankie unlocked a box. 'It don't take long. Here's two hundred and fifty. Don't ever come back.'

'Two-fifty.' JoBeth poked the notes in a pocket. 'Two-fifty. An' you're still patchin' shirts.' Frankie opened the door. 'Why don't *you* marry him?' JoBeth said.

'Because marriage ain't like horse liniment. It don't take the pain away.'

JoBeth paused in the doorway and said, 'The money's for us niggers on the Ridge. To buy a pot still.'

'I never thought it was for baby-clothes,' Frankie said. That was the last time they spoke to each other.

JoBeth went out the back way and left town without delay. She had no wish to meet a Hudd or a Killick, or – worse yet – both at once. Lonzo was waiting in the woods, with the mule. She needed his help to get on its back. 'Let's go slow and gentle,' she said. 'This little 'un's bigger'n I thought.' But after ten minutes she grew impatient and dug her heels into the mule's ribs. 'My tad ain't gonna be born on a mountainside,' she said. 'Besides, I got two hundred an' fifty dollars to give to old Aaron.' Lonzo was surprised but not astonished. White folks always got what they wanted. Just had to ask. Always been that way. Emancipation made no change there.

~

Two days later, JoBeth moved into Martha's cabin, because it was the biggest and best, with a fireplace that rarely smoked, and Martha knew all about birthing. Labour began in the afternoon. 'Ain't this what Mister Doc Brightsides told you?' Martha said. 'That's a smart man.'

'He's an evil greedy connivin' sonofabitch, same as all men,' JoBeth said. 'Oh Jesus ... Why won't it stop?'

'Hey, this is just the beginning,' Martha said. 'Your trouble, always in too big a rush, got no patience. Let happen what's goin' to happen.'

'I never reckoned on this.' JoBeth clenched her teeth and squeezed her eyes tight shut. 'Ooooh ... That hurt. That hurt bad.'

'Well, stop grindin' your pretty little teeth, honey,' Martha said. 'Use your mouth to breathe deep.'

JoBeth tried sucking in air. 'More, honey, more,' Martha said.

'Ain't easy, damn it,' JoBeth gasped.

'Ain't meant to be easy,' Martha told her. 'I had six, so I know.'

The pain receded, and JoBeth wiped snot from her upper lip. 'Six?' she said. 'Where? I never saw six.' At once she knew she'd said the wrong thing.

'Five got sold south. Only child left is Bonny.'

Nothing to be said about that.

An hour later, Bonny was sitting behind JoBeth's head and wiping the sweat from her brow before it could sting her eyes. JoBeth felt as if a cannonball was trying to get out of her and splitting her body in half in the process. She had screamed until she was too hoarse to scream any more. 'This creature,' she whispered huskily, 'must weigh twenty pounds at least.' She was going to die, she knew that for certain, and Martha didn't seem to care.

'Push, honey,' Martha said. 'Push hard.'

'I am, godammit,' JoBeth wheezed.

'No you ain't,' Bonny said. 'You ain't pushin' near hard enough.'

JoBeth squinted at her upside-down face. 'Shut your fool mouth, child.'

'I seen plenty of babies born, an' you ain't pushin' near hard enough,' Bonny said.

'This is over, I'm gonna strangle you,' JoBeth said; but she pushed harder.

Bettsy was leaning in the doorway, picking her teeth with a splinter, watching. 'I see the head,' she said.

'That's what hard pushin' does,' Bonny told JoBeth. JoBeth hated her so much that she made one last, supreme, agonizing effort, and the baby slid out, all wet and bloody.

'You got a boy child,' Martha said, busying herself. 'That what you wanted? Boy?'

'Anythin',' JoBeth said weakly. 'Just so long as it's outside of me.' But she thought for a moment and asked: 'Is he okay? Ain't damaged, is he?'

'Looks kind of like a skinned rabbit,' Bonny said.

'They all do,' Bettsy said. 'Black or white.'

'He's a fine baby,' Martha said. She had him loosely wrapped and she held him up for JoBeth to see.

'Jesus!' JoBeth said. 'Did I make that? He's so *small*.' The boy was bawling.

'You didn't think he was so small a couple minutes ago,' Bonny said. 'Couple minutes ago he weighed twenty pounds, you said.'

'I got cornbread bakin',' Bettsy said. 'I better go.' She left.

'Can I hold him?' JoBeth asked.

'Not until ma's cut the cord an' tied it,' Bonny said. 'Don't you know *nothin*'?'

'Hey!' Martha said. 'Shut your mouth, girl. Go fetch some more water.'

'He looks like Jack,' JoBeth said. 'Well, thank God that's over.'

'Ain't over,' Martha said. 'Just beginnin'. Any time now, he's gonna want the tit.'

'Well, that's just like his father too. Jack could never get enough of my buzoom.' She accepted the boy from Martha, and found herself weeping. 'What's wrong with me?' she demanded. 'What's wrong?'

'Ain't nothin' wrong, honey. Your body just been to hell an' back. Nobody can't say it ain't got the right to cry some tears.' Martha turned her head and sniffed. 'Hot cornbread,' she murmured. 'Ain't that nice?'

~

The boy survived and thrived. Josh took this to be a sign that God wanted Hudd Ridge to survive, too. Nobody denied this, but nobody felt sure of it, either. Everything depended on moonshine, and even Josh couldn't bring himself to say that God was hot for corn liquor, especially made in secret.

Lonzo chose a moonlit night and took a bunch of strong niggers down the Ridge. He paid Irish Tom what he was owed, and some of the gypsies helped carry the job up to the colony. A long and heavy haul. The last mile was through the tired and misty light of dawn. The men made for the glow of the campfires and the smell of coffee.

Ate, slept till noon, ate again. The gypsies went home, all but Tom. The only colonist who knew how to work a pot still was Aaron, and Aaron was sick, so sick that his voice was almost gone; and when he spoke his whispers made no sense. Tom stayed and showed them what to do.

They chose a hard-to-find hollow where a stream came out of a split in a rock. 'First you build your firebox,' he said. They made it out of fieldstone, and shaped it to carry the still, and then bedded more masonry around the base. 'Now, from your still you go down into your thump-keg,' he said. Tubing was led from the top of the still to the thump-keg. 'And from there you go down through your flakestand.' This was a bigger barrel, and the tubing spiralled all through it. 'Which brings us to our glorious conclusion,' Tom said. 'The catch-can.'

'That all there is?' Lonzo asked. The whole assembling had taken only a couple of hours. 'Ain't so hard.'

'That, my boy, is the simple part. You've got yourself a piano. Now you learn to make music. That's not so simple, not so quick. We'll start with making the mash.'

The next few days they spent learning about mash. Tom taught the best mix of malted corn and hard white cornmeal. He showed how to get the right heat, by burning the right wood. Chestnut or ash was best. He explained exactly how and when to stir the mash barrel. 'And especially,' he said, 'when to have the courage to leave it alone. Mash is like a woman. Can't be hurried. Needs time to think.' He noticed JoBeth standing nearby, holding her baby. 'Beg pardon, ma'am.' he said.

'Don't worry about me. I spent nine months thinkin' about this happy little bundle. How long d'you reckon that mash might take before it's ready?'

'Five days.'

'That's faster'n trappin' beaver,' Lonzo said. 'Easier'n cuttin' down timber. Safer'n cheatin' old man Stackmesser with Indum silver mines.'

'Hope you're right,' she said. 'Winter's comin' fast. I surely do hope you're right.'

After five days, Tom found the perfect moment when the mash in the barrels had all turned to still-beer. 'This is where you need to be clever,' he said. 'Get your heat just right, so when you pour this beer in the still it won't scorch or stick.' He let them do all that. He stood back and watched while they kept the still hot enough to boil off the alcohol, and also kept the flakestand cool enough to turn the steam to liquid. There was universal joy at the sight of the first liquor dribbling into the catch-can, and universal gloom when Tom dumped it. 'That's foreshots,' he told them. 'Not fit to be drunk. The real stuff comes later.'

The real stuff arrived in plenty, and when they all tasted it they knew it was no damn good.

Tom was not discouraged. 'Pull the fire,' he said. 'Drain the still. Make fresh beer. We'll do it all over again. This pot-still ain't comfortable yet. She needs to get herself settled into the mountain.' The second attempt was no better. The third effort was a brilliant success. 'Now she's comfortable,' Tom said. 'Now you're starting to play music.' He took a gallon of the liquor and went home.

Everyone had a good taste. It seemed a good time for a party, but Lonzo sent them back to the camp. 'This liquor ain't for drinkin',' he said. 'Not by us.'

~

Lucy worked the spigot while Lonzo half-filled three pint bottles from the same barrel. He whacked the corks in.

'How you gonna remember which is which?' she asked.

It made him laugh. 'I forgot, you married a real dumb nigger. Listen, I get it wrong, they kill me, I want a big funeral. *Big*. Lots of whoopin' an' hollerin'. You fetch that brass band from over at Barber's Landin'. Hear me?'

'Dunno. Where you hid the money?'

'Ain't gonna kill me.' They hugged and kissed. 'Too dumb to get killed.' He took the mule and rode down to the Killick farm.

The brothers saw him coming and left the fields and gathered on the porch.

'That all you brung?' Devereux said.

'This is tastin' whiskey,' Lonzo said. 'This is for you to choose from, boss.'

'Choose what?' Dan asked.

Lonzo lined up the bottles on a table. 'Which you want to buy, Mister Killick. See, I brung a taster of my real strong four-dollar whiskey, an' a taster of my smooth-sippin' five-dollar whiskey, an' this here on the end is a taster of my special Kentucky straight old Southern Dixie six-dollar whiskey. We ain't made a whole lot of that one.'

'Six dollars a jug?'

'Yessir.'

'Gallon jug,' Stanton said.

'Yessir.' Lonzo nudged the four-dollar bottle forward.

The brother each took a big mouthful, swilled it around their

513

teeth, gargled a little, swallowed slowly. 'That's horse-piss,' Stanton said. 'An' if I ain't mistook, the horse has got the staggers somethin' terrible.'

'Ain't buyin' that,' Dan grunted.

'Only way you could get four dollars for that,' Dev said, 'is you give us five dollars first.'

Lonzo was wearing his Cherokee face, carved in mahogany.

They each took a longer swig from the five-dollar bottle. 'Gettin' there,' Dan said.

'Well, it sure ain't horse-piss,' Devereux said.

'Somethin' funny about it,' Stanton said.

They tried it again. 'Good enough for women or Indians,' Stanton said.

'We ain't buyin' neither of them,' Dan said. He picked up the six-dollar bottle and poured a little onto his palm, sniffed it hard. 'You just maybe saved your black life, boy,' he said. He took a long, slow sip, and kept it on his tongue before he swallowed. 'I was gonna beat you bloody for wastin' my time.' He passed the bottle to Stanton, who drank.

'Uh-huh,' Stanton said. 'Yup. Yes sirree.'

Dev drank. 'Gets my vote,' he said. 'Give a swaller to that horse with the goddamn staggers,' he told Lonzo.

They ordered a keg of the six-dollar stuff. 'You pay cash on the barrelhead,' Lonzo said. They stared at him, a nigger giving orders. 'No dollar, no liquor,' he said. He didn't blink. Dan sighed, and nodded.

When Lonzo had gone, Dev said, 'One of these days, gonna take my rifle up that Ridge an' get me a nigger.'

'Sure,' Stanton said. 'So then we got to go to Tennessee to buy corn liquor ain't half as good as these niggers are makin'.'

'Asshole,' Dan told Dev. Already the whiskey was working and Dev threw a punch. 'Oh, shit,' Stanton said. Another fight. He walked away.

Lonzo went into Maggie's tavern by the back door and waited for her in the kitchen. By now he had tipped what remained of the whiskey into one bottle.

'I stick to beer,' she said. 'This could be snake oil for all I know. See what you think,' she told the cook.

He drank half a cupful, very slowly, sucking it through the gaps between his teeth. 'Pure nectar,' he said, and swallowed the last mouthful.

'Hell, you don't know what that word means.'

'Means winter ain't goin' to be so bad, if you can get regular supplies of this.'

'How much you want?' Lonzo asked.

'Just keep sendin' it, I'll tell you when to stop,' she said. 'Folk around here are real sick of drinkin' my coffee.'

'Cash on the barrelhead.' Lonzo enjoyed saying that.

'You're an uppity nigger, ain't you?' the cook said.

'Ain't uppity,' Maggie said. 'Just smart. Smart enough to make a livin' in that howlin' wilderness, which makes him twice as smart as anyone in this town.'

'Four dollars a gallon,' Lonzo said. 'That's if you give me all the empty bottles you got.'

'See?' Maggie said. 'Smart as a fox.'

There was enough left for Lonzo to give Doc Brightsides a taste. He ordered four bottles. 'I hear the baby was delivered satisfactorily,' he said.

'Called Jack.'

'First of many, I expect.'

'My Lucy's carryin' right now.'

'Congratulations.' They shook hands. Lonzo was surprised how strong the doc's grip was. 'She needs any help,' Brightsides said, 'bring her to me. No charge.'

Lonzo smiled: a rare and intimidating sight. 'She needs help, we'll send for you. We got money.'

'My apologies,' Brightsides said. 'I mean no offence. You niggers are emancipated, but us whites take a while longer to get a hold of the idea.'

'Time is what we all got plenty of. That Ridge ain't goin' nowhere.'

Hudd Ridge whiskey was good, and Lonzo sold every drop they made. Well, nearly every drop. The dollars did the colony a power of good. The other side of that coin was everyone in the county knew.

Dundee County enforced the dry vote with religious enthusiasm. This pushed up the value of Hudd Ridge whiskey; and that, in turn, encouraged the law officers to put the still out of business. In this contest the colonists had one unbeatable advantage: the Ridge itself. It was a wilderness that baffled all the sheriff's deputies and revenue agents that tried to creep up its flanks. The tracks they used were no help to anyone trying to reach the top in a quiet hurry: too many streams, thickets, rocks, landslips, dead-ends. Law officers hated climbing Hudd Ridge. If they went on foot their progress was painfully, wearyingly slow. If they took their horses they made so much noise that they knew the raid had failed and the still was hidden before they were halfway up, so they might as well turn back.

They couldn't beat the Ridge. One day, as the colonists were listening to law officers blundering about, far below, Lonzo said to JoBeth, 'Ain't it peculiar? Whitey breaks all kinds of law, tryin' to knock us off this Ridge. Now whitey's gone an' made a new dry law, which we gotta break so we can stay here. Peculiar, ain't it?'

'Certainly looks that way.'

'Maybe this dry vote is one piece of good luck for us niggers.'

'You had enough of the other kind. I guess even Providence runs out of bad luck sometime.'

PEACEFUL

Lonzo had a son, who had a son, who had a son. The Ridge was their home, which doesn't mean it was always a good place to live. Anyone who admires or envies those who live close to Nature should try it. Hudd Ridge was a free community but sometimes it was narrow and suspicious. Sometimes it was unhealthy and violent too. A lot of whiskey got made up there, and a lot of it got drunk. This led to fights over dice, women, anything, nothing. There were murders and often they were messy, bloody killings that no lawman was ever told about.

Then – nobody knew why – the colony would find peace, and for many years it might be a pleasant place to live. Down below, the Hudds and the Killicks still shot at each other occasionally, but the whites forgot to hate the colony and they even grew to like and help its members. Blacks and whites were no threat to each other. If the Hudd niggers ever felt threatened, they withdrew to their Ridge. If they needed money, they made whiskey. They were outlaws. Good. They never wanted the damn law anyway.

Then in the late 1930s, some of FDR's New Deal dollars leaked down into Kentucky and the first road got bulldozed along the Ridge.

It wasn't a good road but it was bad enough for the Hudd colony. It let the revenue agents' cars arrive so fast there wasn't time for anyone to shout 'Fire in the hole!' or make a yodelling hog call or let off a shotgun twice: all those warnings which, for generations, had given the moonshiners ample time to hide the still and its makings. It meant the government had won. The colony crumbled. If they couldn't live on the Ridge in secret, they couldn't live at all. Moonshining was all they knew to do; all the whites had allowed them do.

When the bulldozer came, the law followed it and half Hudd

Ridge wound up in court. The stills were smashed. There was no living up there any more.

Some hunters drove up to the Ridge, too. They shot three panthers in five days. Panthers were vermin, ate cattle, needed to be wiped out. Well-known fact.

Today, everyone has gone. The Ridge is almost back to being wilderness again. Every winter the roads get half-washed away; best for everyone if the county just let them go completely. You can still find one place left over from the colony, if you search hard: the graveyard under the big cedar. A score of headstones still stand. Not in lines, and not chiselled, professional slabs; just natural stone pointers fixed here and there in the ground. It's a pretty spot. Peaceful.

THE END

AUTHOR'S NOTE

Kentucky Blues is fiction, written around a framework of fact. The reader is entitled to know where fact ends and fiction begins.

All the characters (historical figures excepted) are my invention. As far as I know, there is no such river as the Cameron, and no such town as Rock Springs at its navigable end, largely inhabited by folk whose dreams and ambitions have also come to their navigable end. However, I have tried to make my picture of southern Kentucky – its terrain and wildlife, the outlook and beliefs of its people – true to the realities of the nineteenth century.

Kentucky Blues is, I hope, reasonably good history. For instance, southern Kentucky was opened up by settlers in much the way I describe; and Kentucky – midway between North and South – was torn in its loyalties during the Civil War. Emancipation created as many problems as solutions, and Hudd's slaves (ex-slaves) were not alone in finding that their freedom meant they were free to be rejected, hungry and homeless. More than one band of ex-slaves retreated into what white people regarded as wilderness, and survived against the odds.

I have not attempted to tell the story in the pure, authentic language of those times; to do so would have made for very hard reading. But where possible, my characters speak in their own true fashion. For instance, when Kentuckians spoke of a 'tide' on a river, they meant what we would call a flood or a spate; so I kept the word 'tide'. And I make no apology for using the word 'nigger'. At that time, everyone in America, black or white, used it. Not to have used 'nigger' in *Kentucky Blues* would have been as inaccurate and as dishonest as to have ignored the gruesome examples of brutality, even of atrocity, by white slave-owners. My job was to make the story as true as possible. If some readers find that truth unacceptable, they are free to stop reading.

Life in a small, remote town like Rock Springs could be both dull and dangerous. The grind of work was dominant but violence was never far away, whether it was the explosive pastime of anvil-flying (which actually went on) or the disguised banditry of the 14th Pennsylvania Rifles. I created that particular outfit, but they are typical of the outlaw activity that flourished in the aftermath of war. Conflict with law officers was inevitable, too, when several Kentucky counties voted themselves 'dry'. (Some are still dry today.) In the backwoods of Kentucky, strangers were not always welcome. (Not much has changed in that respect, as I found when researching this book.) It is a fact that during log runs on the big rivers, men on clifftops sometimes hurled rocks at the rafts, either to discourage the boatmen or to steal their logs or purely for the hell of it. Life was hard; there was not a lot to laugh about. The problems of existence filled most people's minds. The task each day was to earn a dollar and be alive tomorrow. In particular, the job of a cowboy was far from romantic – long periods of boredom broken by brief spells of intense risk – and I tried to make my account of a cattle drive as accurate as possible. Similarly, I drew on fact when I described riverboat gamblers who were known to improve their luck by wearing hidden machinery which terminated in their sleeves and dispensed extra cards.

Other parts of the story – the events in Texas, the idea of a woman deputy, de Glanville's theatrical frauds, and so on – I made up. Which is not to say they never happened.

D.R.